WARRIORS
OF
GOD

WARRIORS
OF
GOD

ANDRZEJ
SAPKOWSKI

Translated by
DAVID FRENCH

First published in Great Britain in 2021 by Gollancz
an imprint of The Orion Publishing Group Ltd
Carmelite House, 50 Victoria Embankment
London EC4Y 0DZ

An Hachette UK Company

1 3 5 7 9 10 8 6 4 2

Published by arrangement with the Patricia Pasqualini Literary Agency.

A CIP catalogue record for this book is
available from the British Library.

ISBN (Hardback) 978 1 473 22616 6
ISBN (Export Trade Paperback) 978 1 473 22617 3
ISBN (eBook) 978 1 473 22619 7
ISBN (Audio) 978 1 409 18528 4

Typeset by Input Data Services Ltd, Somerset

Printed in Great Britain by Clays Ltd, Elcograph S.p.A

MIX
Paper from
responsible sources
FSC   FSC® C104740
www.fsc.org

www.gollancz.co.uk

Prologue

The world, noble sirs, has lately grown bigger. And shrunk at the same time.

You laugh? Do I seem to talk nonsense? Does the one contradict the other? I shall soon prove it does not by any means.

Look out of the window, gentlemen. What view meets your eyes? The barn, you answer truthfully, and the privy beyond it. And what lies beyond the privy? Heed, if I ask the wench hurrying here with the ale, she will say that beyond the privy is a field of stubble, then Jachym's homestead, the tar kiln and finally Mała Kozołupa. If I ask our innkeeper – a more worldly man – he will add that beyond Mała Kozołupa is Wielka Kozołupa, then the hamlet of Kocmyrów, the village of Łazy, then Goszcz, and beyond Goszcz there's Twardogóra, I believe. But heed: more learned fellows with more enlightened minds – like you, for example – know that the world doesn't end at Twardogóra, either; that beyond it is Oleśnica, Brzeg, Niemodlin, Nysa, Głubczyce, Opava, Nový Jičín, Trenčín, Nitra, Esztergom, Buda, Belgrade, Ragusa, Ioannina, Corinth, Crete, Alexandria, Cairo, Memphis, Ptolemais, Thebes ... Well? Isn't the world growing? Doesn't it become ever larger?

Yet that *still* is not the end. Going beyond Thebes, up the Nile – which issues from its source in the Garden of Eden as the River

I

Gihon – we come to the lands of the Ethiopes, and thence, as we know, to barren Nubia, sun-baked Kush, gold-bearing Ophir and the whole of vast *Africa Terra, hic sunt leones*. And beyond that is the ocean that surrounds all the Earth. But in that ocean, of course, are islands like Cathay, Taprobana, Bragine, Oxidrate, Gynosophe and Zipangu, where the climate is wonderfully fertile and jewels lie around in heaps, as described by the scholar Hugh of Saint Victor and Pierre d'Ailly, and also by Sir John Mandeville, who saw those marvels with his own eyes.

Thus, we have proved that over the course of those few centuries the world has grown markedly. For even if the world hasn't increased in terms of matter, the number of new names certainly has.

How then, you ask, can we reconcile the claim that the world has also shrunk? I shall tell you and prove it. I only entreat you first not to mock or jibe, for what I shall say isn't a figment of my imagination, but knowledge gleaned from books. And it doesn't do to mock books, since their writing is the result of somebody's arduous labour.

As we know, our world is a small piece of land, shaped like a round pancake with its centre in Jerusalem and all engirdled by the ocean. At the Occident, the edge of the Earth is formed by Calpe and Abila – the Pillars of Hercules – with the Strait of Gades between them.

And to the south, as I have just said, the ocean extends beyond Africa. In the south-east, the end of the mainland is marked by *India inferior*, which belongs to Prester John, as well as the lands of Gog and Magog. In the septentrional of the Earth is Ultima Thule, and there, *ubi oriens iungitur aquiloni*, lies the land of the Mongols, or Tartary, while to the east the world ends some way beyond Kiev, with the Caucasus.

And now we come to the crux of the matter. By which I

mean the Portuguese. But more specifically the Infante Dom Henrique, Duke of Viseu, the son of King John. Portugal, it can't be denied, is by no means a large kingdom, and the king's infant was his third son in a row. So, unsurprisingly, Henry gazed more often and with greater hope from his palace in Sagres towards the sea than at Lisbon. He invited to Sagres astronomers and cartographers, wise Jews, navigators, sea captains and master boatbuilders. And thus it began.

In the Year of Our Lord 1418, the explorer João Gonçalves Zarco reached some islands called the *Insulae Canariae*, so called because of the vast multitudes of dogs found there. Soon afterwards, in 1420, the same Gonçalves Zarco and Tristão Vaz Teixeira sailed to the island christened Madeira. In 1427, the caravels of Diogo de Silves reached some islands which were named the Azores – only God and Diogo know why. But a few years ago, in 1434, another Portuguese, Gil Eanes, rounded Cape Bojador. And rumour has it that Infante Dom Henrique – who some are now beginning to call *El Navegador* or 'the Navigator' – is planning his next expedition.

Truly do I admire those seafaring explorers and hold them in great esteem. They are intrepid men. After all, it is terrifying to venture onto the ocean under sail. Why, there are squalls and storms, hidden rocks, magnetic mountains, rough and sticky seas. If there aren't whirlpools, then there's turbulence, and if not turbulence, then currents. It teems with a plenitude of sea monsters and serpents, tritons, hippocampi, mermen, dolphins and flatfishes. The sea is awash with diverse *sanguisugae, polypi, octopodes, locustae, cancri, pistrixi et huic similia*. The most dreadful place is at the end – for where the ocean finishes, beyond its edge, begins Hell. Why do you think the sun is so red when it sets? Because it reflects the infernal fires. What is more, there are holes spread over the entire ocean, and when a caravel

3

imprudently sails over one, it tumbles straight into Hell. It is clear it was created in such an image to stop mortal man sailing the seas. Hell is the penalty for those who break the rules.

But, from my experience, it won't stop the Portuguese, since *navigare necesse est* and there are islands and lands beyond the horizon that need discovering. Distant Taprobane must be drawn on maps, the route to mysterious Zipangu described on *roteiros*, and *Insulae Fortunatae* – the Isles of the Blessed – marked on portulan charts. One must sail ever further, in the wake of Saint Brendan along the route of dreams, to Hy-Brasil, towards the unknown. In order to make the unknown known.

And that is why – *quod erat demonstrandum* – our world is diminishing and shrinking, because soon everything will be visible on maps, portulan charts and *roteiros*. And suddenly everywhere will be close.

The world is shrinking and becoming depleted of one thing: legends. The further the Portuguese caravels sail, the more islands discovered and named, the fewer legends there will be. Another one vanishes like smoke. We have one less dream. And when a dream dies, darkness fills the place orphaned by the dream. Then monsters awake at once in that darkness, particularly when our minds are lulled. What? It has been said before? M'lord! Is there anything that has not already been said?

Oh, but my throat is dry . . . What would I say to a beer, you ask? By all means.

What do you say, devout brother of Saint Dominic? Aha, that it is time I stopped digressing and took up the story again? Of Reynevan, Scharley, Samson and the others? You are right, Brother. It is. Thus do I resume it.

Anno Domini 1427 dawned. Do you remember what it brought? Indeed. It cannot be forgotten. But I shall remind you nonetheless.

That spring, in March, I believe, certainly before Easter, Pope Martin V announced the papal bull *Salvatoris omnium*, in which he declared the need for another crusade against the Czech heretics. Pope Martin named Henry Beaufort, the Bishop of Winchester, the brother of the King of England, cardinal and *legate a latere* in the stead of Giordano Orsini, who was elderly and dreadfully feeble. Beaufort took up the matter vigorously. Soon a crusade was declared, meant to punish the Hussite apostates with fire and sword. The expedition was diligently prepared; money, of prime importance in a war, was meticulously collected, and this time – *mirabile dictu* – no one stole the cash. Some chroniclers believe the crusaders had become more honest. Others that the cash was guarded better.

The Diet of Frankfurt proclaimed Otto of Ziegenhain, Archbishop of Trier, commander-in-chief of the crusade. Everyone who could be was called to arms and soon the armies were ready. Frederick Hohenzollern the Elder, Elector of Brandenburg, reported with a force of soldiers. The Bavarians arrived under the command of Duke Henry the Rich, and Count Palatine John of Neumarkt, and his brother Count Palatine Otto of Mosbach also answered the call. The juvenile Frederick of Wettin, son of the infirm Frederick the Belligerent, Elector of Saxony, came to the rallying point. Raban of Helmstatt, Bishop of Speyer; Anselm of Nenningen, Bishop of Augsburg; and Frederick of Aufseß, Bishop of Bamberg – each came with a sizeable regiment. And Johann of Brunn, Bishop of Würzburg. And Thiébaudde of Rougemont, Archbishop of Besançon. Plus contingents from Swabia, Hesse, Thuringia and the northern Hanseatic cities.

The crusade set off at the beginning of July, in the week after the Solemnity of Saints Peter and Paul, crossed the border and marched into Bohemia, leaving corpses and conflagrations behind it. On the Wednesday before the Feast of Saint James, the crusaders, reinforced by men of the Bohemian Catholic Land-fried, stopped at Stříbro, which was occupied by the Hussite Sir Přibík of Klenové, and surrounded it, battering it cruelly with heavy bombards. Sir Přibík held on valiantly and thought not of surrender. The siege dragged on; time passed. The Elector of Brandenburg Frederick became impatient. *Why, this is a crusade!* he roared, advising that they proceed without delay to march on Prague. *Prague*, he said, *is* caput regni: *whoever has Prague, has Bohemia . . .*

The summer of 1427 was unbearably hot.

And what, you ask, did the Warriors of God say to that? What of Prague, you ask?

Prague . . .

Prague stank of blood.

Chapter One

In which Prague stinks of blood, Reynevan is followed, and then – by turns – becomes bored by routine, is full of recollections and longing, celebrates, fights for his life and drowns in a feather bed. And all the while, Europe turns somersaults, gambols and frolics.

Prague stank of blood.

Reynevan sniffed both sleeves of his jerkin. He had only just left the hospital, and while there – as is usual in a hospital – blood had been let from almost everyone, boils were regularly lanced and amputations took place with a frequency worthy of a better cause. His clothing might have absorbed the smell; there'd have been nothing unusual about that. But his jerkin just smelled like a jerkin. And nothing else.

He raised his head and sniffed. From the north, over on the left bank of the River Vltava, came the smell of dried weeds being burned in orchards and vineyards. Moreover, from the river came the smell of mud and rotting flesh – the weather was hot, the water level had dropped considerably and the exposed banks and dried-out sandbars had for some time been supplying the city with unforgettable olfactory impressions. But this time it wasn't the mud that stank. Reynevan was certain of it.

A light and changeable breeze was blowing intermittently

from the Poříčí Gate to the east. From Vítkov. And the ground at the foot of Vítkov Hill might indeed have been giving off the smell of blood, since plenty of blood had soaked into it.

But that couldn't be possible. Reynevan adjusted the shoulder strap of his bag and walked briskly down the lane. The smell of blood couldn't be coming from Vítkov. Firstly, it was quite far away. Secondly, the battle had been fought in the summer of 1420. Seven years before. Seven long years before.

He passed the Church of the Holy Cross, making good speed, but the stench of blood hadn't faded. On the contrary, it had had grown more intense. For now, all of a sudden, it was coming from the west.

Ha, he thought, looking towards the nearby ghetto, *stones aren't like soil; old bricks and plaster remember much, much lingers on in them. What they absorb stinks for a long time.* And over there, outside the synagogue and in the streets and houses, blood flowed even more copiously than in Vítkov, and a little more recently. In 1422, during the bloody pogrom, at the time of the upheaval that erupted in Prague following the execution of Jan Želivský. Enraged by the execution of their popular tribune, the people of Prague had risen up to seek revenge, to burn and kill. The Jewish district, as usual, took the brunt of it. The Jews had nothing at all to do with Želivský's death and weren't in any way responsible for his fate. But who cared?

Reynevan turned beyond the graveyard of the Church of the Holy Cross, passed by the hospital, entered the Old Coal Market, crossed a small square and ducked into the gateways and narrow backstreets leading to Dlouhá třída. The smell of blood had faded into a sea of other scents, for the gateways and backstreets bore every imaginable stench.

Dlouhá třída, however, greeted him with the powerful and heady aroma of bread. As far as the eye could see, celebrated

Prague bread and rolls lay golden and fragrant on bakers' stalls and counters. Although he had breakfasted in the hospital and wasn't hungry, he couldn't resist and bought two fresh rolls at the first stall he came across. The rolls – called *caltas* – were shaped so erotically that, for a while, Reynevan wandered along Dlouhá třída in a dream, bumping into stalls, lost in thoughts that raged like desert winds about Nicolette. About Katarzyna of Biberstein. There were several extremely attractive women of various ages among the passers-by he bumped into and jostled, lost in thought. He didn't notice them. He apologised absent-mindedly and went on, by turns chewing a *calta* and staring at it spellbound.

The stench of blood in the Old Town Square brought him to his senses.

Ah well, thought Reynevan, finishing the *calta*, *perhaps that's not so strange – blood is nothing new for these streets. Jan Želivský and nine of his companions were executed right here, in the old town hall, having been lured here that Monday in March. After that treacherous deed, the town hall floor was washed, and red foam streamed under the doors and flowed – it was said – all the way to the pillory in the centre of the town square, where it formed a huge puddle. And soon after, when the news of the tribune's death provoked an outburst of fury and the lust for revenge in Prague, blood flowed along all the surrounding gutters.*

People were walking towards the Church of Our Lady before Týn, crowding into the courtyard leading to its doors. *Rokycana will be preaching*, thought Reynevan. *It'll be worth listening to what Jan Rokycana has to say*, he thought. *It's always paid to listen to Jan Rokycana's sermons. Always. Particularly now, at a time when the current events are supplying subject matter for sermons at a simply alarming rate. Oh, he has plenty to preach about. And it's worth listening to.*

But there's no time. There are more pressing matters, he thought. *And there's a problem. Namely, that I'm being followed.*

Reynevan had become aware of being followed quite some time before. Right after leaving the hospital, by the Church of the Holy Cross. His pursuers were cunning, kept out of sight and hid themselves very adeptly. But Reynevan had cottoned on. Because it wasn't the first time.

He knew – in principle – who was following him and on whose orders they were acting. Although it wasn't especially important.

He had to lose them. He even had a plan.

He entered the thronged, smelly, noisy Cattle Market and mingled with the crowd heading towards the Vltava and the Stone Bridge. He needed to vanish and there was a good chance of doing so in the crowded bottleneck on the bridge, in the narrow corridor linking the Old Town with the Lesser Quarter and Hradčany, in the hubbub and crush. Reynevan wove through the crowd, jostling passers-by and earning insults.

'Reinmar!' One of the people he bumped into, instead of calling him a 'whoreson' like the rest, greeted him with his baptismal name. 'By God! You, here?'

'Indeed. Hey, Radim . . . What's the bloody stink?'

'It's clay and sludge.' Radim Tvrdík, a short and not very young man, pointed at the bucket he was lugging. 'From the riverbank. I need it . . . For you-know-what.'

'I do.' Reynevan looked around anxiously. 'I do, indeed.'

Radim Tvrdík was – as the enlightened few knew – a sorcerer. Radim Tvrdík was also – as even fewer members of that enlightened circle knew – obsessed with the idea of creating an artificial person, a golem. Everybody – even the more poorly enlightened – knew that the only golem ever to have been created was the work of a certain Prague rabbi whose name, probably misspelled, was given as 'Bar Halevi' in surviving documents. Long ago, that

Jew, so the story went, used clay, sludge and mud scooped from the bottom of the Vltava to make the golem. However, Tvrdík – and he alone – presented the view that the causative factor was played here not by ceremonies and spells, which were in any case well known, but rather by a specific astrological configuration that acted on the sludge and clay in question and their magical properties. However, having no idea what the precise planetary configuration might be, Tvrdík operated using trial and error, gathering clay as often as he could, hoping one day to finally chance upon the right kind. He also took it from various places. But that day he had gone too far; judging from the stench, he had taken it straight from near some shithouse or other.

'Not working at the hospital, Reinmar?' he asked, rubbing his forehead with the back of his hand.

'I took the day off. There was nothing to do. It was a quiet day.'

'Let's hope it's not one of the last,' said the magician, putting down his pail. 'Times being what they are . . .'

Everybody in Prague understood, knew what 'times' were being discussed. But they preferred not to talk about it and would cut short their speech. Cutting off one's speech suddenly became widespread and fashionable. The custom demanded that the listener assume a thoughtful expression, sigh and nod meaningfully. But Reynevan didn't have time for that.

'On your way, Radim,' he said, looking around. 'I can't stop here. And it'd be better if you didn't, either.'

'Eh?'

'I'm being followed. Which is why I can't go down Soukenická Street.'

'Being followed,' said Radim Tvrdík. 'By the usual chaps?'

'Probably. Cheerio.'

'Wait.'

'What for?'

'It isn't wise to try to lose your tail.'

'What?'

'To the tailers, attempts to lose the tail are a clear sign that the tailee has a guilty conscience and something to hide,' the Czech explained most astutely. 'Only a thief fears the truth. It's sensible not to go down Soukenická Street. But don't dodge, don't weave around, don't hide. Do what you usually do. Attend to your daily activities. Bore the trackers with your boring daily routine.'

'Meaning?'

'I've developed quite a thirst digging up sludge. Come to the Crayfish. Let's have a beer.'

'I'm being followed,' Reynevan reminded him. 'Aren't you afraid—'

'What's there to be afraid of?' The wizard picked up his pail.

Reynevan sighed. Not for the first time, a Prague magician had surprised him. He didn't know if it was their admirable calm or simply a lack of imagination, but some of the local wizards often appeared unbothered by the fact that Hussites could be more dangerous than the Inquisition to anyone who indulged in black magic. *Maleficium* – witchcraft – was among the deadly sins punishable by death in the Fourth Article of Prague. The Hussites were no laughing matter where the Articles of Prague were concerned. Self-proclaimed 'moderate' Calixtines from Prague were the equal of radical Taborites and fanatical Orphans in that respect. Any sorcerer who was caught was put in a barrel and burned at the stake in it.

They turned back towards the town square along Knifemakers Street, then Goldsmiths Street and finally St Giles Street. They walked slowly. Tvrdík stopped by several stalls and shared some gossip with the stallholders he knew. As was standard, sentences were cut short more than once with 'times being what they are ...' which was received with wise expressions, sighs and knowing nods. Reynevan looked around but couldn't see his pursuers. They were keeping well out of sight. He didn't know how it was for them, but he was beginning to find the boring routine deadly boring.

Fortunately, soon after, they turned from St Giles Street into a courtyard and passed through a gateway to emerge opposite the House at the Red Crayfish. And a small tavern named identically by the innkeeper without a scrap of imagination.

'Well I never! Just look! Why, if it isn't Reynevan!'

Four men were sitting at a table on a bench behind the pillars on the ground floor. They were all moustachioed, broad-shouldered and dressed in knightly doublets. Reynevan knew two of them, so he also knew they were Poles. Even if he hadn't, he could have guessed. Like all Poles abroad, these men were conducting themselves noisily and arrogantly, with ostentatious boorishness that in their opinion would emphasise their status and elevated social position. The funny thing was that since Easter, the status of Poles in Prague was extremely low and their social position even lower.

'Good day! Welcome, noble Asclepius!' One of the Poles, whom Reynevan knew as Adam Wejdnar, bearing the Rawicz coat of arms, greeted him. 'Sit you down! Sit you down, both of you! Be our guests!'

'Why are you inviting him so readily?' said another of the Poles, grimacing with feigned disgust. He was also a Greater Pole, known to Reynevan as Mikołaj Żyrowski and sporting the Czewoja coat of arms. 'Do you have a surfeit of cash or something? And besides, the quack works with lepers! He's liable to infect us with leprosy – or something even worse!'

'I'm not working in the lazaretto now,' explained Reynevan patiently, not for the first time. 'I'm working at Bohuslav's hospice now, here in the Old Town by the Church of Saints Simon and Jude.'

'Yes, yes.' Żyrowski, who knew everything, waved a dismissive hand. 'What are you drinking? Oh, blow it, forgive me. Let me introduce you. My lords Jan Kuropatwa of Łańcuchów bearing the Szreniawa arms and Jerzy Skirmunt bearing the Odrowąż. Excuse me, but what is that fucking smell?'

'Sludge. From the Vltava.'

Reynevan and Radim Tvrdík drank beer. The Poles were drinking Austrian wine and eating stewed mutton and bread. They were talking ostentatiously loudly in Polish, telling each other funny stories and responding to each one with thunderous guffaws. Passers-by turned their heads away, swearing under their breath. And occasionally spitting.

Since Easter, specifically since Maundy Thursday, the Czechs' opinion of the Poles hadn't been too high. Indeed, their position in Prague was also pretty low and evincing a downward trend.

Around five thousand Polish knights the first time, and around five hundred the second, had come to Prague with Sigismund Korybut, Jogaila's nephew, pretender to the Bohemian crown. Many had seen in Korybut hope and salvation for Hussite Bohemia, and the Poles had fought valiantly for the Chalice and Divine Law, shedding blood at the Battles of Karlštejn, Jihlava, Retz and Ústí. In spite of that, even their Czech comrades-in-arms didn't like them, in part because the Poles routinely found hilarious the Czech language in general and Czech names in particular, but also because Korybut's treachery had seriously damaged the Polish cause. The hope of Bohemia was thus a total failure: for the Hussite king *in spe* was in cahoots with Catholic lords, had betrayed the matter of *sub utraque specie* Communion and broken the Four Articles he had sworn to uphold. The plot was uncovered and foiled, Jogaila's nephew found himself in prison rather than on the Bohemian throne, and the people began to treat Poles with downright hostility. Some of them left Bohemia at once. But some remained, thereby apparently showing their disapproval of Korybut's treachery and their support for the Chalice, and declaring their readiness to fight on for the Hussite cause. And what of it? The Czech people continued to dislike them. It was suspected – not without reason – that the Poles couldn't give a stuff about the Hussite cause. It was claimed they'd stayed because, *primo*, they had nothing and nowhere to go back to. They had marched to Bohemia as wastrels pursued by courts and warrants, and now, to make matters worse, they had all – Korybut included – been saddled with curses and infamy. And because, *secundo*, they were only fighting in Bohemia in the hope of lining their pockets and gaining spoils and land. And because, *tertio*, they weren't actually fighting, but rather taking advantage of the absence of the Czechs to fuck their wives.

All of those claims were genuine.

Hearing Polish spoken, a passing Praguian spat on the ground.

'My, they really don't seem to like us,' observed Jerzy Skirmunt, in his comical accent. 'Why's that? How odd.'

'I couldn't give a tinker's cuss.' Żyrowski stuck out his chest, displaying the silver horseshoe of the Czewoja arms to the street. Like every Pole, he subscribed to the ridiculous view that as a nobleman, even though a totally impoverished one, he was equal in Bohemia to the Rožmberks, Kolovrats, Šternberks and all the other wealthy families put together.

'Perhaps you couldn't,' said Skirmunt, 'but it's still odd, my dear.'

'The people are astonished.' Radim Tvrdík's voice may have been calm, but Reynevan knew him too well. 'Astonished to see armed knights carelessly making merry at a tavern table. These days. Times being what they are . . .'

He trailed off in accordance with the custom. But the Poles weren't in the habit of observing customs.

'Meaning when the crusaders are marching on you, eh?' Żyrowski chortled. 'With a great force, wielding fire and sword, leaving only scorched earth behind them? And any moment—'

'Quiet,' Adam Wejdnar interrupted him. 'I shall reply thus to you, m'Lord Czech: your reprimand is misplaced. For the New Town is indeed quite empty, for when, as you said, those days came, the New Town followed Prokop the Shaven in great numbers to defend the country. So if any New Town citizen were to scoff at me, I'd keep my counsel. But not a soul went from here, from the Old Town. That's the pot calling the kettle black.'

'A great force is coming from the west,' repeated Żyrowski. 'The whole of Europe! You won't hold out this time. It'll be your end, your demise.'

'Ours,' repeated Reynevan with a sneer. 'But not yours?'

'Ours, too,' Wejdnar replied morosely, gesturing for Żyrowski to be quiet. 'Ours, too. Regrettably. It turns out we made a rotten choice of sides in this conflict. We should have listened to what Bishop Łaskarz said.'

'Aye and I should have listened to Zbigniew Oleśnicki,' said Jan Kuropatwa, sighing. 'And now we're stuck here like beasts in a shambles waiting for the butcher to come. May I remind you, gentlemen, that a crusade the like of which has never been seen is heading towards us. An army of eighty thousand men. Electors, herzogs, counts palatine, Bavarians, Saxons, soldiers from Swabia, Thuringia, the Hanseatic towns, on top of that the Landfried of Plzeň – why, even some mavericks from overseas. They crossed the border at the beginning of July and besieged Stříbro, which will soon fall; perhaps it already has. How far is

Stříbro from here? Just over twenty miles – they'll be here in five days, by my reckoning. It's Monday today. On Friday, mark my words, we'll see their crosses outside Prague.'

'Prokop won't stop them; they'll defeat him in battle. They are too numerous,' said Żyrowski.

'When the Midianites and Amalekites attacked Gilead,' said Radim Tvrdík, 'they were like grasshoppers in their multitude, and their camels were as numberless as the grains of sand by the sea. But Gideon, commanding barely three hundred warriors, defeated and dispersed them. For he was fighting in the name of the Lord of Hosts with His name on his lips.'

'Yes, yes, indeed. And the shoemaker Skuba defeated the Wawel dragon. Don't mix fairy tales up with reality, m'lord.'

'Experience teaches us,' added Wejdnar with a sour smile, 'that if the Lord takes sides, it is usually with the more powerful army.'

'Prokop won't hold back the crusaders,' Żyrowski repeated pensively. 'Ha, this time, m'Lord Czech, even Žižka himself wouldn't save you.'

'Prokop doesn't have a chance!' snorted Kuropatwa. 'I'd wager anything. This host is too mighty. Riding with this crusade are knights from the Jörgenschild, the Order of the Shield of Saint George, the flower of European knighthood. And the papal legate is reportedly leading hundreds of English bowmen. Have you heard, O Czech, of English bowmen? They have bows the height of a man, shoot from five hundred paces and from that distance pierce armour and puncture mail as though it were linen. Why! Such archers can—'

'Do such archers,' Tvrdík interrupted calmly, 'stay upright after being struck over the head with a flail? Various fine men have come here, the flower of knighthood of all descriptions, but thus far none of their heads has withstood a Czech flail.

Will you take a wager on that, m'Lord Pole? I, mark you, state that when an Englishman gets whacked on the head with a flail, that Englishman won't bend his bow a second time, because that Englishman will be a deceased Englishman. If there's any other result, you win. What shall we wager?'

'They'll crush you.'

'They've already tried,' observed Reynevan. 'Last year. On the Sunday after Saint Vitus's day. At Ústí. But you were at the Battle of Ústí, Sir Adam.'

'Aye,' admitted the Wielkopolanin, 'I was. We were all there. You, too, Reynevan. Surely you haven't forgotten?'

'No. I haven't.'

The sun was beating down mercilessly and visibility was poor. The dust cloud kicked up by the hooves of the attacking knights' horses was mixed up with the thick gunpowder smoke that had filled the entire inner square of the wagon fort following the salvo. Suddenly, the crack of breaking wood and triumphant cries rose above the yelling of the soldiers and squealing of horses. Reynevan saw men in flight spilling from the smoke.

'They've broken through,' gasped Diviš Bořek of Miletínek loudly. 'They've rent open the wagons ...'

Hynek of Kolštejn cursed. Rohač of Dube tried to bring his snorting horse under control. The face of Prokop the Shaven was set hard. Sigismund Korybut was very pale.

Yelling, armoured cavalry poured out of the smoke, the knights falling upon the fleeing Hussites, knocking them over with their horses, smiting and hacking any men who hadn't managed to shelter in the inner square of the wagons. A wave of heavy cavalry poured into the breach.

Then suddenly fire and lead spurted from cannons and trestle guns; hook guns rattled, handgonnes roared and a thick hail of bolts rained from crossbows into the throng compressed and crowded in the breach, straight into the faces of the riders and horses. Riders crashed from their saddles, horses tumbled over, men with them. As the cavalry teemed and swarmed, another salvo exploded into the mass with even deadlier effect. Only a handful of cavalrymen rode into the smoke-filled inner square and they were immediately felled with halberds and flails. At once, the Czechs flooded out from behind the wagons with savage cries, catching the Germans by surprise with a sudden counter-attack and driving them from the breach in an instant. The breach was immediately barricaded with wagons, to be manned by crossbowmen and flailmen. Cannons roared again and hook-gun barrels belched smoke. A monstrance raised above the wall of wagons flashed bright gold and a standard bearing the Chalice gleamed white.

Who are the Warriors of God
and His law!
Help right from God
And Trust in Him

The singing rose about the *wagenburg*, growing louder, more powerful and triumphant. Dust settled behind the retreating cavalry.

Rohač of Dube, knowing it was the moment, turned towards the mounted Hussites waiting in formation and raised his mace. A moment later, Dobko Puchała gestured likewise towards the Polish cavalry. A sign from Jan Tovačovský set the mounted Moravians at battle readiness. Hynek of Kolštejn slammed his visor shut.

From the battlefield, the cries of the Saxon commanders ordering their knights to begin another charge could be heard. But the cavalry were falling back, turning their horses around.

'They're running awaaay! The Germans are running awaaay!'
'After them!'
Prokop the Shaven breathed out and raised his head.
'Now . . .' he said, panting heavily. 'Now their arses are ours.'

Reynevan abandoned the company of the Poles and Radim
Tvrdík quite unexpectedly – he simply stood up abruptly, said
goodbye and left. A short, meaningful glance at Tvrdík signalled
his intentions. The sorcerer winked. And understood.

The stink of blood was all around again. *Surely*, thought
Reynevan, *it's coming from the nearby shambles, from Kotce Street
and the Meat Market. But perhaps it isn't? Perhaps it's different
blood?*

Perhaps it was the blood that foamed in these gutters here
in September 1422, when Ironmongers Street and the streets
around it were witness to fratricidal fighting, when the antagonism between the Old Town and the Tábor once again led
to bloodshed. Much Czech blood had flowed in Ironmongers
Street then. Enough for it to still stink.

And it was the stench of blood that sharpened his vigilance.
He hadn't seen his trackers, wasn't noticing anything suspicious
and none of the Czechs walking along the streets looked like a
spy. Despite that, Reynevan permanently felt someone's eyes on
his back. The men trailing him, it appeared, weren't yet bored
with the boring routine. *Very well*, he thought, *very well, you
good-for-nothings, I'll treat you to some more of this routine. Until
you're sick of it.*

He went down Glovers Street, crammed with workshops and
stalls. He stopped several times, feigning interest in the goods
and looking around furtively. He didn't see anyone following
him, but he knew they were somewhere around.

Before reaching Saint Gall's Church, he turned, entering a

backstreet. He was heading towards the Karolinum, his alma mater. He enjoyed attending university debates and quodlibets as part of his routine. After having received Holy Communion under both kinds on *Quasimodogeniti* Sunday, the first after Easter in 1426, he had begun to regularly attend the *lectorium ordinarium*. Like a true neophyte, he wanted to learn the mysteries and complexities of his new religion as fully as possible, and he acquired them most easily during the dogmatic debates which were regularly organised by members of the moderate and conservative wings, grouped around Master Jan of Příbram, and members of the radical wing, drawn from men of the circle of Jan Rokycana and Peter Payne, an Englishman, Lollard and Wycliffite. But those disputes became truly impassioned when they were attended by genuine radicals, men from the New Town. Then things became thrilling indeed. Reynevan witnessed someone defending one of Payne's Wycliffite dogmas being called a 'fucking Englishman' and having beetroots thrown at him. The elderly Křišťan of Prachatice, the university's distinguished rector, was threatened with being drowned in the Vltava. And a dead cat was flung at the venerable Petr of Mladoňovice. The audience gathered there often resorted to fisticuffs; teeth were knocked out and noses broken in the Meat Market near the Karolinum, too.

But some changes had occurred since those times. Jan of Příbram and his followers were revealed to have been involved in Korybut's plot and punished by banishment from Prague. Since nature cannot bear a vacuum, the debates continued, but after Easter, Rokycana and Payne suddenly started to be considered moderates and conservatives. The men from the New Town – as previously – were considered radicals. Uncompromising radicals. There was still fighting during the debates; insults and cats were still tossed around.

'M'lord.'

He turned. The short individual standing behind him was all grey. He had a grey physiognomy, a grey jerkin, a grey hood and grey hose. The only vivid accent about his entire person was a brand-new truncheon turned from light-coloured wood.

Reynevan looked back, hearing a slight noise behind him. The other character blocking the exit to the alley also had a truncheon. He was only a little taller and only a little more colourful than his companion, but his face was much more repugnant.

'Let us go, m'lord,' said Grey, without raising his eyes.

'Where to? And what for?'

'Don't offer any resistance, m'lord.'

'Who ordered this?'

'Lord Neplach. Let us go.'

They didn't have far to go, as it happened, just to one of the buildings on the southern frontage of the Old Town Square. Reynevan couldn't work out exactly which one; the spies led him in from the back, through gloomy arcades stinking of mouldy barley, through courtyards, hallways and staircases. The interior was quite sumptuous – like most houses in that quarter, it had been taken over when the wealthy Germans who had owned it fled from Prague after 1420.

Bohuchval Neplach, called Flutek, was waiting for him in the drawing room beneath a light-coloured, beamed ceiling. A rope was tied to one of the beams. A dead man was hanging from the rope. With the toes of his elegant slippers touching the floor. Well, almost. They were about two inches shy.

Without wasting time on greetings or other outdated bourgeois customs, barely glancing at Reynevan, Flutek pointed at the hanged man. Reynevan understood.

'No ...' He swallowed. 'That's not him. I don't think ... No, no it isn't.'

'Take a closer look.'

Reynevan took a closer look, good enough to be sure that the rope digging into the swollen neck, contorted face, bulging eyes and black lolling tongue would come back to haunt him during his next few meals.

'No. That's not him ... In any case, I can't be sure ... I saw him from the back ...'

Flutek snapped his fingers. The servants present in the drawing room turned the hanged man so that his back was towards Reynevan.

'That man was sitting. Wearing a cloak.'

Flutek snapped his fingers. A moment later, the corpse, now cut down, was draped in a cloak and sitting in a curule chair – striking quite a macabre pose, bearing in mind the rigor mortis.

'No.' Reynevan shook his head. 'Don't think so. That man ... Hmm ... I'd definitely recognise him by his voice—'

'Regrettably, that's not possible.' Flutek's voice was as cold as the wind in February. 'If he could speak, I wouldn't be needing you at all. Go on, get that carcass out of here.'

The order was carried out at great speed. Flutek's orders always were. Bohuchval Neplach was the head of the Tábor's intelligence and counter-intelligence operations, reporting directly to Prokop the Shaven. And while Žižka was alive, directly to Žižka.

'Be seated, Reynevan.'

'I'm afraid I can't—'

'Be seated, Reynevan.'

'Who was that—'

'The hanged man? It doesn't matter in the slightest now.'

'Was he a traitor? A Catholic spy? He was, I gather, guilty?'

'Eh?'

'I asked if he was guilty.'

'In the eschatological sense?' Flutek shot him a nasty look.

'The Final Judgement and all? If so, I can only refer to the Nicene Credo: Jesus, crucified by Pontius Pilate, died, but rose and will come in glory again to judge the quick and the dead. Everyone shall be judged for their thoughts and deeds. And then it shall be established once and for all who was guilty.'

Reynevan sighed and shook his head. He only had himself to blame. He knew Flutek. He shouldn't have asked.

'Thus, it doesn't matter who he was,' said Flutek, nodding towards the beam and the severed rope. 'What matters is that he managed to hang himself while we were breaking the door down. That I didn't manage to force him to speak. And that you didn't identify him. You claim it wasn't him – not the man you allegedly eavesdropped on when he was plotting with the Bishop of Wrocław in Silesia – is that true?'

'It is.'

Flutek cast him a hideous glance. Flutek's eyes, as black as a marten's and which pointed down his long nose like the openings of two gun barrels, were capable of looking extremely hideous. At times, two tiny golden devils would appear in Flutek's eyes which suddenly turned somersaults in unison. Reynevan had seen them before. And they usually heralded something very unpleasant.

'But I think it isn't,' said Flutek. 'I think you're lying. And have been from the start, Reynevan.'

No one knew how Flutek had ended up working for Žižka. Rumours had circulated, naturally. According to some people, Bohuchval Neplach – real name Yehoram ben Yitzchak – was a Jew, a pupil of a rabbinical school, whom, on a whim, the Hussites had spared during the massacre of the ghetto in Chomutov in March 1421. According to others, he wasn't called Bohuchval but Gottlob and was a German, a merchant from Plzeň. Still others said he was a monk, a Dominican, whom Žižka – for unknown reasons – had personally rescued from the massacre of priests and monks in Beroun. Other people claimed that Flutek had been a parish priest in Čáslav, who joined the Hussites just in time and whose neophyte zeal had helped him ingratiate himself so effectively with Žižka that he landed himself a permanent post. Reynevan was in fact inclined to believe the last rumour. Flutek must have been a priest; his outrageous hypocrisy, duplicity, dreadful egoism and almost unimaginable greed spoke in favour of it.

It was indeed to his greed that Bohuchval Neplach owed his nickname. In 1419, Catholic noblemen captured Kutná Hora, the most important centre for extracting ore in Bohemia. Cut off from the mines and mints in Kutná Hora, Hussite Prague began striking its own coin, pennies with such low silver content that were practically worthless. Consequently, the Prague coins were scorned and contemptuously nicknamed 'fluteks'. Thus, when Bohuchval Neplach began to serve as the head of Žižka's intelligence, the nickname 'Flutek' stuck to him in a flash, for it soon turned out that Bohuchval Neplach was prepared to do anything for even a single flutek – even stooping to pluck one from a pile of shit. Bohuchval Neplach never, ever passed up a chance to steal or embezzle one.

How Flutek managed to keep his position with Žižka, who harshly punished embezzlers in his New Tábor and fought thievery with an iron fist, was a mystery. And why Flutek was later tolerated by the no less principled Prokop the Shaven was also a mystery. Only one explanation was possible: Bohuchval Neplach was an expert at what he did for the Tábor. And experts can be forgiven a great deal. *Should* be forgiven. For experts are rare and hard to come by.

'If you want to know,' Flutek continued, 'I have had extremely little confidence in your tale, as indeed I have had in you, from the very beginning. Clandestine meetings, secret counsels and international conspiracies are all very well in literature and suit someone like, let's say, Wolfram of Eschenbach. It's pleasant to read Wolfram's stories of mysteries and conspiracies ... about the mystery of the Holy Grail, Terre de Salvaesche and all sorts of Klinschors, Flagetanises, Feirefizes and Titurels. There was just a bit too much of that literature in your account. In other words, I suspect you were simply lying.'

Reynevan said nothing, just shrugged. Quite ostentatiously.

'There can be various reasons for your confabulations,' continued Flutek. 'You fled Silesia, you claim, because you were persecuted, threatened with death. If it's true, you didn't have any other choice than to curry favour with Ambrož. And how more effectively than to warn him about an attempt on his life? Then you were brought before Prokop. Prokop usually suspects fugitives from Silesia of being spies, so he hangs the lot of them and *per saldo* comes out on top. So, how to save one's skin? Why, for example, by making revelations about a secret counsel and a conspiracy. What do you say, Reynevan? How does it sound?'

'Wolfram of Eschenbach would envy you. And you'd be bound to win the tournament in Wartburg.'

'So you had enough reasons to confabulate,' continued Flutek imperturbably. 'But I think there was really just one.'

'Of course,' said Reynevan, knowing full well what he was getting at. 'Just one.'

The two golden imps appeared in Flutek's eyes. 'The most appealing hypothesis to me is that your chicanery is designed to distract attention from the matter of greatest import. Namely, the five hundred grzywna stolen from the tax collector. What say you, physician?'

'The same as usual.' Reynevan yawned. 'We've been through all this. I'll respond in an unoriginal, boring way to your unoriginal, boring question. No, Brother Neplach, I won't share the money stolen from the tax collector for several reasons. Firstly, I don't have the money, because I wasn't the one who stole it. Secondly—'

'So who stole it?'

'To be boring: I have no idea.'

The two golden imps leaped up and turned a lissom somersault.

'You're lying.'

'Naturally. May I go now?'

'I have proof that you're lying.'

'Oho.'

'You claim,' said Flutek, his eyes drilling through Reynevan, 'that your imagined moot occurred on the thirteenth of September and that Kaspar Schlick took part in it. But I know from first-rate sources that Kaspar Schlick was in Buda on the thirteenth of September 1425. Thus, he couldn't have been in Silesia.'

'You have third-rate sources, Neplach. Wait a moment, it's an entrapment. You're trying to trick me, ensnare me, and not for the first time – am I right?'

'You are.' Flutek did not bat an eyelid. 'Sit down, Reynevan. I haven't finished with you yet.'

'I don't have the money and I don't know—'

'Be quiet.'

They said nothing for some time. The imps in Flutek's eyes calmed down, almost vanished. But Reynevan wasn't deceived. Flutek scratched his nose.

'But for Prokop . . .' he said softly. 'But for the fact that Prokop has forbidden me from laying a finger on you, you and that Scharley of yours, I'd have got what I wanted out of you already. With me, everybody finally talks; not one person has ever stayed silent. You, too, be certain, would tell me where the cash is.'

Reynevan was more experienced now and wasn't to be frightened. He shrugged.

'Yeees,' Flutek continued after another break, looking at the rope hanging from the ceiling. 'And this one would also have talked. I'd have wrung a testimony out of him, too. It's a real pity he managed to hang himself. Know what? For a moment, I really thought he might have been in that grange . . . You really disappointed me by not recognising him . . .'

'I constantly disappoint you. It sorrows me greatly.'

The imps jumped slightly.

'Really?'

'Really. You suspect me, order me tailed, lie in wait for me, provoke me. You question my motives and constantly forget about the single, most important one: the Czech who was plotting in the grange betrayed my brother, turned him over to die at the hands of the Bishop of Wrocław's executioners and even bragged about it to the bishop. So, had it been him hanging from that beam, I wouldn't have skimped a farthing on a thanksgiving Mass. Believe me, I also regret it's not him. Nor any of the others whom you've shown me at other times or asked me to identify.'

'True,' admitted Flutek, in a – probably feigned – reverie. 'I once had my money on Diviš Bořek of Miletínek. My other tip was Hynek of Kolštejn . . . But neither of them—'

'Are you asking or stating? Because I've told you a hundred times it wasn't either of them.'

'Yes, after all, you had a good look at both of them . . . When I took you along with me—'

'At the Battle of Ústí? I remember.'

The entire gentle slope was covered with bodies, but the most macabre site was by the River Zdižnice which ran along the bottom of the valley. There, partly stuck in the bloody mud, towered a mountain of bodies, human corpses mingled with those of horses. It was obvious what had happened. The boggy banks had prevented the men from Saxony and Meissen from fleeing, prevented them long enough for them to be caught first by the Taborite cavalry, and a moment later by the howling horde of infantry rushing after them. The mounted Czechs, Poles and Moravians didn't waste much time and hacked to death anyone in their way, then swiftly set off in pursuit of the knighthood fleeing towards the town of Ústí. Meanwhile, the Hussite infantry – Taborites and Orphans – remained longer by the river. They slaughtered every last German. Systematically, keeping order, they surrounded and crowded them together, then flails, morning stars, clubs, halberds, gisarmes, voulges, bardiches, spears and pitchforks went into action. They gave no quarter. These Warriors of God, covered from head to foot in blood, shouting and singing as they returned from the battle, were leading no captives.

On the other bank of the Zdižnice, in the region of the Ústí road, the cavalry and infantry still had their hands full. The clanging of iron, roaring and yelling could be heard among clouds of dust as black smoke floated over the ground. Předlice and Hrbovice, hamlets on the far bank, were in flames, and judging from the sounds, a massacre was taking place there, too.

Horses snorted, twisted their heads, flattened their ears, shifted uneasily and stamped. The heat was unbearable.

Riders thundered towards them, raising dust, among them Rohač of Dube, Wyszek Raczyński and Jan Bleh of Těšnice and Puchała.

'It's almost over.' Rohač hawked, spat and wiped his mouth with the back of his hand. 'There were some thirteen thousand of them. According to initial estimates, we've dealt with about three and a half thousand so far, but the work's not over yet. The Saxons' horses are weary, so they won't get away – we'll add some more to the reckoning. I'd say we'll be putting up to four thousand to the sword.'

29

'It may not be Grunwald,' said Dobko Puchała with an unpleasant grin. The Wieniawa crest on his shield was almost indiscernible under a layer of bloody mud. 'It may not be Grunwald, but it's still beautiful. What, Your Grace?'

'M'Lord Prokop.' Sigismund Korybut appeared not to have heard him. 'Isn't it time to remember Christian mercy?'

Prokop the Shaven didn't answer. He rode downhill, to the Zdižnice. Among the bodies.

'Mercy's one thing,' said Jakubek of Vřesovic, Hejtman of Bilina, angrily, riding a little to the rear, 'but money's another! Why, it's simply a waste! Look at that one without a head – the crossed gold pitchforks on his shield mean he's a Kalkreuth. A ransom of at least six thousand pre-revolutionary groschen. That one with his guts hanging out, with a pruning knife in a field divided diagonally on his shield, is a Dietrichstein. An eminent family, at least eighteen thousand . . .'

Right by the river, the Orphans stripping the corpses pulled a still-living youngster in armour and a tunic with a coat of arms from under a pile of bodies. The youngster dropped to his knees, put his hands together and begged. Then began to scream, was hit with a battleaxe and stopped.

'Sable, a fess bretessé argent,' Jakubek of Vřesovic observed unemotionally, an expert in heraldry and economics both, apparently. 'So he's a Nesselrode. Of the Nesselrode counts. About thirty thousand for the whippersnapper. We're wasting money here, Brother Prokop.'

Prokop the Shaven turned his peasant's face towards him.

'God is our judge,' he said hoarsely. 'The men lying here didn't have His seal on their brows. Their names weren't in the Book of the Living.'

After a pregnant silence, he added, 'In any case, no one asked them to come here.'

*

'Neplach?'

'What?'

'You keep ordering me to spy, yet your thugs are still following me. Will you continue to have me spied on?'

'Why do you ask?'

'I can't see the point—'

'Reynevan. Do I teach you how to apply leeches?'

They said nothing for a while. Flutek kept looking back at the severed rope hanging from the beam.

'Rats leaving a sinking ship,' he said pensively. 'Not only in Silesia do rats conspire in granges and castles, look for foreign protection and kiss the arses of bishops and herzogs. Because their ship is sinking, because they're shitting themselves, because it's the end of false hopes. Because we're on the rise and they're falling, all the way down to the shithouse! Korybut took a tumble, there was a pogrom and a massacre at Ústí, the Austrians were beaten hands down and slaughtered at Zwettl, Lusatia is aflame right back to Zgorzelec. Uherský Brod and Pressburg are terrified, Olomouc and Trnava tremble behind their walls. Prokop is victorious—'

'For the time being.'

'What do you mean?'

'At the Battle of Stříbro ... Rumour has it—'

'I know what the rumours say.'

'A crusade is marching on us.'

'Nothing new.'

'The whole of Europe, they say—'

'Not all of it.'

'Eighty thousand armed men—'

'Bullshit. Thirty, at most.'

'But they're saying—'

'Reynevan,' Flutek calmly interrupted. 'Think about it. Do you think if things were so dangerous, I'd still be here?'

They said nothing for a while.

'As a matter of fact, any moment now things will become clearer,' said the head of Taborite intelligence. 'Any moment. You'll hear.'

'What? How? Who from?'

Flutek quietened him with a gesture and pointed at the window, then signalled for him to listen carefully. The bells of Prague were speaking.

The New Town began. The Virgin Mary at Trávníček was first, followed soon after by the Emmaus Monastery, a moment later by the bells of Saint Wenceslas's Church at Zderaz, joined by Saint Stephen's, then Saint Adalbert's and Saint Michael's, and after them the melodious bells of Our Lady of the Snows. A moment later, the bells of the Old Town began to sound, first Saint Giles', then Saint Gall's and finally the Church of Our Lady before Týn. Then the bell towers of Hradčany: Saint Benedict's, Saint George's and All Saints'. Finally, the cathedral bell sounded; the most dignified, the deepest, the most brazen, spreading over the city.

The bells of Golden Prague were singing.

There was a terrible confusion and crush in the Old Town Square. People were teeming outside the town hall, pressed up against the gates as the bells tolled on. Caught in the pandemonium, people were pushing each other, shouting over each other, waving their arms; all you could see were sweaty faces flushed with effort and excitement, open mouths and feverish eyes.

'What's happening?' Reynevan caught a tanner stinking of tanning pickle by the sleeve. 'News? Any news?'

'Brother Prokop defeated the crusaders! At Tachov! He beat them hands down, crushed them!'

'Was there a regular battle?'

'Battle?' shouted a character who had clearly just run from a barber, face still half-covered in foam. 'Battle? They fled! The papists ran! For their lives! In panic!'

'They left everything!' bellowed an impassioned apprentice. 'Weapons, cannons, goods, provisions! And fled! From the Battle of Tachov! Brother Prokop victorious! The Chalice victorious!'

'What are you saying? Fled? Without joining battle?'

'Aye, aye! And cut to ribbons by our boys as they ran! Tachov is encircled, the lords of the Landfried surrounded in their castle! Brother Prokop is belabouring the walls with bombards – it'll soon fall! Brother Jakubek of Vřesovic is harrying and routing Sir Heinrich of Plauen!'

'Quiet! Quiet, all of you! Brother Jan is coming!'

'Brother Jan! Brother Jan! And the councillors!'

The town hall doors opened and a group of men came out onto the steps.

They were led by Jan Rokycana, parish priest of Our Lady before Týn, short, with a noble, if not to say otherworldly, look. And quite young. The principal ideologist of the Utraquist revolution at that time was thirty-five, ten years older than Reynevan. Walking beside his now-celebrated pupil and gasping for breath was Jacob of Stříbro, university master. Half a step behind walked Peter Payne, an Englishman with the face of an ascetic. Then came the Old Town councillors: the powerfully built Jan Velvar, Matěj Smolař, Václav Hedvika and others.

Rokycana stopped. 'Brother Czechs!' he cried, raising both hands. 'People of Prague! God is with us! And God is above us!'

The roar of the crowd first intensified, then subsided and quietened down. The church bells stopped ringing in turn.

Rokycana didn't lower his hands. 'The heretics are vanquished!' he cried even louder. 'They who desecrated the Holy Cross by placing it – at Rome's instigation – on their contemptible armour! They have been punished by God! Brother Prokop is victorious!'

The crowd roared in unison and cheered. The preacher hushed them.

'Though the hellish hordes gathered here,' he continued, 'though the bloody talons of Babylon were stretching out towards us, though once again the wrath of the Roman Antichrist threatened the true religion, God is above us! The Lord of the Heavens raised His hand to annihilate the enemy host! The same Lord who drowned Pharaoh's army in the Red Sea, who forced the innumerable army of the Midianites to flee from Gideon. The Lord, who during the course of a single night employed His angel to defeat a hundred and eighty-five thousand Assyrians – that same Lord of the Heavens struck fear into the hearts of our foes! As the army of the blasphemer Sennacherib fled from Jerusalem, so the terrified papist rabble fled in panic from the Battles of Stříbro and Tachov!'

'As soon as the devilish servants saw the Chalice on Brother Prokop's pennants,' chimed in Jacob in a high voice, 'when they heard the singing of the Warriors of God, they bolted in panic to the four points of the compass! They were as chaff scattered on the wind!'

'*Deus vicit!*' yelled Peter Payne. '*Veritas vincit!*'

'*Te Deum laudamus!*'

The crowd roared and howled. It was so loud, Reynevan's ears hurt.

That evening, the fourth of August 1427, Prague thunderously and splendidly celebrated the victory. Praguians reacted to the weeks of fear and uncertainty with spontaneous festivities. They sang in the streets, danced around fires in squares, made merry in gardens and courtyards. The more pious celebrated Prokop's victory at impromptu Masses, said in all of Prague's churches. The less pious had a choice of a great variety of other forms of merriment. Everywhere, in the Old and New Towns, in the Lesser Quarter, which was still largely ashes, in Hradčany, almost everywhere, innkeepers celebrated the triumph over the crusade by treating anyone who wanted it to free alcohol and food. Throughout Prague, bungs and corks popped out of barrels and fragrant smells of cooking drifted from gridirons, spits and cauldrons. As usual, the crafty innkeepers took advantage of the situation – under cover of generosity – to rid themselves of stock that was in danger of going off and any that had spoiled long before. But who cared! The crusade was vanquished! The danger had passed! Let's make merry!

People made merry the length and breadth of Prague. Toasts were drunk in honour of the doughty Prokop the Shaven and the Warriors of God, wishing confusion on the crusaders who had fled from Tachov. In particular, it was hoped that the leader of the crusade, Otto of Ziegenhain, the Archbishop of Trier, would croak on the way home or at least fall ill. Hastily composed couplets were sung telling how the papal legate Henry of Beaufort soiled his britches at the sight of Prokop's banners.

Reynevan joined in the celebrations in the Old Town Square, then moved on to the Bear Inn in Perštýn near the Church of Saint Martin in the Wall with a large crowd of revelling strangers. Then the merry fraternity travelled to the New Town. Gathering up a few drunks on the way from the cemetery of Our Lady of the Snows, they headed for the Horse Market. There they visited in turn two taverns: the White Mare and Mejzlik's.

Reynevan trailed faithfully after the company. Genuinely

delighted by the victory at Tachov, he felt like celebrating and having fun and was worrying less about Scharley. The route suited him, for he lived in the New Town. But he abandoned the plan to go to the apothecary shop in the House at the Archangel in Soukenická Street where he expected to meet Samson Honeypot. He feared compromising the secret location and exposing the Czech alchemists and mages to being unmasked. And even worse. And there *was* a risk. He briefly glimpsed the grey shape, grey hood and grey face of an agent several times in the merry crowd at the White Mare. Flutek, it turned out, never gave up.

So, Reynevan made merry, but sparingly, and didn't drink too much, although the magical decocts he had taken in Soukenická Street made him resistant to all kinds of toxins, including alcohol. Finally, however, he decided to leave the party. The merrymaking at Mejzlik's was beginning to enter the stage that Scharley called: 'Wine, vomit and song.' 'Women' had intentionally been left out of the set.

Reynevan went out into the street and took a deep breath. Prague was quietening down. The sounds of the noisy revelling were slowly being drowned out by the choirs of frogs along the Vltava and the crickets in monastery gardens.

He walked towards the Horse Gate. As he passed taverns and beer cellars, his senses were assaulted by sour smells and the clinking of dishes, girlish squeals, shouts now a little drowsy and increasingly listless singing.

I'm a butcher, you're a butcher, we're both butchers
We'll go off looking for heifers
I'll be buying, you'll be haggling
We'll court pretty maidens

A breeze was blowing, bearing the scent of flowers, leaves, sludge, smoke and God knows what else.

And blood.

Prague still reeked of blood. Reynevan was still being tormented by that stench, still had it in his nostrils. He felt the anxiety it triggered in him. There were fewer and fewer passers-by and no sight or sound of Flutek's spies, but the anxiety didn't diminish.

He turned into Stará Pasířská Street, then into a lane called V Jámě. As he walked, he was thinking about Nicolette, Katarzyna Biberstein. He thought about her incessantly and quickly experienced the effects of that thinking. The images appeared before his eyes so vividly and realistically, in such detail, that at a certain moment it all became unbearable – Reynevan stopped involuntarily and looked back. Involuntarily, because he knew there was nowhere to go anyway. Back in August 1419, barely twenty days after the Defenestration, every last brothel in Prague had been torn down and every last woman of easy virtue driven from the city. The Hussites were very strict regarding the observation of morality.

The realistic and detailed images of Katarzyna also triggered other associations. The rooms in the house at the corner of Saint Stephen's Street and Na Rybníčku Street that Reynevan shared with Samson Honeypot had a landlady, Mistress Blažena Pospíchalová, a widow rich in womanly charms with kind, blue eyes. Those eyes had come to rest on Reynevan in such an eloquent way that he suspected in Mistress Blažena desires that Scharley usually described punctiliously as a 'union based only on lust and not the result of a Church-sanctioned alliance'. The rest of the world defined the activity much more concisely and bluntly. And the Hussites treated such bluntly defined activity with great severity. They usually did it for effect, admittedly, but no one ever knew who or what they might make an example of. So even though Reynevan understood Mistress Blažena's glances, he pretended he didn't. Partly out of fear of getting into hot water and partly – and even more so – out of a desire to remain faithful to his beloved Nicolette.

A furious caterwauling shook him out of his reverie as a large ginger cat dashed out of the dark alley on his right and ran off down the street. Reynevan immediately speeded up. It might have been Flutek's spies who had scared the cat. But it might also have been common cutpurses lying in wait for a lonely passer-by. Dusk was falling, there was almost no one around, and when the backstreets of the New Town were dark and deserted, they stopped being safe. Particularly now, when most of the castle guard had joined Prokop's army, it wasn't advisable to roam around the New Town alone.

So Reynevan decided not to be alone. Two locals were walking about a dozen paces ahead of him. He had to make quite an effort to catch them up as they were walking fast and on hearing his footsteps had clearly speeded up. And suddenly turned into a backstreet. He followed them.

'I say, brothers! Fear not! I only wanted to—'

The men turned around. One had a suppurating chancre just beside his nose and a butcher's knife in his hand. The other – shorter and thickset – was armed with a cleaver with a curved cross guard. Neither of them was Flutek's spy.

The third one, who'd been following him and had scared the cat, had greyish hair and wasn't the spy, either. He was carrying a dagger, slender and razor-sharp.

Reynevan stepped back, pressing himself against the wall. He held out his doctor's bag towards the thugs.

'Gentlemen ...' he gibbered, teeth chattering. 'Brothers ... Take it ... It's all I have ... I ... I beg ... I beg you ... Don't kill me ...'

The thugs' faces, at first hard and set, relaxed and melted

into contemptuous grimaces. Scornful cruelty appeared in their previously cold and vigilant eyes. They advanced, raising their weapons, towards an easy and abject victim.

And Reynevan moved to the next phase. After the psychological ruse à la Scharley, it was time to use other methods learned from other teachers.

The first character wasn't expecting either an attack or that the medical satchel would be slammed straight into his festering nose. A kick to the shins made the second one stagger. The third, the thickset one, was astonished to find his cleaver slicing air and he himself tumbling onto a pile of rubbish, having tripped over a dexterously positioned foot. Seeing the others coming for him, Reynevan dropped the satchel and swiftly drew a dagger from his belt. He ducked under a knife-thrust and twisted the knife-man's wrist and elbow, exactly as explained in Hans Talhoffer's *Das Fechtbuch*. He shoved one opponent into another, dodged and attacked from the side using a feint recommended for such situations in Chapter One of the volume devoted to knife fighting in Fiore of Cividale's *Flos Duellatorum*. When the thug instinctively parried high, Reynevan stabbed him in the thigh, as instructed in the second chapter of the same manual. The thug howled and dropped to his knee. Reynevan dodged, kicked the assailant getting up from the rubbish heap as he passed, side-stepped another thrust and pretended to stumble and lose his balance. The grey-haired thug with the dagger had clearly not read the classics or heard of feints, because he made a sudden, uncontrolled lunge, thrusting at Reynevan like a heron jabbing with its beak. Reynevan calmly knocked his arm up, twisted his wrist, caught him by the shoulder as recommended in *Das Fechtbuch* and shoved him against the wall. The thug, trying to free himself, swung a violent left hook – which landed straight on the point of the dagger, positioned according to the instructions in *Flos Duellatorum*. The slender blade penetrated deep and Reynevan heard the crunch of severed metacarpals. The thug gave a piercing scream and dropped to his knees, pressing his hand, squirting blood, to his belly.

The third assailant, the thickset one, was on him quickly and slashed diagonally with the cleaver from left to right, very menacingly. Reynevan jumped back, parrying and dodging, expecting a textbook stance or position. But neither Meister Talhoffer nor *messer* Cividale were much use to him that day. Suddenly, something very grey, dressed in a grey hood, grey jerkin and grey hose, appeared behind the thug with the cleaver. A truncheon turned from pale wood whistled and a dull thud announced its powerful contact with the back of his head. The grey man was extremely fast. He managed to land another blow before the thug fell.

Flutek and several agents entered the backstreet.

'Well?' he asked. 'Still think there's no reason to keep tailing you?'

Reynevan was breathing heavily, gasping for breath through his open mouth. The terror had only just kicked in and his vision went so dark he had to lean against a wall.

Flutek came closer and bent over to examine the thug with the lacerated hand. He mimicked with swift movements the German block and Italian counter-blow used by Reynevan.

'Well, well.' He shook his head in approval and disbelief at the same time. 'Skilfully done. Who would have thought you'd attain such dexterity? I knew you were taking lessons from a swordsman, but as he has two daughters, I thought you were training with one of them. Or both.'

Flutek gestured for the sobbing and bleeding thug to be bound. He looked around for the one who'd been stabbed in the thigh, but he had furtively slipped away. He ordered the one struck by the truncheon to be stood up. He was still dazed and dribbling. He couldn't look straight ahead – his eyes were still crossing and uncrossing and kept rolling back into his head.

'Who hired you?'

The thug's eyes darted around at random and he tried to spit. Unsuccessfully. Flutek gestured and the thug was hit in the kidneys. When he inhaled with a hiss, he was hit again. Flutek waved a careless hand, indicating that the thug should be taken away.

'You'll speak,' he promised as they marched him down the street. 'You'll tell us everything. No prisoner of mine has ever remained silent.' Flutek turned around to Reynevan, who was still leaning against the wall. 'To ask whether you have any suspicions would be to insult your intelligence. So I shall. Any idea who was behind this?'

Reynevan nodded. Flutek also nodded, in approval.

'The thugs will speak. Everyone talks in the end. Even Martin Loquis finally spoke, and he was a tough and determined little bugger, an idealist and true martyr to the cause. Scoundrels hired for a few pre-revolutionary pence will sing at the very sight of the tools. But I'll still treat them to the red-hot iron. Out of pure affection for you, their would-be victim. Don't thank me.'

Reynevan didn't.

'Out of pure affection,' continued Flutek, 'I'll do something else for you. I'll let you avenge your brother personally, with your own hand. Yes, yes, you heard right. Don't thank me.' Reynevan didn't thank him that time, either. As a matter of fact, Flutek's words hadn't sunk in yet. 'In a short while, my man will report to you. He will instruct you to go to the House of the Golden Horse in the town square, where we spoke today. Go there forthwith. And take a crossbow with you. Have you got that? Good. Farewell.'

'Farewell, Neplach.'

*

There were no further incidents. It was dark by the time Reynevan reached the corner of Saint Stephen's and Na Rybníčku Streets and the house with the room on the first floor that he and Samson Honeypot rented from Mistress Blažena Pospíchalová, the thirty-year-old widow of Master Pospíchal, *requiescat in pace*, may God bless him and keep him, whoever he was, what he did, how he lived and whatever he died of.

He gingerly opened the garden gate and entered the pitch-dark hall. He tried his best to keep the door from squeaking and the old wooden stairs from creaking. He always did when he returned after dark. He didn't want to meet Mistress Blažena. He somewhat feared what a confrontation with Mistress Blažena after dark might lead to.

In spite of his efforts, a step creaked. The door opened and he smelled Hungary water, rouge, wine, wax, plum jam, old wood and freshly laundered bed linen. Reynevan felt a plump arm around his neck and a pair of plump breasts pressing him against the banisters.

'We're celebrating tonight,' Mistress Blažena Pospíchalová whispered into his ear. 'It's a holiday today, my boy.'

'Mistress Blažena . . . But . . . Should one—'

'Be quiet. Come.'

'But—'

'Quiet.'

'I love another!'

The widow pulled him into her chamber and pushed him onto the bed. He plunged into the abyss of the starch-smelling feather bed and sank into it, overpowered by the downy softness.

'I . . . love . . . another . . .'

'No one's stopping you, deary.'

Chapter Two

In which Flutek keeps his word, Hynek of Kolštejn brings peace and quiet to Prague, and history cuts and wounds, keeping physicians very busy.

Flutek kept his word. Which completely astonished Reynevan.

For a month had passed since that conversation, since the revelries celebrating the victory at Tachov. Since the attack. And since the incident with Mistress Blažena Pospíchalová which occurred on the night of the fourth of August. The incident with Mistress Blažena repeated itself, truth to tell, a few more times and, on balance, had more pleasant than unpleasant aspects. The former included – among others – the delicious, hearty breakfasts that Mistress Blažena began to serve her lodgers from the fifth of August. From that day onwards, Reynevan and Samson, who had previously enjoyed rather irregular and meagre meals, walked to their daily duties well fed and content with life; and as they walked, they smiled cheerfully at their neighbours and whistled merrily, remembering the taste of bread rolls, white cheese, chives, liver sausage, gherkins and scrambled eggs with grated celery. Mistress Blažena very often served scrambled eggs and celery. *Eggs*, she would say, shooting Reynevan glances as velvety as Alpine edelweiss, *increase potency. And celery*, she would add, *increases desire.*

A month after those events, on the sixth of September, on the Saturday before the Nativity of the Blessed Virgin Mary, as Reynevan and Samson were finishing their scrambled eggs and celery, a familiar grey character in grey hose appeared in the chamber as quietly as a grey shade.

'The master is waiting,' he said softly and succinctly, 'in the Golden Horse. Shall we go, m'lord?'

The streets of Prague were unusually empty, almost deserted. There was tension in the air, the pulse of the city nervy, anxious and irregular. The roofs shimmered with the rain that had fallen before dawn.

They walked in silence.

Samson Honeypot spoke first.

'Almost exactly two years ago,' he said, 'we were in Ziębice. You arrived in Ziębice on the eighth of September 1425. On a noble mission to liberate your beloved. Do you remember?'

Instead of answering or commenting, Reynevan speeded up.

'In the course of those two years, you've undergone profound metamorphoses,' Samson went on. 'You've changed both your religion and world view: no small thing. To defend them, you sometimes fought with weapon in hand, and were sometimes used by politicians, spies and scoundrels. But your motive now isn't virtuous redemption but quite the reverse: blind revenge. Revenge, which, even if by some miracle should fall upon the men who are actually guilty, still won't bring your dead brother back to life.'

Reynevan stopped.

'We've been through this,' he replied firmly. 'You know my motives. And you promised to help. So I don't understand—'

'Why am I bringing this up again? Because it always bears revisiting something like this. It's always worth trying, because perhaps it will work, and perhaps someone's eyes will be opened and they will see the light. But you're right. I promised to help. And I shall. Let's go.'

Strangely, there wasn't a guard or a soldier to be seen at the Svatohavelská Gate. This was absolutely astonishing, considering that the gate and the bridge over the moat were the main link between the New Town and the Old, and that relationships between the quarters had been tense enough to justify the gate being manned by an armed guard. But there was no sign of the sentry and the gateway stood open. Encouraging anybody to enter. Temptingly. Like a trap.

The streets beyond Saint Gall's, which were usually crammed with stalls, were also nearly empty and a strange silence hung over the Fish Market. And the Old Town Square looked deserted. Two dogs, one cat and about thirty pigeons drank water from a puddle under the pillory in peace and harmony, not even looking back at the few passers-by hurrying around the edge of the square.

The globes on the spires of the Church of Our Lady before Týn glistened from the recent rain. The town hall tower shone like a golden trident.

The astronomical clock on the town hall tower grated as usual, tolled and indicated something – as usual, no one really knew what, why or how accurately. And judging from the sun's position, it was only a little after Terce.

Flutek was waiting in the House of the Golden Horse, in the same room as before, this time, though, without the hanged man.

Standing by the window, the Taborite spy was listening to reports from various men, some of whom looked like agents and some of whom didn't. He saw Reynevan. And grimaced at the sight of Samson.

'You're here.'

'I am.'

'You didn't bring a crossbow,' Flutek remarked sourly. 'Perhaps it's better. You might have shot something. Must that moron of yours be here?'

'No, he mustn't. Go downstairs, Samson. And wait.'

'Stand there,' Flutek instructed him after Samson had left. 'By that window. Stand there, say nothing and watch.'

He stood there, said nothing and watched. The town square was still empty. Beside the puddle under the pillory, one of the dogs scratched itself, the cat licked itself in the region of its tail, broadly speaking, and the pigeons toddled around the edge of the water. A horn sounded somewhere near Týn Yard and the Church of Saint James. A moment later, another was heard from the east, from the ransacked Church of Saint Clement, the former Dominican monastery.

An agent rushed into the room, out of breath. Flutek listened to his report.

'They're coming,' he announced, going over to the next window. 'A force of about five hundred horse. Did you hear, Reinmar? They mean to capture Prague with five hundred horse, the fools. They mean to seize power with five hundred, the conceited asses.'

'Who? Will you just tell me what's going on?'

'Rats leaving a sinking ship. Go over to the window. Have a good look. Look closely. You know who you're looking out for.'

The dogs suddenly fled from the pillory, swiftly followed by the cat. The pigeons flew up in a flapping cloud, frightened by the approaching clatter of horseshoes. A cavalry regiment was approaching from the south, from the moat and the unmanned Svatohavelská Gate. Soon the horsemen – including heavy cavalrymen – began to pour into the square, clanking and rattling.

'The Kolín force of Diviš Bořek,' said Flutek, recognising the livery and emblems. 'Půta of Častolovice's men. The lordlings of Jan of Městecký from Opočno. The knights of Jan Michalec of Michalovice. The cavalry of Lord Otto of Bergow, the Lord of Trosky. And at the head?'

At the head of the regiment rode a knight in full armour, but without a helmet. His white tunic bore a coat of arms – a golden lion rampant on a white field. Reynevan had seen both the knight and the crest before. At the Battle of Ústí.

'Hynek of Kolštejn,' Flutek announced through clenched teeth. 'From the Štěpanice line of the Valdštejns, from the great house of Markvartic. A hero from Vyšehrad, currently Lord of Kamýk and Hejtman of Litoměřice. He's come a long way, from greatness to treachery. Look around among his companions, Reynevan. Look closely. Something tells me you'll see an acquaintance.'

The Old Town Square reverberated with the thud of horseshoes; clattering and clanging echoed against the frontages and rose above the roofs. Hynek of Kolštejn, the knight with the lion, reined in his grey horse before the portal of the Old Town Hall.

'Sacred peace!' he roared. 'It is time for sacred peace! Enough blood, violence and crime! Release the captives! Release Sigismund Korybut, our rightful lord and king! Enough rule by bloody cliques! An end to violence, crime and war! We bring you peace!'

'Sacred peace!' The horsemen took up the slogan in unison. 'Sacred peace! *Pax sancta!*'

'Folk of the city of Prague!' bellowed Hynek. 'O capital of the Kingdom of Bohemia and everyone loyal to the kingdom! Join us! Lord Burgermeister of the Old Town! Gentlemen councillors! Join us! Come to us!'

The doors of the town hall didn't even budge an inch.

'Prague!' screamed Hynek. 'Free Prague!'

And Prague replied.

Shutters banged open, crossbow stirrups and prods peeped out alongside the barrels of hook guns and handgonnes. Suddenly, in unison, the Old Town Square vanished in a deafening thudding of shots, in smoke and the stench of gunpowder. A hail of lead balls and bolts rained down on the soldiers crowded into the square. The screams, roars and yells of wounded men and the neighing and wild squealing of mutilated horses exploded and rose. The horsemen teemed chaotically, bumped into each other, fell over and trampled on any men who fell from their saddles. Some of them immediately urged their horses to a gallop, but there was no escape. The streets had quickly been barricaded with beams and fenced off with chains stretched across them. Bolts rained down from the barricades as soldiers ran into the Old Town Square from all sides, from Iron Street, from Michalská Street, from Dlouhá třída, from Celetná Street and from Týn.

The horsemen, protecting each other with shields, herded together in a huddle in front of the town hall. Hynek of Kolštejn tried to restore order, his voice growing hoarse from yelling. But the firing hadn't let up, balls and bolts still raining down from the windows of the houses surrounding the Old Town Square – from the Unicorn, the Red Door, the Lamb, the Stone Bell and the Swan – from windows, roofs, hallways and gateways. One after the other, knights and esquires tumbled from their saddles onto the ground; horses fell, kicking.

'Good,' Flutek said through clenched teeth. 'Good, Praguians. Keep it up! Oh, you won't get out of this alive, Lord Kolštejn of the Valdštejns. You won't survive.'

As though Hynek of Kolštejn had heard, his regiment suddenly split into two units. One, with around a hundred horses and led by a knight with a silver and black shield, galloped towards the Church of Saint Michael. The other, with Hynek leading, rode at the mob attacking from Dlouhá třída.

Reynevan lost sight of the first unit and could only gather from the yelling and clanking that the horsemen were trying to force their way through the barricades and hack a path to the bridge and the Lesser Quarter. He did see Hynek's unit plough into the armed townspeople, cut down the front rank and break up the next. And saw them stopped by the third, skewered on a wall of gisarmes, spears and pitchforks. The Praguians stood firm, undismayed. There were too many of them. They were strong. Confident.

For reinforcements kept coming.

'Death to the traitors!' they yelled, attacking. 'Into the Vltava with them!'

'Kill them, give no quarter!'

Wounded steeds neighed, rearing up, and their riders fell to the ground, slippery with blood. And from the windows came an unceasing stream of bolts . . .

'Kill the traitors! Into the Vltava!'

The riders retreated, returned to the square, dispersed and re-grouped on their own initiative to force their way through the barricades and chains near the Church of Saint Nicholas and in Michalská Street. But Hynek wasn't with them. The horse of the hero of Vyšehrad had fallen under him, cut down by a scythe blade across the forelegs. The knight managed to jump free in time, his sword still in his hand, and smote those who leaped at him. Back pressed against the wall of the House at the Elephant, he called several men to him. Seeing that they were falling from crossbow belts, he darted into a vaulted hall-way, barging open the door. A mob of Praguians rushed into the house after him. Hynek didn't have a chance. It wasn't long before his bloodied body, shrouded in a tunic decorated with the lion of the Markvartic family, tumbled from a window on the first floor and thudded onto the Prague cobblestones.

'Defenestration!' Flutek laughed, his face contorting demonically. 'A fresh defenestration! That's to my liking, dammit! Justice and symbolism!'

Hynek, having been thrown from the window, was still showing faint signs of life. The Praguians crowded around him. They hesitated for a time. Finally, one man overcame his reluctance and stabbed the knight with a spear. Another hacked at him with a poleaxe. And then all the others fell on him, stabbing and hacking.

'Oh, yes!' Flutek laughed. 'Symbolism! Well, Reynevan? What do you say—'

He broke off. Reynevan wasn't in the room.

It had to be admitted that the knight with the shield divided diagonally into silver and black fields saved himself using good sense and invention. Firstly, while still in the Old Town Square, he discarded the shield identifying him. When the horsemen who had been driven back from the barricades in the Fruit Market regrouped behind the Church of Saint Leonard to attack the Praguians again, the silver and black knight confidently turned his horse around and darted into the narrow streets, tearing off his richly embroidered cloak as he galloped. He rode into the small Puddle Square, frightening ducks and beggars. Hearing the cries of his pursuers, he leaped from the saddle, slapped his steed on the rump and dived into a narrow, dark alley leading towards Swordsmiths Street. The yelling Praguians followed the clatter of hooves towards the Dominican monastery and the Vltava. The river in whose waters – as the shouts of the mob were boringly and monotonously proclaiming – every rebel and traitor would soon meet his end.

The sounds grew fainter and more distant. The knight sighed in relief and smiled faintly to himself. He was already almost certain he would make it. And who knows, perhaps he would have, were it not for the fact that Reynevan knew the area very well. Swordsmiths Street and the backstreets leading from it had been home, in pre-revolutionary times, to several cosy and reasonably priced little brothels, so every student and scholar of Charles University was very familiar with the area. On top of that, Reynevan and Samson Honeypot were using magic – telepathic amulets, very simple ones, but sufficient for rudimentary telecommunication – for tracking and stalking.

The silver and black knight waited for a moment, using the time to drape a piece of cloth he'd found over his armour. He pressed himself against the wall on hearing the thud of horseshoes, but it was only a riderless horse, a dun with blood running down its side. Following the horse came a spotted cow, rocking and mooing – how it got there, God alone only knew.

When it grew silent, the knight quickly headed towards Swordsmiths Street, where he stopped for a moment and looked around, listening to the fading sounds of fighting and slaughter. Then he entered the first arcade and courtyard he came to, where he began removing the treacherous armour. He took down a very frayed and baggy blouse from among other garments on a washing line. It had clearly been made for a pregnant woman or one with a naturally rotund physique. Pulling the blouse down over his head, he couldn't see anything for a moment.

And Reynevan and Samson took advantage of that.

Reynevan slammed the knight hard with a plank picked up from the ground. Samson caught the man by the shoulder, shook him, jerked him up and shoved him hard against the wall.

Astonishingly, rather than sliding inertly down the wall, the knight pushed off against it, jerked a short sword from a sheath and attacked. Samson dodged and Reynevan swung the plank again. The knight parried powerfully, then thrust with the blade so quickly and expertly that had Reynevan not taken lessons from a swordsman, he would have bidden farewell to his liver and his life. The knight nimbly turned the short sword around in his hand and delivered a rapid blow. Had it not been for a dodge Reynevan had learned, the knight's blade would have ended up buried in his cervical vertebrae. Samson neutralised the dangerous situation, knocking the knight's weapon out of his hand with a blow from a stick and felling him with a punch. The punch was powerful, but the knight had no intention of staying down that time, either. He leaped to his feet, seized an empty barrel in both hands, lifted it up, grunted and, red in the face from the effort, threw it like a missile at Samson Honeypot. And here he met his match. Samson caught the barrel in mid-flight and sent it back like a ball. The knight was knocked off his feet and tumbled into a pile of straw.

This time, he didn't manage to get up. Reynevan and Samson were upon him, pinned him down, twisted his arms behind his back and bound them. They wrapped his head around with the blouse to blindfold him and then bound his legs at the ankles with a long rope, which they used to drag him to a nearby cellar. They didn't go easy on him, oblivious of the fact that the knight's head was banging rhythmically against the stone steps and he was groaning and cursing.

Shoved down into a pile of cabbages, he sat up, groaning and fulminating. When Reynevan tore the blouse from his head, he blinked. The cellar had a small window and a little light was coming through. The knight scrutinised Reynevan for a long time, then glanced at Samson, and at once decided that of the two, only one was a partner in negotiations. He looked Reynevan straight in the eye and cleared his throat.

'Sensible,' he forced himself to smile, 'judicious, Brother. Why share with others when you can have everything for yourself? The times are too hard and unpredictable to turn one's nose up at a penny. And you'll end up with a penny, I promise.'

Reynevan surreptitiously sighed with relief. Until that moment, he hadn't been absolutely certain and had felt a gnawing frustration that he might have been mistaken. But when the knight spoke, there was no chance of a mistake. He had heard that voice two years before, on the thirteenth of September, in the Cistercian grange in Dębowiec, Silesia.

'You deserve . . .' The silver and black knight licked his lips and glowered at Reynevan. 'You deserve a reward. If only for your cunning. You caught me craftily, what can I say? You've got your head screwed on—'

He broke off. He realised he was talking in vain, and that his words weren't making any impression on his listener. He immediately changed tack. His face assumed a proud expression and his tone became lordly and imperious.

'I am Jan Smiřický of Smiřice. Understand, lad? Jan Smiřický! The ransom for me—'

'The corpse of your comrade, stripped naked, is already hanging from the pillory in the Old Town Square. There's room beside it.'

The knight didn't lower his eyes. Reynevan knew who he was dealing with but kept to the strategy he'd chosen. He continued trying to frighten and intimidate him.

'Of your comrades, the only ones to survive are those who Father Rokycana defended, shielding them with his own breast from the spears of the rabble. They were dragged to the town hall dungeon. After having to run an impromptu gauntlet of two rows of men wielding clubs and axes. Not all of them came out of it alive. The others are still being hunted and the mob is still waiting outside the town hall. Are you wondering why I'm saying this? For I have a dreadful desire to drag you into the town square, hand you over to the Praguians and watch you dash between the clubs. Do you know where that desire comes from? Can you perhaps guess?'

The knight narrowed his eyes. And then opened them wide.

'It's *you* . . . Now I recognise you.'

'You betrayed my brother, O Jan Smiřický of Smiřice, you turned him over to die. You will pay for that. I'm wondering how. I could, as I said, hand you over to the Praguians. I could stick a knife between your ribs myself, here and now.'

'A knife?' The knight swiftly regained his aplomb and pouted contemptuously. 'You? Between my ribs? Ha, go on then, young Lord of Bielawa. Stab away!'

'Don't provoke me.'

'Provoke you?' Jan Smiřický snorted and spat. 'I'm not provoking you. I'm mocking you! I'm a good judge of character, I can look straight into the soul. I've looked into yours and I shall tell you: you couldn't even kill a chicken.'

'I can, as I said, drag you to the town hall. To a crowd of less sensitive fellows.'

'You can also kiss my arse. I invite you. And I wholeheartedly recommend it.'

'Or I can let you go.'

Smiřický turned away. But not quickly enough for Reynevan not to notice the glint in his eye.

'So, then,' Smiřický asked a moment later, 'a ransom?'

'If you like. You'll give me the answers to a few questions.'

The knight looked at him, saying nothing for a long while.

'You squirt,' he said at last, curling his lip and drawling. 'You

Silesian German. You quack doctor! Do you know who I am? I am Jan Smiřický of Smiřice, a Czech nobleman, a knight, the Hejtman of Mělnice and Roudnice! My ancestors fought at Legnano and Milan, at Ascalon and Arsuf. My great-grandfather covered himself in glory at Mühldorf and Crécy. Answer questions? *Your* questions? Go fuck yourself, dolt.'

'You, Lord Smiřický, plotted treachery against your own countrymen like a common thug. The men who made you hejtman entrusted you with Mělnice and Roudnice. In gratitude, you conspired against them with Konrad of Oleśnica, Bishop of Wrocław, in the Cistercian grange in Silesia two years ago. Two whole years have passed, but you no doubt remember every single word spoken there. Because I do.'

Smiřický fixed his eyes on him. He said nothing for a while, swallowing a few times. When he spoke, apart from astonishment, there was genuine admiration in his voice.

'So it was you ... You were there. You eavesdropped ... The Devil take it! You move widely and ambitiously in the world, I must confess. I admire you. But I feel sorry for you at the same time. Men like you die young. And usually violently.'

Samson Honeypot sent a mental signal using the magical amulet. But although the communication had functioned tolerably during the chase, now, at a distance of two paces, the signal was quite incomprehensible. Although the intent was clear, the content was unintelligible. Reynevan took it as an urge to act decisively.

'You will answer my question, Lord Smiřický.'

'No, I won't. Think you have something you can frighten or blackmail me with? You haven't got shit, young Lord Bielawa. Know why? Because a historical moment is upon us. Each day brings changes. At times like these, you quack blackmailers have to act very quickly or your blackmail becomes a laughing stock. Didn't you see what happened in the streets today? I rode into Prague beside Hynek of Kolštejn. We came straight from Kolín, from Lord Diviš Bořek, who gave us his soldiers. Devout Catholics and Hussite killers like Půta of Častolovice and Otto of Bergow marched shoulder to shoulder with us. Our aim was no secret. We intended to capture the town hall and take control, because Prague is *caput regni*: whoever has Prague has Bohemia. We wanted to free Korybut and make him king. A true king, meaning with Rome's approval. We meant to come to an agreement with the Pope, who is inclined, rumour has it, to compromise regarding the liturgy, and prepared to yield regarding the Chalice and Communion *sub utraque specie*. Prepared to negotiate. But not with the Tábor, not with radicals, not with people who have the blood of priests on their hands. United with Oldřich of Rožmberk and the lords of the Landfried, we meant to finish off the radicals, destroy the Orphans, eliminate the Tábor and restore order to the Kingdom of Bohemia. Understand?

'We entered Prague openly and with visors raised,' Smiřický said, not waiting for Reynevan's response. 'I couldn't have shown more clearly whose side I'm on, what I want and what I am against. Everything was revealed and demonstrated today. So what do you wish to do? Now, with the cat out of the bag, you'll go to the Tábor and announce: "Listen, brothers, I'll tell you some news: Jan of Smiřice is your enemy, he's plotting with the Catholics against you." Old hat, Lord Bielawa, old hat! You've bungled it, you're too late. Indeed, a year, or even a month ago—'

'Even a month ago,' Reynevan finished his sentence, smiling nastily, 'I could have unmasked you. I was dangerous, so you sent assassins to kill me. Most chivalrous, Lord of Smiřice, most noble. Indeed, your glorious ancestors, those heroes of Ascalon and Crécy, must be proud.'

'If you think I'm going to apologise to you for that, you are fucking mistaken.'

'Answer my questions.'

'I believe I've already suggested you kiss my arse? I repeat the invitation.'

Samson Honeypot suddenly stood up. And Reynevan would have sworn that Jan Smiřický took fright.

'It's war!' he cried, confirming Reynevan's suspicion. 'War, lad! Whoever can harm you is your enemy, and you destroy your enemies! Your brother worked for the Tábor, for Žižka, for Švamberk and Hvězda, so he was my enemy – he could and did do harm. And the Bishop of Wrocław, on the contrary, was a valued ally, worth winning over. The bishop wanted the names of Taborite spies operating in Silesia, so he was given a list. In any case, the bishop had been suspicious of your brother for a long time and would have caught up with him eventually without my help. The Bishop of Wrocław has his means and methods. You'd be astonished how effective they are.'

'I wouldn't – I've seen a few things and I don't deny the effectiveness of his actions. After all, now neither Jan Hvězda – whom you mentioned – nor Bohuslav of Švamberk is alive. And you, in the Cistercian grange, put forward both those names as targets for the bishop's killers. Švamberk was from a noble family, perhaps from a nobler and older one than yours, though you boast about your forebears. The scaffold awaits you for Bohuslav Švamberk, his kinsmen will see to that now.'

Samson sent another signal. This one Reynevan understood.

'Hvězda and Švamberk died from wounds sustained in battle,' Smiřický stated meanwhile. 'Talk, accuse me, no one will believe—'

'No one will believe in black magic?' finished Reynevan. 'Is that what you mean?'

Smiřický pursed his lips. 'What the Devil do you want?' he suddenly exploded. 'Revenge? Go on, then – avenge yourself! Kill me! Yes, I betrayed your brother, though he trusted me like Christ trusted Judas. Happy? Of course I'm lying, I never clapped eyes on your brother, I heard about him from ... Never mind. But I turned him over to the bishop and he died because of it. I reckoned you a spy of Neplach, an agent provocateur and a possible blackmailer. I had to do something about you. A hired crossbowman, unbelievably, missed. I tried to poison you twice, but poison probably doesn't work on you. I hired three killers, but I don't know what happened to them. They vanished. All lucky coincidences, young Lord of Bielawa. Very odd, lucky coincidences. Didn't somebody refer to black magic just a moment ago?'

Flutek forced the arrested thugs to confess, thought Reynevan. *He had certainly heard reports about an assassination attempt being prepared, and the thugs revealed the rest under torture, confirming his suspicions. A trap was set for the conspirators, they didn't have a chance. By setting murderers on me, Jan Smiřický lost Prague. And Hynek of Kolštejn lost his life.*

'Rats leaving a sinking ship,' he said, more to himself than to the knight. 'After Tachov, in the face of the growing power of Prokop and Tábor, it was your only chance. The coup, the seizure of power, the release and placement of Korybut on the throne, the negotiations with the papacy and the Landfried. You staked everything on one card. But it didn't work.'

'Aye, it didn't,' the knight replied without much emotion, still staring not at Reynevan, but at Samson. 'I lost. Whichever way you look at it, it appears I'll lose my life. Very well, let what will be, be. Kill me, turn me over to Neplach, throw me to the mob, as you wish. I've had enough of all this. I shall make but one request, beg for one thing ... I have a maiden in Prague. A commoner. Give her my ring and cross. And this pouch. I know, these things are your spoils ... But she's a poor wench—'

'Answer my questions,' Reynevan said, again following Samson's telepathic instruction, 'and you can give her everything yourself. Today.'

Smiřický lowered his eyelids in order to hide the glint in his eye.

'You're ensnaring me. You won't forgive me. You won't renounce your revenge for your brother—'

'You only betrayed him. Others stabbed him with their swords. I want to know their names. Go on, betray them, gain something for something. Give me the opportunity to take my revenge on them and I'll renounce revenge on you.'

'What guarantee do I have that you won't deceive me?'

'You have none.'

The knight said nothing for some time, and all that could be heard was him swallowing.

'Ask,' he finally said.

'Hvězda and Švamberk. They were murdered, weren't they?'

'They were ...' stammered Smiřický. 'Unless ... I don't know. I have suspicions, but I don't know. It's possible.'

'Black magic?'

'Probably.'

'One other person took part in the conversation with the bishop. Tall. Slender. Black, shoulder-length hair. Birdlike face.'

'The bishop's advisor, assistant and confidant. Don't stare at me. You must know or have guessed. He does the bishop's dirty work for him. There's no doubt he murdered Piotr of Bielawa. And many others. Remember the Ninetieth Psalm—'

'The arrow that flieth by day. *Timor nocturnus*. The destruction that wasteth at noonday ...'

'You said it,' Smiřický replied, grimacing. 'You uttered that word. And I think you hit the target. Do you want some good advice, lad? Stay well away from him. From him and from—'

'The black horsemen calling *"Adsumus"*. Intoxicating themselves like assassins, with mysterious Arabic substances. Using black magic.'

'You said it. Don't go after them. Believe me and follow my advice. Don't even try to go near them. And if they try to get near to you, flee. As fast and as far away as you can.'

'His name. The bishop's confidant.'

'It's certain that the bishop himself fears him.'

'His name.'

'He knows about you.'

'His name.'

'Birkart of Grellenort.'

Reynevan drew a dagger. The knight's eyes closed involuntarily, but he opened them immediately and looked boldly at Reynevan.

'That's all, Sir Jan Smiřický. You're free. Farewell. And don't try to threaten me any more.'

'He won't,' said Samson Honeypot suddenly.

Jan of Smiřice's eyes opened wide.

'You have no luck with treason and conspiracy, Jan of Smiřice,' continued Samson calmly, taking no pleasure from the impression he was making. 'Not at all. They don't pay. It will be the same in the future. Beware of conspiracy and treachery.

'So many ideas and plans inside you. So much ambition. In truth, you could benefit from someone to stand behind you, to advise you in hushed tones, make suggestions and remind you. *Respiciens post te, hominem memento te, cave, ne cadas. Cave, ne cadas*, Sir Jan of Smiřice.

60

'Listen, if you have ears to hear. *Nescis, mi fili, diem neque horam.* Your ambition, Lord Smiřický, will be your downfall. You don't know the day or the hour of that downfall.'

When Reynevan left the cellar, Samson had vanished somewhere, but reappeared a moment later. The two of them walked along backstreets towards Swordsmiths Street.

'Do you think that was wise?' began Reynevan. 'Your closing speech? What was it? A prophecy?'

'A prophecy?' Samson turned his idiotic face towards Reynevan. 'No. I just came out with it. But was it wise? Nothing is wise. At least not here in this world of yours.'

'Aha. Funny I didn't guess at once. Speaking of which, are you going to Soukenická Street?'

'Of course. Aren't you?'

'No. There are probably plenty of casualties. Knowing Rokycana, he'll have ordered them taken to the church. There'll be heaps of work, every doctor will come in handy. Furthermore, Neplach will be looking for me. I can't risk him finding me in the House at the Archangel.'

'Of course.'

They entered the Old Town Square. The naked and bestially mutilated body of Hynek of Kolštejn, the Lord of Kamýk, Hejtman of Litoměřice, knight of the Štěpanice line of the Valdštejns, from the family of the great Markvartices was no longer hanging from the pillory. Father Rokycana must have ordered it taken down. Although it pained him, Father Rokycana tolerated killing and officially even approved of it, within certain limits, obviously – only for a good cause, and only when the ends justified the means.

But he never allowed corpses to be desecrated. Well, let's say, almost never.

'Farewell, Reinmar. Give me the amulet. You're liable to lose it and then Telesma will tear my head off.'

'Farewell, Samson. Oh – I forgot to thank you for sending me the telepathic hints. Thanks to them, it went so smoothly with Smiřický.'

Samson glanced at him, and his dopey face suddenly lit up in a broad, dopey smile.

'It went smoothly thanks to your cunning and intelligence,' he said. 'I didn't help or contribute much, apart from chucking a barrel at Smiřický. And as far as suggestions go, I didn't send you any. I just hurried you along telepathically because I was dying to take a leak.'

There really was plenty of work, and it turned out that every pair of hands with healing skill was needed and came in useful.

The wounded filled both aisles of Our Lady before Týn, and from what Reynevan had heard, there were also numerous patients at Saint Nicholas's. Almost until dusk, Reynevan and the other physicians set fractures, stemmed bleeding and sewed back on what needed sewing on.

And when he finished, when he stood up, when he straightened his aching back, when again he fought down the nausea brought on by the stench of blood and incense, when he was finally about to go and wash, the grey character in grey hose appeared as if from nowhere, like a ghost. Reynevan sighed and followed him, neither questioning nor asking anything.

Bohuchval Neplach was waiting for him in the Bohemian Lion tavern in Celetná Street. The tavern brewed its own excellent beer and was famed for its cuisine, but its fame was calculated into the prices of its dishes, hence Reynevan didn't frequent it, for he couldn't afford it either during his undergraduate days or

now. That day, for the first time, he had the chance to familiar-
ise himself with the décor and the fragrances from the kitchen,
which were, indeed, quite delicious.

The head of the Taborite intelligence service was dining alone
in a corner, skilfully and attentively working on a roast goose, completely ignoring the fact that the grease was staining his sleeves
and dripping down the front of his silver-braided doublet. He
saw Reynevan and indicated for him to sit, making the gesture,
incidentally, using a mug of frothing ale he was washing the goose
down with, then went on eating without raising his eyes. It didn't
even occur to him to offer Reynevan any food or drink.

Flutek ate the entire goose, even the parson's nose, which he
left for last. *Where does he put it,* wondered Reynevan, *when he's so
skinny? Though he does have the appetite of a crocodile. Ha, probably
it's his stressful work. Or parasites.*

Flutek briefly inspected the remains of the goose and decided
it was now so unattractive that he could direct his attention to
something else. He looked up.

'Well?' he asked, wiping grease from his chin. 'Have anything
to tell me? To pass on to me? To report to me? Let me hazard a
guess: you don't.'

'You guessed right.'

The two golden imps appeared in Flutek's black eyes. Both
leaped up and turned somersaults as soon as they appeared.

'I was trailing one fellow,' said Reynevan, pretending not to
notice. 'I almost had him, but I lost him near Saint Valentine's.'

'What bad luck,' said Flutek unemotionally. 'Did you at least
recognise him? Would it be the one who was conspiring with
the Bishop of Wrocław?'

'It would, I believe.'

'But he gave you the slip?'

'He did.'

'So you lost another chance to get your revenge,' said Flutek, taking a sip from his mug. 'You really are unlucky. Fate doesn't go your way – indeed, fate doesn't want to favour you in any way. Many a man would break down with such endless bad luck, but I look at you and see that you put up with it manfully. All I can do is admire and envy you.

'But,' he went on, without waiting for a reaction, 'I have some good news for you. I managed to do something you didn't. I caught up with the rascal, quite close to the Church of Saint Valentine, which very nicely confirms your honesty. Are you glad, Reynevan? Are you grateful? Enough, perhaps, to talk frankly about the tax collector's five hundred grzywna?'

'Have mercy, Neplach.'

'My apologies, I forgot that you know nothing about the affair with the tax collector, that you're innocent and uninformed. So let's return to the rascal I apprehended. Imagine, it's none other than Jan Smiřický of Smiřice, Hejtman of Mělnice and Roudnice. Can you imagine?'

'I can.'

'Well?'

'Nothing.'

Reynevan thought the imps would turn a somersault. But they didn't.

'Your reports about the involvement of Jan of Smiřice in the Silesian conspiracy are now, regrettably, old news,' Flutek went on a moment later. 'A historical moment has dawned and much is happening. Every day brings change; what was significant yesterday means nothing today, and tomorrow will be worth less than dog shit. You do understand, don't you?'

'Oh, but I do.'

'Good. Actually, in the broad scheme of things, it's meaning-less – what does it ultimately matter what Smiřický is convicted of? He'll be condemned to death and executed, for conspiracy, treason, revolt – same bloody difference. What is to be, will be. Your brother will be avenged. Are you glad? Are you grateful?'

'I beg you, Neplach, just don't talk about the tax collector's five hundred grzywna.'

Flutek put down his mug and looked Reynevan straight in the eyes.

'I shan't. It pains me to say it, but Smiřický has scarpered.'

'What?'

'You heard. Smiřický has legged it. He escaped from prison. I don't have all the details yet, just one thing is known: his lover, the daughter of a Prague weaver, helped him to escape. An appalling affair indeed, judge for yourself. A knight from a noble family and his mistress, a plebeian, a weaver's daughter. She must have known she was only a plaything to him, that nothing would come of their liaison, but she still risked her life for her lover. Did he serve her lovage or something?'

'Or perhaps humanity sufficed?' Reynevan maintained eye contact. 'A voice beyond him, whispering: *Hominem memento te?*'

'Is everything all right, Reynevan?'

'I'm weary.'

'Would you like a drink?'

'Thank you, but on an empty stomach . . .'

'Ha. Precisely, Doctor. I say, innkeeper! Over here!'

On the Thursday after the Nativity of the Blessed Virgin Mary, the eleventh of September, five days after the attempted coup, Prokop the Shaven, the victor of Tachov and Stříbro, reached Prague. He arrived with an entire army, the Tábor, the Orphans, Praguians and their supporters, war wagons, artillery, infantry and cavalry. There were twelve thousand soldiers *in toto*.

Among them was Scharley.

Chapter Three

In which Reynevan finds out he must beware of an Old Woman and a Maiden.

'Those scrambled eggs were pretty decent,' said Scharley, 'although I have to say the celery spoiled it a little. It doesn't go with eggs at all. Who, for God's sake, puts grated celery into scrambled eggs? And why? It's some bizarre culinary fantasy of the dear landlady. But let's not gripe, the main thing is my belly's full. The landlady, incidentally, isn't at all bad-looking . . . Junoesque curves, pantherine movements, a gleam in her eye – ha, perhaps I'll also rent a room and stay here for a while? I'm thinking about the winter. I won't be here long now because if not tomorrow, then the day after, Prokop will give us our marching orders. We're heading, so I hear, to Kolín to pay Lord Bořek of Miletínek back for his treachery . . . I say, Reinmar, are we going the right way? I don't know Prague very well, but oughtn't we to go in that direction, beyond the new town hall, towards the Carmelite monastery?'

'We're going through Zderaz to the jetty below the Timber Market. We're taking a boat.'

'Across the Vltava?'

'Absolutely. I've been doing it the whole time lately. I told you, I'm working at Bohuslav's Hospital – it's not far from Saint

Francis's, so you have to hoof it through the entire town to get there. It's more than half an hour's walk, and on market days you have to add another half-hour's waiting in a crowd outside the Svatohavelská Gate. It's quicker by boat. And more comfortable.'

'So you bought a boat.' Scharley nodded with poorly feigned seriousness. 'I see physicians are prospering here. They dress elegantly, live in luxury and breakfast in style, served by attractive little widows. Each of them, like Venetian patricians, has his own gondola. Let's go, let's go, I'm dying to see it.'

The broad-bottomed boat moored to the bank in no way resembled a Venetian gondola, perhaps because it served to ship vegetables. Scharley didn't show his disappointment, but hopped nimbly aboard and sat back comfortably among the baskets. Reynevan greeted the boatman. Six months before, he had treated his leg, which had been horrifically crushed between two barges. In return, the boatman, who rowed every day between Psáry and Bubny, repaid him with free transport. Well, let's say *almost* free transport – during the last half-year, Reynevan had also managed to treat the boatman's wife and two of his six children.

A moment later, the old tub, weighed down by carrots, turnips and cabbages and sitting low in the water, cast off from the bank and sailed down the Vltava.

The water, apart from wood shavings and dead trees, was bearing masses of colourful leaves. It was already September, Reynevan thought, although it was unusually warm.

They moved away from the bank, then sailed across a weir and some faster-flowing water, around which perch were chasing shoals of bleaks.

'Among the numerous virtues of this kind of river navigation,' Scharley observed keenly, 'not least important is the chance to talk with no fear of being eavesdropped. So we can resume our chat from yesterday evening.'

The chat from the day before – beginning in the evening and continuing deep into the night – naturally mainly concerned the events of the previous months, from the Battle of Tachov to the recent coup attempt by Hynek of Kolštejn and its consequences. Reynevan repeated to Scharley everything he had learned from Jan of Smiřice a week earlier and told him of the plans that had been adopted. Predictably, Scharley didn't approve of them at all.

'It's a completely idiotic idea,' he stated. 'It's utter madness to return to Silesia in search of revenge. If I didn't know better, I'd think you haven't grown any wiser during the last two years – why, I'd say you've become even stupider. But that's not true, after all. You have grown wise, Reinmar, proof of which is your deed with Smiřický. You had him in your clutches, at your mercy. And then what? You released him. You're embittered by your brother's death and vengeful, but you released him. Because – even with him in your grasp – you understood the pointlessness of that kind of revenge. For Smiřický isn't to blame for your brother's death; nor that Birkart of Grellenort, although perhaps he killed Peterlin with his own hands; nor, paradoxically, Konrad, Bishop of Wrocław, although he gave the order. For what killed Peterlin is the historical moment. It was the historical moment in the winter of 1425 that took Ambrož to Radkov and Bardo. It was history – not the citizens of Kutná Hora – who threw those captured Hussites down the mineshafts. It wasn't Sigismund's Hungarians but history that raped and butchered the women in captured Louny. It wasn't Žižka but history that murdered and burned alive the people in Chomutov, Beroun and Český Brod. It was also history that killed Hynek of Kolštejn. Are you seeking revenge on history? To be like King Xerxes, lashing the sea?'

Reynevan shook his head but didn't say anything.

They sailed to the island of Trávník. A smell of burning was still drifting from the left bank. In May 1420, during fierce battles with the army loyal to the king, the Lesser Quarter was almost entirely reduced to ashes, and so it remained. There had, admittedly, been attempts to rebuild it, but they somehow lacked passion and enthusiasm. For there were countless other worries; history was doing its best to make sure there were plenty.

'In the light of historical processes,' Scharley continued, looking at the blackened remains of the riverside mills, 'one can thus assume you've already avenged your brother, since you are following in his footsteps and continuing the work he left incomplete. As part of your brother's inheritance, you've received Communion *sub utraque specie* and you're a Hussite. Peterlin, I happen to know, because information has reached me, was indeed a loyal Utraquist and served the cause of the Chalice with real conviction. I say it because there's no shortage of people who've done it for other reasons, sometimes very base – and always very prosaic – ones. But, I repeat, that doesn't apply to your brother, nor, I believe, to you. After all, you – sincerely, devotedly, without a trace of cynicism – are fighting for the cause and the religion for which your brother ended up dead.'

'I don't know how it happens, Scharley, but in your mouth the loftiest ideas end up sounding like vulgar jokes. I know you don't usually hold anything sacred, but—'

'Hold anything sacred?' the penitent interrupted. 'Reinmar? Do my ears deceive me?'

'Don't impute to me perfidy or the lack of my own opinion, please,' Reynevan said through pursed lips. 'Of course I was brought closer to the Hussites by the fact that Peterlin died for them. I know what kind of person my brother was, and I stand without hesitation on the side he supported. But I still have my own mind. I thought the matter through and weighed it up in my heart. I received Holy Communion from the Chalice with complete conviction, for I support the Four Articles, I support the teachings of Wycliffe, I support the Hussites in the matter of liturgy and interpretation of the Bible. I support their world view and their plans to establish social justice.'

'Excuse me, *what* kind of justice?'

'*Omnia sunt communia*, Scharley! "Everything shared" – the whole of divine justice is contained in those words. There are no superiors, no inferiors, no wealthy people, no poor people. Everything is shared! Communism! Doesn't it sound splendid?'

'I haven't heard anything so splendid-sounding for a long time.'

'Why the sarcasm?'

'Don't worry about it. Go on. How else did the Wycliffites endear themselves to you?'

'I support the principle of *sola Scriptura* heart and soul.'

'Aha.'

'One needn't add anything to the Bible and neither can one, for the Bible is sufficiently lucid for every believer to be able to understand it without commentary from the pulpit. There's no need for mediators between the faithful and God. Everybody is equal before the Creator. The authority of the Pope and the church dignitaries can only be accepted when it accords with the will of God Most High and the Holy Bible. In particular, wealth was entrusted to the clergy with the aim of carrying out the obligations imposed by Christ and the Bible. If priests don't carry out those responsibilities, if they sin, their wealth ought to be confiscated.'

'Ah!' said Scharley, livening up. 'Confiscated? I like that. I like the sound of that!'

'Don't sneer. Have you never wondered why such a fire flared up from a spark that leaped from the pyre in Constance here in Prague, in Bohemia? I'll tell you. Do you know how many priests there were in the Prague diocese? Six thousand. How many monasteries? A hundred and sixty. Do you know that in Prague itself, every twentieth person wore a habit or a cassock? And how many parish churches were there in Prague? Forty-four. Wrocław, I remind you, has nine. In Saint Vitus's Cathedral alone, there were exactly three hundred ecclesiastical positions. Can you imagine the fortune taken from prebendaries and annats? No, Scharley, it could not and cannot go on like that. The secularisation of church property is absolutely necessary. The clergy has control over too much worldly property. Such an immense concentration of wealth and power can only cause anger and social tensions. It has to end: their wealth, their tyranny, their hubris, their arrogance, their power. They must return to what Christ instructed them to be: poor and humble servants. And it wasn't Joachim of Fiore who came up with it first, not Ockham, not Waldhauser, not Wycliffe and not Huss, but Francis of Assisi. The Church must be transformed. Reformed. From a church of magnates and politicians, braggarts and fools, obscurantists and hypocrites, from a church of Inquisitors, from a church leading a crusade of criminals, of creatures like, for example, our own Konrad, Bishop of Wrocław, it must transform into a church of Francises.'

'You're wasted working in hospitals. You ought to be a preacher. With regard to me, you can ease off a little. We have enough – a surfeit, even – of preachers in the Tábor, and some of their sermons are enough to make one bring up one's breakfast. So have mercy on the scrambled eggs and celery and rein it in a little. You'll be denouncing simony and debauchery next.'

'Indeed! No one observes church vows or rules! From Rome down to the bottom, to the remotest parish, nothing but simony, dissipation, drunkenness, demoralisation. Is it any wonder there are comparisons with Babylon and Sodom and thoughts of the Antichrist? That the saying *"omne malum a clero"* is doing the rounds? That's why I'm in favour of reform, even of the most radical kind.'

Scharley tore his eyes away from the burned-down Knights Hospitaller's priorate and the charred walls of the Church of Our Lady at the End of the Bridge.

'You're in favour of reform, you say? Then I'll gladden your ears with a story of how we, the Warriors of God, put theory into practice. In May of this year – the news of this probably reached your ears – we set off under Prokop the Shaven on a plundering raid to Lusatia. We sacked and burned down quite a few places of worship, including some churches and monasteries in Hirschfeld, Ostritz and Bernstadt, and also – which might interest you – near Frydland, on the estates of Ulrik Biberstein, your beloved Katarzyna's uncle, I believe. Although we stormed Zgorzelec, we didn't manage to capture it, but in Lubań, taken on the Friday before *Cantate* Sunday, we fell upon a dozen priests and monks, including refugees from Bohemia, Dominicans who had sought refuge in Lubań. Prokop ordered them executed without mercy. So we did. The Czech priests were burned to death, the German ones clubbed to death or drowned in the Kwisa. We organised a massacre of a similar scale four days later in Złotoryja ... You have a strange look on your face. Am I boring you?'

'No. But I think we're talking about completely different things.'

'Indeed? You wish to change the Church, you say. So I'm telling you how we are changing it. You claim to want reforms, even the most radical. I remind you that several kings – such as the Polish Bolesław the Bold, the English Plantagenet Henry the Second, and Wenceslaus the Fourth here, in Prague – have already reformed unruly prelates. But what did it achieve? One rabble-rousing Stanisław of Szczepanów executed, one turbulent priest Thomas à Becket stabbed, one troublemaker John of Nepomuk drowned. A drop in the ocean! Not radical enough. Small scale instead of wholesale. For me, I prefer the methods of Žižka, Prokop and Ambrož. The results are definitely more noticeable. You said that every twentieth Praguian wore a cassock or a habit before the revolution. And how many will you encounter in the street today?'

'Not many. Beware, we're going under the Stone Bridge, they always spit from it. And occasionally piss.'

Indeed, the bridge's balustrades were teeming with street urchins trying to spit or piss on every boat, barge or punt passing beneath. Fortunately, too many vessels were gliding by down below for the street urchins to manage to insult more than a few. Reynevan and Scharley's boat had luck on its side.

The current was carrying them nearer to the left bank. They sailed past the badly damaged archbishop's palace and the ruins of the Augustinian monastery. And beyond, above the charred remains of the Lesser Quarter and the river, the rock of Hradčany rose impressively, proudly crowned by the Hrad and the soaring spires of Saint Vitus's Cathedral.

The boatman shoved the vessel into the current with a boathook and they picked up speed. The right bank, beyond the city wall, was covered with the dense buildings of the Old Town, while the left bank was more rustic – almost entirely taken up by vineyards that at one time, before the revolution, mainly belonged to the monasteries.

'Ahead of us is Saint Francis's, if I'm not mistaken.' The penitent pointed to a church tower on the right bank. 'Shall we disembark?'

'Not yet. We'll sail over to the weir – it's a stone's throw to Soukenická Street.'

'Scharley.'

'Yes.'

'Slow down for a moment. We're in no hurry, and I'd like to ...'

Scharley stopped and waved at the girls in the soapmaking workshop, causing a concert of giggles. He shook a fist at some kids who were sticking out their tongues and shouting childish insults. He stretched and glanced at the sun peeping out from behind the church spire.

'I can guess what you want,' Scharley said.

'I listened to your reflections about historical processes,' replied Reynevan, 'although Samson tells me every day that revenge is a vain thing. King Xerxes lashing the sea is pathetic and ridiculous. All the same ...'

'I'm listening with attentiveness. And growing anxiety.'

'I'd love to get my hands on the whoresons that killed Peterlin. That Birkart Grellenort in particular.'

Scharley shook his head and sighed. 'I was afraid you'd say that. Do you recall, my dear Reinmar, Silesia two years ago? And the black riders shouting: "We are here!"? The bats in the Cistercian forest? Huon of Sagar saved our arses then. Had Huon not made it in time, the hide from our arses would be hanging today, beautifully dried, above Birkart's fireplace. I pass over the minor fact that Birkart is clearly a minion of Bishop Konrad, the most powerful individual in the whole of Silesia, a man who merely has to bend his little finger to have us impaled. And that Grellenort himself isn't just some ordinary thug, but a sorcerer. The fellow can turn into a bird, and you want to catch him, you say? And how, I wonder?'

'A way could be found. It always can; all that's needed are good intentions. And a little cunning. I know it's madness to return to Silesia, but even insane enterprises can succeed if the plan is feasible. Am I right?'

Scharley looked at him keenly. 'I observe,' he announced, 'the evident and fascinating influence of your new connexions. I have in mind, naturally, the notorious company from the House at the Archangel apothecary shop. I don't doubt that one can learn an enormous amount from them. The snag is to select something worth learning from that wealth. How does that apply to you?'

'I'm doing my best.'

'You deserve credit. So tell me, how did you fall in with them at all? It can't have been easy.'

'It wasn't.' Reynevan smiled at the recollection. 'To tell the truth, an almost miraculous accident – a coincidence – was required. And just imagine, one occurred. On a certain very hot July day, *Anno Domini* 1426.'

Svatopluk Fraundinst, chief physician of the hospital of the Knights of the Cross with the Red Star, was a man in his prime, well built and handsome enough without special effort. Whenever the opportunity presented itself, he seduced and fucked the pre-revolutionary Benedictine nuns who had been driven by the Hussites from their own convent and were working in the hospital. Hardly a week went by without the doctor dragging a sister into a cubbyhole, from which groaning, moaning and appeals to the saints could soon afterwards be heard.

Reynevan had suspected that Svatopluk Fraundinst was a sorcerer from the very beginning, from the first day he took up work at the hospital and began assisting the surgeon with operations. Firstly, Svatopluk Fraundinst was a Vyšehrad canon, a *doctor medicinae* from Charles University with *licentia docendi* in Salerno, Padua and Krakow. He had been a student of Matěj of Bechyně and a close associate of the famous Bruno of Osenbrughe. In his day, Master Bruno of Osenbrughe had been a living legend of European medicine, and Matěj of Bechyně was strongly suspected of a fondness for alchemy and magic, both white and black. The very fact that Svatopluk Fraundinst earned his living as a surgeon was also significant – university physicians didn't engage in surgery, leaving it to executioners and barbers; they did not even stoop to phlebotomy, which was extolled in their own faculties as a remedy for everything. Physicians who were also sorcerers, however, didn't shun surgery and were good at it – and Fraundinst was quite simply an extremely able surgeon. If you added the typical mannerisms of speech and gesture, the ring with a pentagram he wore quite openly, and the seemingly unimportant and casual allusions, one was left almost without any doubt that Svatopluk Fraundinst had more than a nodding acquaintance with magic, and that he was trying to sound Reynevan out regarding the same matter. Reynevan, of course, was very much on his guard, bluffing and avoiding traps as cleverly as he could. Times were hard and one couldn't be certain of anyone or anything.

Until one day in July, on the eve of Saint James the Apostle's Day, it so happened that a sawyer was brought from a nearby lumber mill, seriously wounded by a saw blade. Blood was gushing out and Fraundinst, Reynevan and a pre-revolutionary Benedictine nun were doing what they could to staunch the flow. It was going poorly, perhaps because of the wound's size, perhaps because they were simply having a bad day. When, yet again, blood from an artery squirted into his eye, Doctor Svatopluk swore so crudely that the Benedictine nun first reeled and then ran away. After her departure, the doctor used a ligating spell, also called 'Alcmena's charm'. He did it with a single gesture and word and Reynevan had never in his life seen a spell cast so efficiently. The artery closed up immediately and the blood began to darken and clot. Fraundinst turned his blood-spattered face towards Reynevan. It was obvious what he wanted. Reynevan sighed.

'*Quare insidiaris animae meae?*' he muttered. 'Why layest thou a snare for me, Saul?'

'I've revealed myself, so you must, too,' the wizard said, grinning. 'Come on, O cautious Witch of Endor. Fear not. *Non veniet tibi quicquam mali.*'

They both cast the spell simultaneously, and the power of the collective magic ligated and sealed up all the blood vessels.

'And that same *doctor medicinae*,' Scharley said, 'introduced you to the congregation of sorcerers who gather at the House at the Archangel apothecary's shop. The one we are approaching right now.'

Scharley had guessed right. They were in Soukenická Street and the apothecary's shop was now visible behind a row of spinners' and weavers' workshops and mercers' shops. Over the entrance, high above the door, hung a bay window with narrow panes decorated with the wooden figure of a winged archangel. The figure was quite battered by age and it was impossible to say which archangel it was. Reynevan had never asked. Neither the first time, when he was taken there by Fraundinst in August 1426, on a Thursday falling on the day of the Beheading of Saint John the Baptist, nor subsequently.

'Before we enter, one more thing.' Reynevan stopped Scharley again. 'A request. I'd be grateful if you would restrain yourself.'

Scharley stamped to dislodge from his boot some shit – at first glance probably canine, although there was no certainty, as some children were hanging around the area.

'We owe it to Samson,' Reynevan continued with emphasis.

'Firstly,' Scharley raised his head, 'you've already said it. Secondly: it is beyond question. He is our comrade, and those four words suffice.'

'I'm glad you see it like that. Believe in it or not, doubt it or not, but resign yourself to the fact that Samson is imprisoned in our world. He is, like an incluse, locked in a foreign mortal shell, and not the most beautiful, you'll admit. He's doing what he can to free himself, he's searching for help ... Perhaps he'll finally find it here, in Prague, at the House at the Archangel, perhaps this very day ... Because this very day—'

'This very day,' interrupted the penitent with a faint tinge of impatience in his voice, 'a world-famous mage, *magnus nigromanticus*, has come from Salzburg to stay in the House at the Archangel. Perhaps he will succeed where the Prague sorcerers failed. You've already told me. A good few times.'

'And you snorted each time and made mocking faces.'

'It's instinctive with me. I react like that when I hear about magic and incluses—'

'So please would you control your instincts today.' Reynevan cut him off quite sharply. 'Would you, mindful of your friendship with Samson, not snort or make faces. Do you promise?'

'Yes, I do. I won't make faces. I'll be serious. I shall not once, may God punish me, roar with laughter when you start discussing witchcraft, demons, parallel worlds and existences, astral bodies—'

'Scharley!'

'I'll hold my tongue. Are we going in?'

'We are.'

It was dark inside the apothecary, and the impression of darkness was intensified by the colour of the wood panelling and furniture. When you entered from the sunlight – as they had – you couldn't see a thing for a moment. You could only stop, blink and breathe in the heady scent of dust, camphor, mint, honey, amber, saltpetre and turpentine.

'At your service, m'lords . . . At your service . . . M'lords would like . . . ?'

Just as he had over a year before, on the Beheading of John the Baptist, Beneš Kejval appeared behind the counter, bald pate gleaming in the semi-darkness.

'How may I help you?' he asked, exactly as he had back then.

'Does m'lord possess *Cremor tartari?*' Svatopluk Fraundinst asked casually.

'*Cremor*,' said the apothecary, wiping his pate, '*tartari!*'

'Precisely. I also need a little *unguentum populeum.*'

Reynevan swallowed in amazement. From what he'd heard, Svatopluk Fraundinst ought to be a famous and respected guest at the House at the Archangel, but the bald apothecary gave the impression he'd never seen him before.

'We have *unguentum*, freshly prepared . . . But *cremor tartari* is harder to come by just now . . . How much do you need?'

'Ten drachmas.'

'Ten? I may be able to find that much. I'll have a look. Come through, gentlemen.'

Only much later did Reynevan find out that the apparently inane welcoming ritual had its purpose. The congregation of the House at the Archangel apothecary's shop operated in utter secrecy. If everything was in order, the customer asked for two – always two – medicines. If he asked for one, it would mean he was being blackmailed or being followed. If, however, a trap had been set in the apothecary's shop itself, Beneš Kejval would give a warning by saying he only had half of one of the quantities.

The actual apothecary's shop was concealed beyond the oak door behind the shop counter. It was furnished in typical fashion for an apothecary's shop: there were cabinets with dozens of small drawers, numerous dark glass jars and bottles, brass pestles and mortars and weighing scales. A dried monster – standard decoration for sorcerers' workshops, apothecaries' shops and conjurors' booths – hung on a string from the ceiling. It looked like a mermaid, half-young woman, half-fish, but in reality, it was a fabricated fish, dried and split open. A ray, stretched out on a board, had convincingly taken on a mermaid's shape: its nostrils imitated eyes and the broken cartilage of its fins, arms. The fakes were manufactured in Antwerp and Genoa, where the rays found their way via Arab merchants or ever-present Portuguese mariners. Some of them were so skilfully made that only with the greatest difficulty could they be distinguished from genuine mermaids. But there was a fail-safe touchstone of authenticity – namely that genuine mermaids were at least a hundred times more expensive than fakes and no apothecary's shop could afford them.

'Antwerpian work.' Scharley sized up the dried monstrosity with an expert eye. 'I once flogged a few of them myself. They sold like hot cakes. There's still one in the Golden Apple apothecary's shop in Wrocław.'

Beneš Kejval glanced at him with interest. He was the only sorcerer at the Archangel who didn't teach at the university. He hadn't even studied. He had simply inherited the shop. But he was an unparalleled pharmacist and a master at mixing medicines – magical and ordinary. His speciality was an aphrodisiac made from powdered agaric, pine nuts, coriander and pepper. It was joked that after consuming that medicine even a corpse would leap up from his bier and bound towards a brothel.

'Go down to the lower chamber, gentlemen. Everybody's there. They're waiting for you.'

'What about you, Beneš? Aren't you coming?' Reynevan asked.

'I'd like to,' said the apothecary, sighing, 'but someone has to mind the store. People are coming in all the time. It doesn't bode well for the world if there are so many sick people dependent on medicine.'

'Or perhaps,' Scharley replied with a smile, 'it's only hypochondria?'

'Then it bodes even worse. Make haste, gentlemen. Aha, Reynevan! Watch out for the books.'

'I shall.'

The apothecary's shop led out into a courtyard. A well, green with moss, suffused the air with an unhealthy dampness, bravely aided by a misshapen elder bush overshadowing the wall that appeared to grow not out of the ground but from a pile of rotting leaves. The bush effectively concealed a small door. The lintel was almost entirely covered in cobwebs. Thick, dense cobwebs. It was clear no one had passed through the door in years.

'An illusion,' Doctor Svatopluk explained calmly, plunging a hand into a cocoon of cobwebs. 'Illusory magic. Straightforward. Quite primitive.'

When pushed, the door opened inwardly – along with the illusory cobwebs, which, after it opened, looked like a thick piece of felt cut with a knife. Beyond the door was a spiral staircase leading upwards. The staircase was steep and so narrow that anyone climbing it would inevitably rub off plaster from the wall onto their shoulders. After several minutes of panting, they stood outside another door. Nobody had bothered camouflaging that one.

There was a library on the other side, full of books, scrolls, papyri and various other strange exhibits. There was no room for anything else.

Piles of incunables were lying simply everywhere; you couldn't take a step without tripping over something like Nicolas Flamel's *Le sommaire philosophique*, Rhazes's *Kitab al-Mansuri*, Morien's *De expositione specierum* or Gervase of Tilbury's *De imagine mundi*. Every incautious step risked a painful bang on the ankles from a metal-edged edition of a work of the renown of Albertus Magnus's *Semita recta*, Witelo's *Perspectiva* or Caesarius of Heisterbach's *Illustria miracula*. It was enough to bump imprudently into a bookshelf for Artephius's *Philosophia de arte occulta*, William of Auvergne's *De universo* or Thomas of Cantimpré's *Opus de natura rerum* to fall on one's head in a cloud of dust.

In all this confusion, one could unwittingly bump into something or accidentally touch something that shouldn't have been touched without exercising great caution. For it happened that grimoires, treatises about magic and compendiums of spells could spontaneously cast spells themselves – all one had to do was make a careless movement, knock or tap something and an accident was waiting to happen. Particularly dangerous in this regard was *The Grand Grimoire*, and *Aldaraia* and *Lemegeton* could also be extremely dangerous. As early as his second visit to the House at the Archangel, Reynevan had the misfortune of toppling a thick book which was none other than *Liber de Nyarlathotep* from a table piled up with books and scrolls. As the ancient incunable, sticky with greasy dust, slammed onto the floor, the walls shuddered and four of the six jars containing homunculi on top of the cupboard exploded. One of them turned into a featherless bird, another into something like an octopus, a third into an aggressive scarlet scorpion, and a fourth into a miniature Pope in pontifical vestments. Before anyone could react, all four of them melted into green, foul-smelling slime, while at the same time the midget Pope managed to squawk: '*Beati immaculati, Cthulhu fhtagn!*' There had been an awful lot of cleaning up to do.

The incident amused most of the Archangel's sorcerers, although several of them weren't blessed with a sense of humour and Reynevan wasn't elevated much in their estimation, to put it mildly. But only one of the mages continued to glower at him long after the incident and let him feel keenly what antipathy meant.

That man was – as can easily be guessed – the librarian and caretaker of the book collection.

'Greetings, Štěpán.'

Štěpán of Drahotuše, the librarian, raised his head from the sumptuously illuminated pages of Apollonius of Tyana's *Archidoxo magicum*.

'Greetings, Reynevan.' He smiled. 'Nice to see you again. You haven't been here in ages.'

Reynevan had devoted considerable effort to healing his relationship with Štěpán of Drahotuše following the gaffe in the library. But he accomplished it and with results that exceeded expectations.

'Could this be the Master Scharley,' said the librarian, scratching his nose with dusty fingers, 'about whom I've heard so much? Welcome, welcome.'

Štěpán of Drahotuše, who was descended from old Moravian nobility, was a monk, an Augustinian and – naturally – a sorcerer. He had been friends with the mages of the Archangel's congregation for many years at the university, but had moved permanently to the hiding place in the apothecary's shop in 1420 after his Hradčany monastery had been sacked and burned down.

Unlike the rest of the mages, he almost never ventured out of the apothecary's shop – or, more precisely, its library – and he didn't visit the city. He was a walking library catalogue, knew every book and could quickly locate them, which, in the conditions of the chaos prevailing there, was a simply inestimable skill. Reynevan was very happy to be friends with the Moravian and spent long hours in the library. He was interested in herbal medicine and pharmaceutics and the Archangel's library was a veritable mine of information in that regard. In addition to the famous classic herbals and pharmacopoeias like those of Dioscorides, Strabo, Avicenna, Hildegard of Bingen and Nicolaus the Superior, the library contained some real treasures. There was Geber's *Kitab Sirr al-Asrar* and Shabbethai Donnolo's *Sefer ha-Mirkahot*; there were unknown works by Maimonides, Hali, Apuleius and Herrad of Landsberg, as well as other *antidotaria, dispensatoria* and *ricettaria* that Reynevan had never seen or heard of before. And he doubted that they had been heard of at the university.

'Very well.' Štěpán of Drahotuše closed a book and stood up. 'Let's go down to the lower chamber. I believe we'll arrive right on time, for they'll probably be finishing soon. In any case, it's quite extravagant to begin conjuration not at midnight, like any normal, self-respecting sorcerer, but at the first hour of the day, but, well ... It's not my business to criticise the actions of somebody like *valde venerandus et eximius* Vincent Reffin Axleben of Salzburg, a living legend, a walking celebrity. Ha, I cannot wait to see how the master among masters is doing with Samson ...'

'Did he arrive yesterday?'

'Yesterday afternoon. He dined, drank and was curious to discover how he could help us, so we introduced Samson to him. Venerandus sprang up and was about to leave, convinced we were mocking him. Samson used the same trick he treated us to last year: he greeted us in Latin and repeated it in Koine and Aramaic. You ought to have seen the honourable Master Vincent's face! But it worked, as it had with us. The honourable Vincent Reffin looked at Samson kindlier, with more interest – why, he even smiled, as much as the muscles of his face permit, which are fixed in a permanent grimace as sombre as it is arrogant. Then the two of them locked themselves away in the *occultum*—'

'Just the two of them?'

'The master among masters,' replied the Moravian with a smile, 'is also extravagant in this regard. He values discretion, even if it borders on tactlessness, not to say rudeness. The old quack is a guest here, dammit. It doesn't bother me, I don't give a hoot, and Bezděchovský is above that kind of thing, but Fraundinst, Teggendorf and Telesma are ... furious, to put it mildly, and sincerely wish failure on Axleben. That wish will be fulfilled, in my opinion.'

'Eh?'

'He's making the same mistake we did at Epiphany. Do you remember, Reinmar?'

'I do.'

'So let's make haste. This way, Master Scharley.'

From the library, they went out into the cloister, and from the cloister, they went downstairs to the ground floor, where they stood before an iron-bound door. An oval plaque on the door depicted a bronze serpent of Moses, *serpens mercurialis*. Above the serpent was a chalice with the Sun and Moon rising from it. Beneath it shone the letters V.I.T.R.I.O.L., an abbreviation of *Visita Interiora Terrae Rectificando Invenies Occultum Lapidem*, a secret transmutational formula used by alchemists.

Štěpán of Drahotuše touched the door and uttered a spell.

The door opened with a grinding and a scraping. As they entered, Scharley sighed deeply.

'Not bad,' he muttered, looking around. 'Not bad . . . I have to admit.'

'I was also speechless the first time I saw it,' said Reynevan, smiling. 'Then I grew accustomed to it.'

The work of the alchemic laboratory, which filled an enormous wine cellar, never stopped; something was happening there every single day. The stoves and athanors were never extinguished, relentlessly pouring out heat, which was appreciated in the winter and also on cold summer days. Calcination and annealing were carried out in the athanors, where all sorts of substances were transformed from the *albedo* to the *nigredo* phase, giving off dreadful smells. Something was constantly being filtered, distilled or extracted in flasks, accompanied by turbulent effervescence and even more overpowering stenches. Acids acted on metals in large aludels, leading to the transmutation of base metals into noble ones, with varying results. Mercury – or *argentum vivum* – bubbled in crucibles, sulphur was melted in cupolas, nitro was liberated and salt was deposited in retorts, with fumes making the eyes water. Substances were dissolving, coagulating and sublimating, and acid spurted all over the place, burning holes in the pages of priceless specimens of Ramon Llull's *De quinta essentia*, Roger Bacon's *Speculum alchemiae* and Arnaldus de Villa Nova's *Theatrum chemicum* lying open on tables. Foul-smelling pails of *caput mortuum* littered the floor.

There were usually at least three or four alchemists at work in the laboratory, as there had been when Svatopluk Fraundinst brought Reynevan there for the first time. That day – unusually – there was only one.

'Hello, Master Edlinger!'

'Don't come any closer,' growled the alchemist, keeping his

eyes on a large flask nestling in hot sand. 'It's liable to explode!'

Duke Wenceslaus, the son of Přemek of Opava, had made the acquaintance in Mainz of Edlinger Brehm, a bachelor of science from Heidelberg, and invited him to Głubczyce. Master Edlinger accepted and spent some time familiarising the young duke with alchemic theory and practice. Wenceslaus – like many of his contemporary dukes – was obsessed with alchemy and the philosophers' stone, so Brehm lived in splendour and prosperity until the Inquisition started to take an interest in him. When the threat of the stake began to hang over Głubczyce, the alchemist fled to the university in Prague, where the turbulent year of 1419 found him. A foreigner, a German who stood out by speaking poor Czech, would certainly have had a hard time, but the mages from the Archangel recognised his skill and saved him.

Edlinger Brehm seized the flask in iron tongs and poured the gurgling blue liquid into a bowl full of something that looked like frogspawn. It hissed, smoked and gave off a foul smell.

'*Sakradonnerwetterhimmelkreuzalleluja!*' There was no doubt that the alchemist had expected a better result. '*Eine total fucking Sache! Scheisse, Scheisse und noch einmal Scheisse!* Are you still here? I'm busy! Aha, I understand . . . You've come to see how Axleben has got on with Samson?'

'Precisely,' confirmed Štěpán of Drahotuše. 'Let's go. Aren't you coming?'

'Actually,' said Edlinger Brehm, wiping his hands on a rag and glaring at the bowl of smoking frogspawn with eyes full of regret, 'actually, I can. There's nothing keeping me here.'

There was a small door in an inconspicuous corner of the alchemic laboratory behind an inconspicuous curtain. For an uninitiated person – if one were ever to make it there – the door appeared to open onto a storeroom full of crates, barrels and bottles. Those in the know moved a lever hidden inside one of the barrels, uttered a spell and the wall slid open to reveal a dark opening that smelled of graveyards. At least, it gave that impression the first time.

Edlinger Brehm lit a magical lantern with another spell and led them on. Štěpán of Drahotuše, Reynevan and Scharley followed him onto steps leading downwards in a spiral around the walls of a dim and apparently bottomless shaft. Cold and damp rose up from the bottom.

Štěpán of Drahotuše turned around. 'Remember, Reynevan?'

It was no palace hallway where we were,
but just a natural passage under ground,
which had a wretched floor and lack of light.

'Samson Honeypot,' Scharley guessed immediately. 'I meant to say: Dante Alighieri. *The Divine Comedy*. Our comrade's favourite work of poetry.'

'There's no doubt it's his favourite,' said the Moravian, smiling, 'for he quotes it extremely often. Your comrade has recalled many a quotation from the *Inferno*, on these stairs in particular. You, sir, I see, know him well in that respect.'

'I'd know him by that at the end of the world.'

They didn't go far down the staircase, only two floors, although the shaft was much deeper and the steps vanished into a blackness from which the splashing of water could be heard. It was a natural cavern, whose history was lost in oblivion, extending down to the Vltava. Nobody knew who had discovered the cave or when, nor who used it or for what purpose, nor who had left this building that had stood there for centuries concealing the entrance to the cavern. Most clues pointed to the Celts – the cavern's walls were covered in partly rubbed-off, moss-obscured reliefs and paintings, which were dominated by typical intricately interwoven ornaments and circles filled with meandering lines. Here and there appeared no less typical wild boars, red deer, horses and horned human figures.

Edlinger Brehm pushed open a heavy door. They entered.

In the underground – so-called 'lower' – chamber, at a table laden with food, sat the rest of the Archangel mages: Svatopluk Fraundinst, Radim Tvrdík, Jošt Dun and Walter of Teggendorf. And Jan Bezděchovský of Bezděchov.

Jošt Dun, called Telesma, like Štěpán of Drahotuše, had once been a monk – which was betrayed by his hair. After his tonsure had grown back, unruly strands stuck out above his ears, making their owner look a little like an eagle owl. From what Reynevan knew about him, since his early years, Telesma had practised *ora et labora* in the Benedictine monastery in Opatovice, where he had also first come into contact with the secret arts. He had then studied in Heidelberg, where he perfected his magical knowledge. He was an absolute authority regarding talismans in terms of theoretical knowledge about them and also with respect to their practical construction. He also cast quite accurate horoscopes, which he traded, selling them to various false prophets, pseudoastrologers and fake fortune tellers, and making tidy profits from doing so. Beside the takings from the apothecary's shop, Jošt Dun's earnings were the congregation's chief source of income.

Walter of Teggendorf, who was now getting on in years, had been a student at Vienna, Bologna, Coimbra and Salamanca, and had *facultas docendi* at all those schools. He was marked by an immense reverence for medicine, alchemy and Arabic magic, particularly for Geber and al-Kindi, that is, as he said himself, for Abu Musa Jabir ibn Hayyan and Abu Yusuf Ya'qub ibn Ishaq al-Kindi. Teggendorf's fascinations found their expression in his approach to the Samson affair. In his opinion, jinn were to blame for everything. He claimed that in his current shape, Samson was a *majnun*, or a person in whose body a more powerful jinn had imprisoned as a punishment an inferior jinn that he had vanquished. There was nothing to be done with imprisonment like that, pronounced the German sorcerer. All that remained was to conduct oneself well and wait for an amnesty.

The *Reverendissimus Doctor* Jan Bezděchovský of Bezděchov was the oldest, most experienced and most respected of the Archangel sorcerers. Hardly anyone knew any personal details about him as he didn't like to talk about himself. He was at least seventy, which, with respect to his youthful appearance, testified to considerable magical powers. It was known he had lectured at the Sorbonne during the reign of King Charles V the Wise, who died in 1380, and in accordance with the regulations, a university lecturer had to be at least twenty-one years old. The universities he had studied and taught at certainly included Paris, Padua, Montpellier and Prague; and those four definitely didn't exhaust the list. It was rumoured that in Prague Bezděchovský became involved in a serious quarrel and a bruising personal feud with the rector, the celebrated Jan Šindel. The basis of the conflict, about which Reynevan had already heard during his studies at the academy, wasn't known, but was behind Bezděchovský's departure from the university and his severing of all contact with it. After 1417, Bezděchovský simply vanished. People wondered long and hard about what had become of him, Reynevan among them. And now he knew.

'Greetings, young man,' said Bezděchovský. Only he among the entire company didn't address Reynevan by his first name. 'Greetings to you, too, Master Scharley. Your fame goes before you. We heard it's your second year with the Taborites. So how is the war going? What's new?'

He was the only member of the company not to interest

himself in politics. The old man was quite indifferent to the events of the war that occupied the interest of the whole of Prague. He only asked about them out of politeness.

'Aye, the war's going well,' Scharley replied politely. 'The right cause is winning, the wrong one losing. Our chaps are beating the foreigners. I meant to say: the good are beating the bad. I mean: Order is triumphing over Chaos. And God rejoices.'

'Oh, oh,' said the old wizard happily. 'How wonderful! Sit beside me, Master Scharley, tell me . . .'

Reynevan joined the other mages. Radim Tvrdík poured him some wine, Spanish Alicante judging from the bouquet.

'How are things?' asked Štěpán of Drahotuše, nodding towards the closed door leading to the *occultum*, the room of divination and conjuration. 'Any results? Or at least some heavenly or earthly signs?'

Svatopluk Fraundinst snorted. Telesma did, too, although he didn't raise his head from the talisman he was polishing with jeweller's rouge.

'*Herr Meister* Axleben prefers to work alone,' said Teggendorf. 'He doesn't like people looking over his shoulder. He guards his secret methods closely.'

'Even from those who play host to him,' Fraundinst remarked sourly, 'thus showing what he thinks of them – as nothing but thieves, out to steal his secrets. He probably hides his pouch and poulaines under his pillow before going to sleep so we can't steal them, either.'

'He began at sunrise,' interjected Radim Tvrdík, seeing that Reynevan was more interested in Samson Honeypot than opinions about Axleben. 'Indeed, all alone with the object, meaning Samson. He didn't want any help, although we offered it. He didn't ask for anything, neither instrument, nor incense, nor *aspergillum*, so he must be wielding some powerful artefact.'

'Or it's true what they say about *Manusfortis*,' added Brehm. 'He shouldn't be underestimated.'

'We aren't underestimating him,' assured Telesma. 'It is, after all, in spite of everything, Vincent Axleben, *magnus experimentator et nigromanticus*, in person. He's certainly not short on magical knowledge. He's a master. So he's entitled to be somewhat extravagant.'

'What a grand word,' said Fraundinst, grimacing. 'In my village, Malá Smědava, people wouldn't call someone like Axleben "extravagant". They'd call him – simply, coarsely and bluntly – an ignorant fucking swine.'

'No one's perfect,' noted Teggendorf. 'Including Vincent Axleben. And the fact that his working methods are bizarre? Why, we'll judge how effective they are. We'll find out and judge them as the Bible instructs: *a fructibus eorum*.'

'I'll wager,' Svatopluk went on, 'that the *fructus* will be sour and misbegotten. Who wants to bet?'

'I definitely don't,' said Štěpán of Drahotuše with a shrug. 'For men do not gather grapes of thorns, or figs of thistles. Axleben won't succeed with Samson and it'll end as we did at Epiphany. In other words: in a failure. Axleben will be undone as we were – by his pride and vanity.'

A delicate trail of smoke spiralled up from the fumigating incense – the classic blend of aloes and nutmeg recommended by most grimoires – smouldering in a cast-iron tripod. Samson, having been put into a trance, was lying on a large oaken table. He was completely naked and on his enormous, almost hairless body could be seen numerous magical and Kabbalist signs, written in magical ink made of cinnabar, alum and vitriol of Cyprus. He had been arranged with his limbs spread out so that his head, arms and legs were touching the appropriate points on the Circle of Solomon – the Hebrew letters Lamed, Vav, Yodh, Kaf and Nun. He was surrounded by nine black candles, a bowl of salt and a goblet of water.

Teggendorf and Brehm, standing at opposite corners of the table and both wearing flowing ceremonial robes, intoned in hushed voices the psalms demanded by the ritual. They had just finished *Ecce quam bonum* and were beginning *Dominus inluminatio mea.*

Bezděchovský went closer. He was wearing a white robe and pointed hat measuring about a cubit and marked with hieroglyphs. He was holding an athame, a double-edged dagger with an ivory handle, which was a prerequisite during goetia.

'Athame,' he said loudly, 'you, who are Athanatos, who knows not death, and who are *al-dhame*, the sign of blood! *Conjuro te cito mihi obedire! Hodomos! Helon, Heon, Homonoreum! Dominus inluminatio mea et salus mea, quem timebo? Dominus protector vitae meae a quo trepidabo?*'

Bezděchovský touched the flame of each candle, the water and the salt in turn with the athame's blade.

'I curse you,' he said each time, 'O Creature of Fire, in the name of the Power: may the apparition and the nocturnal spectre fly from you. I curse you, O Creature of Water, in the name of the Power: expel from yourself impurity and all blemish. In the name of the Power, in the name of Ambriel and Ehesatiel, be blessed, O Creature of Salt, may the ill will of demons leave you. And may the good of the Creator return in its place.'

Svatopluk Fraundinst, who was assisting the old man, approached and handed him a boline, a knife with a crescent-shaped blade. Bezděchovský made four ritual movements in the air with it.

'By all the names of God, by Adonay, El, Elohim, Elohe, Zebaoth, Elion, Escerchie, Jah, Tetragrammaton, Sadai, we command you, demons circling here and present in your astral form, to appear before us in human shape, untainted by any corruption or monstrousness, able to speak plainly and comprehensibly, able to reply to the questions that will be posed to you. Come and be obedient to us, I command you by Daniel, Gediel and Theodoniel, by Klarimum, Habdanum and Inglotum! Come!'

Nothing happened, naturally. No one came and no one appeared. But that was quite normal at that stage of the conjuration.

'*Ego vos invoco,*' Bezděchovský continued, lifting up the boline, '*et invocando vos conjure, per eum cui obediunt omnes creaturae, et per hoc nomen ineffabile, Tetragrammaton Jehovah, in quo est plasmatum omne saeculum, quo audito elementu corruunt, ar concutitur, mare retrograditur, ignis extinguitur, terra tremit, omnesque exercitus Coelestium, Terrestrium et Infernorum tremunt et turbantur! Venite, venite, quid tardatis? Imperat vobis Rex regum!* Titeip, Azia, Hyn, Jen, Minosel, Achadan, Vay, Ey, Haa, Eye, Exe, El, El, Va, Vaa, Yaaaaa!'

The mage's voice rose as the spells were uttered, reaching higher and higher registers, until it became almost a wailing, an inhuman, unnatural keening. The air vibrated perceptibly, the candles sparked and dimmed. Suddenly there was a smell of wild animals, the stench of decay and lion's urine. The darkness that filled the chamber thickened, took on shapes and swelled like a cumulus. Something moved inside the cumulus, brimmed over, writhed like an eel in a sack, like a tangle of vipers. Reynevan saw bloodshot eyes suddenly flash in the tangle, saw dreadful toothy jaws snap, saw monstrous physiognomies looming. His amazement quickly changed into panic. Not just out of fear of that nightmarish monstrousness, but also at the thought that Samson might indeed have something to do with it.

But Jan Bezděchovský of Bezděchov was a powerful mage and had everything in hand. Under the force of his spell, plaster fell from the ceiling and the candle flames turned red and then blue. A roar and boom reverberated and the macabre tangle hardened into a sphere as black as anthracite whose surface appeared to absorb all light. After the next spell, the sphere vanished with a hiss. Samson Honeypot, lying on the table, stiffened and trembled, then went limp and lay motionless.

'By Cratares,' said Bezděchovský. 'By Capitel! I summon you, O Creature! Say who you are. Plainly and without lies, say who and what you are!'

Samson's body trembled powerfully again.

'*Verum, sine mendacio, certum et verissimum,*' he said in a somewhat altered voice. '*Quod est inferius est sicut quod est superius, et quod est superius est sicut quod est inferius, ad perpetranda Miracula Rei Unius.*'

Radim Tvrdík, who was sitting beside Reynevan, gasped aloud and Štěpán of Drahotuše swore under his breath.

'That is the *Emerald Tablet,*' he explained in a whisper, seeing Reynevan's enquiring expression. 'He is speaking the words of Hermes Trismegistus. As though ... As though—'

'As though he were mocking us.' Jošt Dun completed his sentence in a whisper.

'By Alpharoz!' Jan Bezděchovský raised his hands. 'By Bedrimubal! *Per signum Domini Tau!* Who are you? Speak! Where is the truth?'

'Separate earth from fire,' Samson's voice replied almost immediately. 'Separate with great care that which is subtle from that which is gross. And the Power will rise up from Earth to Heaven, then will descend to the Earth again and draw into itself all higher and lower creatures. Then you will possess the glory of this world. And all darkness will flee.'

'Vazotas, Zamarath, Katipa!' cried Bezděchovský. 'Astroschio, Abedumabal, Asath! Speak! I summon you to speak!'

There was a long silence, interrupted only by the sizzling of candles.

'*Completum est . . .*' Samson's calm voice finally sounded. '*Completum est quod dixi de Operatione Solis.*'

Neither the spells nor the names of God helped, neither Astroschio nor Abedumabal helped. The ritualistic gestures made over Samson using the athame and the boline didn't help. Fumigation with incense didn't help. The aspergillum of verbena, periwinkle, sage, mint and rosemary didn't help. Both the *Greater* and the *Lesser Keys of Solomon* proved to be powerless, and the *Enchiridion* and *The Grand Grimoire* fared no better. Magic had almost destroyed the building, but Samson didn't say another word.

The wizards of the Archangel pretended they weren't bothered by the fiasco, saying, *Never mind, we've made a start and we'll see happens next.* Jan Bezděchovský, who found it hardest to put on a brave face, only managed to cite several similar cases of change of personality – he had in mind among others the *casus* of Poppo of Osterna, the Grand Master of the Teutonic Order. Pessimism was in the air, since in that case all the efforts of the Prussian sorcerers had come to nothing. To the end of his life, until his death in 1256, Poppo of Osterna had been 'different' – which no one minded, for the real Poppo had been an awful whoreson.

Teggendorf looked on the bright side, attributing the *infortunium* to simple bad luck, invoked al-Kindi and tirelessly told stories about shaytans, ghouls, jinn and ifrits. Fraundinst and Edlinger Brehm blamed the *dies egiptiaci*, the unlucky Egyptian days, to which in their opinion belonged that memorable Friday, the thirty-first of August 1425, the day of the exorcism in the Silesian Benedictine monastery. The evil 'Egyptian' aura, they said, had tainted the exorcism and its results, and the matter had become singularly abnormal and difficult to reverse because of it. Telesma then remarked that nothing would be achieved without talismans and promised to manufacture some suitable ones. Radim Tvrdík, before he was shouted down, mumbled something about golems and shems.

Štěpán of Drahotuše meanwhile criticised *in toto* the strategy and tactics adopted by the mages. The error, he claimed, lay not just in the method, because that was of lesser import, but in the goal they had set: on the simple and indisputable assumption that Samson Honeypot's personality and spirit were transplanted by an unknown power into the body of a dopey giant. Steps ought to be taken towards reversing the process – in other words, towards discovering the causative factor, since *nihil fit sine causa*. Having discovered that *causa efficiens*, it might be possible to reverse it. But what were the mages of the Archangel doing? Concentrating on attempts to solve the mystery, to unlock the secret that Samson himself clearly didn't want to or could not reveal. In trying to investigate who – or what – Samson was, the sorcerers were striving to satisfy their own curiosity and vanity, behaving like doctors, diagnosing and examining a mysterious illness just to learn about it, without a trace of consideration or sympathy for the person afflicted by that illness.

The mages bridled at and shouted down the Moravian. Before one can begin a treatment, they said – referring to the metaphor – one must acquaint oneself thoroughly with the illness. *Scire*, they said, quoting Aristotle, *est causam rei cognoscere*. Thus, a key element was finding out who – or what – Samson was. Continuing to use medical comparisons – Samson's secret and mystery were not merely symptoms, they were the *nexus* itself, the crux, the essence of the illness. If the illness was to be cured, the secret had to be revealed.

So they made efforts to uncover it. Eagerly and with fervour. And with not a trace of effect.

Samson, meanwhile, had made friends with all the mages of the Archangel. He debated for hours with Jan Bezděchovský about God and Nature. He and Edlinger Brehm stood for days on end beside alembics and retorts with the slogan *solve et coagula* on their lips. He discussed the theories of Arab hakims and Jewish Kabbalists with Teggendorf. He pored over unknown and seriously damaged manuscripts by Pietro di Abano and Cecco d'Ascoli with Štěpán of Drahotuše. He and Jošt Dun made talismans which they later tested in the city. He and Radim Tvrdík walked beside the Vltava, collecting sludge for making golems. Posing as an idiot, he carried out interventionist shopping trips for Beneš Kejval at rival apothecaries.

He played cards, drank and sang with all of them.

The sorcerers had taken a liking to Samson Honeypot. Reynevan couldn't rid himself of the thought that they liked him so much, they had utterly abandoned any efforts that might result in his leaving them.

The door leading to the *occultum* opened and Vincent Reffin Axleben emerged. Gathering up the folds of his black robe, he sat down at a table and downed a glass of Alicante in a single draught. He sat in the silence, without contributing anything himself. He was pale and sweaty; the sweat had stuck his thin hair to his temples and the back of his head.

Vincent Reffin Axleben was a temporary guest in Prague. He was travelling from Salzburg, where he lived, to Krakow for a series of lectures at the academy there. From Krakow, the sorcerer was planning to go to Gdańsk, then on from there via Königsberg to Riga, Dorpat and Pernau. From what Reynevan had heard, Axleben's ultimate destination was Uppsala. He had also heard other things. That Axleben, though a powerful, able and famous sorcerer, was not respected since he practised necromancy and demonomancy, which were deemed controversial. His fun and games with corpses and evil spirits had brought him social ostracism from many circles. Rumours attributed to him the knowledge of and ability to use *Manusfortis*, the Mighty Hand, an extremely powerful spell which could be cast with a single movement of the hand. Gossip had also turned Axleben into one of the leading ideologists of the eastern-European Waldensians and adherents of Joachim of Fiore, and he was also linked to the Lombardist Stregheria. Axleben's very close ties with the Brethren and Sisterhood of the Free Spirit were also no secret – it had greatly astonished the sorcerers of the Archangel that during his stay in Prague, Axleben was staying with them and not at the House of the Black Rose, the Brethren's secret Prague headquarters. Some people attributed it to Axleben's amical relationship with Jan Bezděchovský. Others suspected that the necromancer wanted to pursue his own goals.

'It would be out of the question for me to have this Samson of yours for ever, would it?' asked Axleben, finally raising his head and looking around the assembled company.

Reynevan was already getting up with a sharp retort on his lips, but a poke from Scharley restrained him. The necromancer didn't even notice and appeared only to be looking for an answer in the eyes and face of Jan Bezděchovský. He saw the answer and grimaced.

'Of course, I understand. Pity. I'd love to talk to this . . . gentleman. A well-read individual . . . An elegant speaker . . . And very witty. Very, very witty.'

'Bravo, Samson,' whispered Fraundinst.

'Samson treated him,' Telesma whispered back, 'to the *Emerald Tablet* . . .'

'You won't believe,' Axleben decided to pretend not to hear the whispers, 'what he told me when he was under. Which is also why I'll keep it to myself. Why blab it out, since you won't believe it? I'll only say he gave me various pieces of advice when he was in a trance. I shall, indeed, try to employ them and we'll see with what results.

'This polymath and polyglot with the face of a dimwit,' he continued after a moment devoted to the Alicante, 'regaled me with – among others – a longish quote from *The Divine Comedy*. He cautioned me against submitting to temptations of vanity. To remember that everything is vanity and no misdeed will go unpunished. For among sorcerers, admittedly, Albertus Magnus meets Dante in Paradise, but Michael Scot, Guido Bonetti and Asdente, punished for necromancy, are damned in the Eighth Circle of Hell, Malebolge, the Evil Ditches, in the Fourth Cavern. They groan and weep there, shedding copious tears, and devils torment them by twisting their necks and heads backwards so that their tears pour down their arses. A fine prospect, eh? And this was recited, it should be added, by your Samson in a perfect Tuscan accent.'

Štěpán of Drahotuše and Scharley exchanged smiles and meaningful glances. Axleben swept his dark-circled eyes over them and indicated to Tvrdík to charge his glass again.

'For a moment,' Axleben announced, 'the thought occurred to me: perhaps he is the Devil? The very Devil incarnate? Ha, don't say it hasn't occurred to you, either. Why, it's a veritable textbook devilish trick: beguile, entice, deceive with appearances. *Diabolus potest*, as the classicists would have it, *sensum hominis exteriorem immutare et illudere*. He can achieve it in many ways, for example by transforming the very organ of sense, meaning our eye, by adding something to the ocular substance, owing to which the object we are looking at is seen as the Devil would have us see it. Bonaventure, Psellos, Pierre Lombard all wrote about it years ago, as did Witelo and Nicholas Magni of Jawor, so it would be no bad thing to revisit the works I've mentioned.'

'Blockhead,' whispered Fraundinst.

Axleben again pretended not to hear. 'I nonetheless pronounce,' he said, banging a hand down on the table, 'that we aren't dealing with the Devil here, nor with a case of devilish possession. The interference of demons in people's lives is possible and occurs quite often; we have seen enough of it not to doubt it. But it's a phenomenon in line with the will of the Creator, who allows *ad gloriae sue ostensionem vel ad peccati poenitenciam sive ad peccantis correccionem sive ad nostram erudicionem*. A demon is not in itself a perpetrator. A demon is an *incentor, excitator* and *impellator*, a helper, an instigator and a persuader, one who heightens the evil slumbering in us and incites our sinful nature to evil deeds. And I,' he finished, 'find nothing evil in this person whom you asked me to examine. I know this sounds ridiculous, but there isn't a single trace of evil in him.

'Besides, I see written all over your faces that you yourselves have come to similar conclusions. And I saw something else written there: a great desire for me to finally admit defeat. Accept that I have been bested. Declare that I have achieved nothing. Thus do I declare: I have suffered a defeat, I've achieved nothing. Satisfied? Splendid. So, let's go to some tavern, for I'm hungry. Since my last visit to Prague I've been dreaming of your dumplings and cabbage ... Why the long faces? I thought my defeat would delight you.'

'The very thought, Master Vincent,' said Fraundinst, smiling insincerely. 'Something else bothers us. If you weren't able to discern the essence of the phenomenon—'

'Who said I wasn't?' the necromancer replied, straightening up. 'I was and did. A positive perispirit,' he added, greatly enjoying the pregnant, suspenseful silence. 'Does that expression tell you anything? I ask you needlessly as it most certainly does. You have also most certainly heard that something called a "circling per-ispirit" exists. The matter is quite thoroughly dealt with in the specialist literature, which I heartily advise you to consult.

'I advise you,' continued Axleben, utterly unmoved by the vengeful expressions of the Archangel wizards, 'to study the case of Poppo of Osterna, Grand Master of the Order of Brothers of the German House of Saint Mary in Jerusalem, and that of Lucilla, the daughter of Marcus Aurelius. Perhaps you can recall it? No? Well, you ought to. The same thing happened to your ... Samson as it did to Lucilla and Poppo. The essence of the phe-nomenon is the positive perispirit and the circulating perispirit. Precisely that. I know it. Unfortunately, knowledge is insuffi-cient. I'm unable to do anything with it. I mean I wasn't able and am unable to help this fellow Samson. Let's go for luncheon.'

'If *you* aren't able,' said Štěpán of Drahotuše, squinting, 'who will be?'

'Rupilius the Silesian,' Axleben replied at once. 'And no other—'

'Is he still alive?' Teggendorf interrupted the quite confounded silence.

'Does he exist at all?' Tvrdík whispered to Telesma.

'He is alive,' said Axleben, 'and is the greatest living specialist in the field of astral bodies and beings. If anyone can help here, it's him. Let's go for luncheon. Oh ... I almost forgot ...' The necromancer met Reynevan's gaze and looked him in the eyes. 'You are his friend, young man,' he stated rather than asked, 'and your name is Reynevan.'

Reynevan swallowed and nodded in confirmation.

'While in a trance, Samson prophesied,' said Axleben unemo-tionally. 'A distinct, clear, precise prophesy was repeated several times. Which applied to you. You are to beware of a Woman and a Maiden. It so happens,' the necromancer threw a chilling look at Scharley and Tvrdík, who were smiling scornfully. 'It so happens that I know what it's all about. The Old Woman and the Maiden are two famous towers, in the no less famous castle of Trosky, in the Podkrkonoší. Beware of Trosky Castle, young man called Reynevan.'

'Luckily,' Reynevan mumbled, 'I have no plans to go there.'

'The luck here,' Axleben said over his shoulder as he walked towards the door, 'is that Rupilius the Silesian, the only person in my opinion capable of helping your Samson, has been residing in Bohemia for over a decade. In Trosky Castle.'

Chapter Four

A month later. In which bombards fire and roar at the battle of Kolín and plans are devised: some large, others smaller, more or less utopian and fantastic. But only time will tell what is really utopia and what is fantasy.

'Brother Prokop! Brother Prokop! The bombard has cooled! Shall we fire it again?'

The man to whom the master gunner addressed his question was well built and broad-shouldered. His ruddy, simple-featured face, bulbous nose and black, drooping whiskers gave him the look of a peasant, like a farmer happy with the harvest.

Reynevan had already seen that man. Several times. Reynevan always looked at him with interest.

Before the revolution, Prokop had been a priest. It was said he came from Prague, from a family of Old Town patricians. He joined the Hussites right after the Defenestration, but before 1425 had merely been one of many Taborite preachers – among whom he stood out not only for his good sense, cool head and tolerance, but also by the fact that contrary to Hussite liturgy he didn't wear an apostolic beard, but pedantically shaved every morning, cultivating only his famous moustaches. This daily ritual had earned him the nickname 'the Shaven'. Following the death of Bohuslav of Švamberk, Prokop was quite unexpectedly voted Head Hejtman, supreme commander and chief *director operationum Thaboritarum*, or 'Operational Director of the Tábor' as the title was translated. Soon after his nomination, Prokop acquired another nickname: the Great. Which didn't just refer to his build. Prokop turned out to be a truly formidable leader and strategist, proved by spectacular victories at the battles of Ústí, Zwettl, Tachov and Stříbro. Prokop the Shaven's star was shining brightly.

'Brother Prokop!' the gunner repeated. 'Do we blast?'

Prokop the Shaven looked at the walls and towers of Kolín, the red tiles merging prettily with the autumn colours of the leaves in the neighbouring forests and thickets.

'Why are you in such a hurry to blast?' he replied with a question. 'To demolish? It's a Czech city, by God! Patience, we'll soon go to neighbouring lands where you can have a good blast, flatten a few buildings. But I need Kolín intact and negligibly damaged. And that's how we'll take it.'

Kolín, quite as though wanting to express its opposition and disapproval, replied. There was a booming and crashing from the walls, belches of smoke appeared on the battlements and stone balls whistled, all ploughing into the ground about twenty paces from the earthworks of the first line of the siege. Lord Diviš Bořek of Miletínek, trapped in Kolín, was lacking neither powder nor the will to fight.

'We shall compel Sir Diviš Bořek to surrender,' said Prokop, anticipating the question. 'And we'll capture the town without destruction, without slaughtering after we storm it and without plundering so that the people of Kolín will think well of Brother Hertvík, who will soon be hejtman here.'

The Hussite commanders surrounding Prokop guffawed in chorus. Reynevan knew many of them, but not all. He didn't know Jan Hertvík of Rušinov, who it turned out was already certain of the nomination for Hejtman of Kolín. Among the other Orphans, he had seen Jan Královec of Hrádek and Jíra of Řečice before, and guessed that the fair-haired and cheerfully smiling giant was Jan Kolda of Žampach. Among the Tábor commanders, he recognised Jaroslav of Bukovina, Jakub Kroměšín, Otík of Loza and Jan Bleh of Těšnice.

'Thus.' Prokop straightened up and looked around, indicating he wasn't only talking to the gunner, but to the others as well. 'Thus, please don't rush, don't be hasty, don't waste powder—'

'Are we just to wait outside these walls?' Jan Kolda asked with audible disapproval. 'Stand idly by?'

'Who said idly?' Prokop said, leaning against the stockade. 'Brother Jaroslav!'

'Yes, sir!'

'Has Flu— Has Brother Neplach finally sent his Stentorians?'

'He has,' confirmed Jaroslav of Bukovina. 'Ten of them. Ugly buggers all ... They stink so foully of booze and onions they could knock a big man over. But they have wonderful voices ...'

'Then send them to the walls to yell. Day and night. Particularly at night, it works best at night. Does Lord Bořek have children in Kolín?'

'A daughter.'

'Have them shout about the daughter, too. And you, Brother Kolda, since you don't like to stand idly by ...'

'Yes, sir!'

'Take your cavalry and patrol the villages on both sides of the Labe. Warn the locals one more time that if anybody tries to supply food to the town, they will sorely regret it. If we catch anyone with even a single scone, with even a single sack of kasha, we'll cut off both their hands and both their feet.'

'Yes, sir, Brother Prokop!'

'Get to work, then. Back to your men, I won't keep you any longer ... And you, Brother, why are you still here?'

'We could fire the large bombard ...' grunted the gunner beside the cannon. 'Just one more time ... Before evening ...'

'I knew you'd not bear it.' Prokop sighed. 'Very well. But first come with me, I'll inspect your position to see what you have your cannons trained on. Greetings, Scharley. And greetings to you, Brother Bielawa. Come with me. I'll soon devote some time to you.'

Reynevan was racking his brains trying to figure out how they had met. Prokop the Shaven and Scharley had appeared already to know each other at that first meeting at Shrovetide in 1426, in Nymburk, to where their company was sent from Hradec Králové. Who knows if it hadn't saved all their lives, when first the Hradec Králové Warriors of God and then the ones from Nymburk, who were seeing spies and provocateurs everywhere, were becoming ever more suspicious and ill-tempered? Invoking Peterlin and Horn hadn't helped, since it turned out they had been such secret collaborators that their names didn't mean much and offered no protection. God only knew what would have happened if Prokop hadn't appeared. He didn't fall on Scharley's neck or greet him effusively, but it was obvious they knew each other. How remained a secret that neither of them was inclined to explain or discuss. It was known that Prokop had studied at Charles University and at foreign schools. Reynevan assumed he had met Scharley during one of those journeys.

Reynevan, Scharley and Samson followed Prokop and the gunner along a line of trenches, stockades and fascines. Prokop inspected the bombards and mortars, spoke to gunners and pavisiers, patted crossbowmen on the shoulder, shared earthy jokes with flailmen beside campfires and asked the halberdiers if they were short of anything. He found time to talk to the women busying themselves around cauldrons, tasted the troops' kasha and ruffled the fair hair of children hanging around the kitchen. And to raise his arms modestly when the Warriors of God cheered in his honour.

It lasted quite some time. But Prokop hadn't forgotten about them, either.

They returned to face the town walls.

Prokop's army had arrived at Kolín more quickly than expected, giving the residents of the cottages outside the town little time to save themselves by fleeing inside the walls with whatever they could carry, leaving the Taborites and Orphans considerable stores of food, plenty of livestock and cottages with almost all the necessary tools and utensils. It was thus no surprise that the Warriors of God built their main camp there, surrounded by a barricade of wagons and a corral for the horses. Numerous campfires were burning between the cottages and shacks, hammers clanged in forges and tools clattered in wheelwrights' workshops. Clothes dried on washing lines. Pigs squealed and sheep bleated. Unsavoury smells drifted from the latrines.

'Why are you here, Brother Bielawa?' Prokop suddenly asked.

Reynevan sighed furtively. He'd been expecting that question.

Reynevan had decided to undertake an expedition to Trosky Castle. He'd made the decision quite spontaneously, it should be said, with the unbounded and passionate enthusiasm of a young widow. That enthusiasm and spontaneity didn't especially please the sorcerers from the Archangel, Fraundinst and Štěpán of Drahotuše in particular. They both had their doubts, not just concerning Axleben's information but also the legendary abilities of the legendary Rupilius the Silesian. Axleben, they claimed, was confabulating to distract attention from his embarrassing failure with Samson. Rupilius the Silesian was most probably not at

Trosky Castle. And even if Rupilius the Silesian happened to be there, then the chance he would be able to help was precisely zero – for, according to rough calculations, Rupilius the Silesian was about ninety, and what could one expect from such a fossil?

Telesma, however, took Reynevan's side. Telesma had heard about Rupilius the Silesian, had even met him briefly, and considered his qualifications in the field of spiritualism and astral beings to have been confirmed and verified half a century before. No harm in trying, he pronounced. An expedition to Trosky was an opportunity for Samson Honeypot that ought to be taken, and quickly at that. Rupilius, it was true, was aged four score years and ten, and at that age it's a well-known fact: you catch a chill, sneeze and fart, and without knowing it you are passing into the astral plain.

Telesma was backed up by Bezděchovský. The venerable sorcerer had not only heard of Rupilius, but had met him personally, years before, in Padua. Rupilius, he announced, might indeed help Samson. But no one knew if he'd agree to, because in Padua he'd proved himself to be an arrogant and unobliging arsehole.

Astonishingly, Samson himself treated the project quite sceptically and coolly. Samson hardly participated in the discussion, just grunting now and then. He didn't argue for or against and said nothing most of the time. But Reynevan now knew him too well. Samson simply didn't count on the expedition's success. When he finally agreed to take part, Reynevan couldn't help but get the impression he was doing it out of politeness.

That left Scharley. Reynevan knew Scharley's opinion about the venture before asking him. But he did so, for form's sake.

'It's simply idiotic,' Scharley said calmly. 'Furthermore, it's beginning to remind me of Silesia two years ago and the memorably enthusiastic odyssey to rescue Miss Adèle. An expedition to Trosky looks similarly devised and would probably be carried out similarly, and I can already see the result in my mind's eye. You'll probably never grow wise, Reinmar.

'You claim that we have obligations regarding Samson, that we owe him something,' he continued, a little quieter and more seriously. 'Perhaps you're right, I don't deny it. But life remains life, and the chief rule of life requires us to forget about debts like that, strike them from our memory. The thing with life is that you should look after number one. Love thy neighbour by all means, but not to one's own disadvantage. I claim we've done plenty for Samson, and if the opportunity arises, we'll do more. And the opportunity *will* occur, I'm certain, sooner or later. All we must do is sit down and wait patiently for that opportunity. Why bother looking for it, which sounds suspiciously like looking for trouble? Let's look after number one, Reinmar, because that's of prime importance. And what risk are you exposing us to, laddie? Where do you plan to lead us? There's turmoil, war, fire, chaos, disorder and lawlessness around us. It's not a good time for madcap expeditions. Never mind unprepared ones.'

'You're mistaken,' replied Reynevan. 'I disagree with you entirely. And not just concerning your cynical philosophy of what's most important in life. I disagree with your assessment of the situation. For time is not only on our side, it's also running out. Podještědí and the Jičín Hills are controlled by our army, and the few Catholic lords of that region are intimidated, their morale crushed by the defeat of the crusade at Tachov. They're like smoked bees. So if we're to launch an expedition, let's do it now, before they recover and start stinging again. What do you say to that?'

'Nothing.'

'Regarding preparations, you're right. Let's set about them. What do you suggest?'

Scharley sighed.

*

Reynevan and Samson left Prague on the tenth of October, a Friday, which happened to be the day that the holiday of Saint Gereon and his companion martyrs fell on that year. They left the city in the early morning. When they rode through the Poříčí Gate, the sun came out from behind the clouds, flooding Vítkov and the Hospital Field in a fabulous blaze. Reynevan took the heart-warming sight as a good omen.

Both he and Samson were feeling rough. They had partaken in an effusive farewell with the mages from the House at the Archangel apothecary's shop that was celebrated long into the night. Reynevan was sighing and fidgeting in the saddle – he'd also had to celebrate an additional farewell with Mistress Blažena Pospíchalová.

They were heading for Kolín, which had been besieged by the Tábor, Orphans and Praguians since the middle of September. The siege was being led by Prokop the Shaven. Scharley was in Prokop the Shaven's army. Scharley was meant to have spent the month that had passed since parting from them preparing the expedition. He claimed he had the capabilities. Reynevan believed him. Scharley was both capable and resourceful. The penitent didn't hide the fact – why, he even boasted about it – that he was fighting in the Taborite army for spoils and profit, and that he had already plenty squirrelled away in various hiding places. The sun disappeared behind black clouds coming from the north. It was sombre and gloomy. Not to say ominous.

Reynevan thought that the signs were foolish superstitions.

Prokop gave the impression he wasn't listening. But that was deceptive.

'Give Brother Scharley leave,' he repeated. 'Release him from service in the army during wartime. For your private affairs, Brother Bielawa. In other words, self-interest comes first, and duty to God and the fatherland are second. Is that it?'

Reynevan didn't reply. He just swallowed loudly. Prokop snorted.

'Agreed,' he said. 'I give my permission.' Clearly enjoying their astonishment, he continued, 'There are three reasons. Firstly, Brother Scharley has served in the Tábor's ranks for over a year now and has earned his leave. Secondly, Brother Neplach has informed me of your contributions, Brother Bielawa. You have battled the enemies of our cause with dedication and you apparently fought heroically against the rebels in Prague on the sixth of September. You have treated the wounded, without eating, drinking or sleeping. That unquestionably deserves a reward. And thirdly and most importantly ...'

He stopped and turned around. They were outside a granary, currently serving as headquarters and the organisational centre of the siege staff.

'You'll find out later what is third and most important; we'll return to it, but right now I have other matters to attend to. You'll hear what those matters are because I'm keeping you beside me.'

'Brother—'

'That's an order. Let us go. And your servant ... Oh, I see he has occupied himself with something. Good. He won't do any harm.'

Samson Honeypot, pretending as usual that he couldn't hear or understand anything, had sat down at the foot of the granary wall, taken out a pocketknife and begun whittling a scrap of wood. Samson often whittled. Firstly, he explained, it was a perfect activity for the idiot he appeared to be. Secondly, he went on, whittling was calming and beneficial to the nervous and digestive systems. Thirdly, he added, carving wood helped him when he was forced to listen to discussions about politics and religion, since the scent of fresh wood shavings alleviated the vomiting reflex.

They went into the granary, entering a large room which still smelled pleasantly of grain despite being converted into a staff headquarters. Inside, two men were bent over maps spread out on a table. One was short and thin, dressed in the fashionable black of Hussite priests. The other, younger, in knightly garb, was more powerfully built and fair-haired, with a somewhat cherubic, somewhat harsh and weary face, calling to mind Flemish miniatures of the *Très Riches Heures du Duc de Berry*.

'At last,' said the smaller one in black. 'We've had quite a wait, Brother Prokop.'

'Duties, Brother Prokop.'

Unlike his namesake, the other Prokop had a beard, if a spare, unkempt and rather comical one. By virtue of his size, he had also been singled out with a nickname – he was called Little Prokop. Also a preacher among preachers at the beginning, he made a name for himself with the Hussites – or more specifically the Orphans – after the death of Jan Žižka of Trocnov. Little Prokop had been with Ambrož of Hradec Králové at Žižka's deathbed, and the Orphans considered the witnesses of the final moments of their venerated leader virtually saints – they would even kneel before him and kiss the hem of his robes, and mothers brought their feverish children to him. This esteem elevated Little Prokop to the position of chief spiritual leader – thus he held an analogical office among the Orphans to the one Prokop had performed in the Tábor before he took up the position of Director.

'Duties,' repeated Prokop the Great, pointing vaguely towards the besieged town. His words were accompanied by a powerful roar; the wall shuddered and dust fell from the ceiling. The senior gunner was finally able to fire his two-hundred-pound bombard. It meant at the same time peace until the morning – a bombard had to cool for a minimum of six hours after being fired.

'I apologise for making you wait, Brother. And you, Brother Wyszek.'

Reynevan had met Wyszek Raczyński earlier, at the Battle of Ústí, in the cavalry of Jan Rohač of Dube. The Pole's route to the Hussites was untypical – Wyszek had come to Prague in 1421 as an envoy of the Lithuanian Duke Witold, in whose service he remained. The mission concerned – as it later emerged – Korybut's attempt to gain the throne. The Czech revolution appealed to Raczyński, especially after contact with Žižka, Rohač and the Taborites, who took the Pole's fancy much more than the moderate Calixtines with whom he had discussed Witold's mission. Raczyński quickly joined the Taborites, and there was a genuine bond of friendship between him and Rohač.

At Prokop's signal, everybody took their seats at the map-covered table. Reynevan felt self-conscious and was aware how much of an intruder he was, ill-fitting to the company. His mood wasn't helped by the relaxed nonchalance of Scharley, who felt at home always and everywhere. Also problematic was Little Prokop and Raczyński's apparently unreserved approval of their presence. They were accustomed to it. Prokop always had within reach a wide variety of intelligence agents, emissaries, envoys and men on special – and even very special – missions with whom they were not personally acquainted.

'It won't be a short siege.' Prokop the Shaven interrupted the silence. 'We've been camped outside Kolín since the Exaltation of the Cross, and I'll consider it a success if the town surrenders before Advent. You might end up finding me still here after your return from Poland, Brother Wyszek. When are you setting off?'

'Tomorrow at daybreak. Across the Odra, then via Cieszyn and Zator.'

'Aren't you afraid to go? Now in Poland not only Oleśnicki but any old starosta might lock you up in a dungeon, according to the laws Jogaila has enacted. Caused by his bellyache, no doubt.'

Everybody, including Reynevan, knew what he meant. After April 1424, the Edict of Wieluń – forced on Jogaila by Bishop Oleśnicki, Sigismund and the papal legates – was in force in the Kingdom of Poland. The edict – although neither the name 'Huss' nor the word 'Hussite' were cited – still talked *expressis verbis* about Bohemia as a region 'infected by heresy'. It forbade Poles from trading with Czechs and travelling to Bohemia at all, and ordered any Poles there to return immediately. The disobedient could expect *infamia* and the confiscation of their estates. Furthermore, regarding heretics, the edict fundamentally changed heresy from an offence punishable in Poland by ecclesiastical courts into a crime against kingdom and king, a *crimen laesae maiestatis* and high treason.

This categorisation set in motion the entire state apparatus in pursuing and punishing heresy, and anyone found guilty would be put to death.

The matter naturally infuriated the Czechs – they considered Poland a kindred and amicable country, and now instead of a common front against the Germanic world suddenly came an insult; instead of a front – an affront. However, most people understood Jogaila's reasons and the rules of the complicated game he had to play. It soon became apparent that the edict was only dangerous on paper – and there it remained. So when a Czech mentioned the 'Edict of Wieluń', he usually winked knowingly or added a sneer. As Prokop did that time.

'Never mind, as soon as the Teutonic Knights cross the Drwęca, Jogaila will forget about his high-sounding edict. For he knows that if he has to search around for help against the Germans, it won't be found in Rome.'

'Ha,' replied Raczyński. 'It's true, I don't deny it. But I still have to say I'm afraid. I'm riding in secret, true. But you know yourselves what it's like with a new law: everyone's suddenly vying with each other, everyone wants to demonstrate his zeal and show off, for perhaps it'll be seen and lead to a promotion. So Zbigniew Oleśnicki has an army of informers at his service. And that Jędrzej Myszka, the bishop's *vicarius*, that little squirt, son of a dog, has a dog's nose and is sniffing to find out if there are any Hussites around King Władysław ... Forgive me, I meant to say—'

'You meant to say "any Hussites".' Prokop cut him off coldly. 'Let's not split hairs.'

'Yes, indeed ... But I would rather not go near the king. I'm meeting Sir Jan Mężyk of Dąbrowa, a supporter of our cause, in Zator. Together we shall ride to Pieskowa Skała, where I will meet in secret Sir Piotr Szafraniec, the Chamberlain of Krakow. And Sir Piotr, a fellow favourably inclined towards us, will convey our message to King Władysław.'

'Well, well,' said Prokop pensively, twisting his moustache. 'Except that Jogaila isn't in the mood for envoys now. He has other worries at present.'

The other men exchanged meaningful glances. They knew what he meant, for the news had spread quickly and widely. Queen Sophia, Jogaila's wife, had been accused of marital infidelity and adultery. It was rumoured she had shared her bedchamber with at least seven different knights. Arrests and investigations were ongoing in Krakow, and Jogaila, usually calm, was said to be furious.

'A great responsibility rests on you, Brother Wyszek. Our missions to Poland have come out pretty poorly up until now. Suffice to recall Hynek of Kolštejn. Therefore, first inform Lord Szafraniec, please, that if King Władysław permits, a Czech mission will soon come to the Wawel to pay its respects to His Majesty, which will be led by me, in person. That is the most important thing in your mission: to prepare for mine. You are, you will say, my authorised envoy.'

Wyszek Raczyński bowed.

'I shall leave it to your judgement and intuition,' continued Prokop the Shaven, 'regarding whom you talk with in Poland and whom you approach and sound out. For you must know that I have not yet decided to whom I shall take my mission. I'd like to go to Jogaila. But in adverse circumstances I don't rule out Witold.'

Raczyński opened his mouth but said nothing.

'We share common ground with Duke Witold.' Little Prokop cut in. 'We have similar plans.'

'In what way similar?' Wyszek asked.

'Bohemia stretching from sea to sea. That is our plan.'

Wyszek's face must have expressed a great deal, because Little Prokop immediately hurried to explain.

'Brandenburg,' he declared, pointing a finger at the map, 'is a land that historically belongs to the Bohemian Crown. The Luxembourg dynasty simply traded Brandenburg to the House of Hohenzollern; it won't be difficult to invalidate that transaction. We invalidated Sigismund as a king; we will invalidate his dealings, too. We shall take back what is ours. And if the Teutons fight back, we'll drive our wagons there and tan their hides.'

'I see,' said Raczyński. But the expression on his face barely changed. Little Prokop saw it.

'Having Brandenburg,' he continued, 'we shall set about dealing with the Order, the Teutonic Knights. We shall drive the damned Teutons from the Baltic. And then we'll have the sea, won't we?'

'What about Poland?' Wyszek asked coldly.

'Poland doesn't care about the Baltic.' Prokop the Shaven joined in serenely. 'That was apparent after Grunwald. It was apparent after the Treaty of Melno. It can be clearly seen from Jogaila's current politics, or rather Witold's, for Jogaila ... Ha, I'm sorry to say, but that's life, we'll all grow old one day. And regarding Witold's interests, they are in the east, not the north. So we shall take the Baltic, since ... What is it you say, Scharley?'

'*Res nullius cedit occupanti.*'

'Of course.' Wyszek nodded. 'So that's one sea. And the other?'

'We'll defeat the Turks and that's the Black Sea,' said Little Prokop, shrugging. 'Bohemia will be a maritime power and that's that.'

'As you see, Brother Wyszek,' said Prokop the Shaven with a sneer, 'we're very useful allies. We share common ground with everybody and anyone who joins us profits and benefits. We'll guarantee Jogaila peace from the Order, we'll give Witold a free hand in the east – he can conquer and appropriate anything he wants there, even Moscow, Veliky Novgorod and the Principality of Ryazan. I think the Pope will also benefit when we eradicate the Teutonic Knights, who are now overly unbridled and haughty. We shall fulfil the prophecy of Saint Bridget, this time utterly and completely. And when we crack down on the Turks, the Holy Father will also be more pleased than alarmed, won't he? What do you think?'

Wyszek Raczyński kept his thoughts to himself. 'Am I to repeat that to Szafraniec?' he asked.

'Brother Wyszek.' Prokop became serious. 'You know very well what to say, for you are our man, a righteous Christian, you take Communion from the Chalice like us. But you're also a Pole and a patriot, so proceed such that Poland also benefits. The Teutonic Knights are still a threat to Poland – Grunwald didn't help much and the Teutonic Order still hangs over us like the Sword of Damocles. Should King Władysław choose to hear the Pope's complaints and pleas, he'll join the crusade and send a Polish army against us, and the Teutonic Knights will immediately strike from the north. The House of Brandenburg and the Silesian dukes will attack and Poland will fall. Poland will fall, Brother Wyszek.'

'King Władysław knows this,' replied Raczyński. 'I can't imagine he'll join the crusade. But the Polish king cannot blatantly oppose the Pope. In any case, satires proliferate and Malbork claims Jogaila is a secret pagan and idolater, claims he is in league with pagans, in cahoots with the Devil. Thus, the Polish king will strive for peace. For a settlement between Bohemia and Rome. And Rome is eager for such a settlement—'

'"Eager",' Little Prokop sneered. 'The harder we tan the hide of the Roman crusaders, the more eager it'll be.'

'That's the sacred truth,' agreed the Pole. 'If the Pope could take you – I mean *us* – with fire and sword, he would. He'd torture, execute, impale, burn alive and drown, singing *Gloria in excelsis* all the while. They'd do to us what they did to the Albigensians, then announce it was "to the glory of God". But it turns out they cannot. They're too weak, so they want to parley.'

'I know they do.' Little Prokop snorted contemptuously. 'But why do *we* have to want that? We're kicking their arses, not they ours.'

'Brother.' Raczyński raised his hands in a desperate gesture. 'Brother, you're repeating to me what I know. If you'll allow, I'll tell you what the Polish King Władysław knows. What every Christian king in Christian Europe knows. For the time being, the Church rules the world and wields two swords: the spiritual and the secular. Put more simply: the Pope wields secular power and the king is merely his plenipotentiary. Put even simpler: the Kingdom of Bohemia won't be a kingdom until the Pope approves the King of Bohemia. Only then will peace and order arise and Bohemia return to Europe as a Christian kingdom.'

'To Europe? You mean Rome?' exclaimed Little Prokop. 'Very well, we shall return, but not at the cost of losing our sovereignty! Or our religion! Or our Christian values! First of all, Rome – I mean Europe – must adopt Christian values. To put it bluntly: must accept the true faith. Meaning: ours. So then, *primo*: Europe must accept and receive Holy Communion from the Chalice. *Secundo*: Europe must swear the Four Articles of Prague. *Tertio*—'

'I rather doubt that Europe will comply,' said Raczyński, not waiting for *tertio*. 'Still less the Pope.'

'We shall see!' said Little Prokop indignantly. 'How far away is Rome from here? Two hundred miles? We could be there in a month at most! And then we'll talk! When the Roman Antichrist sees our wagons in Trastevere, he'll soon draw in his horns!'

'Keep calm, Brother, keep calm.' Prokop the Shaven pressed his fists on the table. 'We are for peace, have you forgotten? Our learned friend Petr Chelčický teaches that nothing can justify breaking the Fifth Commandment. "Thou shalt not kill" is sacred and inviolable. We don't want war, we're ready to negotiate.'

'That readiness will gladden the Polish king,' said Raczyński.

'I should think so,' said Prokop the Shaven, 'but Rome ought not to strut so haughtily, nor put itself on a pedestal, nor witter on about two swords. For it is difficult for us, faithful Czechs, Brother Wyszek, to accept that the Popes – whether of the Roman or any other obedience – who have been multiplying like rabbits lately, are competent vicars of God on Earth and that good and virtuous hands wield those two swords. For in recent times, every next Pope turns out to be a worse oaf than the last. If not a moron, then a thief; if not a thief, then a rascal; if not a rascal, then a soak and a lecher. And sometimes all at once. For all my good will, although I'm as docile as a lamb, I shall not be obedient to such shepherds. I won't recognise men like them as the head of the Church, I won't accept such omnipotence, even if I were shown a hundred Donations of Constantine. Master Jan Huss taught that a Pope who lives according to habits which are opposed to Peter the Apostle may not be Peter's true successor. A Pope like that is not the vicar of Christ but of Judas Iscariot. So instead of being obedient to one like that, he should be seized by the scruff of the neck and cast from the pulpit, and his privileges and wealth confiscated! And likewise, from the Vatican to each village parish.

'You say, Brother Wyszek, that the *curia Romana* would welcome back and forgive the Czechs like a prodigal son, receive them again into the European Christian fold? And we are eager to do so. But first of all, they must change their habits and their faith. To the true one. To the faith that Christ taught and Peter professed. That Master Wycliffe and Master Huss taught. For true faith, apostolic faith, in accordance with the letter of the Bible, is the one we faithful Czechs profess. Will the European *christianitas* receive us into its bosom? Then let it first cleanse it.

'There are men like Petr Chelčický, like Mikuláš of Pelhřimov. Like your countryman Paweł Włodkowic, defending freedom of conscience. God willing, the Roman Church, understanding its errors, will turn towards just those men. God willing, it'll heed their teachings.'

'And if it doesn't,' Little Prokop finished with a cold smile, 'it'll heed our flails.'

The silence lasted a long time. It was interrupted by Wyszek Raczyński.

'I'm to repeat all that to Szafraniec,' he stated. 'Is that what you want?'

'If I didn't, would I be speaking about it?' Prokop twirled his moustaches.

*

Jan Rohač of Dube, the famous Hejtman of Čáslav, was waiting for Raczyński outside the granary with a mounted escort.

The Pole swung himself into the saddle of the steed offered to him and took a wolfskin coat from a servant. Then Prokop walked over to him.

'Farewell, Brother Wyszek,' he said, holding his hand out. 'May God guide you. And please pass on my good wishes to King Władysław through Szafraniec. May he fare well—'

'In his marriage with Sophia,' said Little Prokop, grinning, but Prokop the Shaven quieted him with a sharp look.

'May he fare well in the chase,' he finished. 'I know he's fond of hunting, but he should be vigilant. He's seven and seventy – at that age, it's easy to catch a chill and expire from it.'

Raczyński bowed and clicked his tongue at his horse. They were soon trotting towards the crossing on the Labe, he and Jan Rohač of Dube. Two close friends, comrades, companions, brothers in arms. Rohač and Wyszek, the Pole and Czech, still had before them many battles, skirmishes and clashes, during which they would fight together, side by side, horse beside horse, thigh by thigh, shoulder to shoulder. They would also die together – on the same day, on the same scaffold, first cruelly tortured and then hanged. But at that time no one could have predicted it.

The huge bombard had cooled down by morning, and the eager gunner didn't fail to fire it right at sunrise. The roar and the trembling of the ground were so intense that Reynevan fell from the narrow pallet he was sleeping on, and fragments of straw and dust fell from the ceiling for some time.

Smaller bombards were fired after the large one, hurling one-hundred-and-fifty-pound balls. The bombards boomed. The ground trembled. After being woken, Reynevan brooded over his dreams, and there was much to brood over: he'd dreamed of Nicolette, Katarzyna of Biberstein, again. In detail.

The cannons roared. The siege went on.

Around noon, Prokop gave the third and most important reason for agreeing to Scharley's leave. Their spirits sank at once.

'I'll be needing you in Silesia. Both of you. I want you to return to Silesia. In August, when we repulsed the crusade at Stříbro,' Prokop continued, ignoring their expressions and not waiting for a response, 'the Bishop of Wrocław once again stabbed us in the back. The army of the bishop and the Silesian dukes, traditionally supported by Albrecht of Kolditz and Půta of Častolovice, attacked the Náchod region again. Yet again, much Czech blood flowed. Yet again, fire destroyed homes and farms. Yet again, indescribable atrocities were perpetrated on defenceless people.

'For at least a year, a wave of appalling terror has passed through Silesia. Pyres blaze everywhere. The Teutons are cruelly tormenting our Slav brothers. We will not stand idly by. We will march to Silesia and lend a brotherly hand with a peaceful, stabilising mission. But a mission like that has to be prepared.' Prokop still didn't allow them to get a word in. 'And that will be your task. Once you have sorted out your private interests, the ones I've generously given you permission for, you will join Brother Neplach on White Mountain. Brother Neplach will prepare you for the task. Which you will accomplish, I have no doubts, with great dedication: for God, religion and the fatherland. As befits Warriors of God ... I see you want to say something, Scharley. Speak.'

'We are known in Silesia,' said Scharley after clearing his throat.

'I'm aware of that.'

'Many people know us there. Many think ill of us. Many would like to see us dead.'

'Good. That will ensure you are cautious and sensible.'

'The Inquisition—'

'And that you won't betray us. End of discussion, Scharley. Enough! You have your orders. You have a task to accomplish. And now go on leave and sort out your private interests. I advise you to sort out all of them, very thoroughly. Your task is, I accept, risky and perilous. It's right to take care of personal matters before something like that. Pay off one's debts to friends and loved ones. Become indebted to others—'

He suddenly broke off.

'Reinmar of Bielawa,' he said a moment later, and his expression sent shivers running down Reynevan's back. 'Your private interests don't by any chance have anything to do with avenging your brother's death?'

Reynevan shook his head, for his mouth had suddenly gone so dry he couldn't utter a word.

'Ah,' said Prokop the Shaven, putting his hands together. 'Very good. That's excellent. May it thus remain.' A moment later, he continued, 'The Bible says: trust in the Lord. And regarding your brother, you can additionally trust in me, Prokop. I shall take care of it personally. I already have. Your brother, whose memory I respect, was only one of many of our allies killed in Silesia. A murderous hand fell on scores of people who sympathised with us and who helped us. Those crimes will not go unpunished. We shall answer terror with terror, in accordance with God's order: an eye for an eye, a tooth for a tooth, a hand for a hand, a leg for a leg, a wound for a wound. Your brother will be avenged, you can be certain of that. But I forbid you from private acts of revenge. I understand your feelings, but you must restrain yourself. Understand that there's a hierarchy here, a queue for revenge, and you are far from the top of that hierarchy. And do you know who is at the top? I'll tell you: I am! Prokop, called the Shaven. The Silesian wrongdoers have added me to their list, so do you think I'll let them get away with it? That I won't give them an example of terror? I swear by the Father and the Son that they who have spilled blood will pay with their own. As the Bible says: I shall beat them as small as the dust of the earth, I shall stamp them as the mire of the street. I will send a sword after them, till I have consumed them. They who have made a pact with the Devil, who have plotted crimes in secret, dealt murderous blows, now look back anxiously, now feel eyes on their backs. Now those creatures of darkness are afraid of what is lying in wait in the darkness for *them*. They saw themselves as wolves, spreading terror among defenceless sheep. And now they themselves tremble to hear the howling of wolves on their trail.

'Conclusion: the preparation of our attack on Silesia is at this moment a matter of vital consequence for our entire cause. It is an operation as important even as the current siege of Kolín or the attack on Hungary planned for the end of the year. I repeat: if as a result of your attempts at private revenge the operation ends in fiasco, I shall take appropriate measures. Appropriate and harsh measures. I shall not show mercy. Remember that. Will you?'

'I shall.'

'Splendid. And now ... Reinmar, Brother Neplach informs me that you're an expert at ... hmm ... unconventional medicine and I have terrible pains in my bones ... Can you make magic? Cure it with a spell?'

'Brother Prokop ... Magic is forbidden ... Witchcraft is a *peccatum mortalium* ... The Fourth Article of Prague—'

'Stop talking nonsense, will you? I asked if you can cure it.'

'I can. Show me where it hurts.'

Chapter Five

In which we leave our heroes for a short time and move from Bohemia to Silesia, to see what some of our old – and new – friends were up to at more or less the same time, give or take a month or so.

Haven't I seen him somewhere before? thought Wendel Domarasc, *magister scholarum* of the Collegiate School at the Church of the Holy Cross in Opole, looking at his guest. *Haven't I seen him somewhere? And if so, where? In Krakow? In Dresden? In Opava?*

The voices of pupils came drifting in from outside the window, chorally reciting stanzas from Statius's *The Thebaid*. Every now and then, the recitation was interrupted by a yell – the usher supervising the class was correcting a pupil's Latin using a rod and encouraging him to try harder.

The guest was tall and slim to the point of thinness, but strength could be sensed in him. He wore his greying hair in the fashion of a clergyman and his felt cap – Wendel Domarasc would have bet any money – concealed a tonsure or the remains of one. The magister was also willing to bet that the visitor might also have lowered his eyes, humbly bowed his head, put his hands together and mumbled a prayer like a monk. He could have. If he'd wanted to. Now he clearly didn't want to. He looked the magister straight in the eye.

The visitor's eyes were most strange. Their unmoving keenness was unnerving and sent tingles down Domarasc's neck and back. But their strangest feature was their colour – that of iron, the colour of an old knife blade, darkened by use. The realism was enhanced by reddish spots on the irises, just like flecks of rust.

'*Ecce sub occiduas versae iam Noctis habenas astrorumque obitus, ubi primum maxima Tethys imu . . . impulit . . .* Ouch! Oh, Good Lord Jesus!' The young pupil blew on his stinging hands.

Wendel Domarasc, *magister scholarum* of the Collegiate School at the Church of the Holy Cross in Opole and main sleeper agent of the Taborite intelligence service, head and co-ordinator of the spy network in Silesia, sighed softly. He knew who the visitor was – he'd been warned he would come. He knew on whose orders the visitor was there and whose authority he represented. He knew what authorisation the visitor had to give orders, and also the penalty for failing to carry them out. That was all Domarasc knew. Nothing more. In particular, not the visitor's name.

'Well, yes, m'lord.' He finally decided on a form of address as courteous as it was neutral. 'Hard times have come to us lately in Silesia. Hard times, indeed . . . I don't say that, please understand, to shirk my duties or to justify idleness, no, not at all. I make efforts, Brother Prokop need not worry—'

He broke off. The visitor's iron-grey gaze, it turned out, also had the remarkable ability to stem garrulousness.

'In February of last year,' Wendel Domarasc shifted to shorter and more precise sentences, 'the Union of Strzelin was established, as you surely know. Silesian dukes, the starostas and councils of Wrocław, Świdnica, Jawor and Kłodzko. Its aim: to eliminate Czech networks operating in Silesia and then to mobilise their armies to strike Bohemia.'

The visitor nodded to indicate that he knew. But the expression didn't change in his iron-grey eyes.

'They smote us hard,' continued the spy without emotion. 'The bishop's Inquisition and the counter-intelligence of Albrecht of Kolditz and Půta of Častolovice. The abbots of Henryków, Kamieniec and Krzeszów. The Świdnica sleeper agent and several of our people in Wrocław were arrested in the autumn. Somebody was made to testify, or somebody betrayed us, for by the second Sunday of Advent, the Jawor cell had been reeled in. Most of our agents from the Nysa region were arrested in the winter. And this year, not a month has gone by without somebody being caught . . . Or killed. Terror is spreading. People well disposed to us are dying. Merchants collaborating with us are dying. The people are in the grip of fear. It's difficult to recruit new agents in these circumstances. It's difficult to infiltrate – the risk of betrayal and entrapment is growing . . . Brother Prokop, I realise, isn't interested in the difficulties, but in outcomes, results . . . Please report that we're doing what we can. We're doing our jobs. I'm observing the rules of the trade and doing my—'

'I didn't come here to inspect you,' the man with the iron-grey eyes interjected calmly. 'I have my own tasks to accomplish in Silesia. I visited you for three reasons. *Primo*, you're the safest cell and my own safety matters to me somewhat. *Secundo*, I need your help.'

The magister breathed out, swallowed and raised his head more boldly.

'And *tertio*?'

'You need Prokop's help. Here it is.'

The iron-grey-eyed man unfastened his bundle and drew from it a large package wrapped in sheepskin and tied with a leather strap. The package thumped down heavily on the table, announcing its contents with a muffled clank. The spy held out a bony hand covered in liver spots that looked like a hawk's talons.

'This is precisely what we need,' Wendel said, feeling the package. 'Gold and the spirit of victory. If Prokop gives me more gold and a few more victories like Tachov, Silesia will be his in a year.'

'*Numquam tibi sanguinis huius ius erit aut magno feries impre* . . . *imperdita Tydeo pectora; vado equidem exsul* . . . *exsultans* . . . Ow! Ouch!'

'You mentioned,' the *magister scholarum* said as he closed the window, 'that you are counting on my help.'

'Here's a list of what I'll need. Please get it quickly.'

'Hmm . . . It'll be arranged.'

'I must also meet Urban Horn. Please inform him. Have him come to Opole.'

'Horn's not in Silesia. He had to flee. Someone informed and they were almost upon him. He killed one of the bishop's thugs and heavily injured another in Milicz . . . Ha, just like in a knightly romance . . . I think he's in Greater Poland now. I don't know exactly where. As a special agent, Horn isn't subordinate to me and doesn't report to me.'

'Tybald Raabe, in that case. Get him here.'

'There'll be a problem with that, too. Tybald is imprisoned.'

'Where? Who has him?'

'He's at Schwarzwaldau Castle. Sir Herman Zettritz the Younger has him.'

'Organise a swift horse for me.'

Sir Herman Zettritz the Younger, the Lord of Schwarzwaldau, sat sprawled on a chair resembling a throne. The wall behind his back was covered with a slightly sooty tapestry depicting, according to all the signs, the Garden of Eden. Two filthy hounds lay at the knight's feet. Alongside, at a table covered in food, sat the knight's entourage, who were only slightly cleaner than the hounds and consisted of five armed burgmen and two women whose profession wasn't too difficult to guess at.

Herman of Zettritz shook breadcrumbs from his belly and the family arms – a red and silver aurochs' head – and looked down at the priest standing before him in the humble pose of a supplicant.

'Right then, laddie,' he said. 'What was your name again, priest? I've forgotten.'

'Father Apfelbaum,' said the priest, raising eyes the colour of iron, Zettritz noted.

'So he is.' He stuck out his jaw. 'So he is, laddie. The Tybald Raabe you ask about is in my dungeon. I locked the rat up, for he's a heretic.'

'Is that so?'

'He sang rude songs about priests and made fun of our Holy Father, the Pope. He was showing around this amusing picture, here, with Pope Martin V in a pigsty tending swine. The Pope is the one wearing the tiara, third from the left. Haa-haa-haa!'

Zettritz was weeping with laughter and his burgmen joined in. One of the hounds barked and was kicked. The grey-eyed visitor smiled affectedly.

'Though I warned him not to incite my subjects.' The knight grew serious. 'Sing any fucking songs you like about Wycliffe and the Antichrist, I told him, call priests leeches, because they are. But don't fucking tell the peasants that everyone's equal before God and soon all property will be common, including my estates, my burg, my granary and my treasury. Or that they don't have to pay duty because a just, divine order is coming to abolish all duties and rents. I tried to dissuade him, I warned him. He didn't listen, so I threw him into the dungeon. I haven't decided what to do with him yet. Perhaps I'll have him hanged. Or just flogged. Perhaps I'll tie him to the pillory in the town square in

Landeshut. Perhaps I'll turn him over to the Bishop of Wrocław. I need to improve my relationship with the episcopate since it's soured a little lately, haa-haa-haa!'

The grey-eyed priest knew, of course, what it was all about. He knew about the attack on the Cistercian abbey in Krzeszów that Zettritz had committed the year before. The guffaws of the knights at the table suggested that they must also have taken part in the robbery. Perhaps he was looking on too intently, perhaps there was something in his face, because the Lord of Schwarzwaldau suddenly straightened up and punched the armrest of his throne.

'The Abbot of Krzeszów burned three of my farmhands to death!' he bellowed, with a roar the aurochs in his arms would have been proud of. 'He acted against me. He fucking crossed me, though I warned him he wouldn't get away with it! He accused the men of supporting the Hussites without any proof and sent them to the stake! And all in order to show me disrespect! He thought I wouldn't dare, that I wasn't strong enough to strike at the monastery! So I taught him a lesson!'

'The display took place,' said the priest, raising his eyes again, 'if I recall, with the help and complicity of the Trutnov Orphans under the command of Jan Baštín of Porostlé.'

The knight leaned over and his eyes bored into the spy's.

'Who are you, you damned priest?'

'Haven't you guessed?'

'I have indeed,' rasped Zettritz. 'And it's also true that I taught the abbot a lesson with your invaluable Hussite help. But does that make me a Hussite? I take Communion in the Catholic way, I believe in Purgatory and I call on the saints in need. I have nothing in common with you.'

'Apart from the spoils plundered from Krzeszów and split half-and-half with Baštín. Horses, cattle, swine, coin in gold and silver, wine, liturgical vessels . . . Do you think, m'lord, that Bishop Konrad will absolve you in exchange for any old troubadour?'

'You comport yourself too brashly here.' Zettritz squinted his eyes. 'Beware! Or I shall add you to the reckoning. Oh, the bishop would be glad of you indeed . . . For I see you are a man of substance, not some oaf. But don't raise your eyes or your voice. You stand before a knight! Before a lord!'

'I know. And I suggest a knightly way of resolving the matter. An honest ransom for a squire is six hundred groschen. A troubadour's worth no more than a squire. I'll pay for him.'

Zettritz looked at the burgmen and they all grinned menacingly.

'Did you bring silver here? In your saddlebags, is it? And the horse is in the stable? In my stable? In my castle?'

'Indeed.' The grey-eyed man didn't flicker an eyelid. 'In your stable, in your castle. But you didn't allow me to finish. I'll give you something else for the goliard Tybald.'

'I'm intrigued.'

'A guarantee. When the Warriors of God come to Silesia, and it'll happen soon, when they burn everything to the ground, no ill will befall either your stable, your castle or your subjects' belongings. On principle, we don't burn the property of people who are friendly to us. Not to mention our allies.'

It was quiet for a long time. So quiet that the sound of the flea-ridden hounds scratching themselves could be heard.

'Everybody out!' the knight suddenly roared at his entourage. '*Raus!* Begone! All of you! This instant!'

'As regards an alliance and a friendship,' said Herman Zettritz the Younger, the Lord of Schwarzwaldau, once they were alone. 'As regards future collaboration . . . Future collaboration and brotherhood of arms . . . And the division of spoils, naturally . . . May we discuss details, Brother Czech?'

*

Immediately outside the gate, they spurred the horses into a gallop. The sky in the west darkened, literally turned black. A strong wind blew and whistled in the tops of firs, tore dry leaves from oaks and hornbeams.

'M'Lord Vlk!'

'What?'

'Thanks! Thank you for freeing me!'

The grey-eyed priest turned around in the saddle.

'I need you, Tybald Raabe. I need information.'

'I understand.'

'I doubt it. Ah, Raabe, one more thing.'

'Yes, m'Lord Vlk.'

'Don't ever utter my name aloud again.'

The village must have been right on the route taken by the troops of Baštín of Porostlé, who, following the previous year's robbery of the Krzeszów abbey, had plundered the land between Landeshut and Wałbrzych. The village must have offended the Hussites somehow, for all that remained was black, scorched earth, with odd timbers and stones sticking up here and there. Not much was left of the local church, either – just enough to see there had once been a church. The only thing that had survived was a roadside cross and the graveyard beyond the embers of the church, hidden among the alders.

The wind blew, combing the forested mountainside, covering the sky with a blue-grey curtain of cloud.

The grey-eyed priest reined in his horse, turned around and waited for Tybald Raabe to ride up.

'Dismount,' he said dryly. 'I told you I need certain information. Here and now.'

'Here? In this fell wilderness? Right beside a boneyard? At

dusk? Under those clouds, which will any moment burst? Can't we talk in a tavern, over a beer?'

'I've already unmasked myself sufficiently because of you. I don't want anyone to see me with you and put two and two together. For which reason—'

He broke off, seeing the goliard's eyes growing wide in fear.

What they first saw was an explosion of black birds, flying up from the thicket surrounding the graveyard. It was then that they saw the spectral dancers.

One after the other, in a line; holding hands, skeletons appeared from behind the graveyard wall, cavorting in strange and grotesque strides. Some naked, some incomplete, some adorned in ragged shrouds, they danced, rocking and hopping, lifting high their bony feet, shin bones and thigh bones, snapping their gap-toothed jaws rhythmically. The wind blew, groaning like the damned, whistling through ribs and pelvises, playing through skulls like flutes.

'*Der Totentanz* ...' Tybald Raabe gasped. '*La Danse Macabre* ...'

The procession of skeletons went around the cemetery three times and then, still holding hands, they passed into the forest on the hillside, dancing all the while, jiggling and swaying. They walked, hopping and clattering, in a cloud of leaves and ash blown up from the burned-down houses. The flocks of black birds accompanied them the whole time, and even when the ghastly dancers vanished among the thicket, the confusion of birds above the treetops signalled their route.

'It's a sign ...' mumbled the goliard. 'An omen! A plague will come ... Or a war ...'

'Or both,' said the grey-eyed man, shrugging. 'It turns out that the chiliasts were right. This world has no chance of surviving to the end of the second millennium. Judging by all the visible signs, it will be destroyed long before that. Quite soon, I'd even say. To horse, Tybald. I've changed my mind. Let's search for an inn. Well away from here.'

'Why, m'lord,' said Tybald Raabe, his mouth full of peas and cabbage. 'Where will I get my hands on information like that? I shall indeed tell you what I know, in detail. About Peterlin of Bielawa. About his brother Reynevan and Reynevan's romance with Adèle Stercza and what came out of it. About what happened in the Raubritter settlement of Kromolin and at the tournament in Ziębice. About when Reynevan . . . How is Reynevan, anyway, m'lord? Is he well? What of Samson? And Scharley?'

'Don't change the subject. But since you mention him, who is he, that Scharley?'

'Don't you know, m'lord? He's said to be a monk or fallen priest, reportedly fled from a monastery prison. A certain Tassilo of Tresckow told me that Scharley took part in the Wrocław sedition of 1418. You know, the eighteenth of July, when the rebellious butchers and shoemakers killed Burgermeister Freiberger and six councillors. Thirty rebellious heads rolled for that in Wrocław town square and thirty were banished. And the fact that Scharley's head is still on his shoulders suggests he was one of those banished. I think—'

'Enough,' interrupted the grey-eyed man. 'Give me the information I asked for, about the attack on the tax collector and his convoy. The convoy Reynevan was part of. And you, too, Tybald.'

'Aye, aye.' The goliard ladled up a spoonful of peas. 'What I know, I know. And I'll tell you, why not? But about those other things—'

'Like black horsemen screaming: "*Adsumus*"? Clearly under the influence of the Arabic substance called hash'eesh.'

'Indeed. I didn't see that and know naught at all about it. Where am I to obtain information like that? How?'

'Try looking in the bowl you have in front of you.' The grey-eyed man's voice grew menacing. 'Among the peas and pork pieces. If you find it, it'll be your gain. You'll save time and effort.'

'I understand.'

'Very good. All the information, Tybald. Everything you can find. Facts, gossip, rumours, what's talked about at markets and fairs, in taverns, monasteries, barracks and whorehouses. What priests prattle on about in sermons, the faithful during processions, councillors in town halls and women by town wells. Clear?'

'As the day.'

'It's Saint Hedwig's Eve today, Tuesday, the fourteenth of October. In five days, we will meet in Świdnica on Sunday after Mass, outside the parish church of Saints Stanislaus and Wenceslaus. When you see me, don't approach me. I'll walk away and you'll follow. Understood?'

'Yes, Master Vlk . . . Ahem . . . I beg your pardon . . .'

'I'll forgive you one last time. Next time I'll kill you.'

'Tempora cum causis Latium digesta per annum lapsaque sub terras ortaque signa canam . . .'

The pupils of the Collegiate School at the Church of the Holy Cross in Opole were studying Ovid's *Fasti* that day. The shouts of fishermen and shrieks of washerwomen arguing could be heard from the Młynówka. Wendel Domarasc, *magister scholarum*, put some reports from agents in a hiding place. The content of most of them was worrying.

Something was afoot.

The fellow with the iron-grey eyes, thought Wendel Domarasc, *there'll be problems because of him. As soon as I saw him, I knew. It's clear why he was sent. He's a murderer. An assassin, a killer. He was sent here to eliminate somebody. And after something like that there's always a witch-hunt; panicked terror erupts. And it's impossible to work peacefully. Espionage likes calm, it can't bear violence and commotion. It particularly can't bear people with special assignments.*

The magister rested his chin on his interlaced hands. *Why oh why did he ask about the Vogelsang?*

'The Vogelsang. Does that name mean anything to you?'

'Naturally.' Domarasc overcame his surprise and didn't even raise an eyebrow.

'Of course it does.'

'Go on.'

'The code name "Vogelsang",' said the magister, trying to make his tone matter-of-fact, his voice indifferent, 'was given to a secret group with special tasks, directly responsible to Žižka. The group had a co-ordinator and a liaison officer. When the latter met his death in strange circumstances, contact was lost. The Vogelsang simply vanished. I received orders to find the group. I made efforts. And searched. Unsuccessfully.'

He didn't look down, although the iron-grey eyes bored into him.

'I know the facts.' The visitor's voice didn't betray a trace of emotion. 'What I'm asking for is your opinion on this matter. And your conclusions.'

Conclusions, thought Domarasc, *were drawn long ago. By Flutek, Bohuchval Neplach, who is now feverishly hunting the guilty parties. For the Vogelsang – it's no secret – were given funds from the Tábor. Huge sums of money, meant to serve the financing of 'special operations'. There was clearly too much money, and the men recruited to the Vogelsang were clearly too special. The result: the money vanished and so did the men. Probably for ever.*

'As I said, the Vogelsang's liaison officer and co-ordinator were murdered,' he said, urged on by the look. 'The circumstances of the murders weren't just mysterious, they were alarming, and then gossip literally turned them into a nightmare. Fear of death can supersede loyalty and devotion to the cause. In great terror and fear for one's life, loyalty is forgotten.'

'Loyalty is forgotten,' the visitor repeated slowly. 'Have you forgotten yours?'

'Mine is unswerving.'

'I understand.'

I hope he did, thought Domarasc. *I hope he understood. Because I know the rumours circulating close to Prokop and Flutek about betrayal and a conspiracy. A conspiracy, that's a good one. A secret 'special force' is created, recruiting to it scoundrels of the deepest dye who desert at the first sign of danger, stealing the money put into their care. And then conspiracies are looked for.*

And a killer is sent to Silesia.

The washerwomen by the Młynówka argued and accused each other of prostitution. The fishermen swore. The pupils recited Ovid.

'*Adnue conanti per laudes ire tuorum*
deque meo pavidos excute corde metus . . .'

I wonder, thought the *magister*, closing the window, *where that character is now?*

'Do you know that woman?' Parsifal Rachenau asked his comrade. 'And that maiden?'

'You saw me greeting her,' snapped Henryk Baruth, called Starling, loosening his belt. 'Saw me kissing her hand. Do you think I usually kiss unknown women on the hand? It's my aunt, Hrozwita, travelling somewhere. The chubby one is her maidservant and the one in the cap is her housekeeper.'

'And the maid?'

'My aunt's daughter, who's my cousin. My aunt's husband is my uncle. But not Uncle Henryk, Lord of Smarchowice, who's also known as Heineman, nor Henryk called the Crane, from Bald Mountain, but the third, my father's youngest brother, who's called—'

'Henryk,' guessed Parsifal Rachenau, staring at the fair-haired girl.

'Do you know him? Well, you do now. So he's my uncle, my aunt's his wife and the girl's their daughter. Her name's Ofka. And why are you staring at her like that, eh?'

'I . . .' said the boy, blushing. 'Nothing . . . I only . . .'

Ofka of Baruth was only pretending to be absorbed in fidgeting on the bench in the tavern, kicking her legs, tapping a spoon on a bowl, staring at the ceiling and tugging at the end of her plait. Actually, she'd noticed the squire's interest long before and had suddenly decided to react. By sticking her tongue out at him.

'Silly goose,' Starling commented in disgust. Parsifal didn't comment. He was quite fascinated. The only thing that bothered him was the question of kinship. The Rachenaus were related to the Baruths; one of Uncle Gawein's sisters was probably the cousin of an aunt of the wife of Henryk called the Crane. A thing like that probably demanded a dispensation, which might be hard to get. Parsifal thought of marriage as a disagreeable duty, if not literally a punishment, but now he understood beyond reasonable doubt that if he had to, he much preferred Ofka of Baruth to the thin-as-a-rake and pimply Zuzanna, whose father, old Albrecht of Hackeborn, Lord of Przewóz, was obstinately trying to arrange to marry into the Rachenaus. Parsifal was resolutely determined to delay the marriage as long as possible. For over the years, Zuzanna Hackeborn might at most accumulate more pimples, while Ofka had the makings of a comely maiden. A *very* comely maiden . . .

The comely *in spe* maiden, clearly happy with the attention, first bared her lower teeth at him and then stuck out her tongue again. The matron in a bonnet sitting beside her rebuked the girl sharply. Ofka bared her teeth, this time her upper ones.

'How old might she be . . . ?' mumbled Parsifal Rachenau.

'Of what interest is it to me?' Starling said gruffly. 'Or you, for that matter? Get that kasha down you, we must away. Sir Pŭta will be cross if we don't arrive in Kłodzko on time.'

'Why, if it's not Sir Henryk Baruth and Sir Parsifal of Rachenau,' came a voice beside them.

They looked up. Beside them stood a priest, tall and grey-haired. His eyes were the colour of iron. Or perhaps it only appeared so in the smoke-filled tavern?

'Indeed.' Parsifal Rachenau bowed his head. 'Indeed, Father. It is us. But we aren't knights. We're not yet knighted—'

'Oh, that's just a matter of time,' said the priest, smiling, 'and a short one, I'm certain. If I may: I am Father Schlossknecht, servant of God . . . Oh, it's chilly today . . . Mulled wine would go down well . . . Would you honour me, good sirs, by accepting a mug each? Are you eager?'

Starling and Parsifal looked at each other and swallowed. They were most eager. Cash was the problem.

'Father Schlossknecht, God's servant.' The priest repeated the introduction as he placed the mugs on the table. 'Presently of the Brzeg Collegiate Church. At one time chaplain to Sir Otto Kauffung, may God have mercy on his soul—'

'The chaplain of Lord Kauffung!' Parsifal Rachenau tore his eyes away from Ofka of Baruth and almost choked on his mulled wine. 'By the head of Saint Tiburtius! Why, he died in my arms after being felled in battle. It was two years since, in September, in the Goleniowskie Forests. I was in his entourage when we were attacked by brigands! When the brigands abducted two maidens, the daughters of Lords Biberstein and Apolda, in order later to ravish them both, poor things.'

'God be merciful.' The priest put his hands together in prayer. 'Innocent maidens ravished? How much evil there is in the world . . . How much evil . . . How much sin . . . Who could have dared to do such a thing?'

'Brigand-knights. Their ringleader was Reinmar of Bielawa. A scoundrel and a sorcerer.'

'Sorcerer? It can't be!'

'You'll believe it when I tell you. I saw it with my own eyes . . . And heard much . . .'

'I could also tell you a few things!' said Starling, sipping from his mug. His cheeks were already quite flushed. 'For I also saw that Bielawa's witchcraft! I saw witches flying to a sabbath! And people killed on the road near Frankenstein, at the foot of Grochowa Mountain!'

'It can't be!'

'Oh, indeed,' Starling assured boastfully. 'I speak the truth! The Black Riders killed the men of Lady Dzierżka of Wirsing, the horse trader. The Company of Death. Devils! That Bielawa is served by actual devils! You won't believe it when I tell you!'

The grey-eyed priest assured him that he would. The mulled wine went to their heads. And loosened their tongues.

'What did you say, Reverend?' asked Fryczko Nostitz, frowning as he tossed his saddle over the beam. 'What's your name?'

'Father Haberschrack,' the priest repeated in a soft voice. 'Canon at the Church of the Blessed Virgin Mary in Racibórz.

'Aye, aye, I've heard of you,' Fryczko confirmed with an absolutely certain expression. 'And what brings you to me? Something so urgent you intrude on me in the stable. If it's about Hedwiśka, Strauch's daughter, from Racibórz, I swear – and may Saint Anthony burn me to death – that she's lying. I cannot, by any means, be the father of her bastard, for I only fucked her once and that was in the arse.'

'No, no,' said the priest quickly. 'It concerns something quite different from Strauch's daughter. Though just as delicate, I would say. I would like to know ... Hmm ... I would like to know the circumstances of the death of a close relative. Oh, but perhaps not ... I'd rather ...'

'What would you rather?'

'I'd rather talk to somebody else. For you see—'

'You're not being straight, Pater. Speak or get out of here! I'm late for the tavern, my comrades are waiting. Do you know what comrades are? My fellows? Go on! Now say what this is about!'

'But will you answer, if I ask?'

'That all depends.' Fryczko Nostitz pouted. 'For you, damned priests, too often stick your noses in other people's affairs instead of busying yourselves with your own. And the breviary. And praying to God, and helping the meek, as the rule instructs.'

'As I thought,' the priest replied calmly, raising his eyes, which turned out to be the colour of iron. 'I expected you'd say that. Which is why I'd only ask you to liaise. For I'd rather talk to your comrade, that Italian ... He was explicitly commended to me. Since he is the wisest and most adept among you.'

Fryczko burst out in such loud laughter that the horses began to snort and stamp.

'Well I never! They were mocking you, Pater, joking with you. Vitelozzo Gaetani, the most adept? At what? Boozing, probably. Wisest? He's a Piedmont oaf, a right clot, an ignorant block-head. The only thing he'd tell you is his customary: *cazzo, fanculo, puttana* and *porca madonna*. He knows nothing else! Do you want to find out the truth? Then ask a sharp-witted man! Me, for example.'

'If it be your will,' the priest replied, squinting, 'then I shall. What were the circumstances of the death of Master Hanusz Throst, killed two years ago in the region of Silver Mountain?'

'Ha,' snorted Fryczko, 'I guessed as much. But I promised, so I shall tell.'

He sat down on a bench and gestured at another for the priest.

'It was in the month of September, two years since,' he began. 'We left Kromolin, and all of a sudden I see that we're being followed. We set a trap and caught the fellow. And who's fallen into our hands? You'll never guess: Reynevan of Bielawa. That sorcerer and criminal, ravisher of maidens. Have you heard about Reynevan of Bielawa, ravisher of maidens?'

'What does a ravisher of maidens have to do with Throst's death?'

'I shall tell you. Oh, I'll astonish you, Pater. Astonish you . . .'

'Brother Kantor? Andrzej Kantor?'

'It is I.' The deacon of the Church of the Elevation of the Holy Cross had started on hearing a voice behind him. 'It is I . . .'

The man behind him was wearing a black cloak with flowery embroidery, a waisted grey doublet and a beret decorated with feathers, in the fashion of wealthy merchants and patricians. But there was something about the man that didn't suggest commerce or the bourgeoisie at all. The deacon didn't know what. Perhaps the strange grimace of his mouth. Perhaps the voice. Or the eyes. Strange. The colour of iron.

'I have your payment here.' The grey-eyed man took a pouch from inside his doublet. 'For turning Reinmar of Bielawa over to the Holy Office. Which took place, according to our records, here in the town of Frankenstein, *quintadecimo die mensis*

Septembris Anno Domini 1425. The payment is somewhat delayed, regrettably, but that's how our bookkeepers work.'

The deacon had no intention of asking what 'our records' and 'our bookkeepers' meant. He could guess. He took the pouch from the man. It was much lighter than he'd expected, but he didn't think there was any sense arguing over trifles.

'I . . .' He plucked up courage. 'I always . . . The Holy Office can always rely on me . . . If ever I see someone suspicious . . . I report it at once . . . I hasten to the prior . . . Why, only last Thursday, a stranger was hanging around in the cloth halls—'

'We are especially grateful for that Bielawa,' interrupted the man with eyes the colour of iron. 'He was a dreadful criminal.'

'Indeed!' Kantor said excitedly. 'A brigand! A sorcerer! He's said to have killed people. Poisoned them, so they say. He raised his hand against the Duke of Ziębice himself. He beguiled married women in Oleśnica, then ravished them, then used magic to wipe clean their memory. And he took and kidnapped Sir Jan Biberstein's daughter and raped her by force.'

'By force,' repeated the grey-eyed man, sneering, 'when as a sorcerer he could have beguiled her using magic, ravished her any way he liked, then used magic to wipe clean her memory. It seems to lack logic, doesn't it, my friend?'

The deacon said nothing, mouth open. He wasn't quite sure what 'logic' meant. But he suspected the worst.

'And if you're as vigilant as you boast,' continued the grey-eyed man, quite indifferently, 'did anyone ask about Bielawa? Later, after his arrest? It might have been an accomplice, a Hussite, a Waldensian or a Cathar.'

'There . . . was . . . one . . .' Kantor mumbled despite himself. He was afraid of further questions. In particular: why hadn't he already informed on the man who asked? And the reason was fear. The terror aroused in him by the man who had asked.

Black-haired, dressed in black, with a kind of birdlike physiognomy. And the gaze of the Devil.

'What did he look like?' the grey-eyed man asked sweetly. 'Describe him. As precisely as possible. Please.'

To the delight of the man with the iron-grey eyes, there wasn't a living soul in the parish church. The church's patron, Saint Catherine of Alexandria, looked down from the central panel of a triptych surrounded by chubby little angels peeping from behind clouds in the empty chancel reeking of incense.

The grey-eyed man knelt in front of the altar and the tabernacle lamp, then stood up and walked quickly towards a side confessional hidden in the darkness of the aisle. But before he managed to sit down in it, from the vestry came the sound of a loud sneeze, a slightly quieter curse, and after the curse a remorseful: 'God forgive me.' The grey-eyed man also cursed. But didn't bother with the 'God forgive me'. He reached under his cloak for a small pouch, for it looked as though a bribe would be inevitable.

The man approaching turned out to be a hunched old priest in a well-worn cassock, probably the confessor, since he was shuffling towards the confessional. At the sight of the grey-eyed man, the priest stopped dead and opened his mouth.

'Praise the Lord,' the grey-eyed man greeted him, putting as kind a smile as he could on his face. 'Greetings, Father. I have a—'

'Brother ...' The confessor's face suddenly softened, sagging in surprise and disbelief. 'Brother Markus! Is it you? It is! You're alive! You survived! I don't believe my eyes!'

'Rightly so,' the priest with eyes the colour of iron said coldly. 'Because you are in error, Father. My name is Kneufel. Father Jan Kneufel.'

'It's me, Brother Kajetan! Don't you recognise me?'

'No.'

'But I do you.' The old confessor placed his hands together. 'After all, we spent four years in the monastery in Chrudim ... Every day, we prayed in the same church and ate in the same refectory. Every day, we passed each other in the cloisters. Until that dreadful day when those hordes of heretics arrived at the monastery—'

'You confuse me with somebody else.'

The confessor said nothing for a time. Finally his face lit up and a smile contorted his lips.

'I understand!' announced. 'You're incognito! You fear the Devil's servants and their long and vengeful arms. Needlessly, Brother, needlessly! I don't know, O divine vagabond, what roads led you here, but now you are among your own. There are many of us here, a whole group, a whole *communitas* of poor refugees, *exuls*, driven from the fatherland, exiled from our plundered monasteries and desecrated churches. Among them Brother Heliodor, who barely escaped with his life from Chomutov; then there's Abbot Wetzhausen from Kladruby; and the fugitives from Strahov, Břevnov and Jaroměř ... The lord of these lands, a noble and pious gentleman, is merciful to us. He lets us run a school here and preach about the heretics' crimes ... He protects and defends us. I know you've been sorely tried, Brother, I understand you don't want to reveal yourself. If such be your will, I'll keep your secret. I shan't breathe a word. If you wish to go on, I won't tell anyone I saw you.'

The grey-eyed priest looked at him for a while.

'Indeed, you will not,' he said finally.

A lightning-fast movement, assisted by all the strength of his shoulder. The fist, armed with studded brass knuckles, struck the confessor straight in the Adam's apple and penetrated deep to crush the windpipe and larynx. Brother Kajetan rasped, brought his hands up to his throat and his eyes bulged. He had survived the massacre that Žižka's Taborites committed on Chrudim Dominican monastery in April 1421. But he couldn't survive that blow. Saint Catherine and the chubby little angels looked on indifferently as he died.

The priest with the iron-grey eyes took the brass knuckles from his fingers, bent over, seized the corpse by the cassock and dragged it behind the confessional. And sat down on the bench, covering his face with the hood. He sat in complete silence, in the aroma of incense and candles. He waited.

Katarzyna of Biberstein, daughter of Jan Biberstein, the Lord of Stolz, was due to come with her child to confession at the parish church dedicated to her patron. The grey-eyed priest was curious as to the sinful thoughts of Miss Katarzyna Biberstein. Her sinful deeds. And certain extremely sinful facts from her biography.

In the town of Świdnica, on Sunday the nineteenth of October, soon after the Mass, the singing and sounds of a lute lured passers-by to Kotlarska Street, near a potter's stall located right by the lane leading to the synagogue. Standing on a barrel, the not-so-young goliard in a red hood and a jerkin with an ornately trimmed edge strummed and sang.

> *Do not bow before the bishops,*
> *With their piles of gold,*
> *For they have corrupted our faith,*
> *May they redress, for God's sake . . .*

The number of listeners increased with each verse until a small crowd surrounded the goliard.

It's true there were also those who vanished hurriedly when

they found out that the goliard wasn't singing about sex, as they had expected, but about politics, which had lately become dangerous.

The lords have ruined the chaplains,
Canons and deans;
Everything in the church is corrupt,
Piety is in short supply . . .

'It's the truth! The honest truth!' shouted several voices from the crowd, and a dispute commenced. Some began to fiercely criticise the clergy and Rome, while others stood in their defence, asking astutely: if not Rome, then what? And the goliard took advantage of the situation to steal away.

He turned into the Chmielne Arcades, then into Castle Street, heading towards the area by the town walls at the Grodzka Gate. He soon saw his destination: a sign to the beer cellar called the Red Gryphon.

'You sang nicely, Tybald,' he heard behind him.

The goliard pulled his hood aside and looked quite provocatively straight into eyes the colour of iron.

'I waited two hours for you outside the parish church after the Mass,' he said reproachfully. 'You didn't deign to show yourself.'

'You sang nicely.' The grey-eyed man, wearing the mendicant habit of a Friar Minor, didn't bother either making excuses or apologising. 'Nicely, upon my soul. Just a little dangerously. Aren't you afraid you'll be thrown into the tower again?'

'Firstly,' Tybald Raabe pouted, '*pictoribus atque poetis quodlibet audendi semper fuit aequa potestas*. Secondly, how else am I to work for the cause? I'm not a spy who hides in the shadows or in disguise. I'm an agitator, it's my job to move among the people—'

'Very well, very well. Information.'

'Let's sit down somewhere.'

'Must it be here?'

'The ale's first class here.'

When they were sitting at the table, the goliard said, 'The black horsemen you asked about have been seen in Silesia several times. In particular, curiously, they were seen both in Strzelin, where Master Bart was killed, and in the region of Sobótka, where Sir Czambor of Heissenstein fell. In the first case, the witness was a half-witted herdsman, in the second a drunk organist, so – as one might surmise – neither was believed. I consider more reliable the stablemen and grooms of Lady Dzierżka of Wirsing, the horse trader, whose entourage was attacked and routed by knights in black armour near Frankenstein. Many witnessed that occurrence. The Inquisition's servants also say interesting things—'

'You questioned the servants of the Inquisition?'

'Of course not. Not myself. Through confidants. The servants said that the papal Inquisitor, the Reverend Grzegorz Hejncze, has been conducting an intensive investigation into the case of some demonic horsemen who've been prowling around Silesia on black horses for at least two years. They've even been christened the Company of Death, or, more biblically, the Demons at Midday. They're also called ... the Avengers. But out of the Inquisitor's earshot. Why, it became obvious some time ago that the Company of Death kills people suspected of aiding the Hussites, trading with them, supplying them with food, weapons, black powder, lead ... Or horses, like the above-mentioned Dzierżka of Wirsing. So the Black Knights are our allies and not our enemies, the Inquisitor's men whisper behind his back. Why pursue them, why hamper them? Thanks to them we have less work.'

'And the attack on the tax collector? Carrying taxes destined, after all, for the war against the Hussites?'

'It's not known if the Company attacked the tax collector. Nothing is known about that case.'

The grey-eyed man said nothing for a long time.

'I'm curious whether anyone might have survived that robbery,' he said at last.

'I doubt it.'

'You did.'

'I am skilled.' Tybald Raabe smiled slightly. 'I'm always either hiding or running away, so I've developed a sixth sense. Ever since I left my alma mater in Krakow to wander with my lute and songs. You know how it is, Master: a poet is like a devil in a women's convent, everyone always blames him for everything. You have to know how to run away. Instinctively, like a hart. If anything happens, you don't think, you flee. As a matter of fact ...'

'What?'

'I had plenty of luck back then, in Ścibor's Clearing. I was afflicted by the trots.'

'Eh?'

'There was a maiden in the entourage, I told you, a knight's daughter ... I couldn't do it in the proximity of a maid, the shame ... So I went far away to defecate, into the bulrushes right beside the lake. When the robbery occurred, I fled through the marsh. I didn't even see the assailants ...'

The grey-eyed man was silent for a long time.

'Why,' he finally asked, 'didn't you tell me earlier there was a lake?'

The drowner was very vigilant. Even dwelling in a small lake, deep in the forest near Ścibor's Clearing, in the wilderness, even at dusk when the chances of encountering anybody were almost none, it was extremely cautious. Emerging from the water, it made no more ripples than a fish and had it not been for the fact that the surface was as smooth as glass, the grey-eyed man hidden in the undergrowth might simply not have seen the spreading circles. Coming out onto the bank among the reeds, the creature barely splashed, barely rustled; you'd have said it was an otter. But the man with eyes the colour of iron knew it wasn't.

Standing on dry land and having made sure it wasn't in danger, the drowner became more confident. It straightened up, stamped its large feet, hopped up and down, and each time, water and slime splashed copiously from under its green frock coat. Now quite emboldened, the drowner squirted water from its gills, opened its frog-like mouth and croaked sonorously, informing the surrounding fauna who was in charge.

The fauna didn't react. The drowner pottered around a little in the grass, rummaged in the mud and finally walked uphill, towards the forest. Straight into a trap. It croaked, seeing a semicircle of sand in front of it. It moved a flat foot closer and withdrew it, amazed. It suddenly realised what was happening, squawked loudly and turned around to flee. But it was too late. The grey-eyed man jumped out of the undergrowth and magically closed the circle with sand tossed from a sack. Having done so, he sat down on a stump.

'Good evening,' he said courteously. 'I'd like to talk.'

The drowner – the grey-eyed man already knew that the name 'vodnik' was more appropriate for the creature – tried several times to hop out of the magical circle, but without success, of course. Resigned, it shook its flat head energetically and water gushed from its ears.

'Breckkreck,' it croaked. 'Breckkreckeckecks.'

'Spit out the mud and repeat that, please.'

'Breckeckreckkreckkreck.'

'Are you making a fool of yourself? Or me?'

'Quackskvaaacks.'

'A waste of your talent, Master Vodnik. You won't take me in. I know perfectly well you can understand and speak in human tongue.'

The vodnik blinked its double eyelids and opened its wide, toad-like mouth.

'Human tongue . . .' it gurgled, spitting water. 'Human tongue, of course. But does that have to mean German?'

'Touché. How's your Czech?'

'Better.'

'What's your name?'

'Will you let me go if I tell you?'

'No.'

'Fuck off, then.'

There was silence for some time. It was interrupted by the grey-eyed man.

'There's a matter to be sorted out, Master Vodnik,' he began gently. 'I want you to give me something. No, not give. Let's say . . . make available.'

'Bollocks to that.'

'I never imagined for a moment,' the grey-eyed man said, smiling, 'that you'd agree at once. I assumed we'd have to work on it. I'm patient. I have time.'

The drowner hopped and stamped. Water poured from its frock coat again; apparently there was a considerable reserve inside.

'What do you want?' it croaked. 'Why are you tormenting me? What have I done to you? What do you want from me?'

'From you, nothing. Rather from your wife. As a matter of fact, she can hear our conversation – she's there, right by the water's edge, I can see the reeds moving and the water lilies trembling.

Good evening, Mistress Vodnik! Please don't go away, I'll be needing you!'

There was a loud splash near the bank, as though a beaver had dived in, and ripples spread out over the water. The entrapped drowner boomed like a bittern when it calls with its beak in the mud, then puffed up its gills and uttered a loud croak. The grey-eyed man watched it without emotion.

'Two years ago,' he said calmly, 'in the month of September – which you call *Mheánh* – a robbery, a fight and several deaths occurred here, in Ścibor's Clearing.'

The vodnik frowned again and snorted. Water flowed profusely from its gills.

'What's it got to do with me? I don't meddle in your affairs.'

'The victims, weighted down with stones, were thrown into this pond. I'm certain that one of the victims was alive when they were thrown into the water and only died as a result of drowning. And if so, you have it at the bottom in your *rehoengan*, your underwater lair and strongroom. You're keeping it there as a *hevai*.'

'As a what? I don't understand.'

'Oh, but you do. The *hevai* of the one that drowned. You're keeping it in your strongroom. Send your wife to get it and ask her to bring it here.'

'You're talking nonsense, human,' the creature said, wheezing exaggeratedly, 'and my gills are drying up . . . I'm choking . . . I'm dying . . .'

'Don't try making a fool of me. You can breathe air as long as a crayfish, you won't be harmed. But when the sun rises and the wind gets up . . . When your skin begins to crack . . .'

'Jadziaaa!' yelled the vodnik. 'Fetch the *hevai*! You know which one!'

'So you speak Polish, too.'

The vodnik coughed and squirted water from its nose. 'My wife's Polish,' it reluctantly replied. 'From Gopło. Can we talk seriously?'

'Naturally.'

'Then listen, mortal fellow. You guessed right. Of the sixteen that were killed and thrown into the pond, one – although quite full of holes – was still alive. His heart was still beating, and he went down to the bottom in a cloud of blood and bubbles. His lungs filled with water and he died, but ... which you also guessed ... I managed to get to him before it happened and I have his ... his *hevai*. If I give it to you ... do you promise you'll release me?'

'I promise. I swear.'

'Even if it turns out ... For if you know so much, it means you don't believe in fairy tales and superstitions. You won't bring the drowned man back to life by destroying the *hevai*. It's nonsense, superstition, fabrication. You won't achieve anything; you'll just dispel his aura. You'll make him die again, in enormous suffering, so enormous that the aura may not withstand it and will perish. So if it was somebody close to you—'

'It wasn't,' the grey-eyed man cut him off. 'And I don't believe in superstitions. Bring me the *hevai*, just for a few moments. Then I'll return it to you, untouched. And I'll release you.'

'Ha. If so,' asked the vodnik, all its eyelids blinking, 'why the hell did you need the trap? Why did you capture me, putting me through stress and nerves? You should have come and asked—'

'Next time.'

Something smelling of sludge and dead fish splashed by the bank. A moment later, approaching slowly and apprehensively like a mud turtle, the vodnik's wife was beside them. The grey-eyed man examined it with interest, seeing a *goplana* for the first time in his life. At first sight, it didn't differ much from its husband, but the priest's expert eye was capable of spotting even the least significant details. While the Silesian vodnik resembled a frog, its Polish wife called to mind a princess magicked into a frog.

The vodnik took something from its wife that resembled a large freshwater mussel, covered in a beard of algae. Light shone through the algae – the mussel was glowing. Phosphorescing. Like rotten wood. Or a fern flower. The grey-eyed man scattered the sand of the magical ring, freeing the vodnik from the trap, then took the *hevai* from it. And he suddenly felt the container pound and tremble, felt the pulsing and shivers pass from his hands to his entire body, penetrating and piercing, until they finally crawled into his neck and then his brain. He heard a voice, first soft, insectile, then more and more distinct and louder.

'—the hour of our death . . . Now and at the hour of our death . . . Elencza . . . My child . . . My child . . .'

It wasn't anybody's voice, for it wasn't a creature capable of conversing, of whom one could, following the example of necromancers, ask questions. Like Egyptian canopic jars, or the *anguinum*, the druidic egg, or the crystal *oglain-nan-Druighe*, a *hevai* imprisoned the aura, or rather a fragment of it, remembering only one thing – the moment preceding its death. For the aura, that moment lasted an eternity.

'Save my child! Have mercy! Now and at the hour . . . Save my child . . . Help my daughter . . . Run, run, Elencza, don't look back! Hide, hide, run into the bushes . . . Or they'll find and kill you . . . Have mercy on us . . . Pray for us sinners, now and at the hour of our death. My daughter . . . Blessed Virgin Mary . . . At the hour of our death . . . Elencza! Run away, Elencza! Flee! Flee!'

The priest bent over and placed the *hevai*, throbbing with inner light, down on the lake shore. Delicately and carefully. So as not to break it. Not to disturb it. Not to disrupt the everlasting peace.

'Sir Hartwig Stietencron,' Tybald Raabe guessed at once. 'And his daughter. But does that mean she survived? That she managed to escape or hide? They might have killed her later, after drowning him.'

'It doesn't add up,' the grey-eyed man pronounced coldly. 'The drowner counted sixteen bodies dumped in the lake. The tax collector, Stietencron, the six-man escort, four monks and four pilgrims. One body is missing. That of Elencza of Stietencron.'

'They might have taken her with them. You know, for sport . . . Played with her, slit her throat and tossed her into a pit in the forest somewhere.'

'She survived.'

'How do you know?'

'Don't ask questions, Raabe. Find her. I'm going now and when I return—'

'Where are you going?'

The grey-eyed man gave him a look. And Tybald Raabe knew not to repeat the question.

Gregorz Hejncze, *Inquisitor a Sede Apostolica specialiter deputatus* at the Wrocław Diocese, pondered long over whether to go to the execution, weighing up the benefits and costs. There were definitely more costs – if only the fact that the execution was the result of the bishop's Inquisition, and therefore represented competition. There was actually only one benefit: it was nearby. The people found guilty of heresy and aiding the Hussites were going to be burned in the usual place on a piece of hard, bare ground behind Saint Adalbert's Church, compacted by the hundreds of feet of people keen to watch others being tortured and killed.

Weighing up both sides, and somewhat surprised at himself, Gregorz Hejncze finally went to the execution. Incognito, he mingled among a group of Dominicans, with whom he took a place on the platform meant for clergymen and spectators of superior social or financial status. Among them, in the central stand, on a bench covered in crimson satin, lounged Konrad of Oleśnica, Bishop of Wrocław and the initiator and sponsor of the day's spectacle. He was accompanied by several clergymen – including the venerable notary Jerzy Lichtenberg and Hugo Watzenrode, who had recently replaced Otto Beess as provost of Saint John the Baptist's following the latter's removal. There was, of course, also Jan Sneschewicz, the bishop's assistant curate *in spiritualibus*, and the bishop's bodyguard, Kuczera of Hunt. Birkart Grellenort was not present.

Preparations for the executions were at an advanced stage, and the condemned people – eight of them – were already being dragged up ladders and chained to stakes piled high with faggots and logs by the executioner's servants. The pyres, in accordance with the recent fashion, were extremely high.

If Gregorz Hejncze had been deluding himself for so much as a moment regarding Bishop Konrad's intentions, it was time he stopped.

But the Inquisitor hadn't. From the beginning, he knew that the bishop's spectacle was directed against him personally. Recognising some of the condemned people at the stake, Gregorz Hejncze was confirmed in his opinion.

He knew three of them. One, the altarist at Saint Elisabeth's, had spoken a little too much about Wycliffe, Joachim of Fiore, the Holy Spirit and Church reform, but during the investigation had swiftly nonetheless quickly renounced his error, regretted it and after a formal *revocatio et abiuratio* was condemned to wearing penitential robes and carrying a cross for a week. The second, one of the painters of the exquisite polyptychs adorning the altar at Saint Giles', came before the tribunal owing to a denunciation, and when it proved to be groundless was released. The third – the Inquisitor barely recognised him since his ears had been mutilated and his nostrils slit open – was a Jew who had once been accused of blasphemy and profanation of the Host. The accusation was false, so he had been released. Nonetheless, news must have reached the bishop and Sneschewicz, for all three of them were standing chained to stakes, with no idea that they owed their fate to the antagonism between the bishop and the papal Inquisition. And that a moment later, the bishop would order the faggots beneath their feet to be lit. To spite the papal Inquisitor.

Hejncze didn't know how many of the remaining condemned were to die that day just to make a statement. He didn't remember any of them. Not a single face. Not the woman with hair cropped short and cracked lips, nor the beanpole with his legs bound up in bloodstained rags. Nor the white-haired old man with the appearance of an Old Testament prophet, struggling to break free and yelling . . .

'Your Reverence.'

He looked back. And drew the edge of his hood from his face.

'His Eminence Bishop Konrad,' said a very young seminarist, bowing, 'asks you to join him. If Your Reverence would follow me, I'll take you.'

What to do?

The bishop made a curt and rather disdainful wave of the hand and indicated the seat beside him. He keenly sized up the Inquisitor's face, searching for a sign of anything that would amuse him. He found nothing, since Gregorz Hejncze had spent time in Rome and was able to put on a brave face in any situation.

'In a moment,' snarled the bishop, 'we shall delight Jesus and the Blessed Virgin. And you, Father Inquisitor? Are you glad?'

'Inordinately.'

The bishop snarled again, inhaled and swore under his breath. He was clearly angry and the reason was equally clear. Being on public display, he couldn't drink and had already endured a few agonising hours.

'Then look, Inquisitor. Look. And learn.'

'Brothers!' yelled the white-haired old man thrashing around at the stake. 'Awake! Why do you murder your prophets? Why do you stain your hands with the blood of your martyrs? Broooothers!'

One of the servants casually elbowed him in the belly. The prophet folded up, spluttered and was quiet for a while. But not for long.

'You will perish!' he howled, to the delight of the crowd. 'You will peeeerrish! And the pagan hordes will come and kill some of you and take the others captive. Ravenous wolves and darkness will multiply against you and plunge you into the ocean depths. The Lord says: therefore, I will cast thee out of the mountain of God . . . I will destroy thee from the midst of the stones of fire. I will lay thee before kings . . .'

The mob roared with laughter and staggered in delight.

'The Lord shall rain snares upon the wicked! The hail shall sweep away the refuge of lies, and the waters shall overflow the hiding place!'

'Can't that madman be gagged?' asked the Inquisitor in exasperation. 'Or otherwise silenced?'

'But what for?' Konrad of Oleśnica grinned. 'Let the people listen to this drivel. Let them have a laugh. The people toil by the sweat of their brow. Pray zealously. Don't have enough to eat, particularly during fasts. They deserve some diversion. Laughter relaxes them.'

The crowd clearly agreed with him, and each subsequent ex-
clamation of the prophet was greeted with roars of hilarity. The
front rows of onlookers were bent double with mirth.

'You wiiiill peeeriish!'

'Will no one,' Gregorz Hejncze said, unable to remain quiet
and seeing what was afoot, 'will no one be shown any mercy?
Were the executioners not given instructions?'

'Oh, but they were.' The bishop finally rewarded him with a
look, a look of triumph. 'And they are carrying them out to the
letter. For we are strict here, Grzesiu, my boy.'

The servants removed the ladders and withdrew. The executioner approached with a torch lit from a brazier. As he lit the
fires in turn, flames flickered and cracked among the brushwood
and smoke curled upwards. The condemned reacted in various
ways. Some began to pray. Others to howl like jackals. The altarist from Saint Elisabeth's struggled and strained, howled and
banged the back of his head against the stake. The eyes of the
painter of the polyptychs brightened, lit up as the sight of flames
and the smell of burning tore him out of his torpor. The shaven-
headed woman began to wail, a long string of snot hanging from
her nose and saliva dripping from her mouth. The prophet went
on bawling his nonsense, but his voice had changed. The further
the flames crept up, the higher and squeakier it became.

'Brothers! The Church is a harlot! The Pope is the Antichrist!'

The crowd howled, roared and cheered. The smoke grew
thicker, obscuring the view. The flames crept over the wood,
wandering upwards. But the pyres were high. They had been
built like that deliberately. In order to prolong the spectacle.

'Look! See the Antichrist approaching! Look! Don't you see!
Or are your eyes blind? He is from the tribe of Dan! He shall
reign for three and a half years! His church shall be in Jerusalem! His number is six hundred three-score and six, his name

is Evanthas, Lateinos, Teitan! His face is as of a wild beast! His right eye is as a star rising at dawn, his mouth is a cubit in width, his teeth a span in length. Brothers! See you not! Broooo—'

The fire finally defeated and overcame the passive resistance of the damp wood, burst through aggressively, flared up and roared. A horrendous, inhuman screaming rose above the fires. A hot wave drove the smoke away and for a moment, for a very brief moment, human shapes could be seen thrashing around at the stakes in the crimson inferno. It was as though the fire was shooting straight from their screaming mouths.

The wind, mercifully for Gregorz Hejncze, drove the stench in the opposite direction.

The four sides of the garth overshadowed by arcades at the monastery of the Premonstratensians in Ołbin were meant to assist with meditation by recalling the four rivers of Paradise, the four Evangelists and the four cardinal virtues. That 'barricade of discipline', as Saint Bernard called it, was a picture of order and aesthetics. It emanated peace and quiet.

'You're somewhat taciturn, Grzesiu,' remarked Konrad of Oleśnica, Bishop of Wrocław, watching the Inquisitor intently. 'As though you are ailing. Is it your conscience or your stomach?'

The monastery. The garth. The garden. Humility. Calm. Keep calm.

'Your Eminence takes the liberty of addressing me in a particularly familiar manner with admirable unswervingness and unyieldingness. I shall also take the liberty of being unswerving: I shall remind you once again that I am a papal Inquisitor, delegate of the Apostolic See for the Wrocław Diocese. By virtue of my position, I deserve respect and the appropriate title. Your Eminence may call your minions, canons, confessors and dogsbodies "Grześ", "Jaś", "Paś" or "Piesio".'

'Your Inquisitorial Reverence,' said the bishop, putting as much scornful exaggeration into the title as he could, 'need not remind me what I can and can't do. I myself know best. It's easy: I can simply do what I like. In order for there to be no misunderstandings, I will tell Your Reverence that I'm in the process of exchanging letters with Rome – with the very Apostolic See, as it happens – the consequence of which could be that Your Excellency's wonderfully promising career may turn out to be as perishable as a fish's bladder. Pop! And it's gone. And then, the highest office Your Excellency can expect in this diocese is to work for me as a servant, canon or dogsbody, with all its obligations, including the familiar term of address "Grześ". Or "Piesio", if I so wish. For the alternative will be the name "Brother Gregorius" in some remote monastery, among picturesque, dense forests, in a location as far from Wrocław as Armenia.'

'Indeed.' Gregorz Hejncze interlaced his fingers and also leaned against the arcade, without lowering his gaze. 'Indeed, Your Eminence hasn't left much room to be misconstrued. But your efforts were in vain, since the exchange of letters between Your Eminence and Rome is very familiar to me. I also know, indeed, that the result of that correspondence is actually nil. No one, naturally, can forbid Your Eminence from sending further epistles. Little by little does it – who knows, perhaps one of the cardinals will finally succumb, perhaps they'll finally dismiss me? Personally, I doubt it, but everything is in the hands of God, after all.'

'Amen.' Bishop Konrad smiled and breathed out, happy that the level of the conversation had settled down. 'Amen, Grzesiu. You're a bright lad, do you know? It's what I like about you. Pity there's nothing more.'

'A pity indeed.'

'Don't make faces. You know perfectly well what I dislike in you and why I'm trying to have you removed. You're too soft, Grzesiu, too merciful. You act too indecisively, sluggishly and without a plan. And time doesn't favour that. *Haereses ac multa mala hic in nostra dioecesi surrexerunt.* Heresy and heathenism are spreading. The world is teeming with Hussite spies. Witches, kobolds, phantoms and other hellish monsters are mocking us, holding their sabbaths on Ślęża, five miles from Wrocław. Vile practices and the cult of Satan are conducted by night on Grochowa Mountain, on Kłodzko Mountain, on Żeleźniak beneath the peak of the Pradziad, and in hundreds of other places. The Beguines are active again. The godless sect of the Sisterhood of the Free Spirit mocks the law, unpunished, because it's full of and led by noblewomen, patrician matrons and the abbesses of the wealthiest convents. And you, Inquisitor, of what can you boast? Though you had Urban Horn – apostate, traitor and Hussite spy – in your grasp, he slipped out of it. Though you had Reinmar of Bielawa – sorcerer and criminal – in your grasp, he slipped out of it. One after another, petty merchants who trade with the Hussites have slipped through your fingers. I mean: Bart, Throst, Neumarkt, Pfefferkorn and others. They were prosecuted and punished, of course, but not by you. Someone disburdened you. Someone keeps having to. Should somebody be taking over the Inquisitor's work? Well? Grzesiu?'

'I assure Your Eminence that I shall put an end to that.'

'You keep assuring me. Two years ago, in December, you supposedly found a witness whose testimony was to uncover some dangerous, literally demonic organisation or sect, guilty of numerous murders. You unearthed that witness, reportedly a deacon from the Namysłów Collegiate Church, in a madhouse of all places. I was waiting in suspense to listen to the testimonies of that lunatic. And then what? You didn't manage to get him to Wrocław.'

'I didn't manage,' Hejncze said, 'because he was assassinated on the way. By somebody who uses black magic.'

'Indeed. Black magic.'

'Which proves that somebody wanted him silenced,' the Inquisitor continued calmly, 'for had he spoken, his testimony would have seriously harmed somebody. He was an eyewitness to the murder of the merchant Pfefferkorn. Perhaps he would have identified the murderer if he'd been shown a suspect?'

'Perhaps. Or perhaps not. We don't know. And why don't we know? Because the papal Inquisitor is incapable of protecting a witness, even if he's a nutcase from the Tower of Fools. A disgrace, Grzesiu. A fiasco.

'Crime is flourishing under your very nose; no one is safe,' continued the bishop, without waiting for a reaction. 'Robber knights in league with Hussites sack monasteries. Jews desecrate Hosts and graves. Heretics steal taxes, the hard-earned money of the poor. The daughter of Jan Biberstein, knight and magnate, is kidnapped and raped openly by Hussites as revenge for Biberstein being a good Catholic. And where were you? Somebody had to intervene. I, Bishop of Wrocław, with my hands full of endless matters regarding the faith, have to burn the guilty for you.'

'Were there any guilty people among those burned today?' asked the Inquisitor, raising an eyebrow. 'I can't say I noticed.'

'Noticing isn't your strongest suit, Grzesiu,' the bishop retorted. 'You fail to notice far too many things. With injurious results for Silesia, regrettably. For the Church. And for the *Sanctum Officium*, which you serve, after all.'

'Empty and ostentatious executions are injurious to the Holy Office. Injustice is injurious. Such things cause dark legends to arise, myths about the cruel Inquisition, grist to the mill for heretical propaganda. In a hundred years – the thought horrifies me – only the legends will remain, dark and horrific tales of dungeons, torture and fires. Legends that everybody will believe.'

'You understand neither people nor historical processes,' replied Konrad of Oleśnica coldly, 'which writes you off as an Inquisitor. You ought to know, Grzesiu, that there are always two sides. If horrendous legends arise, there'll be anti-legends. Counter-legends. Even more horrendous ones. If I burn a hundred people, in a hundred years they'll be saying I burned a thousand. And others will say I didn't burn a single person. In five hundred years, if this world lasts that long, for every three people talking excitedly about dungeons, torture and fires, there'll be at least one fool claiming there were no dungeons, torture wasn't used, the Inquisition was as compassionate and fair-minded as a good father, penalties were light, nothing more than a ticking off, and all those fires were a fabrication and heretical libel. So do your job, Grzesiu, and leave the rest to history. And to the people who understand it. And please don't drivel on about justice. The institution you work for wasn't founded for justice. Justice is *droit du seigneur*. *Ergo*, justice is me, because I am the senior person here. I am a lord, a Piast, a duke – a Prince of the Church, to be sure, but one who *habet omnia iura tamquam dux*. You, meanwhile, Grzesiu, are, forgive me, a servant.'

'Of God.'

'Bullshit. You're a servant of the Inquisition, an institution meant to strangle thought at birth and intimidate people who think, rebuke and oppress minds, sow fear and terror, and make sure the mob are afraid to think. Because that institution was founded with that purpose. Pity so few people remember that, which is why heresy is spreading and flourishing. It is flourishing thanks to people like you, fanatics with their eyes fixed on Heaven, barefoot and begging, in imaginary imitation of Christ. They who talk of faith, of humility and of divine service allow birds to perch on them and shit on them and from time to time receive the stigmata. Do you have the stigmata, Grzesiu?'

'No, Your Eminence. I do not.'

'Well, that's something, at least. To continue: what you see around you, Father Inquisitor, is not God's plaything but a world that needs to be governed. Ruled. And power is a privilege of princes. Of lords. The world is a dominium that has to surrender to rulers, bowing low to accept *droit du seigneur*, the right of the lord. It's the natural order that power is wielded by the Princes of the Church. And then their sons. Yes, yes, Grzesiu. We rule the world and our power will be inherited by our sons. The sons of kings, princes, popes, cardinals and bishops. And sons of mercers, forgive my frankness, are – and will be – vassals. Subjects. Servants. They are meant to serve. Serve! Do you understand, Gregorz Hejncze, son of a Świdnica merchant? Do you see?'

'Better than Your Eminence realises.'

'Then go and serve. Be as vigilant towards signs of heresy as your name – Gregorikos – ought to suggest. Be uncompromising towards heretics, heathens, deviants, monsters, witches and Jews. Be merciless to those who dare to raise their minds, eyes, voices and hands against my power and my possessions. Serve. *Ad maiorem Dei gloriam.*'

'Regarding the latter, Your Excellency may count on me absolutely.'

'And remember.' Konrad raised two fingers, but there was no trace of a blessing in the gesture. 'Remember: he who is not with me *contra me est*. Either with me, or against me, *tertium non datur*. He who is tolerant of my enemies is himself my enemy.'

'I understand.'

'Good. We shall draw a thick line through what has been. Let's turn over a new leaf. *Sapienti sat dictum est*, to begin with let's agree on this: next week you will send another ten to their deaths at the stake, Inquisitor Grzesiu. May Silesia hold its breath for a moment. May sinners recall the fires of Hell. May the hesitant redouble their faith, having seen the alternative. May informers recall that they must inform – actively and on anybody they can, before somebody informs on them. A time of terror and fear has come! The heretical viper must be seized by the throat in an iron hand and a spiked glove. Seized and held, not released! For it is because the grip was once loosened, because weakness was shown, that heresy is on the march now.'

'Heresy has existed in the Church for centuries,' said the Inquisitor softly. 'For ever. For the Church has always been a rock and a haven for people who profoundly believe, but who also have lively minds. But also, unfortunately, always a refuge, a fertile breeding ground for the displays of such creatures as Your Eminence.'

'I admire in you your intelligence and frankness,' the bishop said after a long silence. 'A true pity that I admire nothing else.'

Father Felicjan – known to the world once as Hanys Gwisdek and nicknamed Little Louse – was basking in a sunny spot at the end of the garth, observing behind a blackthorn bush the bishop and the Inquisitor deep in a hushed conversation. *Who knows*, he thought, *perhaps soon I shall be allowed to take part in conversations like that? As an equal? For I am advancing.*

Father Felicjan was indeed advancing. The bishop had promoted him for his services, which mainly consisted of informing on the previous superior, Canon Otto Beess. When Otto Beess fell out of favour after being denounced, Father Felicjan began to be treated differently at the bishop's court. Quite differently. Father Felicjan thought it was with admiration.

I'm advancing. Ha. I'm advancing.

'Father.'

He shuddered and turned around. The monk who had approached him so soundlessly was not a Premonstratensian, but wore a white Dominican habit. Father Felicjan didn't know him. Which meant he worked for the Inquisitor.

'Go away, Father. There's nothing for you here. Begone!'

The Inquisitor's man, thought Father Felicjan, as he hastily withdrew. *A Dominican, one of those famous unchecked and all-powerful 'white eminences'. That voice, imperious, like that of the very bishop . . . Those eyes . . .*

Eyes the colour of iron.

The poorhouse of the Divine Heart of Jesus was located outside the town walls, near the Weavers Gate. The meal was being served as they arrived. Gaunt paupers covered in suppurating sores dragged themselves out of bed, took bowls in their trembling hands, dipped bread in them and crammed it, now softened, into their toothless mouths. Tybald Raabe cleared his throat, looked away and covered his nose with the cuff of his glove. The grey-eyed priest didn't even notice. Poverty and suffering made no impression on him and had stopped interesting him long ago.

They had to wait. The girl they had gone to see was busy in the poorhouse kitchen.

A foul smell was emanating from there.

They had to wait a while before she joined them.

So that's Elencza of Stietencron, thought the grey-eyed man. *None too appealing. Stooped, grey, thin-lipped. With an empty gaze. And her hair mercifully hidden by a cap and wimple. With her once-fashionable plucked eyebrows slowly growing back.*

Elencza Stietencron, a survivor of the massacre where sixteen men – including soldiers – were killed. The only person to get out alive. The stooped plain-looking girl survived. The conclusion suggested itself. The stooped plain-looking girl was no ordinary stooped plain-looking girl.

'Noble Miss Stietencron—'

'Please don't address me like that.'

'Hmm ... Miss Elencza ...'

Elencza. An unusual name, too. Rarely encountered. Tybald Raabe tracked down its origin – the daughter of Władysław, Duke of Bytom, bore that name. The grandfather of Hartwig Stietencron, who served the Bytom duke, gave that name to one of his daughters. A tradition was established, in accordance with which Hartwig had christened his only child.

The grey-eyed man signalled something to Tybald Raabe with his eyes. The goliard cleared his throat.

'Miss,' he spoke seriously. 'I forewarned you last time. We must ask you a few questions. Regarding ... Ścibor's Clearing.'

'I don't want to talk about it. I don't want to remember.'

'You must,' said the grey-eyed man sternly – too sternly. The girl cringed, quite as though he had raised a hand or shaken a fist at her.

'You must.' The priest softened his tone. 'It's a matter of life and death. We have to know. The young nobleman who joined your party two days before the robbery and soon left it – was he among the robbers in the clearing? Miss Elencza! Was Reinmar of Bielawa among the assailants?'

'A young nobleman,' Raabe explained, 'whom you know as Reinmar of Hagenau, miss.'

'Reinmar Hagenau ...' Elencza Stietencron's eyes widened. 'That ... was ... Reinmar of Bielawa?'

'The very same.' The grey-eyed man did his best to control his impatience. 'Did you recognise him? Was he among the assailants?'

'No! Of course not—'

'Why "of course"?'

'Because ... Because he ...' the girl stammered and looked beseechingly at Tybald. 'It couldn't have ... Master Raabe ... There are rumours ... About Reinmar of Bielawa ... That ... he harmed ... the daughter of Lord Biberstein ... Master Raabe! It cannot be true!'

Fascination, thought the grey-eyed man, suppressing a grimace. *The fascination of the unremarkable girl, in love with a dream, with a painting, with a stanza from Tristan or Erec. Yet another girl who dotes on that Bielawa. One more for his collection. What do they see in him? I'll never understand women.*

'So Reinmar of Bielawa wasn't among the assailants?' he asked again.

'No, he wasn't.'

'Are you certain?'

'I am. I'd have recognised him.'

'Were the attackers wearing black armour and cloaks? Were they crying "*Adsumus*" or "We are here"?'

'No.'

'No?'

'No.'

They fell silent. One of the beggars suddenly began to weep. A nurse, a stout nun in the habit of the Poor Clares, calmed him.

The grey-eyed man didn't turn his head. Or even glance in their direction.

'Miss Elencza. Does your mother ... Your stepmother ... Does your father's widow know that you're here?'

The girl shook her head and her mouth twitched visibly. The grey-eyed man knew what that was all about, for Tybald Raabe had poked around and arrived at the truth. On that ill-fated day, Sir Hartwig Stietencron was taking his daughter to relatives in Bardo, having removed her from his humble estate in order to liberate her from the envious and malicious tyranny of his second wife, her stepmother. In order to save her from the sweaty paws of the stepmother's two sons, ne'er-do-wells and sots who, after bedding all the local and neighbouring serving wenches, had begun to send lustful glances at Elencza.

'Haven't you thought about returning?'

'I like it here.'

She likes it here, he repeated in his mind. *She didn't stay long with the relatives she went to after escaping and wandering. She didn't have time to settle down, accustom herself to it, never mind come to like it. For in December, Bardo was captured, pillaged and burned down by the Hussites, Ambrož's Orphans from Hradec. Her two relatives, the husband and wife, were killed in the massacre.*

Bad luck dogs the girl. Misfortune. Ill fate.

Elencza went to the poorhouse in Ziębice from the embers of Bardo. She stayed for a long time. Arriving as a patient, she plunged into a deep apathy bordering on stupor. Then, after getting better, she began to serve as a nurse to the other sick people. Recently – the intrusive and inquisitive Tybald Raabe had found that out, too – the Strzelin Poor Clares had taken an interest in her and Elencza was being seriously considered for a novitiate.

'And so,' concluded the grey-eyed man, 'you will stay here.'

'Yes, I will stay.'

Stay, thought the grey-eyed man. *Stay. Much depends on your staying.*

Elencza Stietencron.

'Brother Andrzej Kantor?'

'I ...' The deacon of the Exaltation of the Cross started on hearing an unexpected voice behind him. 'It is I ... Oh ... My goodness! It's you!'

The man standing behind him was dressed all in black, with a black cloak, black doublet, black trousers and black, shoulder-length hair. A birdlike face and a nose like a bird's beak.

And the look of a devil.

'It is us,' he confirmed with a smile, and the sight of the smile froze the blood in the deacon's veins. 'It's been a long time, Kantor. I stopped by in Frankenstein to find out if . . .'

The deacon swallowed.

'Has anybody been asking after me lately?' finished the Wallcreeper.

It was a strictly observed custom that if Konrad of Oleśnica, Bishop of Wrocław, was residing at Otmuchów Castle for his amusement, the door to the bishop's bedchamber was closely guarded and absolutely no one was permitted to open it or enter the chamber. So the bishop was dumbfounded when the door suddenly opened with a boom and a small group swept in.

The bishop cursed extremely coarsely. One of the nuns, freckled, red-haired and with cropped hair, jumped with a squeal from between his thighs. The other nun, also quite naked, concealed her head and her identity beneath the feather quilt, at the same time putting on public display something of much more interest than her identity.

Meanwhile, the crowd on the floor separated into Kuczera of Hunt, the bishop's bodyguard, two Otmuchów guards and Birkart Grellenort.

'Your Eminence . . .' panted Kuczera of Hunt. 'I tried . . .'

'He did,' confirmed Wallcreeper, spitting blood from a cut lip. 'But the matter I come with brooks no delay. I told him, but he wouldn't listen—'

'Get out!' roared the bishop. 'Everybody out! Only Grellenort remains!'

The guards followed Kuczera of Hunt out, limping. Behind them, bare feet slapping, ran the two nuns, trying to hide as much of their charms as possible behind their shifts and habits. The Wallcreeper closed the door behind them.

The bishop didn't get up but lay sprawled, only covering the very crux; that which the red-haired nun had been working on so devotedly a moment before.

'Let's hope it is indeed urgent, Grellenort,' he warned ominously. 'Let's hope it is indeed important. In any event, I'm beginning to tire of your impudence. You don't even bother to fly through the window or pass through the walls now. You must cause a sensation. So be it. What is the matter?'

'Oh, no. I'm waiting.'

'What?'

'Does Your Excellency,' drawled the Wallcreeper, 'have anything to tell me?'

'Have you lost your mind, Birkart?'

'Are you by any chance concealing something from me, Father? Something important? Something which, though it is a closely guarded secret, may at any moment be revealed to the whole world?'

'This is nonsense! I will not listen to this!'

'Have you forgotten the Bible, Bishop? The words of the Evangelist? *Non enim est aliquid absconditum quod non manifestetur, nec factum est occultum sed ut in palam veniat.* For nothing is secret that shall not be made manifest. It's my pleasure to inform you that a witness has been found to the robbery of the tax collector, carried out near Bardo on the thirteenth of September, *Anno Domini* 1425.'

'Well, well,' said Konrad of Oleśnica, grinning unpleasantly. 'A witness has been found. And what did they testify? Who, I wonder, robbed the tax collector?'

The Wallcreeper's eyes flashed. 'Revealing the culprit is just a matter of time,' he growled. 'It so happens that this witness was found by people hostile to us. Having the witness, they'll get to the bottom of it and it will come out. Beautifully. So moderate your tone a little, Bishop!'

Bishop Konrad eyed him evilly for some time, then clambered out of bed and hid his nakedness with a mantle. He sat down on a curule chair and was silent for some while longer.

'How could you, Papa?' the Wallcreeper, sitting down opposite, said reproachfully. 'How could you? Without telling me anything? Or informing me?'

'I didn't want to bother you,' Konrad lied smoothly. 'You had so much to do . . . How do you know about the witness?'

'Thanks to magic. And informers.'

'I understand. Using magic and informers, one will be able, I presume, to track down that witness . . . And, hmm, eliminate him? Generally speaking, that witness can go and boil his head and those hostile people can fuck themselves. They cannot do shit to me. But who needs trouble? If it's possible to break the witness's neck . . . Eh? Birkart, my son? Can you help?'

'I have enough to deal with already.'

'Of course, *mea culpa*,' the bishop reluctantly admitted. 'Don't be cross. You're right. I concealed it! What of it? Do you never conceal anything from me?'

The Wallcreeper preferred not to admit that he did indeed, so answered the question with one of his own: 'Explain to me, Father Bishop, why did you steal money that was meant to serve a sacred cause – the war against Czech heresy, a crusade you continue to call for?'

'I saved that money,' Konrad replied coldly. 'Thanks to me, it will serve what it's supposed to serve. It will be spent on what it ought to be spent on. On mercenaries, horses, arms, cannons, guns, gunpowder. On everything we can use to beat, grind down and destroy the Czech apostates. And it is certain that no one will embezzle that coin. If the money had gone to Frankfurt, it would simply have been stolen. As usual.'

'Quite convincing reasoning,' said the Wallcreeper with a smile, 'but I doubt it would convince the papal legate.'

'The legate is the biggest thief of them all. In any case, the legate and the princes already have their silver, for we collected the tax again after the robbery. Everyone saw how it was spent – at the Battle of Tachov! What didn't go into their pockets remained on the battlefield from which they fled in disarray, leaving everything to the Hussites! And that other tax? They've already forgotten about it. It's history.'

'Unfortunately, it isn't,' the Wallcreeper calmly countered. 'The second tax was ratified by the Reichstag. Whoever stole the money played a trick on the Holy Roman Empire's Prince-Electors, made a fool of the archbishops. They won't just drop the matter. They'll sniff around, delve into it. They'll get to the bottom of it eventually – or harbour justified suspicions.'

'What will they do to me? What can they do? They're unable to harm me. This is Silesia! My power and might are here! *Maior sum quam cui possit Fortuna nocere!*'

'*Quem dies vidit veniens superbum, hunc dies vidit fugiens iacentem.*' The Wallcreeper retorted with an equally classical quotation. 'Don't be too cocksure, Papa. Let us be cautious. Even when the matter of the inconvenient witness is solved, one ought to think about finally closing the investigation into the theft of the tax – not by discontinuing it, but rather by capturing and punishing the guilty party.'

'Actually, I think likewise,' admitted Konrad. 'According to the prevailing rumour, the tax collector was attacked and the money stolen by Reinmar of Bielawa, the brother of Piotr of Bielawa, a

Hussite spy. Reinmar fled to Bohemia, to his fellow heretics. So let's lure him to Silesia, capture him and put him on trial. Proof of his crimes will be found.'

'Naturally.' The Wallcreeper smiled. 'Do we need anything more than the accused's confession of his guilt? And Reinmar will confess to all the crimes we accuse him of. Everyone confesses in the end, after a suitably lengthy period of persuasion. Unless he unluckily dies before confessing.'

'Why "unluckily"? I regard it as obvious and normal that Bielawa will give up the ghost in the torture chamber. After having confessed to the robbery of the tax collector. But before revealing where the stolen silver is hidden.'

'Ah. Of course. I understand. But . . .'

'But what?'

'The people interested in the fate of that money might still have their doubts, I fear . . .'

'They won't. They'll find other irrefutable proofs of guilt. An empty trunk will be discovered, the same one the tax collector carried the money in, during a search of the house of Bielawa's accomplice.'

'Brilliant. Who will that be?'

'I don't know yet, but I have a list. What do you say to the papal Inquisitor, Grześ Hejncze?'

'Hey, not too fast.' The Wallcreeper frowned. 'Everything in moderation. I've already told you a hundred times: desist from an open war with Hejncze. A war with Hejncze is a war against Rome and that antagonism can only harm you. *Irritabis crabrones*, you'll stir up the hornets. Although you think yourself superior to and stronger than Fortune and don't fear harm, it doesn't only concern your bishop's arse. By fighting the Inquisitor, you demonstrate to people that, firstly, there's no unity between you, that you're divided and conflicted. Secondly, that the Inquisition needn't be feared. And when people stop fearing, you damn priests could be in deep trouble.'

The bishop said nothing for a while and looked at him through lowered eyelids.

'Son,' he finally said, 'you are precious to us. We need you. You're actually most good to us. But don't growl at us, for we may lose patience. Don't bare your fangs at us, for in spite of the truly paternal love we feel for you, when we lose patience, we'll have your teeth knocked out. All of them. In turn. With long breaks, so that you can suitably enjoy your treatment.'

'And who, then, will solve the matter of the inconvenient witness?' replied the Wallcreeper with an unpleasant smile. 'Who will lure Reynevan of Bielawa to Silesia and capture him?'

'Exactly.' The bishop lifted his mantle and scratched a hairy calf. 'We're jabbering on, bandying words, and the most important things are slipping by. See to it, son. That witness must vanish. Without a trace. Like the other one Hejncze unearthed in the Tower of Fools two years ago.'

'Consider it done.'

'What about Reinmar of Bielawa?'

'He'll also be seen to.'

'Then let's have a drink. Hand me a cup. But first smell the bouquet. Moldavian! I was given six barrels by way of a bribe, for the position of scholaster in Legnica.'

'Bribery for giving out prebends? Tut, tut, Papa.'

'They don't offer monetary bribes because they can't afford it, the paupers. Should I be filling ecclesiastical posts with paupers? Well? While we're on the subject, would you like a church position, Grellenort?'

'No, Father Bishop, I wouldn't. The priesthood sickens me.'

*

The grey-eyed man, noted Wendel Domarasc, had changed his clothes and completely changed his appearance. Today, instead of a cassock, a habit or a patrician's doublet, he was wearing a short leather jacket, tight hose and high boots. He wasn't carrying a visible weapon, but in spite of that looked like a mercenary. The camouflage was an effective disguise – Silesia had recently been crawling with mercenaries. There was great demand for men who could wield a weapon.

'I shall soon carry out my task,' began the grey-eyed man, 'but after doing so I shall immediately vanish. Thus, I'd like to say farewell to you today.'

'May God keep you.' The *magister scholarum* linked his fingers. 'May we meet in better times.'

'Let's hope. I have a final request.'

'Consider it done.'

'I knew and saw for myself,' the grey-eyed man began a moment later, 'that you are a master among masters in the art of underground activities, who can hide what should remain hidden. I believe you can also cause the opposite to happen.'

'Make something secret stop being secret?' Domarasc smiled. 'Give out information and disinformation?'

'You read my thoughts.'

'What or whom does this concern?'

The grey-eyed man explained. Wendel Domarasc said nothing for a long time, then confirmed that he would execute it. But not using words. With a nod of his head.

Through the small open window came a chorus of voices of the pupils from the Opole Collegiate Church school, reciting the beginning of *The Metamorphoses*.

Aurea prima sata est aetas, quae vindice nullo,
sponte sua, sine lege fidem rectumque colebat.

Poena metusque aberant, nec verba minantia fixo
aere legebantur, nec supplex turba timebat
iudicis ora sui, sed erant sine vindice tuti . . .

'The words of Naso were wise.' The grey-eyed man interrupted the long silence after listening. 'The first age was golden,
a timeless spring of the world. But that age won't return. And
the silver age passed after it, and the bronze, too. Now has come
the fourth age, the final age of hard iron, *de duro est ultima ferro*.
The final age is one of blood and destruction. A plague of crime
has erupted into the world. Faith and truth have fled before
war, killing and conflagration. Treachery and violence triumph.
Horrified by what is happening, Astrea, the last of the deities, is
abandoning the Earth. And when the deities are gone . . . What
then? A deluge?'

'No,' countered Wendel Domarasc. 'There will be no deluge.
And it won't be the last age. A guarantee of that is, for example,
those whippersnappers reciting Ovidius Naso. We, the people of
the darkness, people of violence and treachery, we, indeed, will
pass along with the age of bloody steel. But they will survive.
They are the future and hope of the world. What we are doing,
we are doing for them.'

'I thought the same once.'

'And now?'

The grey-eyed man didn't reply. He fingered the knife kept
in a sheath attached to his forearm hidden in the sleeve of his
jacket.

'You were betrayed,' Tybald Raabe repeated, impatiently, bored
by having to repeat it. 'You were sold. You were made into bait.
You're in mortal danger. You must run away at once. Do you
understand what I'm saying?'

Now – only now – did Elencza of Stietencron confirm with a nod; something indeed shone in the watery blue of her eyes. Tybald was cross.

'Don't go home,' he said firmly. 'Don't go home under any circumstances. Don't say goodbye to anyone, don't say anything to anyone. I've brought you a horse, a chestnut, it's behind the hospital laundry. In the saddlebags there's everything you might need on the road. Into the saddle and away, at once. It doesn't matter that night's falling. You'll be safer on the road than here in Ziębice.

'Don't go to the Strzelin nuns, they'll look for you first on that road. Ride to Frankenstein, and from there take the main highway towards Wrocław. Head for the customs post in Muchobór. There everyone you ask will show you the way to Skałka. Ask for the stud belonging to Lady Dzierżka of Wirsing. Lady Dzierżka will recognise the horse, she'll know I sent you. Tell her everything. Understood?'

A nod.

'You'll be safe . . .' The goliard looked around anxiously. 'You'll be safe with Dzierżka. Afterwards, when everything quietens down, I'll take you to Poland. If you desire it so much, you'll become a Poor Clare nun, but in Stary Sącz or Zawichost. Poland isn't Silesia, but, well, it's nice there, too. You'll grow accustomed to it. And now farewell. May God keep you, girl.'

'And you,' she whispered in answer.

'Remember: don't go home. Set off at once.'

'I'll remember.'

The goliard vanished into the gloom as suddenly as he had appeared. Elencza of Stietencron slowly unfastened her apron. She looked through the window where the dark of the night was softening, had almost erased the outlines of the forested hills.

She took a cape from the cloakroom, wound a scarf around

her head. And ran. But not to the moat beyond the laundry. She ran in the opposite direction.

In the tiny room over the hospital where she lived, there was nothing she wanted to take with her. Nothing she could call her own. Nothing she would have missed.

Apart from a cat.

She treated the goliard's warning seriously. She knew what danger meant.

She understood its source, remembered the iron-grey eyes of the priest who had questioned her, recalled the fear he evoked in her. *But it's only a moment*, she thought as she ran, *only a moment, I'll just take the cat, nothing more, what could happen to me, it's only a second* . . .

'Here kitty . . . Here kitty . . .'

The window was slightly open. *He's gone*, she thought with growing terror, *he's vanished into the night in his usual feline way . . . How will I ever find him . . . ?*

'Here kitty-kitty . . .' She ran out onto the landing, getting tangled up in the sheets hanging there. 'Kitty . . . Kitty!' She ran down the stairs. And realised at once that something was wrong. The cold night air had suddenly become even colder, choking her as she breathed in. The cold wasn't fresh and invigorating now; it had become heavy, as dense as phlegm, as mucus, as clotted blood. It was suddenly full of coagulated, concentrated evil.

A bird alighted three paces in front of her. A large wallcreeper.

It appeared to Elencza as if it had taken root in the earth. She couldn't move, couldn't even tremble. Not even when the wallcreeper began to grow in front of her eyes. And change shape. Change into a man.

And then two things occurred at once. A cat mewed loudly. And a huge wolf ran out of the black of the night.

It speeded up, suddenly lengthening its steps into great

bounds and then leaped. But the wallcreeper had become a bird once more, grown blurred, shrunk rapidly, flapped its wings and flown up. It croaked triumphantly when the white fangs of the leaping wolf snapped shut just beyond its tail feathers, missing the target. After it leaped, the wolf landed softly and took off at once into the darkness, in pursuit of the fleeing bird.

Elencza seized the cat and ran. The tears drying on her cheeks.

The Iron Wolf gave chase like every normal wolf does, loping along at a steady, fast, relentless pace. Its nose, lifted from time to time, unerringly caught the magically imbued draught of the soaring wallcreeper. The wolf's eyes glowed in the darkness.

The chase – a pursuit to the death – was on. Through the Niemcza Hills. Along the Oława, Ślęża and Bystrzyca valleys.

Children in their cradles awoke, cried and choked on their tears. Horses in stables fidgeted anxiously. Cattle banged against one another in cowsheds.

A knight in a stone watchtower sat up, awoken by a nightmare. A breviary fell from the trembling hands of a village priest as he recited the *Nunc dimittis*. Soldiers in guardhouses rubbed their eyes.

The chase went on. Before it – announcing it like an outrider – sped Horror. And Terror settled behind it like dust.

There was an ancient place of worship nearby, a flat hummock with a magical solar circle marked out by a ring of polished stones inside which, in days gone by, people prayed to gods older than humankind. It was also a burial ground, a cemetery, a necropolis of folk – and also non-folk – the names of whom were long forgotten. In 1150, as part of the fight against heathenism and superstition, the stones were scattered and in their place Bishop Walter of Malonne had built a small wooden church – or rather an oratory, for the surrounding area was a wilderness. The oratory barely lasted a year – it burned down after being struck by lightning, and fire consumed all the subsequent churches built on the site of the ancient necropolis. The fight lasted twenty years until the death of Bishop Walter himself. People began to whisper that it was better not to fall foul of the Old Gods, and the new bishop, Żyrosław, took the only sensible decision: he chose a completely new, distant, prettier and more favourably situated place for the location of the next church. No one prevented the new church from standing there and attracting large congregations, while invisible hands returned the ancient stones to their former positions in the old cemetery. With time, the place was ringed by a circle of stunted, skeletal trees and, in places, a tangled hedge of blackthorn armed with murderous thorns.

The place was bathed in moonlight.

Trotting over to the first stones and the blackthorn hedge, the Wolf suddenly stopped and its hackles rose as though before fladry lines. It sniffed out the stench of the funereal decay which still hung over the hummock, although the dead hadn't been buried there for centuries. It registered the lodes of ancient magic gathered over the centuries and preventing the enchanted creature from entering. The Wolf shimmered and changed shape. And became a human being. A tall man with eyes the colour of iron.

The cold night air appeared to have set hard. Not a single dry leaf or a single blade of sedge trembled. The silence was deafening.

The sound of steps, a soft grating on the gravel, disturbed the silence. The Wallcreeper passed between the standing stones.

The Iron Wolf moved forward and also entered the circle. The circle came alive at once. Beyond the stones, under them, among them, from the thicket of entangled grass and brushwood, dozens – hundreds – of eyes suddenly flashed like lanterns, lively, twitching and nervous as fireflies. The quiet of the night was filled with a disturbing melody of whispers, a vague murmur of high-pitched, non-human voices.

'They've come.' The Wallcreeper gestured with his head. 'To see you and me. Two of perhaps the last polymorphs in this part of the world. They saw us shape-shifting. Now they want to watch us kill each other.'

He moved his forearm and hand and a knife slid into his fingers. The nine-inch Toledo blade gleamed in the moonlight.

'Let us serve them up a decent spectacle, then,' the Iron Wolf replied huskily, 'something worth telling tales about.'

He brandished the knife which had shot straight into his hand from his sleeve.

'Prepare to die, O Wolf.'

'Prepare to die, O Bird.'

They began to circle the ring, slowly, treading cautiously, eyes never leaving each other. They moved around the circle twice. And then sprang at each other, aiming lightning-fast blows. The Wallcreeper stabbed from above, aiming for the face; the Wolf moved his head a quarter of an inch as he stabbed from below towards his enemy's belly. The Wallcreeper avoided the blow by twisting his hips, then slashed diagonally from the left. Again, the Wolf saved his throat with a faint dodge and jumped clear. He turned the knife in his hand, feinting, slashing upwards from below, the blade clanging against the Wallcreeper's similarly positioned edge. They traded several rapid strokes and jumped aside.

Neither of them was even scratched.

'Prepare to die, O Bird.'

'Prepare to die, O Wolf.'

The lights of non-human eyes flickered and swayed in the gloom, the mumbled and excited murmur rose and fell.

This time, they circled each other for longer, now shortening, now lengthening the distance.

The Wolf attacked, slashing diagonally with his knife held straight out, then turning the blade and dealing a treacherous blow to the neck.

The Wallcreeper dodged, himself thrusting from the left, then from below to the right, then quite low with a sweeping blow that ended in a direct lunge and thrust. The Wolf parried the blow with his knife, dodged the thrust with a half-turn, then lunged forward, feinting and leaping to jab from above to the side of the neck. This time, the Wallcreeper didn't dodge. He parried with his forearm, spun around, turned the knife in his hand and, thrusting with the full strength of his shoulder, stabbed the Wolf powerfully right in the solar plexus. The blade entered up to the cross-guard. The Wolf didn't utter a sound. He only gasped when the Wallcreeper pulled the blade from the wound and withdrew, hunched over, ready to deliver another blow. But there was no need. The knife slipped from the Wolf's fingers and he dropped to his knees.

The Wallcreeper approached vigilantly, staring at the fading, iron-coloured eyes. He didn't say a word.

There was utter silence.

The Iron Wolf gasped once more, bent over and slumped heavily to one side. He didn't move again.

In the stone circle of the ancient cemetery, in the place of worship to old, forgotten and eternal gods, pulsating with ancient magic and power, the Wallcreeper raised his arms and the bloody knife. And screamed. Triumphantly. Savagely. Inhumanly.

All life around fell silent, horror-struck.

Chapter Six

In which, in a certain inn at a crossroads, the entertainment industry flourishes and prospers. The dice are cast, as a result of which something – apparently unavoidable and inevitable – occurs. Anyone who thinks it must all mean the start of quite major difficulties will be right.

The inn at the crossroads was the only building left from the village once located there and which signalled its existence with several black stumps of chimneys, the meagre remains of charred joists and a still-perceptible smell of burning. It was unclear who had put the village to the torch. Most of the evidence pointed to the Germans or Silesians, since the village lay on the route of the crusade which King Sigismund of Luxembourg had led to Prague in June 1420. Sigismund's crusaders had burned down anything that could catch fire but endeavoured to spare inns. For obvious reasons.

This inn was quite typical – low, squat, with a thatched roof that contained as much hard, old moss as it did straw, with several entrances and tiny windows in which the light from cressets and candles now flickered in the darkness, as unsteady and fleeting as will-o'-the-wisps over swamps. Smoke crept out of the chimney, trailed over the thatch and drifted across the meadows. A dog was baying.

'We've arrived,' said Scharley, reining in his horse. 'According to my information, Mr Fridusz Huncleder has temporarily settled here.' Although no one had asked a question, the penitent continued, 'Fridusz Huncleder is a man of affairs, an entrepreneur. He ingeniously fills the gap that, as a result of certain non-economic reasons, has opened up in the relationship between supply and demand. He supplies certain ... what we shall call "services" that are in demand—'

'He runs a travelling whorehouse,' interrupted Samson Honeypot, as quick-witted as ever. 'Or gambling den. Or possibly the former and the latter.'

'Indeed. The military statutes introduced by Žižka are strictly observed in the Hussite army. Drunkenness, gambling and debauchery are prohibited and punished severely, even by the death penalty. But the army is the army, and the men in the camps want to booze, play cards and go whoring. But nothing doing, it's forbidden. To everyone. Žižka's statutes are horribly democratic – they punish everyone regardless of position and rank. It has its benefits, too: it doesn't result in the weakening and loss of combat readiness. The hejtmans understand it, approve of the statutes and severely and ruthlessly execute them. But what's for show is for show ... A halberdier, flailman, crossbowman, wagoner – he, indeed, should be flogged or hanged for dice, whoring or theft; that is right and proper and has a good effect on morale. But a hejtman or a captain—'

'We've come, to put it bluntly, to an illicit establishment serving to sate the illicit cravings of senior officers,' guessed Reynevan. 'How risky is it?'

Scharley shrugged. 'Huncleder operates under the guise of being a military supplier and only allows entry to trusted officers. But in any case, somebody will one day turn him in and then he'll swing. It's also possible that a few of the men they catch here will also swing as a warning and an example ... But first of all, what's life without risk? And second of all, in the event, Prokop and Flutek will back us up. I trust.'

If his voice betrayed a faint note of hesitancy, the penitent drowned it out at once.

'Third of all,' he said, waving a hand, 'we have something to take care of here.'

Right outside the inn, the dog barked at them again, but ran away as they dismounted.

'I don't think I need to explain to you the main principles of how the business functions,' said Scharley, tying the reins to a stake. 'It's a den of unhealthy and forbidden pleasures. You can get blind drunk here. You can admire nude girls and sample sex for money. You can indulge in serious gambling. Great caution is advised in what one says and does. As a matter of fact, just to be clear, only I shall talk. And if it comes to cards or dice, only I shall play.'

'Naturally.' Samson picked up a stick from the ground. 'Naturally, Scharley.'

'I wasn't talking to you.'

'I'm not a child,' Reynevan said, frowning. 'I know how, what and when to speak. And I also know how to play dice.'

'No, you don't. Not with Huncleder and his cheaters. And that's final. Do as I say.'

The hubbub quietened down as they entered. Silence fell and several pairs of nastily staring eyes stuck to them like leeches to a dead cockroach. The moment was unpleasantly worrying, but happily didn't last long.

'Scharley? Is it you?'

'Glad to see you, Berengar Tauler. Greetings to you, too, Master Huncleder. Our host.'

At the table, in the company of three characters in leather jerkins, sat a broad-shouldered, pot-bellied man with a large nose and a chin disfigured by an ugly scar. His face was densely covered in pockmarks, but curiously only on one side, the left – quite as if the scar above his nose, the nose itself and his deformed chin described a demarcation line which the illness hadn't dared to cross.

'Master Scharley,' he answered. 'I don't believe my eyes. What is more, in the company of men I don't know. But since they are with you, sir … We are keen to have guests here. Not because we like them. Ha, we often don't like them at all. But we live off them!'

The men in the leather jerkins guffawed. The rest of those present didn't manifest their merriment, no doubt having already heard Huncleder's joke many times. The beanpole with a red chalice on his doublet at the counter didn't laugh, nor did the bearded man standing next to him wearing black, the absolute archetype of a Hussite preacher. Unsurprisingly, none of the scantily dressed young women moving around the room carrying flasks and pitchers smiled.

Neither did the man with a dark, several-day-old beard nursing a mug, in a jerkin rusty from armour, the man Scharley had greeted as Berengar Tauler right after they entered. The penitent headed towards Tauler's table, where three other men were sitting.

'Welcome and sit you down.' Berengar Tauler gestured to a bench and cast a curious glance towards Reynevan and Samson. 'Introduce us to your … friends.'

'No need,' a fat, ginger-haired man said over his mug. 'I've seen the younger gentleman before. At the Battle of Ústí, with the hejtmans. They said he was their personal physician.'

'Reinmar of Bielawa.'

'We are honoured. And 'im?'

''Im,' replied Scharley with his usual carefreeness, 'is 'im. He does no harm, doesn't interfere. 'Im works with wood.'

Indeed, Samson Honeypot had assumed the expression of an idiot, sat down by the wall and begun whittling a stick.

'If the presentations are underway,' said Scharley as he sat down, 'then be so good, Berengar . . .'

The three men at the table bowed. The fat, ginger-haired man was accompanied by a proud-looking young lord dressed quite richly and colourfully for a Hussite, and a short, thin-faced, swarthy character of Hungarian appearance.

'Amadej Baťa.' The fat man introduced himself.

'And I am Sir Manfred of Salm,' pronounced the colourful lordling, and the exaggerated conceit with which he said it revealed that it was utter balderdash, that he'd probably been christened 'Zdeněk', and had probably never stood near, much less sat beside, a member of the house of Salm.

'István Szécsi.' The dark man confirmed his identity as a Hungarian. 'Will you take a drink? I warn you the prices are outrageous here: a pint of wine costs three groschen and a half-pint of beer five skojeces.'

'But the wine is good.' Tauler sipped from his mug. 'For a secret brothel and gambling den. While we're on the subject, which of those diversions brings you to Huncleder's?'

'None of them, actually.' Scharley nodded towards a wench with a jug and sized her up when she approached. 'Which doesn't mean we won't sample one of them. Will there be a performance today, for example? A *tableau vivant*?'

'Naturally.' Tauler smiled. 'Naturally there will. I'm largely here for that reason. I'm not even going to play, out of fear they'll fleece me for the florin I need for the price of the show.'

'The others.' The penitent nodded. 'Who are they?'

'The one by the bar,' said Amadej Baťa, shaking beer foam from his moustache, 'with the Chalice on his chest is Habart Mol of Modřelice, one of Rohač's captains. The bearded man who looks like a priest is his comrade – they arrived together. The men at the table with Huncleder are his dealers, I only remember the name of one. They call him Jeřábek . . .'

'Come on, gentlemen!' Huncleder called from the table, rubbing his hands together vigorously and enthusiastically. 'To the table, let us play! A fortune awaits!'

Manfred of Salm was the first to be seated, Scharley followed his example, and István Szécsi and Amadej Baťa pulled chairs over. They were joined by Rohač's captain with the Chalice tabard, and his comrade resembling a priest moved away from the bar. Reynevan, mindful of Scharley's warning, stayed put. Berengar Tauler didn't move from the table, either, but gestured towards the nearest wench with his head. She was red-haired and freckled; even her exposed forearms were covered in freckles. She didn't appear as worn out as the others, but her face was strangely hardened.

'What shall we play?' Huncleder, dexterously shuffling the cards, asked the men gathered at the table. 'Piquet? Ronfle? *Trentuno? Menoretto?* It's your choice, your choice, whatever you want, it can be *cricca*, or *bassetta* . . . Or it can be *trappola*, or *buffa aragiato*, or perhaps you prefer *ganapiérde*? I know all the *genera ludorum fortunae*! I'll agree to any. The customer is king. You choose.'

'There are too many of us for cards,' said Baťa, 'and we should all join in. I suggest dice. To begin with, at least.'

'Dice? The noble *tesserae*? The customer is king. I'm ready for any game—'

'Especially using the dice you're turning over in your hand,' István Szécsi said unsmilingly. 'Don't treat us like idiots, friend.'

Huncleder laughed hollowly, tossed the distinctively yellow dice he'd been fiddling with into a mug and shook them. His hands were small and squat, his fingers short and lumpy. Quite the opposite of what one expected from the hands of a cheat or a swindler. But once in action they were skilful and nimble – as agile as a monkey's.

The yellow dice, tossed with a dexterous movement from the mug, rolled a short distance and both came to rest with sixes uppermost. Face still twisted in a grimace that mimicked a smile, Huncleder gathered up the dice in a single, swift movement, as though catching flies. He shook the mug in a sudden *acozzamento* and tossed them again. Two sixes again. Jeřábek chuckled. Rohač's captain swore.

The quick movement, the *acozzamento*, the throw. Again, the double *sexta stantia*, twice *sex puncti*. The throw. A double six. The throw. Same again. The throw. The captain swore again.

'That was only a joke.' Huncleder's half-pockmarked face broke into a grin. 'Just a little joke.'

'Indeed.' Scharley retaliated with a smile. 'A tasteful little joke. Most diverting. Once, in Nuremberg, I witnessed a swindler's hands being broken for the same "little joke" during a game for money. On a stone threshold, using a blacksmith's hammer. We laughed our heads off, let me tell you.'

Fridusz Huncleder's eyes flared up unpleasantly. But he regained control and the grin returned to his pockmarked face.

'A joke's a joke,' he repeated, 'and it'll stay a joke. We'll use other dice for the game. I'll put these away—'

'But not into your pocket, by the Devil,' growled Manfred of Salm. 'Put them on the table. As an exhibit. We'll compare the others with them from time to time.'

'As you wish.' Huncleder raised his hands to indicate he agreed and accepted everything and that the client was indeed king. 'What game suits you? Fifty-six? Sixes and sevens?'

'*Glückhaus*, perhaps,' suggested Scharley.

'Let it be *Glückhaus*. Make haste, Jeřábek!'

Jeřábek wiped the table with his sleeve and drew a rectangle divided into eleven fields in chalk.

'Ready.' Huncleder rubbed his hands. '*Faites vos jeux* ... And you, Brother Berengar? Won't you do us the honour? Pity, pity—'

'Your pity's not sincere enough, Brother.' Berengar Tauler took pains for the 'brother' to sound anything but fraternal. 'You can't have forgotten that last Saturday you fleeced me like a tup in May. I shall sit out for a lack of funds, wait for the *tableau vivant* and amuse myself with this beaker. And possibly discourse, since m'Lord Reinmar isn't keen on dice, either, I see.'

'As you will.' Huncleder shrugged. 'But for us, m'lords, here is the plan: we'll first play dice. Then, when there are fewer of us, we shall play piquet or another *ludus cartularum*. And during it we'll have the spectacle. I mean the artistic interlude. And now, come on, m'lords! *Glückhaus*! Place your bets. Fortune, smile on us!'

For some time, all that could be heard were curses, the *chink* of coins thrown onto the fields, the rattle of *acozzamento* and the sound of the dice rolling on the table.

'Something tells me,' said Berengar Tauler, taking a sip from his beaker, 'that Amadej will lose his shirt in a trice and return here. So if you have anything to say in confidence, do it now.'

'And why do you suppose I do?'

'Intuition.'

'Ha. Very well. Trosky Castle, in the Jičín hills, near Turnov—'

'I know where Trosky Castle is.'

'Have you been there? Do you know it well?'

'I've been there many times; I know it very well. Why do you ask?'

'We want to gain access.'

Berengar Tauler took a sip. 'What for?' he asked, seemingly carelessly.

'Oh, you know, for amusement,' Reynevan answered, his tone similarly careless. 'It's our caprice and favourite pastime: finding our way into Catholic castles.'

'Understood. No further questions. So Scharley is subtly reminding me of the debt I owe him. Am I to pay off my debt like that? Very well, I'll think it over.'

'Is that a "yes" or a "no"?'

'It means I'll think it over. Hey, Marketa! Wine, if you please!'

The ginger-haired, freckled girl with the lifeless face and empty eyes filled his cup. Her figure more than made up for her lack of good looks, and as the girl moved away from the table, Reynevan couldn't restrain himself from looking at her waist and hips, rocking in a gentle, swaying and quite hypnotic walk.

'I see that your eye is pleased by our Marketa,' observed Tauler with a smile. 'Our *tableau vivant*. Our Adamite.'

'Adamite?'

'You mean you don't know anything? Scharley didn't say? Or perhaps you've never heard of the Adamites?'

'It rings some sort of bell. But I'm a Silesian, I've been in Bohemia but two years . . .'

'Order something to drink. And make yourself comfortable.'

Once Reynevan had been served, Berengar Tauler began his tale. 'When the Czech revolution occurred, a considerable number of cranks and crazies emerged from the shadows. In 1419, a wave of religious hysteria, lunacy and mysticism passed through the country. Fanatical prophets were everywhere, warning of the end of the world. People abandoned everything and went into the mountains in large numbers, to wait for the second coming of Christ. All this was grist to the mill to old, forgotten sects. Various fucked-up chiliasts, Adventists, Nicolaites, Paternians, spiritualists, Waldensians, Beghards and the Devil knows who else – it was impossible to count them – crawled out of their burrows ...'

A heated exchange had begun at the dice table, various words were used, some of them coarse. Manfred of Salm was fulminating the loudest.

'And then sermons, prophecies, predictions, omens and apocalypses began,' continued Tauler. 'Some proclaimed the coming of the Third Age, but that the old world had first to be consumed by fire. And then Christ would return in glory, the Divine Kingdom would come, the saints would be resurrected, evil men would inevitably suffer eternal damnation and the good would live in heavenly bliss. Everything would be shared; all personal property would disappear. There would be no rich or poor, no poverty or oppression. A state of universal perfection, happiness and peace would reign. There would be no more misfortune, wars or persecution. Nobody would ever attack another or lead him into sin. Nor covet his wife. Because wives would also be for common use.

'But the world didn't end, as we know, Christ didn't descend to Earth, people came to their senses and chiliasm and Adventism began to lose their followers. The dreams of equality were shattered, like the fantasies about the elimination of all power and all obligation. The revolutionary Tábor restored state structures and by the autumn of 1420 began to gather duties and taxes. Obligatory ones, naturally.

'The structures of church authority were also reconstructed, as were those of the Taborites. The leader of the Hussites, Bishop Mikuláš of Pelhřimov, proclaimed from the pulpit the canon of true faith and accused anyone who didn't respect it of being an apostate and a heretic. And thus the Hussites, the greatest

195

heretics in Europe, found their own heretics, their own dissidents. Their own Picards.'

'The name, I believe, is a corruption of "Beghard"?' Reynevan interjected.

'Some would say so,' Tauler replied, nodding, 'but it's more likely from Picardy and the Waldensians, who came here in 1418, finding in Bohemia sanctuary and an astonishing number of adherents. The movement grew in strength and followers, led by the Moravian Martin Húska, called "Loquis" for his eloquence. To call them radicals would be quite an understatement. They exhorted people to demolish churches, since the true church of God, they claimed, is a pilgrim church. They utterly rejected the Eucharist. They renounced the significance of all the objects of religion, destroyed every monstrance and every Host they got their hands on. Everything that exists is God, they proclaimed, ergo, man is also God. Holy Communion can be given by anyone, they claimed, and it can be received under any kind. That claim particularly annoyed the Calixtines. "What do you mean?" the latter howled. "Master Huss was burned and we spill blood for Holy Communion *sub utraque specie*, in bread and wine, and here some Martin Loquis gives it under the kind of kasha, peas and sour milk?"'

Samson diligently whittled away in his corner. Beautiful, coiled shavings curled over the blade of his pocketknife.

'By February 1421, they'd had enough of the sectarians. They were expelled from the Tábor and sent away. Around four hundred Picards left the mountain and founded their own fortified camp in nearby Příběnice—'

'What are you talking about?' Amadej Baťa asked curiously, returning from the card table with the forced cheerfulness of a fellow who has lost all his money.

'The Picards.'

'Aah? The nudes? Ho-ho . . . I understand . . .'

Tauler took up his tale again. 'Húska Loquis was no longer among the Příběnice outcasts – they were now led by the preacher Petr Kániš and his cronies Jan Bydlín, Mikuláš Slepý, Trsáček and Burján. They announced the abolishment of all family ties and invalidated marriage. They proclaimed brotherly equality and absolute sexual freedom. They claimed that they were pure, like Adam and Eve, and among the pure there was no room for sin. They cast off their robes and paraded naked, like Adam's state before the fall, and soon acquired the popular nickname of "Adamites". They began to indulge enthusiastically in mass orgies. However, internal squabbles and differences soon emerged among their ringleader priests – it seems the conflict was less about religious questions and more about the division of their harems. Several ringleaders left, taking with them small gaggles of followers and flocks of young women. As a matter of fact, most of the women were happy in the Picardian communes, where the idea of complete sexual equality was promoted. It was presented, *nota bene*, in such a way that any woman could sleep with and fuck whoever she wanted to. That freedom was actually sham, for Kániš and the other priests played the role of cockerels in those henhouses. But the women were so captivated, so full of promiscuous mysticism, that they vied with each other to serve some "holy man", viewed spreading their legs as a privilege, a religious service, and literally regarded it as grace if in his goodness a "holy man" deigned to sanctify their readily proffered arses—'

'Well,' Amadej Baťa interrupted philosophically, staring at the backside of one of the wenches serving the players, 'such is woman, lust incarnate. And insatiable in her urges. Thus it has been ever since the world began, and will be *in saecula saeculorum* . . .'

'Talking about skirt as usual, are you?' said Scharley, sitting down, evidently bored with the game.

'I'm giving your companion a brief history lesson,' Berengar Tauler replied.

'Then I'll gladly listen.'

Tauler cleared his throat and continued, 'The Picards were still a thorn in Žižka's side. Crusades were being organised against Bohemia and Catholic propaganda was trumpeting about Picardian cultism, so the Adamites were the perfect subject for them. Soon it was believed throughout Europe that all Czechs wandered around naked and fucked each other according to Jan Huss's teachings. In the face of the threat of crusades, anarchy in the ranks could be fatal, and the Picards, let's face it, still had closet supporters in the Tábor. Towards the end of March 1421, Žižka sent a force against Kániš's commune. Some of the sectarians were slaughtered; the rest – a few dozen, including Kániš himself – were captured and burned alive. It happened in the village of Klokoty, on the Tuesday before Saint George's Day in late April. The location was not coincidental. Klokoty is right beside Tábor, so the massacre could be seen from the walls. Žižka was warning the Tábor—'

He broke off and glanced at the corner where Samson Honey-pot was sitting. 'He's a devil for whittling. Look at him – is it safe to give an idiot a knife? Might he cut off his hand?'

'Never fear,' Reynevan said, accustomed to questions like that. 'He is, in spite of appearances, extremely attentive. Go on, Brother Berengar. What happened next?'

'They finished off more sectarians, one after the other, until only one group remained: Burján's commune. They were hiding in the forests by the River Nežárka. It was a dreadful band, the most radical of radicals, absolutely fanatical and certain of their divine mission. They began to rob neighbouring villages and settlements – allegedly to "convert". In reality, they murdered, plundered, burned things down and committed appalling atrocities. They feared no one. Burján, their leader, who was now officially addressed as "Jesus" and "Son of God" – as indeed Kániš had been – vouched that as chosen ones they were immune and immortal, that no blade could cut them and no weapon harm them. He surrounded himself with a harem of about two dozen women and girls. It finally went so far that . . .'

'Well?'

'That he began to administer Communion . . . Erm . . . By means of . . . fellatio. A marvellous sacrament, isn't it? But the end of the Picardian interlude was approaching fast, Žižka was hanging over them like a hawk. In October, they were tracked down and surrounded. Burján's Adamites put up fierce resistance, they fought like tigers. Most were slaughtered and about four dozen taken alive. They were all burned at the stake. Half of them were women, most of them pregnant. Mercy was shown: the male Adamites were cruelly tortured before being burned. The female Adamites were burned without torture.'

'All of them?'

'Not at all,' Amadej Baťa interjected with a lecherous smile.

'Several were left alive,' said Berengar Tauler, nodding. 'It was a closely kept secret, carefully hidden from Žižka. The matter of the Adamites' sexual freedom was then common knowledge. Female Adamites, so ran the rumours, made love after stripping naked and simply adored orgies, particularly in groups, nothing gave them greater pleasure than group sex, with several men on one of them. Well, if that's how they like it—'

'You needn't finish,' said Reynevan through clenched his teeth.

'But I will. For one of the women who was saved, the last alive, is serving drinks here.'

'Marketa,' confirmed Amadej Baťa. 'Said to be the favourite, the pet, of the Adamite Burján. Huncleder bought her from the Taborite brethren when they grew tired of her. Now she is his. His property. Entirely and for ever. Until death.'

'When she joined the sect, she burned her bridges.' Tauler noticed Reynevan's astonished expression. 'There was no way back. The sectarians were disowned by their families . . .'

'And Picards are still being hunted down,' added Scharley, sounding indifferent. 'Almost every day they expose and burn somebody after torturing them. The wench must do what Huncleder orders for she's at his mercy. She's only alive thanks to him.'

'Alive?' Reynevan turned his head. No one reacted.

The red-haired girl called Marketa charged their cups. This time, Reynevan watched her more attentively. This time, as she filled his cup, she looked up. He didn't see in her eyes what he had expected: pain, shame, humiliation, a slave's anxious docility. The eyes of the red-haired girl were despoiled by measureless apathy.

Out of the corner of his eye, he noticed something that surprised him even more.

Samson Honeypot had stopped carving.

'Well, gentlemen and brethren,' said Huncleder, getting up from the table. 'Time to divert yourselves after your hard work. Servants, push the benches together! Move yourself, Jeřábek! Hey, wenches, draw the wine and serve it! And may I remind our guests that you have to pay for the diversion. To feast one's eyes on this spectacle you must part with a florin or a Hungarian ducat. Or its equivalent in value, which means thirty groschen. No one who parts with the sum will regret it! The prospect is worth even ten ducats, I vouch!'

Soon all the guests were sitting in a makeshift auditorium, with the oak table they had been playing on in front of them.

Several candle holders were placed on the table to provide il-
lumination. Suddenly, one of the servants began to rhythmically
beat on a drum. The hubbub subsided.

Marketa emerged from a side room. The drum fell silent.

She walked calmly, barefoot, attired in something that only
after a moment revealed itself to be a surplice, a genuine liturgical robe. A servant offered a hand to help her climb onto the
table. She stood motionless for a time, immersing herself in the
rhythm of the drum. Then she lifted the surplice. A little above
her knees. And then higher. She swayed gently and turned all
around, as ethereal as a scantily clad shepherdess. Manfred of
Salm yelled enthusiastically and clapped his hands, but fell
silent on noticing that the others were utterly absorbed by the
spectacle.

Marketa didn't even react. Each gesture, movement, glance,
twitch of her face and unnatural smile said the same thing: *I'm
utterly alone here. I'm alone, alone, isolated and far from you. From
you and from everything you represent. I'm in a completely different
world.*

Et in Arcadia ego, thought Reynevan. *Et in Arcadia ego.*

The drumbeats quickened, but the girl didn't adapt to the
rhythm. On the contrary, her movements were awkward. Pon-
derous, sluggish. Enticing and hypnotic. And the edge of the
surplice she was lifting crept ever higher, to halfway up her
thighs, higher, higher, finally and eventually revealing what
they had all been waiting for, at the sight of which they reacted with involuntary grimaces, grunts, groans, puffs and loud
swallowing.

The drum beat loud and then stopped. Marketa slowly raised
the surplice. And then quickly pulled it up over her head. Freckles
dotted her arms and shoulders, covering her neck and breasts
in a delicate pattern. There were none lower down. The drum

banged at a quicker rhythm and the girl began to pirouette and sway, like a Bacchante, like Salome. Now they saw that freckles also covered her back and nape. Her shock of hair undulated like the Red Sea just before Moses commanded it to part before him. The drum boomed loudly and Marketa froze in a pose as lascivious as it was unnatural. Among the spectators, Manfred clapped again, Rohač's captain yelled, Amadej Baťa cried out and slapped his thighs. Huncleder cackled. Berengar Tauler began to applaud.

But that wasn't the end of the performance.

The girl knelt and cupped her breasts, squeezing and display-ing them to the audience, swaying and writhing like a snake all the while. And smiled. But it wasn't a smile. It was a spastic contraction, a *spasmus musculi faciei*.

At a signal from the drum, Marketa lithely and sinuously moved from kneeling to a sitting position. The drum began to beat out a frantic, staccato rhythm and the girl writhed like a snake again. Finally, she stopped moving, tossing her head backwards and spreading her legs wide. So wide that no detail escaped the spectators. Nor any details of the details.

The display went on for some time.

Then the girl snatched up the surplice, jumped down from the table and vanished into the side room, pursued by the sounds of applause and cheers. Manfred of Salm and Rohač's captain hooted and stamped, Berengar Tauler stood up and clapped and Amadej Baťa crowed like a rooster.

'Well?' Fridusz Huncleder got up, crossed the tavern and sat down at the table. 'Well? Ever seen such a ginger one? Wasn't the spectacle worth a ducat? While we're on the subject, m'Lord Scharley, I only received two from you, but three of you came in. And here every pair of eyes counts – if you look, you pay. This is a revolution and we're all equal, lord and servant . . . I say! I wasn't talking to you, but to your master! Sit back down, go on carving your stick. As a matter of fact, do *you* have a ducat? Have you ever even *seen* a ducat in your life?'

It was some time before Reynevan realised whom Huncleder was addressing. And some time before he recovered from his astonishment.

'Are you deaf?' asked Huncleder. 'Or just stupid?'

'The girl who danced.' Samson Honeypot brushed shavings from his sleeve. 'I'd like to take her away from here.'

'Whaaaaat?'

'I'd like to assume the right of ownership of her, so to speak.'

'Right of whaaaat?'

'Too complicated?' Samson didn't raise his voice at all. 'Then I'll say it more simply: she's yours, and she's going to be mine. So let's sort it out.'

Huncleder gave him a look, a long look, as though unable to believe his own eyes and ears. He finally burst out laughing.

'M'Lord Scharley,' he said, turning his head. 'What's this pantomime? Is he always like this? Just comes out with it? Or did you make him?'

'"He" has a name.' Scharley proved that even the least-expected incident was incapable of putting him off his stride. 'He's called Samson Honeypot. I didn't tell him to do anything. Nor forbade him. He's a free man. He has the right to carry out independent commercial transactions.'

Huncleder looked around. He didn't like either Manfred of Salm's open chuckling, nor Amadej Bata's snorting, nor the splendidly amused faces of the others. He wasn't pleased. It was easy to see it in his face.

'There'll be no independent transactions,' he drawled. 'The wench isn't for sale, for one thing. And I don't trade with simpletons, for another. Get out of here, dolt. Scram. Groom the horses, clean the latrine or something. This is a gambling house. If you don't gamble, get out.'

'But that's exactly what I had in mind,' replied Samson, as serene as a statue. 'Trading in people is a matter for thugs and bloody whoresons, while gambling, in spite of its many flaws, also has its merits. In a game of chance, as the name indicates, one must rely on unfathomable chance. Aren't you curious about unfathomable chance, Huncleder? You say you're prepared for any game. Go on, then. One throw of the dice.'

Silence fell on the room. Grimaces of wild amusement still contorted the faces of some of the men present, but they'd stopped laughing aloud. Huncleder's pockmarked face set and contracted hideously. With a movement of his head, he ordered his servants out of the shadows. Then he tossed a pair of dice – the same ones they had played with – in front of Samson. And picked up his own, yellow ones.

'So let's play,' he said icily. 'One throw. If you win – the girl's yours. You won't even have to pay extra. But if I throw a higher score than you . . .'

He snapped his fingers. One of the servants handed him a hatchet. Another raised a loaded crossbow. Scharley quickly grabbed Reynevan by the arm.

'If I throw more,' Huncleder finished, putting the hatchet down on the table in front of him, 'I'll chop off as many digits as I score. Fingers first, then toes as well if needs be. Depending on what I throw. And what unfathomable fate demands.'

'Hey!' said István Szécsi angrily. 'What's this? Put down those confounded yellow dice—'

'What butchery are you planning?' interrupted Habart Mol of Modřelice, Roháč's captain.

'The dimwit wants to play!' Huncleder shouted over them. 'So he will! Since he's a free fellow. With the right to be independent.

He can still quit. Admit of his own free will that he made a fool of himself and leave of his own volition. No one's stopping him. If he doesn't delay his departure too long.'

The captain, it was clear, might have challenged that, and the stern faces of the Hungarian and Baťa spoke for themselves. But before anyone could speak or act, Samson had shaken the dice and tossed them onto the table. One of them showed a four, the other a three.

'That's seven,' he said with a horrifying calm, 'if I'm not mistaken.'

'You aren't.' Huncleder rattled his dice in a cup. 'Four and three make seven. And regarding your fingers and toes: ten and ten make twenty. For the present.'

The dice rolled. All the men crowded around gasped in unison. Jeřábek swore.

The two yellow dice landed with the ones uppermost.

'You lost.' Samson Honeypot's bass interrupted the deathly silence. 'Fate's not well disposed towards you. The girl is mine. Thus, I shall take her and be on my way.'

Huncleder attacked across the table with the speed of a wild-cat. The hatchet blade whistled but didn't bury itself in Samson's temple, where it was aimed. The giant was too swift. He moved his head aside, caught Huncleder above the elbow with his left hand and squeezed the fingers holding the weapon with his right. Everybody heard Huncleder's howl and the crunch of the bones. Samson prised the hatchet from his broken fingers, gripped it, bent Huncleder over the table and slammed the butt of the axe down on the fingers of the other hand now pressed against the tabletop. Huncleder howled even louder. Samson struck again. Huncleder fell face first onto the table and fainted.

So he didn't see Reynevan bound nimbly over to the servant holding the crossbow and knock it upwards so that the stock thudded into his lips and teeth. Or Scharley overpower the other servant with his favourite kick to the knee and the punch that broke his nose. Or Amadej Bať a hit one of the swindlers in the lower back with a stool. Or Berengar Tauler use two daggers drawn from God knew where to warn the others not to get involved. Or Reynevan back up the warning with the crossbow he had seized from the servant. Or Jeřábek sitting in shock with his mouth foolishly open, which made him look just like a carved wooden figure from a peasant's cottage. Or Samson walk calmly into the side room and lead out the red-haired, freckled girl. She was pale and moved with reluctance – why, even quite unwillingly – but Samson wasn't in the least bothered by that, unceremoniously using gentle but firm force.

'Let's go,' he said to Reynevan and Scharley. 'Now.'

'Indeed,' agreed Berengar Tauler, still holding the two daggers. 'Let's go, and quickly. Amadej and I are coming with you.'

No more than half a mile from the inn, the track led them out of a dark forest onto a patch of stubble, bright beneath the stars. Berengar Tauler, who was leading the cavalcade, stopped and reined his horse around, barring the others' way.

'Stop!' he called. 'Enough's enough! I want to know what's going on here – what the Devil is this about?'

Scharley's horse tossed its head, neighed and flattened its ears. The penitent calmed it down.

'What the hell was that row about?' Tauler continued. 'A row we might all pay for with our lives? Why the hell do you want that wench? Where are we bloody going? And above all—'

He suddenly forced his horse straight at Samson as though meaning to ram him. Samson didn't even flinch. Neither did the girl with the still indifferent, wooden expression and distant stare riding in front of him.

'Above all,' yelled Berengar Tauler, 'who the bloody hell is that character? Who is he?'

Scharley rode over to him so aggressively that Tauler reined his mount in sharply.

'I'm not riding another furlong with you,' Tauler said, now much more calmly, 'until you tell me what this is about.'

'As you wish,' said Scharley slowly. 'Suit yourself.'

'We helped you in the tavern, didn't we? We got involved, didn't we? We're in difficulty now, aren't we? Don't you think a word of explanation is called for?'

'Yes. I mean, no. It isn't.'

'Then I . . .' Tauler almost choked. 'I . . .'

'I don't know about you,' said Amadej Bat́a, staring at Samson as he walked his horse up on the other side, 'but I know what I want. I want to know how the hell the ones came up on the loaded dice instead of the sixes. I'd gladly learn how to do it – for a fee, naturally. I understand it's magic, but can anyone do it? Or does one need some special power? If so, I wonder what?'

'A mighty power!' Reynevan, who had been listening, finally got his feelings off his chest. 'A great one! An unimaginable one! Such a power that I wonder if there's any point—'

'Restrain yourself.' Scharley quietened him harshly. 'You've said enough!'

'I'll say what I want!'

'I observe,' Berengar Tauler snorted, 'that there's a lack of con-sensus regarding the event among you, too, and that a family squabble is about to erupt. And since Bat́a and I aren't family, we'll ride away a stretch. When you've said all you need to say, call us and we'll decide what to do next.'

There was a pause once they were left alone. Reynevan felt the anger draining from him but didn't know where or how to start. Scharley couldn't be counted on; he never spoke first in situations like that. The horses snorted.

'In the gambling den, what had to happen, happened,' Samson Honeypot finally said. 'It was inevitable. It had to happen because . . . no other course of events was possible, since any alternative course of events would have meant indifference. Consent. Approval. Tolerance. What we saw in the gambling den, what we were witnesses to, ruled out indifference and inactivity, and thus there was really no alternative. Thus, what had to happen, happened. And the dice . . . Why, dice, generally speaking, are governed by similar principles when they roll. They fall as they have to fall.'

Reynevan heard the girl in front of Samson sighing softly.

'And essentially, I have nothing else to add,' continued Samson. 'If you wish to ask anything . . . Reinmar? A moment ago, I had the impression something was vexing you.'

'One thought,' said Reynevan, surprised by his own calm. 'Just one thought. The Prague mages racked their brains for a year wondering how to help you, to enable you to return to your normal form, to your normal world, element, dimension, whatever it is. They failed. Now we've planned quite a risky expedition through Bohemia, heading somewhere near Jičín and Turnov, almost to the very Lusatian border, since we want to help you. After what I saw today, indeed, a certain thought is vexing me. Do you actually need any help at all with anything, Samson? Do you – who's capable of changing the fate of tumbling dice – need the help of ordinary men who are capable of so little? Do you need our help? Does it matter to you?'

'I do,' the giant answered at once, without a second's hesitation. 'And it does.' A moment later, very softly and gently, he added, 'But, Reynevan, you both know that it does.'

The girl – Marketa – sighed again.

'Very well.' Scharley stepped in. 'What happened, happened. Know this, Samson. Your fatalism is alien to me. I believe it's extremely easy to protect oneself from what is inevitable: just don't do it. It's similar with phenomena one cannot gaze on with indifference ... just look away. All the more so since they represent the norm in this world rather than the exception. But it's done, and I can't see it being undone. We did a good deed, but we shall pay for it because one always pays for stupidity. However, before that happens, here's the plan: we need to place the girl somewhere safe—'

'I'll take her to Prague,' announced Samson. 'To Mistress Pospíchalová.'

Marketa shifted ostentatiously in the saddle and growled like a cat. Samson wasn't bothered by the display. Nor, it appeared, by her squeezing his wrist very hard.

'You can't take her there by yourself,' said Scharley. 'Too bad, we'll all go. What about Tauler and Baťa? If the plan to go to Trosky is still on, Tauler might come in useful, since he claims he has a way of getting into the castle. We can't reveal too much to the two of them, but the fact is that they were on our side in the gambling den and may have problems because of us. Huncleder might want revenge. They both serve in the Taborite army, and the Devil only knows which notable hejtmans have gambled – and lost – at Huncleder's place ...'

'No matter how notable a hejtman is,' promised Reynevan, 'he can be taken down a peg or two. The same goes for Huncleder if he kicks up a fuss, for notable men have more notable men above them.'

'Flutek.'

'Exactly. Which is why you'll all go to Prague. And I'll continue on my way. To White Mountain.'

Chapter Seven

In which Reynevan removes a stone from a kidney and becomes a father as a reward. As part of that same reward, he also becomes a spy. And takes the rough with the smooth.

White Mountain was the name of a treeless hill west of Prague, a short distance from the Premonstratensian monastery in Strahov. Armies marching on Prague had used the foot of the hill several times as a camp. As a result, the residents of neighbouring villages, tired of requisitions and robbery, got the hell out and the area became deserted. Armies came and went, but White Mountain had its own permanent residents. Bohuchval Neplach, called Flutek, turned White Mountain into the headquarters and training centre of the Hussite intelligence service. Flutek could have resided in Prague itself, but didn't want to. He didn't like the capital and was afraid of it. Prague – let's face it, even in moments of peace and quiet – was like a slumbering but unpredictable bloodthirsty monster. Praguians were easily moved to anger and their outbursts were terrible to those they didn't like.

Few in Prague liked Flutek.

Which was why Flutek preferred White Mountain. He liked to say that because he, Bohuchval Neplach, resided there, the name 'White Mountain' would go down in the history of

Bohemia. Children, he liked to say, would learn that name.

The day was dawning and it was beginning to rain as Reynevan passed the once wealthy but now plundered and desolate Strahov monastery. When he reached White Mountain, the day had fully dawned and it was raining steadily. The drenched sentries on the stockade ignored him completely, while the guard at the gate waved a hand towards the parade ground. Without being accosted by anyone, he led his horse to the stable. Some men in the stable eyed him up, but none of them asked him anything.

The espionage centre was being enlarged. The rain further intensified the pervasive smell of recently sawn planks and planed beams, and shavings littered the ground. Behind the old cottages and barns peeped new buildings, bright with fresh planks and beams, oozing resin from their ends. Without arousing anybody's curiosity, Reynevan went over to one of the new buildings, which was long and low and resembled a large granary. He entered the hallway, then a large room full of smoke, steam and damp. And men, eating, talking and drying their clothing. They stared at him. Wordlessly. He withdrew.

And looked into another large room. Around forty men were sitting on benches, listening attentively to a lecture. Reynevan knew the lecturer, an elderly man, a spy, rumour had it, who'd been in the service of Charles IV. The old codger was so decrepit that the rumour was plausible. Why, judging from his age and appearance, the old man could even have spied for the House of Přemyslid.

'And if something should go wrong . . .' he lectured, coughing. 'If you are ever cornered, then remember: it's best to start yelling in a crowded place that it was the Jews, the Jews caused it all, it was a Jewish plot. Put a piece of soap in your mouths, get a good lather up with water at the town well, spit and cry: "Save me, help, I'm dying. The Jews have poisoned me, it's the Jews." The people will at once attack the Jews, a disorderly confusion will begin and the Inquisition, having abandoned your trail, will pursue the Jews instead, while you can flee in peace. Do the same if you are captured and taken to be tortured. In that instance, play the fool, protest your innocence, say that you're an unwitting instrument and that the Jews are guilty. "They forced me, they bribed me with gold." You will be believed, be sure. They always fall for it.'

'My, my! Reynevan!'

The man who shouted to him was Slavík Candát, whom Reynevan knew from his university days. When Reynevan was just beginning his education, Slavík Candát had already been studying for at least eight years and was older than most of the doctors, never mind the magisters. 'Studying' was actually stretching it a bit – Slavík Candát did visit the academy from time to time and was even seen there occasionally. But he could be found much more often in one of the whorehouses in Na Perštýně or Krakow Street. Or in the town jail, where he was often put for taking part in drunken brawls and causing disturbances after dark. Although no longer a youngster, Candát adored brawling, so it was no surprise when he enthusiastically joined the revolutionary movement after the Defenestration. Reynevan hadn't been at all surprised to see him working for Flutek in the spring of 1426, during his first visit to White Mountain.

'Greetings, Slavík. What, have you become a secretary?'

'Eh? You mean these?' Candát indicated the sheets of paper and quill pens he was carrying. 'They're letters from Heaven.'

'From where?'

'I've been promoted,' boasted the eternal student, pulling his fingers back over a bald pate as though combing his hair. 'Brother Neplach transferred me to the propaganda department.

I've become a scribe. An artist. Almost a poet. I write letters that fall from Heaven. Do you understand?'

'No.'

'Then listen.' Candát took one of the sheets and squinted at it through weak eyes. 'A letter by Our Lady from Heaven. Which I wrote yesterday: "Faithless folk, base and perverse generation," he began, his voice transforming into preacherly exaltation as he read, "God's wrath and calamities will fall on you, your labours and your flocks. Since you do not profess the true faith but listen instead to the Roman Antichrist, I shall turn my face from you. My Son shall judge you for the evil you have committed in His holy Church and destroy you as He destroyed Sodom and Gomorrah. And there will be a weeping and gnashing of teeth, amen."

'Letters from Heaven, get it?' explained Candát, seeing that Reynevan didn't get it at all. 'Letters from Jesus, letters from Mary and Peter. We write them as propaganda. Agitators and emissaries learn them by heart and go to enemy countries to propagate them to the locals. In order – as our director says – to confuse the local folk so they don't know who's a friend, who's an enemy or what's what. That's what letters from Heaven are, get it? Like this letter by Jesus, listen. Note how beautifully written it is—'

'Slavík, old chap, I'm in a bit of a hurry—'

'Listen, listen! "Sinners and scoundrels, your end is nigh. I am patient, but if you do not abandon Rome, the Beast of Babylon, I, my Father and all my angels will curse you—"'

'Brother Bielawa?' A voice from behind Reynevan saved him. 'Brother Neplach urgently requests your presence. If you would follow me.'

One of the freshly erected buildings was imposing and resembled a manor house. It had several rooms on the ground floor and several austerely equipped chambers on the first floor. One of the chambers contained a large and not at all austere bed in which Flutek was lying, covered with an eiderdown and groaning.

'Where've you been?' he howled wildly at the sight of Reynevan. 'I sent men to Prague and Kolín in search of you! And you . . . Ooh . . . Ooooh . . . Aaaaagh!'

'What's the matter? Oh, don't say anything. I know.'

'You do, do you? Impossible! What's wrong with me, then? What am I suffering from?'

'Kidney stones, generally speaking. But at this moment you have colic. Sit up. Lift your shirt and turn away. Does it hurt? Here?'

'Ooouuuch! Fuck me!'

'There's no doubt it's renal colic,' Reynevan announced, 'which you are well aware of as it's certainly not the first time and the symptoms are typical: acute pains shooting downwards, nausea, pressure on the bladder—'

'Stop talking and start treating me, you damned quack.'

'You've unexpectedly found yourself in quite good company.' Reynevan smiled. 'Jan Huss suffered from severe stones and very acute attacks of renal colic while in prison in Constance.'

'Ah.' Flutek covered himself with the eiderdown and gave a pained smile. 'Undoubtedly a sign of saintliness . . . On the other hand, I'm not surprised Huss didn't recant . . . He preferred the stake to the pain . . . Christ, Reynevan, do something, I beg you . . .'

'I'll give you something to relieve the pain in a moment, but the stones must be removed. A barber-surgeon is necessary. Or ideally a specialist lithotomist. I know one in Prague—'

'I don't want one!' bellowed the spy, either from pain or fury. 'There was one here! Do you know what he wanted to do? Cut open my arse! Understand? Cut open my arse!'

'Not your arse – your crotch. You have to be cut open to reach the stones. Long forceps are inserted through the cut to access the bladder—'

'Stop!' bellowed Flutek, paling. 'Not another word! That's not why I brought you here, why I sent relays of horses after you . . . Cure me, Reynevan. With magic. I know you can.'

'You must be delirious. Witchcraft is a *peccatum mortalium* . . . The Fourth Article of Prague orders the death penalty for sorcerers. For now, I'll prepare you a potion to relieve the pain. And *nepenthes*, an intoxicating medicine for later. You'll take it when the lithotomist arrives. You'll barely feel it when he makes the incision, and you'll endure the forceps going in. Just be sure to grip a wooden peg or leather belt in your teeth—'

'Reynevan.' Flutek went as white as a sheet. 'Please. I'll cover you with gold—'

'Aha, of course you will. For a moment, because sorcerers sent to the stake have their gold confiscated. You must have forgotten that I worked for you, Neplach. I've seen a lot. And learned a lot. Besides, it's vain talk. I can't remove the stone using magic because, firstly, an operation like that is risky, and secondly, I'm not a sorcerer and don't know any spells—'

'You do,' Flutek interrupted coldly. 'I know very well that you do. Heal me and I'll forget that I know.'

'Blackmail, is it?'

'No. Minor cronyism. I'll be indebted to you. As part of paying off the debt, I'll erase certain matters from my memory, and if you're ever in need, I'll be able to repay you. The Devil take me if—'

'He's taking you anyway.' It was Reynevan's turn to interrupt. 'We'll carry out the operation at midnight. Without any witnesses, just you and me. I'll need boiling water, a silver jug or goblet, a bowl of hot coals, a copper cauldron, honey, birch and willow bark, some fresh hazel rods, something made of amber—'

'They'll supply it all for you,' Flutek assured him, biting his lips in pain. 'Whatever you want. Summon servants, issue orders. Whatever you need will be supplied. I've heard that for necromancy, human blood or organs are occasionally necessary ... Brains, livers ... Don't hesitate to ask for them. If needs be ... we can eviscerate somebody.'

'I'd like to believe,' Reynevan said as he opened a casket of amulets, a present from Telesma, 'that you've gone insane, Neplach. That the pain has muddled your mind. Tell me that what you're saying is insanity. Say it, please.'

'Reynevan?'

'What?'

'I really won't forget this. I'll be indebted to you. I promise, I'll grant your every wish.'

'Every one? Splendid.'

Reynevan had every reason to be proud. First of all, he was proud of his foresight, for badgering Dr Fraundinst so long that the latter had – despite his initial reluctance – revealed to him his professional secrets and taught him several medical spells. He was also proud of the fact that he had knuckled down over the translations of Geber's *Kitab Sirr al-Asrar* and Rhazes's *Al-Hawi*, that he'd studied *Regimen sanitatis* and *De morborum cognitione et curatione* thoroughly, and that he'd paid close attention to the illnesses of the kidneys and bladder, especially regarding the magical aspects of therapy. He was also proud of the fact that he had aroused sufficient affection in Telesma for him to give Reynevan over a dozen very practical amulets as a farewell gift. But Reynevan was naturally proudest of the result. And the result of the magical operation surpassed all expectations. The stone in Flutek's kidney, treated with a spell and the action of an amulet, disintegrated. A simple relaxing spell usually applied during labour cleared the ureter, while powerful diuretic spells and herbs completed the job. Woken up from the deep anaesthesia brought on by the *nepenthes*, Neplach expelled the remains of the stones with bucketsful of urine. There was, admittedly, a brief crisis – at a certain moment, Flutek began to pee blood and before Reynevan could explain that it was a perfectly normal symptom after the operation, the spy roared, fulminated and hurled insults at the physician, which included expressions such as '*verfluchter Hurensohn*' and 'fucking meshugenah wizard'. Neplach stared at his member squirting blood, called for soldiers and threatened the physician with being burned at the stake, impaled and flogged, in that order. He finally grew weary and fell asleep, exhausted. He slept for more than half a day.

It kept on raining. Reynevan was bored. He dropped in on the lectures of the elderly man who had once been a spy for Charles IV. He visited the men writing letters from Heaven and the Apocalypse and was forced to listen to a few. He looked into the barn where the Stentorians practised, a special intelligence service department consisting of bruisers with loud – or Stentorian – voices. The Stentorians were trained for psychological warfare: they were tasked to undermine the morale of the defenders of besieged castles and towns. They practised far from the main camp because when they trained, their voices were deafening.

'Surrender! Lay down your arms! Otherwise! You! Will all! Perish!'

'Louder!' yelled their instructor, directing them with hand gestures. 'All at once and louder! One-two! One-two!'

'Your! Daughters! Will be! Dishonoured! Your! Children! Will be! Slaughtered! We will! Impale! Them! On spears!'

'Brother Bielawa.' One of Flutek's adjutants tugged him by the sleeve. 'Brother Neplach asks to see you.'

'We will! Flay! You! Alive!' yelled the Stentorians. 'We will! Cut! Off! Your balls!'

Bohuchval Neplach was now feeling splendid, nothing was bothering him, and so he was back to his nasty and arrogant old self. He listened to what Reynevan had to tell him. The expression he wore while listening didn't augur particularly well.

'You're an idiot,' was his comment about the brief and general account of the to-do in the gambling den. 'To take such a risk and for whom? A common prostitute! They could have cut all your throats; I'm actually astonished they didn't. Huncleder had probably given his best bodyguards the day off. But don't worry, my physician, so dear to my heart and kidneys. The swindler won't endanger you or your company of misfits. He will be warned of the consequences.

'And regarding the other matter,' continued Flutek, interlacing his fingers, 'you're even greater idiots. The Podkrkonoší is in flames, the Lusatian borderland is burning. The Vartenberk, Biberstein and Dohn families and various Catholic magnates are relentlessly waging what they call a "gallows" war with us. Otto of Bergow, the Lord of Trosky, has already acquired the nickname of "Hussite-killer". And my promise to fulfil your request? I revoke it. *Primo*, you tricked me despicably; *secundo*, your request is idiotic; *et tertio*, you refuse to tell me what you mean to search for there. Having considered everything, I decline. Your death on a Catholic gibbet would be a loss to us, all the worse for being senseless. And we have plans for you. We need you in Silesia.'

'As an intelligence agent?'

'You declared your support for the cause of the Chalice. You asked to join the ranks of the Warriors of God. Good for you! Everybody should serve the best he can.'

'*Ad maiorem Dei gloriam?*'

'Something like that.'

'I'll serve the cause much better as a physician than as a spy.'

'Leave that to my judgement.'

'I'm counting on it. Because it was your kidney I removed a stone from.'

Neplach said nothing for a long time, scowling.

'Very well.' He sighed, looking away. 'You're right. You cured me. You relieved my torment. And I promised to fulfil your request. If you so desire it, if it's your greatest dream, you can go to the Podkrkonoší. I, meanwhile, will not only *not* ask you what it's all about, but will furthermore aid you in the escapade. I'll give you men, an escort, money and contacts. I repeat: I won't ask what you plan to deal with there. But you are to make short work of it – you must be in Silesia by Christmas.'

'You have hundreds of spies at your disposal,' Reynevan said, 'trained in the trade, spying for cash or the cause, but always willingly and of their own free will. But you insisted on me, a dilettante with no expertise who is unsuitable for spying and about as effective as a lame horse. What logic is there in that, Neplach?'

'Would I bother you if there wasn't? We need you in Silesia, Reynevan. You. Not hundreds of ideologically committed or professional spies trained in the craft. You, and you alone. For matters that no one but you is capable of accomplishing. And for which you can't be replaced.'

'Details?'

'Later. Firstly, you're heading into a dangerous place and may not return. Secondly, you didn't share the details with me, so I return the favour. Thirdly, and most importantly: I don't have time now. I'm leaving for Kolín to see Prokop. As regards the escapade, talk to Hašek Sýkora. He will give you men, a special unit. And remember: make haste. Before Christmas—'

'I'm to be in Silesia, I know. Although I don't want to be – and it's a poor agent who acts unwillingly under duress.'

Flutek said nothing for a while.

'You cured me,' he finally said. 'You rescued me from the clutches of agony. I shall repay you. I'll see to it you go to Silesia without being forced. Why, willingly even.'

'Eh?'

'You've become a father, Reinmar.'

'Whaaat?'

'You have a son. Katarzyna Biberstein, daughter of Jan Biberstein, Lord of Stolz, gave birth to a child in June 1426. To a boy, born on the holiday of Saint Vitus and christened with that saint's name. He is now, as one can easily calculate, a year and four months old. According to my agents' reports, a bonny lad, the spit and image of his father. Don't tell me you wouldn't like to see him.'

'Splendid,' Scharley repeated. 'Splendid twice over.'

'I must have sent her ten letters,' Reynevan said bitterly. 'More than ten, I'd say. I know we're at war and times are uncertain, but one of the letters must have reached her. Why didn't she reply? Why didn't she send word? Why did I have to find out about my own son from Neplach?'

The penitent tugged on the horse's bit. 'The conclusion suggests itself,' he said, sighing. 'She has no desire to see you at all. It might sound cruel, but it's only logical. Perhaps even—'

'Perhaps even what?'

'Perhaps he isn't even your son? There, there, calm down, control yourself! I was only thinking aloud. But on the other hand—'

'On the other hand, what?'

'It might be that . . . Oh well, no! Never mind. If I say it, you'll do something foolish.'

'Speak, damn it!'

'You might not have received answers to your letters because old Biberstein is ashamed and furious and has locked his daughter and the little bastard up in the tower . . . Why, no, that's utterly banal and sentimental. Like *Aucassin et Nicolette* . . . By the saints, don't make faces like that, laddie, you're frightening me.'

'Don't talk nonsense and I won't. Agreed?'

'By all means.'

After taking a detour around Prague, they headed north. Rain was falling relentlessly; when it stopped pouring, it began to spit, and when it stopped spitting, it began to drizzle. The mounted squad became bogged down in the mud and was making slow progress – in two days they had only reached the Labe and the bridge linking Stará Boleslav to Brandýs. The following day, having skirted around the town, they continued on their way towards the Nymburk road.

Samson Honeypot – riding behind Scharley and Reynevan – said nothing, but sighed from time to time. Berengar Tauler and Amadej Baťa, riding behind Samson, were deep in conversation. The conversation – perhaps because of the weather – quite often descended into a quarrel, which was fortunately as short-lived as it was sudden. And bringing up the rear, wet and gloomy, rode the Cherethites and Pelethites. Unfortunately.

Scharley, Samson, Tauler and Baťa had arrived at White Mountain on Saint Ursula's Eve, the day after the departure of Flutek, who had set off for Kolín, having been summoned by Prokop the Shaven. Red-haired Marketa, they reported, had remained in Prague, successfully billeted in the house on the corner of Saint Stephen's and Na Rybníčku Streets with Mistress

Blažena Pospíchalová. Mistress Blažena took in the girl, for she had a warm heart, a heart Scharley additionally appealed to, admittedly, with the sum of a hundred and twenty groschen in cash and promises of further funding. Thus Marketa – the girl clearly preferred not to reveal her surname – was tolerably safe. The two ladies, Samson Honeypot assured them, had taken a liking to each other and ought not to tear each other's eyes out during the next few months. And afterwards, he concluded, we shall see.

The fact that Berengar Tauler and Amadej Baťa had remained with the company was somewhat astonishing, frankly; Reynevan hadn't expected to see them after they parted. Tauler often conferred with Scharley, quietly and secretly, so Reynevan suspected that the penitent had tempted him with some fibs, the confabulated prospect of imagined loot. When asked directly, Berengar smiled mysteriously and declared that he preferred their company to Prokop's Taborites, whom he had abandoned because war was a thing without a future, and soldiering a thing without prospects.

'To be sure,' added Amadej Baťa, 'shoemaking has a real future. Everybody needs footwear, don't they? My father-in-law is a shoemaker. I'll just save up a few pennies, let order return to the world, then I'll go into business and expand my father-in-law's workshop into a manufactory. I shall manufacture poulaines. On a large scale. Soon the whole world will be wearing Baťa poulaines, you'll see.'

It had stopped raining and begun drizzling. Reynevan stood up in the stirrups and looked back.

The Cherethites and Pelethites, wet and gloomy, were following them. They hadn't got lost in the pouring rain and the fog.

Unfortunately.

*

As it turned out, Flutek had been behind the gift of that hideous company, that motley and foul-smelling rabble. Indirectly. The pleasure was directly due to Hašek Sýkora, the deputy head of the propaganda department.

'Ah, good day, good day,' Hašek Sýkora greeted them when Reynevan appeared before him with Scharley and Tauler. 'Ah, I know. The expedition to Podještědí. I've received my instructions. Everything is prepared. First, I must finish these woodcuts ... Ah! I must finish, for the emissaries are waiting—'

'May I take a look?' asked Scharley.

'Ah?' Sýkora clearly loved that interjection. 'Ah! A look? By all means. Go ahead.'

The propaganda woodcut, one of many lying on the table, portrayed a monster with a horned goat's head, a tuft of hair on its chin and a hideous, scornful goat's face. The monster was wearing something like a dalmatic on its shoulders, a flaming tiara on its horned head and slippers with crosses on its feet. It held a pitchfork in one hand and was holding the other in a gesture of benediction. There was an inscription over the beast: EGO SUM PAPA.

'Few people can read,' said Scharley, pointing at the words. 'And the picture isn't that distinct. How are simple folk to know it's the Pope? Perhaps it's Huss?'

'May God forgive your blasphemy!' Sýkora choked. 'Ah ... Folk will know, never fear. They – I mean the papists – print pictures of Huss. They – the blasphemers – depict him in the form of a goose with teeth. It has become established. Simple folk know: Beelzebub, a horned, goat-like devil, means the Roman Pope, while a goose with teeth means Huss. Ah, and there's your escort, reporting for duty.'

The escort had lined up on the parade ground in a somewhat ragged line. It consisted of ten thugs. Their faces were loathsome.

The rest of them, too. They resembled a pack of thieves and marauders armed with whatever they could scrounge and dressed in whatever they could filch. Or find on a dust heap.

'Ah, here are your men, at your command from now on,' the deputy head of the propaganda department said, pointing at them. 'From the right: Jewel, Cheapjack, Warrior, Dung, Beetle, Ostrich, Dunnock, Bag, Pea-Muncher, Mořic the Scrapper.'

'May I,' Scharley said in the baleful silence, 'request a word in private?'

'Ah?'

'I won't ask,' the penitent drawled when they were alone, 'if these gentlemen's names are their own or aliases. Although in principle I ought to look into it, since one can judge bandits by their nicknames and *noms de guerre*. But never mind. I wish to ask about something else: I know from Sir Reinmar Bielawa that Brother Neplach promised us a solid and reliable escort. An escort! What kind of a rabble is lined up over there? Is it the bloody Cherethites and Pelethites? Dick, Prick, Shitter and Crapper?'

Hašek Sýkora's jaw jutted out menacingly. 'Brother Neplach ordered me to give you men,' he snapped, 'and what are they, eh? Birds of the sky, perhaps? Or fish of the sea? Frogs of the marsh? Not at all. They are men. The men I can spare at the moment. There aren't any others. You don't like them, ah? You'd prefer, ah, big-breasted women? Or Saint George on a horse? Lohengrin on a swan? I'm sorry, nothing doing. They've all gone.'

'But—'

'Are you taking them or not? Make your mind up.'

The following day, amazingly, it stopped raining. The horses, trudging through the mud, were walking a lot more energetically

and briskly. Amadej Baťa began to whistle. Even the Cherethites and Pelethites – the squad of ten men led by Mořic the
Scrapper that Scharley had christened with biblical names – had
become animated. The previously gloomy, morose slovens who
had appeared to be constantly at odds with the world began to
converse, swap lewd jokes and chuckle. And finally, to everyone's
amazement, sing. In Czech.

> *The skylarks are calling me high above the moors,*
> *Saying my true love cavorts with vulgar boors.*
> *I should let her tarry and take my feather bed,*
> *To lay it neath a tree and rest my tired head . . .*

A son, thought Reynevan. *I have a son. His name's Vitus. He
was born a year and four months ago on Saint Vitus's Day. Exactly
the day before the Battle of Ústí. My first great battle. A battle I
might have died in if things had gone differently. If the Saxons had
destroyed the wagon fort and scattered us, there would have been a
massacre and I might have died. My son would have lost his father
the day after his birth . . .*

And Nicolette . . .

*The ethereal Nicolette, Nicolette as slender as Masaccio's Eve, as
one of Parler's Madonnas, had a swollen belly. Because of me. How
can I look her in the eye? And will I even be able to look her in the
eye at all?*

Oh, never mind. It has to work out in the end.

It was the Thursday after Saint Ursula's Day when they reached
Krchleby and rode towards Rožďalovice on the Mrlina, a right-
bank tributary of the Labe. They were still, in accordance with
the earlier advice of Flutek and Sýkora, avoiding busy highways,
particularly the major trade route leading from Prague to Leipzig
via Jičín, Turnov and Žitava. They were only around three miles

from Jičín, where they intended to conduct reconnaissance outside Trosky.

The terrain around the upper Mrlina warned them at once that they were entering a dangerous region, one of conflict, a still-burning strip of borderland separating feuding religions and nations. 'Burning' was utterly appropriate, for charred remains suddenly became the defining element of the landscape, the blackened ruins of homesteads and cottages, of large and small villages. The scene was almost identical to the remnants of the village near Huncleder's gambling den, the scene of recent fateful events. The same soot-covered stumps of chimneys, the same piles of fused ash, the same blackened skeletons of beams and roof timbers. The same acrid stench of burned-down buildings.

The Cherethites and Pelethites hadn't sung for some time and were attending to their crossbows. Tauler and Baťa, who were leading the cavalcade, had theirs at the ready. Reynevan followed their example.

On the fifth day of their journey, a Saturday, they came to a village the ashes of which were still hot and smoking. That wasn't all – over a dozen corpses could be seen at various stages of carbonisation. Mořic the Scrapper tracked down and dragged out from a nearby potato cellar two living people – an old man and a young girl. The girl had a blonde plait and a grey frock full of holes burned into it by sparks. The old man had two teeth – one above, the other below – in a bushy white beard.

'Fell on us,' he explained incoherently in answer when asked what had happened.

'Who?'

'Them ones.'

Enquiries into who 'them ones' were achieved nothing. The mumbling old man was unable to describe or name 'them ones' beyond calling them 'rascals', 'rogues', 'devils' and 'God strike them down'. Once or twice, he also used another expression – 'martauz' – that Reynevan had never encountered before and didn't know.

'It's from Hungarian.' Scharley frowned and surprise could be heard in his voice. 'They call slave traders and kidnappers "*martahuzes*". The old man probably meant that the villagers were abducted. Taken into captivity.'

'Who could have done it?' said Reynevan, sighing. 'The papists? I thought we controlled this region.'

Scharley bristled somewhat at the 'we'. And Berengar Tauler smiled.

'Our destination, Trosky Castle, is barely two miles from here,' Tauler calmly explained, 'and not without reason do they call Lord Bergow a Hussite-killer. Also nearby are Kost, Hrubý Rohozec, Skála and Frýdštejn – all bastions of the lords of the Catholic Landfried. The seats of knights loyal to King Sigismund.'

'You know both the locality and those knights,' said Reynevan, watching the old man and the little girl with the plait ravenously gulping down the pieces of bread Samson was giving them. 'You're pretty well informed. Isn't it time you revealed your information source?'

'Perhaps it is,' Tauler agreed. 'It's like this: my family have been vassals of the Bergows for years. We travelled with them to Bohemia from Thuringia, where the Bergow family supported the Lord of Lipa in a rebellion against King Henry of Bohemia. My father served Sir Otto the Senior of Bergow, the Lord of Bílina. I served Otto the Younger at Trosky for some time, but no longer. That, though, is a personal matter.'

'Personal, you say?'

'I do.'

'Then we'd like you to lead the march, Brother Berengar,' said

Scharley coldly. 'Up to the front with you – to the place reserved for experts in the land and its inhabitants.'

The following day was Sunday. Being completely preoccupied with other things, they would never have realised. Not even the distant sound of some bells tolling aroused any associations, nor reminded them of anything – neither Reynevan, nor Samson, nor Tauler and Baťa, never mind Scharley, for Scharley usually made light of both holidays and the Third Commandment. Unlike, it turned out, the Cherethites and Pelethites, in other words Mořic the Scrapper *et consortes*. All ten of them, having seen a cross at a junction, rode over to it, dismounted, knelt down in a circle and began to pray. Very zealously and very loudly.

'That bell may be Jičín.' Scharley gestured with his head, without dismounting, 'Tauler?'

'Perhaps. Let's be cautious. We must avoid people recognising us.'

'More specifically, recognising you,' the penitent snorted, 'and recalling those personal matters. I wonder how grave they were.'

'That's not your concern.'

'Oh, but it is,' countered Scharley, 'because it determines how Lord Bergow remembers you. If unfavourably, as I suspect—'

'Not your concern,' Tauler interrupted. 'What's important is what I promised you. I know how to get into Trosky.'

'How is that?'

'There is a way. If nothing's changed—'

Tauler broke off on seeing Amadej Baťa's face. And his eyes grow wide.

The road heading north vanished between two hillocks, from where several horsemen, until then unseen, were riding slowly out. Plenty of horsemen, actually, riding as a party numbering at least twenty horse, and the hillocks could easily have been hiding the same amount again.

The detachment consisted mainly of foot soldiers, grey crossbowmen and lancers led by eight knights and esquires, two of whom were dressed in full plate. One of them bore a large red cross on his breastplate. Scharley swore.

Tauler swore. Baťa swore. The Cherethites and Pelethites looked on open-mouthed, still kneeling and with hands held together in prayer.

To begin with, the knights in armour were just as astonished as them but took a little longer to come to their senses. Before the one with the cross – no doubt the commander – had raised a hand and shouted a command, Tauler, Baťa and Scharley were already riding hard, Samson and Reynevan were spurring their horses, and the Cherethites and Pelethites were swinging themselves into the saddle. The knight's order was directed mainly at the crossbowmen. Before Mořic the Scrapper's men were able to get away, a hail of bolts fell on them. One man tumbled from his horse – it might have been Warrior, or possibly Dung, Reynevan couldn't tell. He was too busy saving his own skin.

He hurtled on at breakneck speed through a grove and a clump of birch trees; the white trunks flashed by. One of the Cherethites overtook him, galloping frantically after Tauler, Scharley and Baťa. Samson's horse was wheezing alongside. Behind them came the thudding of hooves and the shouts of their pursuers. And suddenly the high-pitched, dreadful cry of somebody being caught. A moment later, another man was intercepted.

They hurtled into a ravine, narrow but widening and leading towards a small river. Just ahead of him, Scharley, Baťa and Tauler were splashing through it. They climbed up the far bank and then the side of the ravine. The slope turned out to be muddy and Tauler's horse slipped, sliding back onto its haunches, neighing in fear. Tauler fell from the saddle but immediately sprang up, yelling for help. Mořic the Scrapper and several of his men passed him at a gallop without even lifting their heads from their horses' manes. Reynevan reached down from the saddle, held out a hand and Tauler seized it, swinging himself up behind him. Reynevan shouted and jabbed the horse with his spurs. He appeared to have overcome the steep, slippery slope.

But he had not.

His horse slid back down the muddy ravine and toppled over, kicking frantically and unseating both riders. Reynevan shielded his head with both hands, tried to roll away but didn't manage to. His foot was caught in the stirrup and being squeezed painfully as the horse thrashed about. Tauler, who had been dazed by the fall, got to his feet only to be kicked in the head. Hard. With a resounding thump.

Somebody grabbed Reynevan by the arm and tugged him. He cried in pain, but his foot was jerked out of the twisted stirrup leathers. The horse struggled to its feet and ran away. Reynevan stood up, saw Samson on his feet and then, to his horror, a group of horsemen splashing through the river. They were almost upon them. So close that Reynevan could see their contorted faces. And their bloodied spear blades.

They were saved from death by the Cherethites and Pelethites, Mořic the Scrapper *et consortes*. They hadn't fled but stopped at the edge of the ravine and now released a salvo from their crossbows. They fired accurately. Horses and riders splashed into the water. The Cherethites and Pelethites rode down the slope, yelling, brandishing swords and maces, and fell on the lancers.

With the advantage of surprise and determination, they stopped the pursuers in their tracks. For a while. But it had been, in fact, a suicidal attack. They were facing a larger force, and more heavy cavalry was arriving to aid the lancers and bowmen.

The Cherethites and Pelethites fell from the saddle one by one. Stabbed, hacked, pierced, Dunnock, Beetle and Bag – or perhaps Dunnock, Ostrich and Pea-Muncher – tumbled into the water and the bloody mud, one after another. The last to fall was the valiant Mořic the Scrapper, who was knocked from his saddle by the battleaxe of the knight with a cross and stonemason's pliers on his breastplate.

Reynevan and Samson, naturally, didn't wait for the predictable outcome of the engagement. They fled up the hillside. Samson was carrying the still-unconscious Tauler. Reynevan was carrying a crossbow which he'd had the presence of mind to pick up. Sensibly, as it turned out.

They were being chased by two riders – esquires, judging from their armour, steeds and trapping. When the esquires were almost upon them, Reynevan raised the crossbow to his shoulder. He aimed at the rider's body but, mindful of the lesson once given him by Dzierżka of Wirsing, changed his mind and sent a bolt into the horse's chest. The horse – a fine pale grey – dropped as though poleaxed and the rider turned a somersault that an acrobat would have been proud of.

The second esquire reined his horse around, pressed his head to the mane and galloped away. It was the correct decision. Cavalry flooded out of the wall of trees. At least four dozen armoured riders, most with the red Chalice on their chests or the Host on their shields.

'They're ours!' yelled Reynevan. 'Ours, Samson!'

'Yours,' Samson Honeypot corrected him, sighing. 'But I must admit it's a welcome sight nonetheless.'

The cavalrymen with the Chalice rode down the slope en masse with a yelling, clanging and thudding resounding above the river. The esquire, the youngster whose horse Reynevan had shot, leaped to his feet, looked around and ran away on unsteady legs. He didn't get far. One of the riders caught up with him and struck him on the back of the head with the flat of his blade, knocking him down. He then reined his horse around and walked over to Reynevan, Samson and the still-unconscious Tauler. He wore a coat of arms with crossed truncated boughs on his chest, partly obscured by a red cloth Chalice.

'Greetings, Reynevan,' he said, raising the moveable visor of his sallet. 'How go you?'

'Brázda of Klinštejn!'

'Of the Ronovic family. Good to see you, too, Samson.'

'The pleasure is mine.'

There were about a dozen bodies lying in the ravine, in the river and on the banks. It was difficult to guess how many the water had carried off.

'Whose men were they?' asked the commander of the relief, a long-haired, moustachioed youth as thin as a rake. 'They sped away too fast for me to identify them. You saw them close up. So? Brother Bielawa!'

Reynevan knew the man asking the questions. He had met him in Hradec Králové two years before. It was Hejtman Jan Čapek of Sány, who was advancing rapidly through the Orphans' ranks. The cavalry bearing Chalices on their chests who had come to their aid were Orphans. The Warriors of God thus christened themselves after having been 'orphaned' when their beloved and revered leader, the great Jan Žižka of Trocnov, died.

'Reynevan! I'm talking to you!'

'Apart from the foot soldiers, there were eight more armoured men,' he calculated. 'Two knights and six esquires. That's one of them, over there, being bound. The commander had a cross on his armour, and pliers or pincers on his shield ... Black on a silver field ...'

'As I suspected.' Jan Čapek of Sány grimaced. 'Bohuš of Kováň, the Lord of Frýdštejn. A brigand and traitor! Oh well, pity he managed to escape ... I'd have flayed him ... And what are you doing here? Where did you come from? Eh? Brother Scharley?'

'We're travelling.'

'Travelling,' repeated Čapek. 'Well, you were fortunate. If we hadn't arrived in time, you'd have travelled vertically for the last leg of your journey, dropping from a branch with a rope around your necks. Lord Bohuš likes to trim trees with hanged men. We have scores to settle with him, oh yes—'

'Does this Lord Bohuš,' Reynevan suddenly recalled, 'by any chance trade in people? Slaves? Is he what they call a *martahuz*?'

'A queer name.' The Hejtman of the Orphans frowned. 'It's true that Bohuš of Kováň shows no mercy to folk of our faith. Anyone he catches alive he strings up at once from the nearest tree. If he manages to catch one of our priests, he burns him at the stake, publicly, as a terrible warning. But I've never heard of him taking slaves. You, let me tell you, were lucky. You escaped with your lives—'

'Not everyone.'

'That's life.' Čapek spat. 'In a moment we'll make a burial mound. How many can that be? The Czech lands are so full of burial mounds and graves, we're beginning to run out of space ... That one there? Also dead?'

'He's alive,' replied Amadej Baťa, who was kneeling beside Tauler with Samson, 'but each time he opens his eyes he closes them again ...'

'A horse kicked him.'

'Well,' said Čapek, sighing, 'that's his misfortune. And we don't have a medic.'

'We do.' Reynevan unfastened a bag. 'I'll tend to him.'

*

Although he didn't usually, Reynevan fell asleep in the saddle. He would have fallen had Samson, who was riding beside him, not held him up.

'Where are we?'

'Almost there. There's a castle tower up ahead.'

'What castle?'

'A friendly one, I think.'

'How's Tauler? Where's Scharley?'

'Scharley's riding at the head with Čapek and Brázda. Tauler's unconscious, slung between two horses. And you'd better wake up now, Reinmar. It's no time to doze.'

'I'm not dozing. I wanted . . . I wanted to ask you something, friend Samson.'

'Ask away, friend Reinmar.'

'Back in the gambling den, why did you step in? Why did you stand up for that girl? And please don't serve me empty platitudes. Tell me the real reason.'

'*I found myself within a forest dark* . . .' The giant answered with a quotation. 'What a prophetic phrase. As though the master Alighieri had sensed I would one day find myself in a world where one can only communicate using lies or deceit and the pure truth is taken as an empty platitude or evidence of mental deficiency. You'd like to hear the real reason, you say. Why right now? You've never before asked me to explain my actions.'

'So far I've understood them.'

'Indeed? I envy you, for I haven't always. And still don't. The incident with Marketa fits that pattern. To some extent, for there are other reasons, indeed. I'm sorry, but I can't tell you them. They are, *primo*, too personal. *Secundo*, you wouldn't understand them.'

'Because they're unfathomable, naturally. Otherworldly. Not even Dante could help me?'

'Dante can always help.' The giant smiled. 'Very well. If you want to know ... In the gambling den, during that repulsive show, my spirit was yearning.'

'Hmm ... A little more?'

'With pleasure.'

E lo spirito mio, che già cotanto
tempo era stato ch'a la sua presenza
non era di stupor, tremando, affranto,
sanza de li occhi aver più conoscenza,
per occulta virtù che da lei mosse,
d'antico amor sentì la gran potenza.

Neither of them said anything for a long time.

'*Amor?*' Reynevan finally asked. 'Are you certain it's *amor?*'

'I'm certain it's *gran potenza.*'

They rode on in silence.

'Reinmar?'

'Go on, Samson.'

'It's high time I was going home. Let's make an effort, shall we?'

'Very well, friend. We shall. I promise. Is that the bridge? Yes, I think it is.'

Hooves thundered on the timbers and planks as the horsemen rode onto a bridge spanning a deep canyon. The castle – their destination – stood atop a steep precipice that plunged straight down to a river, probably the Jizera. Beyond the bridge there was a solid gate, and beyond the gate an extensive bailey over which the castle's mighty bergfried towered.

'We're home!' Jan Čapek of Sány announced loudly from the head, his mount's horseshoes ringing on the cobbles of the bailey. 'In Michalovice. I mean, *I'm* home!'

Chapter Eight

In which the reader, although they make the acquaintance of several historical figures and persons important to the story, in principle doesn't find out much apart from that you know a good bird by its song. But, all in all, the most important thing they learn in this chapter is which crowned heads and prominent notables fucked a wench in 1353 who is now an old woman.

Reynevan and Scharley were invited to supper. Berengar Tauler, in spite of the medical attention, was still lying unconscious. Amadej Baťa offered to watch over him. Samson – as usual – was quartered in the stable. As usual, he was playing dice with the stablemen, who were keen to fleece the simpleton. It probably needn't be stated who finally lost their shirt to whom.

Supper was served in the main chamber of the upper castle, decorated with a wooden figure of the Archangel Michael, a tapestry with a unicorn and a large red coat of arms depicting a silver lion rampant hanging just below the ceiling. In the corner, a fire roared in a hearth and beside it on a stool sat a hunched old woman, absorbed with a spinning wheel, a distaff and a merrily hopping spindle.

All the Hussite hejtmans – both local and neighbouring ones visiting the castle by chance – were dining. In addition to Jan

Čapek of Sány and Brázda of Klinštejn, sitting at the table was a tall, swarthy man with a hooked nose and evil, piercing eyes, his neck encumbered by a heavy gold chain, a decoration more usually worn by town councillors than soldiers. Reynevan knew him and had seen him among the Orphans in Hradec Králové. But only now were they introduced to each other: it was Jan Kolúch of Véska.

On Kolúch's left sat Štěpán Tlach, the hejtman of an outpost in nearby Český Dub, a not old, yet very grey-haired man with a red, plebeian face and the gnarled hands of a carpenter, wearing a padded and richly embroidered knightly doublet in which he clearly felt uncomfortable. Seated beside Tlach was a scrawny, fair-haired man with a scar on his cheek. The scar looked menacing, but it was a souvenir of a simple, amateurishly incised boil. The scar's owner introduced himself as Vojta Jelínek.

As was customary among the Orphans, there was a priest at the hejtmans' table – so between Čapek and Brázda sat a short, stout, bearded man dressed in black, presented as Brother Buzek, servant of God. The servant of God had evidently begun dining earlier, for he was already more than tipsy.

No delicacies were served. The large dishes of mutton and beef chops and ribs were served only with large quantities of roast turnip and a basket of bread. Several kegs of Hungarian wine were brought to the table, all with the lion of the Markvartic family branded onto them. The sight of them reminded Reynevan of Prague, as did the coat of arms hanging from the ceiling. The sixth of September. And Hynek of Kolštejn falling onto the cobblestones from the window of the House at the Elephant.

Before they began dining in earnest, there were, it turned out, several official matters to be dealt with. Four Hussites shoved a prisoner into the room – the esquire captured beside the river.

The one whose horse Reynevan had shot from under him with a crossbow.

The youngster's hair and clothes were dishevelled and a large bruise on his cheekbone was swelling and assuming a beautiful colour. Jan Čapek of Sány glared at the escort but said nothing. He only gave a sign for the captive to be unhanded. The esquire pushed away the hands gripping him, stood erect and looked at the Hussite commanders proudly, but Reynevan could see his knees were trembling somewhat.

There was silence for a while, only disturbed by the soft whirring of the spinning wheel of the old woman in the corner.

'Sir Nikel of Keuschburg,' said Jan Čapek. 'Welcome, we're glad to have you. You shall remain under our roof until a packhorse shows up here with a ransom. You know that in any case, m'lord – you know wartime customs.'

'I serve Sir Friedrich of Dohna!' said the esquire, raising his head. 'Sir Friedrich will pay my ransom.'

'Are you certain?' said Jan Kolúch of Véska, pointing a bone stripped of meat at him. 'For, you see, rumour has is that you are fond of Barbara, Sir Friedrich's daughter, that you are courting her. And who knows if Lord Dohna approves of your advances? Perhaps he's rubbing his hands together, glad to be rid of you? Pray, my son, for it to be otherwise.'

The esquire first paled and then flushed red.

'I have other kin!' he declared. 'I'm a Keuschburg!'

'Then pray that miserliness hasn't got the better of them, for you won't eat at our table for nothing. At least not for long.'

'Not for long,' confirmed Jan Čapek. 'Or perhaps long enough for you to see your error? Perhaps you'll spurn the Roman farce and turn towards the true faith? Don't make a face! It's happened to better men than you. Sir Bohuslav of Švamberk, may God rest his soul, changed his life almost from one day to the

next, being promoted from a captive to the Tábor's chief hejtman. When brother Žižka took him prisoner and threw him
into a dungeon in Příběnice, Sir Bohuslav saw his mistake and
received the Chalice. We have a priest here, as you see. And so?
Shall I ask for the Chalice?'

The squire spat on the floor. 'Shove your Chalice, heretic,' he
answered back proudly. 'You know where.'

'Blasphemer!' yelled Father Buzek, leaping up and spilling
wine on himself and his neighbours. 'To the stake with him!
Have him burned, Brother Čapek!'

'Burn money?' Jan Čapek of Sány smiled hideously. 'You must
be drunk, Brother Buzek. He's worth at least four thousand groschen. While there's the faintest chance they'll pay a ransom
for him, no one will lay a finger on him – even were he to pro-
claim Master Huss himself a leper and a sodomite. Am I right,
Brethren?'

The Hussites agreed enthusiastically, roaring and banging
their mugs on the table. Čapek gestured to the guards to escort
the captive out. Father Buzek glared angrily at him and then
poured close to half a quart of Hungarian wine into himself in
a single draught.

'You lust after a mean penny, like the Pharisees!' he said,
and his words were already quite slurred. 'And P-Paul wrote to
Timothy: The love of money is the root of all evil. Which while
some coveted after, they have erred from . . . Hic . . . The faith
. . . And no covetous man hath any inheritance in the kingdom
of Christ and of God . . . You cannot serve God and Mammon!'

'We'd rather not,' said Jan Kolúch of Véska, laughing, 'but we
have to! For let me tell you, there's no life without Mammon.'

'But there will be!' The preacher filled his cup and emptied it
in one gulp. 'There will be! When we triumph! Everything will
be shared; all ownership and property will vanish. There will be

no rich or poor, no poverty or oppression. Happiness and divine peace will reign on Earth.'

'What nonsense,' said the stooped old woman spinning in the corner. 'Pious old soak.'

'We shall secure divine peace with our swords,' Jan Čapek said seriously. 'We shall buy it with our blood. And we deserve a just reward for it, including Mammon. We didn't fight a revolution, Brother, to return to that miserable hole, Sány. And to my sorry excuse for a stronghold, to my watchtower, which a hog almost knocked over by rubbing against it. Revolutions are fought in order for things to change: for the worse for the losers, for the better for the winners. Do you see, honoured guests, honourable Reinmar and Scharley, that coat of arms high up on the wall? It's the crest of Sir Jan of Michalovice, known as Michalec. The castle where we are feasting, Michalovice, was his family seat. And then what? We seized it from him! We were victorious! When I find the time, I'll get a ladder, take down that shield and hurl it on the ground; why, I'll even piss on it. And I'll hang my heraldic stag on the wall on a shield twice as large! And I shall rule here! Sir Jan Čapek of Sány! Lord of Michalovice!'

'Indeed, indeed!' Štěpán Tlach joined in from the dish of ribs. 'The revolution is victorious, the Chalice triumphs. And we shall be great lords! Let's drink to it!'

'Great lords! Only for hens to laugh at,' said the old woman by the spinning wheel with venomous contempt as she adjusted the bobbin on the flyer. 'You're bare-arsed brigands. Parvenus whose coats of arms drip paint when it rains.'

Štěpán Tlach threw a bone at her but missed. The other Hussites paid no attention to the old woman.

'But Mammon . . .' continued the preacher, pouring wine copiously and becoming increasingly incoherent. 'Mammon ought not to be served. Yes, yes, the Chalice will triumph, the true way will be victorious ... But the covetous shall not inherit ... the Kingdom of God. Listen to me ... Hic—'

'Enough.' Čapek waved a hand. 'You're drunk.'

'I am not! I'm sober ... hiiic ... And thus do I say to you: Let us venerate ... Let us venerate ... *Pax Dei* ... For they shall be damned ... The Chalice will triumph ... Triuuumph ... Eeey ...'

'Didn't I tell you? Drunk as a lord!'

'I'm sober!'

'You're drunk!'

'To prove you're not drunk,' said Jan Kolúch, twirling his moustache, 'do as I say. Stick two fingers down your throat and say: Grrr! Grrr! Grrr!'

Priest Buzek managed the first 'Grrr', but on the second choked, rasped, goggled and vomited.

'Go on and puke,' said the old woman scathingly over her distaff. 'Hope you puke your own arse out.'

Once again, she was ignored; the company was clearly accustomed to it. The vomit-spattered preacher was shoved out of the hall. There was a thudding as he fell down the stairs.

'In actual fact, honoured guests,' said Kolúch, wiping the table with a hat left behind by Father Buzek, 'we're some way short of outright victory. We're sitting and feasting at Michalovice, which was seized, as Brother Čapek said, from Sir Jan Michalec. We've captured Mladá Boleslav, Benešov, Mimoň and Jablonné. But Michalec didn't flee far, only to Bezděz. And where is Bezděz? Go over to the window and look northwards and you'll see it, a mere two miles away, over the river. Two miles! When one of us sneezes, Lord Michalec in Bezděz shouts, "Bless you!".'

'Unfortunately,' Štěpán Tlach said gloomily, 'Lord Michalec has no blessings for us, but would rather wish us damnation. But we cannot march on Bezděz, it's impregnable. We'd barely chip its walls.'

'That is the truth, unfortunately,' Vojta Jelínek said over his shoulder as he pissed into the hearth. 'And there's no shortage of other castles and lords nearby who wish us a cruel death. Petr of Vartenberk menaces us every other day from Děvín, a stone's throw away. Six miles from here is Ralsko, lorded over by Sir Jan of Vartenberk, known as Chudoba . . .'

'You've met Bohuš of Kováň, Lord of Frýdštejn,' added Čapek. 'You know what he's capable of. And there are others . . .'

'Aye, there are,' Kolúch growled. 'We do hold the more strategic castles: Vartenberk, Lipý, Český Brod, Bělá pod Bezdězem and of course Michalovice. Most of the length of the trade route is still controlled by the papists and the Germans. The Lords of Dohna control Falkenberg and Grabštejn castles. Mikuláš Dachs, a client of the Lusatian Bibersteins, is the burgrave of Hamrštejn. That old brigand Hans Foltsch, a mercenary from Zgorzelec, has designs on Roimund Castle. The brothers Jan and Jindřich Berk of Dubá control Tolštejn—'

'Kinsmen,' boasted Brázda of Klinštejn. 'The Ronovic family, as I am.'

'Kinsmen like you exercise the Berks' hounds,' interrupted the old woman at the spinning wheel.

'Of the brothers from Dubá,' snorted Jan Kolúch, 'Jindřich is particularly ill-disposed to us, for we took Lipý from him. It's said he vowed in the church in Žitava that he wouldn't eat meat until he ejects us from Lipý Castle. I'd say his fast will last a long time.'

'Indeed!' shouted Štěpán Tlach, slamming his fist down on the table. 'Damned be any man who tries to remove us. Just let him try! We, the Orphans, stand firm here!'

'Aye! We stand firm!'

Čapek frowned. 'It's not enough just to be here and bay like dogs on a chain. That's not how Brother Žižka taught us. The best form of defence is attack! Strike the foe, give him no rest! Wait not until the foe arrives with his rabble but march on him, enter his domain with fire and sword. Strike them, the Lord said to the Israelites. And it is time to strike! It is time to muster and strike: Frýdštejn, Děvín, Ralsko, Roimund, Tolštejn—'

'And beyond,' interrupted Kolúch with a wicked grin. 'Lusatia! Grabštejn, Frydland, Žitava, Zgorzelec! But we cannot do it alone. We lack forces. For where can we look to for support? To Prague? Prague, if it isn't planning treachery, is playing at revolutions and street brawls. To the Tábor? The Tábor is besieging Kolín, a Czech town. As if there were no Hungarian, Austrian or German ones.'

'They say,' said Scharley, 'that Prokop is planning something of that kind now. That his gaze turns towards Hungary and Austria.'

'God willing. But meanwhile you've seen for yourselves what manner of neighbours we have here.'

'One name hasn't been uttered yet,' said the penitent, seemingly casually. 'Does he not trouble you? I have in mind Otto of Bergow at Trosky Castle, some four miles from Michalovice. What kind of neighbour is he, I wonder?'

'A thorn in the arse.' The old woman, fiddling at the spindle, spoke before the Hussites. 'That's what Lord Bergow is to you, gentleman brigands, isn't he? A thorn in the arse!'

There was a long silence, indicating that the old woman had touched a nerve. Jan Kolúch of Véska broke the silence.

'We are Warriors of God,' he said, playing with a knife. 'We are mindful of the Lord's word when He spoke through the mouth of the prophet Jeremiah: The most proud shall stumble and fall, and none shall raise him up. I will kindle a fire in his cities, and it shall devour all round about him.'

'Give him according to his deeds,' added Čapek, also clearly versed in biblical quotations.

'Render to him all that he has done.'

'Amen.'

'Bergow has a winged fish on his coat of arms,' added Štěpán Tlach, ominously and to the point. 'Neither fish nor fowl. The day will come when we'll scale that little fish. And pluck that little bird.'

'Amen to that.' Vojta Jelínek stood up. 'I'm drowsy, Brethren.'

'I also.' Jan Kolúch stood up, too, and Brázda of Klinštejn and Štěpán Tlach followed his example.

'Indeed, the day was hard . . . Are you going, Brother Čapek?'

'I shall sit a while yet. With our guests.'

The fire crackled. Tawny owls hooted around the tower. The old woman's spinning wheel rattled softly.

'We are alone,' said Jan Čapek of Sány, interrupting the long silence. 'Speak.'

They did so.

'A wizard,' the Hejtman of the Orphans said in disbelief. 'You are searching for a wizard? You? Serious men?'

After the serious men had confirmed their intentions, he said, 'I've never ever heard of Rupilius the Silesian, but there's a seer, alchemist or mage in almost every castle here, so it's quite likely that Lord Bergow has one as either a guest or a prisoner. The problem lies elsewhere—'

'You are the problem,' said the old woman, demonstrating her good hearing. 'Hanging's too good for you!'

'Pay her no heed.' Čapek grimaced. 'Treat her like a piece of furniture. When Lord Michalec fled before us, he left a great many things. Furniture, livestock, ham in the smokehouse, wine in the cellar. A coat of arms on the wall. And that old crone. In that very corner. I wanted to pack her and her bloody spinning wheel off to the servants' quarters but was unable to, she kicked up such a row. But I can't drive her from the castle, she'd die of hunger. I let her stay there, spinning—'

'I'll sit and spin,' the old woman snapped. 'I'll sit here until Lord Michalec returns and drives you from here, bare arses.'

'Where was I?'

'With the problem,' Scharley prompted him.

'Yes, indeed. It lies in the fact that Trosky Castle, where your Rupilius may reside, is unassailable and cannot be penetrated. It's impossible to get into it.'

'There's a man in the company who knows how to do it,' said Scharley, lowering his voice.

'Aha – those two,' guessed Čapek. 'That Tauler with the bandage and the other one. Well, I advise not putting too much hope in them. Be particularly heedful if an underground passage is mentioned. Know that all secret passages and tunnels supposedly linking Trosky Castle to other places in the area, even as far as a quarter of a mile away, are legends and fabrications. Fairy tales. If that Tauler promises to deliver you into the castle using a secret tunnel, then he's either a trickster and a liar himself, or has swallowed somebody else's lies. Either possibility is perilous to you. If you wander around searching for a "secret passageway", you'll finally fall into German or papist hands.

'We Orphans,' he continued, 'have been here in Podještědí since spring 1426. If there'd been any secret passages, we'd have found them. Were it possible to get into Trosky, we'd have done so. For the old woman spoke honestly: Trosky and that damned German, Bergow, are thorns in our arses. We never stop looking for a way to rid ourselves of that thorn.'

'The passage may be magical,' Reynevan remarked. 'Do you believe in magic?'

'What's to believe?' Jan Čapek pouted. 'There's no such thing.

But if by some chance it did exist, it would be utterly baffling and out of reach of ordinary mortals. Magic would be of no benefit to an ordinary fellow like me. Which means if something were magical it might as well not be. Is that logical?'

'Stunningly.' Scharley smiled. 'It's hard to argue with logic like that. Would you thus advise us, Hejtman, to drop our plans and return home?'

'I would indeed. Return home. And wait patiently. Rumour has it that Bergow was in league with Hynek of Kolštejn in Prague on the sixth of September. Prokop the Shaven won't forgive anyone who supported the plot. He's now laying siege to Bořek of Miletínek, it'll soon be the turn of others. Any moment now, Bergow will get his just desserts and Trosky will be ours. And everything that Trosky contains. Including your sorcerer.'

'Wise advice,' said the penitent, without taking his eyes off Reynevan. 'Isn't it, Reynevan?'

'You called Lord Bergow a "damned German",' said Reynevan unexpectedly. 'There aren't any other German-born families in the area, are there? Aside from the Lords of Dohna in Falkenberg and Grabštejn?'

'Aye, there are only those two families. What of it?'

'Nothing. For now.'

'For now,' said Čapek, standing up, 'I'm going to bed. Goodnight, Brethren.'

'And to you, Brother.'

The fire in the hearth wasn't crackling any longer but just flickering, now flaring up, now dying down. The spinning wheel had stopped tapping, too. The old woman wasn't spinning but sitting still.

'What has befallen this castle?' she suddenly said. 'Dedicated to Archangel Michael, it's stood for a hundred and fifty years, and for a hundred and fifty years the Markvartic family have been the Lords of Michalovice. But now ... Such a rabble ... Oh my days ... I recall when kings stayed here ... And today? It's a shame!'

'Don't lie, Grandmama.' Scharley's reaction slightly surprised Reynevan, who was now a little sleepy. 'It's unseemly, in the winter of your life. You've never seen a king, old woman – unless it was Herod in a nativity play.'

'Who are you calling old? May your tongue shrivel up. And I've seen more kings than you've had hot dinners.'

'Where, may I ask?'

'In Vienna.'

'Where?'

'In Vienna, fool!' The old woman straightened up on her stool. 'At Easter *Anno Domini* 1353, the monarchs of this world gathered in Vienna. Emperor Charles, whose wife Anne of Bavaria had just died, was arranging to marry the young Anne, niece of Bolko II of Świdnica-Jawor. Oh, the kings and lords that came to Vienna then—'

'And you were there, were you, Grandmama? An invited guest?'

'What would you know, boor? Fool! For I ... I was pretty then ... Young ... First Emperor Charles caught me in the cloisters of an evening, bent me over the banister, lifted up my shift. He tickled my neck with his beard and I laughed so loud he almost popped out ... He was furious, so I took him in hand and put him back where he belonged. Oh, then he said, I'm fond of you, little Moravian, I can give you in marriage to a knight ... But I wasn't thinking of marriage then, when there were so many comely lads around ...

'The second,' the old woman said dreamily, 'was Ludwik, the King of Hungary. How eager was that young man ... ? Then I

caught the fancy of the King of Poland, Casimir the Great ...
His nickname was apt, let me tell you—'

'You're lying, old woman.'

'Ruprecht, Count Palatine of the Rhine ... Getting on a bit
and a German to boot. Don't expect any sweet nothings or com-
pliments, he just barked: *Mach die Beine breit!* While Arnošt of
Pardubice, the Archbishop of Prague, hey, he had a silver tongue
and was well-versed ... Oh, he knew various tricks and ingen-
ious mischief ... Przecław of Pogorzela, Bishop of Wrocław, a
Pole, he was also handy, knew his way around a woman, but his
footwraps stank to high heaven ... Albrecht, Duke of Austria—'

The old woman choked and had a coughing fit. It was some
time before she went on.

'But the one who satisfied me most wasn't a king or a bishop,
but a poet, a Tuscan,' she said, drooling a little. 'He was a dream
of a man. Not just hot-blooded but could talk the most beautifully of them all. Ha, you know a good bird by its song. Oh,
how he could talk ... In rhyme, even. They called him ... Erm
... His Christian name was like that saint from Assisi ... But
his surname ... Let me think ... What the Devil ... Raucous?
Petraucous?'

'Perhaps it was ...' Reynevan stammered. 'Perhaps it was
Petrarca? Francesco Petrarca?'

'Perhaps.' The old woman nodded. 'Perhaps, son. The memory
fades after all those years.'

Chapter Nine

In which a brilliant idea occurs to Reynevan. As a result, he finds out how much it's worth to various people. The fact that towards the end of the chapter its value grows at lightning speed ought in principle to please him. But it doesn't.

Scharley utterly surprised Reynevan. Having heard the premises of the brilliant plan, he by no means mocked, or jeered, or called him a clown or an idiot – why, he didn't even tap his forehead, which he did quite often in discussions. Having heard the premises of his brilliant plan, Scharley calmly put down the mug of beer he was drinking with his breakfast, stood up and left the room without a word. He didn't respond to being called, didn't even turn his head. He didn't even kick the dog that had got caught up in his feet but stepped over it with menacing calm. He didn't even slam the door as he went out. He simply walked away.

'I do understand him a little,' said Jan Čapek of Sány, who had appeared in the castle kitchen at just the right time to hear the premises of the brilliant plan. 'You are a dangerous man, Brother Bielawa. I once had a comrade who often entertained similar ideas. Often. He was a serious threat. Until recently.'

'Until recently?'

'Indeed. As a result of his last idea, he was broken on the wheel in Loket town square a year ago, as part of the Saint Ludmila's Day celebrations. Two others were also executed with him. There are ideas which don't just harm the author but the people around him, too. Regrettably.'

'My plan will certainly not harm anybody,' said Reynevan, slightly irked. 'If only because I shall undertake and execute it myself, alone. Only *I* will be taking a risk.'

'But a great one.'

'Do we have a choice? No, we don't! Tauler is still unconscious, and even if he comes round, you said yourself, Brother Čapek, that the secret underground passage to Trosky is an illusion and nothing will come of it. Time is short. We must take action. I consider my plan for entering the castle quite feasible, with a good chance of success.'

'My, oh my!'

Reynevan bristled. 'Lord Bergow is a German.' He began counting on his fingers. 'Lord Dohna, too. The Hussites who captured the young Keuschburg, indeed also a German, are much closer to Trosky than to Falkenberg. It's normal and logical that they would send an emissary with a demand for a ransom to Lord Bergow. It is clear and obvious that Lord Bergow would inform Lord Dohna, his fellow countryman, about it.'

'Lord Bergow,' said Čapek, shaking his head, 'would seize the Hussite emissary by the arse and chuck him into the dungeon. As he usually does.'

'The Hussites know he does that.' Reynevan smiled triumphantly. 'They have learned that oaths mean nothing to him, that knightly parole may be violated. For which reason they will use a completely chance person as an emissary. A foreigner. An itinerant poet from Champagne wandering aimlessly around the countryside.'

Čapek said nothing. He just raised his eyes towards the heavens. Or actually towards the kitchen ceiling.

'An itinerant poet from Champagne.' Samson shook his head. 'Oh, my, Reinmar, Reinmar ... And do you know even three words of the tongue of the Franks?'

'I know more than three. Don't you believe me?'

Par montaignes et par valees
Et par forez longues et lees
Par leus estranges et sauvages
Et passa mainz felonz passages
Et maint peril et maint destroit . . .

'Quite fluent,' admitted Samson with a sigh. 'The accent, I must admit, is also half-decent. And the choice of an excerpt from a romance ... Why, most apt and fitting for the circumstances.'

'So fitting,' interjected Scharley, who had just entered the kitchen soundlessly, 'it couldn't be more so! All you need, O itinerant poet from Champagne, is to think up a suitable name. A *nom de guerre* that is equally fitting and aptly characterises you. I suggest Yvain Le Cretin. When do we set off?'

'*I'm* setting off. By myself.'

'No.' Samson Honeypot shook his head. 'I am. This matter concerns me and only me. I don't want to put any of you at risk because of me. It's high time I took my own affairs into my own hands. Assuming that Reinmar's idea is a good one, it can be slightly modified: in order to deliver to Trosky a ransom demand for the young Keuschburg, they might make use of an itinerant idiot. I think it's quite a decent cover, and my appearance—'

'Your appearance is indeed breathtaking,' interrupted Scharley, 'but it's not quite enough. The mission needs someone with skill in the fields of fraud, deceit, leading people by the nose and pulling the wool over their eyes. No offence, but there's only one of us here who deserves to be called a specialist.'

'The idea was mine,' Reynevan calmly replied, 'and I won't give it up. It's rightfully mine and I'm setting off alone. And I'm certain I'm the most suitable of us for this enterprise.'

'Not at all,' Scharley objected. 'You're the least suitable. It was you and not us whom the augury told to beware of the Old Woman and the Maiden. But you, of course, don't believe in auguries. When it suits you—'

'I've learned that from you.' Reynevan cut him off. 'Enough talking, I'm leaving. Alone. You're staying. For if—'

'Yes. If what?'

'If something goes wrong . . . If I were to be . . . I'd like to be able to count on having you both at the ready. And that you'd come to my aid and get me out of trouble.'

Scharley said nothing for a long time.

'I'm tormented by the thought,' he finally said, 'that if I were to wallop you on the head, Reinmar of Champagne, then tie you up and lock you in a cellar for a while, you'd thank me for it one day. So I wonder why I don't do it.'

'Because you know I wouldn't thank you.'

The execution of the plan went smoothly. Hejtman Vojta Jelínek, who was still residing at Michalovice, when informed about the venture in general terms, offered his help eagerly and at once. Intending to set off towards Roimund with a small reconnaissance party, he declared his readiness to take a more roundabout route and escort Reynevan to the Jičín highway, where he could easily join a merchant caravan.

They set off later that very day. Around noon.

Berengar Tauler awoke and came to sometime in the afternoon.

He had stopped vomiting and could stand fairly straight and even walk. He went to the latrine by himself and returned without anyone's help, so it appeared that he had recovered. Enough for Scharley and Jan Čapek to nail him down regarding the secret underground passage leading to Trosky. Assuming the stern faces of Inquisitors, they showered the now healthy man with questions intended to corner him and catch him out.

'What passage?' The pale Tauler paled even more and blinked but was by no means frightened. 'What underground corridor? What are you talking about?'

'How did you plan to get us into Trosky? Using a secret passage, wasn't it?'

'No, damn it! I don't know anything about a passage! I have – or rather had – a comrade at Trosky, the head groom ... I counted on his helping us ... He owed me a favour ... He'd have got us into the castle or found out what we'd need to do ... What the bloody hell is this?'

Scharley and Čapek didn't answer. They rushed out of the room and ran downstairs, issuing orders as they ran.

They nearly exhausted their mounts trying to get there before sundown. They covered practically the entire Jičín highway, almost reaching Kost Castle. They encountered two merchant caravans, a coppersmith with a wagon containing copper products and a troupe of wandering acrobats, a beggar and an old woman with a basket of penny buns.

But none of them had seen a poet from Champagne. Or anyone answering the description. Not that day, not any day.

Reynevan had vanished. As though the ground had swallowed him up.

Scharley insisted they follow Vojta Jelínek and his troop and catch up with them to find out what had happened and where they had left Reynevan. Jan Čapek firmly refused. There was no chance of catching up with Jelínek's troop, which had several hours' start on them. Night was falling and the area was dangerous. Too close to Catholic castles. Too close for a detachment numbering only twenty horse. ·

They retraced their steps along the same road, looking around attentively. Searching for a lone rider. And when it grew dark, the glow of a campfire.

They saw nobody.

There was no sign of Reynevan.

The first sensation he felt after waking was biting cold, all the more acute since he couldn't move at all, couldn't curl up to protect what remained of the warmth in his body. It was as though he were paralysed.

Then, in turn, his other senses awoke and he realised the position he was in. His open eyes showed above him stars against a black October sky: Polaris, the Greater and Lesser Bears, Arcturus in the Herdsman, Vega, Castor and Pollux and Auriga. His sense of smell was assaulted by a stench, vile and overpowering in spite of the cold and the obvious fact of lying under the open sky, on hard, bare, frozen ground. His sense of hearing registered desperate screams coming from somewhere nearby. And guffawing.

His neck was terribly sore, regardless of which he wriggled and struggled – he had worked out that he could not adjust his position because he was being immobilised by several bodies pressed hard against him, and that it was those bodies that were giving off the noisome odour. The bodies reacted to his movements by pressing even closer and tighter. One voice moaned, another groaned, a third called on God. A fourth cursed.

On his left – meaning towards Vega and the constellation

Lyra – flickering flashes of fire lit up the black of the night. The smell of smoke finally overcame the stench of human bodies. It was from the campfire that the desperate cries – which had now become groans and sobbing – were coming. He thrashed around again and with great effort freed a hand, forcibly pushing one of the bodies – clearly a woman's and by no means a skinny one – away from him. He swore and drew up a knee.

'Leave it, m'lord,' somebody just alongside whispered. 'Don't do anything, sir. Woe on us if they hear—'

'Where am I?'

'Quiet. If they hear they'll thrash us—'

'Who?'

'Them. The *martahuzes* . . . For God's sake, be quiet . . .'

Footsteps, the creaking of wood. The flare of a brand. A cackle. He turned his head and looked.

The face of the man holding the torch was thickly covered in pimples. He had almost no forehead. His stiff, black hair appeared to grow straight from his eyebrows and the bridge of his nose. Reynevan had seen him before.

There were three more. One was carrying a lantern and holding something in his other hand. Two of them were frogmarching a teenage boy. He was sobbing.

They pushed him down brutally onto the ground, bent over and shone the torch on the people lying down – now Reynevan saw that they were crowded inside an enclosure ringed by a sparse palisade. They selected somebody. A voice screamed in desperation, another howled, another appealed once again to God and the saints. A whip whistled and the disjointed screams were drowned by the sounds of blows. The boy dragged from the enclosure – who was even younger than the previous one – was weeping and begging for mercy. From beyond the palisade soon resounded his piercing cries. And the cackling of the *martahuzes*.

Reynevan swore and clenched his fists helplessly. *I'm in it*, he thought. *I really am.*

Memories began to return.

He had a premonition when the pimply-faced man with hair growing from his eyebrows rode out of the forest at the crossroads on a shaggy piebald. When he smiled, revealing blackened stumps of teeth. When another four men emerged after him from the trees, just as repugnant-looking and smiling.

Reynevan's premonition was confirmed when Pimple-Face gestured a greeting at Hejtman Vojta Jelínek, glanced at Reynevan and eyed him up appraisingly and repulsively. Hejtman Vojta Jelínek also looked at him with a scornful grimace, which said all too clearly: 'There's one born every minute.'

Reynevan pretended to be adjusting a stirrup and suddenly spurred his mount and dashed into the forest. They were expecting it. They barred his way with their horses, kicked him down from the saddle and held him on the ground. And then bound him. Jelínek, the scoundrel, watched, smiling, from the height of his saddle.

'It's someone of note,' he said to Pimple-Face. 'Somebody important, not just any pipsqueak. You'll give me six hundred groschen for him, Hurkovec.'

'Like hell,' retorted Pimple-Face. He had pimples everywhere, even on his eyelids, even on his lips, why, he even had pimples on his pimples. 'Important, indeed! Judging from his dress, he's some fucking minstrel. How much will I get for him? God only knows. I'll give you a hundred and twenty. Well? Too little? Go fuck yourself, Jelínek. Have his throat slit and toss him into the bushes—'

'Give me five hundred, at least! He's a high-ranking fellow, I tell you!'

'Two.'

'You make plenty of money thanks to me! I keep up a good supply of people for you. I've rounded up whole villages for you, you skinflint!'

'Three hundred.'

'Ha. It'll be my loss. Hey, why's he thrashing about? Choke him a little! Just gently!'

Reynevan tried to break free. Vainly. A strap was thrown around his neck. He was choked gently and kicked gently in the belly a few times. Then struck on the head. He lost consciousness. For a long time.

They heard the screams and sobs of the boy being raped beyond the palisade, by the campfire. The one that had been raped earlier was groaning and whimpering.

'What will they do to us?'

'Sell us,' whispered back his neighbour, the one who had earlier quietened and warned him. 'They'll sell us to our deaths. They're *martahuzes*, sire. Man traders.'

At dawn, Reynevan used all his strength to press himself against and cuddle up to the others crowded on the dirt floor in a moaning and trembling swarm. He had no inhibitions. What mattered was every little scrap of warmth. Even if it stank. In any case, he wasn't worth any more than the stinking rest.

For he was only worth three hundred Prague groschen. Or around ten Hungarian ducats. Or about as much as two cows, with a sheepskin and a gallon of beer thrown in.

At daybreak, there were shouts, curses, foul insults, kicks and blows of whips. The people crammed into the enclosure were driven out one by one through the gate in the palisade and then put into wooden yokes with holes for their heads and hands.

They were driven, blows of whips raining down on them, into a marching column.

Reynevan's yoke stank of vomit. No wonder. It bore the dried remains of it.

Pimple-Face, in the saddle of the shaggy piebald, whistled through his fingers. Whips cracked. The column set off. The captives were praying aloud. Whips cracked again.

The nightmare had its good side. Urged by blows to trot, he began to feel warmer.

Judging by the sun, they were heading east. The pace was easier than it had been at daybreak; they weren't being forced to trot, but not owing to mercy or compassion. Two people – an older man and a woman – had fallen and couldn't stand up, even though the man traders hadn't spared blows or kicks. The column was driven on, so Reynevan didn't see what happened to the pair, but he had his forebodings. He heard Pimple-Face angrily calling Hejtman Jelínek every name under the sun for supplying him with 'cadavers' and cursing his men for 'damaging the goods'. The result of the incident was that they were allowed to walk more slowly. And were flogged more seldom.

Reynevan was limping, had bruised a heel; he hadn't walked such a distance for a long time. To his right, a young man, his equal in years, panted under the weight of the yoke. In the night, being decidedly less numb than the others, he had introduced himself in snatched sentences as a carpenter from Jaroměř on his journeyman years, moving from village to village perfecting his craft. He'd been assailed on the way from Jičín to Žitava and captured. Through sobs, the journeyman begged Reynevan that if by some miracle he should escape to inform Alžběta, the daughter of master Růžička, a Jaroměř tailor. He declared that if he got away, he would inform anyone Reynevan wanted.

Reynevan didn't suggest anyone. He lacked trust. And didn't believe in miracles.

They walked along ravines, through forests following tracks between shady spruce, among groves of sycamore, ash and elm. They passed slender, autumnal roadside birches, as beautiful as queens attired in cloth of gold. A sight indeed to please the eye and fill the heart with joy. But there was no pleasure. And no joy.

The sun had already tracked a long way across the sky when men shouted and horses neighed at the head of the column. Reynevan's heart leaped in his breast at the sight of soldiers in kettle hats, pointed hoods and cherry tunics. Which made the sight of Pimple-Face shaking the hand of the corporal commanding the soldiers in an effusive greeting all the more unpleasant and painful.

The meeting of obvious comrades took place at a crossroads from which the now enlarged escort drove the column towards the south. The forest soon ended, the trees thinned out and the sandy track began to wind among fantastically shaped rocks. The sun, high in the sky, shone behind fluffy clouds gliding across the blue.

Suddenly, their destination came into view. Clearly visible. Leaving no doubt.

'Is that . . .' groaned Reynevan, trying to move the edge of the yoke away from his chafed neck. 'Is that . . . ?'

'Aye . . .' confirmed the journeyman carpenter. 'Aye, indeed it is . . .'

'Trosky . . .' groaned someone behind them. 'Trosky Castle . . . God, have mercy on us . . .'

A lone, bizarre, two-horned rock, like a devil's head, like the protruding ears of a crouching wolfhound, stuck up from a sparsely tree-covered hill. The rock – Reynevan didn't know and couldn't have known – was made of hardened magma, an exposed outpouring of volcanic basalt. The magnificent rock towering over the surrounding area had, not unsurprisingly, appealed to somebody as the obvious foundation for a stronghold. That person – as Reynevan knew, since he had acquired some information before the expedition – was the celebrated Čeněk of Vartenberk, the Burgrave of Prague during the reign of King Wenceslaus. The builders employed by Čeněk took advantage of the volcanic formation: they set the castle in the saddle between the basalt horns and built towers on the actual horns. The taller of the two, built on the eastern horn, slenderer and four-sided, bore the name of the Maiden. The western, lower, squat and five-sided one was called the Old Woman.

In 1424 – when the castle's lord was Otto of Bergow, the sworn enemy and cruel tormentor of adherents to the Chalice – the castle was besieged by furious Taborites. A lengthy assault by catapults and bombards achieved nothing, however, with the storm ending in failure and the Warriors of God having to withdraw. From then on, Trosky was considered unassailable. Thus, Lord Bergow felt invincible and went on tormenting the neighbouring Hussites with iron, fire and the noose.

'Get a move on there!' yelled Pimple-Face from the front. 'The castle is before us! Drive those swine uphill, it's about time they moved their legs!'

Whips whistled. Blows and curses rained down.

They were driven through a narrow gate into a walled outer bailey which narrowed towards the west, overshadowed by the walls of the upper castle. The yokes were removed. Reynevan felt the back of his neck with a numb hand to discover it had been rubbed raw. The journeyman carpenter began to say something to him but broke off with a cry when the thong of a whip struck his back.

'Line up, curs!' Pimple-Face roared. 'Stand in line! Keep your traps shut!'

Pushed and prodded, they lined up by the wall. There were thirty-three people with him – Reynevan was only now able to count exactly – including seven women, four old people and three striplings. Neither the old people nor the boys appeared fit for slave labour. He wondered why they'd been captured.

He had no more time to wonder further.

The way to the gate leading to the upper castle from the outer bailey was up a wooden, partially roofed staircase. A group of richly attired men was descending it, to be greeted by the captain of the guard and several vassals at the bottom.

'And what do we have here, Hurkovec?' asked a well-built man with a fair moustache leading them. There was no doubt who he was: his loose-fitting *haqueton* was decorated with the motif of a winged fish, the crest of the Bergow family. The man was the Lord of Trosky Castle, Otto of Bergow in person.

'What do we have here?' he repeated. 'A few peasants, beggars, women and children. I thought, Hurkovec, I'd made a few things clear to you. You were meant to supply me with Hussites, you good-for-nothing. Hussites, not peasants caught at random. Think I shall pay you for peasants? Most of whom are probably mine anyway?'

'As God is my judge.' Pimple-Face beat his breast and bowed low. 'May I not live to see tomorrow, Your Lordship! They are Hussites, most surely Hussites. Heretic scum, one and all, true sons of Huss.'

'They don't look it,' said another knight, young and handsome, wearing a bell-shaped cap over curled hair. Almost every hem of his clothing was finished with rounded serrations, as fashion demanded. 'They don't look it,' he repeated, approaching, covering his nose with a serrated sleeve, 'but let us ask for form's sake. I say, old woman! What are you? Do you venerate Huss as your god?'

'I am innocent! Good sir! I am a poor widow!'

'And you, peasant? Do you receive communion under both kinds?'

'I am not guilty! Mercy!'

'They lie, Your Lordship,' Pimple-Face assured him, bowing. 'They lie, the heretical swine, trying to save their skins. Wouldn't you, in their place?'

The handsome knight glanced at him with vicious contempt, looking as though he'd strike him for such a suggestion. But he confined himself to spitting.

And then turned to Bergow and an older knight in a quilted doublet standing alongside, with a dignified face and proudly pouting mouth. Reynevan was certain he'd seen him before somewhere. After a moment's thought, he realised he also knew the man in the bell-shaped cap.

'I don't know, I truly don't know, Sir Otto.' The dignified man turned to Lord Bergow, spreading his arms. 'We have orders from the patriciate of the Six Cities. Bautzen placed an order with me. Sir Hartung Klüx of Czocha, here present, represents the interests of Zgorzelec; Sir Lutpold of Köckeritz, who will soon be here, represents Löbau. But our orders are for Hussites. Not some chance and lamentable rabble.'

Otto of Bergow shrugged. 'What can I say, noble Sir Lothar of Gersdorf? Just one thing: this chance rabble will be begging for mercy in Czech before they burn at the stake in Bautzen or Zgorzelec. Like genuine Hussites. Indistinguishable.'

Lothar Gersdorf nodded in understanding and in agreement with the logic. And Reynevan now recalled where and when he'd seen him and the handsome, serrated Hartung Klüx in the bell-shaped cap. He'd seen both of them two years before. In Ziębice. At the tournament on the Feast of the Birth of the Virgin Mary.

Gersdorf, Klüx and several of the other knights stepped aside to confer. A handful of knights who had previously been silent also approached the prisoners. Two of them didn't bear coats of arms. The third, dressed most richly, had on his doublet a shield divided into six vertical silver and red bands, the universally known coat of arms of the Schaff family. Reynevan also remembered seeing Gocze Schaff, the Lord of Gryf Castle, at the Ziębice tournament. So, the man at Trosky must have been his brother Janko, the heir and Lord of Chojnik Castle.

A clanging and thudding of hooves resounded from the gate and guardhouse as a detachment of soldiers rode into the outer bailey. They were preceded by two heralds. One, dressed in white, was carrying a blue standard with three silver lilies. The yellow standard of the other herald bore a red stag's antler. Reynevan felt a lump in his throat. He knew that coat of arms. More acquaintances had arrived. The new arrivals reined in their horses and dismounted, carelessly tossing the reins to panting servants, then walked up to the lord of the castle and bowed with respect, but proudly. Apart from the pikemen and bowmen, only a young page wearing a large beret with three ostrich plumes remained in the saddle. Indifferent to being thought of as a rogue, a jester and a fool, the page led his horse through a sequence of dressage steps. Horseshoes rang on the cobbles.

'Lord Bergow. We cordially greet you!'

'Lord Biberstein, Lord Köckeritz. May I welcome you warmly.'

'If I may: Lord Köckeritz's and my knights and clients: Sir Mikuláš Dachs, Sir Henryk Zebant, Sir Wilrych Liebenthal,

Piotr Nimptsch, Jan Waldau and Reinhold Temritz. Are we in
time for the banquet?'

'Both for the banquet and for business.'

'So I see.' Ulrik of Biberstein, Lord of Frydland, cast his eyes
over the captives against the wall. 'Though it is a third-rate sight.
Unless it's what's left after the Six Cities creamed off whatever
decent goods there were. Greetings, Lord Gersdorf. Lord Klüx.
Lord Schaff. How goes it? Has the deal been struck?'

'Not yet.'

'So conclude it.' Biberstein rubbed his hands. 'And to the
banquet, to the banquet! By Saint Dionysius, I'm dying for a
drink!'

'That can easily be done.' Otto of Bergow nodded towards the
pages.

Reynevan remembered from the accounts of the Hussite
hejtmans that Mikuláš Dachs – who had arrived with the Lord
of Frydland and went back to him after inspecting the captives
– was a client of the Bibersteins. His expression was eloquent. A
shake of the head expressed the rest.

'It gets ever worse, I see,' said Biberstein, taking a large goblet
from a servant. 'The goods become poorer and poorer, Sir Otto,
the quality becomes more and more inferior. A sign of the times,
a *signum temporis*, as my chaplain would say. Oh well, we'll pay
what they're worth, so let's talk prices. In the year of our Lord
1419, one paid in Kutná Hora sixty groschen for a Hussite seized
and meant for torture and execution, and three hundred for a
heretical preacher—'

'But it was a buyer's market then,' Bergow interrupted him.
'In 1419 it wasn't difficult to catch a Hussite, for the Catholics
were winning. Now the Hussites are on top and the Catholics are losing, so a Hussite captive is a rarity, a veritable rarity.
And therefore dear. And the lords of the Landfried inflate

the prices themselves, creating precedents. Oldřich of Rožmberk pays nine thousand groschen ransom. After the Battle of Tachov, the Bavarians and Saxons bought back their own men even more dearly. For as much as twelve thousand groschen a head.'

'As I listen,' Lothar Gersdorf said as he approached and raised his head proudly, 'I truly wonder who has lost his mind: me or you. Lord Rožmberk and the Germans were paying for gentlemen, for noblemen, for knights. And what are you selling here? Motley beggars! Go on, catch and offer me Rohač of Dube, give me Ambrož, Královec, the Zmrzlíky brothers, Jan Černín, Kolúch or Čapek of Sány. I'll spend my silver on them. But I don't intend to waste my money on these beggars. What good are beggars to me?'

'These beggars,' Lord Bergow said without lowering his gaze, 'will scream and howl for mercy in the Czech language at the stake. That's what you want, isn't it?'

'Indeed,' said Biberstein, nodding coldly. 'In our towns and cities, people tremble with fear before Czechs, fall into panic. They remember what happened in May.'

'Agreed,' Lutpold Köckeritz confirmed gloomily. 'The people of Frydland, Žitava, Zgorzelec and Lwówek looked at the Hussites from the walls. But though the towns were defended and the attacks successfully repulsed, people still fall silent in horror whenever somebody mentions the dreadful fate of Ostritz, Bernstadt, Lubań and Złotoryja. One must show these people something to raise their spirits. The best thing being the sight of a Czech Hussite on the scaffold. Go on then, Otto, name your price. If it's sensible, I'll consider it ... I say! I say! Control that mare, Douce!'

The page, the boy in the beret with feathers showing off on a horse, had trotted over to the group so fast she almost rode right into the knights. No page, squire or cadet would have dared to make such a display, conscious of the consequences, which included a flogging. The page in question evidently wasn't afraid of the consequences. Probably because she wasn't a page.

Under the rakishly tilted beret, blue eyes the colour of a mountain lake, bold to the point of insolence and framed by what must have been half-inch eyelashes, peeped at the knights. The rapaciously retroussé nose clashed somewhat with the blonde locks, ruddy cheeks and cherubic lips, but the overall effect caused a strange sensation in the region that poets used to call euphemistically *circa pectora*.

The girl – who was fifteen at most – was wearing a white hem-stitched blouse and a waistcoat of scarlet satin. A man's jerkin with a sable collar in the most fashionable style completed the outfit, with her arms stuck through the side seams so that the sleeves hung freely to the back and waved behind delightfully in the gallop.

'If I may, noble gentlemen.' Lutpold Köckeritz presented her with a slight sneer. 'This knave juggling a horse is my niece, the gentle-born Miss Douce of Pack.'

The knights – all of them, including the older and more dignified – fell silent and goggled. Douce of Pack reined around her mount, an elegant dark bay mare.

'You promised, Uncle dear,' she said loudly. Her voice was not especially pleasant. Eliminating – although not for everyone – the charm and effect caused by the first impression.

'I made a promise and I shall keep it,' said Köckeritz, frowning. 'Be patient. It doesn't do to—'

'You promised, you promised! I want to now, this minute! I'm bored!'

'The Devil take it! Very well. I shall give you one. Choose. Sir Otto, I'll take one of them. Without haggling. I'll pay whatever price you name. We'll settle up afterwards. I promised the wench I'd give her one and you see for yourselves how fussy she is . . . So, no matter the cost . . .'

Lord Bergow tore his gaze from the girl's thigh and cleared his throat, finally understanding what it was all about.

'There is no cost,' he said, bowing. 'Let it be a gift from me. In honour of her beauty and grace. Please choose, m'lady.'

Douce of Pack returned the greeting from the saddle and smiled. With seductive charm. Then paraded before the dumbstruck knights, making the mare take small steps as she rode over to the captives.

'That one!'

She has taken a vow, thought Reynevan, watching the servants pull the apprentice from Jaromierz out of the row. *She has taken a vow of charity and promised to free somebody. The carpenter is lucky. It's a sheer miracle . . . And I could have asked him to inform Scharley. Pity . . .*

'Flee,' hissed the lass, leaning down from the saddle and pointing to the gate. 'Run!'

'No!' yelled Reynevan, understanding too late. 'Don't—'

He broke off as one of the *martahuzes* hit him with the back of his hand. And the journeyman carpenter set off at a run towards the courtyard. He ran fast. But didn't get far. Douce of Pack seized a javelin from one of the mounted lancers at full gallop, caught up with the apprentice almost at the gate and hurled the weapon in full flight, powerfully, from the shoulder. The javelin struck him in the middle of his back, between the shoulder blades, the tip emerging beneath his breastbone with a fountain of blood. The apprentice fell, legs kicking, curled up and stopped moving. The girl reined her horse around indifferently and paraded across the courtyard. The horseshoes rang rhythmically on the stone flags.

'Is that usual for her?' Ulrik Biberstein asked, curiously but coldly.

'Was she born like it?' Lothar Gersdorf asked, by no means more warmly. 'Or did she acquire it?'

'She ought to be sent into the forest after wild boar.' Janko Schaff cleared his throat. 'What she kills could at least be eaten ...'

'She lost interest in boar long ago,' said Köckeritz gloomily. 'Young people today ... But what to do, she's kin ...'

Douce of Pack trotted closer. Close enough for them to see the look in her eyes.

'I want one more, Uncle dear,' she said, shoving her crotch against the pommel. 'One more.'

Köckeritz looked even gloomier, but before he could say anything, Hartung Klüx forestalled him. The Lord of Czocha Castle was still staring at Douce as though bewitched. Now he stepped forward, removed his bell-shaped cap and bowed low.

'I would be honoured to give the noble lady what she requests,' he said, 'in homage to her beauty. Sir Otto?'

'Of course, of course.' Lord Bergow waved a dismissive hand. 'Please choose. You can pay me later.'

The women behind Reynevan began to sob. And he knew. Before he felt the horse's hot breath over him. Before he saw the eyes above him. Eyes the colour of a mountain lake. Beautiful. Enchanting. And absolutely inhuman.

'This one.'

'He doesn't come cheap,' said Pimple-Face, bent over in a bow. 'He's the dearest ... A singular Hussite, so the price is singular ...'

'I shall not bargain with you, boor.' Klüx clenched his jaw. 'You will not name the price. And for the maiden I shall pay any price. Seize him!'

The pikemen dragged Reynevan out, pushed him right in front of the dark bay mare's chest and its ornate peytral shot with gold thread.

'Run.'

'No.'

'Oh, he resists?' Douce of Pack leaned down from the saddle and fixed him with a piercing gaze. 'You won't run? Stay there then. Think it makes any difference to me? I'll ride up and run you through. But I'll wager you won't stand still; you'll be off like a shot. And then you'll pay for your pride. I'll stick you like a pig!'

'Two thousand four hundred groschen?' Lord Bergow suddenly roared. 'Two thousand four hundred? You've lost your fucking mind, Hurkovec! Lice must have sucked the sense out of your dull head! You're either bereft of your senses or you take me for a fool! If it's the first, I'll only have you flogged; if the second – you'll be hanged like a dog!'

'A single Hussite ...' Pimple-Face grunted. 'That's why the price ... But we can bargain—'

'I'll give two thousand four hundred for him without bargaining.' Janko Schaff unexpectedly joined in. 'But not as a gift. I bow before m'Lady Pack's beauty, but let her run someone else through. I want him in one piece.'

'Which suggests that you know who it is, Lord Schaff,' said Köckeritz, arms akimbo, 'and how much he's worth. But won't share the information, eh?'

'He doesn't have to,' said Lothar Gersdorf, 'for I also know who it is. I recognise him. He's a Silesian, Reinmar of Bielawa. Said to be a sorcerer. An alchemist. A heretic and a Hussite spy to boot. He made an attempt on Duke Johann's life in Ziębice when I was present. He was allegedly hired by the Hussites to commit that crime, but I'm inclined to believe it was the result of crazed jealousy and concerned a lady. The Devil only knows where the truth lies, but the fact is that Bielawa is wanted throughout Silesia. And there must be a bounty on his head since Sir Janko is ready to pay two thousand four hundred for him without even haggling. But nothing will come of it. The Hussite spy will make a pretty bauble on the scaffold in Bautzen town square, it will be a beautiful execution. Folk will flock from miles around to see it. I'll beat down your price, Schaff. Bautzen, gentlemen, gives three thousand!'

'What is a sorcerer, a Hussite spy and a hired killer doing in my castle?' asked Lord Bergow slowly and forcibly. 'At whose instigation is he here? Eh?'

'I've offered that Silesian of yours to m'Lady Douce as a gift,' said Hartung Klüx, as though he hadn't heard. 'And I'll pay—'

'I doubt you have coin enough,' interrupted Gersdorf.

'This concerns my honour and knightly virtue!' roared Klüx. 'I'm ready to lay down my life, never mind the three thousand groschen! I shall easily find the sum, if necessary!'

'But will you find six?' asked Ulrik of Biberstein, who hadn't spoken for some time. 'For I top that. I'll give six thousand groschen for him. And let no one bleat about honour, for this is a matter of honour. Don't ask me to explain. But if this is indeed Reinmar Bielawa, he must be mine. I'll give six thousand for him. Sir Otto of Bergow? What say you?'

Bergow looked at him for a long time. Then swept his gaze over them all.

'I say: nothing doing.' He raised his head. 'I annul the transaction and withdraw this Bielawa from sale.'

'But why?' Biberstein asked.

'Because,' said Otto of Bergow, with a steady gaze, 'it pleases me to do so.'

'Very well.' Biberstein hawked at length and spat. 'It's your castle, your will, your right. Except if that's your will, I've lost interest in being your guest. Let's thus finish the business and be gone.'

'Indeed.' Lothar Gersdorf nodded.

'Agreed,' said Janko Schaff, also nodding. 'I'm also somewhat in a hurry, so let's strike the deal and say our farewells.'

'In that case, so that you won't think badly of me,' declared Lord Bergow, clearly appeasing them, 'there'll be a rebate. A special price, as I'd give a brother. Like it was in Kutná Hora eight years ago. Sixty groschen a head. I'll throw the women and youngsters in for nothing.'

'And let's not beat each other down but divide them among us,' suggested Gersdorf. 'Bautzen, Zgorzelec, Löbau, Frydland and Jelenia Góra. First of all, we'll divide up the women and striplings evenly, two a head, and the rest—'

'The rest can't be divided evenly.' Köckeritz quickly reckoned up. 'It won't be fair.'

'It will, upon my soul,' said Bergow, beckoning his soldiers towards him. 'It will be bloody fair, no one will lose out. Hey, take them! Those three! Bind them!'

Before Pimple-Face's *martahuzes* could react, they were tied up. Only when they had been shoved over to join their recent captives did they begin to struggle, yell and rage, but blows from truncheons, whips and spear shafts quickly and brutally quelled them.

'Sire ...' whined Pimple-Face, whom no one had touched. 'What ... What ... Why, they're my men—'

'Perhaps you'd like to join them? Do you wish to?'

'No, not a bit of it.' Pimple-Face's mouth twisted into a broad and repulsive grimace. 'Not at all! Do they mean anything to me? I'll find new ones.'

'Indeed, one always can. So go. Ah, I almost forgot ...'

'Eeeh?'

Otto of Bergow smiled at him, then nodded towards Douce of Pack, who was holding a javelin across her saddle. Douce flashed her teeth and her blue-green eyes.

'You brought a spy and a murderer to my castle. Run to the gate. Fly! Swiftly!'

Pimple-Face blanched, turning as white as a fish's belly. He quickly recovered his senses, spun on his heel and dashed towards the gate like a whippet. He ran fast. Very fast. It looked like he might make it.

But he didn't.

Chapter Ten

In which it turns out that nothing sharpens mental processes like hunger and thirst. But when it becomes necessary to solve a mystery, pissing on human remains gives the best results. Especially on All Souls' Day.

'Reinmar of Bielawa from Silesia.' Otto of Bergow, Lord of Trosky Castle, eyed Reynevan from head to foot and back again. 'Sorcerer. Alchemist. Hussite spy. And on top of that a hired killer. A wide range of skills, if I may say so. Which skill did you bring to my castle? You do not answer? Never mind. I know anyway.'

Reynevan said nothing. He had a lump in his throat, couldn't swallow. The dungeon was dreadfully cold and stank horribly. The stench, it appeared, came from an opening in the floor covered by a heavy iron grating. Although the descent beneath the tower down a winding staircase had taken quite some time, the level they found themselves on wasn't the lowest. There was something even lower. The dungeons beneath the Maiden must have extended down to the very guts of the Earth.

Servants stuck their torches into iron cressets. The grating in the floor scraped as it was opened. They lowered a ladder into the musty-smelling, dark opening.

'Climb down.' Bergow confirmed Reynevan's hunch. 'Be quick.'

They didn't let him climb down to the very bottom. Instead they shook the ladder hard and Reynevan fell from a height, landing heavily on the compacted, rock-hard floor. The fall knocked the wind out of him.

'I once had here an arrogant mage, well read and smooth-tongued, who claimed that a dungeon like this one is called an *oubliette*,' shouted Lord Bergow from above, blocking off the scrap of light entering through the opening. 'I've never heard anyone apart from that wizard use the word. It's meant to derive from the word for "forget" in Gallic, ho-ho. I shall enlighten you as to why: the grating will soon be replaced and you will be forgotten. Quite forgotten also as far as bread and water are concerned. Which is why I prefer the local Czech name *hlado-morna* over the Gallic one. You will be starved to death, Lord of Bielawa. Unless you smarten up and reveal to me who hired you; on whose orders you were to kill me. I warn you, lies and deceit won't help. I already know who's behind the assassination attempt. You only have to supply the details. And the proof.'

Reynevan groaned and changed his position. He was bruised, but probably nothing was broken. He heard the grinding and scraping of the grating being closed.

'Ah, I almost forgot,' Bergow added from above. 'Magic, if you are indeed a sorcerer, won't help you. That cocksure mage I mentioned put special protection spells on the *hladomorna*. He claimed that not even Merlin himself could undo them. It turned out he wasn't lying, which he found out to his cost. He perished down there and will now keep you company. Thus, if Rupilius the Silesian couldn't escape from there, you have no chance, either. Farewell. And since soon you'll be drinking your own piss, let me wish you *prosit* in advance.'

The footsteps and clanking of metal faded. The echoes died away. And a deep, dull silence fell.

It took some time for Reynevan's eyes to adapt to the darkness. Enough to notice the grinning white skull of a skeleton chained to the wall in the corner of the dungeon.

The rumour was true. The sorcerer Rupilius really had resided at Trosky Castle. And still did. For ever and ever.

The fundamental problem of magical amulets, Telesma, the Prague sorcerer from the Archangel, had once explained to Reynevan, *is a matter of size. The matter of size is even more significant than that of price. Everyone knows that the more valuable the material a talisman is made from, the more powerful it is. But it was the Phoenicians who came up with the principle that good means dear. Buy cheap, buy dross – that axiom was also said to have been conceived among the merchants of Tyre and Sidon.*

The claim that the more substantial the mass of the amulet, the greater its power was a truism, and an extremely problematic one at that, for the very nature of magical periapts demanded that they be handy. A talisman was useful if it could be carried on one's person – in a pocket, inside a jacket, on a finger. So what if a dried and pressed stork allowed one to easily read a stranger's thoughts? said Telesma. *Or a mummified corpse's leg could reliably protect one against spells. Where is one to carry it? On a string around one's neck? It looks ridiculous.*

All one can do, the sorcerer finished his theorising with a practical conclusion, *is to reconcile oneself with the fact that amulets, talismans and suchlike are only suitable for weak magic, for lower-level sorcery. Having reconciled oneself thereto, one should do what one can – which means to miniaturise. If it can't be more powerful, let it at least be more convenient to carry around.*

So Telesma experimented thoroughly – with varying results. And when Reynevan left Prague, he received as a gift a small copper casket no larger than two human fists. The satin-lined compartments concealed no fewer than twenty small objects: miniaturised amulets with various uses.

Naturally, Reynevan guarded the box carefully and didn't expose it to any risk. Since the expedition to Trosky Castle was damned risky, the box had remained in Scharley's care. With certain exceptions. He took two amulets with him: a ring for healing wounds and a periapt for detecting magical activity. Aside from being useful, the two talismans also had the virtue of being inconspicuous. The healing ring, cast in tin, concealed a large diamond. The magic-detecting periapt was made of gold wire masked by entwined horsehair.

Its inconspicuousness hadn't protected the ring – everything had its value to Hurkovec's *martahuzes*, even tin. When stripped of his sheepskin coat, hat, pouch, belt and Venetian dagger, Reynevan had also lost the ring – he'd been fortunate not to lose the finger as well. However, the horsehair-covered magic-detecting periapt fastened around his arm above the elbow had escaped the attention of the men who searched him. And was now the only thing Reynevan could count on.

And Reynevan had to count on something – and fast. He realised that two days had passed since his last meal. He hadn't eaten for forty-eight hours. And hardly drunk anything.

'*Visum repertum, visum repertum, visum repertum.* Cabustira, bustira, tira, ra.'

When he repeated the spell, it achieved no more than he had the first time. The walls of the *oubliette* – or as Bergow preferred, the *hladomorna* – glowed like phosphorous, emitting light like rotting wood in the forest and confirming the depressing truth that the dungeon was indeed set about with a powerful protective spell. However, the skeleton chained to the wall, in whom Reynevan must have seen Rupilius the Silesian, the illustrious theoretician and practitioner of the sorcerer's arcana, wasn't shining or giving off the tiniest glow. Illustrious or not, Rupilius in the form of a merrily grinning skeleton, unlike the walls, wasn't emitting any magic, which was incontrovertible proof that the works of sorcerers endure longer than they themselves do.

Reynevan somewhat lost heart, since he had harboured a faint hope that the periapt would enable him to detect something that would prove useful in his situation. For, being a sorcerer, Rupilius could have smuggled some magical objects into the dungeon, for example in his rectum, as the mage Circulus had done when he was imprisoned in Narrenturm. But Rupilius the Silesian had brought nothing with him. And there he was, common sense suggested, sitting in the corner and grinning among his other decaying and crumbling bones. If he'd had other options, common sense went on, it wouldn't have ended like that.

After telling common sense to shut up, Reynevan put the amulet to his lips, then to his forehead.

'*Visum repertum, visum repertum, visum repertum . . .*'

His hands were trembling slightly and he had difficulty uttering the whispered spell. He was famished. And dreadfully thirsty. A strange, very unpleasant feeling began to grip him.

The feeling of desperation.

He didn't know how much time passed, how long he'd been imprisoned. He was quickly losing track and would fall asleep from time to time, now in a nervous and short-lived doze, now in a deep sleep, close to lethargy. His senses beguiled him, he heard voices, whining, moaning, the scraping of stone against stone, the clanking of metal against metal. Far away – he could have sworn – a girl was laughing. He could have sworn that somebody was singing in what sounded like German.

The forests are all a-greening
Why is my beloved far away?
He rode away on his horse
Oh, who will love me?

Typical symptoms, he thought. *Hunger and dehydration are beginning to take effect. I'm losing my mind. I'm going mad.*

And suddenly something occurred that confirmed to him that he was indeed mad.

The opposite wall of the dungeon moved.

The lines of mortar clearly bowed and rippled like patterned fabric blown by the wind. The wall suddenly billowed like a sail, swelled in a large and quickly growing bubble. The bubble burst stickily. And something emerged from it.

That something was invisible, evidently concealed beneath a spell. Dumbfounded, frozen and curled up in a ball in the corner, Reynevan observed the outline of a shape, a transparent shape, metamorphosing, bulging as it moved, like water. He guessed why he was able to see it at all: the remains of the spell emitted by the magic-detecting periapt still hung in the air.

The transparent shape moving smoothly towards Rupilius's skeleton hadn't noticed him. But Reynevan suddenly understood with blinding certainty that this might be his only chance.

'*Video videndum!*' he yelled with the amulet in his hand. 'Alef Tau!'

The shape materialised so suddenly that it shuddered, which made Reynevan's task much easier. He leaped at the newcomer like a lynx, grabbed him and flung him down onto the dirt floor, then punched him under the ribs with all his strength. It forced the air and a foul curse from the visitor and Reynevan seized him by the throat. Or tried to, for he was suddenly butted in the face. Although he saw stars, he returned the blow, cutting his forehead on the newcomer's teeth. The latter swore again on being struck and yelled something incomprehensible. The magic-detecting amulet reacted automatically and the dungeon filled with light. *Of course*, Reynevan managed to think, feeling a dreadful force lifting him up in the air. *There's no doubt he's a sorcerer. Somebody who knows magic*, he thought as he levitated. *I've taken on a mage*, he thought just before slamming into the wall with great force. He crumpled and curled up in a ball, unable to take any further action.

The arrival nudged him with the tip of his shoe. 'Are you injured?' he enquired softly.

Reynevan didn't answer.

'Who the Devil are you?'

Reynevan didn't answer that time, either, but curled up in an even tighter ball. The stranger bent over and picked the amulet up from the floor.

'A Visumrepertum periapt,' he said with some admiration in his voice. 'Quite well made. And you saw through my fe-fiada using the Spell of True Seeing ... Are you a Toledo?'

'*Alma* ...' grunted Reynevan, feeling his head and neck. *Mater ... Nostra. Clavis ... Salomonis?*

'Yes, yes, we'll get by without the declamation. Who made the Visumrepertum? You?'

'Teles— Jošt Dun. From Opatovice.'

'And from Heidelberg,' the stranger added carelessly. 'How is he?'

'They are all well.'

The visitor shifted his weight from foot to foot. He was a man of around forty, short, pot-bellied, very broad-shouldered and seemingly bowed over under the weight of his shoulders. The clothes he wore were the grey, simple and none-too-clean apparel of a servant. But Reynevan would have bet any money that the stranger was not a servant.

'Do you give your word,' the visitor asked again, feeling his nose, 'that you won't attack me again?'

'No.'

'Eh?'

'I have to get out of here.'

The man said nothing for a while.

'I understand,' he finally said, hoarsely. 'You're in an *oubliette* and I know its purpose. I shall supply you with vittles and beverages. But don't read too much into that.'

Reynevan devoured the bread, sausage and cheese almost without taking a breath and almost choked on the watery ale. Having appeased the first pangs of hunger, he ate more slowly, chewing more thoroughly. The man in the grey servant's costume watched him with interest. After Reynevan had eaten and drunk his fill, he also began to take interest in his visitor.

'Otto of Bergow,' said the man. 'The man who imprisoned you in here. Is he aware of your magical abilities?'

'Only sketchily.'

'How long have you been here?'

'What day is it today?'

'Samh—' the man stammered. 'I mean All Souls'. *Commemoratio animarum.*'

Reynevan drained the last drops of ale from the jug and stowed away a bread crust in his jacket.

'You can come clean,' he declared. 'When you went to get the food, I had a look at the objects you brought, the ones lying over there – mistletoe, birch bark, a sprig of yew, a candle, an iron ring, a black stone, typical attributes of a ceremony for the dead. And today, as you let slip, is the Feast of Samhain. You passed through this wall to pay your respects to those bones according to the ritual of the Older Tribes.'

'Correct.'

'So he was your kinsman. Or friend.'

'Incorrect. But let's attend to more important things. I'll advise you how to avoid death by starvation. You aren't the first. Plenty have been put in this *oubliette*, and you see yourself that there's only one skeleton, not counting those very ancient bones. Listen carefully. Are you?'

'I am.'

'The son of Otto of Bergow, Jan, is an Utraquist and hejtman in the Tábor. Otto somehow got the crazy idea that his Hussite son is plotting against him and wants to take his life and fortune. Although to me it's utter rot, it has acquired the characteristics of a persecution complex. He senses paid killers around every corner, smells poison at every meal. He sees his parricide son in every Hussite, which explains his hatred of the Calixtines. The matter is simple: you'll have to confess to being an assassin hired by Jan of Bergow who has come to Trosky to murderer Otto.'

Reynevan snorted. 'Delighted with my frank admission, Otto of Bergow will have me broken on the wheel. Assuming he believes me. It would suffice to ask me what his son looks like and the lie will be revealed.'

'You are a mage. Don't you know any persuasive or empathic spells?'

'No.'

'Well, bad luck.'

'Damn it!' Reynevan exploded. 'Stop deceiving me! I don't want to read too much into it, but you came in here through the sodding wall! So open it and let me leave!'

The visitor said nothing for a long time, not looking at Reynevan, but at the skeleton.

'Unfortunately, that outcome is not possible,' he finally replied.
'What?'

'I cannot do that ... Sit quietly or I'll cast the *Constricto* on
you. For you've already learned the hard way that your magic's
no match for mine.'

There was a note of conceit in the visitor's voice – and that
conceit helped Reynevan solve the mystery, played the role of
a catalyst which made the hazy solution become transparent.
Hunger may also have been sharpening his perception.

'Well, well,' he said slowly. 'Just to think, my reason for coming
to Trosky was to meet you. You and no other.'

'What are you saying?'

'I cannot compete with you in magic,' Reynevan drawled, 'for
you are a truly powerful sorcerer. And on top of that, a polyglot,
for no one else in the locality knows the word "*oubliette*". Were
I to escape through a magical passage, were I to vanish mysteriously, the alarm would be sounded: a sorcerer must be hidden at
Trosky. A sorcerer who is capable of overcoming the dungeon's
magical protection. For he himself installed it. I got into Trosky
in order to meet you, Master Rupilius. To ask for your advice.'

'I congratulate you on your imagination,' snapped the man.
'You ought to write romances ... What are you bloody doing?'

'I need to relieve myself.' Reynevan stood astride the skeleton.
'Why do you ask?'

'Get the fuck away from there!' yelled the visitor. 'Get away, do
you hear? Don't you dare desecr—'

He broke off, choking on the unuttered word. Reynevan
turned around, smiling triumphantly.

'As I thought,' he said. 'Not a kinsman, not a friend, but he
comes with a candle and mistletoe on All Souls' Day to visit
his *own* remains. And falls into a frenzy when somebody makes
to piss on them, because I'd be pissing on your very own bones,

wouldn't I? For it's your bones lying here, Master Rupilius the Silesian, O expert in bodies and astral beings. Your body may have died in this dungeon, but not your essence. You passed astrally into someone's else's physical form. Into the form of the person whose spirit you displaced into your own body. And whom hunger killed here, rather than you.'

'It doesn't bear thinking about,' said Rupilius the Silesian after a long pause. 'It doesn't bear thinking what bloody titans of intellect are wasting away in dungeons these days.'

Reynevan remained alone for a long time. Long enough to decide the rainy day had come and gnaw on the bread crust he had been saving for that day.

After vanishing into the wall, Rupilius the Silesian left him to a terrible loneliness, awful anxiety and the even more awful torture of hope. *He'll return*, lingered the hope wailing in his head. *He won't return, he'll leave me to my fate*, the logic in his skull came to life, *why should he return, what will he gain by helping me? He'll forget the man left in the* oubliette, *erase me from his memory* . . .

Light flashed above; the clanging metal reverberated. *They're getting me out of here*, thought Reynevan. *There's hope . . . Unless Bergow has become impatient.* Anxiety froze the hope. *And has decided to drag a testimony out of me by other means. They'll release me from here, but only to haul me off to the torture chamber* . . .

Something boomed thunderously, a clanging from above; the grating opened with a grinding sound, followed by a clattering and a scratching. Somebody blocked out the light and suddenly the shape of a ladder being lowered emerged from the darkness.

'Out you come, Reynevan,' sounded the voice of Rupilius the Silesian from high up. 'At the double, at the double!'

I didn't reveal my identity to him, he realised, scrambling up the smoothly worn rungs. *I didn't tell him my given name, much less my familiar nickname. He's either a telepath, a psychic or* . . . At the top, it turned out to be the 'or'. And Reynevan grunted as he was embraced in a powerful bear hug.

'Samson!'

'Aye, Samson,' Rupilius the Silesian, who was standing beside them, confirmed with a slight sneer. 'I envy you your comrades, lad. Could be worse, could be worse. And now be off, time to go.'

'But how—'

There's no time!' The sorcerer cut him off. 'Time to go! You've a long journey ahead of you.'

They climbed up some stairs, from where a metal-bound door led them to the torture chamber, full of spine-chilling instruments and tools. In a corner, barely visible, was a small door leading to a narrow corridor. They passed more doors and Rupilius only stopped at the fifth or sixth.

'*El Ab! Elevamini ianuae!*'

The door yielded to his gesture and biblical spell and they entered. The room was full of chests and cases. Rupilius placed a lantern on one and sat down on another.

'Let's get our breath back,' he ordered. 'And talk.'

The chest that Reynevan sat down alongside was full of books. He wiped off the dust. Averroes' *Culliyyat*. Ramon Llull's *Ars Magna*. Bernard of Clairvaux's *De gradibus humilitatis et superbiae*.

'These are my belongings,' said Rupilius, making a sweeping gesture towards the cases. 'Books and other things I need for my work. Some of them have a price. Most don't. Most of them are priceless, if you understand what I mean.

'You, Reynevan, are Toledo. What you are, Samson, I don't fully know, but you, too, undoubtedly guess the essence of the matter, which will save us time and trouble. Thus, without details – which, if you don't mind, are none of your bloody business

– I'll tell you: Otto of Bergow, for ten years my sponsor and benevolent master, suddenly stopped being benevolent and began
making demands that I couldn't fulfil. Or didn't want to. It was
thus planned for me to starve to death in the *oubliette*, having
fallen out of favour with my master. In the dungeon, I managed
to end the existence of my good old body, and of the soul of the
other person that I separated from its body, the one I currently
use. The transfer took place in some haste, and I also chose my
object in haste. The result is that I am only a servant at Trosky.
As such, I cannot remove my effects from here. Effects I am very
attached to. Very attached, do you understand? So the agreement is this: I'll help you escape from the castle. In return, you
must come back in two years and help me to move out. Agreed?
I'm waiting.'

'One thing first of all, Master Rupilius,' said Reynevan, stroking the metal binding of *The Enchiridion of Pope Leo*. 'I entered
Trosky in order to—'

'I know why you're here,' interrupted the sorcerer. 'Samson
and I have already chatted briefly about that. And we know a
little.'

'It's true,' said the giant, smiling at Reynevan's expression. 'We
know a little. Not everything. But there is some progress.'

'I'm not interested in "some progress",' said Reynevan, biting
his lip, 'but in finding a way to solve the problem once and for
all. You said it's high time you returned home, Samson. You
asked me to do what I could. And now, when a chance is within
reach—'

'Weren't you listening?' Rupilius didn't let him finish again. 'I
said that we have spoken, and that we know a little. But nothing
is yet within reach, regrettably. Not yet.'

'We already know a little,' replied Reynevan. 'Vincent Axleben
took an interest in Samson in Prague – and he's a master among

masters, after all. He claimed it concerned the astral body. And the *perispirit*. The *perispirit* . . . Hm . . . Positively circling.'

'A circulating perispirit.' Rupilius grimaced. 'Well, well. Indeed, one knows the master by his hypotheses. But did the master among masters ever explain what it's all about?'

Anyone who had any contact with magic and occult knowledge, even in passing, knew what the perisprit was. Every novice of the esoteric arts was regaled at the very start of his education with a long, convoluted disquisition, given in an extremely obscure way, about the construction of the human creature. Human beings, the disquisition explained, consist of the physical aspect – the material body – through which they interact with the external material world surrounding them. Human beings also have a spirit, built from immortal ether. There also exists something that connects and binds the spirit to the body, something that mediates between the spirit and the body, and that something is the fluid body, known as the perispirit, blah, blah, blah.

Although the matter appeared simple, it was difficult to find two mages who agreed regarding the perispirit. There were argu-ments about whether the perispirit was coarser or more ethereal, or, in accordance with the *Emerald Tablet*, grosser or subtler. There was no agreement as to whether the perispirit was permanent or changeable, nor what the perispirit did and didn't influence.

There was a theory that attributed quite an enormous role and capabilities to it. According to this theory, the perispirit – being by nature a bond between the material body and the ethereal spirit – determined both the strength and the quality of the bond. In other words, it gives the body more or less spirit. But not all perispirits are alike. Some are given a proverbial 'great soul', making artists of them. Others are given great analytic abilities, making them into scientists and inventors. Those granted the ability to control other souls become leaders and statesmen. It allows a select few to see what is unseeable, to gaze into the abyss of astral beings, making them great mages, spiritualists, prophets and psychics. But the perispirit is so stingy with the rest that even though they have a spirit, the only thing they can do is sit in a tavern drinking one beer after another.

Reynevan had known all that for a long time. As it's been said before, it was elementary knowledge. After the examination of Samson carried out in Prague, Axleben had, however, used the term 'positive perispirit' and 'circling perispirit'. This was advanced knowledge and the mages of the Archangel only explained it to Reynevan later. According to most theories, the bond between the perispirit and the spirit was unbreakable, but the bond with the body was not. The perispirit, it was claimed, can decide at any moment that the bond between the spirit and a given body didn't suit it and sever it. As a rule, it was claimed, the perispirit did that at the moment when the bond was being formed, in other words just after birth or in the first weeks of the infant's life, explaining the high infant mortality rate.

On severing the bond, the perispirit frees the spirit and passes with it into the ethereal – astral – sphere, and remains there for eternity, being similar to the spirit itself: hostile to the material world and negatively predisposed towards it. It can happen, it was claimed, that the perispirit is able to separate itself not only from the body but also from the spirit. That occurs when, unlike the spirit, the perispirit is predisposed positively to the world of matter. This kind of perispirit then circulates in a peculiar 'twilight zone' between the material and the astral worlds, looking for the chance to bond an unoccupied body to a temporarily un-assigned spirit. In his present spiritual-corporeal form, Samson was a typical example of that kind of bond.

The problem was that no one knew whether the perispirit

bonded at random, or whether it was guided during the bonding by some kind of logic. Who today is able to fathom out the logic of a perispirit of that kind? And until someone can, nothing will be achieved. What the perispirit has joined mortal man cannot rend asunder.

'It would seem,' Reynevan said with resignation in his voice, 'that we are at the point of departure. We needlessly dragged ourselves a great distance and needlessly put ourselves at risk—'

'Another specialist who is my equal in the matters of interest to you lives in Grenada.' The sorcerer interrupted once more. 'It's a little further away than Trosky. And the emirs there aren't too fond of Christians. They tend to impale them on stakes. Or flay them alive. Unlike Axleben, I don't promote myself as a master among masters, but I know my job. I also know how to formulate a hypothesis, which differs somewhat from the one the master among masters proposed, mainly regarding what is possible, what is not, what is achievable and what is not. One can achieve anything, as long as one knows how to carry it out—'

'Without meaning to cause offence,' Reynevan interrupted this time, 'I think we've heard enough hypotheses. What about Samson?'

Rupilius didn't even look at him as he replied, 'Samson knows my hypothesis, which differs somewhat from Axleben's. It's a radical and risky one, I admit, and I wouldn't be surprised if he didn't accept or attempt it. But if he does, he'll have to wait. I shall penetrate the essence of the matter and find a more reliable way of carrying out a repeat transmogrification, but I need up to two years. Why do you think I asked you to return after that period of time? Out of a predilection for even numbers? Which brings us back to our agreement. So I ask: are we in agreement?'

'We are.'

'By the end of two years?'

'Agreed.'

'Then let's go.'

Samson brightened up the wearying trek along the narrow corri-
dors and cramped stairways for Reynevan with a tale. Reynevan
had already worked out some of it, but he listened eagerly.

Samson had found out by sheer accident that Reynevan had
fallen into the hands of the Catholics at Trosky. The Hussites
had a spy at Tolštejn Castle which was occupied by the brothers
Jan and Jindřich Berk of Dubá. Sir Lothar Gersdorf had visited
the castle with seven prisoners in tow. While Lord Gersdorf was
dining with the brothers, the spy questioned the prisoners. One in
particular – allegedly a former *martahuz* – turned out to be particularly talkative and revealed something significant. As a result
of that information, Hejtman Vojta Jelínek was seized and thrown
into a dungeon, accused of treachery, espionage and criminal private interests. With the help of red-hot irons, Jelínek shed light on
many matters in the dungeon. Including Reynevan's case.

After learning that Reynevan was at Trosky, in the grip of
Lord Bergow, Jan Čapek and the Hussite hejtmans wrote him
off as missing and wouldn't hear of a rescue mission. So Scharley,
Samson, Tauler and Baťa took the matter into their own hands.
After all, Tauler still had in reserve his erstwhile comrade, the
head groom. It was thus decided that Samson, not Tauler, would
go to the castle. It was observed that peasants often visited
Trosky with supplies, not only on wagons, but also on foot. The
guards never interfered on condition that the provisioner fitted
the image of a peasant, meaning he was very shabby, smelled
strongly and had the face of a country bumpkin or idiot. Samson
Honeypot fitted. Perfectly. Equipped for the mission with a
goose, a barrel of butter and a trug of mushrooms, he entered the

lower castle, where, having lost himself in the crowd, he began to search for the head groom. Before Samson found him, he himself was found.

Rupilius the Silesian had quickly learned about the events of a few days before. About the visit of the Silesian and Lusatian lords and knights, about the sale of prisoners. And about some psychic or charmer who'd been put in the *hladomorna*. Certain that somebody would come looking for the prisoner, Rupilius kept watch on all visitors to the castle by magical means. The magic swiftly uncovered Samson.

'I was speechless,' Samson confessed, 'when he surprised me in the stable . . .'

'I was speechless,' Rupilius was equally frank, 'when he seized me by the throat. Fortunately, we quickly recognised each other . . .'

Neither of them was especially forthcoming regarding the details, and Reynevan didn't insist. He decided to question Samson later on the details of that rapid mutual recognition. Now he listened to the next stage – about how, having seen through each other, Rupilius and Samson Honeypot decided to free Reynevan from the *oubliette* and do it without magic in order not to arouse suspicion – namely by destroying the padlock to the grating with a blacksmith's hammer. Now, Samson finished in a whisper, they were nearing the secret passageway connecting Trosky Castle to the outside world.

Because such a passage *did* exist. And contrary to the legend, it wasn't legendary.

'Quickly, quickly,' Rupilius urged them. 'We must hurry. Something evil is circling above the castle, I can feel it.'

The spiral staircase was steep and the steps extremely uneven. They descended for a long time until their way was blocked by a rough, solid rock wall. There was no sign of a door or an entrance. For Rupilius, though, it didn't represent a problem.

'Yashiel, Vehiel, Baxasoxa! Effetha! *Ecce cecidit paries!*'

The rock wall, as the biblical text of the spell would suggest, didn't crumble, but parted and drew aside like a curtain. Beyond it was a black gulf emitting a foul odour.

'From here you proceed alone,' pronounced Rupilius the Silesian, handing Samson a lantern. 'An hour's march – not more – and you ought to emerge before dawn. The lantern is magical and will give you sufficient light, but I suggest you hurry. It's something of a labyrinth, but it's easy; whenever it branches, you turn right. You'll cope. Don't ferret around in side passages, don't stop for too long, try not to touch anything if there's no need. Be on your guard. I've already said: something evil is hanging above the castle. Farewell.'

'Where will we come out?'

'Oh.' The sorcerer slapped his forehead. 'I almost forgot. The exit is located to the north-east of the castle. Near the exit, there'll be a stream, and by following it downstream you'll reach a settlement called Ktová. It's almost right by the Žitava road . . . And where are your comrades waiting?'

'In the forests to the north of the castle. We'll find them.'

'Then Godspeed. Farewell, Samson. Farewell, countryman Reinmar. Don't forget about our agreement.'

'We shan't. Thanks for everything, master and countryman . . . If I may ask: what part of Silesia are you from?'

'Poznań. Go now. The lantern is magical, but not everlasting.'

The corridor they were walking along was without doubt of natural origin, hollowed out by water. Only the first section, under Trosky itself, bore the marks of human interference. The walls had, however, been worked so primitively and the remains of pickaxes and other tools lying around here and there were so corroded that it was apparent it had been excavated centuries before. Trosky Castle, the beginning of the construction of which dated back more or less to 1370, wasn't built on virgin rock. There was no doubt that the Old Woman and the Maiden had been erected on some ancient construction reaching deep into the earth.

The further they went, the fewer were the traces of mining activity, until they finally vanished altogether. The floor became uneven and they had to walk more slowly and carefully. Until, yet again, something crunched under Samson's foot and the giant bent over and brought the lantern closer. And gasped.

The traces of human activity had vanished. But not the traces of humans themselves. Or more precisely their remains. They were treading on scattered human bones.

For some time, Reynevan had been keeping the Visumrepertum periapt at the ready and now he activated it with a slightly trembling hand and a spell.

He wasn't mistaken – the subterranean cavern lit up with an intense blaze. The light of the lantern cast baleful shadows, flickering on the walls like great bats. Paintings covering the walls could now be discerned. Dizzying spiral meanders whirled around, horses and stags seemed to rear up and tangles of snakes coiled and uncoiled. Horned people danced.

'Celts,' said Samson. He was probably right.

'Let's not tarry here.'

Human skulls rattled under their footsteps and shinbones crunched.

Another high-ceilinged cavern opened up in front of them, so high that the roof faded into the darkness. The light of the lantern and the glow of the periapt illuminated another rock relief. They gasped in unison.

Under a burial mound built of skulls, a horrendous face, a
demonic mask, the horned visage of the Devil himself grinned
and goggled at them. The faded red pigment which had once
coloured the macabre idol shone through a layer of pale moss.
Human bones were lying around, piled up.

'It isn't the Celts.' Reynevan swallowed.

'No,' Samson agreed. He spoke with effort, as though greatly
fatigued. 'Let's not stay here. It's time we left. Some kind of evil
is hanging over this place. Over the entire area.'

They walked on, acutely mindful to turn right, always right,
and the forks multiplied as the corridor grew narrower.

Finally, it became so cramped they had to walk in single file.
Reynevan clearly heard the sound of running water somewhere
behind the rock wall.

It might have been the stream Rupilius had mentioned. They
had been walking underground, he calculated, for well over an
hour and must have been a considerable distance from Trosky
Castle, at least a quarter of a mile, perhaps even more.

'I believe I can feel a breeze on my face ...' he said, suddenly
stopping. 'Cover the lantern. Perhaps we'll see light?'

'We won't. It's still dark outside.'

The tunnel was becoming narrower and narrower. They
couldn't even walk in single file now but had to shuffle sideways,
step by step. Reynevan kept scraping his belly against the rock,
scratching the buttons of his jerkin. For someone much bulkier
like Samson Honeypot, the cramped conditions of the passage
must have been sheer hell. Reynevan could hear the giant moaning and cursing.

'Samson?'

'Go on, go on ... I'm behind you ...'

'Will you get through?'

'I will ... Somehow ... You go on ... Find the exit ... Let me know ... When you're close ...'

The cold current of air on Reynevan's face became so tangible he thought he could also smell the scent of a forest, fir needles and pine cones. He began pushing his way through more quickly, making more and more vigorous movements. Suddenly, the passage widened and he saw stars. He felt he was barely a step from the exit.

'It's the cave mouth!' he yelled. 'Samson! I made it! I got thr— Aaaagh!'

He lost his footing and tumbled downwards with a cry. Fortunately, he only fell a short distance onto stony scree. Pebbles worn smooth by water shot out from under him. He carried a landslide down the steep slope with him, tumbled off a precipice, banged against a boulder as he fell and finally landed on some moss with both hands in the foaming and icy water of a stream.

And realised at once that he wasn't alone.

He understood before he even heard the wheezing of a horse and the clatter of a horseshoe against stone. And a voice.

'Reinmar of Bielawa. Welcome. How glad I am to see you.'

He recognised the voice. The moon emerging into a gap between the clouds gave enough light for Reynevan to be able to see a black horse with a gleaming coat and the silhouette of a man holding the reins, his pale, birdlike face shining in the darkness and his shoulder-length hair. Reynevan had seen that man and heard that voice before. And Jan Smiřický of Smiřice had disclosed his name. It was Birkart Grellenort, the bishop's confidant and thug. The man who had killed Peterlin. Reynevan grew anxious.

'Does it surprise you?' asked the Wallcreeper, grinning. 'That I'm waiting here? I've known of this passage for years, you poor fool. I knew you'd try to escape this way. And I was informed that you were at Trosky. I have ears and eyes everywhere. And I have caught you, Bielawa. I've finally caught you—'

The scree rattled and Samson Honeypot came hurtling down the slope. Like a hurricane. An avenging angel. Suddenly, there was a flash of lightning and a crack of thunder – in November! The Wallcreeper's horse reared up, neighing frantically, and Grellenort jerked his sword out of its scabbard. And in front of Reynevan's eyes dropped it, taking several rapid steps backwards.

'Reayahyah!' he bellowed. 'Bartzabel! Ha-Shartatan!'

Lightning flashed again. Before he was temporarily blinded, Reynevan saw the Wallcreeper's face contort in panic-stricken fear, squint his eyes and wave his arms clumsily. And suddenly begin to shrink, melt, change shape, until finally he flew away in the form of a loudly croaking bird.

'*Adsuuumus!*' resounded from somewhere nearby, and other voices answered the call from nearer and further away. Neighing and the thudding of hooves reverberated.

'*Adsuuumuuuus! Adsuuumuuuuus!*'

'Take the horse,' panted Samson, pressing the reins of the black steed into his hands. 'Into the saddle and ride . . .'

'And you?'

'Don't worry about me. We have to split up. We'll find each other at dawn. Flee! Ride!'

Reynevan swung himself into the saddle, Samson slapped the horse's rump and the black horse neighed and galloped off between the firs. Although galloping through a dark forest could have been fatal, Reynevan, stupefied by recent events, knew how to adjust his riding to the conditions and cope with obstacles. Somewhere behind, and then to the side, he heard the tramping of hooves and wild cries. Reynevan pressed his cheek against the mane.

'*Adsuumuus! Adsumuus!*'

The moon went behind the clouds, plunging the world into impenetrable darkness. Only then did Reynevan begin to slow the steed down, without difficulty, as a matter of fact, for the gallop had exhausted the black horse and it was wheezing, covered in foam. Reynevan reined it in and listened. Cries were still drifting through the forest. And whistles. The black horse snorted.

At the sound of a piercing whistle close by, the horse tossed its head and whinnied. Reynevan caught it by the nostrils, but it didn't help. The black horse just jerked its head and neighed even louder. Understanding that the horse was reacting to a call, Reynevan instinctively dismounted and lashed the black horse's rump with an osier ripped from a bush. The horse leaped away with a squeal and Reynevan ran through the forest. In the opposite direction. As far away as he could. He ran blindly, without stopping, terror giving him strength and fleetness of foot.

His way was first barred by a rushing stream, then a hill and ravines among bizarrely shaped rocks. He waded through the thigh-high water of the stream without thinking and ran towards the ravines. And suddenly changed his plan. The ravines were too obvious an escape route, they might furthermore drive him into a trap, into a cul-de-sac with no way out. He began to scramble quickly up the steep slope, soon reaching a treeless summit where he sat down, trembling, squeezed between two rocks. A few short heartbeats later, the stream was churned up by snorting horses and about a dozen horsemen in black cloaks. Having crossed the stream, the pursuers rode deep into the ravine.

The sky to the east had begun to lighten a little. Reynevan was trembling, his teeth chattering. The wet clothes stiffened on him, freezing, and the cold nipped like a fierce dog.

It was utterly silent.

Chapter Eleven

In which Reynevan is – by turns – attacked, rescued, captured, fed and finally abducted, while owing to a certain priest, mandrake is sown on the southern foot of the Karkonosze Mountains.

The only thing moving in the area was a murder of crows circling over the trees. The only thing that could be heard was their plaintive cawing.

There wasn't a trace of the black riders and the wind had stopped carrying the cries of '*Adsumus*'. He appeared to have lost his pursuers. In spite of that, Reynevan didn't leave his hiding place on the hill for a long time. He wanted to be utterly and completely certain. Furthermore, the hill offered the opportunity to get his bearings in the forested, rocky wilderness.

The hill wasn't high enough, though, to command an extensive enough view from the top since it was obscured by other, higher hills. To be more precise, he couldn't see the Old Woman or the Maiden, the towers of Trosky Castle, the sight of which would have given him his bearings.

He calculated that he had walked for more than an hour underground from Trosky, which gave a distance of around a quarter of a mile. Then there was the gallop through the trees, followed by the lengthy escape on foot. Assuming he had galloped and run in a straight line, he had covered ten furlongs at most. So he couldn't have been far from where he left the underground tunnel, where Grellenort had surprised him. Where Samson . . .

Grellenort, he thought, *had been frightened by Samson. Birkart Grellenort, Peterlin's killer. The sorcerer capable of changing into a bird, the* timor nocturnus, *the destruction that wasteth at noon, the bishop's thug, the thug whom Jan Smiřický claimed in Prague that the bishop himself feared. And a character like that is panic-stricken at the sight of Samson Honeypot, the giant with an idiot's face.*

So it is indeed true. Samson Honeypot is not of this world. Huon of Sagar recognised him right away, as did the mages from the Archangel, Axleben and Rupilius. Only I continue to treat Samson as a good and jovial companion, as a comrade. I have scales over my eyes that won't let me see it.

He sighed, but also felt relief at the same time. Previously, he had been pricked by his conscience for listening to Samson and fleeing, leaving his comrade in need. Now he understood that Samson had coped wonderfully without his help. *He probably escaped from the Black Riders easily*, he thought, *and joined Scharley and the rest of the company long ago. They must be searching for me now.*

Despite that, I have to get moving, he thought. *My clothing didn't dry at all in the night, and it's fast clouding over and growing cold. If I stay here, I'll fall asleep and freeze to death. Walking will warm me up. If I don't encounter Samson and Scharley, I'm sure to come upon someone else, I'll bump into a good soul and ask around. I'll chance upon a track or road; I'll emerge onto the highway. Trosky Castle lies near the busy road leading from Prague to Žitava via Jičín and Turnov, while to the south of Trosky there's another highway, a back road leading to Žitava via Mimoň and Jablonné. I know the other road, I rode from Michalovice that way; it was there that Jelínek sold me to Hurkovec's* martahuzes. *Jelínek . . . Wait till I get my hands on you, you bastard . . .*

Rupilius said that the way out of the underground passage led north-east from the castle, in the vicinity of the village of Ktová or something. We were meant to follow a stream after leaving the cavern. There is a stream. But is it the right one? The stream, whose icy waters almost caused my death by hypothermia during the night, flowed in broad meanders and vanished into a winding ravine. God only knows where it ends up. Despite that, it must be the only sensible route. The stream has to join a river somewhere. Even if I'm totally lost, sticking to the bank means I won't be walking around in circles. There are villages beside streams, and charcoal burners, tar makers and woodcutters build their settlements next to streams.

He was already walking by the time he got to the final reflections about the stream's virtues.

Reynevan was walking very fast, as fast as the rough terrain permitted. He was exhausted and panting but had warmed up enough for his wet clothing to be literally steaming on him; it was drying fast and not so unpleasantly cold any more. Although he had covered quite a considerable distance, he didn't find any tracks by the stream, not counting paths trodden by deer and depressions in the mud made by wild boar.

As he had predicted, it became overcast and a light snow even began to fall.

The forest thinned out abruptly and Reynevan saw the outlines of wooden buildings looming beyond the last maples. Heart beating, he speeded up and almost ran into the clearing.

The buildings turned out to be huts covered in tree bark, most of them tumbledown. There was no point even looking inside. All traces of humanity were covered by grass and weeds. Great stretches of blackened wood shavings and sawdust lay around, no longer even smelling of resin. A long-forgotten axe driven into a tree stump was red with rust. The woodcutters – for the huts had undoubtedly belonged to them – must have abandoned the glade many years before.

'Anybody here?' Reynevan preferred to be certain. 'I say! I saaaay!'

Something rustled behind him. He quickly spun around, but in spite of his speed he only managed to catch a fleeting glimpse of a shape vanishing around the corner of a hut. The shape was small. The size of a child.

'I say!' he said, running after it. 'Stop! Wait! Fear not!'

The small creature wasn't a child. Children aren't shaggy and don't have dogs' heads. Nor arms reaching to the ground. Nor do they run away in strange leaps and bounds, swaying on short, crooked legs, croaking loudly as they do so. Reynevan set off in pursuit. Towards a gap in the wall of trees. And a road. When he came out onto the road, the shaggy creature stopped. Looked back. Stared goggle-eyed. And bared its doglike teeth.

'Fear not . . .' Reynevan panted. 'I won't—'

The creature – a forest kobold, a *waldschrat* – interrupted him with a loud and strangely scornful-sounding croaking. It was answered by a chorus of similar squawks. Coming from all directions. Before Reynevan realised what he was mixed up in, about twenty of them attacked.

He kicked one, felled another with a punch and then found himself on the ground. The kobolds swarmed over him like lice. Reynevan yelled, kicked out, punched blindly, even bit, ineffectively. Each time he threw one off, two more took its place. The situation was beginning to become perilous. Suddenly, one of the kobolds dug its claws into his hair and ears and another landed on his face, stopping up his nose and mouth with its hairy behind. He began to suffocate and panic seized him. He felt teeth clamping onto his thighs and calves. He kicked out clumsily, but the kobolds clung on tightly to his legs. Reynevan jerked his head out from under the hairy backside smothering him and howled. Desperately and inhumanly.

And just like in a fairy tale – help was at hand. The track suddenly resounded with shouts, neighing and the thudding of iron-shod hooves. Something swept the kobold from his face and the weight on his legs also vanished. Reynevan saw above him a horse's belly and an iron sabaton in a stirrup, caught sight of the flash of a sword and watched blood gush from the severed doglike head. Right beside him, another *waldschrat* was thrashing about and squirming, pinned to the ground by a bear spear. Hooves were thudding all around him, spraying wet sand. He heard cursing, laughing, guffawing. As though there was a reason for merriment.

'Get up,' he heard from above. 'We've driven the devils away.'

He got to his feet. He was surrounded by armoured men on horseback. Among them was the knight who had told him to stand up, wiping the blood from his sword blade. Reynevan saw a moustachioed face shaded by a raised hounskull helmet. It was strangely familiar.

'In one piece? They didn't bite anything important off?'

The armoured men guffawed when he involuntarily ran his hands over his now ragged trousers. The knight removed his helmet. Reynevan recognised him right away.

'So it was worth it,' said Janko Schaff, Lord of Chojnik Castle, resting a fist on the pommel of his saddle. 'It was worth hanging around here for a few days. I felt you'd abscond from Trosky, Reynevan of Bielawa.'

They made a stop close by the track, under a grove of large oaks. Several of the soldiers had set off on a pretty hopeless pursuit of the kobolds. The rest spent some time looking in amazement at the corpses and talking. Finally, the remains of four of the dead *waldschrats* were hanging by their legs from branches, and the esquires and servants had begun to skin them as trophies and proof of the victory. Reynevan watched gloomily. He wasn't sure if they wouldn't start skinning him, too. Jan Schaff's apparently benign but at the same time mischievously cunning expression didn't bode well. Reynevan didn't let the feigned cordiality delude him.

'Lucky for you that you were yelling and we heard you,' said the Lord of Chojnik, 'otherwise you'd have been in deep trouble. We know those shaggy beasts, there are plenty of them in the wilds of the Karkonosze. In winter, hunger drives them nearer to human homesteads. They attack in packs and eat people alive, stripping the flesh to the bone. Some say the local highlander women give birth to them after mating with dogs, yuck, foul idea. Others that they are *simiae*, foreign beasts once bred by the Knights Templar. Yet others think they are devils that have emerged from hellholes. Right, Zwicker?'

'What is evil comes from the Devil,' responded the priest walking alongside and casting Reynevan an extremely venomous glance from under his hood, 'and every sin demands punishment.'

'Idiot,' commented Schaff in hushed tones. 'I say, m'Lord Bielawa! The danger has passed yet you're still downcast. Fed, in fresh raiment, yet you're still out of sorts. Why's that?'

'You planned to buy me at Trosky.' Reynevan decided to make things clear. 'You meant to spend two thousand four hundred Prague groschen, no doubt in order to sell me on at a profit. Whom, I wonder, had you chosen as a buyer, m'lord? The Inquisition? The Bishop of Wrocław?'

'Damn the bishop.' Schaff spat. 'The Inquisition, too. I wanted to buy you out of the goodness of my heart. Out of affection.'

'Affection for what? We don't even know one another.'

'We know each other better than you think. Your brother Piotr, may the Lord keep him, was a decent man. He never refused anyone in need of help. Or a loan. When we, the Schaffs, were in need, who helped us? Piotr of Bielawa!'

'Aha.'

'And who now has it in for Reinmar, Piotr's brother? Who seeks his downfall? The bishop? Damn him, I said! The Sterczas? The Sterczas are common brigands. Jan, the Duke of Ziębice, irked that Reinmar bedded his lover because she preferred a younger and a more red-blooded one? And finally, Jan Biberstein of Stolz. Said to be a most gentle lord, but what does he do? Sets a bounty for the capture of a nobleman as though for a fugitive servant. And for what? For seducing his daughter? Jesus Christ! Why, that's what maidens are for, the Good Lord created them to be seduced, and in order for them to yield to seduction he gave them a whorish nature. Am I right?' Without waiting for agreement, Schaff continued, 'After you were recognised at Trosky, I thought to myself, "I'll rescue that lad, I won't give him to the Six Cities, I won't let the executioners torture Piotr of Bielawa's brother on the scaffold for the mob's pleasure. I'll buy the poor wretch," I thought to myself . . .'

'Many thanks. I'm in your debt, m'lord—'

'Two thousand four hundred groschen.' Janko Schaff appeared not to have heard. 'Not such a great sum, I thought. The late Sir Piotr loaned us much more in days gone by. And m'Lord Reinmar, plucked from the clutches of the Lusatian murderers, I thought to myself, will be able to return the favour. For Master Reinmar has five hundred grzywna which he robbed from the tax collector two years ago. He'll be able to repay it. And share it out.'

'Oh, Lord Schaff.' Reynevan sighed, apparently nonchalantly.

'Do you believe rumours? You've just said that those men have designs on me, that they're using underhand methods. That they don't shrink from slander and calumny, that they spread vile rumours about me in order to denigrate me. For it's a calumny and an untruth that I robbed the tax collector. A calumny and an untruth, do you understand? I'm grateful for the rescue, I shan't forget you, m'lord. But now, if you don't mind, I must bid you farewell. I have to find my companions, who—'

'Not so fast.' Schaff glanced at his men and gave a signal. They moved in at once. 'Not so fast, Lord Bielawa. You wish to bid me farewell? So swiftly? Where's your gratitude? I didn't buy you out at Trosky, agreed, though good intentions count. But I did save you from the wild monsters, you can't deny that. If not for me, you'd be dead. So when we divide up the tax collector's grzywnas, you take three hundred and I'll take the rest. That'll be fair.'

'I didn't rob the tax collector and don't have that money!'

'We'll talk more at Chojnik Castle about whether you have it, how much you have and where it is.' Schaff squinted slightly. 'Whence we shall soon set off. If you give me your knightly parole that you won't try to escape, I won't order you bound. In any case, where could you escape to? The forests are teeming with those hell hounds. Bergow is certainly on your trail. Ulrik Biberstein – who can't wait to get his hands on you – is also sniffing around near Trosky. No harm will come to you while you're with me. I'll even leave you some of the tax collector's money, I'll only take . . . Four hundred grzywna. For which reason—'

Before the heir to Chojnik could finish, the Visumrepertum periapt quivered on Reynevan's arm. Spontaneously.

The magic that triggered the amulet was so powerful, Reynevan didn't have the slightest difficulty in determining the direction from which it was emanating. Taking both Schaff and

his men by surprise, he ran across the track through some juni-
per bushes, cleared a hollow and without a second thought fell
on a man in a hood crouching behind a fallen tree. Reynevan
knocked a box resembling a small reliquary out of his hands
with a sweeping punch, kicked it, punched him in the nape and
again in the ear. The hood fell and a tonsure shone. Reynevan
would have punched the priest again, but Schaff's men caught
him and seized him in an iron grip.

'What the Devil are you playing at?' yelled Schaff. 'Are you
insane? Or demented?'

'Look what he had,' yelled Reynevan even louder. 'Ask him
what he was doing!'

'What are you talking about? That's Father Zwicker, my
chaplain!'

'He's a traitor! That casket is a magical communicator! He was
sending a signal, trying to contact somebody and summon them
here using magic! And I know who!'

Schaff bent down to the box lying on the ground, but stepped
back suddenly on hearing a buzzing sound. Without thinking
twice, he crushed the box with a mighty blow of his boot, grinding it into the sand with his heel. The chaplain uttered a stifled
cry at the sight.

'Would you like to explain this to me, Zwicker,' said Schaff,
approaching him. 'Eh?'

'I can explain,' Reynevan shouted, still being held by the
soldiers. 'The damned priest has betrayed me! He has brought
tormentors down on me – it was owing to him that they almost
caught me yesterday! Ask him about the sorcerer Birkart
Grellenort! Ask him how long he has served Grellenort, how
long he has informed for him! How long he has been betraying
you, too!'

'Birkart Grellenort,' Janko Schaff repeated ominously, seizing the chaplain by the collar of his vestments. 'The bishop's confidant. Is that so? Is it? You're his spy? You use magic to report to the bishop? Telling him everything I say, do and think? Are you betraying me?'

The chaplain pursed his lips and turned his head away.

'Answer the accusation, wretched priest. Defend yourself. Swear you are innocent. That you are my obedient servant. That you pay with loyalty for the bread you eat thanks to my grace, and for the money I graciously permit you to steal!'

The priest still said nothing. Schaff pulled the priest towards him. And then shoved him away, casting him down onto the ground.

'Bind the scum,' he ordered. 'The executioner will have words with him.'

'Apostate!' bellowed Zwicker from the ground. 'Heathen! You are not my master; I do not serve you! I serve God and those who act on God's orders! They will catch up with you, you hell spawn, and my martyrdom will be avenged! You shall know my masters' wrath; you'll howl like a whipped cur when they come on their black horses! And you, Bielawa, unchaste scoundrel, you'll find no refuge on this Earth! There is already a place for you in Hell! But here, on Earth, you will taste agony! You will be flayed—'

One of the soldiers quietened him with a powerful kick. The chaplain curled up, wheezing.

'To horse,' Janko Schaff commanded without looking at him. 'On we go!'

Schaff's party numbered nine horsemen – two burgmen, two esquires, three bowmen and two armed servants. There must have been more with him at Trosky – the seven slaves that Schaff received in the division weren't with them. An escort had probably driven them towards the Silesian border. Now the only captives were the chaplain and Reynevan. Unlike the priest, Reynevan's arms hadn't been bound nor his legs tied under the horse's belly. He had been coerced into giving his parole that he wouldn't try to escape, sealed by a vow on his honour and the cross. He naturally planned to escape at the first opportunity, but Scharley would have been proud of him – neither his face twitched nor his voice trembled when perjuring himself. He almost believed the oath himself. Schaff, however, wasn't so gullible; he had certainly dealt with oaths before, and with people of Scharley's ilk. Reynevan wasn't tied up, but his horse was led by the bridle and a bowman riding behind kept a keen eye on him. And a loaded crossbow trained on him.

They rode quite quickly, without dallying, heading towards the north and the mountains. The route led through a barren and remote area, indicating that Schaff was deliberately avoiding main roads. Reynevan didn't know the Podkrkonoší at all and was quite lost. He did know the destination, though: Chojnik Castle near Jelenia Góra. It was on the Silesian side of the Karkonosze, so it could be presumed that the detachment would head for a pass. Reynevan's knowledge of the area was too poor to know which one.

Although he didn't really know the Karkonosze or the surrounding region, he had heard various tales about Chojnik Castle, and he knew enough about the place to be anxious. The ancient stronghold, already shrouded in numerous legends, stood at the top of a steep, high mountain, rising over a bottomless abyss reputedly strewn with human bones, and known – in order to avoid unfortunate misunderstandings – as 'Hell's Valley'. The modern stone castle, built by the Świdnica-Jawor Piasts, had been captured around fifty years earlier and added to his already very wealthy estates by Gocze Schaff, Burgrave of Jelenia Góra. The castle was inherited by his elder son Janko. His other son,

Gocze junior, was the lord of nearby Gryf Castle. The brothers ruled the entire surroundings with iron fists, including part of the important trade route running along the bank of the River Bóbr.

While the genealogy and wealth of the Schaff family didn't interest Reynevan greatly, the same couldn't be said for Chojnik Castle. Most of the horrible stories about the stronghold were most likely apocryphal, but the fact remained: Chojnik was a difficult castle to enter and even more difficult to leave. An escape, were it to succeed, would have to be attempted before they entered the castle.

There was one more important reason for doing so.

The frozen ground on the track and the moss on the roadside clearing were churned and torn up by many hooves. Schaff's soldiers created a circle and looked around with their hands on their sword hilts. The bowmen loaded their crossbows, observing the road and the edge of the forest attentively.

'There was a brawl here,' said Gwido Buschbach, a short, stocky and not so young esquire and the detachment's guide and tracker. 'Around thirty horse. They fought, then went their separate ways. Yesterday, judging from the horse shit.'

'Who fought whom?' asked Schaff. 'Are there any clues?'

'Naught but this.' Buschbach shrugged. 'It was hanging on a snag. Don't tell us much.'

'On the contrary,' said Reynevan, paling slightly as he looked at the shred of black fabric. 'It does. I know who wears cloaks like that.'

'What are you waiting for?' snapped Schaff. 'Speak!'

'You won't be inclined to believe it.'

'I'll be the judge of that.'

*

Janko Schaff listened, attentively and with a knitted brow, to the story of the Wallcreeper and the black horsemen. Although Reynevan suitably shortened and edited his account, the Lord of Chojnik had no problem with it. Reynevan saw a flash in his eye several times which might have signified that the knight had already heard this and that about black horsemen, murdered merchants, terrors by night, demons destroying at noon and other peculiarities mentioned in Psalm Ninety-One.

'The Company of Death,' he muttered. 'Riders on black horses. The same ones the infernal priest was threatening me with. They fell on somebody here. I wonder who.'

'Lord Bergow has apparently sent out a party,' Reynevan casually reminded him. 'Lord Biberstein, too—'

'I know.' Schaff cut him off. 'You are being hunted, and Grellenort and his black horsemen are hunting the hunters to take the spoils from them. You're their target. They want you.'

'Undoubtedly. Which is why—'

'I should set you free?' The Lord of Chojnik smiled evilly. 'Out of concern for my safety? Nice try, Bielawa, nice try. You'll have to do better than that.'

'Well, at least be on your guard—'

'Don't instruct me.'

The entire affair had fatal consequences for Father Zwicker. Brought before Schaff and bombarded with questions, the priest gritted his teeth and didn't utter a word, not even when his face was slapped a few times.

'Bielawa!' Schaff gestured him over. 'You've shown me you know some magic. So tell me: is it possible that this damned priest, although in fetters, might have saddled us with that Grellenort using witchcraft?'

Reynevan spread his arms and shrugged. Which was sufficient for Schaff. A rope was tossed over a horizontal bough and before he could say the Lord's Prayer, Chaplain Zwicker was hanging from a noose, convulsively tensing and relaxing his legs, observed by the bored looks of the entire company.

'We'll have to come by here again,' said Gwido Buschbach. 'The damned priest released his seed here, look. Mandrake will sprout here for certain.'

Schaff indeed needed no instruction on how to behave in perilous situations. They continued to ride along forest tracks, carefully avoiding the more travelled ones. They were moving slowly, with two foreriders posted ahead: Gwido Buschbach and a bowman. The Lord of Chojnik grimly ordered the rest to be quiet, alert and attentive. The detachment began to look so combative that the fear of the Wallcreeper almost left Reynevan, and he no longer cowered in the saddle whenever a bird flew over the track or squawked nearby.

It cut both ways, unfortunately. In the face of such vigilance, it was difficult even to think about escaping. In spite of that, it was constantly on Reynevan's mind.

They stopped for the first night in an abandoned colliers' settlement, where ore was extracted and smelted in the summer. For the second stop, soon after fording a river which Gwido Buschbach called the Mumlava, he chose for them a small, godforsaken mountain village, remote and hidden in a deep ravine, called Mumlavský Důl. Reynevan had heard and noted the settlement's name from Schaff's conversation with the headman, who had a shock of shaggy, grey hair, like a wolverine. He was clearly scared, in such a panic that Schaff took pity on him. Rather than yelling and punching him in the usual knightly manner, he decided to play the role of the benevolent and generous lord. Having been given a small handful of pennies, the

Wolverine cheered up and an almost frightening smile split his unshaven face in half. He immediately invited the knight to his farmyard, stammering out an explanation on the way as to why he was so anxious and the whole village terrified. Some *hrozne*, very *hrozne* gentlemen had passed by that way several times, he explained, very mounted and very well armed and God-'elp-us and mercy-me. It took some time to determine when those awful cavalcades occurred, but finally it was established that it was two nights ago and the early morning after that. But describing what the horsemen looked like and what they were wearing apparently went well beyond the peasant's abilities.

Schaff's face clouded over and he bit his moustache, but his mood suddenly improved. And not only his. For from the Wolverine's farmyard wafted something extraordinarily pleasant, something divine and blissfully inviting, something tenderly and lovingly home-made, something wistfully and touchingly motherly. A marvellous, familiar aroma, deeply etched in the subconscious, called forth everything that was pleasant, good and joyous, making one want to sit down and weep with contentment. To restate it more concisely: the fragrance of onions and meat fried in melted lard drifted from the cottage. Tears began flowing from the eyes of Schaff, his brawlers and Reynevan, and saliva dripped from their mouths with the force of a mountain waterfall.

'We butchered a hog,' explained Wolverine. 'It being the season, see, m'lord—'

The Lord of Chojnik didn't let him finish. And reached into his pouch. At the sight of the pennies in his fist, the fellow staggered, opened his mouth and for a moment appeared about to howl. But he quickly calmed down.

'Come in ...' he panted, stowing the money into his jacket. 'For a little something ...'

*

'The men who are said to have ridden through,' said Janko Schaff, shooing a hen from the table, 'might have been the Black Riders, the Company of Death. But it might also have been Biberstein's men. Or Bergow's from Trosky . . . The Devil take them! I hadn't counted on them being so determined to get their hands on you, Bielawa.'

Werner Dorfinger, one of the Chojnik vassals, cast Reynevan a grim look. 'If, God save us, they come for us . . . Are we going to fight over him or what?'

'What will be, will be,' Schaff interjected. 'And what will be is what I decide. Clear?'

They devoured such quantities of the meat scraps fried in lard that they could barely move and felt they had no room for anything else. That state endured until the housewife began to spoon boiled *jitrnice* liver sausage and blood pudding stuffed with barley groats out of a cauldron. Barely had it cooled a little than they fell on it like wolves.

'Christ the Lord . . .' Dorfinger loosened his belt by another two holes. 'It's a long time since I tasted such *jitrnice* . . . Ha, I'll have some more, but I must just go behind the barn.'

'Take your sheepskin,' advised Ralf Moser, the other vassal from Chojnik, as he emerged from the vestibule, shaking snow from his hat and collar. 'It's snowing out. And the wind's howling like a damned soul.'

'Well, it's true.' Schaff grinned. 'Zwicker was hanged, after all. And the wind doesn't know, either, that it wasn't of his free will.'

'Damned priest . . .' Moser choked on the steam and smoke and coughed. 'Damned priest can still do us some mischief beyond the grave . . .'

'Help us, I'd say,' said Gwido Buschbach, disagreeing, giving an intrusive goat trying to nibble his boot a kick. 'For if somebody has it in for us, they'll easily guess which way we're headed. They might waylay us on a mountain pasture below Szrenica. They might be waiting for us at Borówczane rocks. They might plan to catch us near the upper reaches of the Szklarka, before we ride down into the Wrzosówka valley … But in a raging blizzard, God willing, we might slip through somehow … Pass me the blood pudding …'

'I'll have some, too,' Schaff said. 'By Saint Maurice, patron saint of knights … Delicious. Is there none left?'

'There is, m'lord, there is.'

'There you are, good fellow, another penny … I say! Where are you going, Bielawa?'

'I have to go behind the barn.'

'Go with him, Moser. So he doesn't get any foolish ideas.'

'But I'm back in the warm,' the burgman protested. 'Where can he go? In a snowstorm, in the winter? Among wolves and monsters? To a certain death? He's not a fool, after all!'

'Go, I said.'

Snowstorm or not, wolves or not, Reynevan didn't care. He had to escape and this was the only chance. Now, at night, when Schaff and his men were sated, indolent and drowsy. While Moser was exchanging a few words and coarse jokes with Dorfinger as they passed each other in the dark of the hallway, Reynevan grabbed his sheepskin. And a heavy weight from a set of scales standing there.

In the courtyard, they were greeted by cold air and a snowstorm. And darkness. They almost groped their way behind the barn.

'Beware,' warned Moser from the front. 'There's a plough here somewhere …'

He stumbled and fell over. When he raised himself onto his

hands and knees, swearing vehemently, Reynevan was already swinging the weight towards him, intending to slam the poor wretch in the back of the head. At that moment, swift shadows flashed against a snow-covered manure heap, a dull clatter resounded and Moser grunted and fell flat on the ground. The next moment, a hundred candles flared up before Reynevan's eyes and a hundred thunderclaps boomed in his head. The courtyard, the cottage, the barn and the manure heap spun around and turned a somersault, and the earth and sky changed places several times.

He didn't fall, for he was being held up by several pairs of strong arms. A coarse sack was pulled over his head. His arms were bound. He was dragged. He was tossed onto the saddle of a snorting, stamping horse. The horse set off immediately at a gallop, hooves striking the stones. Reynevan's teeth snapped and rang under the sack and he was afraid he would bite his tongue off.

'On we go!' commanded somebody with a hoarse, hideously evil voice. 'Ride, ride! Gallop!'

The gale howled and whistled.

Chapter Twelve

In which Reynevan returns to Silesia. Facing the perspective of a life as long as a mayfly's but armed with more reason for revenge.

When the sack was violently tugged from his head, Reynevan cowered and cringed, screwed up his eyes and grimaced as the sparkling whiteness of the snow painfully and completely blinded him. He smelled smoke and horses' sweat, heard their stamping, snorting and neighing, the clank of tackle and murmuring, and understood that he was in the midst of a large group of men.

'Congratulations,' he heard, before he began to see. 'Congratulations on a successful bag, Master Dachs. Difficult job?'

'Seen worse,' replied from behind his shoulder a familiar voice, the evil and hoarse one, now with a note of obsequiousness. 'I've known worse, honourable Sir Ulrik.'

'Were any of Schaff's men injured? Did they come to any harm?'

'Nothing a dab of ointment won't put right.'

Reynevan cautiously opened his eyes.

They were in a large village; a church tower rose up above the thatched roofs of cottages, barns and granaries. The streets were full of horsemen, at least forty of them. Among them were mounted knights in white plate armour. There were pennants, including a golden one with a single red stag's antler. Indeed, before he even saw the crest, Reynevan had already guessed who had caught him this time.

'Head up!'

Ulrik of Biberstein, Lord of Frydland and Żary, the uncle of Nicolette, loomed over him on a war horse.

Rather than being frightened, he was relieved. Not to see Birkart Grellenort.

'Do you know who I am?'

He nodded stiffly, for a moment unable to utter a word, which was read as insolence. The man with the evil voice punched him in the region of the kidneys. Reynevan had also seen him at Trosky. *Mikuláš Dachs*, he recalled. *A client of the Bibersteins. The burgrave of some castle or other. I forget which.*

'I know . . . I know who you are, Lord Biberstein.'

Ulrik Biberstein sat upright in the saddle, in so doing appearing even taller. He rested a fist in a steel gauntlet on the faulds of his Nuremberg armour.

'You will be punished for what you have done.'

Reynevan didn't answer, in so doing risking another thump. But this time Mikuláš Dachs let it go.

'Prepare him for the road,' ordered Biberstein. 'Give him some warm things so he won't expire. He's to arrive at Stolz in one piece and sound in body.'

Three knights rode slowly over from the group near the cottage and came closer. Two were wearing full plate armour, modern and white, with large reinforced left pauldrons and rerebraces, allowing them to do away completely with shields. The third, the youngest, wasn't wearing plate armour; all he had on under his wolfskin coat was a quilted, slightly grubby doublet. Reynevan recognised him at once.

'The wheel of fortune turns!' Nikel of Keuschburg, the former prisoner at Michalovice Castle, snorted contemptuously. 'You had me and now I have you! How do you like it, m'lord heretic? I'm free today, bought out of captivity. And you're in fetters! With a rope round your neck! Soon to meet the hangman!'

Making his steed take short steps, the youngster rode closer. He clearly intended to force his horse between the Lord of Frydland and Reynevan, but Mikuláš Dachs barred the way.

'What right do you have to take this prisoner, Lord Biberstein?' cried Keuschburg.

Ulrik of Biberstein pouted his lips, with no intention of answering. The squire flushed with anger.

'Yours is a poor example!' he yelled. 'An example of private interest! You put the country at risk for some obscure family feud, for personal vengeance and self-seeking scores. It is a shameful deed! Shameful!'

'Master Foltsch,' Biberstein interrupted in a calm voice. 'You are a serious fellow, known for your consideration and famed for your good advice. So advise this young pup to shut his trap.'

Keuschburg reached down to his side, but one of the riders caught his arm in an iron gauntlet and squeezed so hard the youth cringed in the saddle. Reynevan guessed who it was; he remembered the stories heard at Michalovice. Hans Foltsch from Roimund Castle. A mercenary from Zgorzelec.

'How can I counsel him when he speaks the truth?' Foltsch said slowly. 'Your prisoner, Sir Ulrik, is a senior Hussite, a comrade of notable local hejtmans, allegedly on good terms with them. He surely knows much about the heretics' designs and their secret plans. War is upon us, and whoever sees through the enemy's designs wins out. This captive should be taken to Zgorzelec or Žitava, to be questioned a little and have everything he knows patiently wrung out of him. Thus, I also say: hand him over. For the good of the country, renounce your feud and give him up.'

Ulrik of Biberstein glanced left, glanced right, and the knights, esquires and pikemen responded to his glance by urging their horses ever closer. A squire approached Mikuláš Dachs, who was standing beside Reynevan, with a mighty Zweihänder sword, holding the sheathed weapon so that the hilt was at comfortable arm's reach. Hans Foltsch saw it all.

'And if I don't wish to renounce it,' drawled Ulrik of Biberstein with his fist still resting on his side, 'what then? Will you strike at me? For the good of the country?'

Foltsch didn't even twitch. But the burgmen of Roimund and the Zgorzelec men moved their horses closer, directly facing Biberstein's men. There were a few more of them, Reynevan observed. Swords could be heard grating in scabbards, but Hans Foltsch's calm was holding everyone back.

'No, Lord Biberstein,' said the Zgorzelec mercenary coldly. 'We shall not, for it would please our foes inordinately – when we take up arms against each other, the Hussites rub their hands together. I've said what I meant to say.'

'And I heard you.' The Lord of Frydland raised his head. 'And so it ends. Farewell. M'Lord Foltsch. M'Lord Warnsdorf.'

Keuschburg disdainfully ignored the farewell and paled with fury.

'Oh no it isn't!' he yelled. 'It's not the end at all! It will not be left like that! You will answer for this, Lord Biberstein! If not before the courts, then on the duelling ground!'

'I'm accustomed to having people who threaten me with the courts flogged like dogs.' Ulrik Biberstein raised his voice. 'So restrain yourself, pup, if you want to keep the skin on your back. I'll have you beaten here in the mud, not on the duelling ground. You young upstart! What of it, if you mean to marry into the Dohnas? Even if you took a Dohna for your wife you wouldn't amount to anything. How dare you thus address ancient nobility,

O son of a freed peasant servant of the Merseburg bishops. You're ridiculous!'

Keuschburg's pale face flushed as red as a sliced beetroot and it looked as though he would charge Biberstein with his bare hands. Foltsch grabbed him by the shoulder and the knight addressed as Warnsdorf seized his horse by the bridle. But the rest of the Zgorzelec soldiers were spoiling for a fight. There was a shout, then another, and swords and battleaxes flashed. Spurred horses neighed and blades flashed in the hands of Biberstein's men. Mikuláš Dachs grasped and raised the two-handed sword.

'Stop!' roared Hans Foltsch. 'Stop, dammit! Put away your weapons!'

The men of Roimund and Zgorzelec obeyed him. Reluctantly. Horses snorted, trampling the snow into mud.

'Be on your way,' Ulrik Biberstein said ominously. 'Be on your way, Master Foltsch. Right now. Before anything evil happens.'

The snow thawed in no time when a little sunshine came through the clouds. The wind dropped. It became warmer.

Autumn had returned.

Szklarska Poręba – Reynevan now knew the name of the village with the church – emptied somewhat after Foltsch and Warnsdorf's detachment disappeared into a ravine leading towards Jakub's Pass, which he had heard separated the Karkonosze from the Izera Mountains. For some time, Mikuláš Dachs watched gloomily as they went and said something to Biberstein, pointing by turns at the men riding away and at Reynevan. Biberstein pouted, eyed the prisoner up and down evilly and nodded. Then issued orders. Dachs bowed.

'Lord Liebenthal!' he called, approaching. 'Lord Stročil, Lord Priedlanz, Lord Kuhn! If you would.'

Four knights stepped out from the gathering and walked over, clearly interested but haughtily reluctant. Which didn't bother Dachs in the slightest.

'The Honourable Sir Ulrik of Biberstein has ordered this rascal delivered to Silesia, to Stolz Castle,' he said, pointing at Reynevan, 'and turned over to Sir Jan Biberstein, the brother of the Honourable Ulrik. The prisoner is to arrive there no later than five days' time, on Monday, for today is Thursday. He is to be delivered alive, healthy and undamaged. Lord Biberstein has entrusted Lord Liebenthal with command of the escort, but all of you will answer for the carrying out of the order with your lives. Do you understand, gentlemen? Lord Liebenthal?'

'Why us?' Liebenthal asked brusquely, rubbing his very well-defined, stubbly black chin. 'And why only we four?'

'Because that is what Sir Ulrik ordered. And because I advised him to do so.'

'We thank you warmly,' sneered another of the four, dressed in a beaver hat worn at a rakish angle. 'You mean we are to deliver him to Stolz hale and hearty. And if we don't, we lose our heads. Splendid.'

'And if he tries to flee?' A third man, a beanpole with a fair moustache, gloomily eyed Reynevan up and down. May we at least lame him?'

'You'd then risk the Lord of Stolz having you lamed, too.'

'Then what?' the moustachioed man continued. 'Are we to bind him and deliver him in a sack? Or maybe shove him into an iron barrel like the one Konrad of Głogów kept Henry the Fat in? Or perhaps—'

'Enough!' Dachs cut him off. 'The captive is to arrive at Stolz, hale and hearty, in five days. It's up to you to do it and that's that. I'll add that he'd have to be insane to try to escape. Plenty of parties are after him and if caught by any of them he can expect death. And by no means a swift nor an easy one.'

'And what will they do at Stolz? Cover him in blossom, will they?'

'None of my business what they cover him in.' Dachs shrugged. 'But I know what awaits him in Zgorzelec, Žitava or Bautzen: torture and the stake. If Bergow or Schaff seize him again, he will surely suffer a nasty death. Thus, I don't imagine that he'll try—'

'I shall not try,' announced Reynevan, tired of being silent. 'I can give you my word. Swear on the cross and all that is sacred!'

The knights roared with unrestrained and hearty laughter. Tears were running down Dachs' face.

'Ooh, Lord Bielawa,' he said, wiping the tears from his cheeks. 'You've amused me splendidly. You'll swear, you say? Feel free! But in the meantime, we'll bind you with a length of stout rope. And we'll put you on a peasant's bow-legged nag so you won't start thinking about galloping. All just to be on the safe side. Nothing personal.'

They set off soon after. In accordance with Dachs' promise, Reynevan's arms were tied up, without excessive cruelty but firmly and tightly. In accordance with the promise, he was put on a horse, or rather a hideous, lumbering nag with crooked hind legs, a horse in name only, which was clearly incapable not only of galloping but even trotting. Naturally, there was no point thinking about escaping on such a steed – it wouldn't have been possible even to overtake a pair of yoked oxen on it.

They rode east. Towards Jelenia Góra. Towards the road linking Zgorzelec with Świdnica, Nysa and Racibórz.

I'm going to Silesia, thought Reynevan, rubbing his itching nose against the fur collar of his cloak. *I'm returning to Silesia, as I promised. As I vowed. To myself and others.*

If Flutek knew, he'd surely be glad. It's the beginning of November, a mere four days after All Souls' Day. It's a long time until Christmas, and I'm already in Silesia.

They rode east. Towards Jelenia Góra. Towards the Sudety highway, which linked Zgorzelec with Świdnica, Nysa and Racibórz. Which passed through Frankenstein on its way. And the area of Stolz Castle.

The castle, thought Reynevan, wiping his nose on his collar, *where my Nicolette is. And my son.*

They reached the village of Hermsdorf around noon. They speeded up, spurring the horses, anxiously glancing towards the granite rock and tower of Chojnik Castle rising above the village. Mikuláš Dachs, warning against possible tricks by potential pursuers, ordered them to be particularly vigilant in the vicinity of Chojnik. Common sense suggested that Janek Schaff couldn't be in the castle as his trip through the Karkonosze wilderness and valleys must have taken him considerably longer than their route along the highway. But their anxiety didn't begin to leave them until the castle vanished from sight.

In the valley, they passed Cieplice, a village well known for its warm springs and healing waters. They soon saw Jelenia Góra, the spire of the parish church and the tower of the castle rising above the town, which was allegedly built by Bolesław the Wrymouth, Duke of Lesser Poland, three hundred years earlier and enlarged two hundred years later by his great-great-something grandson.

The escort's leader, Liebenthal, reined his horse around, rode over and rested his stirrup against Reynevan's. Then drew a knife and cut the rope binding his wrists.

'We're going through the town,' he said dryly. 'I don't want people to stare. Or for tongues to wag. Do you understand?'

'I understand and thank you.'

'Thank me tomorrow. For know this: any tricks and I'll use this blade to cut off your ears. I swear on the Holy Trinity that I will. Even if I am punished by the Bibersteins, I'll cut off your ears. Beware.'

'Beware also,' added Priedlanz, the one with the fair moustache, 'that even though we hold you captive, you can expect worse treatment from the others. Remember what Dachs said – the men who are pursuing you are planning torture and death for you. And can we be sure who's following us? Foltsch, perhaps, and the other one, Warnsdorf of Rohožec. Bergow, perhaps? Klüx? Janko Schaff? And these lands, know this, are the estates of Schaff and his relatives and comrades – the Nimpcz, Zedlitz and Redern families. Even if you escaped from us you wouldn't get far. You'd be caught by peasants and they'd turn you over to their masters.'

'Without a doubt,' said the third member of the escort, nodding in agreement. 'In sooth, better let us deliver you to Stolz. And count on Sir Jan Biberstein's mercy.'

'I shan't try to escape,' Reynevan assured them, rubbing his wrists. 'I'm not afraid of Jan Biberstein, for I don't consider myself guilty. I shall prove my innocence.'

'Amen,' summed up Liebenthal. 'Let us ride, then.'

They stopped to rest and make camp a short way beyond Jelenia Góra, in the village of Maywaldau. They ate whatever was to hand and slept in a shed, the wind blowing down from the mountains again whistling through the many holes in the walls and roof.

Reynevan, exhausted by the hardships, fell asleep quickly. So quickly that wakefulness passed smoothly into sleep and, imperceptibly, dreams replaced reality. *Ooh, ooh, gentlemen, but I long for a woman. Damn you, Priedlanz, for mentioning it, I won't get to sleep now. Never mind, we'll soon be in Świdnica and I know a little brothel there ... And near the castle in Rychbach I know two merry maids ...*

Nikel Keuschburg foams at the mouth, waving a gnawed bone: *He killed my horse Sturm under me, shot him with a crossbow, the whoreson, forty grzywna I gave for him, but I never regretted it, for he was fleet ... No, not the Hussite! The horse was fleet! My Sturmie ... And that Hussite, Reinmar of Bielawa, may he meet a bad end ...*

Run, hisses Douce of Pack, narrowing her blue-green eyes. Hefting a javelin. *Flee*, adds Birkart of Grellenort, standing alongside her. *I'll catch you whatever happens. I have ears and eyes everywhere. In every monastery.*

He'll find a way out of it, says Gregorz Hejncze, *Inquisitor a Sede Apostolica specialiter deputatus* at the Wrocław Diocese. *And then there's a chance he'll lead us to ...*

I'm interested in birdsong, says Konrad of Oleśnica, the Bishop of Wrocław. *Reinmar of Bielawa will lead me to the trail of birdsong.*

The rider gallops into the night through forests and rocky canyons. He bangs on the iron-bound gate of the monastery, reinforced like a stronghold. It's opened by a monk in a white habit and a black scapular decorated with a cross and the letter 'S' winding around the base.

Hans Foltsch, the Zgorzelec mercenary at Roimund, fulfilled his responsibilities completely – he personally delivered Nikel Keuschburg, who'd been bought out of Hussite captivity, to Falkenberg Castle, located at the top of Falcon Mountain, one of the Dohna family's residences. The now-liberated youth was greeted at the castle with unalloyed joy, and fourteen-year-old Barbara of Dohna wept with happiness, as did her thirteen-year-old sister Eneda. After all, an identical misfortune might happen, if not that day, then the day after, to Eneda's suitor,

Kasper Gersdorf. Barbara and Eneda's mother, Her Ladyship Margareta of Jenkwicz, also wept, to keep them company. As did their grandfather, old Sir Bernhard of Dohna, but he was elderly, and although he often laughed and wept, he seldom knew why.

Friedrich of Dohna, Lord of Falkenberg, son of Bernhard, husband of Margareta and father of the girls, didn't display any joy. He tended to smile wryly and only feign happiness. He hadn't just been impoverished by the ransom of four thousand eight hundred groschen. By paying the Hussites for Keuschburg, he had officially declared him as the official candidate for son-in-law, and he was certain Barbara could have done better. So he chewed his moustache, smiled affectedly and couldn't wait for the banquet at which he meant to drink himself stupid in order to forget.

Among the remaining people, one of the few to be genuinely pleased was Hans Foltsch. He had received the sum of six thousand groschen from Friedrich of Dohna for Keuschburg's ransom. He had knocked Hejtman Jan Čapek down to three thousand six hundred. But told Sir Friedrich it had been four thousand eight hundred. When the story of Nikel Keuschburg's adventures had circulated throughout both the upper and lower castles, the rider surreptitiously left Falkenberg.

He rode his horse hard. After just under an hour's ride, a little after midnight, he banged on the iron-bound gate of the Celestine monastery in Oybin, which was reinforced like a stronghold. In the monastery, no one was still in bed – the severe Celestine rule ordered the monks to rise at midnight and begin their prayers and labours.

'Where did the news come from?'

'From Oybin, Your Excellency. From the Celestines. From Prior Burchard.'

'How old is the news?'

'It reached Oybin last night, *post sexta die mensis Novembris*, at the third night vigil. And now it is the night of the seventh of November and the first vigil has just passed. The messenger, may I remark, rode day and night, not sparing his horse. The tidings he brought can be considered absolutely fresh.'

Gregorz Hejncze, *Inquisitor a Sede Apostolica specialiter deputatus* to the Wrocław Diocese, lounged comfortably, stretching out the soles of his boots towards the heat coming from the hearth.

'It ought to be expected,' he murmured. 'It ought to be expected that Reinmar of Bielawa won't sit still, particularly when he finds out about . . . certain matters. It was to be predicted that the Bibersteins would catch him. Are they indeed taking him to Stolz?'

'Of course,' confirmed Łukasz Bożyczko, a Pole, a deacon at Saint Lazarus's Church who worked diligently and very committedly for the Holy Office. 'They are taking the Sudety road, naturally, and at this moment must be in the vicinity of Bolków. They certainly don't journey at night and the day is short at present. Your Excellency? We could seize them in Świdnica. We have people there—'

'I'm aware of that.'

'If he . . .' The deacon coughed into his fist. 'If Reinmar of Bielawa ends up in Stolz, he won't leave alive. If he falls into the clutches of Jan Biberstein, he'll be tortured to death. He ravaged Sir Jan's daughter and Sir Jan will visit cruel revenge on him—'

'If he's guilty,' interrupted Hejncze, 'he deserves to be punished. Are you sorry for him? He's a heretic, a Hussite, after all, his death is a joy, a pleasure and a delight to us good Catholics. The crueller the death, the greater the delight. You took an oath, after all, like the whole of Silesia. Must I remind you of it? *Die*

*Ketzer und in dem christlichen Glauben irresame Leute zu tilgen und zu verderben . . . * That was it, wasn't it?'

'I merely . . .' the deacon mumbled, quite put off his stroke by the Inquisitor's sarcasm. 'I merely wanted to mention that this Reinmar might know a great deal . . . If Biberstein tortures him to death, then we—'

'Lose the chance to torture him to death ourselves,' Hejncze finished. 'Well, there is that risk.'

'I'd say it was a certainty.'

'The only certainties are taxes, and that the Church of Rome is everlasting.'

The deacon had no further arguments.

'Send the messenger on to Świdnica,' the Inquisitor said a moment later. 'To the Dominicans. Have them send their best agents to tail him and observe him discreetly. For I think . . .'

Hejncze realised he was talking to himself. He tore his gaze away from the stain on the ceiling and looked at the somewhat pale deacon.

'I think that Reinmar of Bielawa will get himself out of trouble,' he finished. 'I think there's a chance he'll lead us to—'

'—lead me to the Vogelsang,' finished Konrad of Oleśnica, Bishop of Wrocław. 'The matter of the robbed tax is small beer; we'll solve it somehow or other, there's no rush. But the Vogelsang . . . Were I to get my hands on the Vogelsang, now that would be something. And that infernal Reynevan of Bielawa, he's becoming more and more fascinating, I do declare . . . He might lead me to the Vogelsang.'

The bishop finished a glass of Rhenish wine. Since the morning worship he had already drunk three quarts of various wines, at the very least. Wine ensured health, drove away melancholy, increased potency and protected from disease.

'From what Prior Burchard reports from Oybin,' he continued, pouring himself more wine, 'it appears that this Bielawa
must be in the vicinity of Bolków, so we should assume he will
reach Świdnica in two days, on Sunday, *nona die Novembris*.
Hmm. I have agents with the Świdnica Dominicans, but I fear
that many of them work for both sides, which means they work
for Hejncze, too . . . I'll have to send one of my own bodyguards
. . . Hmm. I give up my bodyguards reluctantly, for I've received
reports that my murder is being planned. By Hussites, naturally.
Ah well, I'd show them, if I caught the men from the Vogelsang
. . . If I talked them round, turned them, if they began to work
for me . . . Ha! Do you understand my plan, Birkart, my son?'

The Wallcreeper didn't reply. He had wrapped himself tightly
in a fur, for it was chilly in the chamber, the wind from Rychleby
whistling through the cracks in Nysa Castle's walls.

'You do,' Konrad answered himself. 'Thus, you'll also understand the order I hereby issue to you: leave Reynevan alone. And
incidentally, how the hell did he manage to escape from you in
the Karkonosze?'

'It was miraculous.' Either the Wallcreeper's face twitched or
it was the flickering of the candle. 'Miracles happen. Does Your
Eminence doubt that?'

'Indeed I do, for I have seen them fabricated. But now isn't
the time to quibble. Clearly providence meant for Reynevan
to escape from you. Don't take a stand against providence, son.
Call your dogs, your ill-famed company, your Black Riders, off
the scent. Let them sit tight in Sensenberg and wait for orders.
They'll be needed when – following Reinmar of Bielawa – we
track down the Vogelsang. While you, Birkart of Grellenort,
will be ever with me, by my side. Here, in Nysa. In Otmuchów
Castle. In Wrocław. In short, wherever I happen to be, I
want you close to me. Always and everywhere. I told you, the

Hussites are after me, are planning an attempt on my life . . .'

The Wallcreeper nodded. He knew perfectly well that the 'attempt on his life' was humbug; the bishop himself had invented it to create a pretext for intensifying terror and oppression. The matter of linking Reynevan of Bielawa with the secret Hussite organisation code-named 'Vogelsang' was also extremely doubtful. Bishop Konrad had, in truth, numerous sources of information, but they weren't always reliable. Too often the obsequious informers told the bishop what the bishop wanted to be told.

'In the event of an assassination attempt,' he said, 'perhaps it would be better if my Horsemen—'

'Your Horsemen,' said the bishop, slamming a fist down onto the table, 'are to sit tight in Sensenberg! I've told you! People are talking too much of the Company of Death! Hejncze has his eye on me and would be pleased to be able to link me with the Horsemen, with you, black magic and witchcraft! You're being talked about too much, too many rumours are circulating!'

'We took pains that they would,' the Wallcreeper reminded him calmly. 'To sow terror. It is, after all, our joint initiative, my dear bishop. I did what we agreed. And what you personally ordered me to do. For the cause. *Ad maiorem Dei gloriam.*'

'For the cause?' The bishop gulped wine from a goblet and grimaced as though it were gall, not Rhenish. 'Hussite spies and sympathisers who possessed valuable information you murdered in cold blood. For pleasure. For the pleasure of killing. So don't say it was to the glory of God. For God is liable to be annoyed.'

'We'll leave that matter to divine judgement.' The Wallcreeper's face didn't even twitch. 'I shall carry out your order, Bishop. My men will remain in Sensenberg.'

'I understand that. I understand that, my son. They'll remain in Sensenberg. And should you need men, draw them from my mercenaries. Be my guest.'

'I'm grateful.'

'I should hope so. And now go. Unless you have something to say.'

'It so happens that I do.'

'What might it be?'

'Two things. The first is a warning, the second a request, a humble supplication.'

'I'm all ears.'

'Don't underestimate Reinmar of Bielawa, Bishop. You don't believe in miracles, you mock Arcane Knowledge, you shrug magic off with a wry smile. That's foolish, Bishop, if I may say so. *Magna Magia* exists and miracles happen. I saw one lately. In the vicinity of Reynevan, actually.'

'Indeed? What did you see?'

'A creature that shouldn't be. That shouldn't exist.'

'Ha. Perhaps you looked into a mirror by accident, my son?'

The Wallcreeper turned his head away. The bishop, although pleased with his spitefulness, didn't smile. He inverted the hourglass – *media nox* had passed and in around eight hours it would be *officium matutinum. It's high time I retired to bed*, he thought. *I work too much. And what do I have to show for it? Who appreciates it? Pope Martin, that whoreson*, zum Teufel mit ihm, *still won't hear of an archbishopric for me. The diocese is still formally under Gniezno's authority!*

He turned towards the Wallcreeper, his face grave. 'I understood the warning. I shall bear it in mind. And the request? You mentioned a request.'

'I don't know what plans you have, Father, but when the time comes, I'd like to deal with this Reynevan . . . with my own hands. Him and his companions. I'd like Your Eminence to promise me that.'

'I promise,' said the bishop, nodding. 'You will.'

If it's in my interest and that of the Church, he added in his mind.

The Wallcreeper looked him in the eyes and smiled.

They were riding down a road beside the rapidly flowing Bóbr, along an avenue of alders and elms. The weather had improved, the sun even shining occasionally. Seldom and briefly, unfortunately, but why, it was November. The seventh of November, to be precise. *Septima Novembris*. Friday.

The family of Wilrych of Liebenthal, singled out by Biberstein to command the escort, had come from Meissen. He was said to be distantly related to the powerful Liebenthals of Liebenthal near Lwówek. He liked to boast about it. Which was actually one of his few defects.

The other members of the escort couldn't be accused of much, either. Deep down, Reynevan thanked providence, aware that he might have ended up much worse off.

Bartoš Stročil considered himself a Silesian. Reynevan vaguely recalled that a Stročil kept an apothecary's shop in Wrocław, but he preferred not to delve into it.

'I know a fine little brothel in Świdnica,' repeated Stročil yet again, rocking in the saddle. 'And near the castle in Rychbach I knew two merry maids, seamstresses . . . It was two years ago, in truth; they might have got married, the whores . . .'

'We could stop off there and find out . . .' said Stoss of Priedlanz with a sigh.

'We ought to.'

'*Jo, jo*,' said Otto Kuhn. 'We ought to.'

Stoss of Priedlanz, a Lusatian but of Czech descent, was a client of the Bibersteins – like his father, grandfather and probably great-grandfather. Otto Kuhn came from Bavaria. He didn't brag about it, being a man of few words, but when he did speak, the guttural sounds left no doubt: only the Bavarians could butcher the beautiful German tongue like that.

'Ha!' said Liebenthal, spurring his horse. 'Then we shall stop, methinks, at that Świdnica brothel. I've also been feeling strong urges recently. And when I think about carnal urges I become poetical. A second Tannhäuser.'

'It's the same with me. Just without the Tannhäuser.'

'I say!' Priedlanz stood up suddenly and turned back. 'Did you see? Over there?'

'What?'

'A rider! Someone was watching us from that hillock! High up, behind those firs. Now he's gone. He's hidden ...'

'Dammit. That's all we need. Did you recognise his colours?'

'Dressed in black. And his horse was black.'

'A Black Horseman!' cackled Stročil. 'Again! Lately it's been nothing but Black Riders, black apparitions, the Company of Death. The Company of Death here, the Company of Death there, the Company rode by, the Company attacked Lord Bergow's men over the Izera ... And now you're affected, Priedlanz?'

'I saw him, strike me dead! He was there!'

'Urge on the horses,' Wilrych Liebenthal ordered dryly, without taking his eyes from the edge of the trees. 'And be heedful.'

They did so and rode quicker, with their hands on their sword hilts. The horses snorted.

Reynevan felt waves of fear flowing over him.

The anxiety spread to the others. They rode vigilantly, looking around intently. No one was jesting now, quite the opposite – the incident was being taken extremely seriously, to such an extent that they set up an ambush, cunningly and efficiently. In one of the ravines they passed, Stročil and Kuhn dismounted and hid in the undergrowth with crossbows at the ready. The others rode on, making an excess of noise and talking loudly.

The Silesian and the Bavarian waited concealed for almost an hour. In vain. No one was trailing them. But even then, the tension didn't diminish. They were still riding cautiously and often glanced back.

'I think we've lost him . . .' Stročil sighed.

'Or Priedlanz really was seeing things,' stammered Kuhn.

'Neither the one nor the other,' growled Liebenthal. 'The scoundrel's behind us, I just saw him. On the hill to the left. Don't look around, dammit.'

'He's a cunning bastard.'

'He's following us . . . What does he want?'

'Who the hell knows . . .'

'What do we do?'

'Nothing. Keep your weapons at the ready.'

They rode on, tense and downcast, along a road running through ravines beside the bank of the Bóbr, the water foaming in rapids among alder, elm, maple and frequent groves of old, sometimes enormous oak trees in autumn foliage. The view was glorious and should have calmed them. It didn't. Reynevan glanced surreptitiously at the knights and saw the anger growing in them. Kuhn, examining his crossbow, ground out some guttural Bavarian curses. Priedlanz spat. The usually garrulous Stročil was as quiet as the grave. Liebenthal kept up the appearance of calm for a long time, but finally exploded, too.

'And him,' he wheezed out, casting a hideous look at Reynevan. 'And him, he was sent to us from Hell, riding that half-dead nag, slowing us down! We're crawling along like fucking snails because of him.'

Reynevan looked away, determined not to be provoked.

'Damned heretic!' Liebenthal accosted him again. 'What

bloody well made you renounce the true faith? Forsake Our Lady? Venerate that devil, Huss? Blaspheme against the sacraments?'

'Let him be, Wilrych,' Stoss of Priedlanz calmly advised. 'Let him be.'

Liebenthal was still huffing but obeyed. They rode on in an uncomfortable silence.

And Reynevan, previously undecided, resolved to take action. He had to run away. It turned out that Birkart Grellenort hadn't lied – he did indeed have eyes and ears everywhere. The chaplain Zwicker hanged at the foot of the Karkonosze wasn't his only spy; it turned out there was also an informer in Ulrik Biberstein's entourage. The escort taking him to Silesia had been easily tracked down and didn't stand much of a chance in a dangerous confrontation with the Black Riders. *Alone*, he thought, *I'd more easily manage to hide, more easily lose my pursuers.*

The knights' experience hadn't escaped his attention. He couldn't just run away from those men. A method was needed. A ruse.

After covering more or less a mile, they entered Janovice, a large village on the Bóbr, just as the church bell was tolling noon. Around an hour later, they reached a junction – their route crossed a highway leading from Świerzawa to Landeshut. The previously empty road was now teeming with travellers and the escort's mood clearly improved. The knights stopped looking around, knowing that now, among a group of people, they were much safer than in the wooded wilderness of the Karkonosze hills. Priedlanz once again complained that he was itching for a woman, and Stročil resumed praising various whorehouses he had once visited. Otto Kuhn was singing Bavarian songs under his breath. Only Liebenthal was still nervous, irritable and cross. Almost every traveller he passed was treated to muttered abuse.

A Jewish hawker became 'murderer of Christ', 'bloodsucker' and – of course – 'Jew boy'. All merchants were naturally 'thieves' and the miners from the nearby copper mine were 'Walloon vagabonds'. A group of Friars Minor were awarded the label of 'fucking slovens' and some Knights Hospitaller riding under arms were called a 'gang of sodomites'.

'Know what?' Stročil suddenly spoke, accurately sensing the reason for the mood. 'I don't think it was human, that character in black who was tracking us.'

'So what can it be?' asked Liebenthal.

'A spirit. A demon. Why, this is the Karkonosze, have you forgotten?' said Stročil.

'The Rübezahl . . .' guessed Kuhn. *'Jo, jo . . .'*

'The Rübezahl has deer's antlers and wears a long beard,' Priedlanz said with conviction. 'That one didn't.'

'The Rübezahl can take on any form.'

'Fuck . . . A crucifix would come in handy. Or any kind of cross. Anybody got one? What about you, Bielawa? Don't have a cross, do you?'

'No.'

'All that's fucking left is to pray to the saints . . . But which ones?'

'To the Fourteen Holy Helpers,' suggested Stročil. 'All of them at one go. There are a few bold 'uns among them. Saint George, for example, obviously. Apart from him, Cyriac kept the Devil on a chain, Margaret tamed a dragon and Eustace tamed lions. Vitus . . . I can't recall what Vitus did. Must have been something.'

'Vitus cavorted amusingly,' interrupted Kuhn.

'You see. What did I say?'

'Shut the fuck up, will you!' yelled Wilrych of Liebenthal. 'It makes my blood boil to listen to it!'

*

'Look, at that wealthy party.'

Indeed, one had to admit that the entourage passing them heading from Bolków looked magnificent. At the head rode an outrider in blue and silver livery, with a similarly chequered pennant. He was followed by armed riders and ornately dressed courtiers surrounding a carriage pulled by four greys, upholstered with patterned fabric and decorated with blue ribbons. A corpulent matron in a mob cap and wimple, emanating an aura of dignity, was seated on the carriage surrounded by ladies-in-waiting.

'Rosamunde of Borschnitz,' said Priedlanz, bowing.

'Née Bolz,' confirmed Stročil in hushed tones. 'Ha, she's said to have been a veritable beauty once. My late papa told me that in his younger days half of Silesia was in love with her – bachelors chased after her like dogs after a bitch, for apart from being comely she was also well dowered. She finally wed Kuno Borschnitz, the one who—'

'Dragons were still walking the Earth when your papa was young,' Liebenthal interrupted scathingly. 'It was so long ago that the Wrocław bishops still obeyed the Gniezno Archdiocese, the Duchy of Świdnica was ruled by the Piasts and the King of Bohemia, Wenceslaus IV, was still in nappies. That old crone Lady Borschnitz must be well over sixty by now – it's a marvel she hasn't turned her toes up yet. Crack the whip, it enrages me when we crawl along like this! Hey, heretic, spur that mare! I say! One of you whack that nag on the rump!'

'Calm yourself, Wilrych.'

They made camp in Bolków, a small town lying at the foot of a mountain, at the top of which towered a celebrated and menacing castle.

This time they slept in an inn – Liebenthal finally decided to delve deeper into the purse Dachs had given him to cover the costs of the journey. They also treated themselves to supper in the form of tasty cabbage and mushroom pierogi.

Reynevan – hunger satisfied – fell into a dreamless sleep.

The following day, low clouds covered the sky and it began to drizzle. They rode on, seldom breaking the silence. They were vigilant, but there was no sign of the rider tracking them. He had vanished. Like a ghost. Perhaps it really had been a ghost? Perhaps it really had been the Rübezahl, the demon of the Karkonosze? Perhaps it had disappeared because they were further away from the Karkonosze?

It went on drizzling.

It only cleared up in the late afternoon. When they reached Świebodzice.

They stopped at the tavern called the Bearded Goat. *It's late,* said Wilrych Liebenthal, *and there's a risk that we won't reach Świdnica before dusk and the closure of the gates. And since Świdnica observes the one-mile law, you won't find a tavern within a radius of one mile from the town. And there's a pleasant smell coming from that Bearded Goat.*

The smell, it turned out, was cabbage, onion, kasha and rye soup made with smoked bacon, but above all roast goose. The holiday of Saint Martin was coming and he made his presence felt. There were several wagons outside the tavern located close to the Bolków Gate and plenty of horses in the stable. The guests might have been enticed by the Goat's kitchen – or they were forced to stay there owing to Świebodzice's travel laws.

'Busy here today?' Reynevan said to the stable boy. 'Rushed off your feet, are you? And whose are those horses?'

The boy told him. He was very excited. And very talkative. They would have talked longer but for Liebenthal.

'I say! You! Bielawa! What's this chit-chat? Not another word and get over here! Look lively!'

The tavern, full of smoke, the smell of a fire and pleasantly warm, was crowded. Peasants predominated, observing the ancient rural tradition that demanded they get blind drunk on a Saturday night. There were also merchants and pilgrims from Compostela with scallop shells sewn onto their cloaks. There were Cistercian questors emptying bowls and jugs with gusto. On a bench by the hearth sat six pikemen in leather jerkins and beside them at the table sat four glum characters dressed in black.

Liebenthal and the others ordered food and drink in the loud, brusque tones expected of knights. Liebenthal again decided to deplete the funds he had received for the journey, so their table was soon filled with dishes of meat and troughs of kasha, jugs of wine and demijohns of cider.

'Aah ...' Priedlanz groaned after some time. 'This food isn't half-bad ... And the drink's passable.'

'*Jo, jo.*' Kuhn belched. 'Good, *gut. Wia sih's g'hört.*'

'Down the hatch!'

'Good health! Charge our glasses, Bartoš!'

'Your good health!'

'Pity that after the eating and drinking we won't get a fuck.' Bartoš Stročil sighed. 'But tomorrow, dammit, it'll be different, you'll see. When we stop in Świdnica. At the mercy of Saint Gregory the Miracle-Worker! I know a little whorehouse in Świdnica, the whores there are like hinds—'

'I trust,' said Liebenthal, twisting his moustaches, 'that your information comes from more recent times. What, Stročil? How long ago did you know those hinds? Let's hope it doesn't turn out they're the same age as old Madam Borschnitz now. More old crones!'

'Temper what you say, m'lord,' said Reynevan. 'I believe, what's more, that you insult the honour of the ladies here.'

'Who asked you?' roared Liebenthal. 'Why do you open your trap?'

'Hush, gentlemen,' hissed Priedlanz, glancing around restlessly. 'A little quieter. People are beginning to stare. And what is it, Bielawa?'

'Lady Borschnitz isn't by any means old. My father is her age and is not an old man.'

'Who? What?'

'Sixty years isn't old.' Reynevan raised his voice. 'My father—'

'Fuck your father!' roared Liebenthal. 'The Devil take your father! Sixty years isn't old? You clod! Whoever passes sixty is a decrepit, senile, doddering old fool! And that's that! And you sit quiet and don't argue, or I'll punch you in the face!'

'You're growing ever louder,' snarled Priedlanz. 'Not everyone has heard you yet. Take that filthy wretch by the door. I believe he hasn't.'

'And further,' said Reynevan softly, looking Liebenthal straight in the eyes. 'Further, I don't like the way you refer to ladies, gentlemen. How dishonourably you treat them. One could think you measure all ladies with the same yardstick. Thinking them all alike.'

'Strike me down!' Liebenthal slammed his fist onto the table, making the dishes bounce. 'For God's sake! I can't stand it!'

'Will you be quiet! Dammit—'

'Lord Bielawa.' Stročil leaned across the table. 'What's come over you, m'lord? Are you drunk or what? Or perhaps sick? First your father, now ladies . . . What's the matter?'

'I deny that all ladies are alike.'

'Indeed, they are!' roared Liebenthal. 'They are all the fucking same! And serve the same purpose!'

'I don't believe it!' Reynevan leaped to his feet and waved his arms. 'No, gentlemen! I refuse to listen to this! I barely endured it,' he said, his voicing growing louder and higher in pitch, 'when you insulted the Holy Father, Pope Martin V, comparing him to an arsehole, calling him a decrepit, senile, doddering old fool! But refusing to revere Our Lady? Saying she doesn't merit reverence? Saying she's the same as all women and conceived and gave birth *sicut ceterae mulieres*? No, I will not listen to this placidly! I'm compelled to take my leave of your company!'

Liebenthal's and Priedlanz's jaws dropped. But not all the way. While they were still dropping, the four glum men at the table in the corner leaped to their feet, along with the pikemen in leather jerkins.

'In the name of the Holy Office! You are arrested!'

Liebenthal pushed the table away from him and grabbed his sword as Stročil kicked the bench over, and Priedlanz and Kuhn flashed half-drawn blades. But the four glum men found unexpected allies. A clay pot, thrown with great accuracy and force by one of the pilgrims decorated with scallops, smashed against Kuhn's forehead. The Bavarian's back slammed against the wall, and before he came to his senses, he was being held in the powerful grip of two Cistercians. The third Cistercian, a short fellow but stocky and strong, shoulder-barged Liebenthal and punched him with a short but accurate left hook and then with a right. Liebenthal punched back, the monk dodged – minimally, but enough for the punch to barely brush his tonsure – then hit Liebenthal with a nice uppercut, followed by an even nicer straight right. Right in the nose. Liebenthal, blood covering his face, vanished under the swarm of pikemen who had set about him. Other men had already overpowered Stročil and Priedlanz.

'You are arrested,' repeated one of the glum men, none of whom had participated in the brawl. 'You are arrested in the name of the Holy Office. For blasphemy, sacrilege and offending religious feelings.'

'Fuck your arses!' roared Priedlanz, face down on the ground.

'That will be noted.'

'Fucking whoresons!'

'That, too.'

It probably doesn't need adding that Reynevan had long since left the tavern. As soon as the row began, he ran for it.

The stable lad had fulfilled his request and left one of the horses saddled. It was still long enough before sundown for the gate not to be locked, but near enough for there not to be a soul on the road, no one who could give the pursuers any directions. And Reynevan didn't doubt that he would be followed as soon as the matter was explained. He would be followed, he knew, not only by his recent escort, but all the glum men he unerringly recognised as servants of the Inquisition. He had to increase the distance as quickly as possible, get as far away as he could in order for the approaching dusk to hinder his pursuers. When darkness fell, he had to be far away. At all costs. Even if he had to ride his horse into the ground.

Luck continued to help him; for the time being, the horse wasn't showing any signs of fatigue in the gallop. It only began to lather up and pant when they reached the forest. Reynevan had to slow down there anyway. In the forest, it was almost completely dark.

His luck ended once it became totally dark. As he rode across a bridge over a stream, the thud of hooves echoed on the timbers, drowning out the thudding of other hooves. A rider, dressed in black and invisible in the gloom, emerged from the darkness like a phantom. Before Reynevan could react, he was pulled from the saddle. He fought back but the black rider had literally super-human strength. He lifted him up and cast him down onto the rocky ground.

There was a flash, pain, paralysis. Then the hard ground appeared to melt beneath him, sucking him into a billowing silence. Into a bottomless abyss of soft oblivion.

He regained consciousness in a semi-supine position. And in fetters. His wrists were tied on his lap, his legs bound at the ankles. *During the course of the last ten days*, he thought, *it's the fifth time someone has seized me, the fifth time I've been somebody's prisoner. It must be a record.*

That was his first thought. Which preceded a more sensible one, considering the situation: *Who actually caught me this time?*

His back was resting against something that was probably a wall, for it was hard and gave off the smell of old lime plaster. There was also a crumbling wall beside him, shielding a blazing bonfire from the wind. The wind was blowing fiercely, stronger gusts howling. Fir trees soughed and creaked. Reynevan had a strong impression that he was somewhere high, at the top of a mountain or hill.

'You're awake?'

The powerful man who had seized and bound him was wear-ing a coarse, black woollen cloak. He also sported armour. And a knightly belt. He didn't resemble Birkart Grellenort or any of his Black Riders. Reynevan's astonishment was even greater than his sense of relief; he had thought it was Grellenort who had caught him. Then why had this strongman in armour kidnapped him and who was he? For it couldn't be the Rübezahl, the spirit of the Karkonosze, could it? Reynevan swallowed. He didn't believe in the existence of the Rübezahl. On the other hand, during the course of the last two years, he had encountered and seen plenty of things the existence of which he didn't believe in.

'Are you Reinmar of Bielawa? Confirm it. I wouldn't like to make an error.'

'I am Reinmar of Bielawa. Who are you?'

'Who am I?' The voice of the knight in the black cloak changed a little, and not encouragingly. 'Let's say I'm a consequence.'

'A consequence of what?'

'Your past deeds. And misdeeds.'

'Oh. An avenging angel? An emissary of doom? The relentless long arm of the law?'

Reynevan himself was surprised by how easily he assumed an easy tone. *Routine*, he thought. *I'm quite simply good at it now.*

'You demanded I confirm my identity,' he went on, still careless, 'so you don't know me. I've never clapped eyes on you before. Thus you are acting, obviously, on behalf of somebody and on somebody's orders. Whose? Who has reason to judge my past misdeeds? Let me guess. I know the men who are after me.'

'You are awfully verbose.'

'Jan of Biberstein and the Inquisition? Out of the question. It's unlikely to be Lord Bergow and the Lusatians. Who does that leave? Konrad, Bishop of Wrocław? The Sterczas? Duke Jan of Ziębice? Buko of Krossig? Adèle Stercza, perhaps?'

The black knight sat down opposite. Fire lit up his face and flickers of flame were reflected in his armour.

'Interesting names. Interesting persons. Particularly the last one, Adèle of Stercza. Would it surprise you if I were acting on her behalf? On her orders?'

'And are you?'

'Take a guess.'

They both said nothing. The wind blew and whistled, smothering and fanning the fire by turns.

'There is no shortage of pretty maids in Silesia,' the knight said. 'Nor is there a lack of comely, free-spirited women. And lately, the population of beautiful, willing and relatively unexploited widows has been quickly growing in strength. And you, Bielawa, took the very worst virago, Adèle of Stercza, from that horn of plenty. What exactly drew you to her? What did you see in her that the others didn't have?'

'You are awfully verbose.'

'Did it arouse you that she was married? That her husband was far away, in foreign lands? That he wasn't satisfying his wife as he ought? That she would only know true pleasure with you? What did she say to you? What did she whisper into your ear? Did the two of you mock the cuckolded husband during your amorous frolics in her chamber? I think—'

'I don't care what you think.' Reynevan cut him off sharply. 'You speak of things about which you had, have and will have no idea. Thus, let it lie.'

'Aha! It hurts when I touch that place, does it? It was amusing to mock the cuckold, but the amusement ended when you became a cuckold oneself. That harlot led you a merry dance . . . Half of Silesia roared with laughter to hear how you went to the tournament in Ziębice and professed your love for the slut in front of Duke Jan. Oh, how the beautiful Adèle blemished your knightly honour . . . And exposed you to ridicule! You must indeed hate her, I think. But I shall console you . . . Delight your soul—'

'You ought to know that I don't feel injured by any means. And don't call her a "harlot" again in my presence. You feel safe because my arms are bound. So don't look to my honour, but rather look to your own, for you cheapen it. And I can manage without being consoled. But just out of interest: how did you intend to console me?'

The black knight said nothing for a long time, looking on with a strange expression. He finally spoke.

'Adèle Stercza is dead.'

Silence reigned again for a long time. And, again, it was the knight who broke it.

'Duke Jan, Lord of Ziębice,' he said, weighing his words, 'decided to strengthen the alliance of his duchy with Kłodzko, with Sir Půta of Častolovice. They both judged that the best way to do so would be for Jan to wed Anka, Půta's youngest daughter. But there was a problem, and the problem's name was Adèle. Adèle of Stercza, who was already strutting around Ziębice like the lady of the manor and a duchess. Who, when she was informed about Duke Jan's marriage plans, created such a stink that the walls shook. It became clear that she wasn't just another mistress, not one of those innumerable lovers who could be urged, bribed or ceded as a vassal. It was clear that if ditched, Adèle would cause a great fuss and create an enormous scandal. So Půta of Častolovice pulled a sour face, anxious to avoid a scandal, and assured Jan he would not expose his Anka to any unpleasantness. There would be no betrothal, he vowed on all the saints, until the suitor became blameless, and order and piety had returned to the Ziębice court. He would not send his daughter to Ziębice until he was certain that she wasn't threatened by any gossip, mockery or slights.

'Jan of Ziębice quite swiftly found a way of getting rid of the problem, allegedly at the instigation of his confessor. It may interest you to hear that you contributed to the plan in some small way, m'lord, for the herzog recalled that the Burgundian was once in collusion with Reinmar of Bielawa, the notorious sorcerer. You have a most strange expression. I thought you'd be delighted to hear of her taming, that the news that you are partly responsible for the Jezebel's fall would gladden you . . . I thought—'

'You thought wrongly. Go on.'

'It was additionally proved that Adèle had indeed tried to beguile the duke using love witchcraft. She was accused of black magic and of making a pact with the Devil. The case was investigated by the most distinguished specialist in witchcraft in the region, Mikołaj Kappitz, abbot of the abbey in Kamieniec. He found Adèle guilty, revealed in and around her devilish practices and scents. They say he disclosed it all for the one hundred Hungarian ducats the duke paid him. They arrested a herbalist and scorched her heels . . . She confessed that Adèle had bought love potions and other things from her. That she plotted her revenge in advance out of fear that Herzog Jan would abandon her by ordering a devilish decoct which would have caused the permanent impotence of the duke's male member. And, just in case, also poisonous herbs. For Anka of Častolovice.

'Adèle was shown the herbalist's testimony and an agreement proposed, but the Burgundian was unafraid. A trial for witchcraft? By all means. I'll have plenty to testify at the trial; the judges, canons and abbots will have plenty to listen to. I know a lot and am only too happy to share it. We shall see if Duke Jan is pleased when it is trumpeted.

'Jan, who believed the case concluded, was furious. He issued orders. Before she knew where she was, the beautiful Burgundian was thrown into the town hall dungeon. She went from eiderdowns and satins to rotten straw . . .'

'Was she . . .' Reynevan relieved his tight throat by coughing. 'Was she tortured?'

'Not a bit of it. She was a noblewoman, after all. Jan of Ziębice didn't dare to stoop to villainy of that kind on a noblewoman. He wished only to frighten her with imprisonment. Force her to be subservient, to leave Ziębice politely and without making a fuss on her release. He didn't know—'

'What . . .' Reynevan felt a hot flush rush to his cheeks. 'What didn't he know?'

'A gang operated in the town hall gaol.' The knight's voice changed and Reynevan thought he heard the soft grinding of teeth. 'Guards, hangman's assistants, ruffians from the castle guard, a few commoners, a few apprentices . . . In brief, they had set up a free brothel in the prison. When a woman – especially one suspected of witchcraft – was imprisoned, the rogues visited by night—' He broke off, then continued in an even more altered voice. 'Once, one of the scoundrels left the belt from his britches in the cell in the haste and confusion. They found Adèle in the morning. Hanged with that belt.

'No action was taken, naturally. No one was punished. Jan of Ziębice feared publicity. The Burgundian, it was proclaimed, had been killed in the cell by the very Devil after betraying him, for she meant to renounce him and had asked for the sacraments. That was all confirmed and imparted from the pulpit by that same Mikołaj Kappitz, the abbot from the Cistercian abbey in Kamieniec. He mentioned you again then, as a matter of fact, as a warning about what consorting with sorcerers can lead to.'

'And no one . . .' Reynevan overcame the lump in his throat. 'No one—'

'No one,' the knight finished. 'Who cared? And today everybody has forgotten about it. Aside from Sir Půta of Častolovice, perhaps. Sir Půta is still on good terms and allied with Duke Jan, but Jan's marriage to Anka keeps being postponed.'

'And it will not come to pass,' rasped Reynevan. 'I'll kill Jan. I'll ride to Ziębice and kill him. In the church, if needs be, but I shall. I'll avenge Adèle.'

'Avenge her?'

'Indeed. So help me, God and the Holy Cross.'

'Don't blaspheme,' the knight admonished him dryly and

347

hoarsely. 'One doesn't seek God's help in vengeance. Revenge, if it be true revenge, must be cruel. He who avenges must turn from God. And is accursed. For ever.'

He swiftly drew a misericorde, leaned over, seized Reynevan by the shirt front, tugged him up, choking him, and brought the blade to his throat, his face to Reynevan's face and his eyes to Reynevan's eyes.

'I am Gelfrad of Stercza.'

Reynevan closed his eyes and twitched, feeling the blade of the misericorde cutting the skin on his neck and hot blood dripping down inside his shirt. But it only lasted a moment, a fraction of a moment, and the blade was withdrawn. He felt the bonds yield as they were cut.

Gelfrad of Stercza, Adèle's widower, straightened up.

'I had resolved to kill you, Bielawa,' he said hoarsely. 'Having learned who you were in Szklarska Poręba, I tracked you, waiting for an opportunity. I know you were not guilty of Nicolaus's death. Two years ago, you spared Wolfher's life. Had it not been for your nobleness, I'd have lost two brothers instead of one. In spite of that, I resolved to take your life. Yes, yes, you suspect correctly . . . I wanted to kill you because of my wounded male pride. I wanted to wash away the filth of notoriety from my coat of arms with your blood. Drown – in your blood – the disgrace of a wretched *cocu*, a king among cuckolds.

'Ah well . . .' he ended, replacing the misericorde in its sheath. 'Much has changed. No one knows I'm alive and in Silesia, not even Apeczko, now the family's senior member, nor my brothers Wolfher and Morold. And I won't stay here long. I'll sort out what I must and never return. I now reside in Lusatia, in the service of the Six Cities . . . I'm also going to marry a Lusatian girl. Soon. I'm already courting, don't you know? If you could see her . . . Cornflower-blue and none-too-quick eyes, a snub nose covered in freckles, short legs, a big arse, nothing French, nothing Burgundian ... So perhaps something will change for the better in my life. With any luck.

'I shall treat what you said as your word of honour,' he said, turning around. 'Know that I'm going to Ziębice. You can guess why. I'm going to Ziębice to fulfil a duty. I shall carry it out, may the Devil help me. But if by a stroke of luck I don't ... If I don't succeed ... Then I shall hold you to your word, Bielawa. To your *verbum nobile*.'

'I vow,' Reynevan said, rubbing his numb wrists, 'here in the face of these ancient mountains, I vow that Adèle's tormentors and murderers will not sleep peacefully or enjoy impunity. I swear that before Jan of Ziębice dies, he will know for what he is dying. I take this oath and shall discharge it, even if I sell my soul to the Devil.'

'Amen. Farewell, Reinmar of Bielawa.'

'Farewell, Gelfrad of Stercza.'

Chapter Thirteen

In which the Green Lady – no less mysterious than the Green Knight from the well-known legend – demands various services of Reynevan, including that of giving her pleasure.

Reynevan waited for them in Mokrzeszów, a village about half a mile outside Świebodzice, by the highway leading to Świdnica. He didn't have to wait long. The knights who'd been escorting him until the day before must have left Świebodzice in the early morning. When he saw them coming down the road, the Sunday Mass in the Mokrzeszów church was still in progress, the parish priest having reached the *postcommunio*.

When they saw him, they were dumbfounded and reined in their mounts. Reynevan had time to have a good look at them. The brawl with the Inquisition – although it had probably been quickly explained – had left its marks. Priedlanz had a black eye. Kuhn's head was bandaged. Liebenthal's nose, likely broken, was red and blue and piteously swollen.

The latter was first to shake off his astonishment. And react. Exactly as Reynevan had expected. The knight dismounted and attacked him with a cry.

'Leave him, Wilrych!'

'I'll kill the whoreson!'

Reynevan shielded himself from the punches, retreating and

covering his head. He didn't even try to fight back. In spite of that – quite by chance – his fist somehow made contact with the knight's swollen nose. Liebenthal howled and fell to his knees, cradling his face in both hands. But Stročil and Priedlanz lunged for Reynevan, catching him by the arms. Kuhn, convinced that Reynevan intended to attack the kneeling Liebenthal, shielded his comrade with his body.

'Gentlemen . . .' Reynevan uttered. 'Why this violence . . . I've returned, haven't I? I shan't try to escape any more. I yield to being delivered to Stolz without resisting.'

Liebenthal stood up, wiping the tears from his eyes and the blood from his moustache, and drew a knife.

'Hold him!' he bellowed, or rather boomed. 'Hold the bastard tight! I'll cut off his ears! I swore I would! And I will!'

'Leave it, Wilrych,' repeated Priedlanz, looking back at the people now leaving the church. 'Control yourself.'

'You can see he came back,' added Stročil. 'He promised he won't try to escape again. Besides, he'll be trussed up like a turkey.'

'One ear at least!' Liebenthal struggled to break free of Kuhn, who was trying to restrain him. 'Just one! As a punishment!'

'No. He's to be delivered whole.'

'A piece of ear, then!'

'No.'

'Well, at least a punch in the face!'

'That you may do.'

'I say! Gentlemen! What's going on here?'

The woman who had uttered those words was tall, and her imperious pose made her appear even taller. She was wearing a travelling *houppelande*, simple of fashion and grey, but made of delicate cloth of high quality, trimmed with a dormouse collar and gloves edged with the same fur. The woman's calpac was also made of dormouse, worn over a muslin *couvre-chef* covering her hair, cheeks and neck. A pair of eyes looked out from under the calpac. Eyes as blue and cold as a bright January morning.

'Are you staging a nativity play, gentlemen?' asked the woman. 'Though Advent hasn't even begun?'

Liebenthal stamped his foot, frowned angrily and lifted his head, but quickly restrained himself. He was aided in his decision by, among other things, the sight of soldiers emerging from the vestibule behind the woman. Among others. But not only.

'Lord Liebenthal, am I right?' The woman eyed him. 'You were my guest in Żary Castle last summer, and in the party that was subsequently assigned to me. I recognise you, although your nose had a different shape and colour then. Do you remember me? Do you know who I am?'

Liebenthal bowed low. Priedlanz, Stročil and Kuhn followed his example. Reynevan also bowed.

'I await an answer. What is occurring here?'

'We must urgently deliver this man to Stolz,' said Liebenthal, pointing to Reynevan, 'on the orders of His Grace Ulrik Biberstein. We must deliver him to the castle—'

'Bruised and battered?'

'I have orders.' The knight cleared his throat and blushed. 'I gave my word—'

'Your word,' interrupted the woman, 'won't be worth a row of buttons if this young man arrives at Stolz with even a single bruise. Do you know the Lord of Stolz, Sir Jan Biberstein? For *I* do. And I warn you: he can be hot-headed.'

'What can I do,' roared Liebenthal pugnaciously, 'when he defies me and tries to flee?'

The woman waved a hand. She was wearing rings with gemstones in gold settings, the total value of which was too high to permit a rapid valuation. Servants and soldiers approached, followed by bowmen led by a fat corporal in a brass-studded brigandine with a broad short sword at his side.

'I happen to be making for Stolz now,' said the woman. Addressing her words more to Reynevan than to Liebenthal. 'My party will guarantee you safety on the road,' she added freely – casually, even – 'and the appropriate execution of Sir Ulrik's orders. I, for my part, promise you a reward, a generous reward, which Jan Biberstein will not refuse when I praise you before him. What do you say to that, m'Lord Liebenthal?'

Liebenthal had no choice but to bow again.

'I, myself, shall guarantee the good treatment of the prisoner,' added the woman, still looking at Reynevan. 'Meanwhile, you, Reinmar of Bielawa, will repay me with pleasant conversation on the route. I await an answer.'

Reynevan straightened up. And bowed. 'I'm honoured.'

'Naturally you are.' The woman gave a studied smile. 'So let us be off. Give me your arm, young man.'

She held out a hand and the gesture revealed from under the dormouse cuff a close-fitting sleeve of green velvet cloth of a vivid, gorgeous, intense shade. He took her hand. The touch made him tremble.

'You know me, Madam,' he said. 'You know who I am. You have a considerable advantage over me.'

'You don't even know how considerable.' She smiled rapaciously. 'And you may call me . . .'

She hesitated and glanced at her sleeve.

'. . . the Green Lady. Why do you look so? Because only you, knights errant, are allowed to appear incognito, under romantic sobriquets? I'm the Green Lady to you and that's that. The thing is not in the colour of the robe. I boldly compare myself to that Green Knight. Men have been ready to put their heads on the block for a single glance from me. Perhaps you doubt it?'

'I wouldn't dare. Should such an opportunity arise, I won't hesitate, either.'

'An opportunity, you say? Who knows? We shall see. For the time being, assist me into the saddle.'

They rode on, with the ridges of the Sudety Mountains blue against a background of clouds on their right. The Green Lady and Reynevan were preceded only by the outriders: a fat sergeant and two bowmen. Following the Lady and Reynevan came the rest of the soldiers, plus servants leading reserve and packhorses. Liebenthal *et consortes* formed the procession's rearguard.

They weren't alone, for the road was actually quite busy. It was unsurprising – they were riding along a busy trade route, well travelled since ancient times, linking the West with the East. The section to Zgorzelec was known as the *Via Regia*, the royal road, which passed through Frankfurt, Erfurt, Leipzig and Dresden to Wrocław. In Zgorzelec, the road forked into the so-called Sudety Highway, which ran along the foot of the mountains through Jelenia Góra, Świdnica, Nysa and Racibórz, to connect with the Wrocław road again in Krakow and head east towards the Black Sea. No wonder that wagon after wagon and caravan after caravan were moving along the Sudety Highway. Traditionally, oxen, rams, swine, leather, furs, wax, potash, honey and suet journeyed from east to west, towards Germanic countries. Wine was traditionally transported in the opposite direction, and goods manufactured by the advanced industry in the west, which in the east traditionally never gained a foothold to develop.

The Green Lady tugged on the reins of a shapely white mare and rode close enough to brush her knee against Reynevan's.

'I see dried blood on your collar,' she remarked. 'Whose work is it? Liebenthal and company?'

'No.'

'A short answer.' She pouted. 'Painfully succinct. And to think, I had *so* hoped you'd elaborate on the subject, regale me with a thrilling tale. You were to amuse me, I remind you. But since it's not to your liking, I shan't insist.'

He didn't answer, being simply tongue-tied. They rode on in silence for some time. The Green Lady gave the impression of being utterly absorbed by the views. Reynevan kept glancing across at her. Furtively. She eventually caught him at it, caught his gaze like a spider ensnares a fly. He fled from her look. It sent shivers up his spine.

'If I understood rightly,' she resumed the conversation quiet carelessly, rupturing the silence hanging between them, 'if I understood right, you managed to flee from your guards. In order to return the following day. Voluntarily. You enjoyed one mere night of freedom. And now you're heading to Stolz Castle, into the hands of Sir Jan Biberstein. You must have had a reason to act thus. Did you?'

He didn't answer, but merely nodded. The Green Lady's eyes narrowed dangerously.

'A significant reason?'

He was about to nod again but restrained himself in time.

'Indeed, m'lady. But I'd prefer not to talk about it. With respect. But if I offend, I apologise and beg forgiveness.'

'I forgive you.'

He stole a glance at her again and she caught him again in the snare of her eyes, the expression in which he could not decipher.

'I felt and still feel like a tête-à-tête. I meant only to use questions to coax you towards garrulousness. For, in any case, I know the answers to most of the questions.'

'Indeed?'

'You are giving yourself up to Sir Jan to make a point. Endeavouring to convince him that you have a clear conscience. In the case of Kasia Biberstein, naturally.'

'You astonish me, m'lady.'

'I'm aware of it. I'm doing so deliberately. Let's return, though, as my confessor often says, to the *meritum*. Your efforts won't impress Sir Jan, believe me. Quite disagreeable procedures await you at Stolz Castle, I think, which are likely to end wretchedly. You ought to have fled while you had the chance.'

'Escape would confirm the legitimacy of the charges. It would be an admission of guilt.'

'Oh. Then you are innocent? With a clean conscience?'

'You've heard plenty of rumours about me.'

'I have indeed,' she admitted. 'There were plenty of them. About you. And your exploits. And conquests. I listened, whether I liked it or not.'

'You know, m'lady,' he cleared his throat, 'how it is with gossip. It makes a mountain out of a molehill—'

'I also know there's no smoke without fire. Don't quote any more proverbs, I beg you.'

'I didn't commit the crime I'm accused of. To be precise, I didn't attack and rob the tax collector. And I don't have the stolen money. If that interests you.'

'It does not.'

'What, then?'

'I already said: Katarzyna Biberstein. Are you innocent with regard to her? Your conscience isn't burdened by any sins? Or even peccadillos?'

'I'd rather not converse on that particular subject,' he said through pursed lips.

'I know you wouldn't. Świdnica's ahead of us.'

*

They entered the town through the Strzegom Gate and left through the Lower Gate. As they passed through, Reynevan sighed several times, seeing and recognising familiar and well-liked places – the Golden Lindworm apothecary's shop, where he had once trained; the Crusader Tavern, where he had once drunk Świdnica March ale and tried his luck with the local girls; and the vegetable stalls which he visited to try his luck with the maids bringing their goods from the countryside. He looked longingly towards Kraszewice Street where Justus Schottel, an acquaintance of Scharley's, had printed playing cards and dirty pictures.

Although preoccupied by his memories, he kept furtively glancing at the Green Lady riding on his right. And when he did so, he suffered pangs of conscience. *I love Nicolette*, he repeated. *I love Katarzyna Biberstein, who bore me a son. I'm not thinking about other any women. None at all. I should not.*

Yet he did.

The Green Lady also gave the impression of being lost in contemplation. She kept silent. She only spoke after they passed through the village of Boleścin, when the thudding of the party's hooves had quietened after crossing the bridge over the Pilawa.

'In around a mile,' she said, 'we'll come to Faulbrück. Then the town of Rychbach. Then Frankenstein. And after Frankenstein, Stolz Castle.'

'I know the area a little.' He allowed himself a slight teasing tone. 'The villages of Kopanica and Koziniec lie between Rychbach and Frankenstein, I believe. Is that of any great significance?'

'None at all to me.' She shrugged. 'But in your place, I'd devote more attention to the route. Every mile we cover and every town and village we pass through brings you closer to Sir Jan

Biberstein and his righteous indignation. If I were you, I'd be on the lookout for a chance in each of them.'

'I've already said I don't mean to escape. I'm not a criminal. I'm not afraid of standing before Biberstein. Nor his daughter.'

'Well, well.' She fixed him with a piercing gaze. 'What a sincere outburst. What would you have me think, my boy? That you're as pure as a babe in arms? That there was nothing between you and Kasia Biberstein? That though they flay you and break your bones, you won't own up to the plump child hanging on to Kasia's skirts at Stolz?'

'I do feel ...' Reynevan felt himself blush and it annoyed him a little. 'I do feel responsible. Yes, that's it: responsible. Not guilty. But as I said earlier, I'd rather not talk about that. We may converse on other topics. The landscape, for example. That small river is the Pilawa and those are the Owl Mountains.'

She laughed. He sighed softly, having feared a different reaction.

'I am trying,' she said, 'to understand the motives of your conduct. I'm curious – why, it's a foible of my female nature. I like to know, connect cause to effect, comprehend. It gives me pleasure. Give me pleasure, Reinmar. If not out of sympathy, then at least out of politeness.'

'Madam ... If you wouldn't mind ...'

'Just one thing, one matter, answer one question. How can it be you don't fear the dungeons of Stolz? Biberstein's fury? After raping his only daughter?'

'I beg your pardon?'

'Righteous indignation again? You took Katarzyna Biberstein by force. Against her will. Everybody knows that.'

'Everybody?' He swung around in the saddle. 'Meaning who?'

'You tell me.'

'I didn't start this.' He felt the blood rushing to his face again. 'With all due respect, it wasn't me who started this conversation.'

She was silent for a long while.

'The facts are as follows,' she suddenly began. 'Two years ago, on the fourteenth of September, in the morning, you and your comrades attacked a party in Goleniowskie Forests, in which Lady Katarzyna of Biberstein, the daughter of Jan Biberstein of Stolz, was journeying with Jutta of Apolda, daughter of the Schönau Cup-Bearer. You seized the reinforced wagon the maidens were travelling inside. The pursuers who set off a few hours after you found the conveyance. There was no trace of the maidens.'

'I beg your pardon?'

'The two maidens had vanished, I said.' The Green Lady fixed him with a piercing glance. 'Do you have anything to add? Any comments?'

'No. Nothing.'

'The pursuers followed your trail, but they lost it near Nysa and it was already afternoon. Only then was it decided to send a rider to Stolz Castle. The news arrived in the evening. Sir Jan Biberstein sent out a call to arms to his vassals but couldn't take any concrete measures before dawn. Before the soldiers had gathered, the Cistercians in Kamieniec were already ringing the Sext. And when they were ringing the Nones, the two maidens, Katarzyna and Jutta, suddenly appeared at Stolz in the convoy of an Armenian merchant. Both in one piece, healthy and at first glance inviolate.

'As a result,' she continued in the face of Reynevan's silence, 'it was one of the briefest kidnappings in the history of Silesia. The commonplace affair bored everybody and was soon forgotten. Or at least until Candlemas. Meaning until Katarzyna Biberstein's delicate condition could no longer be concealed.'

Reynevan's face gave nothing away. The Green Lady watched him beneath her eyelashes.

'Only then,' she continued, 'did Jan of Biberstein go truly berserk. He offered a reward of a hundred silver grzywna to whoever found and turned in the kidnappers, and if they were themselves embroiled in the affair, an additional amnesty to avoid punishment. Sir Jan also put the screws on his daughter, but Kasia dug in her heels: she knew nothing, remembered nothing, had been unconscious and nauseous, blah, blah, blah. Jutta of Apolda, who was suspected not to have escaped with her maidenhood intact, either, also dug in her heels.

'Time passed, Katarzyna's belly grew quickly and beautifully, and the direct creator of that wonder of nature still remained unknown. Jan Biberstein raged and the whole of Silesia enjoyed the rumours. But a hundred grzywna is a considerable sum. Someone appeared who cast light on the affair – a participant in the robbery and kidnap, a certain Notker Weyrach. He wasn't stupid enough to believe in the pledges of immunity, preferring to conduct the case from a distance via his kinsmen – the Bolz family of Zeiskenberg – before whom, in the presence of a priest, he swore on the cross and gave testimony. And the cat was out of the bag. Or rather you were, my ephebe.

'The noble daughter of the noble Jan, swore Weyrach, was shown respect by the kidnappers, no one laid a finger on her or offended her honour with even a bold glance. Unfortunately, there happened to be in the honourable Raubritter company, quite by accident, a certain avowed miscreant, good-for-nothing debauchee and sorcerer to boot. He, bearing a grudge against Sir Jan, used magic to seize his daughter from the kidnappers and assuredly raped the poor child. Doubtless making use of black magic, so the poor thing remained unaware of what went on. The scoundrel and rapist went by the alias of Reinmar of

Hagenau, but news travels fast, people put two and two together and the truth always comes out. It was revealed to be none other than Reinmar of Bielawa, known as Reynevan.'

'And that was sworn on the cross? The heavens are indeed forbearing.'

She snorted. 'Weyrach's revelations would have been believed without a cross, too. The reputation of Reinmar of Bielawa was already established in Silesia. He had already used witchcraft to coerce women ... Suffice to recall the affair with Adèle of Stercza ... You've paled a little, I see. Out of fear?'

'No. Not out of fear.'

'I thought not. Returning to the matter in hand: no one questioned the Raubritter's testimony, no one had any doubts. No one thought twice. Save me.'

'Indeed?'

'Weyrach swore that only one maiden had been kidnapped: Biberstein's daughter, to be precise. Only her. The second maid remained with the strongbox; she was ordered to pass on the ransom demand ... Do you have anything to add?'

'I do not.'

'And nothing surprises you about the story?'

'Nothing.'

'Even that the pursuers didn't find the other girl, Jutta of Apolda? And that the following day both maidens returned to Stolz? Together, even though, if Weyrach is to be believed, one was kidnapped twice in one day and the other not once? Doesn't even that astonish you?'

'Not even that.'

'You can't be so resistant to astonishment,' she suddenly sneered, and anger flashed in her blue eyes. 'Thus, you mock me.'

'You do me an injustice, madam, imputing that to me. Or – which is more likely – you're toying with me.'

'You know best what happened to the maids, first-hand. You were there, you don't deny it, you took part in the robbery. Weyrach's account points to you as the father of Katarzyna Biberstein's child, and you indeed do not deny it, you appear only to suggest that the commerce occurred with her consent. Which seems strange, if not quite improbable . . . But also conceivable . . . You are paling and blushing by turns, my boy. Which makes one think.'

'Naturally,' he blurted out. 'It must. I was found guilty in advance. I'm a rapist, which was determined by the testimony of a person as credible as Notker Weyrach, a brigand and a bandit. Biberstein will order me executed as his daughter's molester and rapist. Without giving me, naturally, the chance to defend myself. And the fact that I shall pale and blush by turns while being dragged to my death, protesting my innocence? Every rapist does the same. But who would lend credence?'

'You are so righteously and sincerely indignant that *I* almost do—'

'Almost?'

'Almost.'

She spurred on her mare and rode ahead. And waited for him. Watching him with a smile he couldn't decipher.

'Faulbrück is up ahead.' She pointed to a church steeple sticking above the trees. 'We shall stop here. I am hungry. And thirsty. Neither should you disdain the chance to drink, Reinmar. *Carpe diem*, my boy, *carpe diem*. Who knows what tomorrow may bring? And thus . . . let us make merry as my kinsman, the Bishop of Krakow, Zawisza of Kurozwęki, used to say. Does that surprise you? I am, know you, of the Greater Polish Topór coat of arms, related to the bearers of the Różyc. Spur on your horse, Sir Knight. Let us make merry.'

*

362

The Green Lady's decisive movements, the way she held her head – proudly yet naturally – and particularly the way she drank – gracefully and easily, cup after cup – in all that, there was indeed something that brought to mind Zawisza of Kurozwęki. The Green Lady might, the suspicion grew somewhat in Reynevan's mind, simply be confabulating regarding her consanguinity. A good five hundred families in Poland bore the Topór coat of arms, and all of them, as was normal in Poland, could prove all sorts of family ties. Kinship with the Bishop of Krakow paled in the face of the blood ties declared by some families with King Arthur, King Solomon and King Priam. But looking at the Green Lady, Reynevan couldn't rid himself of associations with Zawisza, the now legendary hell-raising bishop. And other associations following on from them, for the bishop had died as a consequence of immoral desires – he had been battered to death by a father whose daughter he had tried to ravish. And the lecher's soul had been transported straight to Hell by devils, calling in wild voices, heard by many: 'Let us make merry!'

'I drink to you, Reinmar.'

'Your good health, madam.'

She had changed for dinner. Her dormouse calpac had been replaced by a velvet rondlet with a band and a muslin *liripipe*. Her dark blonde hair, now revealed, was gathered on the back of her neck in a golden net. A modest string of pearls shone on her quite boldly bare neck. The white *cotehardie* worn over the green gown had plunging slashes at the sides, allowing one to admire her waist and the pleasing curves of her hips. Those extremely fashionable slashes were called by their critics *les fenêtres d'enfer*, for it was claimed they tempted one to mortal sin. There was indeed something in it.

Liebenthal and his company were occupying a bench in

the corner behind the fireplace and getting drunk in brooding silence.

The innkeeper moved to and fro, serving wenches hurried busily back and forth with dishes, and the Green Lady's servants also helped, which meant the food and drink arrived quickly. The food was simple but tasty, the wine tolerable; surprisingly good for an inn of that class.

They said nothing for a time, a taut energy sparking between them, turning their attention to beer soup with egg yolks, local trout from the Piława, wild boar sausages, hare in cream and pierogis.

Then there was caraway cake and Cypriot Malvasia, ginger-bread and more Malvasia, the fire in the hearth crackled, the servants stopped interfering and Liebenthal and company went to bed in the stables. It was now very quiet and warm, hot even, the blood pulsed in the temples and burned on the cheeks. The fire was reflected in flaming glances.

'Your good health, dear ephebe.'

'And yours, madam.'

'Drink. Do you want to say anything?'

'I've never . . . I've never ravished a woman. Neither using violence, nor magic. Never, ever. Believe me, madam.'

'I do. Though it's difficult to admit it . . . You have the eyes of Tarquin, gorgeous boy.'

'You're making fun of me.'

'Not a bit of it. Sometimes, neither violence nor magic are needed to seduce a woman.'

'What do you mean by that?'

'I'm a riddle. Solve me.'

'Madam—'

'Don't say anything. Drink. *In vino veritas.*'

*

The fire in the hearth had died down and was glowing red. The Green Lady rested an elbow on the table and her chin on her knuckles.

'Tomorrow,' she said, and her voice vibrated throatily and enticingly, 'we shall arrive at Stolz. Whichever way you look at it, you know perfectly well, tomorrow will be for you . . . an important day. We can't know or predict what will happen, for God moves in mysterious ways. But . . . Perhaps this night . . .'

'I know,' he replied when she paused, then stood up and bowed low. 'I am aware, O gracious lady, of the gravity of this night. I know it may be my last. Which is why I wish to spend it . . . in prayer.'

She said nothing for a while and drummed her fingers on the table. She looked him straight in the eyes. For so long that he eventually lowered his.

'In prayer,' she repeated with a smile, and it was a smile worthy of Lilith. 'Ha! That is also a way to drive off sinful thoughts . . . Oh well, then I, too, shall spend the night in prayer. And contemplation. On transience. On how *transit gloria*.'

She stood up and he knelt down. At once. She touched his hair and then quickly withdrew her hand. He thought he heard a sigh. But it might have been his own.

'Beautiful lady.' He lowered his head still further. 'Green Lady. Your *gloria* will never pass. Neither your *gloria*, nor your beauty, neither of which have their equal. Oh . . . If only fate had brought us together in other—'

'Say nothing,' she murmured. 'Say nothing and go now. I will also go. I must to my prayers.'

They reached Stolz the following day.

Chapter Fourteen

In which various facts come to light at Stolz Castle. Including the fact that to blame for everything are, respectively: the perversity of women and Wolfram Pannewitz.

Jan of Biberstein, Lord of Stolz Castle, was almost identical to his brother Ulrik. It was known that the Lord of Stolz was much younger than the Lord of Frydland, but it wasn't conspicuous. It was caused by the knight's appearance, which was truly Homeric. He had the height of a titan, the build of a hero and shoulders worthy of Ajax. In order to utterly exhaust the Homeric comparisons, the faces and Greek noses of the two Biberstein gentlemen instantly brought to mind Agamemnon the Atreides, ruler of Mycenae. Grave, proud, lordly, noble – but not in the best of humour that day.

Jan of Biberstein was waiting for them in the chamber armoury, a high-ceilinged, harshly cold chamber stinking of ironmongery.

He was decidedly *not* in the best of humour.

'Everybody out!' he commanded right to begin with, in a voice that shook the spears and glaives on stands by the wall. 'Private and family matters are going to be discussed here! I said, everybody out! This does not apply to m'Lady Cup-Bearer, naturally. You are welcome here and your presence is desired.'

The Green Lady nodded slightly and adjusted her sleeve with

a gesture indicating mild interest. Reynevan didn't believe it. She was interested. Very interested, probably.

The Lord of Stolz crossed his arms on his chest. Perhaps it was by chance, but he was standing such that the shield with the red horn on the wall was positioned directly above his head.

'It must have been the Devil,' he said, looking at Reynevan as Polyphemus must have looked at Odysseus and his companions. 'The Devil must have tempted me to go to Ziębice for the tournament on the Birth of the Virgin Mary. The Devil was embroiled in it, without a doubt. But for devilish forces, none of those misfortunes would have happened. I never would have heard of you. Wouldn't have known you exist. Wouldn't have to fret over the fact that you exist. Wouldn't have had to go to such trouble to finally stop you existing.'

He was silent for a time. Reynevan was quiet. He was even breathing quietly.

'Some say,' Biberstein continued, 'you defiled my daughter out of revenge, for a grudge you bore against me. The Bishop of Wrocław, gracing the affair with his attention, declares that it was because of Hussite and heretical instigation to maltreat me, a Catholic. Duke Jan of Ziębice claims, however, that you are a degenerate and have a criminal nature. It is also said that you are in league with the Devil and the Devil procures your victims. It is all one to me, frankly speaking, but just out of interest: why did you do it? Answer me when I question you!'

Reynevan suddenly realised he had completely and absolutely forgotten the defence summation he had composed in advance for that circumstance and which was intended to eclipse that of Socrates. He realised that with a feeling closer to horror.

'I do not mean . . .' He put all his effort into making his voice sound strong. 'I do not mean to lie or put on a good front. I take responsibility for . . . For what happened. For the results . . . Miss Katarzyna and I . . . Sir Jan, it is true that I am at fault. But I am not a criminal, I have been slandered in your eyes. What happened between myself and Miss Katarzyna . . . There was no evil intent. I swear on my mother's grave, neither evil intent, nor premeditation. It was determined by chance—'

'Chance,' Biberstein repeated slowly. 'Let me guess: you're walking along without evil intent, returning home, let's suppose, from a tavern. The night is dark, pitch black. In the gloom, by chance, my daughter bumps into you and wallop! Quite by chance, she impales herself on your cock, which by chance is sticking out of your britches. Was it thus? If so, you are absolved in my eyes.'

'I am prepared,' Reynevan took a breath, 'to make amends—'

'It is to your credit that you are. For you shall. Today.'

'I'm prepared to wed Miss Katarzyna.'

'Oh!' Biberstein turned his head towards the Green Lady, who appeared preoccupied with contemplating her fingernails. 'Did you hear, m'Lady Cup-Bearer? He is ready! On hearing that *dictum*, should I be beside myself with joy? Knowing the bastard will have a father and Kasia a husband? Has no one explained the situation to him? That all I need do is snap my fingers and a queue of forty suitors will form. And that I, Biberstein, can take my own sweet time choosing a husband for my daughter. Listen, you pup. You don't fulfil the conditions to be Kasia's husband. You are an outcast. You are a heretic. And if that wasn't enough, you're a pauper. A beggar. Yes, yes, Jan of Ziębice has confiscated the entire patrimony of the Bielawa family. For treason and heresy.

'But above all else,' the Lord of Stolz raised his voice, 'an example is needed. Quite a palpable one. One that will be talked about in Silesia. One that will be long remembered. When there is a lack of terror, when crimes go unpunished, society becomes demoralised. Am I right?'

No one challenged the statement. Jan Biberstein went closer and looked Reynevan in the eyes.

'I have thought long and hard ... about what I would do to you when I finally caught you. I have studied much, and without affronting antiquity, recent history has proved to be the most instructive when it comes to novel punishments. In 1419, barely eight years ago, when Catholic Czech lords caught Calixtines, they executed them in imaginative ways, trying to outdo each other with their invention. In my estimation, the victor's laurel must go to Sir Jan Švihovský of Rýzmberk. Lord Švihovský ordered that a Hussite he caught have black powder stuffed into his mouth and down his throat and then be set alight. Eyewitnesses claim that when it exploded, fire and smoke belched out of the heretic's backside.

'When I heard about that,' Biberstein continued, clearly delighting in Reynevan's horrified expression, 'I received enlightenment. I was certain what to have done to you. I shall go further than Lord Švihovský, however. Having stuffed you full of powder, I shall have a lead ball shoved up your arse and measure how far it flies. A rear-end shot like that ought to satisfy both my paternal feelings and my scientific curiosity. What do you think?

'I must declare to you, not without satisfaction,' he went on, not waiting for an answer, 'that I shall beset you terribly after your death, too. I considered it idiotic and a waste of effort, but my chaplain insisted. You are a heretic, so I shan't bury your remains in holy ground, but rather order them tossed somewhere for the ravens to eat. Since, if I remember rightly: *quibus viventibus non communicavimus mortuis communicare non possumus.*'

'I am in your hands, Lord Biberstein,' said Reynevan, and

resignation helped him gather the remains of his courage. 'At your mercy. Act with me as you deem fit. If you want to act like a butcher, who will stop you? Or perhaps you're frightening me with torture in the hope that I'll begin to beg for mercy? Not a bit of it, Sir Jan. I am a nobleman. And I shall not demean myself before the father of the maiden I love.'

'Nicely put,' the Lord of Stolz said coldly. 'Nicely and boldly. You again arouse scholarly curiosity in me: how long will your courage last? Ha, let's not waste time; the gunpowder and ball are waiting. Do you have any last requests?'

'I should like to see Miss Katarzyna.'

'Ah! And what else? Rut her one last time?'

'And my son. You cannot forbid me that, Sir Jan.'

'I can. And I shall.'

'I love her!'

'I shall soon remedy that.'

'Sir Jan,' spoke the Green Lady, and the timbre of her voice called to mind various things, including honey. 'Display magnanimity. Show chivalry, with examples of which recent history also abounds. Even the Czech Catholic lords granted the last requests of the Hussites, I believe, before stuffing them with gunpowder. Grant the request of the young Lord of Bielawa, Sir Jan. The lack of examples of magnanimity, I observe, demoralises society no less than undue leniency. Furthermore, I ask you on his behalf.'

'And that decides it.' Biberstein bent his head. 'That decides it, m'lady. It shall be thus. Hey there! Servants!'

The Lord of Stolz issued orders and the servants ran away to execute them. After a painfully lengthy period of waiting, the door creaked. Two women entered the armoury. And one child. A little boy. Reynevan felt a wave of heat run through him and the blood rushing to his cheeks. He also noticed his mouth had dropped open. He clamped it shut, not wanting to look like a dumbstruck moron. He was not certain of the result. He must have looked like one. For that was how he felt.

One of the women was a matron, another a young maid, and the difference in age and the striking similarity left no doubt – it was a mother and daughter. Nor was it difficult to place their origin, particularly for somebody who – like Reynevan – had once heard a lesson about the typical hereditary traits of women and maids of the most notable Silesian families, a lesson given by Lady Formosa of Krossig at the Raubritter Bodak Castle. Both the matron and the maiden were rather short and rather stocky, wide in the hips like women from the Pogorzela family who had married into the Biberstein family long before. Their small, snub and very freckly noses also testified irrefutably to the Pogorzela blood flowing in their veins.

Reynevan didn't know and had never seen the matron. The maiden he had seen sometime before, and only once. The little boy clutching her skirt had light-coloured eyes, plump hands, a head covered in golden curls and generally speaking was a silly little thing – in other words: a small, gorgeous, chubby, freckled cherub. Reynevan had no idea who he had inherited his looks from. And all in all, it didn't concern him much.

Reynevan only needed a moment for the above-mentioned observations and reflections, which required several sentences to describe. For according to the more learned astronomers of that age, an hour – *hora* – was divided into *puncta*, *momenta*, *unciae* and *atomi*, so one could conclude that Reynevan's reflections took no more than one ounce and thirty atoms.

Sir Jan Biberstein required more or less the same number of ounces and atoms to analyse the situation. His face darkened dangerously, his Homeric brow frowned threateningly, the nostrils of his Greek nose flared and his moustache bristled

371

ominously. That angelic grandson had for a grandfather, it turned out, an evil old devil. And at that moment, the Lord of Stolz of resembled one so faithfully that you could have painted him on a church fresco.

'It's not this maiden,' he stated, and when he spoke, there was a growling in his throat. 'It turns out it isn't that maiden at all. Somebody is trying to make an idiot out of me. Lady wife.' His voice rumbled in the armoury like a wagon laden with empty coffins. 'Would you mind taking our daughter to the ladies' chambers and talking some sense into her, in any manner you consider appropriate. For my part, I suggest applying a birch switch to her bare backside until you succeed in obtaining some information. When you come into possession of that information, my dear lady wife, and are able to share it with me, appear before me. And don't try to do so any earlier, nor for any other reason.'

The matron paled slightly but only curtsied, without uttering a word. Reynevan caught sight of her expression as she tugged her daughter by a white sleeve peeping out from under a green *cotehardie*. It wasn't an especially kind expression. The daughter – Katarzyna of Biberstein – also looked on. Through tears. There was reproach in her eyes. And sadness. He could only guess at what saddened her and what she reproached him for. But he didn't feel like guessing. It no longer interested him. Katarzyna of Biberstein no longer interested him. All his senses flew towards another person. About whom, he suddenly realised, he knew nothing. Apart from her name, which he now knew.

When the women had left with the little boy, Jan of Biberstein swore. Then he swore again.

'*Nec cras, nec heri, nunquam ne credas mulieri*,' he growled. 'Why is there so much perversity in you women? M'Lady Cup-Bearer?'

'We are contrary.' The Green Lady smiled the lethal, charming smile of a demoness. 'We are devious. For we are the daughters of Eve. After all, it's said we were formed from a crooked rib.'

'You said it.'

'However,' said the Green Lady, glancing at Reynevan under her eyelashes, 'in spite of appearances, it isn't so easy to delude us. Or seduce us. Ever since the Garden of Eden, we have been known to succumb to serpents, that's true. But never snakes in the grass.'

'What do you mean by that?'

'I'm a riddle. Solve me, Sir Jan.'

The gleam in Jan Biberstein's eye dimmed as soon as it appeared.

'My esteemed Lady Cup-Bearer,' he said, stressing her title more than before, 'is being playful. But it's no time for mischief. Am I right, Lord of Bielawa? Or perhaps I'm mistaken? Perhaps you are joyous? Perhaps you think you're out of the soup? Wriggled out of trouble like an eel? It's a long way from that, believe me. Lucky for you, you didn't impregnate my Kasia. But you fell on her like a brigand, and for that alone you ought to be quartered. Or, since you're a heretic, you should be turned over to the bishop so he can roast you at a stake in Wrocław. Perhaps you wanted to say something, madam? Or am I mistaken?'

'You are.'

The door creaked and the matron entered the armoury. Without her cap. A little flushed. Chest heaving.

'Oh,' said Sir Jan, pleased. 'So soon?'

Lady Biberstein glanced at her husband with forgiving superiority, went up to him and whispered into his ear for a long time. The longer she whispered, the more Sir Jan beamed.

'Ha!' he finally cried, beaming all over his face. 'Young Wolfram Pannewitz! Ha, 'pon my soul! I know him! He was wandering around Goleniowskie Forests, playing at being a knight errant.

He must have chanced upon her when she fled from the strong-box ... Ha, by a hundred horned devils! Why, I remember! And when he came here later, do you remember, wife, how he shot glances, flushed and slavered ... Brought gifts! Ha! But there was no desire to wed! Now there will be. For he's a decent match, my dear wife, quite decent. I'll soon visit old Lord Pannewitz in Homole and we'll converse, father to father, about our children's japes. We shall converse about honour—'

He broke off, glanced at the Green Lady and Reynevan, as though astonished that they were still there. He scowled.

'I should—'

'You shouldn't do anything,' the Green Lady interrupted sternly. 'I shall deal with the matter. I'll take him with me and leave right away.'

'Won't you stop the night, m'lady? It's a long way to Schönau—'

'I'm leaving right away. Farewell, Sir Jan.'

The Green Lady hurried, forcing her entourage to make haste. They headed north, towards the rocks and hills. They rode swiftly, the misty Ślęża massif ahead of them and the blue Rychleby and Jeseníky behind them. Reynevan rode at the end of the procession, not really knowing where to or why. He hadn't yet recovered his composure. The ride didn't last long, however. The Green Lady suddenly gave the order to stop, then indicated with a movement of her head for Reynevan to ride behind her.

There was a penitentiary cross standing at the foot of the hill. Crosses like that usually made Reynevan ponder and prompted him to contemplate. Now the cross didn't evoke anything.

'Dismount.'

He did as he was told. She stood before him, the wind blowing her cape around, making it cling to her.

'We shall part here,' she said. 'I'm going to Strzelin and from

there home to Schönau. Your company would not be politic.
Understand? Cope by yourself.'

He nodded. She moved close to him and looked him in the
eyes. Briefly. And then looked away.

'You seduced my daughter, you scoundrel,' she said softly. 'And
I ... I, rather than slapping you across the face and showing
you contempt, have to blush, and in my heart be grateful that
you ... You know what. Ha, you're also blushing? Good. That's a
comfort, at least. A paltry one, but still.'

She bit her lips.

'I am Agnes of Apolda. The wife of Cup-Bearer Berthold
Apolda. The mother of Jutta of Apolda.'

'I presumed so.'

'Better late than never.'

'I wonder when you guessed.'

'Earlier. But never mind. Fortune favours you,' she continued.
'You're a perfect example of fortune's darling. But stop tempting
fate. Flee. Vanish from Silesia, for ever if possible. You're not safe
here. Biberstein wasn't your only enemy. You have plenty, and
sooner or later one of them will catch you and kill you.'

'I have to stay,' he said, biting his lips. 'I won't go until I see—'

'My daughter, yes?' She squinted dangerously. 'I forbid you.
I'm sorry, but I won't consent to the liaison. You aren't a worthy
match for Jutta. Jan of Ziębice has indeed confiscated everything
you owned. I'm not as calculated as Biberstein and could survive
having a pauper for a son-in-law, wealthy only in heart, may love
conquer all, but I won't let my daughter marry a hunted outlaw.
You, if you have any decency at all – and I know you do – won't
allow your enemies to follow your trail to her. You won't expose
her to danger and harm. Confirm that.'

'I confirm. But I'd like to—'

'Don't,' she interrupted at once. 'There's no point. Forget her.

And let her forget. It's already been two years, my boy. I know this will hurt you, but I'll say it: time has tremendous healing powers. Cupid's arrow sometimes penetrates deep, but even those wounds heal in time, if you don't pick at them. She'll forget. Perhaps she already has. I'm not saying that to hurt you. On the contrary: to allay the pain. You're fretting with thoughts of responsibility, of duty. Of your debt. You have no debts, Reinmar. You're free of obligations. Perhaps I'll be bluntly prosaic – why poeticise it? The fact that you slept together is a meaningless episode.'

Reynevan didn't answer. She went close to him, very close.

'The encounter with you . . .' she whispered, gingerly touching his cheek. 'The encounter with you was a pleasure. I shall remember it. But I wouldn't want to meet you again. Or see you. Never and nowhere. Is that clear? Answer me.'

'It is.'

'Just in case fresh ideas occur to you, know this: Jutta isn't at Schönau. She's gone away. There's no sense asking anybody at the castle or in the vicinity, for no one knows her whereabouts. Do you see?'

'I do.'

'Then farewell.'

Chapter Fifteen

In which Reynevan – thanks to a certain anarchist – finally meets his beloved.

The innkeeper's wife passing by his table glanced at him enquiringly, her eyes indicating the empty mug. Reynevan shook his head. He'd drunk enough. Besides, the beer was nothing special. To be precise, it was lousy. Like the food. The fact that there were plenty of guests despite that could only be down to the lack of competition. Reynevan himself had stopped there, in Ciepłowody, on learning that the next inn was in Przerzeczyn, on the Wrocław road, but it was just over a mile to Przerzeczyn and dusk was falling.

I need some help, he thought.

He'd been analysing the situation for almost an hour and trying to work out a sensible plan of action. Each time, he came to the conclusion that he wouldn't achieve much without help.

After parting from Agnes of Apolda, the Green Lady, and overcoming the dejection her words had caused him, he rode to Powojowice. What he found there disheartened him even more. The steward whom Duke Jan of Ziębice had appointed to Peterlin's confiscated estate needed barely two years to utterly ruin the famous and prospering fulling mill. Nicodemus Verbruggen, the Flemish dyeing master, had uprooted, it turned out, to somewhere in Greater Poland, unable to endure the harassment. New payments kept being added to Duke Jan's ledger. *The time will come*, thought Reynevan, grinding his teeth, *when accounts will be settled, Your Grace. A time for accounting. And payments.*

For the time being, though, I need help. I won't get much done here without help.

Two inconspicuous men were sitting in one corner, hunched over beer mugs. They were dressed simply and meagrely but were too clean for ordinary vagabonds, and nor did their faces bear the mark of chronic undernourishment. One had very bushy eyebrows, the second a ruddy and shining face. They were both wearing hoods. Both, Reynevan observed, often – too often – glanced towards him.

I need help. Who can I ask? Canon Otto Beess? I'd have to go to Wrocław and that's risky.

To the monks of the monastery of the Holy Spirit in Brzeg? It's doubtful they still remember me; five years have passed since I worked in the hospital. Furthermore, Birkart Grellenort might have eyes and ears there, too. Perhaps, then, I should go to Świdnica? Justus Schottel and Simon Unger, Scharley's friends from the printing works in Kraszewice Street, will certainly remember me – I helped them for four days with their obscene paintings and woodcuts.

That's probably the best plan, he thought. *Scharley and Samson, who will be searching for me in Silesia – there's no doubt about that – will surely end up at the printing works. Until that time, I'll hide there, think up other plans, including . . .*

Including a plan of how to get closer to Nicolette in secret.

The two men in the corner were talking softly, leaning over the table and drawing their hooded heads close. For some time, they hadn't looked towards Reynevan once.

Perhaps I'm imagining it, he thought, *perhaps my suspicions are now becoming pathological? I see and smell eavesdroppers every-where. Like now, for example, that tall character at the bar, swarthy and dark-haired, resembling a journeyman, is looking at me surrep-titiously. Or so it seems, at least.*

To Świdnica, then, he decided, standing up and tossing a few coins on the table from what the Green Lady had given him when they parted. *To Świdnica, via Rychbach.* Riding the horse that the Green Lady had lent him.

After leaving the smoky tavern, he breathed in the November evening air, which now carried a boreal scent of winter, a harbin-ger of frosts and snowstorms.

It's the twelfth of November, he thought, *the day after Saint Martin's Day. It'll be Advent in three Sundays. In another four, it'll be Christmas.* He stopped for a moment, looking up at the sky, streaked fiery-purple in the west. *I'll set off with the dawn*, he decided, entering a lane and heading towards the stable where the horse was being kept and where he planned to sleep. *If I don't dawdle, I'll make it to Świdnica before the gates are closed . . .*

He tripped. On a body. Lying on the ground, right by the threshold to a cottage, was a man. Reynevan recognised him at once. It was one of the men from the tavern, the one with the bushy eyebrows. Now that the hood and hat had fallen off, a tonsure was visible, shaved down all the way to a thin ring of hair above the ears. He was lying in a pool of blood. His throat had been cut from ear to ear.

A crossbow bolt slammed into the beam above Reynevan's head with such force that straw fell from the roof of the porch. Reynevan jumped aside and cowered as another bolt thudded into the whitewashed wall right beside his face, sprinkling him with lime dust. He fled in panic; seeing to his left the black abyss of the lane, he ducked into it without hesitation. The fletching of a third bolt hissed beside his ear.

He cleared some barrels and a muck heap and ran into an arcade. And collided with somebody. So hard that they both fell down.

The stranger was first to his feet. It was the other man from the tavern, the one with the shiny face. He also had a tonsure. Reynevan picked up a thick log from a pile by the wall and aimed a blow at him.

'No!' cried the fellow with the tonsure, retreating against the wall. 'No! I'm not—'

He spluttered and puked blood. He didn't fall but remained suspended. A bolt was sticking out under his chin, pinning him to a post. Reynevan hadn't even heard the whistle. He cowered and rushed into the lane.

'You! Stop!'

He stopped so abruptly that he skidded over the slippery grass, straight in front of a horse. His very own horse. The bay from the Green Lady whose reins were being held by the tall, swarthy character resembling a journeyman.

'Into the saddle,' he commanded hoarsely, shoving the reins into his hand. 'Into the saddle, Reynevan of Bielawa. Ride! And don't stop.'

'Who are you?'

'No one. Ride! Don't tarry!'

He obeyed.

He didn't ride far; the night was pitch-black and dreadfully cold. After happening on a hayrick by the road, Reynevan buried himself deep in the hay. His teeth were chattering. From cold and fear.

Someone had made an attempt on his life in Cieplowody. But who? Biberstein, having given the matter more thought?

Duke Jan's thugs, who might have been tracking him? The

bishop's servants? The Inquisition? Who were the men with shaved heads who were watching him in the tavern? And why were they killed? Who was the character resembling an apprentice who saved him?

He lost himself in speculations. And fell asleep, utterly confused.

Reynevan was woken by the cold at dawn, and any somnolence was driven away by the tolling of bells. Quite close by, as it turned out. After digging himself out of the hayrick, he looked around and saw walls and towers. The view was familiar. In the misty and unearthly morning light, Reynevan recognised the town as Niemcza, where he had gone to school, where he had acquired learning and beatings.

He rode into town among a group of wayfarers. Hungry, he was drawn by kitchen smells, but the crowd moving along the streets dragged him instead towards the town square. It was full of people, crowded shoulder to shoulder.

'They're going to torture somebody,' stated with certainty a powerful fellow in a leather apron on being asked the reason for the gathering. 'They'll probably break him on the wheel.'

'Or shove 'im on a spike,' said a skinny woman in an apron, looking like a peasant, licking her lips.

'They'll be giving out alms, I've 'eard.'

'And indulgences. Not for nothing, but cheap, they say. For the bishop's priests have come. From Wrocław itself!'

Four people were standing on the scaffold towering above the crowd: two monks in Dominican habits, an elderly gentleman in black who looked like a clerk and a burly soldier in a kettle hat and a red and yellow tunic worn over armour. One of the Dominicans was speaking, hands raised theatrically. Reynevan listened carefully.

'This loathsome Czech heresy deranges order! It preaches evil and perverse teachings about the sacraments! It condemns marriage. Eyes fixed on carnal pleasures and bestial desires, it does away with all the legal bonds and public order that once kept crimes in check. And more than anything, craving Catholic blood, it compels anyone who doesn't agree with its errors to kill and burn with bestial cruelty: cutting off the lips and noses of some, the hands and members of others and quartering still others. Orders pictures of Jesus Christ, His Holy Mother and the other saints destroyed and despoiled—'

'When will the alms be given out, eh?' called a voice from the crowd. The soldier on the scaffold straightened up and stood with arms akimbo, scowling. The heckler was quietened down.

'In order to better explain the gravity of the matter, good folk,' said the clerk in black, meanwhile, 'in order to open your eyes to the vileness of Czech heresy, a letter from Heaven will be read. It fell from Heaven on the city of Wrocław, in front of the very cathedral, and is written in the hand of Jesus Christ, our Lord, amen.'

A whispered prayer passed through the crowd and people crossed themselves, elbowing one another. There was some confusion. Reynevan began to withdraw, pushing through the mob. He'd had enough.

On the scaffold, the other Dominican unrolled a parchment.

'Oh, you sinners and scoundrels,' he read solemnly. 'Your end is nigh. I am patient, but if you don't sever your ties with Czech heresy, if you continue to offend the Mother Church, I will curse you for ever. I shall send down on you hail, fire, thunderbolts and tempests to destroy your work. I shall lay waste your vineyards and seize all your flocks. I shall punish you with bad air and bring great poverty down on you. Thus do I admonish you and forbid you from listening to Hussites, heretic masters and other whoresons, the servants of Satan. And whoever betrays Me will not see eternal life, and blind and deaf children will be born to him—'

'Fraud!' shouted somebody from the throng in a thunderous bass. 'Swindling papist falsehood! Don't believe that, brothers, good folk! Don't give credence to fraudulent bishops!'

The soldier on the scaffold ran over to the edge and shouted some orders, pointing to where the voice came from, and the crowd swayed as halberdiers marched in, jostling people with their pikestaffs. Reynevan stopped. Things were becoming interesting.

'"Mother",' someone yelled from a completely different part of the square, in what sounded like a familiar voice. 'The Roman Church calls itself the "Mother"! But it is a cruel serpent and spat poisonous venom onto Christianity when it raised a vicious cross in its bloody hands against the Czechs and proclaimed from its venal mouth a crusade against true Christians! Priestly immorality dripping with mendacity wants to kill in Bohemia God's immortal truth, which considers God Himself its prolif-erator and defender! And whoever raises a hand against God's truth will suffer death and the torment of damnation!'

The clerk on the scaffold issued orders and pointed, and mournful bruisers in black jerkins began to force their way through the crowd towards the voice.

'Rome is a venal harlot!' bellowed a new voice from a fresh location. 'The Pope is the Antichrist!'

'The Roman Curia is a gang of thieves!' sounded a similar bass voice, but from somewhere else entirely. 'They aren't priests, but sinful scoundrels!'

A lute strummed away and a very familiar voice sang loudly and brightly.

The truth is of Christ
Lies are of the Antichrist
The priests conceal the truth
for they fear it,
Deceiving the common folk!

The people began to laugh and take up the song. The halberdiers and the sorrowful men scurried around in various directions, swearing, poking and striking with their pikestaffs, combing the square in search of the hecklers. In vain.

Reynevan stood a better chance. He knew who to look for.

'God help us, Tybald Raabe.'

The goliard retreated at the sound of the words, backing into a fence and frightening a horse standing on the other side. The horse thudded a hoof against the wall of the stable and snorted and other horses followed it.

'Young Master Reinmar . . .'Tybald Raabe got his breath back, but the pallor didn't leave his face. 'Young Master Reinmar! In Silesia? I don't believe my eyes!'

'I know him,' said the goliard's companion, a hooded dwarf. 'I've seen him before. Two years ago, on Grochowa Mountain, at the sabbath during the holiday of Mabon. Or, as you call it, the *aequinoctium*. He was with a comely maid. It turns out he's one of ours.'

He took off his hood. Reynevan gasped involuntarily.

The creature's oval, elongated head – there could be no doubt that it wasn't a human being – was adorned with short, ruddy bristles as stiff as a hedgehog's spines. The picture was completed by a nose as hooked as the Pope's on a Hussite pamphlet and bulging eyes covered with red veins. And ears. Large ears. So large, the word 'colossal' would have been more accurate.

The creature chortled, clearly amused by the impression it was causing.

'I'm a beguiler,' it boasted. 'Don't say you didn't hear me.'

'I did. A moment ago, in the square. So it's true what they say about you . . .'

'That we can direct sound from anywhere we please?' The beguiler opened its mouth, but its bass voice came from behind Reynevan, who started in astonishment.

'Indeed we can.' The beguiler smiled joyously as its voice issued from somewhere beyond the horses' stalls. 'It's child's play for us. Long ago, we used it to lure travellers into swamps,' the creature went on, its voice emerging from all sorts of places: behind the wall, under a pile of straw, from the attic. 'For amusement. We still do it, but more seldom, for we became bored of that amusement. How fucking long can you keep that up? But the skill occasionally comes in handy . . .'

'I saw and heard.'

'Let's go and have a drink,' suggested Tybald Raabe.

Reynevan swallowed. The beguiler chortled and pulled the tight hood over its head.

'Fear not,' explained the goliard with a smile. 'We've had some practice. If anyone's taken aback, we tell him he's a foreigner. A stranger from distant lands.'

'From Samogitia.' The beguiler sniffed and wiped its nose on its sleeve. 'Tybald even gave me a Samogitian nickname. My right name is Malevolt, Jon Malevolt. But call me "Brazauskas" in company.'

The innkeeper placed another jug on the table and glanced once again with interest at the beguiler.

'What's it like in that Samogitia?' he said, unable to restrain himself. 'As dear as it is here?'

'Even dearer,' Jon Malevolt replied gravely. 'They want fifteen groschen for any old bear now. I'd move permanently to these parts, but they water down the drinks a little too much.'

The innkeeper went away without revealing whether he'd understood the allusion. Tybald Raabe scratched his head. Reynevan had just finished his tale. Tybald gave him his complete attention and didn't interrupt once. He now appeared to be lost in recollections.

'My dear Reinmar,' he finally said, abandoning the annoying mannerism of addressing him as 'young master', 'if you expect any advice from me, it'll be dead simple. Flee from Silesia. I'd warn you that you have plenty of enemies here, but you're perfectly aware of that, after all. For that's why you're here, isn't it? So listen to some good advice: flee to Bohemia. Your enemies here are a tiny bit too powerful for you to harm them.'

'Indeed?'

'Indeed, unfortunately.' The goliard looked at him keenly, fixing him with a piercing gaze. 'In particular Jan, Duke of Ziębice, is a little beyond your reach. I know he plundered your possessions – I saw how he ruined Sir Piotr's fulling mill. And I know sufficient about the circumstances of Adèle Stercza's death to be able to see through your designs. Thus, I advise: abandon them. Duke Jan doesn't give two hoots about your declarations of vengeance against him.'

'Your conclusions are too hasty,' said Reynevan, sipping from a cup of wine, which was indeed a little too watered down. 'Too hasty, Tybald. Perhaps I have other tasks and affairs in Silesia, another mission? Would you dissuade me from them? You? After what I saw in Niemcza town square?'

The beguiler chortled. 'Good, wasn't it?' It grinned, showing crooked teeth. 'They were racing about in the crowd like spaniels, spinning around like turds in an ice hole . . .'

'It's our job,' said Tybald Raabe more seriously. 'Agitation is vital. And Malevolt works with me, helps me, as you saw. Supports our cause. He shares our convictions.'

'Oh!' Reynevan showed his interest. 'Regarding the teachings of Wycliffe and Huss? The abolition of papal primacy? Communion *sub utraque specie* and modifications to the liturgy? The need for reform in the Church?'

'No,' interrupted the beguiler. 'None of that. I'm not an idiot, and only an idiot could believe that your Church is reformable. But I still support every revolutionary movement and insurrection. For the goal is nothing and the movement is everything. The world must be shaken at its foundations. Call forth chaos and confusion! Anarchy is the mother of order, for fuck's sake. Let the old order crumble, let it go up in flames! And in the ashes will remain a shining diamond, the dawn of eternal victory.'

'I see.'

'Like hell you do. Innkeeper! More wine!'

The innkeeper, surprisingly, appeared to have taken to heart Malevolt's snide remark, because he began to serve slightly less watered-down wine. The effects weren't long in the coming – the beguiler posing as a Samogitian was soon leaning against the wall, snoring. And since the inn had emptied, Reynevan decided it was time to talk frankly.

'I need a place to hide, Tybald. And for a longer rather than a shorter time. Until Christmas. Perhaps even longer.'

Tybald Raabe raised an enquiring eyebrow, and, without needing further prompting, Reynevan gave an account of what happened in Cieplowody. In detail.

'You have plenty of enemies in Silesia,' the goliard concluded, none too originally. 'In your shoes, I wouldn't go into hiding but would take to my heels. At least as far as Bohemia. Haven't you considered such a solution?'

'I must . . . hmm . . . stay.' Reynevan avoided his gaze, not certain how much he could reveal. For Tybald Raabe was a sly fox.

'I get it.' The latter winked knowingly. 'Got orders, have we? I knew Neplach would know how to use you. I expected that. Urban Horn did, too. Horn also guesses what this is all about.'

'And what *is* it all about, if one may ask?'

'The Vogelsang.'

'What is the Vogelsang?'

'Hmm, ahem . . .' Tybald coughed unexpectedly and scratched his nose in embarrassment. 'I don't know if I ought to tell you. Since you're asking, it means Flutek didn't tell you. Though I reckon it's better for you not to know.'

'What is the Vogelsang?'

'In 1423,' Gregorz Hejncze said to Łukasz Bożyczko, 'Jan Žižka ordered the creation of special task forces, which were to be sent beyond Bohemia's borders into enemy territory, where Žižka was already planning to transfer the fight for the Chalice. The forces were meant to operate in strict secret, quite independent of the usual spy networks. Their sole task was to prepare the way for aggressive forays into neighbouring countries. They were supposed to help the Taborites with their plundering raid by using sabotage and acts of terror and by spreading panic. The groups were set up and sent out. To Austria, Bavaria, Hungary, Lusatia and Saxony. And Silesia, naturally. The Silesian group received the code name—'

'The Vogelsang . . .' whispered Bożyczko.

'The Vogelsang,' Tybald Raabe confirmed. 'As I was saying, the group reported directly to the commander-in-chief. Contact was maintained using special liaison agents. It happened that the Vogelsang's liaison agent perished – he was murdered – and then contact was lost – the Vogelsang simply vanished. The reason appeared clear: the group feared treachery. Each fresh liaison agent might have been a plant and that suspicion was reinforced by a wave of arrests directed at the networks and sub-groups set up by the Vogelsang. Neplach thought long about whom to send. Someone the Vogelsang would trust.'

'And he did.' Reynevan nodded. 'For Peterlin was the Vogelsang's liaison officer. Am I right?'

'You are.'

'Neplach believes this highly confidential Vogelsang will reveal itself to me? Just because Peterlin was my brother?'

'However faint, there is a chance,' the goliard agreed gravely. 'And Flutek is desperate. It's known that Prokop the Shaven has been planning a plundering raid on Silesia for a long time. Prokop is very much counting on the Vogelsang, it's part of his strategy. He has to know whether the Vogelsang—'

'Whether the Vogelsang has been compromised.' Reynevan finished the sentence, suddenly understanding. 'The group may have been unmasked, its members captured and turned. If the agent seeking contact with the group were to be caught ... I mean, if I were caught, if I were seized and executed, it would be proof of betrayal. Am I right?'

'You are. And now what do you say to my advice? You'll treat it more seriously and vanish while you can?'

'No.'

'They're putting your head on the block. And you're letting them. Like an utter simpleton.'

'What counts is the cause,' Reynevan said after a long pause, and his voice was as solemn as a bishop's at Corpus Christi.

'What?'

'What matters most is our cause,' he repeated, and his voice was as hard as a gravestone. 'When the good of the cause is at stake, individuals matter not. If, thanks to that, the noble cause of the Chalice moves a step closer to victory, since it's meant to be a stone thrown at the ramparts of our ultimate triumph ... I'm prepared for that sacrifice.'

'Not for a long time.' It turned out the beguiler hadn't been asleep at all. 'Not for a long time have I heard anything so inane.'

*

And my dad was a carter
What he earned he spent on whores
And I'm just the same
What I earn I give to them!

The villagers of Mieczniki watched gloomily as the three riders swayed in their saddles. The one who was singing, accompanying himself on the lute, was wearing a red, horned cap with dishevelled grey hair sticking out of it. One of his companions was a handsome young man and the other an ugly dwarf in a tight hood. The dwarf looked the most drunk of the three. He could barely stay on his horse, was roaring in a deep voice, whistling through his fingers and accosting girls. The peasants had fierce expressions but didn't approach or start a brawl. The one in the red cap had a short sword in his belt and looked threatening. The ugly dwarf was patting an ugly club hanging from his saddle, whose thicker end was bound with iron and which was equipped with an iron spike. The peasants couldn't have known the club was a notorious Flemish *goedendag*, a weapon which the French knighthood had been on the receiving end of at the Battles of Courtrai, Roosebeke, Cassel and elsewhere. But its appearance was enough to discourage them.

*

'Not so loud, gentlemen,' hiccoughed the handsome young man. 'Not so loud. Let's not forget the principles of secrecy.'

'Fuck secrecy,' commented the dwarf in the hood in a drunken bass. 'On we go! I say, Raabe! Where did you say that fine tavern was? We've been riding for hours and our throats are dry!'

'About another furlong,' said the grey-haired man in the horned cap, swaying in the saddle. 'Another furlong ... Or two ... On we go! Spur your horse, Reinmar of Bielawa!'

'Tybald ... *Nomina sunt odiosa* ... Secrecy ...'

'Pshaw!'

My mamma was a washerwoman
But never washed a thing
What others washed and hung up
She swiped from the washing lines ...

The dwarf in the hood belched long and loud.

'On we go!' bellowed the bass, patting the *goedendag* at his side. 'On we go, noble lords! And what are you staring at, peasants? Churls? Cowherds?'

The folk of Grauweide looked on sombrely.

When the hour called *nox intempesta* arrived and an impenetrable darkness had absolutely muffled and embraced the monastery village of Gdziemierz, two men stole towards the dimly lit Silver Bell Inn. They were both dressed in black jerkins, close-fitting but still allowing free movement. Their heads and faces were swathed in black kerchiefs.

They circled the inn, found the kitchen door at the back and went noiselessly inside. Hidden in the darkness under the stairs, they listened to the mumbled voices that were still coming from the guest room on the first floor, despite the late hour.

Dead drunk, one of the black-clothed men signalled to the other.

Even better, replied the other, also using shared sign language. *I can only hear two voices.*

The first listened a little longer. *A troubadour and a dwarf*, he signed. *A good thing. The drunk spy is asleep in the next room. To work!*

They cautiously climbed the stairs. Now they could clearly hear the voices of the people talking, mainly a deep voice that was holding forth quite indistinctly. Regular and loud snoring could be heard coming from the chamber alongside. Weapons appeared in the hands of the men in black. The first drew a knight's misericorde. With a swift movement, the second opened a *navaja*, a folding knife with a slender, razor-sharp blade, the preferred weapon of Andalusian Gypsies.

At an agreed sign, they burst into the chamber, bounded over to the pallet, pounced on the person sleeping there and pinned them beneath the eiderdown. They plunged in their knives at the same time. And realised simultaneously that they had been taken in.

But it was too late.

The first, struck in the back of the head by the *goedendag*, was felled like a tree under a woodman's axe. The second was brought down by a blow from nowhere with a table leg. They crumpled but were still conscious, wriggling on the floor like worms, scratching at the floorboards. Until the falling *goedendag* knocked that idea out of their heads.

'Beware, Malevolt,' they heard before they plunged into oblivion. 'Don't kill them.'

'Fear not! Just another tap and that's that.'

One of the men tied up had hair as fair as straw, eyebrows and eyelashes of the same colour, and a stubbly, broad, prominent chin. The other, older man, had very thinning hair. Neither said a word or uttered a sound. They sat, tied up, backs against the wall, staring vacantly ahead. Their faces were lifeless, frozen, without a trace of emotion. They ought to have been a little astonished, if only by the fact that despite the sounds of merrymaking none of their vanquishers was drunk. By the fact that the voices had come from somewhere no one had been. By the fact that they had been expected, that they'd fallen into a precisely devised and laid trap. They ought to have been surprised. Perhaps they were. But they weren't showing it. Only now and again did the flickering of candles appear to make their lifeless eyes react. But that was only an illusion.

Reynevan sat on a pallet, watching and saying nothing. The beguiler was hiding in the corner, resting on the *goedendag*. Tybald Raabe was playing with the *navaja*, opening and closing it.

'I know you.' The goliard was the first to break the lengthening silence, pointing his knife at the balding man. 'Your name is Jakub Olbram. You lease out the mill near Łagiewniki from the Henryków Cistercians. How amusing, people generally had you down as a snitch who reported to the abbot. Was that a cover? Because I see you have other skills. Apparently, you don't shrink from contract killing, either.'

The balding character didn't react. He didn't even glance at Raabe and seemed not to hear his words at all. Tybald Raabe snapped the *navaja* open and kept it open.

'There's a small lake in the forest near here.' He turned towards Reynevan. 'With a nice, thick layer of sludge at the bottom. No one would ever find them. You can consider your mission nonexistent,' he added seriously. 'You found the Vogelsang. But it's not the Vogelsang any longer. It's a gang of thieves prepared to murder in defence of their loot. Don't you understand? The group was equipped with huge funds. A lot of money to set up networks and sabotage groups, to prepare for "special operations". They pocketed the money, embezzled it. They know what awaits them if it comes out and Flutek finds them – that's why they vanished. Now they've taken fright, they're dangerous. It was them and no one else who tried to kill you in Ciepłowody. So I advise you: show no mercy. Stones around their necks and into the lake.'

No traces of emotion appeared on the faces of the two bound men, no traces of life in their vacant eyes. Reynevan stood up and took the *navaja* out of the goliard's hand.

'Who shot a crossbow at me in Ciepłowody? Who killed the monks? You?'

Not a trace of reaction. Reynevan leaned over and cut the men's bonds, one after the other. He tossed the knife down at their feet.

'You are free,' he pronounced dryly. 'You may go.'

'You're making a mistake,' said Tybald Raabe.

'A very stupid one,' added the beguiler from the corner.

'I am Reinmar of Bielawa.' Reynevan spoke as though he hadn't heard them. 'The brother of Piotr of Bielawa, whom you once knew well. I serve the same cause as Piotr. I'm staying here, at the Silver Bell. I'll be here all week. If the Inquisition or the bishop's men appear, news of it will go to Bohemia. If I die one night at the hands of assassins, news of it will go to Bohemia. Prokop will know that the Vogelsang can't be relied upon, because the Vogelsang has ceased to exist.

'If, though,' he continued a moment later, 'it's as Tybald says, make good use of these seven days. I shall not send any reports to Bohemia until a week passes. That ought to suffice you – one can ride a long way in that time. Neplach will find you in any case, sooner or later, but that's a matter for him and you. It doesn't interest me. Now begone.'

The freed men looked at him, but it was as though they were looking at an object, a thing which held no meaning for them, to boot. Their eyes were lifeless and vacant. They didn't say a word, didn't utter a sound. They simply went out.

There was a long silence.

'Just look at him, Raabe,' said Jon Malevolt, ending the silence. 'He sacrificed himself for the cause. Curious, he doesn't look like an idiot. Aren't appearances deceptive?'

'When the Hussites get their own Pope,' added Tybald Raabe, 'he ought to declare you a saint, Reinmar. If he doesn't, it'll mean he's an ungrateful knob.'

Reynevan stayed in the Silver Bell for a week, sitting with a crossbow in his lap during the day and dozing with a knife under his pillow at night. He was alone – Tybald Raabe and the beguiler had gone into hiding. Too great a risk, they explained. Should something happen, it's better to be far away. But nothing *did* happen. No one came to arrest or murder Reynevan. The chances of becoming a martyr were diminishing from one day to the next. Tybald Raabe showed up on the twentieth of November with news and gossip. Jakub Olbram from near Łagiewniki had disappeared. Vanished like a sigh. He had no doubt taken good advantage of the week's delay that Reynevan had given him. Seven days, announced the goliard, was enough to reach Lübeck and from there take a ship to the end of the world, if needs be. In short: the Vogelsang doesn't exist, the Vogelsang can be written off, all hope of the Vogelsang can be forsaken. It would have to be reported to Prokop. Immediately. There was no time to waste.

But to be quite certain, let's wait, suggested Reynevan. Another week. Better yet, a week and a half . . .

Reynevan, however, had already lost hope, to the extent that he stopped loitering in the Silver Bell Inn killing time by reading Henry Suso's *Horologium sapientiae*, which some scholar – unable to pay for his vittles and liquor any other way – must have left there. The next morning, he saddled his horse and rode off. Glancing quite often in the direction of Brzeg and towards the village of Schönau, the estate of Cup-Bearer Berthold Apolda. The Green Lady had claimed that Nicolette wasn't in Schönau, but perhaps he could find out for himself?

Tybald, who had been stopping by in Gdziemierz more and more often, saw through him quite easily. He wasn't to be brushed off with excuses and forced Reynevan to confess. After hearing him out, he grew solemn. *Such things*, he declared, *end badly.*

'You've only just disentangled yourself from an affair with one maid, only just escaped from Biberstein's clutches by a miracle, and you're walking into more trouble again? It could cost you dearly, m'lord. Cup-Bearer Apolda isn't one to be pushed around and the bishop and Grellenort also know how many beans make five; they might already be lying in wait for you near Schönau. As might Jan of Ziębice. Your name is now well known in Silesia.'

'Well known? How so?'

'Rumours are circulating,' answered the goliard. 'It's possible that somebody is deliberately spreading them. Duke Jan has doubled the guard in Ziębice – it's said the court astrologer warned him of a possible attempt on his life. In the city, people are talking openly about an avenger, about revenge being taken for Adèle. The killings carried out in Ciepłowody are being discussed widely. The affair of the attack on the tax collector is coming back to haunt you. Diverse strange people are appearing and asking diverse strange questions. Suffice it to say,' Tybald Raabe concluded, 'it'd be more prudent to ditch your Silesian escapade. And keep well away from Schönau.

'The Vogelsang is no more, but you, Reinmar, still have a mission to accomplish in Silesia. You can expect one of Flutek's messengers before Christmas. There'll be things to do, important things; you ought not to bungle them. And if you do and it gets out it was because of your romancing, you'll answer with your life. Which would be a pity.'

Tybald rode away. But Reynevan – who had previously been undecided – now began to think endlessly about Nicolette.

Jon Malevolt, the anarchist beguiler, appeared in Gdziemierz on the twenty-eighth of November with quite an astonishing proposition. In the nearby forests, he announced, winking and licking his lips meaningfully, reside two sylvan witches, young, curvaceous and friendly, having great needs and scorning monogamy. And serving excellent bigos, what's more. He, Malevolt, was setting off to the witches for a social visit, but, as they say, the more, the merrier. Seeing Reynevan sighing, hesitating and generally squirming, the beguiler ordered a demijohn of three-year-old mead and took him to one side.

'So you're in love.' He summed up what he'd discovered, picking his teeth with a fingernail. 'You adore and long for her, quite in vain, to make things worse. It appears to be a familiar matter, particularly among you humans. I think you even like it and your poets appear unable to pen a couplet without it. But, brother, you're Toledo, after all. What – I ask you – is the purpose of love magic? What is the purpose of *philia*?'

'It would be an insult both to me and to her if I used *philia* to allure her.'

'What matters is the result, young man, the result! It's ulti-mately a question of sexual attraction, which is usually satisfied – forgive my bluntness – by sticking one thing into another. Don't make faces! There's no other way, Nature didn't plan any other. Well, if you're so virtuous, such a *preux chevalier*, I won't insist. Draw her to you, then, in the classical manner. Conjure up some flowers in the winter, a dozen red roses, purchase a dozen iced buns in town and a-courting you will go.'

'The snag is that . . . I simply don't know where to search for her.'

'Ha!' The beguiler slapped his knee. 'We'll solve that problem in a trice! Find the object of your desire? A trifle. We just need a little magic. Get up, we're going.'

'I'm not visiting the witches.'

'It's your loss, bugger you. I'll go and sample the bigos . . . Erm . . . But most importantly, I'll bring back some ingredients for a spell . . . I'll be back soon and we'll knuckle down. In order not to waste time, I'll draw a Scheva on the floor here.'

'You mean the Fourth Pentagram of Venus?'

'I see you know a thing or two. Do you know the inscription, too?'

'Elohim and El Gebil in the Hebrew script and Schii, Eli, Ayib in the Malachim alphabet.'

'Bravo. Very well, I'm off. Expect me . . . What day is it today?'

'The twenty-eighth of November. Friday before the first Sunday in Advent.'

'Then expect me on Sunday.'

The beguiler kept his word. He appeared first thing on the thirtieth of November, the first Sunday in Advent, and got down to work at once. He looked at the pentagram drawn by Reynevan with a critical eye, checked the inscriptions and nodded to indicate his approval of everything. He stood red wax candles at the corners and lit them, then shook the ingredients – mainly bunches of herbs – from his bag. He affixed a small cast-iron bowl to a tripod.

Reynevan couldn't restrain himself. 'I thought you used the magic of the Older Folk. Your own.'

'I do.'

'But the Fourth Pentagram of Venus is from the canon of human magic.'

'And where do you think people got their magical canons from?' said Malevolt, straightening up. 'Thought they invented it?'

'You mean—'

'I mean,' interrupted the beguiler, pouring salt, herbs and powders into the bowl, 'we put what's needed with what's needed. I also possess the Arcane Knowledge of humans. I've studied it.'

'Where? How?'

'In Bologna and Pavia. And how? In the normal way. What did you mean? Ah, I understand. My appearance. It surprises you, does it? Well, I'll tell you: nothing is difficult if you want it. The key is to think positively.'

'One day,' said Reynevan, sighing, 'they'll even start admitting girls to universities . . .'

'That's taking it a little too far,' the beguiler said sourly. 'We won't see girls at varsities, not even if we wait a hundred years. And it's a shame, frankly speaking. But that'll do, enough daydreaming. Let's get down to brass tacks . . . Dammit . . . Where's that flacon of blood . . . Ah, here it is.'

'Blood, Malevolt? What for? Black magic?'

'For protection. Before we begin the Scheva, we must protect ourselves.'

'From what?'

'What do you think? From danger!'

'What danger?'

'By entering the astral realm and touching the ether,' the beguiler patiently explained as though to a child, 'we put ourselves at risk. We lower our guard. We become an easy target for the *malocchio*, the Evil Eye. One may not enter the astral realm without security. I learned it in Lombardy, from the girls of Stregheria. Let us begin, we're wasting time. Repeat after me.'

In the east Samael, Gabriel, Vionarai,
In the west Anael, Burchat, Suceratos.
From the north Aiel, Aquiel, Masagariel,
From the south Charsiel, Uriel, Naromiel . . .

The candle flames pulsated. The red wax spattered.

No one knew what the catacombs beneath the Church of Saint Maciej concealed, not even the oldest and wisest residents of Wrocław. Even the Knights of the Cross with the Red Star, to whom the church belonged and who walked the floor every day, didn't know what was to be found barely a few yards beneath it. To be precise: only two of the crusaders knew the secret. Two of the group of seven Hospitallers served the Wallcreeper and were his informers. Those two knew about the hidden entrance and the magical password that opened it. The two of them – being scholars of the secret arts – also possessed Arcane Knowledge. Their task was to keep the *occultum* in order and as acolytes to assist the Wallcreeper during vivisections, necromantic experiments and demonic conjurations.

That day, only one of them was assisting the Wallcreeper. The other was sick. Or was malingering in order not to assist.

The crypt was flooded by the deathly light of a dozen candles and the devilish, flickering glow of the coals burning on a huge tripod. The Wallcreeper, in a black hooded robe, stood in front of a lectern overlaid with books, turning the leaves of Abdul Alhazred's *Necronomicon*. Beside it lay other, equally well-known and powerful magical grimoires: *Ars Notoria, Lemegeton, Arbatel, Picatrix*, as well as Honorius of Thebes' *Liber Juratus*, a notorious book and so dangerous that few dared to use the spells and formulae it contained.

In the centre of the chamber, a skeleton was lying on a large, flat block of granite resembling a catafalque. It wasn't actually a skeleton, but the detached bones of a human skeleton arranged in the correct configuration: a skull, shoulder blades, ribs, a pelvis, the bones of the upper arms and thighs, and shinbones. The skeleton was incomplete, lacking many of the small bones of the feet – carpals, metacarpals and phalanges – and several cervical and lumbar vertebrae. It was also lacking its right collarbone. All the bones were black and some were very charred. The Hospitaller assisting the Wallcreeper as an acolyte knew that the remains belonged to a certain Franciscan burned alive five years earlier for heresy and witchcraft. The Hospitaller had personally dug the bones from the ashes, then collected, segregated and arranged them by hand. To find the very smallest, he had sifted the cold charcoal through a sieve.

The Wallcreeper moved away from the lectern and stopped over a scroll of pristine parchment lying unfurled on the marble table. Having pushed up the sleeves of his black robe, he raised his arms. In his right hand, he held a wand made from a yew branch.

'*Veritas lux via,*' he began calmly, stooped humbly over the parchment, '*et vita omnium creaturarum, vivifica me.* Yecologos, Matharihon, Secromagnol, Secromehal. *Veritas lux via, vivifica me.*'

You'd have sworn a wind blew through the crypt. The candle

flames flickered and the fire on the tripod suddenly exploded. The shadows on the walls and the vaulted ceiling assumed fantastic shapes. The Wallcreeper straightened up and spread his arms in a sudden movement. '*Conjuro et confirmo super vos, Belethol et Corphandonos, et vos Heortahonos et Hacaphagon, in nomine Adonay, Adonay, Adonay, Eie, Eie, Eie, Ya, Ya, qui apparuis monte Sinai, cum glorificatione regis Adonay, Saday, Zebaoth, Anathay, Ya, Ya, Ya, Marinata, Abim, Jeia, per nomen stellae, quae est Mars, et per quae est Saturnus, et per quae est Luciferus, et per nomina omnia praedicta, super vos conjuro, Rubiphaton, Simulaton, Usor, Dilapidator, Dentor, Divorator, Seductor, Seminator, ut pro me labores!*'

Fire shot up in bursts, shadows danced. On the parchment – virginally pure until that moment – suddenly began to appear hieroglyphics, symbols, sigla and signs, at first pale, but quickly becoming darker.

'Helos, Resiphaga, lozihon,' recited the Wallcreeper, following with movements of his wand the figures as they appeared. 'Ythetendyn, Thahonos, Micemya. Nelos, Behebos, Belhores. *Et diabulus stet a dextris.*'

The Hospitaller shuddered. He recognised the gestures and formulae, enough to guess that Master Grellenort was casting a terrible spell on somebody, a spell capable from a distance of attacking the selected individual with weakness, illness, paralysis – death, even. But there wasn't enough time for dread, or to analyse whom the master had selected as his victim. The Wallcreeper held out his hand in an impatient gesture. The acolyte quickly pulled a white dove from a wooden cage and handed it to him.

The Wallcreeper calmed the fluttering bird with a gentle touch. And wrenched off its head with a sudden movement. Gripping it in his fist, he squeezed it like a lemon, straight onto the *occultum*, the spurting blood describing complicated patterns on the parchment.

'Alon, Pion, Dhon, Mibizimi! *Et diabulus stet a dextris!*'

The Wallcreeper tore the next dove into pieces, holding it by a wing and a leg. And ripped the heads off the next three with his teeth.

'Shaddai El Chai! *Et diabulus stet a dextris!*'

It takes time, thought the acolyte, *for that spell to reach the place it's been sent to. But when it does, the person who is the target will be doomed.*

Feathers and down whirled around the crypt, burned up in the fire, floating up to the ceiling on warm air. The Wallcreeper spat the feathers from his blood-covered lips and placed the wand on the parchment, wet with blood.

'Rtsa-brgyud-blama-gsum-gyaaaal!' he bellowed. 'Baib-kaa-sngags-ting-adsin-rgyaaai! Show him to me! Find him! Kill him!'

In front of the eyes of the horrified acolyte, who was no stranger to dreadful sights, a reddish glow began to veil the charred skeleton on the catafalque. The glow quickly thickened, took on a form, became more and more material and quickly clothed the skeleton in a bright body. Crimson veins and arteries of fire began to curl and spiral around the charred bones.

'N'ghaa, n'n'ghaighaaai! Iä! Iä! Find him and kill him!'

The skeleton shuddered. And moved. Its bones scraped against the granite of the catafalque. The black skull snapped its charred teeth.

'Shoggog, phthaghn! Iä! Iä! Y-hah, y-nyah! Y-nyah!'

'Scheva! Aradia!' Malevolt sprinkled a handful of powder onto the coals, a mixture of dried sagebrush and pine needles, judging by the smell. He poured blood from the flacon into the flame that shot up.

'Aradia! *Regina delle streghe!* May it cloud the eyes of he who

403

lies in wait for me. May dread seize him. *Fiat, fiat, fiat.* Eia!' The beguiler poured three drops of olive oil onto the glowing coals and snapped his fingers. 'Scheva! Eia!'

Con tre gocciole d'olio,
With three drops of olive oil,
I curse you, die, burn up, malocchio,
Vanish by the power of Aradia.
Se la Pellegrina adorerai
Tutto tu otterai!

The candle flames suddenly shot upwards.

The candles went out instantly, filling the crypt with the stench of soot. The fire on the tripod vanished into the embers and smouldered deep within it. With a rattle, the skeleton on the granite catafalque disintegrated once more into a hundred charred, black bones of various sizes.

And the parchment on the lectern covered in necromantic hieroglyphics, stained with blood and caked in dove feathers, suddenly caught fire, curled up, blackened. And disintegrated.

It became horribly cold. The magic which a moment before had filled the crypt like warm glue vanished. Utterly and irreversibly.

The Wallcreeper swore foully.

The Hospitaller gasped. Perhaps a little out of relief.

Magic was occasionally like that. There were days when nothing went right. When everything went wrong. When there was nothing else to do but give up on magic.

Before casting the love spell, Malevolt, as was customary with the Older Tribes, donned a wreath of dried stalks. He looked so ridiculous in it that Reynevan could barely keep a straight face.

The love spell was astonishingly simple: the beguiler merely sprinkled the pentagram with an extract of gentian and probably borage. He tossed some pine needles onto the glowing coals and sprinkled a few crushed whortleberry leaves on them. He snapped his fingers several times and whistled; the former and the latter were both typical for the Old Magic. But when he began the invocation, he used a verse from the Song of Songs.

'*Pone me ut signaculum super cor tuum ut signaculum super brachium tuum quia fortis est ut mors.* Ismai! Ismai! Sun Mother whose body is white from the milk of the stars! *Elementorum omnium domina*, Lady of Creation, Feeder of the World! *Regina delle streghe!*'

Una cosa voglio vedere,
Una cosa di amore
O vento, o acqua, o fiore!
Serpe strisciare, rana cantare
Ti prego di non mi abbandonare!

'Look,' whispered Malevolt. 'Look, Reynevan.'

In the haze that had floated above the pentagram, something moved, quivered, danced in a mosaic of flickering reflections. Reynevan leaned forwards and strained to see. For a fleeting moment, he thought he saw a woman: tall, black-haired, with eyes like stars, the sign of a crescent moon on her forehead, dressed in a many-hued gown shimmering with myriad shades, now white, now copper, now crimson. Before he finally comprehended what he was watching, the apparition vanished, but the presence of Mother Universe was still palpable. The haze above the pentagram grew denser. Then it became clearer again and he saw who he desired to see.

'Nicolette!'

She appeared to hear him; she suddenly moved her head. She was wearing a calpac with a fur trim, an embroidered tunic and a cotton shawl wrapped around her neck. He saw a hundred white-trunked, leafless birch trees behind her. And behind the birches a wall. A building. A castle? A watchtower? A temple?

And then everything vanished. Utterly, completely and definitely.

'I know where that is,' said the beguiler, before Reynevan began to complain. 'I recognise the place.'

'Then speak!'

The beguiler did. Before he had finished, Reynevan was already dashing to the stable to saddle his horse.

The vision hadn't lied. He saw an old black oak woodland set against white-trunked birches, all the whiter against the dark trees. Her grey mare trod slowly, gingerly on the deep snow. He struck his horse with his spurs and rode closer. The mare whinnied and his bay stallion answered.

'Nicolette.'

'Reinmar.'

She was dressed in male attire: a padded jerkin with an embroidered pattern and a beaver-fur collar, riding gloves, thick, coloured woollen *braccae* or leggings and high boots. She wore her fur-trimmed calpac over a silk wimple covering the back of her neck and cheeks, and a woollen shawl had been wound several times around her neck, with the end freely tossed over her shoulder in the manner of a male liripipe.

'You cast a spell on me, sorcerer,' she said coolly. 'I felt it. I was compelled to come here by some force. I couldn't resist it. You enchanted me – confess.'

'I did, Nicolette.'

'My name is Jutta. Jutta of Apolda.'

His memory of her was different. Nothing obvious had changed, not her face, oval like the Madonna of Campin, nor her high forehead, nor the regular curve of her eyebrows, nor the slightly retroussé nose, nor the line of her mouth. Nor the expression of her face, deceptively childlike. Her eyes had changed. Or perhaps they hadn't changed at all, perhaps what he saw in them now had always been there? A cool thoughtfulness hidden in a turquoise abyss, a thoughtfulness and an enigma waiting to be solved, a mystery waiting to be discovered. Things he'd once seen in almost identical blue and similarly cold eyes. The eyes of her mother. The Green Lady.

He rode even closer. The horses snorted, the steam from their nostrils mingling together.

'I'm glad to see you in good health, Reinmar.'

'I'm glad to see you in good health ... Jutta. That's a beautiful name. Shame you kept it from me for so long.'

'And did you,' she said, raising an eyebrow, 'ever ask my name?'

'How could I? I took you for another. You deceived me.'

'You deceived yourself.' She looked him straight in the eyes. 'Your dream deceived you. Perhaps you desired in your heart for me to be somebody else? During the kidnap, it was you who pointed me out to your comrades with your own finger as Biberstein's daughter.'

'I wanted ...' He reined in his horse. 'I had to protect you from—'

'Exactly!' she cut in. 'So what was I to do then? Contradict you? Reveal to your brigand friends who was really who? You saw Kasia; she almost died of fright. I preferred to allow myself to be kidnapped—'

'And to continue to deceive me. You didn't bat an eyelid when I called you "Katarzyna" on Grochowa Mountain. It served you better to be *incognito*. You preferred me not to know anything about you. You deceived me, you deceived Biberstein, you deceived everybody—'

407

'I did so because I had to,' she said, biting her lips and lowering her eyes. 'Don't you understand that? When, in the morning, I descended Grochowa Mountain to Frankenstein, I met a merchant, an Armenian. He promised to take me to Stolz. And right outside the town, not believing my eyes, I meet those two, Kasia Biberstein and Wolfram Pannewitz the Younger. They didn't have to say anything, it was enough to look at them to know that not only I had tasted . . . Erm . . . That not only I had . . . Erm . . . Intriguing adventures. Kasia was terribly afraid of her father, and Wolfram even more of his own . . . So what was I to do? Talk of witchcraft? About a flight through the sky to a witches' sabbath? No, better for both of us to play dumb and claim we'd escaped our kidnappers. I hoped that out of fear of Sir Jan's revenge the Raubritters would run for their lives and that the truth would never out. That no one would even want to investigate it. For how was I to know that Kasia Biberstein was pregnant?'

'And that I'd be accused of raping her,' he finished bitterly. 'You weren't remotely worried by the fact that for me it meant a death sentence. And dishonour worse than death. A stain on my honour. You are a true Judith, Jutta. By staying silent regarding the rape, you condemned me like your biblical namesake did Holofernes. You gave them my head on a plate.'

'Have you been listening?' She tugged at her reins. 'Clearing you of the charge of rape would have meant accusing you of witchcraft. Do you think that your head would have come out of it better? In any case, no one listened to me. What weight does the word of a maid, an irrational maid, carry against the word of a knight making a vow on the cross? I'd have been ridiculed, taken to be suffering from the vapours and palpitations of the womb. While you were safe in Bohemia, no one could get their hands on you there. Until the moment when, as I expected, Wolfram

Pannewitz would overcome his fear and kneel at Biberstein's feet to ask for Kasia's hand.'

'He has still not done it.'

'Because he's an oaf. The world appears to be teeming with them. Everyone is vying to bed some girl or other. And then what? They take fright. They turn tail, flee to foreign lands—'

'Are you referring to me?'

'How astute you are.'

'I wrote you letters.'

'Addressing them to Katarzyna Biberstein. But she didn't receive any of them. The times don't favour correspondence. Shame. I'd have gladly received tidings that you were alive. I'd have gladly read what you wrote . . . My Reinmar.'

'My Nicolette . . . Jutta . . . I love you, Jutta.'

'I love you, Reinmar,' she replied, turning her head away. 'But it changes nothing.'

'Nothing?'

'Did you only come to Silesia for me?' She raised her voice. 'You'll love me till death us do part? You wish to unite with me to the end of your life? If I consent, will you abandon everything and we'll run away somewhere to the far side of the world? Will you drop everything, this moment? Two years ago, having given myself to you, I was prepared to do that. But you were afraid. Now, in turn, no doubt an important mission that you must carry out will interfere. Admit it! Do you have a mission to carry out?'

'I do,' he said, unwittingly blushing. 'A truly important mission, a truly sacred duty. What I'm doing, I'm doing for you. For us. My mission will change the nature of the world, improve the world, make it better and more beautiful. When it dawns, we will live, you and I, live and love to the end of our days in such a world, a truly Divine Kingdom. That is what I desire, Jutta. I dream of it.'

'I'm almost twenty years old,' she said after a long pause. 'My sister is fifteen and will be wed at Epiphany. She looks down on me and would consider me insane if I confessed that I don't in the least envy her wedding, much less her betrothed – an old soak and boor almost three times her age. Or perhaps I really am abnormal? Perhaps my father was right, taking from me and burning the books of Hildegard of Bingen and Christine of Pizan? Why, my darling Reinmar, complete your mission, then, battle for your ideals, search for the Holy Grail, change and improve the world. You are a man, and those are manly things, to fight for dreams, search for the Grail and improve the world. As for me, I return to the convent.'

'Jutta!'

'Don't look horrified. Yes, I'm presently living at the Poor Clare convent in White Church. Of my own free will. When the time comes to decide, I shall also make a decision of my own free will. For the moment, I'm just a *conversa* . . . And not quite that. I'm wondering what to do next—'

'Jutta—'

'I haven't finished. I declared my love for you, Reinmar, because I love you, I love you indeed. Meanwhile, you go and change the world and I'll be waiting. For want of an alternative, frankly speaking—'

He interrupted her, leaning over in the saddle and seizing her around the waist. Taking her in his arms, he pulled her from the saddle, slipping her feet from the stirrups, and they both fell into a deep snowdrift. They blinked, shaking the dry snow from their eyelids and lashes, and looked into one another's eyes. At paradise lost and paradise regained.

With trembling hands, he stroked her jerkin, smoothed the delicate texture and fine weave of the fabric, became drunk on the provocatively sharp roughness of the flowery embroideries, followed with quivering fingers the mysterious pleats and thickness of the seams, brushed with his fingertips, seized, squeezed and caressed the excitingly hard buttons, wonderfully intricate clasps, embellishments and buckles. Sighing, he caressed the thick knotted wool of the shawl which pleasantly irritated the fingers, stroked her wimple, the divine delicacy of the expensive Turkish cloth. He plunged his face into the fur of the collar, breathing in the delicious scents of all Araby. Jutta sighed and moaned spasmodically, tensing up in his arms, digging her fingernails into the sleeves of his jacket, pressing her cheek against the quilted cloth.

He tore off her calpac, with trembling fingers unwound the shawl holding her neck captive and coiled like the Jörmungandr worm, impatiently pulled aside the edge of the silken wimple and arrived – like Marco Polo reaching Cathay – at her nakedness, the naked skin of her cheek and the marvellously lascivious nakedness of her ear, emerging from the fabric. He touched her ear with impatient lips. Nicolette groaned, tensed up, seized him by his padded collar, grabbing with a rapacious hand, squeezing and stroking the shiny, brassy hardness of his belt buckle.

Hugging each other tightly, their mouths met in a long and passionate kiss. A very long and passionate kiss.

Jutta moaned. 'My bottom's cold,' she gasped passionately into his ear. 'The snow is wetting me.'

They stood up, all trembling. From the cold and excitement.

'The sun is setting.'

'Indeed.'

'I must return.'

'Nicolette . . . Couldn't we—'

'No, we couldn't,' she whispered back. 'I live in a convent, I told you, didn't I? And Advent has begun. During Advent, one may not . . .'

'But ... But I ... Jutta—'

'Go, Reinmar.'

When he looked back the last time, she was at the edge of the forest, glowing in the light of the setting sun. In that glow and the winter light, he realised with horrifying certainty that she wasn't Jutta of Apolda, daughter of the Cup-Bearer of Schönau, a *conversa* with the Poor Clares. At the edge of the forest, mounted on a grey mare, was a goddess. A bright figure of rare beauty, an unearthly apparition, *divina facies, miranda species*. A heavenly Venera, lady of the elements. *Elementorum omnium domina.*

He loved and adored her.

Chapter Sixteen

In which numerous encounters occur, the separated friends meet again and *Anno Domini* 1428 – a year that will prove eventful – dawns.

He returned slowly, deep in thought, staring at the horse's mane, letting the animal plod drowsily in the wet snow and virtually find the way itself. After crossing the Wrocław highway, he took a shortcut down the road he had followed on the way to find Jutta. He didn't hurry, even though dusk was falling and the red globe of the sun was already sinking below the treetops.

The horse snorted as hooves clattered on timbers and planks, and Reynevan raised his head and tugged at the reins. Sooner than he had expected, he reached a footbridge crossing a forest ravine, along the bottom of which a swift stream boomed and seethed. The footbridge was none too wide, rickety and quite rotten. Hurrying to Jutta, he had ridden across it. This time he preferred to dismount and lead his snorting horse by the bridle.

He was halfway across when he saw a rider in a black cloak emerging from behind the beeches on the far side.

Reynevan grew anxious. He instinctively looked back, although he had no chance of turning his horse around on the bridge. His instinct didn't disappoint him. There was also a rider behind him. He ground his teeth, cursing under his breath his frivolity and lack of vigilance.

Another rider joined the one standing at the far end. Reynevan held the horse's reins tighter. He felt for the hilt of his dagger. And waited for events to develop.

The men barring his way were evidently also waiting for the same thing, for neither of them said anything or made any movements. Reynevan glanced downwards, under the bridge. He didn't like what he saw. The ravine was deep and the rocks around which the water was foaming had hideously sharp edges.

'Who are you?' he asked, although he knew. 'What do you want from me?'

'It is you who wants something from us,' said the one at the back, removing his hood. 'It's time to say what. And on whose orders.'

Reynevan recognised him right away. It was the tall, swarthy man with the unremarkable face and the look of a journeyman. The one who first watched him in the inn in Ciepłowody and then saved him by giving him a horse.

The others also revealed their faces. He knew one of them, too. It was the pig-like, fair-haired man with the prominent chin, the very same who two weeks before had burst into his chamber holding an Andalusian *navaja*. He didn't know and had never seen the third, whose skinny, bony face resembled a skull. But he guessed who they were.

'Where's the fourth man?' he asked imperiously. 'That Master Olbram, or whatever his name was? The one who tried to stab me while I slept at the Silver Bell?'

Skull-face threw back his cloak, which was draped over the horse's side, revealing a loaded crossbow. The small size and manufacture told Reynevan that it was a hunting weapon rather than a military one. Crossbows like that were no match for military ones in terms of range and penetration but were definitely superior regarding accuracy. A skilled bowman couldn't miss with such a weapon and from a range of up to twenty paces would hit an apple as surely as William Tell from the Canton of Uri.

'I'll graze your horse.' Skull-face appeared to read Reynevan's thoughts. 'I'll just graze him with a bolt. The horse will kick and toss you off the bridge. Your masters from the Inquisition will treat it as an accident when they find your broken corpse at the bottom of the ravine. They'll simply write you off and forget about you.'

'I don't serve the Inquisition.'

'It matters not to me whom you serve. I recognise the stench of a spy. Even from this distance.'

'I have no less sensitive a nose.' Reynevan, though petrified with fear, remained defiant. 'And I can smell a traitor, thief and embezzler, and on top of that a common thug. I don't wish to talk with you further. Shoot, kill me, you venal rogue. Oh, the thought of what Neplach will do to you when he catches you fills me with delight.'

'You're shaking like a leaf, spy,' said the fair-haired man. 'Every spy is a coward.'

Reynevan let go of the bridle and drew his dagger.

'Come onto the bridge, O bold gentleman with his cronies behind him,' he snarled, 'There's room for two here! Come on, have at you! Or do you only use that Spanish knife when your victims are asleep?'

Skull-face lowered the crossbow and laughed dryly. First the swarthy apprentice and then the fair-haired man joined in.

'I swear,' he said. 'The spit and image of his brother.'

'The spit and image,' repeated Skull-face. 'Come to us, Reinmar of Bielawa, brother of Piotr of Bielawa. Let us shake your hand, Reynevan, brother of our comrade, the late lamented Peterlin.'

Reynevan pulled the snorting horse from the bridge. He was scowling, but he had overcome his shaking knees. Skull-face shook his hand and patted him on the shoulder. His thinness and cadaverous complexion were shocking at close quarters.

'Excuse our excessive vigilance,' he said. 'Life has taught us to be so, and thanks to that lesson we are alive. As you've correctly guessed,' he continued, 'we're the Vogelsang. We aren't traitors, we haven't been turned, we haven't changed sides. We didn't embezzle the money entrusted to us. We are ready to take action. We believe that you've come from Prokop and Neplach. We believe that you represent them, that you have their authorisation. That on their orders you are to lead us, because the time has come. Then lead us, Reynevan. We trust you. My name is Drosselbart.'

'Bisclavret.' The fair-haired man introduced himself.

'Rzehors.' The hand of the swarthy apprentice was as hard and rough as an unplaned board.

'Thanks for the horse in Ciepłowody.'

'Don't mention it.' Rzehors's eyes were even harder than his hand. 'We wondered where you were headed on that horse.'

'Have you been following me?'

'We wanted to know where you were going,' repeated the fair-haired man, Bisclavret, like an echo. 'From whom you were seeking help.'

'Those monks—'

'Those Świdnica Dominicans, spies of the Inquisition. They saw Rzehors, we didn't want to take a risk ... Especially because in the tavern there were two more we had our suspicions about. So—'

'So we did what had to be done,' Rzehors finished unemotionally, 'and then we set off after you. Some of us thought you'd fly straight to Świdnica and seek protection under the Inquisitor's wings ... Olbram—'

'Exactly,' Reynevan interjected when the swarthy man broke off. 'And where is that Master Olbram? My would-be murderer?'

Bisclavret was silent for a long time. Rzehors softly cleared his throat. A strange grimace appeared on Drosselbart's narrow face.

'A difference of opinion arose concerning you,' the thin man finally said, 'regarding what ought to be done. We didn't agree with him, so—'

'So he went his way,' Rzehors interrupted quickly. 'Now there are three of us. Let's not stand here, night is falling. Let's ride to Gdziemierz.'

'Why Gdziemierz?' Reynevan asked.

'We've checked Gdziemierz and your Silver Bell Inn,' said Drosselbart. 'It's an entirely decent and safe haven. We want to move there. Do you have any objections?'

'No.'

'Then to horse and let's ride.'

Night had fallen, fortunately a bright one, for the moon was shining and the snow was sparkling and glinting.

'You didn't trust me for a long time,' said Reynevan when they left the forest for the road. 'You almost killed me. I'm Peterlin's brother, and yet—'

'A time has come,' interrupted Drosselbart, 'when a man will betray his brother and become Cain to him. A time has dawned when a son will betray his father, a mother her son and a wife her husband. Subjects will betray their king, soldiers their commander and priests their God. You were under suspicion, Reinmar. There were reasons.'

'What were they?'

'In Frankenstein, you were in the Inquisition's prison,' said Rzehors, riding on his other side. 'Inquisitor Hejncze might have recruited you. Made you collaborate using blackmail or threats. Or simply by bribing you.'

'Precisely,' said Drosselbart seriously, straightening his hood. 'That was the issue. And not just that.'

'What else?'

'Neplach sent you to Silesia as bait.' Bisclavret snorted from the back. 'He was the angler, we the fish, while you were the worm on the hook. We were loath to believe that you were naive enough to consent to an agreement like that. Without your own hidden design, without playing a double game. We weren't certain about your design or your game. And we had every right to suspect the worst. Didn't we?'

'Indeed,' he reluctantly admitted.

They rode on. The moon shone. Horseshoes rapped on the frozen ground.

'Drosselbart?'

'Yes, Reinmar?'

'There were four of you. Now there are three. And at the start? Weren't there more of you?'

'There were. But they evanesced.'

Drosselbart, Bisclavret and Rzehors made themselves comfortable at the Silver Bell Inn with the blithe ease of urbane men of the world Reynevan had only seen before in Scharley. At first, the innkeeper gave them a queer look with restless eyes, but he calmed down on receiving from Drosselbart a handsome pouch filled to metallic hardness. And after Reynevan's assurances that everything was shipshape and in good order.

The innkeeper's reaction and expression were nothing compared to the reaction and expression of Tybald Raabe when he appeared in Gdziemierz the following day. The goliard was literally dumbstruck. Of course, he immediately recognised Bisclavret and knew who he was dealing with, but it took him a long time to relax and shed his mistrustfulness. He needed a long, frank conversation for that. When it finished, Tybald Raabe sighed deeply. And reported the news he had brought.

Any day now, he announced, a messenger from Prokop and Neplach would arrive in Gdziemierz.

'Any day now' turned out to be the fifth of December, the Friday after Saint Barbara's Day. The long-awaited messenger from Prokop and Flutek was – to Reynevan's great amazement, and also great joy – an old friend: Urban Horn. The comrades greeted each other effusively, but soon after it was Horn's turn to be amazed – at the sight of Drosselbart, Rzehors and Bisclavret lining up in front of him.

'I'd have sooner expected my death,' he admitted when they were left alone after the presentation. 'Neplach sent me to help you to search for the Vogelsang. And you – whatever next? – have not only found them, but also clearly won them over. Congratulations, friend, my heartfelt congratulations. Prokop will be pleased. He's counting on the Vogelsang.'

'Who will give him the news? Tybald?' Reynevan asked.

'Of course. Reynevan?'

'Eh?'

'This Vogelsang . . . There's only three of them . . . Not many of them . . . Weren't there more than that?'

'There were. But apparently they evanesced.'

A lie can travel halfway around the world before the truth can get its boots on – spending time with the Vogelsang categorically proved the aptness of that proverb. All three of them lied continuously, always, in every circumstance, day and night, during the working week and on Sundays. They were simply pathological liars, men for whom the concept of truth simply didn't exist. Without doubt, it was the result of a long life embroiled in clandestine activities – feigning, lying and masquerading.

As a consequence of that, one couldn't be sure of them, their life stories or even their nationality. Lying pervaded everything. Bisclavret, for example, introduced himself as a Frenchman, a French knight and a Gallic warrior, a *miles gallicus*. The other two loved to misspeak it as *morbus gallicus*, which didn't bother Bisclavret, who was evidently accustomed to it. He had once belonged, he claimed, to one of the gangs of the notorious *Écorcheurs*, or Flayers, cruel brigands who not only robbed their victims of their riches, but also flayed them alive. That version was, however, contradicted a little by his accent, which was more Cracovian than Parisian. But who knew if his accent was genuine, either?

The cadaverous Drosselbart didn't conceal the fact that he bore an assumed name. *Verum nomen ignotum est*, as he grandly said. Asked about his nationality, he described himself rather vaguely as *de gente Alemanno*. It might have been true. Assuming it wasn't a lie.

Regarding his birth, Rzehors didn't state either the country or the region; he said nothing at all about it. But when he talked about anything else, his accent and colloquialisms formed a mess and hotchpotch so chaotic, so confused and confusing that his listeners were lost after the first few sentences. Which was doubtless the intention.

The trio displayed certain telltale habits, but Reynevan was too inexperienced to decipher them. All three members of the Vogelsang suffered from chronic conjunctivitis, often involuntarily rubbed their wrists, and when they ate always shielded their plates or bowls with a crooked arm. When Scharley saw them later, he deciphered the signals in no time. Drosselbart, Rzehors and Bisclavret had spent a considerable amount of their time behind bars. In dungeons. And fetters.

*

When the conversation shifted to professional matters, the Vogelsang stopped lying and became horrifyingly businesslike and focused. During several conversations lasting deep into the night, the trio reported to Reynevan and Horn on what they had accomplished in Silesia. In turn, Drosselbart, Rzehors and Bisclavret supplied details about the active and sleeping agents they had in most Silesian towns, especially those in the vicinity of the routes the Hussite armies would most likely choose. The Vogelsang were also happy to report on their financial state – exhibiting a certain pride in their trustworthiness – which, in spite of their huge expenses, was still more than satisfactory.

The discussion of plans and strategies brought home to Reynevan that an offensive and a war were actually only weeks away. The three members of the Vogelsang were absolutely certain that the Hussites would attack Silesia when the spring came. Urban Horn neither confirmed nor denied that; he kept his own counsel. Pressured by Reynevan, Horn let him in on a secret. He said that it was more than certain that Prokop would attack Silesia.

'Forces from Silesia and Kłodzko attacked the regions of Broumov and Náchod three times: in 1421, 1425 and this August, right after the victory at Tachov. The atrocities they committed demand equally cruel reprisals. The Bishop of Wrocław and Půta of Častolovice need to be taught a lesson. Thus, Prokop will teach them a lesson they won't forget in a hundred years. It must be done, in order to raise the morale of the army and the people.'

'Aha,' said Reynevan.

'That's not all. The Silesians have sealed the economic embargo so tightly they've practically annihilated trade. They are also effectively blocking the route for goods from Poland. That blockade is proving very costly to Bohemia, and if it lasts much longer may cost the Czechs their lives. The papists and supporters of Sigismund cannot defeat the Hussites militarily and are suffering defeat after defeat on the battlefields. In the economic arena, however, they are beginning to win and are landing painful blows on the Hussites. This cannot continue. The blockade must be broken. And Prokop will do it. Breaking, at the same time, if possible, Silesia's spine. With a crack. In order to cripple it for a century.'

'Was it only about that?' asked Reynevan, disappointed. 'Only that? And the mission? And the message? And preaching the true word of God? And the fight for true apostolic faith? For ideals? For social justice? For a new, better world?'

'Why, of course!' Horn raised his head and smiled with the corners of his mouth. 'Those, too. It's about a better, new world and the true faith. It's so obvious it doesn't bear mentioning. Which is why I didn't.

'An offensive against Silesia is thus certain,' he said, interrupting the lengthy, heavy silence. 'It will occur, beyond reasonable doubt, in the spring. One thing I still don't know is the direction from which Prokop will attack. Which way will he enter: through the Lewin Pass? Through the Mladkov Gate? From Landeshut? Or perhaps he will come from Lusatia, after first giving the Six Cities a hiding. I don't know. But I'd like to. Where the hell is Tybald Raabe?'

Tybald Raabe returned on the twelfth of December, the Friday before the third Sunday in Advent. He didn't bring the information Horn was expecting, but rumours. Queen Sophia had given the King of Poland, Jogaila, a third son, christened Casimir, in Krakow on Saint Andrew's Day. The Poles' joy was somewhat marred by a horoscope created by the famous mage and astrologer Henryk of Brzeg, according to which Jogaila's third son had been conceived and born under a foreboding astral conjunction. During his reign, the astrologer prophesied, misfortune and numerous disasters would befall the Kingdom of Poland. Reynevan rubbed his forehead and pondered. He knew Henryk of Brzeg and that he bought his horoscopes from Telesma at the House at the Archangel. And Telesma's horoscopes always came true. In their entirety.

It was evident that Urban Horn was only mildly interested in the fate of the Jagiellonian Dynasty. He was waiting for other tidings. Tybald Raabe was sent out into the world again, before fully resting.

The first blizzards began after the third Sunday in Advent. In spite of that, Reynevan rode to White Church several times to rendezvous with Jutta of Apolda. Owing to the cold, they couldn't meet in the forest, so their trysts occurred with the permission of the smiling abbess, quite openly, in the convent garden, under the interested gaze of the grey-habited Poor Clares. And naturally had to be limited to holding hands. The abbess pointedly pretended not to see anything, but the lovers didn't dare to be any bolder.

The beguiler Malevolt, who arrived at the Silver Bell Inn on the seventeenth of December, had something to add to Reynevan's growing knowledge of the convent. Like, for example, that the church with whitewashed walls, whose name Alba Ecclesia applied to the entire village beside it, had already stood for over a hundred and fifty years, and that the village belonged to the Lords of Byczeń. When that family died out, Duke Bolko I of Świdnica, the great-great-grandfather of Jan of Ziębice, gave the village to the Poor Clares of Strzelin and founded a convent and provostry in White Church.

'It's not an ordinary nunnery or provostry,' Malevolt informed him with a strange grimace. 'White Church, they say, is a place of punishment, a place of banishment for dissenting nuns. Meaning the kind who think too much, too often, too independently and too freely. It's said a veritable elite of free-thinking nuns is gathered there.'

'What do you mean? And Jutta?'

'Your Jutta must have quite good connections.' The beguiler winked. 'It's the dream of most Silesian nuns and candidates to end up in White Church.'

'In a place of punishment and imprisonment?'

'Are you dim-witted or what? Not long ago we were talking about girls and universities, about how no academy would ever, not for anything in the world, let girls enter their halls. But women's universities already exist. Concealed in convents, like the one in White Church. That's all I'll say. It ought to satisfy you.'

Urban Horn said more, a few days later.

'University?' He grimaced. 'Oh, well, you could call it that. Nonetheless, I've heard that the curriculum there covers learning you won't find at other academies.'

'Hildegard of Bingen? Christine of Pizan? Erm ... Joachim of Fiore?'

'For a start. Add to them Mechthild of Magdeburg, Beatrice of Nazareth, Juliana of Liège, Baudonivia and Hadewijch of Brabant. Add Elsbet Stangl, Marguerite Porete and Heilwige Bloemardinne of Brussels. And the crowning glory is Maifreda of Pirovano, the female Pope of the Guglielmites. Be cautious with the last few names if you don't want to make trouble for your darling.'

The blizzard hadn't let up, the world had vanished in snow, drifts were lying halfway up the walls of the Silver Bell Inn and the roads were absolutely covered. Reynevan, like it or not, had to abandon his visits to White Church to meet Jutta of Apolda. The snowdrifts were so high that their feverish passion was snowbound and had to cool off.

On the last Sunday before Christmas, the blizzards abated, the snowdrifts subsided and the roads became somewhat passable. And then – to Reynevan's delight – Tybald Raabe brought Scharley and Samson Honeypot to Gdziemierz. The friends greeted and hugged each other so warmly they were moved to tears. Why, even Scharley sniffed once or twice.

First one and then another demijohn appeared and with so much to discuss they didn't stop at two.

After fleeing from Trosky, Samson had found Scharley, Berengar Tauler and Amadej Baťa, and the four of them immediately resolved to set off in search of Reynevan. Aware that they wouldn't get far against Grellenort's Black Riders, they rode headlong to Michalovice to ask Jan Čapek for help. Čapek cheerfully agreed – he appeared more interested in the secret underground passage Reynevan and Samson had escaped through from Trosky than in Reynevan's fate. It was easy to imagine the hejtman's irritation when it turned out that Samson had forgotten the location of the cave and couldn't find it. They searched all day, but without success. Čapek's annoyance grew. When Scharley suggested that rather than wandering up and down the stream they finally start to track Reynevan, the infuriated Orphan hejtman sent his men back to Michalovice, declaring to the company that they could continue the hunt alone.

'So we searched alone,' Scharley said, sighing, 'for quite a long time. We went beyond Ještěd, as far as Roimund and Hammerstein. Čapek found us again there, this time in the company of

Štěpán Tlach of Český Dub and an emissary of Flutek who had come from White Mountain.'

Hejtman Tlach, it turned out, had received news from his informer in the Celestine convent at Oybin and the mystery of Reynevan's disappearance was explained. Unfortunately, the company were unable to go after Biberstein's men. The messenger from White Mountain brought with him the order to return at once. The order was categorical, and since the responsibility for its execution fell on the hejtmans, the company set off under escort. Or rather in a convoy.

At White Mountain, only Scharley was retained by Neplach. Samson was raring to head for Silesia alone, but the penitent talked him out of a one-man expedition.

'It didn't take me long,' he said, smiling evilly. 'Our friend Samson had important matters to see to in Prague. All day and every day. Promenading with the red-haired Marketa in Zderaz or Slovany. Or sitting with her in Podskalí, where the two of them spent hours looking at the Vltava and watching the sun go down. Holding hands.'

'Scharley,' said Reynevan.

'What? Isn't that right?'

'*D'antico amor senti la gran potenza ...*' said Reynevan, recalling the quotation and also unable to stop laughing. 'How is she feeling, Samson?'

'Much better. Let's have a drink.'

'There are rumours,' said Scharley, squinting into the sun, 'that a plundering raid is in the offing. A large one. You could call it an invasion. Or better yet: a war.'

'If you were with Flutek at White Mountain you surely know what's afoot,' Reynevan said, stretching. 'Flutek certainly didn't fail to inform you.'

Scharley wouldn't be distracted. 'There are rumours that you've been assigned an important role in that war. That you will, as the poet says, find yourself in the very centre of events. Which suggests that all of us will.'

They sat on the terrace of the Silver Bell Inn, enjoying the sun, which was pleasantly warm in spite of the slight frost. Snow sparkled on the forested hillside and water lazily dripped from icicles hanging from the roof. Samson appeared to be dozing. Perhaps he really was? They had talked well into the night and probably completely needlessly uncorked the last demijohn.

'It's child's play to get your arse kicked when you're caught up in the centre of a war,' continued Scharley, 'especially when you have an important role. Or get another part kicked. When war is waging, it's extremely easy to lose a body part. Which may include your head. And then it's very dangerous.'

'I know what you're getting at. Stop.'

'You appear to be reading my mind, hence I have nothing to add, for you've already arrived at the conclusion, I understand.'

'I have. And I declare: I'm fighting for the cause, I'm going to war for the cause and I shall fulfil the role I've been assigned for the cause. The cause of the Chalice must prevail, all our endeavours are bent towards it. Thanks to our efforts and sacrifices, Utraquism and the one true faith will triumph, an end to immorality will dawn and the world will change for the better. I'm ready to spill blood for it. And give up my life if necessary.'

Scharley sighed. 'But we aren't skiving,' he said calmly. 'We're fighting. You're making a career in medicine and intelligence. I'm moving up through the military hierarchy and quietly amassing loot. I've already put away a pretty penny. We've cheated the Grim Reaper several times in the service of the Chalice. And all we're doing is tempting fate, pushing on blindly from incident to incident, each one worse than the last. It's high time to talk seriously to Flutek and Prokop. Let younger men risk their necks in the field and in the front line. We've earned a rest – we've done enough to be able spend the rest of the war lying around *sub tegmine fagi*. Or alternatively, we've earned the right to cosy positions at headquarters, Reinmar, which, apart from being comfortable and lucrative, have another inestimable virtue. When everything begins to totter, fall apart and disintegrate, posts like that are easy to run from. And then you can take plenty with you—'

'What exactly will start tottering and falling apart?' Reynevan frowned. 'Victory is in sight! The Chalice will triumph and the true *Regnum Dei* will dawn! That's what we're fighting for!'

'Hallelujah,' Scharley summed up. 'It's hard talking to you, lad. So I'll put the arguments to one side and end with a concise and matter-of-fact suggestion. Are you listening?'

'I am.'

Samson opened his eyes and raised his head to indicate he was, too.

'Let's get away from here,' said Scharley calmly. 'To Constantinople.'

'To where?'

'Constantinople,' the penitent repeated in an utterly grave voice. 'It's a large city on the Bosporus. The pearl and capital of the Byzantine state—'

'I know what and where Constantinople is,' Reynevan interrupted patiently. 'I was asking why we have to go there.'

'In order to live there.'

'And why should we live there?'

'Reinmar, Reinmar.' Scharley looked at him pityingly. 'Constantinople! Don't you get it? A glorious world, a glorious culture. A splendid life, a splendid place to live. You're a doctor. We'd buy you an *iatreion* near the hippodrome and you'd soon be a famous specialist in women's complaints. We'd wangle Samson into the Basileus's guard. I, by virtue of my sensitive nature and dislike of effort, wouldn't do any work at all . . . aside from meditation, gambling and the occasional petty swindle. In the afternoons, we'll walk to Hagia Sophia to pray for greater profits, stroll around the Mesa and enjoy the sight of sails on the Sea of Marmara. We'll eat lamb pilau and fried octopus washed down with spiced wine in one of the taverns on the Golden Horn. Heaven on Earth! To Constantinople, lads, to Byzantium. Let's leave Europe behind us, gentlemen, the ignorance and the barbarians. Let's shake that loathsome dust from our sandals. Let's go where it's warm, abundant and blissful, where there's culture and civilisation. To Byzantium! To Constantinople, the city of cities!'

'To foreign lands?' Reynevan knew that the penitent was joking but played the game. 'Abandon the land of our fathers and grandfathers? Scharley! What about patriotism?'

'This is what I think about patriotism.' Scharley made an obscene gesture. '*Patria mea totus hic mundus est.*'

'In other words,' continued Reynevan, '*ubi patria, ubi bene.* That's a philosophy for vagabonds and Gypsies. You have a fatherland, for you had a father. Didn't you take anything from your family home? No lessons?'

'But naturally.' Scharley feigned indignation. 'Plenty. About life and other subjects. All sorts of wise maxims that help me live a dignified life today. To this very day,' he said, wiping a tear away theatrically, 'I can recall my father's virtuous words. I'll never forget his noble teachings, which I remember and which still guide me through life. For example: put on thick hose after Saint Scholastica's Day. Or: you can't squeeze blood out of a stone. Or: a beer in the morning sets you up for the day. Or—'

Samson snorted. Reynevan sighed. Water dripped from the icicles.

Twelvetide – Christmas, *Nativitas Domini, Wynachten* – was observed at the Silver Bell Inn extremely riotously, though only by the small group of companions. After a short-lived thaw, the blizzards returned and the snow-covered roads once again cut the tavern off, and in any case few people travelled at that time. Aside from Reynevan, Scharley and Samson, aside from the Vogelsang, Urban Horn and Tybald Raabe, the innkeeper, Marcin Prahl, also joined in the celebrations. Without regret, he brought up several kegs of Rhenish, Multan and Transylvanian wine to add to the party. The innkeeper's wife, Berta, made sure there was a rich and delicious bill of fare. The only guest from the 'outside' turned out to be the beguiler, Jon Malevolt, who, to everyone's astonishment, didn't arrive alone, but accompanied by the two sylvan witches. The astonishment was great, but by no means disagreeable. The witches turned out to be attractive women with endearing looks and bearing. After the ice was broken, they were accepted by everyone, including Berta Prahl, who was horrified at first.

The witches also honoured the celebration by contributing two huge barrels of bigos. Excellent bigos. The term 'excellent' was utterly insufficient – why, even the name 'bigos' was inadequate. The dish prepared by the sylvan witches was a veritable hymn in honour of stewed cabbage, an ode in praise of smoked bacon and pork fat, a paean to venison and a panegyric to fatty meats, a melodic and loving canzone to dried mushrooms, caraway seed and pepper.

The poetry was enhanced beautifully by the wormwood vodka Malevolt brought, which was prosaic, but effective.

*

The winter, which had seemed harsh in December, only showed what it was capable of after *Circumcisio Domini*. The blizzards grew stronger and for some time it snowed hard day and night. Then the sky brightened up and a somewhat pale sun shone from behind the clouds. And then the frosts came. They gripped with such strength that the earth appeared to groan and froze rock solid.

The frost was so bitter that you came back numb with cold after going out to the privy or for firewood, and any longer expeditions threatened severe frostbite. The others looked at Horn and Tybald – who had decided to leave at Epiphany – as though they were mad. But Horn and Tybald did go. They had to.

It was 1428.

Urban Horn returned on the twenty-eighth of January. The shocking news he brought with him wrenched the company out of its drowsy winter lethargy.

An attempt had been made on the life of Duke Jan of Ziębice at Epiphany, the day of the Revelation of the Lord. When the duke was leaving the church after Mass, the would-be killer forced his way through his guard and attacked him with a dagger. Jan only survived thanks to the sacrifice of two of his knights, Tymoteusz of Risin and Ulrik of Seiffersdorf, who shielded him with their own bodies. Risin even took the blade for the duke, which gave others the chance to disarm the assailant. He turned out to be none other than Gelfrad of Stercza, the knight who had disappeared years before in foreign lands and whom everybody, including his own family, had thought dead.

Rumours about the incident quickly spread through Silesia. Few were in doubt regarding Gelfrad Stercza's motive, since everybody knew about Duke Jan's affair with the knight's wife Adèle, the gorgeous Burgundian. Everybody knew how ruthlessly Duke Jan had treated his lover at the close of the affair; everybody knew the death that Adèle had met owing to that treatment. And although no one, naturally, approved of or tried to justify Gelfrad's deed, the matter was discussed at length and seriously by the knighthood in burgs and watchtowers, and efforts were made to convey information about the discussions to Ziębice. And although the infuriated Duke Jan demanded a cruel and painful execution for the assailant, he had to draw in his horns under the influence of the opinions. Not only his closest kinsmen the Haugwitzes, the Baruths and Rachenaus, but all the other powerful knightly families in Silesia stood up for Gelfrad. Gelfrad Stercza, it was declared, was a knight, and a knight from an old family, who acted blindly to challenge a stain on his honour, and it was known who was responsible for that stain. Duke Jan raged on, but his advisors quickly dissuaded him from a sadistic execution. A time when a Hussite invasion could be expected any moment, they declared, wasn't a good moment to alienate the knighthood. Thus, only the even more resolute Bishop of Wrocław, Konrad, took the side of the resolute duke. The bishop rejected the argument about the defence of honour, turned the entire matter into a political issue, claimed that Gelfrad Stercza had acted from Hussite instigation and demanded for him a cruel death for high treason, witchcraft and heresy. Stercza, roared the bishop, had acted from similarly base motives as the brigand Chrzan, the murderer of the Cieszyn Duke Przemko, and thus ought to be burned with fire and his flesh torn with pincers like Chrzan. The Silesian knighthood, however, wouldn't hear a word of it, dug their heels in and prevailed to such an extent that Gelfrad almost got away with it. He was only to be punished with exile, the Silesian knights refusing to contemplate a harsher punishment to the fury of Duke Jan and the bishop. Gelfrad Stercza would have escaped with his life had it not been for one minor fact. In court, the knight not only did not express remorse, but also declared that no banishment would stop him from further attempts on the life of the duke and that he wouldn't rest until he had spilled his enemy's blood. And refused to take back his words. The powerful men of Silesia no longer had any arguments against such a *dictum*. They washed their hands of it and Jan of Ziębice cheerfully sentenced the knight to death. By beheading.

The sentence was carried out swiftly, on the fifteenth of January, the Thursday before the second Sunday after Epiphany. Gelfrad Stercza went to his death calmly, bravely, but without swagger. He didn't give a speech from the scaffold. He just looked at Duke Jan and uttered a single sentence, in Latin.

'What?' Reynevan asked softly. 'What did he say?'

'*Hodie mihi, cras tibi.*'

Reynevan couldn't hide his dejection, it was too visible and conspicuous. Feeling the need to confide, to unburden himself, he told the company everything. About Adèle, Duke Jan and Gelfrad Stercza. About his revenge. No one said anything. Except Drosselbart.

'Revenge, they say, is a delight,' pronounced the beanpole. 'But usually it's the meaningless delight of a fool, delighting in a dream of delight. Only a fool puts his head on the block when he doesn't have to. *Hodie mihi, cras tibi*, what happens to me today will happen to you tomorrow ... Your eyes shine at the sound of those words, Reinmar of Bielawa, I see it. I know what you're thinking. And I have one request: don't be foolish. Will you promise me? Promise us all?'

Reynevan nodded.

Just as abruptly and suddenly – like the frost before it – came a thaw. Reynevan, missing Jutta, saddled his horse and galloped to White Church. There was actually less galloping and more laborious forcing his way through melting snowdrifts. The expedition lasted several hours, and the result was learning from the nun at the gate that Jutta had gone to her sister's wedding and was in Schönau.

Reynevan couldn't risk the ride to Schönau. He returned to Gdziemierz after dusk. And the following day had to part with Jon Malevolt, the beguiler anarchist.

'Won't you stay with us?' he asked the beguiler as the latter was leading his shaggy horse from the stable. 'Won't you ally with us? What you helped Tybald with has a natural consequence. Wouldn't you like to be part of it?'

'No, Reinmar. I wouldn't.'

'But you claim that you are in favour of revolution, that you support insurrections. That it's time to transform the old order, to shake the world at its foundation. Stay with us. We shall transform the order, and we shall give the world a good shake, believe me. At any moment—'

'I know,' interrupted Malevolt, 'what's going to happen at any moment. I listened to your conversations and looked into your eyes when you talked about war. With all my heart, I'm for revolution and anarchy; I support the movement and transformation utterly. But I won't risk personal involvement in this process. The revolutionary struggle for change changes you. Transforms you. You need great strength to stay in control and not become ... something it is ill to transform into. I'm not sure of my strength or self-control. So, I prefer to step aside. Enough! But I wish you all ... And you, Reinmar ... Success. Farewell, Reynevan.'

The beguiler parted company with them but left something behind him. Several days later, Reynevan saw Samson Honeypot practising blows and thrusts with the *goedendag*, the iron-edged Flemish weapon, on the threshing floor. Samson and Malevolt, having taken a liking to each other, had spent hours playing cards and dice, so the *goedendag* may have been won in a game. It might also have been a present, a parting gift.

Reynevan didn't ask.

On the Feast of Saint Vincent, the joint patron of Wrocław Cathedral solemnly celebrated in Silesia, the goliard Tybald Raabe appeared in Gdziemierz. He had probably visited all his informers, for he finally brought news from Bohemia. Kolín, he reported, had capitulated at last. After eighty-four days of siege, on the Tuesday before Saint Thomas's Day, Sir Diviš Bořek of Miletínek gave up the town on condition that the garrison could leave unharmed. Prokop agreed to the condition. He'd had enough of the siege. And had other plans.

'Prokop,' reported the goliard, 'is now mobilising the Tábor, the Orphans and the Praguians. A plundering raid on Hungary is certain.'

Tybald set off again. He was away for a long time, right up until *Invocavit* Sunday, when he returned with fresh tidings. Just as expected, the army commanded by Prokop and Jaroslav of Bukovina had struck Uherský Brod and from there the Hungarian lands. The towns of Senice, Skalice, Orešany, Modra, Pezinok and Jur were captured and burned down. On Ash Wednesday, however, the eighteenth of February, the Czechs reached Pressburg itself, torching the suburbs and all the surrounding villages. They set off on their return journey with wagons full of spoils. They marched past Trnavy and Nové Město nad Váhom to the great horror of the residents. No one dared to stand in their way or oppose them in battle.

"And in the meantime,' Tybald continued knowingly, 'powerful reinforcements arrived in Moravia: armed units from Nymburk, Slané, Uničov and Břeclav.'

'So it's Silesia's turn,' said Bisclavret, grinning.

'Our time has come,' Drosselbart announced briefly. 'Let's make ready.'

'Let's make ready,' Urban Horn echoed.

They made ready. For whole days and nights, they pored over maps and planned. Bisclavret and Rzehors left with packhorses, returning after two days with a large, clinking load. They must have brought several dozen grzywna.

Reynevan once again set out for White Church, but Jutta wasn't in the convent that time, either. The winter, it turned out, had separated the only recently united lovers a second time.

It was Lent. The Feast of Saint Maciej who breaks the ice passed. The saying didn't lie. The ice was broken and winter no longer had the strength to resist. Caressed by a warm southern wind, the snows melted and snowdrops showed through them. The heady fragrance of spring was in the air.

Tybald Raabe returned with the wind and the fragrance. When they saw him riding up, they knew: it had begun.

'It has begun,' confirmed the goliard with burning eyes. 'It has begun, gentlemen. Prokop has struck. He crossed the boundary of the Duchy of Opava on Shrovetide. We are at war.'

'War,' Urban Horn echoed. '*Deus pro nobis!*'

'And if God is with us,' added Drosselbart dully, 'who can stand against us?'

The wind blew from the south.

Chapter Seventeen

In which the Tábor marches into Silesia, Reynevan begins sabotage activities and Duke Bolko Wołoszek happens fortunately upon the chariot of history.

Reynevan, Urban Horn and Rzehors set off to meet the Tábor. Bisclavret and Drosselbart went to Głuchołazy and Nysa, to spread black propaganda and sow panic. Scharley and Samson remained in Gdziemierz, intending to join them later.

In the beginning, the former group took the Krakow road to Racibórz. Soon, however, just beyond Prudnik, problems began – the road was congested with refugees, mainly from Osoblaha and Głubczyce, where, the refugees claimed, horrified, that the Hussites could already be seen. The confused, fragmented accounts spoke of the burning of Ostrava and the plunder and destruction of Hukvaldy. Of the siege of Opava. The Hussites, the fugitives gabbled in trembling voices, were marching in great force, in an unimaginable horde. Hearing it, Rzehors smiled wolfishly. His time had come. A time for solo acts of black propaganda.

'The Hussites are coming!' he cried to the passing fugitives, feigning a panicked tone of voice. 'A terrible host! Twenty thousand armed men! They're coming – burning and murdering! Flee, people! Death is upon us! They are close at hand! They're in sight! Forty thousand Hussites! None can stand up to them!'

Soldiers appeared on the road behind the fugitives and their wagons laden with whatever they had taken with them. Also clearly fleeing, groups of quite miserable-looking knights, lancers and bowmen listened to the accounts of the approaching fifty thousand Hussites, to stories told in a feigned panic-stricken voice and liberally peppered with mispresented or simply invented quotations from the Apocalypse and the Prophetic Books.

'The Hussites are coming! A hundred thousand! Woe unto us, woe unto us!'

'That'll do,' growled Horn. 'Restrain yourself. A little goes a long way.'

Rzehors restrained himself. In any case, there was no one left to agitate, for the road had emptied. And a little later they saw two similar columns of black smoke rising high into the sky beyond a wall of trees.

'Nová Cerekev and Kietrz.' One of the last refugees pointed with his head. He was driving a wagon bearing his wife and a Minorite monk, their belongings and children. 'They started burning yesterday . . . They say bodies are lying in heaps . . .'

'It's divine retribution,' pronounced Rzehors. 'Run, people. Waste no time! Flee far from here. For verily do I tell you, it'll be like it was two hundred years ago: the invaders will march all the way to Legnica. Thus does God punish us for the sins of the clergy.'

'What are you saying?' The monk bridled. 'What sins? Have you lost your mind? Don't listen to him, Brothers! He's a false prophet! Or a traitor!'

'Run away, good people, run away!' Rzehors spurred his horse onwards but still turned around in the saddle. 'And don't believe monks or priests! And don't drink the water outside the castle walls! The Bishop of Wrocław has ordered the wells poisoned!'

*

They passed Głubczyce, silent in terror, rode on and saw to their right the Opava Mountains and the Hrubý Jeseník massif. Their route was marked by more and more columns of smoke. Not only Nová Cerekev and Kietrz were burning, but at least five other towns and villages.

They rode up a hill and saw the Tábor advancing: a long column of cavalry, infantry and wagons. They heard the singing in Czech.

O knights of God, make ready for the fight!
Sing ye in praise of the Lord's peace!
The Antichrist is abroad, fomenting unrest,
Be heedful, his trickery will never cease!

At the front rode standard bearers with banners fluttering above them, including the pennant of the Tábor – white with a gold Chalice and the motto '*Veritas vincit*' – and a second standard, this one of the field army, also white, with a red Chalice and a gold Host sewn onto it, surrounded by a crown of thorns.

After the standard bearers rode the commanders. Warriors covered in dust and glory; illustrious leaders. Prokop the Shaven, easily recognisable by his frame and huge whiskers. Markolt of Zbraslavice, the celebrated Taborite preacher and ideologist. Like Prokop, dressed in a fur calpac and coat; like Prokop, singing. Also singing was Jaroslav of Bukovina, the commander-in-chief of the Tábor field army. Jan Bleh of Těšnice, the hejtman of the municipal defence army, singing dreadfully out of tune. Beside Bleh, not singing, was Blažek of Kralupy, wearing a tunic with a large red Chalice on his armour and riding a battle stallion. Beside him, Fedor of Ostrog, a Ruthenian prince, warlord and troublemaker, fighting alongside the Hussites. Beyond them followed commanders of the municipal militias: Zikmund of

Vranov, Hejtman of Slaný; and Otík of Loza, Hejtman of Nymburk. Behind them came an ally of the Taborites, Sir Jan Zmrzlík of Svojšín, in full armour, with his coat of arms on his shield: three red stripes on a silver field. The two knights riding side by side with Zmrzlík also bore coats of arms. The Polish Wieniawa, a black buffalo's head, could be seen on the gold shield of Dobko Puchała, a veteran of Grunwald, leading a regiment made up of Poles. Jan Tovačovský of Cimburk, commanding a powerful regiment of Moravians, bore silver and red battlements on his shield.

> *The flowers, the grass and the wind,*
> *weep, O imprudent humankind,*
> *Gold, precious stones, grieve with us!*
> *Angels, archangels, soldiers of Christ's love,*
> *thrones, apostles, grieve with us.*

The wind blew from Jeseníky. It was the eleventh of March, *Anno Domini* 1428. The Thursday before Laetare Sunday.

A mounted troop. Light cavalry in kettle hats and sallets with spears.

'Urban Horn and Reinmar of Bielawa. The Vogelsang.'

'We know who you are.' The troop's commander didn't lower his eyes. 'You've been expected. Brother Prokop is asking if the coast is clear. Where is the enemy army? At Głubczyce?'

'There's no one at Głubczyce.' Urban Horn smiled mockingly. 'The coast is clear, no one will stand in your way. No one in the region would dare.'

The Głubczyce suburbs were burning, fire quickly consuming the thatched roofs. Smoke was completely veiling the town and the castle, drawing the greedy glances of Taborite commanders. Prokop the Shaven noticed them.

'Leave well alone,' he said, straightening up from a table erected in the middle of the forge. 'Don't touch either Głubczyce or any more neighbouring villages again. Duke Wenceslaus will pay, it has been agreed. We shall keep our word.'

'They don't keep their promises to us!' growled Preacher Markolt.

'But we do to them.' Prokop cut him off. 'For we are the Warriors of God and true Christians. We will keep our word to the Duke of Głubczyce, the heir of Opava. At least as long as the heir of Opava keeps his. But if he betrays us, if he takes up arms against us, then I swear on the Lord's name he shall only inherit smoke and ash.'

Some of the commanders present in the makeshift headquarters smiled at the thought of the massacre. Jaroslav of Bukovina openly chortled and Dobko Puchała gleefully rubbed his hands together. Jan Bleh grinned, as if already seeing the fire and killing in his mind's eye. Prokop noticed it all.

'We are entering the bishop's lands,' he declared, resting a fist on the map lying on the table. 'There'll be enough to burn, enough to plunder—'

'Bishop Konrad,' said Urban Horn, 'and Půta of Častolovice are concentrating their forces at Nysa. Jan of Ziębice marches to their aid. Ruprecht, Duke of Lubin and Chojnów, is also approaching, and his brother, Ludwik of Oława.'

'How many of them are there in all?'

Horn looked at Rzehors. Rzehors nodded, knowing that everybody was waiting to see what valuable intelligence the notorious Vogelsang would offer.

Rzehors raised his head after quite a long calculation. 'The bishop, Půta, the dukes. The Knights Hospitaller from Strzegom and Mała Oleśnica. Mercenaries. Municipal militias ... And peasant infantry ... Taken together, seven to eight thousand men. Including about three hundred lances.'

'Young Duke Bolko, the heir of Opole, is approaching from Krapkowice and Głogówek,' interrupted Jan Zmrzlík of Svojšín, who had just returned from a foray. 'His men have reached Kazimierz and occupied the bridge over the Stradunia, a strategic point on the Nysa-Racibórz road. What force might Bolko be commanding?'

'Around sixty lances,' Rzehors assessed calmly, 'and around a thousand foot soldiers.'

'Damn that bloody Opolian!' growled Jaroslav of Bukovina. 'He's cutting us off, threatening our flank. We can't march on Nysa with him behind us.'

'So let's strike straight at him,' suggested Jan Bleh of Těšnice. 'With our full force. Let's crush him—'

'He's lined up in a place that is hard to attack.' Rzehors shook his head. 'The Stradunia has flooded, the banks are marshy—'

'Furthermore,' said Prokop, raising his head, 'time does not permit it. If we get caught up in a fight with Bolko, the bishop will gather more forces and occupy more convenient positions. When she sees we have difficulties, that she-wolf Lady Regent Helena in Racibórz is liable to take action. She and her loathsome son, Mikołaj. Przemko of Opava is likely to decide to do something extremely stupid, and it might also be too great a temptation for Wenceslaus. We would end up encircled, fighting on several fronts. No, Brethren. The bishop is our most bitter foe, so we march as quickly as possible towards Nysa. Let us move out! The main forces by road, towards Osoblaha ... And I'll have other tasks for brothers Puchała and Zmrzlík. But more about that in a moment. Firstly ... Reynevan!'

'Brother Prokop?'

'The young Opolian . . . You know him, I believe?'

'Bolko Wołoszek? I studied with him in Prague—'

'That's wonderful. You'll go to him. With Horn. As envoys. You'll suggest a pact in my name—'

'He won't want to listen to us,' said Urban Horn coldly.

'Put your faith in God.' Prokop looked at Dobko Puchała and Jan Zmrzlík, who were waiting for orders, and his mouth twisted into a grimace. 'In God and in me. I'll make sure he will.'

The Stradunia in spring indeed turned out to be quite a serious natural obstacle. Marshy meadows stood underwater and the current washed the trunks of the riverside willows, silver in their raiment of thick, downy pussy willow. The river marshes teemed with frogs.

Urban Horn's horse danced on the road, kneading the mud with its hooves. Horn tugged on the reins.

'To Duke Bolko!' he shouted at the guards on the bridge. 'Envoys!'

Horn shouted it a third time, but the guards looked on in silence and continued pointing at them their crossbows and harquebuses resting on the bridge's balustrade. Reynevan began to feel anxious. He kept glancing back at the forest, wondering if they would make it into the trees if the need arose.

Four horsemen rode out of the forest on the far bank. Three of them stopped just before the bridge and the fourth, in full plate, rode onto the bridge with a thudding of horseshoes. The coat of arms on his shield was not – as Reynevan had first thought – the Czech Odrzywąs, but the Polish Ogończyk.

'The duke will receive envoys!' called the rider. 'Over here, to our bank!'

'On your knightly parole?'

The Ogończyk lifted his visor, which kept slipping, and stood up in the stirrups.

'Hey!' There was amazement in his voice. 'But I know you! You're Bielawa!'

'And you,' Reynevan recalled, 'are Sir Krzych . . . of Kościelec, aren't you?'

'Will Duke Bolko guarantee us knightly inviolability?' Horn interrupted the exchange of pleasantries.

'His Lordship the Duke gives his parole.' Krzych of Kościelec raised an armoured gauntlet. 'He would never harm young Lord Bielawa. Come hither.'

'Well, well, well,' said Bolko Wołoszek, Duke of Głogówek and heir to Opole, drawling out his words. 'Prokop must respect me since he sends such notable personages to parley. So notable and so celebrated. Not to say notorious.'

The duke's entourage mumbled and muttered. His officers had gathered in a cottage at the edge of the village of Kazimierz and consisted of one herald in a blue tabard adorned with the gold Opole eagle, five armoured knights and one priest, also armoured, in a breastplate and couters. Of the knights, three were Poles; apart from Krzych of Kościelec, the duke was accompanied by a Silesian Nieczuja whom Reynevan knew and a Prawdzic he didn't. The fourth knight had the silver hunting horn of the Falkenhayns on his shield. The fifth was a Knight Hospitaller.

'Sir Urban Horn,' continued the duke, scowling at the emissary, 'is famous the length and breadth of Silesia, mainly from the orders for his capture sent by the bishop and the Inquisition. And who do we have here, gentlemen? That heathen Horn – a Beghard, heretic and spy – acting as emissary in the service of the arch-heretic, Prokop the Shaven.'

The Knight Hospitaller grunted malevolently. The priest spat.

'While you, I see,' Wołoszek continued, shifting his gaze to Reynevan, 'have utterly thrown in your lot with the heretics. You must have sold your entire soul to Satan and serve him devotedly since he sends you as an envoy. Or perhaps the master heretic Prokop thought if he sent you, he would gain something, owing to our old amity? Ha, if he counted on that he is mistaken. For I tell you, Reynevan, that when everybody in Silesia was denigrating you, calling you a thief and a brigand, ascribing to you the foulest crimes – including the rape of a maid – I defended you, not allowing anyone to slander you. And do you know the outcome? I looked a damn fool.

'But I saw my error,' concluded the duke after a pregnant pause. 'I saw my error! The mission of an Antichrist carries no weight, I shall not talk to you. Forward, guards! Seize them! And bind that rascal!'

Reynevan struggled and his knees buckled when Krzych of Kościelec pinned him down from behind, seizing him by the shoulders in his powerful hands. Two servants caught Horn by the arms as a third deftly wound a rope around his elbows and neck, tightened it and tied a knot.

'God sees.' The priest raised a hand in a theatrical gesture. 'God sees, Duke, that you act rightly! *Firmetur manus tua*, may your hand be made strong when it chokes the hydra of heresy!'

'We are emissaries ...' Reynevan grunted in the grip of the Pole. 'You gave your parole—'

'You are emissaries, but of the Devil. And parole given to heretics is empty. Horn is a traitor and a heretic. And you are a heretic. You were once my comrade, Reynevan, so I shall not order you bound. But shut your trap!'

He did as he was told.

'I shall turn *him* over to the bishop,' said the duke, nodding at

445

Horn. 'It is my duty as a good Christian and son of the Church. Where you are concerned . . . I've already saved you once as an old friend. And now I also mean to release you—'

'What?' roared the priest as the Falkenhayn and Knight Hospitaller growled. 'Release a heretic? A Hussite?'

'And you shut your trap, Pater.' Wołoszek flashed teeth beneath his moustache. 'And only open it when requested. I release you, Reinmar of Bielawa, mindful of our erstwhile friendship. But it's the last time, by God's wounds! The last time! Don't come before my eyes again! I'm leading a crusading force. Soon I shall join my company with the bishop's men, and together we shall march to Opava to wipe you heretics from the face of the Earth. God willing, the Bishop of Wrocław will recognise me as a good Catholic! Who knows, perhaps he will cancel my debts. Who knows, perhaps he'll return to me what he once stole from the Duchy of Opole. Thus, let's hold high the cross, God thus wishes, and we march, march on Opava!'

'The wind blows ashes around where once the suburbs of Opava stood,' said Horn, arms bound. 'Yesterday, Prokop was at Głubczyce. Today, he's even closer.'

Bolko Wołoszek leaped forwards and punched Horn hard in the ear.

'I said,' he hissed, 'I won't talk to you, turncoat, much less listen to your prattle.'

'Reynevan!' He turned around violently. 'What was he saying about Opava? Taken? Unbelievable! Let him go, Sir Krzych!'

'Opava held out,' answered Reynevan, rubbing his shoulder, 'but the suburbs went up in smoke. Kietrz and Nová Cerekev also, and before them Hukvaldy and Ostrava. Hradec nad Moravicí and Głubczyce survived only due to the good sense of Duke Wenceslaus. He parleyed with Prokop, paid the ransom and saved the duchy. Or at least part of it.'

'Am I to believe that? Believe that Przemko of Opava didn't join battle with the Hussites? Let his son negotiate with the Hussites?'

'Duke Przemko is crouching behind the walls of Opava Castle as quiet as a mouse, keeping his eyes on the fires that are burning wherever he looks. And the young Duke Wenceslaus clearly has good sense, which is enviable and ought to be imitated.'

'God will punish those who have fraternised with the heretics and parleyed with them,' the priest exploded. 'A pact with a heretic is a pact with Satan! Whoever enters into one is damned for ever. And here, on Earth, while they're alive—'

'Your Grace,' shouted a soldier in a kettle hat, bursting in to the cottage. 'A messenger!'

'Bring him here!'

The messenger, it could be seen – and smelled – hadn't spared himself or his horse. A layer of caked-on mud covered him up to his waist and the stench of horse's sweat was pungent even at a few paces from the man.

'Speak!'

'The Czechs approach . . .' panted the messenger, gasping for breath. 'A great force . . . Burning everything . . . Osoblaha in ashes . . . Prudnik captured—'

'Whaaat?'

'Prudnik taken . . . A dreadful slaughter in the town . . . Czyżowice afire . . . Biała burning . . . Seized . . . The Hussites—'

'Have you lost your mind?'

'Hussites . . . at Głogówek . . .'

'And where are the bishop's men? Where is Jan of Ziębice, where Dukes Ruprecht and Ludwik? Where Sir Pŭta?'

'At Nysa. They order . . . They order Your Lordship the Duke to join them at all speed—'

'Join them?' Wołoszek burst out, clenching a mace stuck into

447

his belt. 'They retreat, leaving my towns and land to be destroyed, and I am to join them? My Głogówek imperilled, and I am to march to Nysa? The Bishop orders it? Konrad of Oleśnica, that thief, old soak and whoremonger, dares to order me? And why do you stare? I need fucking advice! Advice! What to do?'

'Attack!' roared the Knight Hospitaller. '*Gott mit uns!*'

'Perhaps it's false news?' The Silesian with the Nieczuja coat of arms blinked.

'March to Nysa and join forces with Bishop Konrad,' the Falkenhayn said firmly. 'We'll form a great host and defeat the heretics in a general battle. Avenge the towns that lie burned—'

The duke looked at him and ground his teeth. 'Don't advise me how to avenge, but rather how to save ourselves!'

'Parley?' stammered the Ogończyk. 'Pay off the town?'

'I have no money.' Wołoszek ground his teeth again. 'My Prudnik . . . Sweet Jesus! My Głogówek!'

'We must put our faith in God,' said the priest. 'It will be as God decrees . . . Here is the Bible . . . I shall open it haphazardly and what I read will come to pass—'

'And on the strength of the curse,' recited Urban Horn, ahead of the clergyman, 'all were devoted to be destroyed: men and women, young and old, with the edge of the sword—'

Bolko Wołoszek glared at him and Horn fell silent. But Reynevan immediately spoke up.

'And Joshua burned Ai,' he continued, 'and made it a heap for ever, even a desolation unto this day. Think it over, Bolko. Make a decision. Before it's too late. It's a revolution, Bolko,' he went on, seeing that the young Piast wasn't in a hurry to interrupt him. 'The world takes a new form, moves in a new direction. The chariot of history moves apace, no power is capable of stopping it. You can either climb aboard or be crushed by it. Choose.'

'You can be among the victors or among the vanquished,

Duke,' said Horn. 'Woe always betides the vanquished, as the classicists tell us. While the victors . . . To the victors the spoils. For the world also takes on a new form on maps.'

'Eh?'

'*Sapienti sat dictum est.* Border posts, Your Lordship, are shifted to the advantage of the victors. And they who support them.'

'Do I understand that to be a proposal?' A flash appeared in the young duke's eye. 'An offer?'

'*Sapienti sat.*'

'Ha.' The flash was still there. 'And I shall benefit, you say. And how, exactly?'

Horn smiled imperiously and glanced at his bonds. At a gesture from Wołoszek, they were immediately cut. Seeing that, the Falkenhayn growled again and the Knight Hospitaller slapped his sword hilt. And the priest jumped up.

'My lord!' he yelled. 'Don't listen to devilish prodding! These Hussite vipers are dripping venom into your ears! Remember the faith of your forebears! Remember—'

'Shut your trap, damned priest.'

The priest jumped even higher. 'Is this your true nature?' he yelled even louder, waving his arms in front of the duke's nose. 'They recognise you! O apostate! O turncoat! You fraternise with heretics! Knights – have at him, whoever believes in God! I curse you! May you be accursed at home and abroad, may you be accursed at your slumbers, rising, walking—'

Bolko Wołoszek struck him in the temple with a powerful reverse blow. The six-flanged iron head of the mace crushed the bone with an audible crunch. The priest slumped, jerking and trembling. The duke turned around, his furiously contorted mouth about to issue an order. His look was enough and the Poles anticipated their master's intentions. With a powerful blow of a battleaxe, Krzych of Kościelec smashed the skull of the Knight

Hospitaller who was pointing a sword at him, the Prawdzic stabbed the Falkenhayn in the throat with a misericorde, while the Silesian Nieczuja plunged a blade into his back. Bodies were falling onto the dirt floor; blood was forming puddles.

The servants and pages looked on open-mouthed.

'There.' The Ogończyk grinned. 'What a happy day. It's been ages since I last killed a Teutonic Knight.'

'To our soldiers!' cried the duke. 'To our folk! Calm them! Particularly the Germans! If anyone offers resistance, take him down! And prepare to move out!'

'To Nysa?'

'No. To Krapkowice and Opole. That's an order!'

'Yes, sire!'

Bolko Wołoszek turned around and fixed his blazing eyes on Reynevan and Horn. He was breathing rapidly, loudly and irregularly. His hands were shaking.

'*Sapienti sat*,' he uttered hoarsely. 'Did you hear what I ordered? I'm withdrawing my men to avoid contact with your troops. I'm not going to Nysa; I won't support the bishop. Prokop should treat it as an act of alliance. You, in return, will spare my lands. Głogówek ... But that's not all. Not all, by God's wounds! Tell Prokop ...' The young duke raised his head proudly. 'Tell him an alliance with me will warrant substantial changes to maps. To be specific ...'

'Specifically,' Horn repeated, 'Wołoszek demanded a permanent fiefdom of Hukvaldy, Příbor, Ostrava and Frenštát. I promised them to him as we had agreed. But that wasn't enough for him – he also demanded Namysłów, Kluczbork, Gryżów, Rybnik, Pszczyna and Bytom. I promised them to him, Brother Prokop, also pledging them in your name. Was I too hasty?'

Prokop the Shaven didn't answer at once. He was eating while

standing with his back to a combat wagon, scooping up dumplings with a lindenwood spoon and raising them to his mouth.
Milk was drying on his moustache.

Behind the wagon and Prokop, a great fire raged and roared,
the town of Głuchołazy aflame. The wooden parish church
blazed like a torch. As fire consumed the roof and thatch, smoke
billowed in black clouds up into the sky. The screams of people
being killed didn't let up for a moment.

'No, Brother, you weren't.' Prokop the Shaven licked the spoon.
'You acted correctly, promising them in my name. We'll give him
everything we've pledged. Bolko deserves to be compensated for
the damage, for it somehow occurred that Zmrzlík and Puchała,
when putting Biała and Prudnik to the torch, also burned down
his beloved Głogówek in their haste. We shall compensate him
for that offence. In truth, most of the towns he is demanding
still have to be captured. We shall see in the capturing what kind
of ally Duke Bolko is and reward him aptly for his service to the
cause.'

'And service to God,' interjected the preacher Markolt, with
his mouth full. 'The heir of Opole must receive the sacrament
from the Chalice and swear on the Four Articles.'

'There will be time for that, too.' Prokop put down his bowl.
'Finish your food.'

The milk and dumplings were drying on Prokop's moustaches.
Behind Prokop, the town of Głuchołazy was turning to ash. The
townspeople were wailing at various pitches as they were killed.

'Prepare to move out! On to Nysa, Warriors of God! On to
Nysa!'

Chapter Eighteen

In which, on Thursday the eighteenth of March 1428 – or, as it is usually written in chronicles: *in crastino Sancte Gertrudis Anno Domini MCCCCXXVIII* – around 14,000 men go for each other's throats at the Battle of Nysa. Fatal casualties among the defeated number *circa* M. As is customary among chroniclers, the victors' losses are passed over in silence.

'Huss is a heretic!' chanted the front ranks of the bishop's army arrayed on Monk's Meadow. 'Huss is a heretic! Hoo! Hoo! Hoo!'

News of the Taborites marching on Nysa must have reached the Bishop of Wrocław long before – and no wonder, since it's quite difficult to carry out a secretive manoeuvre with an army numbering over seven thousand men and close to two hundred wagons. Particularly if that army is burning every settlement on the route of the march and the surroundings, marking its path clearly with fire and smoke. Thus, Bishop Konrad had enough time to form up his soldiers. Sir Pǔta of Častolovice, Starosta of Kłodzko, had enough time to come to their aid. Having gathered under his command one thousand one hundred horse and nigh on six thousand peasant foot, having a powerful reserve and support in the form of armed Nysa burghers and the town walls, the bishop and Pǔta had decided to join battle in the field. When Prokop the Shaven appeared at Nysa, he found in the region of

Monk's Meadow armed Silesians with standards, arrayed and ready for battle. He accepted the challenge.

As the hejtmans were organising their men – which they did quickly – Prokop set about to pray. He prayed calmly and softly, entirely ignoring the insults being hurled by the Silesians.

'Huss is a heretic! Huss is a heretic! Hoo! Hoo! Hoo!'

'Lord,' he said, putting his hands together. 'Lord of Hosts, we flock to You in our prayers. Be our shield and protector, rock and stronghold in the perils of war and the spilling of blood. May Your grace be with us sinful folk.'

'Devil's sons! Devil's sons! Hoo! Hoo! Hoo!'

'Forgive us our sins. Arm the soldiers with strength, be with them in battle, give them courage and valour. Be our solace and refuge, give us strength to defeat the Antichrists, our foes and Yours.'

Prokop made the sign of the cross, as did the others: Jaroslav of Bukovina, Jan Bleh, Otík of Loza and Jan Tovačovský. Prince Fedor of Ostrog, who had just returned from having burned down Malá Stínava, crossed himself in the Orthodox manner. Dobko Puchała and Jan Zmrzlík, who had returned from burning down Strzeleczki and Krapkowice, crossed themselves. Markolt, kneeling beside a bombard, crossed himself, beat himself on the chest and repeated that it was his *culpa*.

'God in the Heavens.' Prokop raised his eyes. 'Thou rulest the raging of the sea: when the waves thereof arise, Thou stillest them. Thou hast broken Rahab in pieces, as one that is slain; Thou hast scattered Thine enemies with Thy strong arm. May the enemy forces leave the battlefield vanquished today, too. To battle, Brethren. Go forth, in the name of God.'

'Onwards!' bellowed Jan Bleh of Těšnice, riding up before the army on his skittish horse. 'Onwards, Brethren!'

'Onward, Warriors of God!' Zikmund of Vranov brandished

his mace, giving the signal for the monstrance to be raised before the regiment. 'Go forth!'

'Go foooorth!' The captains passed it down the line. 'Go foooorth! . . . Foooorth . . . foooorth . . .'

The mass of Taborite infantry shuddered, their armour and weapons rattling like a dragon's scales, and like a great dragon moved forward. The formation, numbering many thousand men, a thousand and a half paces wide, two and a half paces deep, marched straight towards the Silesian army mustered at Nysa. The wagons within the formation rattled.

Reynevan, in imitation of Scharley, had climbed up into a pear tree for a better view, searched but couldn't locate Bishop Konrad among the Silesians. He only saw the bishop's red and gold standard. He caught sight of the pennant of Půta of Častolovice and the man himself, trotting in front of the knighthood and holding them back from a chaotic charge. He saw the large Knights Hospitaller regiment, among whom must have been Ruprecht, Duke of Lubin, the Grand Prior of the order. He saw the arms and colours of Ludwik, Duke of Oława and Niemcza. He ground his teeth on seeing the banner of Jan of Ziębice, with a half-black, half-red eagle.

The Taborites proceeded, marching with regular, measured step. The wagons' axles creaked. The line of Silesian peasant infantry, hidden behind pavises, blades upright, didn't budge, and the mercenary commanding them, a knight in full plate armour, galloped up and down the ranks, yelling.

'They hold fast . . .' said Blažek of Kralupy to Prokop, and anxiety sounded in his voice. 'They'll wait, letting us open fire . . . The cavalry won't move before that.'

'Trust in God,' replied Prokop, eyes fixed on the battlefield. 'Trust in God, Brother.'

The Taborites marched on. Everybody saw Jan Bleh ride to

the head, in front of the array. Saw him give the signal. All knew what order he was giving. A song rose above the marching companies. A battle chant in Czech.

Ye, who are warriors of God,
And of His law,
Pray to God for help and have faith in Him;
That ever with Him shall you victorious be!

The Silesian line trembled visibly, the pavises wavered, the spears and halberds swayed. The mercenary – now Reynevan recognised the ram's head on his shield and knew that he was a Haugwitz – roared and issued commands. The song rumbled like thunder, rolling above the field.

Christ is worth all your sacrifice,
He will reward you as is foretold
When you give up your life for Him
You shall join the heavenly fold.

The Lord commands you
To disdain all bodily harms,
Thence give up your mortal lives,
For your brothers and take up arms!

Crossbows and harquebuses peeped out from behind the Silesian pavises. The Haugwitz bellowed until he was hoarse, forbade the men from firing, ordered them to wait. That was a mistake.

When the Hussite wagons had approached to a distance of three hundred paces, trestle guns fired and a hail of bullets thudded against the pavises. A moment later, a dense cloud of bolts hissed towards the Silesians. The dead fell, the wounded howled and the line of pavises shook. The Silesian foot soldiers responded with answering fire, but chaotically and inaccurately.

The bowmen's hands were shaking. For on Bleh's command, the Taborite regiment had speeded up. And then began to run. With savage cries on their lips.

'They won't hold . . .' There was first disbelief and then hope in Blažek of Kralupy's voice. And then certainty. 'They won't hold! God is with us!'

Although it appeared unbelievable, the Silesian line suddenly disintegrated as though blown apart by the wind. Dropping their pavises and spears, the peasant infantry bolted to a man. Haugwitz, trying to restrain them, was knocked over along with his horse. In panic and disarray, dropping their weapons, hiding their heads in their hands, the Silesian peasantry fled towards the townspeople's dwellings and the riverside undergrowth.

'Attack!' Jan Bleh roared. 'Have at them! Kill!'

Horns boomed on Monk's Meadow. Seeing that it was time, Půta of Častolovice roused the knighthood. Lowering their lances, a thousand horse and more of iron cavalry moved onto the offensive. The earth began to tremble.

Bleh and Zikmund of Vranov realised the gravity of the situation at once. On their command, the Taborite infantry immediately closed ranks into a tight formation, pavises raised. The wagons were turned broadside, and the barrels of cannons appeared behind the lowered sides.

The iron wave of Silesian knighthood smoothly re-formed, dividing up into three groups. The middle one, under the bishop's banner with Půta himself leading, was meant to drive a wedge into the Taborite array and dismember it; the other two groups were meant to clench it like pliers – Ruprecht's Knights Hospitaller to the right, the Dukes of Ziębice and Oława to the left.

The cavalry gave a battle cry and moved into an earth-shaking gallop. The Taborites, although they saw sallets and the horses' iron chanfrons growing larger, responded with an impudent yell as hundreds of glaives, pikes, bear spears, pitchforks and gisarmes emerged and were lowered through the pavises, while hundreds of halberds, flails and morning stars were raised. Bolts rained down, handgonnes and harquebuses roared, cannons blasted and spat shot. The lethal salvo lacerated Ruprecht's Hospitallers. Wounding and frightening the horses, it also slowed down the cavalry from Ziębice and Oława. The bishop's mercenaries and the iron knights of Půta of Častolovice weren't to be slowed, however, and they crashed into the Czech infantry with full force. Iron thudded against iron. Horses squealed. Men screamed and howled.

'Now! Onwards!' Prokop the Shaven pointed with his mace. 'Attack, Brother Jaroslav!'

An answering shout came from hundreds of throats. The mounted regiment of Jaroslav of Bukovina and Otík of Loza charged onto the battlefield from the left flank, and Tovačovský's Moravians, Puchała's Poles and Fedor of Ostrog's unit struck from the right. Behind them, the infantry reserve – the terrible Slány flailmen – rushed onto the field.

'Haaaave at theeeem!'

They joined battle. The loud, resonant thudding of weapons striking armour rose above the squealing of horses and the yelling of men.

The Knights Hospitaller tried to stop the charge of Otík of Loza, but the Nymburk men wiped them out at the first impact, tunics with white crosses strewing the blood-soaked earth in an instant. The Ziębice men resisted manfully, not only not yielding in the face of the enemy, but actually repelling Jaroslav of Bukovina's lancers. The knights and esquires of Oława also valiantly withstood the impetus of Dobko Puchała and Tovačovský's attack but couldn't endure the blows of the Polish and Moravian swords. They wavered. And when they saw Puchała viciously cleave open with a battleaxe the head of Typrand of Reno, the commander of the mercenaries, they lost hope. The entire left flank wavered and cracked like glass. Půta of Častolovice saw it. Although caught up in the fight with the infantry, although splashed with blood up to his basinet, Půta saw and understood the threat in no time. And when, standing up in his stirrups, he saw Jaroslav of Bukovina's cavalry encircling him from the right, when he saw the armoured troops of Otík of Loza forcing their way through and a horde of flailmen rushing to their aid, he knew he was lost. Shouting commands – his voice now hoarse – he turned around to see the bishop's regular soldiers flee, Marshal of the Court Wawrzyniec of Rohrau run from the battlefield, Hyncze of Borschnitz, Mikołaj Zedlitz and the burgrave of Otmuchów bolt. To see the defeated knighthood of Ziębice flee in confusion. To see the decimated Oława men turn tail in the face of the attack by the Moravians and the Poles. To see Commander Dietmar of Alzey die and the surviving Knights Hospitaller run away on seeing it, see Otík of Loza's cavalry give chase and cut them down cruelly. To see fall from his horse and be caught by a gisarme hook the young squire Jan Czetterwang, son of a Kłodzko patrician. Whom he, Půta of Častolovice, Starosta of Kłodzko, had told he would keep an eye on his only son in the battle.

'To me!' he yelled. 'To me, Kłodzko!'

But battle and warfare have their own rules. When, at his order, the Kłodzko knighthood and the remains of the regular soldiers put up fierce – if desperate – resistance against the Hussites, Půta of Častolovice reined his horse around and fled. He was compelled, he had no choice. Nysa, the still heavily defended bishop's capital, had to be saved. He had to save Silesia. The Kłodzko lands.

And his own skin.

When they were quite near the moat, the town walls and the toll gate, Pŭta's horse, forced into an unforgiving gallop, trampled on the discarded bishop's standard, treading the black eagles and red lilies into the spring mud.

Thus ended the Battle of Nysa, fought on Monk's Meadow and its surroundings the day after Saint Gertrude's Day, *Anno Domini* 1428, in a crushing defeat and another triumph for Prokop the Great. Afterwards, things proceeded as usual. Drunk on victory, masses of Hussites began finishing off the wounded and stripping the dead. The latter numbered around a thousand, but by supper Reynevan had already heard songs swelling the result to three thousand. At dusk, the song had gained two new verses and the number of dead had grown by a further two thousand.

Now it was the turn of the triumphant Czechs to shout insults, threats, derision and filth about the Pope at the foot of Nysa's walls, and the defenders had to sit in silence. Every last cottage outside the town walls was burned down, but the town wasn't attacked. Prokop limited himself to firing bombards, without great conviction, and in the evening, Preacher Markolt organised a torchlit display with the heads of the fallen stuck on spear blades outside the walls.

The following day, before the loot was loaded onto wagons, the Vogelsang – represented by Drosselbart, who had fled from the town – reported to Horn and Reynevan. They immediately went to Prokop. Nysa, reported Drosselbart, was well prepared to be defended. Sir Pŭta had the situation under control, he was maintaining iron discipline, nipping in the bud any manifestations of panic or defeatism. He had enough men and the means for an effective and lengthy defence of the town in the event of a siege, even following the flight of the bishop and the dukes.

'While you were parading around with severed heads on poles,' announced the cadaverous Drosselbart, quite impudently, 'the bishop was fleeing through the Wrocław Gate. And the dukes – Ruprecht, Ludwik of Oława and Jan Ziębice – also made good their escape.'

Prokop the Shaven didn't comment but looked on enquiringly. Drosselbart understood without words.

'You can forget about Ruprecht for the moment,' he announced, 'he will flee all the way to Chojnów, he won't bar your way now. If you want to know my opinion, his uncle, Ludwik of Brzeg, will also flee at any moment. Ludwik, as you've no doubt noticed, didn't take part in the battle, didn't even leave Brzeg, even though the bishop was furious. He has quite a powerful force, something around a hundred lances. But avoids fighting. He's either frit, or ... Other rumours are circulating in this regard ... Should I say?'

'Go on.' Prokop was playing pensively with the end of his moustache. 'I'm listening attentively.'

'Ludwik of Brzeg's wife, as you know, is Elisabeth, the daughter of the Prince-Elector of Brandenburg, Frederick. The Prince-Elector is in cahoots with the King of Poland, Jogaila, and is trying to marry his son to Jogaila's daughter. He knows that the King of Poland is secretly sympathetic to the Czechs, so in order not to annoy him or spoil the chance of a marriage with Poland, he is exerting influence on Duke Ludwik through his daughter, so that Ludwik will avoid—'

'Enough.' Prokop let go of his moustache. 'That's nonsense, I won't waste time on it. But spread that rumour, by all means. Let it circulate. What can you say about Jan Ziębice? And about the young Duke of Oława?'

'Before they fled from Nysa, there was an argument between the two of them and Půta of Častolovice. It's no secret what it was about. Both of them want to save their duchies. In short: they want to negotiate. Pay a ransom.'

'Emperor Sigismund threatens loss of life, honour and estates to anyone who parleys with us,' said Prokop slowly, 'and the Church throws in a curse. Have they forgotten about that? Or do they consider them empty threats?'

'Sigismund is far away.' Drosselbart shrugged. 'Very far away. Too far away for a king. A king should defend his subjects. But what is Sigismund doing? He's in Buda, doing nothing. The dukes used that argument more than once in their dispute with Půta.'

'What say you to that?' Prokop the Shaven raised his head. 'Horn? Bielawa?'

'Jan of Ziębice is a traitor,' Reynevan blurted out hurriedly. 'A mendacious bastard! He fled from Nysa, betrayed and left Sir Půta, his future father-in-law, all alone. He is betraying Emperor Sigismund and only wants to make a pact with us because it's convenient to him today. Tomorrow, he'll betray us for his own convenience!'

Prokop looked at him for a long time.

'I presume,' he said finally, 'that Jan of Ziębice and Ludwik of Oława are undecided and hesitant, not knowing how to approach us. We'll ease their task by taking the first step ourselves. If they really want to parley, they'll seize the chance with both hands. You'll ride to Ziębice and Oława and submit our proposal. If they pay ransom and refrain from armed interventions, I'll spare their duchies. If they don't pay or break the agreement, they won't even rise from the rubble and embers in a hundred years. You'll leave at once. You two. Horn and Brother Drosselbart.'

'What about me?' asked Reynevan.

'Not you,' replied Prokop calmly. 'You seem too excited to me. I sense some private interest in this, some rage, some personal matter. We are carrying out noble aims and ideas in this campaign. We are bringing the true word of God. We are burning churches where, instead of God, they venerate the Roman Antichrist. We are punishing prelates, tyrants and oppressors of the people who have sold their souls to Rome. We are punishing Germans greedy for Slavic blood. But apart from noble ideas, we have business to do. The harvest was meagre and we are beginning to feel the effects of the embargo. Sixteen bushels of rye cost four groschen in Prague, Reinmar. Four groschen! Bohemia is threatened with hunger. We marched on Silesia for plunder and spoils. For money. If I can acquire money without fighting or human casualties, all the better, all the greater our gains. Negotiations and pacts, remember, are as good a way to wage a war as firing bombards. Do you understand that?'

'I do.'

'Splendid. But in any case, I shall wait until it has matured in your breast. Meanwhile, Horn and Drosselbart are riding to Ziębice and Oława. Without you. I have other tasks for you.'

The next day, on the Saturday before *Judica* Sunday, called White Sunday in Silesia and Deathly Sunday by the Czechs, Prokop began negotiations with Půta of Častolovice regarding the ransom for the captives taken in battle. Meanwhile, Jaroslav of Bukovina and Zikmund of Vranov burned down Otmuchów and Paczków, painting the sky with two towering columns of smoke. Otík of Loza, Zmrzlík and Tovačovský hadn't wasted any time, either, burning down Vidnava and capturing Javorník Castle. Puchała didn't fall behind, diligently and methodically burning down the bishop's villages and farmhouses.

But Prokop found some time for Reynevan. He interrupted the negotiations to bid him farewell. And give him his final instructions.

'Your task is of prime importance for the campaign,' he instructed. 'Now, face to face, I'll tell you: it is much more important than the negotiations being conducted by Horn and Drosselbart. I'm telling you this because I see you are still sulking about not being sent with them. I repeat: the task you are receiving is a hundredfold more important. And, I don't deny, a hundredfold more exacting.'

'I shall carry it out, Brother Prokop,' promised Reynevan. 'For the glory of the Chalice.'

'For the glory of the Chalice,' repeated Prokop the Shaven with emphasis. 'Good you understand how closely you are bound to the cause of the Chalice, and that only with us will you avenge your brother and the harm received at the hands of the papists. Only this way – and no other – will you accomplish it. Remember.'

'I shall.'

'Godspeed.'

Five horses rode away in the morning. Carrying Reynevan, Scharley, Samson, Bisclavret and Rzehors. Samson had the Flemish *goedendag* fastened to his pommel, while Scharley was armed with a dangerous-looking weapon called a falchion, a scimitar with a curved blade, widening to the point. Weapons like that, in spite of their Saracen appearance, were forged throughout Europe and were particularly popular in Italy. It was lighter than a traditional sword and considerably handier in combat, particularly in close combat.

They crossed onto the left bank of the Nysa near the smoking ruins of Otmuchów and headed towards the Rychleby range. They travelled along the route that a few days earlier the Hussite units had marched down. Everywhere, as far as the eye could see, were visible tracks of their passing and evidence of the noble aims and ideas upheld by the Tábor. Smouldering embers were all that remained of churches where the Roman Antichrist was venerated. Here and there, a prelate who had been bought by Rome was hanging from a bare branch. Ravens, crows, wolves and wild dogs were feeding on the corpses. Actually, one ought to have assumed that they were all the bodies of Germans and the enemies of the Chalice greedy for Slavic blood, ought to have believed that among the dead there were no completely innocent or chance individuals. One might have believed that. But no one did.

They passed the bishop's town of Javorník and headed for the mountains and the Krutvald Pass. And there, in the spring, winter descended on them.

It began harmlessly, becoming overcast, with a somewhat harsher and colder wind and a few little snowflakes. Without warning, in an instant, the few snowflakes turned into a dense, white blizzard. The snow, falling in large flakes, instantly covered the road, painted the spruce white and filled the ruts. It stuck to the travellers' faces and filled their eyes with water as it melted on their eyelashes. The higher towards the pass they climbed, the worse it became – the ferociously howling gale intensified the blizzard, and they couldn't see anything apart from the manes of their horses, white from snow. Having blinded them, the blizzard toyed with their other senses – you would have sworn you'd heard wild laughter, giggles, cries and howling in the snow. None of the company was especially superstitious, but all at once they began to huddle and cower in the saddle, and without being urged at all, the horses trotted more briskly, giving only the occasional anxious snort.

Fortunately, the road led them into a basin, additionally protected by a beech forest. And then they smelled smoke and saw a small light. It was quiet. In weather like that not even the dogs felt like barking.

In the tavern, apart from beer, they were only serving herring, cabbage and peas without gravy – it was Lent, after all. There were so many guests that Reynevan and company found it hard to get a room. Among the customers, colliers from Złoty Stok and Cukmantl predominated and there were also plenty of refugees – from Paczków, Vidnava and even Głuchołazy. Naturally, the Hussite invasion was the chief topic of conversation, displacing even the economy and sex. Everybody was talking about the Hussites. Rzehors wouldn't have been Rzehors if he hadn't taken advantage of the occasion.

'Let me tell you this,' he began, when he was allowed to speak. 'In this world, some men make an honest and fair living and eat their daily bread. But others devour that bread like thieves and plunderers, for they didn't work for it, and only stole and robbed it from the men that work. And among them are noblemen, prelates, priests, monks and nuns, who suck the people like leeches, who don't follow the word of the Gospel, but in fact act quite the opposite. Thus, they are all enemies of God's law and deserve to be punished. Do you know, Brothers, how the peasants from Ketř and Głubczyce recently saved their homes and chattels? They took the matter into their own hands and resolved it themselves. When the Czechs reached them, they saw the charred ruins of the church and the lord's castle, and the lord and the parish priest dangling from nooses. Think this matter over, Christian Brethren. Think it over well!'

The audience nodded, yes, yes, that's true, he's right, the magnates and masters oppress us, give us a hard time, more beer, innkeeper, and the priests and monks are the worst bloodsuckers, damn them, beer, beer, *mehr Bier*, and taxes, *verfluchte Scheisse*, they'll probably throttle us soon, hard times have come, all our women think about is whoring, the young are ever discontent and don't listen to their elders, it used to be different, more beer, *mehr Bier*, crack open a keg, innkeeper, that herring of yours is damned salty.

Scharley, bent over his bowl, swore under his breath, and Samson whittled and sighed. Reynevan chewed the peas, which tasted like chicken feed without any gravy. Smoke crept under the tavern's low, soot-covered ceiling, cobwebs rippled and illusory shadows played.

They slept in the stable and in the morning continued their journey towards Lądek. Reynevan and Scharley wouldn't let Rzehors forget his performance of the previous evening. Taken to one side, he was made to listen to a few comments, mainly concerning the principles of underground activities. Reynevan reminded him that the Vogelsang were heading for Kłodzko on a secret, important mission, which demanded discretion and secretiveness. Bringing unwelcome attention on them could compromise the mission.

Rzehors sulked a little to begin with, referring to the order given him directly by Prokop, which was to spread propaganda among the peasantry. He boasted that he had shaken the morale of the bishop's infantry at Nysa, and so on and so forth. Finally, he agreed to observe a little more discretion. He held out until the village of Radochów, about half a mile past Lądek.

'Let me tell you this!' he yelled to a gathering of peasants and refugees after climbing up onto a barrel. 'Priests and magnates spread stories about the Czechs bringing war. They lie! This is not war but brotherly help, a peace mission. The Warriors of God are bringing a peace mission to Silesia, because peace, *pax Dei*, is the holiest of holy for good Czechs. But for there to be peace, we must defeat the foes of peace, with arms and force if needs be! It's not the Silesian folk, who are friends of the Czechs, who are the enemy, but the Bishop of Wrocław, a scoundrel, oppressor and tyrant. The Bishop of Wrocław is in league with the Devil – he poisons wells and has decided to spread a plague through Silesia and wipe out the people. Thus, the Czechs only stand against the bishop, the priests and the Germans! The common people must not fear the Czechs!'

When the crowd had grown in size, Bisclavret also found a chance to show what he could do. He read the crowd a letter from Jesus Christ that had fallen from Heaven onto a field near Opava.

'The end is nigh for you, O you sinners and scoundrels,' he read fervently. 'I am patient, but if you do not break away from Rome, from that Beast of Babylon, I, my Father and my angels will curse you for ever and ever. I shall send down on you hail, fire, lightning and storms, so your work will be spoiled. I shall destroy your vineyards and take away all your flocks. I shall punish you with bad air and bring great poverty down on you. Thus do I admonish you and forbid you from paying a tithe to the unworthy papists, priests and bishops, servants of the Antichrist; I forbid you from listening to them. And whoever betrays us will not see eternal life, and in his house will be born blind, deaf and scabrous children . . .'

The listeners crossed themselves, faces contorted in horror. Scharley swore under his breath. Samson kept peacefully silent and acted the idiot. Reynevan sighed but took no action and said nothing.

The valley of the Biała led them straight into the Kłodzko valley, where they stopped to rest in a tavern outside the village of Żelazno. The wealth of taverns and inns wasn't surprising since they were travelling along a trade route particularly popular with merchants wanting to avoid Kłodzko's tolls on the way to Bohemia. Owing to the considerable height of the Krutvald Pass, the road was too arduous for laden-down wagons, but merchants carrying light loads often took that route. The company chose it for other reasons.

In the tavern in Żelazno, apart from merchants, travellers and in recent times war refugees, there was a group of goliards, troubadours and merry scholars making a lot of noise and disturbance. Rzehors and Bisclavret naturally couldn't help themselves. It was too tempting. After telling a dozen obscene stories about the Pope, the Bishop of Wrocław and the clergy in general, a game of political riddles began.

'Why does the Roman Curia tend its sheep?' Rzehors asked.

'To fleece them!' the goliards shouted back, banging their mugs on the table.

'And now heed!' called Bisclavret. 'This'll be about the Roman hierarchy! Who'll guess this? *Virtus, ecclesia, clerus, diabolus! Cessat, calcatur, errat, regnat!*'

'Virtue perishes,' the students deftly paired up the words. 'The Church oppresses! The clergy goes astray! The Devil reigns!'

The innkeeper shook his head and several merchants ostentatiously turned their backs on them. The goliards' amusement was clearly not to the liking of five travellers dressed in dull clothing at a table alongside, particularly a fellow with a complexion as dark as a Gypsy's.

'Keep it down!' demanded the Dark Man finally. 'Keep it down, there are others here! We can't talk for your clamour!'

'Oho!' the goliards shouted back. 'Hark at him! A peasant wishes to object! Well, well!'

'Enough, I said!' The swarthy man wasn't giving up. 'Enough easy manners!'

The goliards drowned him out with whistles and catcalls. They went on revelling, but now a little less exuberantly and with slightly lowered voices. Perhaps that's why what happened, happened. Reynevan's hearing wasn't now dulled or drowned out by the laughter at foolish anecdotes about popes, anti-popes, bishops and priors, and he began to listen for other sounds and noises. All of a sudden, he began to pick out snatches of the five dull travellers' conversation from the bedlam and pandemonium. There was something in their conversation that enticed his ear, some words, syntax, phrases. Or a name, perhaps? Not knowing why, Reynevan wetted a finger in his beer and drew on the table-top the Supirre sign, which was used for eavesdropping. Feeling Samson's astonished eyes on him, Reynevan traced over the sign with a dry finger, deliberately thickening the line. He began to hear more clearly at once.

'Might one ask,' Samson enquired gently, looking up from his whittling, 'what you have in mind?'

'Don't interfere, please.' Reynevan was focused. 'Supirre, *spe, vero. Aures quia audiunt.* Supirre, *spe, vero.*'

He began making out every word before the sound of the spell had faded.

'May I croak if I be lying,' said the swarthy one. 'I ain't never seen such a fine body on a woman, never. Tits like Saint Cecilia's from a church painting, and firm, as though carved from marble. Stuck up even when she was on her back, they did. No wonder Duke Jan lost his head over that Frenchwoman.'

'But he grew wise,' said another with a snort, 'and got rid of her, tossed her into a dungeon.'

'May God reward him for that.' The swarthy man chortled. 'Or we'd not have had our pleasure with her. And such pleasure, you've not known the like ... Every night we gathered in the Ziębice gaol ... And took turns ... She fought back furiously,

I tell you, often scratching our faces like a she-cat . . . But that made the merriment all the greater.'

'Had you no fears? That she'd bewitch you? There was talk of the Burgundian being a witch, in league with the Devil. They say the Abbot of Kamieniec declared—'

'Aye,' admitted the swarthy man, 'I won't lie, I was frit at first. But my urges were stronger, ho-ho. How often do you have the chance to fuck a beauty that Duke Jan of Ziębice used to roll in his satin sheets? Anyhow, the prison guards allayed our fears. For three years they've been fucking all the young wenches who get locked up, and most of them have a delation for witchcraft. They fuck 'em freely. And no 'arm's came of it. Too much is made of sorcery.'

'What did you say at confession?'

'Confession? Fiddlesticks. I'm telling you, you never saw her, that Adèle. If you'd seen 'er, stripped naked, your fear would have vanished at once. Round about the fifth night, we—'

The swarthy man's company were never to find out what happened on the fifth night. Reynevan acted as though in a trance, almost mechanically. He leaped to his feet, sprang forward and punched the storyteller in the face. His nose crunched; blood gushed. Reynevan rocked at the hips and punched him again. The swarthy man screamed so horrifyingly that the tavern fell silent. People began to dash for the door. The traveller's companions sprang up but stood petrified. And when the swarthy man tumbled from the bench to the floor, they fled. Bisclavret and Rzehors pushed the students and goliards towards the door, while Scharley restrained the innkeeper, who had come running. A serving wench began to scream in a high-pitched voice.

The swarthy man on the ground was also screaming. Also in a high-pitched, desperate, pleading voice. He choked as Reynevan kicked him in the mouth with all his strength. When Reynevan jerked him to his feet, the man gobbled, spat blood and teeth, his head lolled, his eyes rolled up, he went limp and hung inertly. Reynevan took aim, but his fist was no longer enough, it was completely inadequate. Everything around him became blindingly bright, clear and white. He shoved the traveller against a post and snatched up a jug from the table, which shattered at the first blow. He then picked up a stout staff from the table and struck the man above the elbow. The bone crunched and the swarthy man howled like a dog. Reynevan struck him once more, with all his might, on the other arm. Then on the leg. Reynevan struck him on the head as he fell, and when he was lying on the ground, he kicked him in the belly, and then again in his groin with his other foot. The swarthy man wasn't screaming now, just shuddering as though in a fever, trembling convulsively. Reynevan was also trembling. He threw down the staff, knelt over the man on the ground, seized him by the hair and began to furiously slam the back of his head against the floor. There was a crunch and he felt the skull crack. Like an eggshell. Somebody caught him, violently tugging him away. It was Samson.

'Enough,' said the giant, holding him in a powerful grip. 'Enough, enough, enough. Control yourself!'

'If that's how you fellows carry out secretive activities and espionage, please accept my warm congratulations,' rasped Rzehors.

'We have a mission to accomplish,' added Bisclavret, 'and now they'll be hunting us for murder. Reynevan! What came over you? Why did you—'

'There was clearly a reason.' Scharley cut him off.

'Aha,' said Rzehors. 'Let me guess. Adèle Stercza. Reynevan! But you promised—'

'Shut up.'

A large, gleaming puddle, black in the light of torches, spread around the head of the man on the ground. Scharley knelt down beside him, seized him by the temples, gripped tightly and twisted suddenly and powerfully. There was a crunch and the fellow tensed up. Then drooped. Reynevan was still seeing everything in shades of bright, violent white. All sounds were muffled. His legs felt like jelly and he would have fallen if not for Samson.

Scharley stood up.

'Well, Reinmar,' he said coldly. 'That was something of a turning point for you. But you still have much to learn. I'm referring to your technique.'

'Let's get out of here,' said Bisclavret. 'Quickly.'

'You're right,' said Samson.

They didn't talk. They fled in silence at a gallop, following the Biała into the Kłodzko valley. Without knowing when, they found themselves at a crossroads, on the road running parallel with the right bank of the Nysa. Since noon, crowds of refugees had been moving along the road. They were being driven on by panic. By desperation.

The companions merged into the crowd. No one paid attention to them. No one showed any interest in them. No one came after them. No one was interested in a common crime, a trivial murder, an unimportant victim, an unimportant perpetrator. There were more important matters. Much more important. Much more dangerous. Sounding in the shaking voices of the refugees from the south.

Bobošov was burned down. Lewin was burned down. Homole and Štěrba Castles were besieged. Mezilesí was in flames. The invaders were marching through the Nysa valley, burning and murdering indiscriminately. A powerful army numbering several thousand Hussite heretics. The notorious Orphans under the command of the notorious Jan Královec.

*

Almost half a century later, fidgeting on a hard stool, an old chronicler monk from the Augustinian monastery in Żagań straightened up the parchment on his lectern and dipped his quill pen in ink.

In medio quadragesime Anno Domini MCCCCXXVIII traxerunt capitanei de secta Orphanorum Johannes dictus Kralowycz, Procopius Parvus dictus Prokupko et Johannes dictus Colda de Zampach in Slesiam cum CC equites et IV milia peditum et cum CL curribus et versus civitatem Cladzco processerunt. Civitatem dictam Mezilezi et civitatem dictam Landek concremaverunt et plures villas et opida in eodem districtu destruxerunt et per voraginem ignis magnum nocumentum fecerunt . . .

The monk jerked up his head in terror on smelling smoke. But it was only weeds being burned in the monastery garden.

Chapter Nineteen

In which Reynevan tries to help in the capture of the town of Kłodzko, insistently, doggedly and using various means, in other words, as the chronicler was to write half a century later, *per diversis modis.*

Kłodzko, whose panorama they saw in the morning, turned out to be a mass of red tiles and golden roofs perching on a hillside, descending to the very waters of the Młynówka Canal which encircled the hill. Reflected in the water of the Nysa, wide at this point, the slope was crowned by the castle hill dominating the town with its towers.

The road was still blocked by the conveyances of refugees, their stinking livestock and stinking young. The closer to the town, the greater the number of wagons, the hubbub became louder, the children appeared to be reproducing spontaneously and the stench suddenly intensified.

'The Old Horse Market is ahead of us.' Rzehors pointed. 'And the Wygon suburb. Soon there'll be the bridge over the Jodłownik.'

The Jodłownik turned out to be a small, fast-flowing river, and the bridge was totally thronged. Reynevan and company didn't wait for the road to free up but copied other riders by urging their mounts into the water and crossed the stream without difficulty. Further on, cottages, shacks and sheds stood on either side of the road and their dwellers busied themselves with everyday tasks, not gracing the travellers with anything more than a passing glance. They rode quite briskly for some time, but soon another obstruction stopped them. This time it was impassable.

'The bridge over the Nysa,' said Bisclavret, standing up in the stirrups. 'That's what is causing the hold-up. There's nothing for it. We'll have to wait.'

They waited. The queue moved forward slowly, at a speed that allowed them to admire the landscape.

'Oho,' muttered Rzehors. 'I see many changes. Walls and towers renovated, new earthworks, *chevaux-de-frise* and stockades on the banks of the Młynówka ... Sir Půta hasn't been idle. He clearly smelled a rat.'

'Ambrož's plundering raid of three years ago taught him something,' mumbled Scharley. 'Do you see that?'

Wagons laden with foodstuffs, stones and bundles of bolts increased the crush on the road.

'They're making ready the defence ... But what's happening over there? Are they knocking down buildings?'

'It's the Franciscan monastery,' explained Bisclavret. 'They're sensibly destroying it. In a siege, it would be an ideal breaching tower and it's built of stone to boot. Cannons are most accurate at four hundred paces, so balls shot from the monastery wall would strike the centre of the town, at the very town hall. It's sensible of them to knock it down.'

'The men demolishing it most energetically are the Franciscans themselves,' observed Scharley. 'I see they're working with great joy and gusto. Quite the symbolic twist of fate. They are smashing up their own monastery and enthusiastically, what's more.'

'As I said, they are acting sensibly,' Bisclavret replied. 'What a throng by the bridge . . . Dammit . . . Could they be searching?'

'If word has got out about—' Rzehors looked at Reynevan, who was still saying nothing.

'It hasn't.' Scharley cut him off. 'It can't have. Don't panic.'

'I won't, because I'm not accustomed to doing so,' Rzehors replied. 'And now I bid you farewell. I won't enter the town; you'll need someone outside the walls. Bisclavret? The usual signals?'

'Naturally. Farewell.'

Rzehors urged on his horse, melted into the crowd and vanished. The others crept on slowly towards the stone bridge. Reynevan was silent. Scharley rode closer and their stirrups clinked.

'You did what you did,' he said coldly. 'It can't be undone. For a few nights, instead of sleeping you'll be staring at the ceiling ravaged by your conscience. But right now, get a grip.'

Reynevan cleared his throat and looked at Samson. Samson didn't return his glance. He nodded, agreeing with Scharley.

Unsmiling.

In front of the bridge stood a squad of halberdiers and a group of monks in black habits with leather belts, identifying them as Augustinians.

'Heed!' shouted the corporals. 'Heed, people! The town is being made ready for defence, so entry onto the bridge is only granted to those skilled in arms and ready to fight! Only them as are skilled in arms! Those as aren't but can labour are to help demolish the monastery and erect a palisade. Their families may stay in Kłodzko. The rest go on, to the Rybaki suburb, where Franciscan friars are making vittles and serving them and tending to the sick. From there, after you've rested, head north, towards Bardo. I repeat, Kłodzko is preparing for a siege, entry only to those who are skilled in arms! They are to report at once in the town square, to receive orders from the guild masters . . .'

The crowd murmured and seethed, but the halberdiers were firm. Soon a division had occurred – some turned towards the bridge and the rest, several of them swearing vehemently, rode on along the Wrocław road leading between the bank of the Nysa and the cottages of the suburb.

It became a little less crowded.

'Heed! The town will be defended! Entry only to those as are skilled in arms!'

Unrest was occurring before the bridge. There was quarrelling; raised voices could be heard. Reynevan stood up in the stirrups. Three clergymen in travelling attire were arguing with a captain with a blue and white shield on his tunic. A tall Augustinian with an aquiline nose and bushy eyebrows walked over to the clergymen.

'Father Fessler?' he asked, recognising one of them. 'Parish priest of Waltersdorf? What brings you to Kłodzko?'

'An amusing jest, indeed,' answered the priest, frowning exaggeratedly. 'As if you didn't know. But we won't bandy words here, in front of these churls. Stand down your soldiers, Frater! You can bar the way to tramps, but not me. I've been travelling all night; I must rest before I continue.'

'And whither does your journey take you, may I ask?' said the Augustinian, slowly.

'Don't play the fool!' The parish priest was still extremely angry. 'The infernal Hussites are coming in a great host, burning, pillaging and murdering. My life is dear to me. I'm fleeing to Wrocław, perhaps they won't get that far. I advise you to do the same.'

'I thank you for the advice.' The Augustinian tilted his head. 'But duty keeps me here, in Kłodzko. We mean to defend the town along with Sir Půta. And shall succeed, with God's help.'

'Perhaps so, perhaps not,' the parish priest rejoined. 'But that's your affair. Out of my way.'

'We shall defend Kłodzko.' The monk had no intention of complying. 'With the help of God and good people. Any help will come in useful. And we shan't spurn yours, Fessler. You left your parishioners in the lurch. Here you have an opportunity to atone for your sin.'

'How dare you mention sin?' the priest yelled. 'And atonement? Out of my way! And watch your words – you insult the Church in my person! And what of it, O barefoot beggar? That I flee? Yes, I do, for it is my duty to save myself, my person and the Church! The heretics are approaching, murdering priests; I am saving the Church in my person, for the Church is me!'

'No,' responded the Augustinian calmly. 'It is not. The Church is faithful Christians. Your parishioners, whom you left in Waltersdorf, though you owe them help and support. It's them, those people yonder, preparing to defend, not to flee. So cast down your bundle, Reverend, seize a pick and get to work. And not another word, Fessler, not another word. I'm humble, but the captain here, God forgive him, is blessed neither with humility nor undue patience. He can order you to work with a flogging. He can also order you hanged. Sir Půta granted him wide powers.'

Fessler opened his mouth to protest, but the captain's expression made him close it quickly. He resignedly accepted the pick handed to him. His companions picked up shovels. They all had the expressions of true martyrs.

'God's grace is found in labour!' the monk shouted after them. 'And I advise you not to shirk or idle! The captain is watching!'

'Oh,' Bisclavret muttered under his breath. 'Oh, it won't be so easy for us, I observe. Hey, good folk! Who's that, the monk? Anyone know him?'

'That's Henryk Vogsdorf,' one of the wagoners shipping a load of stone balls for the bombards informed them. 'The Augustinian prior. The people hold him in high esteem.'

'Indeed.'

A mounted unit trotted over from Rybaki, heading for the Lower Bridge Gate. The halberdiers immediately stopped the column of refugees. As the unit approached, it was clear it consisted entirely of magnates. The wagoner transporting balls for bombards who had accompanied them from the bridge on the Nysa turned out to be well informed and talkative.

'The man at the head is our starosta, the Honourable Sir Půta of Častolovice,' he explained, needlessly. Everybody knew Sir Půta and his coat of arms – diagonal blue bands on a silver field. Reynevan and Bisclavret exchanged glances – the presence of Půta in Kłodzko meant that Prokop had left Nysa.

'Beside the starosta,' the wagoner pointed, 'rides the Deputy Starosta, Sir Hanusz Czenebis. Behind him is Sir Mikołaj Moschen, the leader of the mercenary force, and the Honourable Wolfram of Pannewitz. Yonder is Maltwitz, Lord of Eckersdorf. Gentlemen from the council: Czetterwang, Gremmel, Lischke ...'

Sir Půta's entourage rode through the Lower Gate with a thud, the sound of horseshoes echoing under the vault of the gatehouse. Once the mounted men had crossed the bridge on the Młynówka and disappeared through the Upper Gate, the halberdiers allowed the fugitives to proceed. Bisclavret suddenly cleared his throat, nudging Reynevan's stirrup with a foot. Needlessly. Reynevan had already noticed. Everybody had. A woman gave a soft scream behind them.

Four dead bodies were hanging on hooks from the *avant-corps* of the tower above the Upper Gate. The corpses of four people. To be precise, the remains of the corpses of four people, for the bodies were lacking everything that normally protrudes from a human being, including ears. It was clear that the upper and lower limbs had been worked on lengthily and diligently, for they now only loosely resembled limbs.

'They're Hussite spies!' The wagoner tugged on the reins. 'They caught one and he turned in his accomplices under torture. When the Hussites arrived at Kłodzko, they were meant to open the gates in secret and start fires in the town. They tortured and killed them in the town square two days since. They were cruelly tortured, to discourage others. Flesh torn with red-hot pincers and hooks, bones broken. And now the gates are well guarded by day and by night. You'll see.'

They did indeed. The Upper Gate was being guarded by a garrison of at least thirty well-armed soldiers. Steam belched from a cauldron suspended above a campfire, lifting the lid. The commander of the company, a bruiser with the face of a criminal, was tossing a stick for a dog.

Bisclavret looked on gloomily, saying nothing.

'Did you know any of the men hanging from the gate?' Scharley asked him, apparently unemotionally.

Bisclavret didn't look around. His face was set. Finally, he said, 'Indeed, but we weren't that close.'

The Water Gate was also being guarded by an equally strong garrison. Bisclavret swore softly.

'It won't be easy here,' he finally murmured. 'I'll bet it's the same at the other gates. I don't like the look of it, not one bit. We can bid goodbye to the idea of capturing and opening one of the gates. We need to revise our plans.'

'What do you suggest?' Scharley squinted. 'Turn on our heels and scarper? While we still can?'

'No,' said Reynevan. 'We're staying.'

'Do you have full control of your faculties?' The penitent eyed him up and down. 'Suitable to enable you to make decisions?'

'I'm in control of all my powers. We remain in Kłodzko.'

'Not as part of a penance, I trust? I ask because a short while ago you reminded me of a penitent craving expiation.'

'Never mind what impression I give.' Reynevan frowned. 'I heeded your advice and I've got a grip. And thus, I declare: we have our orders. The Orphans are depending on us, we must help them capture the town. Let us check all the gates.'

They did. Reynevan, Scharley and Samson inspected the wall from the Bridge Gate to the Castle Hill. Their survey left them pessimistic. The Bath Gate was barred securely using stones and timbers and a squad of soldiers was encamped outside the parish church as well. Companies of mercenaries were stationed at the other gates, the Green and the Czech.

They met Bisclavret at the agreed location, in the back of a bakery in Grodzka Street. Apart from news that the Water Gate and the Przyłęcko Gate were manned by large units of guards, Bisclavret brought some rumours, mainly from the front. It was confirmed that Prokop had left Nysa and led the Tábor north towards the Odra. The mission of Horn and Drosselbart must have succeeded, for the Taborites hadn't attacked Ziębice, Strzelin or Oława. That fact was widely commented on and opinions varied. According to some, Jan of Ziębice and Ludwik of Oława had committed treason. By negotiating with the heretics, they had proved to be no better than the traitor Bolko Wołoszek and those spies swinging on nooses from the Bridge Tower. There were also those who thought that the dukes had acted judiciously and by negotiating had saved the goods and lives of many people. If only other men, they added pointedly, though softly, could demonstrate similar good sense. The latter opinion was clearly beginning to prevail when news arrived in Kłodzko of the plunder and utter destruction by fire of Niemodlin after Bernard, the Duke of Niemodlin, Wołoszek's uncle, had rejected the invitation to parley with Prokop the Shaven.

But it was the Orphans marching from the south who worried the townspeople more acutely than Prokop's Taborites. News about the Orphans had just reached them and caused a considerable commotion, for it was understood that the entire country south of Kłodzko was in flames and running with blood, and the Hussites were pushing north unchecked. Refugees and eyewitnesses told in trembling voices of the fall of Homole Castle, which guarded the Lewin Pass and was thought to be impregnable. Two other fortresses that were supposed to have stopped the invaders – Štěrba and Karpno – had been captured and reduced to ashes. Lewin, Mezilesí, Schnellenstein, Lądek and numerous villages had gone up in smoke. Terrified refugees and eyewitnesses told how anybody who hadn't fled was slaughtered and the citizens of Kłodzko were close to sheer panic.

Bisclavret rubbed his hands together, but his joy was short-lived. They arrived at the town square just as Sir Půta of Častolovice addressed the crowd gathered there. Prior Vogsdorf was standing beside him.

'*Necessitas in loco, spes in virtute, salus in victoria!*' yelled Sir Půta. 'I vow, here, before you, on our Lady of Kłodzko and the Holy Cross, that I shall not take a step backwards. I shall defend the town or fall doing so!'

'I shall not leave undefended a single one of you, even the most meagre servant,' added Prior Vogsdorf, without emphasis. 'Not a single one of you. I swear on this Holy Cross.'

'We're out of luck,' said Bisclavret unemotionally. 'It couldn't be worse for us. That sodding Pûta *sans peur et sans reproche* and a bloody valiant and honest priest. What were the chances of that? Bad luck!'

'Bad luck,' Scharley calmly agreed. 'We simply don't have any fucking luck. Let's sum it up. Not a chance of opening any of the gates, and it will be difficult to sow panic among the defenders. What does that leave?'

'Murder.' The Frenchman grimaced. 'Assassination. An act of terror. We can try to eliminate Pûta and the prior. In that regard, we can count on Reynevan, who in Żelazno yesterday demonstrated hitherto—'

'Enough.' Reynevan cut him off. 'Not another word about it. I'm waiting for serious suggestions. What's left to us?'

'Fire.' Bisclavret shrugged. 'To start a fire – or rather several fires. In several locations at once. But that's impossible. Count me out of that.'

'Why?'

'Reynevan.' The Frenchman's voice was cold and his expression even colder. 'Play the idealist if you wish, or if you think it suits you. You may, if that's your will, fight for Wycliffe, Huss, God, the sacrament *sub utraque specie*, the good of the people and social justice. But I am a professional. I want to do my job and get out alive. What, don't you understand? Strategic fires, to be effective, must be started at the very moment of the attack. Understand?'

'I understand,' said Scharley, 'at the very moment of the attack. When there's no chance of fleeing. The men who capture the town with our help will cut us down during the customarily joyful bloodbath.'

'Perhaps we could agree on a signal—'

'By hanging a cord made of scarlet thread like Rachab at

Jericho? You've listened to too many sermons, laddie. Don't mix literature up with serious matters. I'm with Bisclavret and say: I won't take part in any insane schemes like that. I am also a professional, may I remind you. And have several professions. Each of them dear to me. Dear enough to make me love and value life.'

'There may be a way,' said Reynevan after a long pause, 'to start fires here without risking the precious skin of our gentlemen professionals.'

'Oh! Might there?' Scharley said.

'Indeed. For I, gentlemen, am also a professional.'

One might have thought that the apothecary's shop, the House at the Archangel in Prague, the refuge of scholars and philosophers, a temple of thought and progress, would be the last place one could learn how to manufacture magical incendiary bombs. But anyone who thought that would have been in error. It was possible to learn all kinds of arcana and skills at the House at the Archangel. And as luck would have it, Reynevan had personally participated in the process of building a powerful incendiary bomb.

Teggendorf and Radim Tvrdík, furious with a dishonest rival – the former parish priest at Saint Stephen's, a dilettante magician who functioned outside the guild – had decided to manufacture a bomb, called in magical jargon *Ignis inextinguibilis*. At first, they had planned to inform on him anonymously, counting on the local courts to deliver justice, but they regarded that as less than honourable revenge. The sorcerer priest had a beautiful country house in Bubny, to which he would invite maidens and married women for obvious reasons. That house was Teggendorf and Tvrdík's target. Hey, they joked reprehensibly, that damned priest will be dumbfounded when he returns from Prague with another bit of skirt to see a crater in the ground where the cottage used to stand!

The mages quickly got over their anger, however, and the bomb was never used. But the *Ignis inextinguibilis* was built, according to ancient Arabic prescriptions taken from books published in Constantinople. With the active involvement of Reynevan. Who now, over a year later, in Kłodzko, knew exactly what he needed.

'I need,' he declared confidently and emphatically to his companions, who were looking at him quite critically, 'two small barrels of olive oil, a bucket or two of wood tar, a small pail of honey, four pounds of saltpetre, two pounds of brimstone and the same again of slaked lime. On top of that, I must have a skin of resin, ideally pine resin. And two pounds of powdered antimony. It can be had in apothecaries' shops.'

'Is that all?'

'We'll make five bombs, I think. Thus, we need five clay jugs with narrow necks. Straw to wrap them up in. And lots of pitch to pour over them—'

'And a sea monster?' Bisclavret asked calmly. 'And the lance of Saint Maurice? And a flock of popinjays? Some apes? Won't you need them, too? You must have fallen on your head, Reynevan. The town's going to be besieged tomorrow; they're already rationing bread, salt can't be had for love nor money, and you're sending us out to buy brimstone and antimony.'

'I'll also need some sort of workshop.' Reynevan wasn't to be dissuaded. 'So stop bellyaching and get to work. The Vogelsang must have a resident spy in Kłodzko. Perhaps even more than one—'

'You saw those bodies hanging from the gate?' Bisclavret cut him off. 'They were the Vogelsang's resident spies. But yes, you're quite right, that wasn't all of them, we have one more. But contacting him now would mean he'll also hang. People speak during torture, Reynevan. And betray others.'

'Gentlemen.' Scharley joined in. 'You can't assume it'll end in disaster before we even give it a try. Hand over the list, Reinmar. We'll scour the town and see which of those ingredients we can conjure up. We'll find a workshop, too. We have money, we have time—'

'Things aren't so good regarding time,' retorted Bisclavret. 'Today is the twenty-second of March, the Monday after White Sunday. Královec's Orphans will be here on Wednesday. Thursday at the latest.'

'We'll manage,' said Reynevan with conviction. 'To work, gentlemen.'

The Vogelsang's resident sleeper in Kłodzko turned out to be the altarist at the Church of Our Lady, a man by the name of Johann Trutwein. He almost fainted at the sight of Bisclavret. However – and respect is due – he overcame his nerves quickly enough to be able to answer questions coherently. His teeth chattered somewhat when he talked about the fate of the other agents who were first tortured in the town hall's cellars and then in the town square, in full view of the common folk. The altarist himself survived only because the unfortunates didn't know anything about him, the Vogelsang being too shrewd to put all their eggs in one basket. But be that as it may, Johann Trutwein still got the fright of his life.

Bisclavret, however, had a reliable remedy for states of anxiety. At the sight of a pouch stuffed with money, the altarist brightened up, and having heard what they wanted from him acted admirably efficiently. He immediately offered the conspirators a workshop, the chambers in Milk Street of a merchant who had fled the town, entrusting Trutwein with the key and its supervision. He immediately also offered help in the purchase of the raw materials. He didn't ask what purpose they would serve. Just as well, as no one would have told him anyway. The same day, Reynevan, aided by spells and amulets, began to make the magical fuses, called *Ignis suspensus*, in the merchant's chambers. The rest of the squad headed to town to buy what was needed. And then a problem occurred.

The problem, astonishingly, turned out not to be sulphur or saltpetre, which could fairly easily be bought from the local apothecaries; not resin, which the local tar makers who had sought protection in the town had in abundance; nor powdered antimony, which was sold to them by an alchemist fleeing from Bystřice, at an admittedly quite extortionate price. The ingredient you'd have thought would be the least complicated caused the most problems: oil. There was no oil in Kłodzko. It had all been bought.

There were very few specialised oil merchants in Kłodzko since demand for oil was met entirely by the town presses. The manufacture of oil *intra muros* occurred in mills and was carried out by millers' apprentices as a sideline. Now, facing the threat of a siege, some of the apprentices had gone to fight, while those that remained were milling flour for bread day and night.

The invaluable altarist from Our Lady had a solution to that, too. In the parish church, he'd heard the whispered news that one of the local oilmakers had some reserves but was hiding them in order to make a killing at the right moment. Perhaps he might agree to sell a barrel or two. Having declared his readiness to intercede in the negotiations, the altarist went home, for dusk was falling.

The next day, there was a hubbub and excitement in the town. People were hurrying to the Green Gate, so the company also went there. The crowds squeezed onto the walls were pointing at columns of smoke rising to the south. Rengersdorf, Martinov, Hannsdorf and Železno were all burning, the news had it. The black smoke, dispersed by the wind into a ragged plume, soon rose to the west of the town over Schwedeldorf and Roszyce. The townspeople's anxiety rose to fever pitch. Combined with the earlier tidings about the burning down of Kunzendorf, the smoke to the west could mean only one thing: the Hussites were approaching Kłodzko from two sides.

'Tomorrow,' said Bisclavret, looking meaningfully at Reynevan after they returned. 'Královec will reach the town tomorrow.'

'I'll manage.' Reynevan pointed to five jugs wrapped up in straw. 'All we do is add the oil, mix it, bung it and cover it in pitch and it'll be ready. Then all that's left is to plant them in the right places. Have you decided where?'

Bisclavret smiled wolfishly. 'Indeed,' he drawled malevolently. 'It's all planned.'

'Trutwein should be here any moment now. With good news, God willing.'

Johann Trutwein only showed up at the tenth hour of the day, an hour after the Nones were rung at the Augustinian monastery. But he did indeed have good news. The oilmaker, he announced, would sell the oil. But he was asking . . .

Bisclavret scowled furiously when Trutwein whispered in his ear. He took the altarist to one side and the two of them argued at length.

'It's agreed,' he declared after returning. 'We fetch the goods tonight. The oilmaker demands the transaction take place secretly.'

In the evening, the flames of fires could now be seen. Kościelniki, Leszczyny, Pawłów, Ruszowice and the monastery village of

Podzamek were all in flames. The townspeople had been ordered off the walls and their places taken by soldiers. Bombards, catapults and other menacing-looking machines were being set up.

The town bells tolled the Angelus. Bisclavret refrained from comments, but Reynevan saw and understood the same as the others did.

'Frenchman?'

'What?'

'I presume you're able to contact Rzehors?'

'You presume correctly.'

'And our escape route? Have you thought about it?'

'You take care of your bombs, Reynevan. And make sure they explode. And that the spells work at a distance.'

'I am taking great care. You've no idea how much.'

The bell at Our Lady's announced the *ignitegium*, the order to douse fires and lights, with three successive, rapid strikes. It was the signal for decent burghers to go to bed.

Reynevan, Bisclavret, Scharley and Samson weren't decent burghers. Nor could Johann Trutwein, who appeared in Milk Street at dusk, be counted among them. When darkness fell, they began to steal towards the area around the Water Gate and Butcher Street.

Though the *ignitegium* had been announced, the town wasn't asleep, but remained anxiously watchful. No wonder, since to the south and west the sky was bright with the glow of fire and the enemy was almost at the gates. Outside the walls, soldiers' campfires were burning, the guards were shouting to each other on the walls and the footsteps of patrols thudded in the streets. In such conditions, it took them much longer than they had planned. Trutwein began to worry that the oilmaker wouldn't wait, presuming they had given up on the idea.

His fears appeared to be justified. It was dark in Butcher Street; they couldn't see lighted candles or cressets in any of the windows. The gate in the courtyard was open, however.

'Scharley, Samson,' whispered Bisclavret. 'Stay here. Keep your wits about you.'

Scharley placed a hand on the hilt of the falchion and Samson also raised his *goedendag* purposefully. Reynevan felt the hilt of his dagger and followed Bisclavret and Trutwein into the darkness of the gateway reeking of cat.

A candle flame flickered and shone in a window at the very end of the courtyard.

'Over there . . .' whispered Trutwein. 'On we go . . .'

'Wait,' hissed Bisclavret. 'Stop. Something's not right. Something's—'

About a dozen thugs leaped out of the darkness and fell on them.

For some time, Reynevan had been squeezing in his fist one of Telesma's amulets, made from a chip of a belemnite guard. All he had to do was shout out the spell.

'*Fulgur fragro!*'

There was a deafening roar, a blinding flash and the air imploded with a piercing whistle. Reynevan bolted, hard on Trutwein's heels. Bisclavret dashed after them, having first managed to slash several of the bruisers – who were temporarily blinded and deafened – with his Andalusian *navaja*.

The trap had been carefully laid, however, and their escape route was cut off. When they rushed out into the street, they ran straight into a fierce brawl. Scharley and Samson were resisting a massed attack by more thugs.

'Take them alive! Alive!' thundered a command. Reynevan knew that voice.

He felt somebody seize him by the shoulder. He drew his

dagger, slashed vigorously, twisted the hilt in his hand, stabbed from above, spun around, made a powerful reverse cut right after it, using his momentum and position, from right to left. He heard a cry; blood splashed his face and two bodies fell at his feet. Blood spattered his face again, but this time it was the work of Scharley and his curved falchion. Someone grabbed him again, at the same time seizing his wrist above the dagger. There was a hollow thud and the grip loosened. It was Samson, who had appeared at his side, felling the assailants one after another with vicious blows of the *goedendag*. But more attackers kept coming.

'Run for it!' yelled Bisclavret, stabbing and slashing with the *navaja*. 'Fast! Follow me!'

Scharley darted after the Frenchman, wielding the falchion as he ran, attackers quailing before him. Reynevan was grabbed again, but the man howled and recoiled as the dagger plunged into his eye. As Reynevan fought off another attack, knife grated against knife, steel against steel, sending up sparks. Fortunately, the knifeman fell like an ox in a slaughterhouse after a blow from the *goedendag*.

Reynevan snatched a pot wrapped in straw from inside his jerkin. Five bombs were still in the merchant's chambers in Milk Street. That one was the sixth.

'*Ignis! Atrox!* Yah, Dah, Horah!'

There was a hiss, a loud blast and the street was lit up by a powerful explosion that splashed liquid fire in all directions, sticking to everything within range. Everything in the vicinity caught fire. That included a woodpile, the whitewashed wall of a house, the cobbles and the slops in the gutter. And several attackers. The screams of the men being burned rose up to the starry sky. Then Reynevan recognised a familiar shape in the light of the blaze. A black cloak, a black doublet and black shoulder-length hair. An avian face and a nose like a bird's beak.

'Take them alive!' yelled the Wallcreeper, shielding his face from the roaring flames. 'I want them alive!'

'Run!' Samson tugged Reynevan, paralysed by the horror, by the arm. 'Run!'

'Fire! Fire!'

They ran as fast as they could as the lane behind them thundered with the sound of their pursuers' footsteps.

'Take them alive! Aliiive!'

'Fire! Fiiiire!'

They ran as fast as they could, animal fear giving them strength. They knew what being taken alive meant. A long, slow death in a torture chamber, sides burned with red-hot irons, broken joints, bones crushed in pincers and boots. A cruel death on the scaffold. *Anything but him*, thought Reynevan, bounding like a greyhound. *Anything but Birkart Grellenort.*

One of the men was catching up and Samson twisted back to slam him with the *goedendag*. Reynevan stabbed a second from below, in the groin. The man howled and curled up on the cobbles. A third tripped over him. Before he hit the ground, Reynevan slit open his face.

They ran on, having gained a little advantage. They saw Scharley indicating the way – into a narrow alley. They ran. Bisclavret was in front of them. Trutwein had vanished.

'Run! Now left!'

The sounds of their pursuers quietened somewhat; they must have briefly confused them, and they were being hampered by people hurrying with buckets to put out the fire. But Reynevan and Samson didn't stop, they ran without pausing to draw breath. Mud squelched under their feet, water splashed, a dreadful stench assailed their nostrils, an awful fug of urine and faeces. Bisclavret and Scharley broke some planks with a bang.

'Get in! Go on, fast!'

It was some time before Reynevan understood that the Frenchman was instructing them to enter the black, circular hole of a latrine belching out a vile stench. Scharley had just vanished into it with a splash. *Better shit than a torture chamber*, he thought. He took a deep breath. The faeces below greeted him with pleasant warmth. And then a great wave as Samson dropped into it. The stench was overpowering.

'This way, ugh ...' Bisclavret spat out what the wave had carried into his mouth. 'To the canal. Heads up. It soon gets better. There'll be more clearance later.'

They heard their pursuers approaching. Reynevan held his nose between his fingers and dived under.

Reynevan preferred to erase from his memory the trek through the clay-lined sewer on his hands and knees. The clearance to the brick vault increased and diminished by turns, so sometimes his mouth was above and sometimes below the liquid shit. His hands and knees sank into a thick layer with the consistency of potter's clay on the bottom, which was shit that had settled there over the last sixty years, since, as Reynevan found out later, the Kłodzko sewage system dated back to 1368.

It was difficult to say how long their ordeal lasted. It felt like an entire aeon. But suddenly there was the overwhelming joy of fresh air and the delight of fresh water bringing tears to their eyes – they plopped out of the sewer straight into the Młynówka. From there, it wasn't far to the Nysa, where they were able to rinse themselves in the faster-flowing current. They jumped into the water and swam across to the right bank. The surface of the water shimmered in the gold and red of the great blaze consuming the shacks and sheds of Rybaki and Wygon. The shapes of riders flickered.

'Dammit,' said Scharley in a tired voice. 'I had a currant bun in my pocket . . . It must have fallen out. That's breakfast down the drain . . .'

'Who betrayed us? Trutwein?'

'I doubt it.' Reynevan sat down in the shallow water, revelling in the sensation of it washing him clean. 'The bomb I set was thanks to him . . . He supplied me with a little oil. He filched it from the church . . .'

'Oil in a church?'

'For extreme unction.'

Horses' hooves thudded dully on the riverside sand.

'Vogelsang! Good to see you sons of bitches alive!'

'Rzehors! Ha! And Brázda of Klinštejn?'

'You're alive, Reynevan! Greetings, Scharley! Hail, Samson!'

'Berengar Tauler? You, here?'

'In person. I went from the Tábor to the Orphans, but I still maintain that soldiering has no future . . . Oh, you stink to high heaven—'

'To horse.' Brázda of Klinštejn cut off the conversation. 'Královec and Prokop the Small want to see you. They're waiting.'

The Orphans' headquarters was located in a tavern in the Neulende suburb. When Reynevan entered, led in by Rzehors and Brázda, a silence fell.

He knew the commander-in-chief of the Orphans' field army, Hejtman Jan Královec of Hrádek, a sourpuss and evil character, but one who fully merited his reputation as an able commander and was adored by his soldiers almost as much as Žižka had been. He also knew Jíra of Řečice, a hejtman from Žižka's old guard. Naturally, he knew the preacher, Little Prokop, who followed the hejtmans everywhere. He knew the ever-smiling and invariably cheerful Sir Jan Kolda of Žampach. He didn't know the young nobleman in full armour with a shield twice divided into black, silver and red fields. He was informed it was Matěj Salava of Lípa, Hejtman of Polička. He couldn't see Piotr of Lichwin, known as Piotr the Pole, anywhere, and only later found out that he had remained with the garrison in the captured stronghold of Homole.

Královec received calmly the news that the sabotage in the town had failed, that none of Kłodzko's gates had been forced and no fires had been started.

'Oh well, that's life.' He shrugged. 'In any case, I've always thought that Prokop and Flutek hold an inflated opinion of you, Reynevan of Bielawa. You are simply overrated. On top of that, forgive me, you reek.'

'I fled Kłodzko through the sewers.'

Královec was still composed. 'So the town shat you out. How symbolic. Now go and get washed and tidied up. A sizeable job and a serious task await us here. We have to capture that town ourselves, without outside help.'

'In my opinion,' Reynevan blurted out, 'Kłodzko ought to be avoided. The defence is extremely strong, the commanders valiant, the morale of the garrison high ... Wouldn't it be better to go straight to Kamieniec? And the Cistercian monastery? It's very wealthy.'

Jíra of Řečice snorted and Kolda shook his head. Královec said nothing, but he sneered and looked at Reynevan long and unwaveringly.

'When I want your opinion in military matters,' he finally said, 'I'll let you know. Dismissed.'

Grey smoke trailed over the monastery garden and there was a smell of burned weed. The old monk chronicler dipped his quill in the inkwell.

Anno Domini MCCCCXXVIII feria IV ante palmarum
Viclefiste de secta Orphanorum cum pixidibus et machinis
castrum dictum Cladzco circumvallaverunt, in quo castro
erant capitanei dominus Puotha de Czastolowicz et Nicolaus
dictus Mosco, et ibi dictis pixidibus et machinis sagittantes et
per sturm et aliis diversis modis ipsum castrum conabantur
aquirere et lucrare; ipsi vero se viriliter defenderunt . . .

The quill scratched. There was a smell of ink.

'Onwards!' yelled Jan Kolda of Žampach, shouting over the bangs and shouts. 'Onwards, Warriors of God! Up the walls! Up the walls!'

A stone – probably shot from either a catapult or a mounted crossbow – slammed into the barricade with such force it would have knocked it down, along with Reynevan and the rest of the garrison hiding behind it, had Samson not been with them. The giant staggered under the impact but remained on his feet, holding on to the barricade's support. That was fortunate, because missiles were showering ceaselessly down from the walls. In front of Reynevan's eyes, a bowman leaning out from the next pavise was hit straight in the forehead, the ball smashing his skull into pieces.

A wild yell resounded from the Czech Gate – the Orphans had managed to put ladders and branched boughs against it and were now climbing up them and being decimated by the fire from above. Boiling water and molten pitch were poured on them, along with a hail of rocks and spiked timbers. The companies of Jíra of Řečice attacking the section between the Green Gate and the Bathing Gate were faring no better. Twice they had put up ladders and twice been repelled.

Tauler and Samson pushed the barricade forward again.

Rzehors cursed as he fought with the jammed lever of a cross-bow. Scharley and Bisclavret, having loaded a harquebus, poked the barrel out from cover and fired at the same moment as a wagon-mounted twelve-pound cannon was fired from behind the next barricade. Smoke enveloped everything and Reynevan was deafened for a few seconds. He couldn't hear anything, not bangs, not shouts, not blasphemous oaths or the howling of the wounded. Before he was struck in the arm by the handle of a scourge, he hadn't even heard Hejtman Jan Královec, who had ridden up on horseback, showing crazy disregard for the bolts whistling around him.

'. . .'s sake!' Reynevan finally heard. 'Can't you fucking hear? You were forbidden from joining the attack! I forbade you from playing at war! We need you for other matters! Away, to the rear! Everybody to the rear! We're falling back!'

Kolda's soldiers at the wall couldn't hear Královec's order, but they didn't need to. Casting down the ladders, they retreated. Some retreated in orderly fashion, in array, hiding behind pavises and harrying the defenders on the battlements with heavy fire from handgonnes. But others simply fled, flying in panic, just to get away from the walls and the death raining down on them. From outside the Green Gate, Reynevan saw the Orphans of Jíra of Řečice also retreating towards Zarzecze and Neulende. The defenders on the walls yelled triumphantly, brandished their weapons and waved pennants, ignoring the incendiary missiles, balls, bolts and round shot that the attackers were unremittingly shooting at them from below. From the gate tower, the white and blue pennant of Půta of Častolovice and a large processional crucifix were raised and the people roared and sang, crowing in triumph. Although a quarter of the town was in flames, they were exulting.

Bisclavret attached the hook to the edge of the barricade, took aim and brought the fuse to the touch-hole. The harquebus fired with a roar.

'May it fly straight up Sir Pŭta's arse!' growled Bisclavret through the smoke. 'Direct my ball, Our Lady!'

'We're falling back.' Scharley wiped his face, smudging soot. 'We're falling back, lads. The fun's over. Kłodzko has repelled the attack.'

'Jesuuuuuus!' yelled Parsifal Rachenau at the top of his voice as he lay on the floor of the hoard. 'Jesuuuuuus! Chriiiist!'

'Stop it,' hissed Henryk Baruth, called Starling, leaning over him. 'Behave yourself! Don't be a wench!'

'I am . . .' Parsifal sobbed. 'I am a wench now! Chriiiist! It tore off . . . It tore everything off! Oh God, oh God . . .'

Starling stooped over, his nose almost touching his friend's bloody buttock, and expertly examined the wound. 'Nothing's been torn off,' he stated firmly. 'Everything's in its place. The ball's just buried in your arse, and not even that deep. It was shot from distance, had no power . . .'

Parsifal howled, sobbed and burst into tears. From pain, shame, fear and relief. For he had already imagined, clearly and in detail, a truly infernal and hair-raising scene: there he was, speaking in a high falsetto, transformed into a capon like Peter Abélard, like Peter Abélard sitting and writing idiotic treatises and letters to Ofka of Baruth, and Ofka meanwhile indulging herself in the bedchamber with another full-blooded man with everything where it was meant to be. War, the boy realised in horror, was an awful thing.

'Everything's . . . there?' he asked, swallowing back tears. 'Starling . . . Take another look to be sure . . .'

'Everything's there.' Starling calmed him. 'And it's almost stopped bleeding. Hold on. A monk's hurrying here with bandages, he'll soon pluck the ball out of your backside. Wipe away your tears, folk are watching.'

The defenders of Kłodzko weren't watching, though, weren't interested either in the tears or the bloody wound in the bottom of Parsifal of Rachenau. They were busy raising triumphant cheers on the walls. Sir Půta of Častolovice and Prior Vogsdorf were being carried aloft.

'But I wear a blessed gorget with Our Lady around my neck,' Parsifal suddenly groaned. 'I bought it from the monks . . . It was meant to protect me from enemy bullets! How can that be?'

'Shut your bloody mouth—'

'It was meant to protect me!' the boy howled. 'How can it be? What kind of—'

'Shut it,' Starling hissed. 'Shut your yap, or woe on us.'

The quill scratched.

The witnesses of the dicebatur, *like Kralowycz,* capitaneus Orphanorum, *enraged by the doughty resistance of the defender, ordered special criers, called* Stentores, *to shout loudly beneath the walls and threaten the defenders with foul torture if they didn't surrender the town, trying to strike terror in them by that clamour. Seeing how vain were their efforts, he ordered a length of white canvas measuring a dozen cloth-yards and painted on it in great letters: SURRENDER OR DEATH and* demonstrare *to those defenders on that section of wall which* Prior Henricus et fratres canonici regulares *had defended and could read. Howbeit,* Prior Henricus, *the Hector of Kłodzko, being valiant of heart, felt not fear. He ordered the brothers to take a cloth of a dozen cloth-yards also and paint on it in contempt of those Wycliffites: BEATA VIRGO MARIA ASSISTE NOBIS.*

'What?' growled Jan Kolda. 'What have they daubed?'

Brázda of Klinštejn snorted. Jíra of Řečice chortled.

Painted in large letters on the canvas hung on the walls by the yelling and cheering defenders were the words:

DEINE MUTTER DIE HUR

Královec looked at the banner for a long while, long and un-waveringly, as though hoping that the letters would form them-selves into something different. Finally, he turned around and met Reynevan's eyes.

'Kamieniec, you said? The Cistercian monastery? The wealthy Cistercian monastery. Was that it?'

'Aye, it was.'

'Well then ...' Královec looked at Kłodzko once again and sighed. 'Well then, what are we waiting for? Let's go.'

Et sic Orphani, the quill scratched on the parchment, *a Cladzco feria II pasce recesserunt.*

The chronicler made a full stop, grunted and straightened his aching back.

Writing chronicles was hard work.

Chapter Twenty

In which participants, eyewitnesses and chroniclers recall certain events from the period directly preceding Easter, 1428. And again, no one knew who to believe.

'My name, Holy Tribunal, is Brother Zephyrin, from the monastery of the Cistercian Order in Kamieniec. Please forgive my confusion, Reverend Fathers, but it is the first time I am come before the Office . . . Though only to deposit a *testimonium*, but still . . .

'Yes, sir, indeed, I shall get to the point. Which is what happened in the monastery on that tragic day of Holy Tuesday, *Anno Domini* 1428. And which I saw with my own eyes. And shall testify thereto under oath, as God is my— Beg pardon? To the point? *Bene, Bene.* Right away.

'Some of the brethren of the monastery had already fled by the Saturday before the Sunday during the fast, when *Judica me Deus* is sung, when the heretics were burning Otmuchów, Paczków and Pomianów. During the night, we saw fires covering half the sky and at dawn the sun barely broke through the smoke. At that time, as I said, some of the *fratres* had lost heart and fled, taking only what they could gather up in their hands. The abbot fulminated, calling them cowards, threatening them with divine punishment – ha, had I known what was awaiting him, I'd have fled first. And I, too – I shan't lie to the Holy Tribunal – would also have fled, only I had nowhere to go. I am a Lombard from the town of Tortona, and I came to Silesia from Altenzelle, first to Lubiąż, and then from the monastery in Lubiąż wending to Kamieniec. Eh? I should keep to the subject? *Bene, Bene*, I shall. I'll tell you how it was.

'Soon *post dominicam Judica quadragesimalem* I hear from the refugees: the heretics are gone, they headed for Grodków. The relief! I hasten to the church, lie spreadeagled on the floor in front of the altar, *gratias tibi Domine*, thank You, O Great Lord. And, once again, cries, yelling: why, fresh followers of that Satan Huss, called the Orphans, are coming from Kłodzko. They burned down that hapless town Bardo a second time. At first, hope sprang – perhaps they'll pass us by? Perhaps they'll choose Frankenstein? Take the Wrocław road, perhaps they won't think to turn towards Kamieniec. Thus, to the church, to pray in that intention, *Sancta Maria, Mater Christi, Sancta Virgo virginum, libera nos a malo, sancte Stanislaus, sancte Andrea, orate pro nobis* ... But our prayers availed nothing, it was clear our Lord wanted us to taste – like Job ... Ah, yes, indeed. Keep to the subject.

'Thus, in brief: the crux is that the Devil's hordes fell on the monastery on Holy Tuesday itself. They attacked suddenly, like a bolt from the blue; they climbed the walls, beat down the gate and before you could say *peccatores te rogamus* the entire horde was inside. And set to killing ... What horror! *Sanctus Deus, sanctus fortis, sanctus immortalis, miserere nobis* ... They stuck Brother Adalbert with a spear, Brother Pius fell from sword cuts, as did Saint Dionysius ... Brother Mateusz was downed with a crossbow, and many others *graviter vulneratis* ... And the Hussites, may God punish them, began to drive cattle from the cowshed, piglets from the sty, lambs ... They took them all, to the last beast ... Ugh, scoundrels, not only were they *haeretici*, but also *latrones et fures*! From the church they seized vessels, reliquaries, copes, chasubles, a great silver cross, votive offerings, candlesticks . . . They left nothing. They drove those of us who were left alive up against the courtyard wall. The leader of that pack, an ugly fellow, no doubt a heretic, they called him Kralowicz, with another called Kolda, I believe. They called forth peasants. For may you know, Holy Tribunal, that local peasants – damned heathens, turncoats – were marching with those Hussite Czechs. The heretic Kralowicz orders them, go on, show us which of these monks oppressed the people and we'll try them here and now. And he would punish the bloodsuckers – that's what he called us. And those churlish Judases at once pointed out Brother Maternus: he ground us down. Indeed, 'twas true that Frater Maternus could be stern with the peasants, he was wont to say *rustica gens optima flens et pessima ridens*. And for that they hauled him out and beat him to death with flails, the scoundrels. Then *Celerarius* Scholer was killed, the peasants pointed him out because he manhandled wenches, and at times boys, too . . . After him, *Custos* Wencel, Brother Idzi, Brother Laurenty . . . They screamed, moaned, begged, blood spurted, we on our knees, weeping, *ab ira tua, ab odio et omni mola voluntate libera nos, Domine . . .*

'What happened to the father abbot, you ask? I shall tell you. The Hussites were making ready to go when a young lordling hurried up, blond-haired, personable, but with an evil eye, mouth foully twisted. They called him "Renewan". Not at all, Reverend Father, I'm not in error, I heard clearly: Renewan. I can swear on the cross . . . Then that Renewan seized Father Abbot by the habit. This here is Mikołaj Kappitz, Abbot of Kamieniec, he cried, the cruellest oppressor, a knave, an informer and a . . . erm, forgive me . . . cur of the Inquisition. And he bent over to the abbot and said, teeth grinding, *Do you recall Adèle, you whoreson?*

Whom you accused of witchcraft in Ziębice for a hundred ducats? And sent to her death? You'll pay for it now. Recall Adèle as you plummet to Hell, despicable priest. Thus he spoke before hauling the abbot into the courtyard. I heard correctly. Every word. I can swear on the cross …

'Keeping to the point: they beat Abbot Kappitz to death. They beat him with clubs and axes … Now, that Renewan, he just stood and watched.

'And that is everything that happened, Holy Tribunal, on that Holy Tuesday, *Anno Domini* 1428. I have spoken the truth, the whole truth and nothing but the truth, so help me God. The heretics burned down our church and abbey. They set fire to the barns, the mill, the bakery and the brewery, then went away, burning down our monastery village, Radkowice, on the way. But, on leaving, they stripped of our habits those of us who survived. At that time, we didn't understand why they did so. It only became apparent later. When the brigands attacked Frankenstein …'

'Who are you?' yelled the guard at the Kłodzko Gate. Alongside him, several other men with cocked crossbows leaned out from the battlements. 'The gates are locked! We aren't letting anyone into the town!'

'We are from Kamieniec!' crowed Rzehors from beneath his hood. 'Cistercians! We fled from the slaughter through the woods! The monastery is afire! Open the gate, good fellow!'

'Not a chance! It is forbidden! Understand, monk? Orders!'

'Let us in, by God,' Reynevan pleaded. 'Brothers in Christ! The heretics are hot on our heels! Don't leave us to our doom! Do you want our blood on your consciences? Open up!'

'How should I know who you are? Perhaps Hussites in disguise?'

'We are monks, good and devout Christians! Cistercians from Kamieniec! Can't you see our habits? Open up, by the living God!'

A monk appeared beside the captain of the guard, a canon of the Holy Sepulchre, judging from his habit.

'If you are indeed Kamieniec Cistercians,' he shouted, 'what is your abbot's name?'

'Mikołaj Kappitz!'

'What canticle is sung on the *Laudes* on Sunday and on feast days?'

Reynevan and Bisclavret looked at each other vacantly. Scharley rescued the situation.

'The Canticle of the Three Young Men,' he declared confidently. 'Called the *Benedicite Dominum*.'

'Sing it.'

'What?'

'Sing it!' yelled the captain. 'And loud! Or we'll make a fucking pincushion out of you!'

'*Benedicite, omnia opera Domini, Domino!*' bellowed the penitent, out of tune, saving the day again. '*Laudate et superexaltate eum in saecula! Benedicite, caeli, Domino, benedicite, angeli Domini . . .*'

'They are monks, in truth,' said the canon of the Holy Sepulchre gravely. 'We must let them in. Draw back the bolts! Make haste, make haste!'

The Augustinian chronicler leaned over his parchment and resumed writing.

But it proved to be treachery, for they were not monachi *but heretics,* qui se Orphanos appellaverunt, *dressed in habits stripped from the Cistercians, when* in feria III pasce *they attacked the* monasterium Cisterciense de Kamenz, *which* monasterium eodem die efractum et concrematum est. *They were not the Lord's flock but wolves*, lupi in vestimento ovium, *the same notorious traitors who called themselves the Vogelsang: traitors, Judases, scoundrels with neither honour nor faith. Those blackguards forced their way through the imprudently opened gate and fell on the guard. Behind them was a horde of further* Orphani, *previously hidden under a tarpaulin on a wagon like the Achaeans in the wooden horse. The guard having been killed and the gates opened wide, in galloped the heretics'* equites, *behind them rushed the infantry and, in no time, there were five and a half hundred heretics, with more coming anon. And dreadful terror occurred . . .*

No one dared to oppose them as they ran through the new town, down New Street. There were scarcely two dozen of them, but they made enough noise and racket for a hundred. The Hussites yelled and whooped, clattering on wooden clappers. Bisclavret and Rzehors were blowing into brass trumpets and Scharley was beating a metal cymbal. Horror-struck and stupefied by the deafening hullabaloo, the citizens of Frankenstein fled before them, running towards the town square. Only once were crossbows and harquebuses fired at them, from the windows of the brewery, but they didn't even slow or stop making a racket. The yells and gunfire intensified from the Kłodzko Gate, which had been breached deceitfully, to the south, and soon also from the west; the Orphans were evidently storming the castle and the Church of Saint Anne.

They ran. They were shot at again in Lower Bathhouse Street, this time to some effect; two bodies were left lying in the muddy gutter. The small garrison of the Ziębice Gate also greeted them with a chaotic crossbow salvo, but the bowmen's hands were shaking, and no wonder: they had already seen the black smoke rising above the roofs and heard the cries of the slaughtered.

They attacked the guards with fury at once and it appeared as though the Orphans wanted to take out their anger after the reckless run through the streets.

At once, bodies began to fall and blood to stain the cobbles outside the gate. Reynevan didn't take part in the fighting, but, along with Berengar Tauler and Samson, reached the gate and began sliding back the bolts. Scharley was watching their backs and cut down a guard with rapid blows of his falchion who rushed at them.

The bolts and beams clattered down, the double gate pushed from the outside opened wide and cavalrymen rode in with a thud of hooves, followed by a wave of infantry uttering battle cries. Horseshoes boomed on the cobbles and the Orphans poured into the town, straight down Ziębice Street.

'Good work, Reynevan!' yelled Jan Královec of Hrádek, reining in his horse in front of him. 'Good work with that gate! I'm changing my mind about you! They were right to praise you! And now onwards, onwards! The town still isn't ours!'

When they reached the town square, it appeared that Královec was wrong and that Frankenstein was already in the Orphans' hands. The house of the Abbot of Henryków was in flames, the cloth hall in flames, the market stalls in flames; fire and smoke were belching from the windows of the guilds' houses. The town hall was still being stormed, as above the battle cries of the attackers rose the high-pitched screams of the slaughtered. People being tossed from windows were falling directly onto the blades of voulges and halberds held upright. A massacre was taking place in the arcades around the town square. Shots could still be heard from the southern part of the town; the castle, under attack from the forces of Kolda of Žampach, was clearly putting up a fight. But a fire was burning fiercely in the bell tower of Saint Anne's.

Hussite foot soldiers rushed into the town square, followed by the cavalry led by Matěj Salava. The young knight's face was black with soot and his sword dripped blood.

'Over there!' Královec pointed with his mace, trying to bring his horse under control as it slipped on the blood. 'We can cope here. You men, get over there! To the Dominican monastery! To the monastery, Warriors of God!'

'Come on, lads.' Reynevan turned around. 'To the monastery. Quickly. Scharley, Rzehors . . .'

'Let's go, Reinmar the Doughty Gate-Opener,' called Královec.

'Tauler, are you with us? Samson?'

'I'm here, too.'

Salava's mounted troops, quite useless in the fighting to capture buildings, scoured the streets, leaving the storming of the Dominican monastery to the infantry. Numbering over a hundred men, it was being commanded by Smil Půlpán, the Deputy Hejtman of Náchod, a chubby fellow with a shaved head. Reynevan recognised him, having seen him before.

'Have at them!' yelled Smil Půlpán, pointing his short sword in the direction of the attack. 'Have at them, Brothers! Kill them!'

Yelling, the Hussites sprang to the assault, faltering over and over under a hail of missiles, only to spring forth again at once.

'Have at them! Death to the papists!'

Supported by the burghers and guildsmen, the Dominicans bravely and staunchly defended their monastery, but it was a vain attempt. The Orphans' advantage was overwhelming, the virulence of their attack terrible. The monks yielded under the assault, falling back, leaving bodies in white habits, surrendering one building after the next to the Hussites.

The vestibule and barricaded main doors of the Church of the Exaltation of the Cross were the last bastion. The monks fought to the last crossbow bolt and the last harquebus ball. And to the last man.

When, enraged by the rearguard action, the Orphans finally burst into the chancel over the corpses, the rainbow-coloured beams shining from the stained-glass windows revealed only two monks left alive. One, head lowered, was kneeling at the altar, by the *antepodium*. The second was shielding the first with his body and a crucifix.

'*Templum Dei sanctum est!*' His voice, albeit reedy, soared and echoed high up. 'Whoever destroys God's temple destroys God! Withdraw, hell spawn! Withdraw, demons, heretics, before God strikes you down!'

'That's Jan Buda,' explained one of the Silesians allied with the Orphans grovellingly. 'The one kneeling is Mikołaj Karpent-ariusz, their prior. They have both preached against the teach-ings of Master Huss. They finished every sermon "the only good Czech is a dead Czech". Both blessed the weapons of the soldiers marching on Náchod.'

Smil Půlpán's cheek and neck were covered in blood; he was holding his ear, part of which had been torn off by a crossbow bolt. About a dozen of his men had perished and another dozen were injured, but his ear appeared to be infuriating him the most.

'Only good Czech is a dead Czech, eh?' he repeated ominously. 'Then woe is you, you damned priests, for you're in the clutches of living and evil Czechs. We shall show you how evil a living Czech can be. Take them. To the courtyard with them!'

'Don't you dare touch me!' yelled Jan Buda. 'Don't you dare—'

A punch in the face quietened him down. The prior put up no resistance.

'*Vexilla Regis prodeunt* ...' he whimpered as he was dragged down the nave. '*Fulget Crucis mysterium* ... *Quo carne carnis con-ditor* ... *Suspensus est patibulo* ...'

'He's gone out of his mind,' stated one of the Orphans.

'It's a hymn.' Reynevan had heard that Smil Pŭlpán had been a sacristan before the revolution. 'It's the hymn *Vexilla Regis* – it's sung during Holy Week and today is Good Friday. A most apt day for martyrdom.'

A crowd of Orphans gathered around the two monks in front of the church. The first blow fell almost immediately, then the first kick, then more blows and kicks, and then clubs and axe butts. The prior dropped. Jan Buda stayed on his feet, praying out loud and spitting blood from his lacerated mouth. Smil Pŭlpán looked at him with hatred. At a sign, a stump used for splitting logs was brought from the woodshed.

'They say you blessed the weapons of the men marching on Náchod, Papist. We learned the punishment we'll use on you from the bishop's ruffians at Náchod. Bring him here, Brethren.'

Jan Buda was dragged over and one of his legs was placed on the chopping block. One of the Hussites, a powerful bruiser, raised a battleaxe and swung. Jan Buda screamed frightfully and blood shot up in a pulsating fountain from the open wound. The Orphans lifted up the Dominican, jerking spasmodically, and placed his other leg on the block. The battleaxe landed with a dull thud and squelch and the ground shuddered under the impact. Jan Buda screamed even more horrifically.

Berengar Tauler took a few unsteady steps, leaned with both hands against the wall of the church and vomited. Reynevan withstood it, but barely. Samson went very pale and suddenly glanced up at the sky. And remained looking in that direction for a long time, as if expecting to find something there.

On a block used to chop firewood, those butchers, haeretici, *wishing in their rage and wickedness to surpass the very Devil, their master and teacher, severed with axes all the poor wretches'* extremitatis *one after another. My quill cannot describe those atrocities, my hand trembles,* lacrimae *flow from my eyes* ... Nicolaus Carpentarius, Johannes Buda et Andreas Cantoris, martyres de Ordine Fratrum Praedicatorum, *died martyrs' deaths for the Word of God and for their witness. O God, O God, we appeal to Thee!* Usquequo, Domine sanctus et verus, non iudicas et vindicas sanguinem nostrum?

Meanwhile, the Orphans plundered the church of everything of any value. Holy paintings, planks from the choir stalls and the chopped-up remains of the altar – objects without value – were burning on a mountainous pyre. On Půlpán's orders, the two mutilated and dying monks were dragged over to the pyre and tossed onto it. The Hussites, standing in a ring, watched the two limbless torsos clumsily writhing in the flames. In fact, they burned poorly as it had started raining. Smil Půlpán felt his torn-off ear, swore and spat.

'There's one more!' yelled some men hurrying from the vestibule. 'Brother Půlpán! We've caught another! He was hiding in the pulpit!'

'Bring him here! Bring the papist!'

The man whom the Hussites dragged in, howling, wriggling and kicking was – Reynevan recognised him right away – Deacon Andrzej Kantor. He was dressed in nothing but a shirt, for he had clearly been caught trying to discard his Dominican habit. As he was being dragged, he noticed Reynevan.

'M'Lord Bielawa!' he howled. 'Don't let them kill me! Don't leeet them! Save me, m'loooord!'

'You sold me, Kantor. Remember? You sold me to my death. So you will perish like Judas.'

'M'loooord! Have meeercy!'

'Bring him here.' Půlpán pointed at the bloodstained chopping block. 'He'll be the third martyr. *Omne trinum perfectum!*'

Perhaps it was an impulse, some vague recollection. Perhaps it was momentary weakness, fatigue. Perhaps it was catching Samson Honeypot's deeply melancholic expression out of the corner of his eye. Reynevan didn't entirely know what induced him to take that particular action. He snatched a crossbow from the hands of the Czech next to him, took aim and squeezed the trigger. The bolt struck Kantor beneath the sternum with such force that it passed right through him, almost wrenching the deacon from his executioners' grasp. He was dead before he hit the ground.

'I had my own score to settle with him,' said Reynevan in the turgid and dreadfully deathly silence that followed.

'I understand,' said Smil Půlpán, nodding. 'But don't ever do that again, Brother. Because others might not.'

Flames roared across the church roof, the chevrons and beams crashing down into the blazing interior. A moment later, the walls began to crumble and collapse. A column of sparks and smoke shot skywards. Black rags whirled around above the fire like crows above a battlefield.

The Church of Saint Anne caved in completely. Only the stone arch of the portal remained standing and grew black in the flames. Like the gate to Hell.

A rider dashed into the square and brought his foaming horse to a sliding stop in front of the Orphans' hejtmans: Jan Královec, Little Prokop, Kolda of Žampach, Jíra of Řečice, Brázda of Klinštejn and Matěj Salava of Lípa.

'Brother Jan! Brother Prokop has turned back from Oława and is heading via Strzelin to Rychbach. He calls for you there without delay!'

'Did you hear that?' Královec turned towards his officers. 'The Tábor calls!'

'The castle has not yet fallen,' Little Prokop reminded him.

'Lucky for it. Commanders, to your troops! Load the loot onto the wagons, round up the cattle! We are moving out! We march on Rychbach, Brothers! On Rychbach!'

'Greetings, Brethren! Greetings, Tábor!'

'Welcome in God's name, Brethren! Greetings, Orphans!'

There was no end to the cries of greeting; joy and euphoria at the reunion seized them all. Soon, Jan Královec of Hrádek was crushing Prokop the Shaven's right hand, Little Prokop was kissing Markolt's bristly cheek, Jan Zmrzlík of Svojšín was slapping Matěj Salava of Lípa on his iron cuirass and Jaroslav of Bukovina was groaning in the powerful embrace of Jan Kolda of Žampach. Urban Horn hugged Reynevan, Rzehors hugged Drosselbart. The Orphans' flailmen and archers greeted the Taborite lancers, while the Slány voulgemen and the Nymburk axemen hugged the Chrudim bowmen. The drivers of the combat wagons greeted each other, cursing hideously in their customary fashion.

The wind buffeted the banners fluttering beside each other – the Orphans' Pelican shedding drops of blood into a gold Chalice flapped beside the *Veritas vincit*, the Host and the Tábor's crown of thorns. The Warriors of God cheered and threw their hats and helmets into the air.

While behind them, the town of Rychbach, which had been torched by the Taborites after being abandoned by its panicked residents, blazed and belched forth clouds of black smoke.

Prokop, his hand still on Jan Královec's shoulder and a very satisfied smile on his face, looked at the army forming up. Now, gathered together, it numbered over a thousand horse, more than ten thousand foot and three hundred combat wagons laden with artillery. He knew there was no one in the whole of Silesia capable of standing up to that force in the field. All that was left to the Silesians were the walls of their towns. Or – as in the case of the people of Rychbach – flight into the forests.

'Move out!' he yelled to the hejtmans. 'Prepare to move out! We're marching on Wrocław!'

'On Wrocław!' Jaroslav of Bukovina joined in. 'And Bishop Konrad! Moooove out!'

'Today is Easter Day!' cried Královec. *Festum festorum!* Christ is risen from the dead! He is truly resurrected!'

'*Resurrexit sicut dixit!*' Little Prokop joined in. 'Hallelujah!'

'Hallelujah! Let us sing to God, Brethren!'

A thunderous song escaped the lips of the Orphan flailmen and Taborite lancers and soared heavenwards. To be echoed by the voulgemen of Chrudim, the pavisiers of Nymburk and the crossbowmen of Slaný.

Christ the King
Has risen from the tomb!
Let us all sing,
His glory dispels the gloom!
Lord have mercy!
Lord have mercy!

As they set off in turn, the song was taken up by the spearmen of Zikmund of Vranov, the knights of Zmrzlík, after them the crews of the combat wagons, the light cavalry of Kolda of Žampach, the riders of Salava and the Moravians of Tovačovský. Finally, the Poles of Puchała brought up the rear with the thunderous song on their lips.

Our Lord rose from the dead,
After His cruel torment,
For us this is solace indeed,

Christ is our merriment!
Have mercy!

Dust blew up in a cloud over the Wrocław road. Leaving behind the flames of Rychbach, the Taborite–Orphan army of Prokop the Shaven marched north. Towards Ślęża, shrouded in clouds and darkening on the horizon.

Jesus Christ is arisen,
We must his example follow,
Therefore let us hasten,
The Lord God to hallow.
Lord have mercy!

The fires in the town were still raging, while the area outside the walls had almost burned down, was only smoking as dying flames flickered on charred beams and posts. Hearing the Hussite singing fading away in the distance, people began to emerge from their hiding places, to leave the forests and descend from the hills. They looked around, horrified, weeping, seeing the destruction of their town. They wiped the soot and tears from their faces. And sang. For it was Easter, after all.

Christ, He has risen
From all His agony
To praise Him we are bidden,
So let us joyous be!
Lord have mercy!

The Franciscan monks left their hiding places and came down from Winnik Mountain. They walked, weeping and singing, towards the blackened ruins of the town.

It was Easter.

Christus surrexit
Mala nostra texit
Et quos dilexit
Hoc ad celos vexit
Kyrieleison!

The army of Prokop the Shaven marched north. Clouds of fire and columns of smoke rose above the villages burned down by the sorties of Salava and Fedor of Ostrog. The thatched roofs of Útěchov bloomed in crimson flames. Praus, Harthau and Rudelsdorf were on fire. Soon, almost the entire horizon was aflame.

It was Easter.

The Warriors of God were marching north. With a song on their lips.

Ye Saints, please intercede
May our calls not go ignored,
Pray for us we plead
All hail the Almighty Lord!
Lord have mercy!

It was Easter. Christ was truly resurrected.
Fire consumed the land.

Chapter Twenty-One

In which various individuals watch how history comports itself – from various perspectives. History throws off its chains. Lets rip. And shows what it can do.

'Woe is Silesia.'

'Silesia is accursed!'

Located near Środa Śląska, situated by the River Średzka Woda, the refugee camp was overcrowded, simply bursting at the seams. Usually, the rotation of people coming and going meant that conditions were fairly tolerable, but that day Dzierżka of Wirsing was literally horrified by the perspective of new fugitives appearing.

She relaxed when dusk began to fall – people seldom arrived during the night, and she knew that many people were planning to leave at daybreak. The Hussites had gone. They had marched south, taking the route to Kostomłoty, Strzegom, Bolków and Landeshut. Perhaps they had returned to Bohemia? Now the smoke had stopped blackening the sky during the day and the glow of fires wasn't lighting up the night sky. People were tired of wandering, they wanted to go home. Back to their burned-out houses. To the ashes of their towns and villages. To Sobótka, Gniechowice, Górka, Frankenthal, Arnoldsmühle, Woskowice, Rakoszyce, Słup. And many, many others, with names that sounded strange and meant nothing to them.

An ox lowed; a goat bleated. A child started crying some-where among the wagons, and Elencza of Stietencron quickly dashed past beside Dzierżka. Having finished her work with the others in the kitchen, Elencza didn't join them to sleep and rest. Elencza appeared never to rest. For seven days, during which Dzierżka supported the camp organisationally and financially, Elencza only rested when categorically instructed to do so. Dzierżka didn't like to be categorical with Elencza. She saw how the young woman reacted to it. She saw it the first day when Elencza Stietencron arrived in Skałka on Tybald Raabe's chest-nut. When Dzierżka foolishly thought she knew how to shake the young woman out of her torpor and apathy.

'Woe is Silesia,' repeated a stout Wrocław burgher, a merchant whom not even the presence of armed forces could prevent from taking to the road with a cart full of goods.

'Accursed Silesia,' repeated a miller from Marcinkowice.

The refugees gathered around the campfire – a kind of camp council that had spontaneously formed, made up of people with evident authority – nodded and muttered. Dzierżka was the only woman among them. They were mainly grave-looking peasants with the faces and bearing of natural leaders. Aside from the stout Wrocław burgher, there was also the miller from Marcinkowice near Brzeg, a leaseholder from near Kątowy, two mercenaries in livery faded by the dust of many roads and an innkeeper from Górka. There was a barber-surgeon from Sobótka, who was much in demand. He was a Minorite from the monastery in Środa Śląska, a senior monk; the younger ones were tirelessly attending to the sick and wounded. There was a Jew, from God knew where. There was a knight. One of those impoverished ones, but still a remarkable sight among the others.

'Twice in Wrocław we feared for our lives,' said the stout

merchant. 'The first time was on the Thursday before Palm Sunday, when, after sacking Brzeg and burning down Ryczyn, the main Hussite forces stopped outside Oława. The fire and smoke were clearly visible and the stench of burning was being carried on the wind, for it is but a stone's throw from Oława to Wrocław . . . And though the town walls are strong, defended by cannons, with no shortage of soldiers, our legs turned to jelly . . . But God averted it. They departed.'

'Not for long,' observed one of the mercenaries.

'Aye. We'd barely breathed a sigh of relief on hearing that Prokop had turned back towards Strzelin, had barely celebrated an anxious Easter before the bells rang out the warning again. The Hussites are returning! In even greater numbers. Having joined forces with those hellish Orphans, they are burning Rychbach, burning Sobótka, the roads are crawling with refugees. And on the Friday before *Misericordia* Sunday, once again we see smoke from the walls, this time to the west: Kąty is afire. Word gets out that there's a large camp near Środa and Prokop is preparing to attack. The bells toll again, the women and children flee into the churches—'

'But you saw it out again that time,' said Dzierżka. 'There was no attack, as we all know. The Czechs departed two days later, on *Misericordia* Sunday.'

'They set off for Strzegom,' confirmed another soldier. 'Everybody thought they'd attack Świdnica, but they didn't. They clearly feared the fortress—'

'It wasn't that,' said the knight. 'Świdnica made a secret pact with the Hussites a year ago. That's why it survived.'

'And m'Lord Starosta of Kolditz was safe and sound behind Świdnica's walls,' sneered the miller from Marcinkowice. 'What cares he if the land is burning and awash with blood? He won't be harmed – he made a pact. Ugh!'

There was silence for some time. The innkeeper from Górka interrupted it.

'The Hussites headed west from Strzegom,' he said. 'They left Jawor undamaged but sacked Świerzawa and put it to the torch. They utterly plundered and burned down Dobków, the manor of the Lubiąż monks, then went on, towards Złotoryja. And today I met a friend on the highway. He said that Złotoryja is burned down for the second time – it's an unlucky town. And Prokop and the Orphans are said to be marching on Lwówek—'

'Things have changed,' interjected the Sobótka barber-surgeon. 'I also asked the refugees. The Hussites reached Lwówek a week since, on Thursday, but didn't cross the Bóbr. While the Lusatian knighthood, well-armed gentlemen who were meant to come to Silesia with relief, took fright and fled in cowardly fashion to the left bank, to cower there like mice. The Lusatians won't come to our aid. We're alone, children. Woe is Silesia!'

'Accursed Silesia!'

An ox lowed; a dog barked. Another child started crying. Elencza turned her head but couldn't go. She was carrying a little boy and comforting him, and a slightly older little girl was clinging to her skirts. Elencza sighed and sniffed. Dzierżka scrutinised her from under her eyelashes. She'd never given birth, never had her own children, but she never regretted it, it had never been a problem. *Not until today*, she thought in sudden terror, a cold hand seizing her chest and tightening her throat.

'Our only hope is that the plundering raid goes on and on,' said the Wrocław burgher. 'The Hussites must be exhausted, burdened down by all the spoils—'

'Only defeats are exhausting,' said the knight. 'Only those who flee grow weary, their meagre bundles burdening them. Victory gives strength, spoils are as light as a feather! They that conquer are content! Their horses eat wheat from our granaries while ours rummage among ashes. But it is true, they have been fighting for some time. It's not far to the Karkonosze passes and Bohemia from the River Bóbr. God willing, they'll go home.'

'But for how long?' The miller from Marcinkowice grew annoyed. 'After all, they know we're weak and no match for them on the battlefield. They know that we've lost heart and have no one to lead us into battle! That the Silesian knights take to their heels at the very sight of the Hussites, flee like hares! Why, even the dukes flee! What did Ludwik of Brzeg do? He ought to have defended the town and his defenceless subjects. When he ground them down with taxes, they said: "Never mind, we'll pay our hard-earned coin, but our good lord will defend us when the moment comes." But what did the good lord do? Fled like a coward, leaving Brzeg at the mercy of the invaders. The Hussites utterly plundered the town, burned down the parish church and turned the Collegiate Church of Saint Hedwig into a stable, the blasphemers!'

'And why doesn't a lightning bolt strike them down, why doesn't God's wrath fall on them?' The barber-surgeon from Sobótka shook his head. 'It is difficult not to doubt . . . Erm . . . I meant to say: God tries us sorely—'

'Gentlemen, you ought to accustom yourself to being tried,' said the Jew unexpectedly. 'Oi, I tell you it's only difficult at the start. One finally gets used to it.'

There was silence for some time. The knight broke it.

'Going back to Duke Ludwik,' he said, 'in truth, he didn't act chivalrously, leaving Brzeg at the mercy of the Hussites, nor as befits a knight or a duke. But—'

'But it wasn't just him, you meant to say?' the miller interrupted with an angry grimace. 'You are right! For others also turned tail on the enemy, staining their honour. Where are you,

Duke Henryk the Pious, who chose death rather than flee from the field?'

'I meant to say,' the knight stammered a little, 'that the Hussites achieved much by treachery. By treachery and propaganda. Spreading false news and panic—'

'But where does treachery come from?' the Minorite monk suddenly asked. 'Why does that seed sprout so easily and bloom so luxuriantly, why such a harvest? Magnates and knights surrender fortresses and castles without a fight, go over to the enemy's side. The peasantry is drawn to the Hussites, serve them as guides, identify and turn priests over to their deaths. What's more, they attack monasteries and pillage churches themselves. There are plenty of apostates among the clergy, too. But there's no duke prepared – like Henryk the Pious – to fight and die *pro defensione christiane fidei*. It's puzzling to me. How does it come about?'

One of the peasants, a powerful fellow with a shock of hair, spoke up in a deep voice, 'Perhaps because we didn't have to fight the Saracens, the Turks or the Tartars, who invaded Silesia in our great-grandfathers' time. I've heard they were black-faced, red-eyed, fire-breathing, bore devilish marks, used witchcraft and choked our soldiers with hellish fumes. You knew at once what power drove them on. But now? Monstrances swaying over the Czech army, the Host and pious words painted on their bucklers. They sing to God as they march, pray on their knees and receive Holy Communion before the battle. Call themselves "Warriors of God". So perhaps ...'

'Perhaps God is on their side?' The monk finished his sentence with a wry smile.

Only a year ago, thought Dzierżka in the heavy silence that fell, *only a year ago no one would even have dared to think something like that, let alone say it. The world is changing, changing utterly. Why is it, though, that the world must always change in massacres and conflagrations? In trying to renew itself, must it always bathe in blood, like Poppaea in milk?*

'I'm beginning,' announced Scharley from the steps of the altar, 'I'm beginning to support the teachings of Huss, Wycliffe, Payne and the rest of the Hussite ideologists more actively. It is indeed time to begin changing churches ... Well, perhaps not at once into stables, like the Brzeg Collegiate Church, but into lodging houses. Just look how cosy it is here. We're out of the wind and rain, there are hardly any fleas ... Yes, Reinmar. As far as the churches are concerned, I'm going over to your religion, beginning a noviciate. You may treat me as a candidate for membership.'

Reynevan shook his head, tossing wood onto the bonfire that he and Berengar Tauler had lit in the centre of the nave. Samson sighed. He was sitting a little way off, reading a book dug out by candlelight from an enormous pile under the pulpit. When the church was being plundered, no one was tempted by the books. They were of no use, after all.

'We're sitting pretty here.' Drosselbart broke off another board from the matroneum in the chancel. 'There's plenty of firewood. It'll last till summer.'

'And there are things to eat,' added Bisclavret, biting a bone-dry sausage he'd found in the vestry. 'It turns out it's true what they say: *qui altari servit, ex altari vivit.*'

'And one can always find something to drink out of.' Rzehors raised a captured Communion cup full of wine. 'You don't have to lap it up like a dog from a barrel ... And there's reading matter ... Isn't there, Samson? Samson!'

'I beg your pardon?' The giant raised his head. 'Oh, yes ... You won't believe it – I found a sentence in Polish in this Latin work. And the work dates from 1231, from the times of Henry the Bearded. There's a date on the title page, look: *Anno verum Millesimo CCXXXI*, and under it, as clear as day: *benefactor noster Henricus Cum Barba Dei gratia dux Slesie, Cracouie et Poloniae* . . .'

'What does that sentence in old Polish say?' Drosselbart asked with interest. Samson read it aloud.

'Nonsense.'

'Indeed.'

'And a crap rhyme.'

'Agreed.'

Footsteps, clanking, rattling and a hubbub of excited voices echoed from the vestibule. Brands and torches lit up the gloom and the shapes of people entering the church. Scharley swore. It turned out they were being visited by Pešek Krejčíř, a preacher of the Orphans, one of Little Prokop's subordinates. Krejčíř was followed by several youngsters bearing arms. Scharley swore again.

In both the Tábor army and among the Orphans, women always accompanied the marches, mainly taking care of provisioning and cooking, occasionally nursing the wounded and sick. The women, usually widows, took their children with them. When the boys grew up, a new form of unit emerged in the Hussite armies – youth squads. The units grew quickly, absorbing shepherd boys and street urchins on the marches. They also quickly became the mascots and favourites in the army. Pets of the soldiers, favoured and indulged by everyone. Sensing their status and privileged position, the beloved boys became spoiled and unruly. Hussite propaganda, presenting them as the 'Divine Children of the New Order', propagated and nurtured fanaticism and cruelty in the youths, and such seeds – like among any group of children – fell on extremely fertile ground. The merry brood became known as 'sling shooters', for they were mainly armed with slings, the weapons favoured by shepherds and street urchins. Reynevan, however, had never seen the youths use their slings in battle. Or actually fight at all. But he had seen the youngsters in other circumstances. After the Battle of Ústí, the 'Children of God' had cruelly blinded fallen Saxons by thrusting sharpened sticks through the slits in their helmets. Not so long ago, in Głuchołazy, at the Battle of Nysa, in Bardo, in Frankenstein and Złotoryja, they had beaten, kicked, stoned and mutilated the wounded and poured boiling water and milk over them.

'What is this?' Krejčíř asked sternly, pointing at the chalice Rzehors was drinking from. 'Do you break the law, Brother? Do you seek punishment? All spoils are to be put in a common barrel! Whoever keeps even a single trinket will be punished! As the Holy Bible clearly states! Achan, the son of Zerah of the tribe of Judah, who stole a garment and gold from spoils belonging to God, was stoned and burned in the Vale of Achor!'

'It's only silver-plated brass . . .' muttered Rzehors. 'Very well, have it.'

'And what is this?' The preacher snatched the book from Samson's hand. 'What is this? Know you not, Brother, that the New Era dawns? And the New Era has no need of either books or writing, for God's Law will be written in our hearts? And may the old world go up in flames!'

The book with the Polish sentence from 1231 was tossed onto the fire.

'May the old world perish! And with it its false wisdom! Begone! Begone! Begone!'

With each cry, he tossed a book into the flames. First a *Tractatus*, then a *Codex* and a *Cronica sive gesta* flew into the fire as Samson stood by with arms hanging loosely, smiling. The smile made Reynevan feel uncomfortable. Krejčíř brushed dust from his hands, snatched a spiked, metal-headed club from one of the sling shooters, looked around and entered one of the aisles. He spotted a painting. *The Adoration of the Christ Child.*

'The New Era!' he yelled. 'Man shall cast his idols of silver and his idols of gold to the moles and to the bats! Saith the Lord God: turn yourselves from your idols; and turn away your faces from all your abominations!'

He swung and the club shattered the painted board. One of the boys giggled foolishly.

'Thou shalt not make thee any graven image!' the preacher roared, striking more paintings with the club. 'Of any thing that is in Heaven above! Or that is in the Earth beneath! Or that is in the waters beneath the Earth!

The Expulsion from Paradise was reduced to matchwood, a triptych of the Annunciation was split and fell from the wall and *The Adoration of the Magi* was broken in two. *Saint Hedwig*, luminous and misty like the works of the Master of Flémalle, was chopped up. Krejčíř destroyed them with abandon as the sound of wood splintering echoed around the church. He turned his frenzied assault onto some murals and smashed the faces of cherubs on a frieze. And then he saw a sculpture. A painted wooden figure. Everybody saw it. And was dumbstruck.

It stood, head slightly bent, gathering in its delicate hands the drapes of a robe whose every carved fold sang a paeon to the sculptor's artistry. Arched backwards slightly, but proudly, as though wanting to display her swollen belly, the pregnant Madonna looked down on them with carved, painted eyes, and *Gratia* and *Agape* shone from them. The pregnant Madonna smiled, and in her smile the artist had expressed greatness, glory, hope and the light of dawn after the black of the night. And the words *magnificat anima mea Dominum*, uttered softly and with love.

Magnificat anima mea Dominum. Et omnia quae intra me sunt.

'No sculptures!' bellowed Krejčíř, raising the club. 'No statues! I will punish the carved images of Babylon!'

No one saw him move, but Samson was suddenly standing in front of the figure, shielding it from the preacher, barring the way to it with his arms spread in the shape of a cross.

What is he doing? wondered Reynevan, seeing Tauler's horrified expression and Scharley's face frozen in a grimace of resignation. *What the hell is he doing? It means suicide to challenge an Orphan preacher ... In any case, Krejčíř is, by and large, right ... In the New Era, idols and graven images will not be honoured, they will not be bowed down to. Risking his life for a sculpture carved from a lindenwood log? Oh, Samson ...*

The preacher took a step back, astonished, but quickly recovered his composure.

'Would you shield an idol? Defend a graven image? Do you mock the words of the Bible, O blasphemer?'

'Find something else to smash,' Samson answered calmly. 'Not this. You may not.'

'May not? May not?' Foam appeared on Krejčíř's lips. 'I will ... I will ... Forward, children! Have at him! Kill!'

In the blink of an eye, as fast as lightning, Scharley was standing beside Samson, Tauler was beside Scharley, and Drosselbart, Rzehors and Bisclavret were beside them. And Reynevan, too, not knowing himself when, how or why. But he was there. Blocking the way. To Samson. And the sculpture.

'Would you? Would you, heretics?' yelled Krejčíř. 'Idolaters? Forward, children! Have at them!'

'Stop.' A resonant and imperious voice reverberated from the vestibule. 'Stop, I said.'

Prokop the Shaven entered the church, accompanied by Královec, Little Prokop, Jaroslav of Bukovina and Urban Horn.

Their steps thudded and rang out, echoing menacingly as they walked down the nave. The torches cast malevolent shadows.

Prokop came closer, examined and assessed the situation with a rapid, stern glance. On seeing his expression, the sling shooters lowered their heads, all of them vainly trying to hide behind Krejčíř's coat-tails.

'But, Brother, you see ...' mumbled the preacher. 'These men—'

Prokop the Shaven interrupted him with a gesture. Quite firmly.

'Brother Bielawa, Brother Drosselbart.' He summoned them with a similar gesture. 'If you would, there are some things we must talk over before we set off. As for you, Brother Krejčíř ... Be gone from here. Be gone and—'

He broke off and glanced at the sculpture.

'Find something else to smash,' he added a moment later.

An ox lowed; a goat bleated. Smoke hung low, creeping towards the bulrushes by the stream. A wounded man, just sewn up by the barber-surgeon from Sobótka, moaned and groaned. The Minorites glided among the refugees like wraiths, on the lookout for symptoms of a possible epidemic. *God sent those monks,* thought Dzierżka. *They know about epidemics, they'll spot one, if necessary. And they aren't afraid. If it comes to it, they won't run away. Not them. They don't know what fear is. The humble and silent fortitude of Francis lives on in them.*

The night was warm, it emanated spring. Somebody was praying aloud nearby.

Elencza, asleep in Dzierżka's lap, moved and whimpered. *She's tired,* thought Dzierżka. *Exhausted. That's why she sleeps so restlessly. That's why she's being tormented by nightmares.*

Again.

*

Elencza groaned in her sleep. She was dreaming of fighting and blood.

A black aurochs on a gold field, thought Reynevan, looking at a shield half-stuck into the mud. *The technical description of that coat of arms is:* d'or, au taureau passant de sable. *And that other coat of arms on that shield, barely visible under caked-on blood, with red roses on a slanting silver strip, is described as:* d'azur, à la bande d'argent, chargée de trois roses de gueules.

He wiped his face with a nervous movement.

Taureau de sable, *a black aurochs, that's Sir Henryk Baruth. The same Henryk Baruth who three years ago hurled abuse at me, beat and kicked me at the Ziębice tournament. Now it was his turn – a blow from the iron swipple of a flail has so flattened and twisted the armet that I'd rather not imagine what the head inside looks like.* The Hussites had stripped the Bavarian suit of armour from the fallen knight, but not the dented helmet. So now Baruth was lying like some enormous grotesque, in his hose, a shirt, a mail coif, the helmet and the pool of blood that had leaked out from under the helmet.

While the three roses, trois roses, *is Krystian Der, the son of Walpot Der of Wąwolnica. I played with him as a boy, in the woods near Balbinów, by the Frog Ponds, in the meadows of Powojowice. We played at being the Knights of the Round Table, at Siegfried and Hagen, at Dietrich and Hildebrand. And later, we chased the Wąwolnica miller's daughter, rightly expecting that one of us would eventually cop a feel. Then Peterlin married Gryzelda of Der, and Krystian became my brother-in-law . . . And is now lying in the red mud, staring up at the sky through glazed eyes. Utterly lifeless.*

He looked away.

Berengar Tauler claimed that war was a thing without a future

*and soldiering a thing without prospects. Drosselbart tried to prove
– insincerely and because of Mammon – that a Brave New World
would spring from the turmoil of war. All their hopes evaporated
on the twentieth day of the month of April* Anno Domini *1428, a
Tuesday, in the village of Moczydło. Tauler's regarding the future
and prospects, and Drosselbart's regarding whatever he'd hoped for.
Prokop the Shaven ordered them to ride to Moczydło. To agitate.
There was little chance that anyone in Silesia would try to form a
peasant infantry, but Prokop preferred to be cautious. The* well-
agitated peasants fled from Nysa, *he said, twisting his moustache,*
before the fighting occurred. Thus, more agitation is necessary.
With a view to future engagements.

They set off in the morning, a troop of ten mounted men
and one war wagon. The riders were assigned to them by Prince
Fedor of Ostrog. They were, like most of the prince's men, Hungarians and Slovaks. The wagon, pulled like all war wagons by
four horses, belonged to Otík of Loza's Nymburkians and had
a standard crew: a wagon hejtman, two wagoners, four crossbowmen, four handgonners and five men armed with flails,
glaives and voulges. Riding alongside them were Drosselbart as
an agitator, Rzehors as the agitator's assistant, Reynevan as the
assistant's assistant, Scharley as Reynevan's assistant, Berengar
Tauler as a hanger-on and Samson as Samson.

The Hungarian cavalry, contemptuously called 'Kumans'
by the Czechs, drove the residents of Moczydło onto the village green, then quickly rode around between the cottages,
in order – as was their custom – to try to steal or rape what
they could. The Kumans' customs were harshly discouraged in
the Hussite army, hence Ostrog's Magyars dared only to indulge themselves in secret, on distant forays when no one was
looking.

The wagon hejtman decided not to look. His officers also

devoted all their attention to drowsy conversations, scratching their arses and picking their noses.

Drosselbart climbed onto a wagon and agitated. Preached. Saying that what was happening wasn't war at all and by no means a plundering raid, but rather fraternal help and a peace mission, and the armed operations of the Warriors of God were being directed exclusively at the Bishop of Wrocław: a scoundrel, oppressor and tyrant. By no means against our brothers and sisters, the Silesian folk, because we, the Warriors of God, love the Silesian folk very much and have their good at heart. Oh, by God, how we do.

Drosselbart preached with great enthusiasm, giving the impression he believed what he said. Reynevan knew, of course, that Drosselbart didn't believe a word and that it was what Prokop and Markolt had told him to say. How could apparently sensible people, Reynevan wondered, think that anyone would believe anything as obviously and blatantly nonsensical as that 'peace mission' nonsense? For no one with the smallest scrap of intelligence could believe anything like that. Not even a peasant who had spent his life shovelling shit from one place to another would give credence to anything like that. Reynevan couldn't accept Scharley's theory that if you repeat nonsense often enough everybody will finally believe it.

Drosselbart finished his first piece of propaganda and began another. About the dawning New Times. The peasants' faces – which had been deadpan during the 'peace mission' nonsense – suddenly became animated. Unlike the 'peace mission', several aspects of the New Times attracted the peasants' attention.

'When that time comes, there will be no more human government or domination or subjugation on the Earth. There will be no more serfdom or taxes. Kings, princes and prelates will disappear and all exploitation of the poor folk will cease. Peasants will not pay any rent to their masters, nor serve them, and homesteads and fishponds, meadows and forests will become theirs . . .'

The peasants would probably have been given copses and groves, too, but Drosselbart's litany was brutally interrupted. By a crossbow bolt shot from a nearby wood. And as the beanpole was toppled from the wagon by an arrow to his belly, a cavalry unit galloped out of the wood. And they were charged so swiftly that there wasn't much they could do. Some of the Nymburkians simply fled, bolted, trying – following the example of the peasants – to find shelter among the cottages, shacks and wattle fences. They were slaughtered as they ran. The rest were surrounded, either on or around the wagon, and a fierce fight began. Berengar Tauler was one of the first to fall. The remaining Taborites fought like devils, aided by Reynevan, Scharley and Rzehors, Samson wreaking havoc with the *goedendag*. But they were in serious trouble and wouldn't have survived had the Kumans not come galloping out from the cottages. The fighting shifted from the wagon, moved nearer the edge of the village green and turned into a mounted chase and hand-to-hand combat.

'Over there . . .' grunted Rzehors, crawling out from under the wagon and pushing a crossbow into Reynevan's hands. 'See him? Him on that grey, with an aurochs on his shield? He's the commander . . . My arm's injured . . . Shoot him, Reinmar . . .'

Reynevan seized the crossbow, ran closer just to be certain and fired. The bolt deflected off the reinforced spaulder with a loud clang. And the knight turned to look at him. He yelled from behind his visor and pointed out Reynevan with his sword to another rider, and both of them attacked him at full gallop.

Scharley snatched up a handgonne without a fuse. Samson saw it and deftly tossed him a firebrand from a campfire broken up by hooves. The penitent caught the glowing wood just as deftly, spun around and aimed from armpit height. Fortunately, there was still some powder left in the touch-hole. There was a roar, fire and smoke spat from the barrel, and the attacking rider shot from the saddle, straight under the hooves of the Hungarians chasing him. The first knight, with the aurochs in his coat of arms, loomed over Reynevan with his sword raised to strike, and suddenly stiffened and dropped the weapon and the reins as one of the Nymburkians stabbed him under the arm with a voulge. Another ran up with a flail and struck with great force. It split the armet like a dry pea pod and blood spurted out.

'We gave them what for!' said the wagon hejtman, staggering and wiping from his face the blood that was streaming from his crown. 'We gave . . . Them . . .'

The Hungarians were yelling triumphantly on the village green. No one was pursuing the fleeing Silesian knights. It became overcast. Four Silesians had been killed. Five Hussites had fallen and there were twice as many wounded. Before the corpses had been carried outside the wattle fences at the edge of the birch copse, one of the wounded died. A large pit was needed.

Berengar Tauler. Drosselbart of the Vogelsang. Henryk Baruth, with *sable, an aurochs passant*. Krystian Der, *trois roses de gueules*. A mounted crossbowman. An esquire. A Zbořil, an Adamec, a Ráček, for whom a Mistress Zbořilova, a Mistress Adamcová and a Mistress Ráčková would be waiting in vain at home.

'Hand me the spade,' Samson Honeypot said in the silence. 'I'll dig.' He stuck the spade into the ground, pushed down with all his strength, lifted it up and tossed aside a sod. 'I'll dig as a penance. Because I'm to blame! *Iniquitates meae supergressae sunt caput meum!* I went to war! Out of curiosity! I could have stopped others, but I didn't. I could have taught. I could have manipulated. I could have kicked the right people in the arse! I could finally, bugger it all, have sat in Podskalí with Marketa beside me, sat in silence with her and watched the Vltava go by. But I went to war. For the meanest of reasons: curiosity about war itself and human nature.

'So I'm to blame for the deaths of those who lie here. I shall be to blame for the deaths and misfortune that are yet to occur. For that reason, I shall dig this fucking grave. From that pit, *de profundis, clamo ad te, Domine . . . Miserere mei, Deus*, have mercy upon me, O God, according to Thy loving-kindness. According unto the multitude of Thy tender mercies; blot out my transgressions. Wash me thoroughly from mine iniquity, and cleanse me from my sin. . .'

After the third verse, he wasn't praying alone. And others were digging.

Dzierżka had dozed and was woken by raised voices. She jerked her head up, groped around and felt Elencza's forearm under her fingers. Elencza roused herself and started to cough dryly.

'There's news,' said the Franciscan standing inside the circle. His habit was hitched up and he was wearing riding boots instead of sandals. He had clearly ridden straight from the monastery in Środa. 'There's news from our brothers, the monks of the monastery of the Holy Spirit in Lubin.'

'Go on, Frater.'

'The Hussites attacked Chojnów. On the Saturday before *Jubilate* Sunday.

'Barely a few days ago.' Someone quickly totted it up. 'Christ be merciful.'

'And Duke Ruprecht?'

'Fled with his knights to Lubin before the attack. Leaving Chojnów to its fate.'

*

The bombardment using incendiary shells lasting several hours was admirably effective. Fire raged on the roofs of homesteads, and in many places the wooden hoardings on the walls were also burning. The flames drove the defenders from them more effectively than salvoes from crossbows, harquebuses and trestle guns. The people of Chojnów, who were forced to put out the fires, couldn't defend the walls, where Hussites were now swarming – Taborites on either side of the Legnica Gate, and Orphans along almost the entire length of the southern curtain wall.

The battle cries and yells suddenly intensified. Torched and fired on from bombards, the Legnica Gate creaked, one wing drooped and the other tumbled down in a shower of sparks. Foot soldiers – Jan Bleh's flailmen – ran towards the gate roaring savagely, followed by the cavalry – the Czechs of Zmrzlík and Otík of Loza, Tovačovský's Moravians and Puchała's Poles.

Reynevan and Scharley ran with the latter. This time, no one forbade them from fighting – quite the opposite – in order to force the Chojnówians to spread out the defence between all the walls, Prokop and Královec had ordered every man who could to take up arms.

After passing through the gate, they ran straight into the fiery jaws of the conflagration along a narrow street between burning houses. Any defenders who attempted to put up resistance were hacked down in a flash; the rest of them fled. From the north, the shooting quietened down but the yelling increased; the Orphans had clearly breached the wall and forced their way into the town.

They burst into the elongated town square and in front of them rose up the stone shape of a church and a lofty tower, shrouded in smoke. Before they had time to think, the tower spat fire and iron. Reynevan saw around him balls and bolts churning up the ground and men falling. The screams were deafening.

He knelt down. He applied pressure to the carotid artery of one wounded man, hit in the neck by a bolt. Beside him, another man whose leg had been torn off below the knee by a handgonne ball was rolling around and howling. A third was squirming, blood spurting from his belly. A fourth was only twitching.

'On your feet, Reynevan! Onwards, to the tower!' shouted Scharley.

Reynevan ignored him, busy trying in vain to stem the bleeding. When the wounded man choked on his own blood and died, Reynevan moved to the one who'd lost his leg. He tore his shirt into strips, dressed the wound and bound the leg. The casualty wailed.

A man with a spear rushed out of a blazing house and behind him a youth with charred clothes, carrying a small dog. The man's head was crushed with a flail at once. The youth was run through with a pike and pinned to the ground along with the dog. As the youth drooped on the pike, the dog thrashed about, yelping, forepaws flailing.

Reynevan tended to the wounded. Attackers teemed outside the church, which was veiled in smoke and belching fire. They were still being shot at from the tower, balls and bolts whistling through the air.

'Have at theeem!'

Covered in soot and black as devils, Orphans poured out of a side street, driving in front of them and mowing down the townspeople fleeing in panic from them. Scharley tugged Reynevan by the arm. He left the man he was bandaging and ran, jumping over corpses.

The fighting had ceased outside the church in the town square, however. The defenders of the tower – including plenty of women and children – were being dragged from the building and made to stand by a wall. Jaroslav of Bukovina was there, issuing orders. The sounds of slaughter coming from the southern side of the town drowned out his voice, but the gestures he made left no one in any doubt. Once the prisoners were crowded together and pushed against the wall, people were hauled from the crowd in ones and twos. Thrown down on their knees. And killed. Blood poured, flowing in a foaming river, washing chaff and muck from the gutters.

'Mercy! I beg you!' howled a townswoman in a dull grey skirt thrown down onto her knees. 'What have I done? Why? For God's sake—'

The blow of a club split her head in two like an apple. She slumped without a sound.

'Because when I called, ye did not answer,' explained Prokop the Shaven, who was standing nearby. 'When I spake, ye did not hear. But did evil before mine eyes, and did choose that wherein I delighted not. Therefore, will I number you to the sword, and ye shall all bow down to the slaughter.'

'Brethren! Warriors of God!' yelled Královec. 'Give no quarter! Let no one go, put all to the sword! Kill them! And burn down the town! Burn it to the ground! May not even couch grass grow here for the next hundred years!'

Fire shot above the roofs of Chojnów with a roar. And the screams of the people being killed soared even higher. High above the billowing smoke.

'After burning down Chojnów,' the monk continued his account, 'and killing all its residents, the Hussites turned back again, heading towards Bolesław along the Zgorzelec road. On hearing their approach, the people fled into the forests, setting light to the town with their own hands.'

'Jesus Christ . . .' The Wrocław merchant crossed himself, but his face brightened up at once. 'Ha! If Prokop has set off for

Bolesław along the Zgorzelec road, it means he'll leave us alone! He's going towards Lusatia!'

'A vain hope,' countered a Minorite to sighs from the others. 'Prokop will turn back from Bolesław towards Silesia again. And attack Lubin.'

'Christ, be merciful,' sounded voices. '*Gott erbarme . . .*'

'Lubin was still holding out yesterday.' The monk put his hands together. 'The cottages outside the city walls were in flames and the town was ablaze because the assailants were firing burning missiles onto the roofs, but the folk valiantly resisted, repulsing the attack. The news from Chojnów must have reached them; the Lubin people know what awaits them if they surrender, so they are holding out.'

'Moat's deep there,' muttered an elderly soldier, 'walls seven ells high, more than ten towers . . . They'll hold out. If they don't lose heart, they'll hold out.'

'God willing.'

Elencza trembled and moaned in her sleep.

Dzierżka, despite her superhuman efforts, must have dropped off again and was shaken out of sleep. The man tugging her turned out to be her own man, Sobek Snorbein. Snorbein was commanding a group of stablemen, on Dzierżka's order riding all over the vicinity, both on and off the roads, searching for lost and ownerless horses, particularly pedigree stallions and destriers which were good breeding stock for the stud in Skałka. On hearing the instructions given to Snorbein, Elencza had goggled and looked outraged, at which she was told curtly and bluntly by Dzierżka that wasting godsends was a sin, that selfless magnanimity was admirable, but only during holidays, and, generally speaking, the horses would be returned if the owners could be found and could prove their rights. Elencza hadn't asked any questions. Particularly since soon afterwards, Dzierżka had established a refugee camp, wholly dedicating herself to it both on working days and holidays.

'M'lady.' Sobek Snorbein leaned towards the horse trader's ears. 'Things are no good. The Czechs are coming. They've put the outskirts of Ścinawa to the torch. They are also burning down Prochowice. The Hussites are marching on Wrocław ... So they'll pass this way—'

Dzierżka of Wirsing came to her senses at once and sprang to her feet.

'Saddle our horses, Sobek. Elencza, get up.'

'What?'

'Get up. I'm just going to talk to the monks and when I return, you're to be ready. We are fleeing. The Hussites are coming.'

'Is such haste necessary? To Prochowice it's only—'

'I know how far it is to Prochowice.' Dzierżka cut her off. 'And haste is necessary. A Hussite troop may appear here any moment, believe me. Some of the Czechs—'

She cut off and glanced at Snorbein.

'Some of them,' she muttered, 'have damned good horses.'

'Jesus,' sighed Jan Královec. 'Is that town in the middle of the very sea?'

'That's the Odra and a branch of it.' Urban Horn pointed to the broad expanse of water. 'And that's the Oława, which surrounds the town from the south.'

'And well protects access to it,' said Jíra of Řečice, 'as though it had no need of walls.'

'But it has them,' said Blažek of Kralupy, 'and sturdy ones at that. It's not short of towers, either ... Never mind church spires! It's almost like Prague!'

539

'The first,' said Horn, flaunting his knowledge and pointing, 'is Saint Nicholas's in Szczepin, and over there, that's Nicholas's Gate. That large church with the tall tower is Saint Elisabeth's, and the other one, just as imposing, is Saint Mary Magdalene's. That tower is the town hall. And that church there is—'

'Saint Dorothy's,' Prokop the Shaven interjected dispassionately, demonstrating no worse a knowledge of Wrocław. 'And there, on Piasek Island, is the Church of Our Lady. Beyond Piasek is Ostrów Tumski, beyond it the Collegiate Church of the Holy Cross, beside is the cathedral, which is still being built. Over yonder . . . Ołbin, the great Premonstratensian monastery. And over there, Saint Catherine's and the Dominican Saint Adalbert's. Satisfied? Know everything now? Splendid, because you won't see Wrocław's churches close at hand. Not this time, at least.'

'Naturally,' said Jan Tovačovský of Cimburk, nodding. 'It would be madness to attack the city.'

'O thee of little faith!' Little Prokop grimaced and spat. 'Had Joshua thought like you, Jericho would be standing to this day! It is the might of God that brings down walls—'

'Leave God be,' Dobko Puchała interrupted calmly. 'Jericho or not, only a quite deranged fellow would storm Wrocław now.'

The Hussite leaders muttered, in the main agreeing with the opinions of the Moravian and the Pole. The gleam in the eyes of Královec, Jan Bleh and Otík of Loza attested to the fact that they would willingly have tried if they could have.

'But we are here.' Prokop, as usual, didn't miss the gleams. 'From quite far away to this den of the Antichrist. We have journeyed hard and long, and it would be a sin not to give the Antichrist a lesson in religion.'

Before them, at the foot of the hill, the River Ślęza, wide and flooding the meadows, with storks wading in it, flowed along its shallow course. Birch woodland was becoming clothed in a delicate, fresh green. Bird cherry trees were beginning to bloom. Marsh marigolds and buttercups were flowering in the wetlands and dandelions in the meadows. Reynevan looked away from the signs of spring. The main forces of the Tábor and Orphans were crossing the Bystrzyca via the captured bridge in Leśnica, beside the smoking embers of the customs house.

'We'll give the people of Wrocław and the Antichrist bishop a lesson they won't forget,' continued Prokop. 'That small village at the foot of the hill – what's it called?'

'Żerniki, good sire.' One of the obsequious peasant guides hurried over. 'And that 'un is Muchobór—'

'Burn them both down. You deal with it, Brother Puchała. Over there, and I see a mill over there ... And another. And there's a village ... And there's another ... And what's that? A wooden church? Brother Salava!'

'At once, Brother Prokop!'

An hour hadn't even passed before fire and smoke began rising into the sky, the stench of burning making the fresh spring air unbreathable.

I tire of marching with pike and gun,
I would find more joy with my darling one ...

Wistful subject matter was beginning to dominate noticeably in the repertoire of Prokop's army's marching songs. Weariness of war was making itself felt more and more.

Leaving Wrocław behind, they marched southwards, with Ślęża looming up suddenly and menacingly on their right from the flat landscape. The peak of the mountain, though not at all of imposing height, was veiled as usual in elongated clouds – it looked as though the clouds gliding across the sky had snagged on the peak and remained there.

They marched on Strzelin and Ziębice quite quickly, not even doing much pillaging. In truth, there wasn't much left to pillage. Jan Kolda of Žampach, stationed and left at the post on Ślęża, was waiting idly in the castle, but often set forth, plundering anything that was fit to plunder and burning anything that could catch fire. The odd priest or monk hanging by a rope from a roadside tree could usually be put down to Kolda's men, although one couldn't rule out the spontaneous initiatives of the local peasant community, often taking advantage of the opportunity to settle accounts with their parish priest or monastery for old grudges and injustices. Reynevan feared for White Church, pinning his hopes on the agreement reached with the Patriciate of Strzelin and the Duke of Oława. And the dense forests concealing the monastery.

The sight of Ziębice, calling forth memories of Adèle and Duke Jan, was like a red rag to a bull to him. He tried talking to Prokop, hoping to convince him to break the agreement with Jan and attack the town. But Prokop was unmoved.

All he achieved was permission to join Dobko Puchała's cavalry units harrying the vicinity with forays. Prokop didn't protest. He didn't need Reynevan now. While Reynevan took out his anger, burning with the Poles the hamlets and granges surrounding Ziębice.

On the fifth of May, the day after Saint Florian's Day, a strange mission arrived in the Hussite camp. Several richly attired burghers, several high-ranking clergymen, several knights, including – judging from their coats of arms – Zedlitz, Reichenbach and Bolz, and on top of that a Pole bearing the Toporczyk arms. The entire company joined in secret negotiations with Prokop, Jaroslav of Bukovina and Královec long into the night in the only surviving building of the Cistercian grange. When, at dawn, Prokop issued the order to move out, everything was explained. Another agreement had been reached. Following the example set by Jan of Ziębice, Bernard of Niemodlin, Ludwik of Oława, Helena of Racibórz, Przemko of Opava, Kazko of Oświęcim and Bolko of Cieszyn had all decided to save their own estates by entering into negotiations.

The talks with the Silesian dukes had fuelled rumours in the army that it marked the end of the plundering raid and that it was time to go home. Rumours were circulating that the march ordered by Prokop on Nysa would shift to Opava, and from there the army would carry straight on to Odry in Moravia.

'Perhaps we'll be home by Pentecost,' said Dobko Puchała, lending credence to the rumour when asked. 'In that case,' he added, winking at Reynevan, 'we ought to torch something here before we go, hadn't we?'

Oh, my sorrow, my grief!
I cannot find out,
Where I shall spend the first night,
When my soul flees the body . . .

The sky was shrouded in black clouds, a cold wind was blowing and a thin rain fell from time to time, pricking like needles. The weather had a clear influence on the songs sung by the Poles.

This perfidious world told me,
That my life would be long,
Yesterday it did not tell me,
That my life would be long . . .

Puchała's destination was the village of Berzdorf, the grange of the Henryków monastery, which was protected by the Ziębice agreement. Wanting at one fell swoop to send up in smoke the ducal grange in Ostrężna and the little church in Wigandsdorf that had survived by a miracle and not stay too far behind the army moving swiftly towards Nysa, Dobko divided his detachment into three combat squads. Reynevan and Samson remained with the commander. Scharley didn't take part in the operation, since he was suffering from a bout of diarrhoea so severe that even magical medicine was unable to help him.

They rode through rough country, crossing narrow gorges with tributaries of the Oława flowing at the bottom, carrying peat-brown water over rocks and around fallen logs. Beside one such stream, Reynevan saw the Washerwoman.

Only he and Samson noticed her. She didn't raise her head at all, however, even though the detachment had crossed a stream barely twenty paces from her. She was very slight, and the slightness of her figure was additionally accentuated by her clinging dress. Reynevan couldn't see her face – it was completely hidden by her long, straight, dark hair, which fell right down to the water over which she knelt and was being caressed by the slow current.

She was holding a blouse or shift in her wax-white arms, arms up to the elbows in the water, rubbing and squeezing it with eerily slow movements. Small clouds of pulsating blood were drifting from the shift like smoke. The blood floated through the water, colouring it crimson, pink froth bathing the horses' knees.

A strong wind blew; a sudden, fell wind, rattling the now green branches and tearing from the sides of the ravine clouds of last year's dry weeds. Reynevan and Samson squinted. When they opened them, the apparition had vanished.

But blood was still flowing in the water.

They said nothing for a while.

'Are we going?' Samson finally cleared his throat. 'Or turning back?'

Reynevan didn't answer, just spurred his horse, urging it to catch up with Puchała and the Poles who were already vanishing among the greening alders.

*

In the next ravine, they walked into a trap.

Shots were fired and bowstrings twanged from a thicket on the far hillside as a hail of balls and bolts fell on the Poles. Men yelled, horses squealed and several of them reared up and fell to the bottom of the ravine. Among them was Samson's.

'Find cover!' roared Puchała. 'Dismount and find cover!'

The thicket sang again with the clang of bowstrings and the hiss of bolts. Reynevan felt a blow to his shoulder so hard that he fell to the ground, unluckily onto a slope covered in wet fallen leaves as slippery as soap. He slid down them to the bottom of the ravine, and only then, as he tried to stand, did he see the fletching of a bolt protruding below his clavicle. *Christ, not the artery*, he managed to think before weakness overcame him.

He saw Samson free himself from under his dead horse, get to his knees and then his feet. And fall with his head bloodied, even before the deafening roar of a harquebus fired from the thicket had died away.

Reynevan yelled, but his cry was drowned out by another handgonne salvo. The ravine completely filled with smoke. Belts whistled. The wounded groaned.

Although his arms and legs had turned to jelly and every movement was causing him convulsions of pain, Reynevan crawled over to Samson. A large pool of blood had already spread around the giant's head, but Reynevan saw that the ball had only grazed his temple. *The skull*, he thought, *the skull might be damaged. Dammit, it must be. His eyes . . .*

Samson's glazed eyes suddenly rolled back in their sockets. Reynevan watched in horror as the giant's head shuddered, his mouth contorted and saliva ran from it. A strangled cry came from his throat.

'It's dark . . .' he mumbled indistinctly, in a strange voice. 'Dark . . . Black . . . Jesus . . . Where am I? It's night here . . . I want to go 'ome . . . 'Ome! Where be I . . . ?'

Reynevan, horror-struck, pressed a hand to Samson's blood-ied temple and whispered – or rather croaked – the formula of the Alkmena spell. He felt cold overcome him, flowing from his shoulder, from the bolt lodged beneath his clavicle. Samson struggled and waved an arm as though shooing something away. His eyes were suddenly clearer. And more lucid.

'Reynevan . . .' he panted. 'Something . . . Something's hap-pening to me . . . While I still can . . . I'll tell you . . . I have to tell you . . .'

'Lie still . . .' Reynevan bit his lip with the pain. 'Lie still . . .'

In a second, Samson's eyes misted over and terror filled them. The giant whimpered, sobbed and curled up in the foetal position.

The exchange is happening. Recollections and associations flew through Reynevan's spinning head like a gale. *Someone is leaving us; someone is coming to us. The monastery idiot is returning to his mortal shell from the darkness he passed into. The* negotium *that usually comes from the darkness is returning to the darkness. Going back to where it came from. The wanderer, the* Viator, *is going back to where it came from. In front of my eyes, Death is doing what the sorcerers couldn't.*

Pain racked him again, spasms squeezed his lungs and larynx, utterly paralysing his legs. He felt his back with a trembling hand. As he had expected, the point of the bolt was sticking out. And blood was flowing.

'Hey, you whoresons!' yelled someone from the thicket beyond the ravine. 'Heretics! Godless curs!'

'Whoresons yourselves!' Dobko Puchała roared back from the other side of the ravine. 'Sodding papists!'

'Want to fight? Then come over to our damned side!'

'You bloody come over to ours!'

'We'll kick your fucking arses!'

'We'll fucking kick yours!'

It appeared that the none-too-sophisticated and painfully trivial interchange would last an eternity. But it didn't.

'Puchała?' said a voice from the thicket in disbelief. 'Dobko Puchała? Of the Wieniawa?'

'And who's bloody asking?'

'Otto Nostitz!'

'Oh, damn! Grunwald?'

'Grunwald! The Day of the Sending Out of the Apostles, 1410!'

There was silence for some time. The wind, however, was carrying the smell of smouldering fuses.

'I say, Puchała? We won't go for each other's throats, will we? After all, we faced each other in battle. It's not fucking right.'

'Not at all. After all, we crossed swords. Why don't we go our way and you yours? What say you, Nostitz?'

'I say we may.'

'I have casualties down there! If I take them, they'll expire on the way. Will you look after them?'

'My parole. We crossed swords, after all.'

Reynevan, not knowing how he found the strength, finally stemmed the bleeding from Samson's head by repeating a spell over and over. And realised that he was quite awash in blood himself. Everything went black. He stopped feeling the pain.

Because he had lost consciousness.

Chapter Twenty-Two

In which the fever eases and intensifies by turns, but the pain increases. And, to make matters worse, they have to flee.

He regained consciousness in semi-darkness, saw the darkness yield before the light and the light merge into the gloom and combine with it, creating a shadowy, translucent suspension. *Umbram fugat claritas*, flashed through his head. *Noctem lux eliminat.* The Aurora, *Eos rhododactylos*, rose and painted the eastern sky pink.

He was lying on a hard pallet and any attempts to move caused pains to shoot through his shoulder and scapula. Before he even touched the thickly bandaged place, he recalled in detail the bolt that had been there, the fletching of goose feathers at the front, an inch of ash wood and another of iron point sticking out at the back. There was still a bolt in there. An invisible and immaterial bolt of pain.

He knew where it was. He'd been in many hospitals, so the funk of many fevered bodies, the stench of camphor, urine, blood and decay was nothing new to him. And superimposed on it, the unending and intrusive melody of soft snores, moans, groans and sighs.

The reawakened pain in his scapula pulsated, neither subsiding nor easing, radiated across his back, up to his shoulders and downwards to his buttocks. Reynevan touched his forehead, felt the wet hair under his hand. *I'm feverish*, he thought. *The wound is festering.*

Things are looking bad.

'God help us, Brother, may God help us. We're alive. We've made it through another night. Perhaps, dammit, we'll get out of this ...'

'You're Czech?' Reynevan turned his head towards the pallet on his right, from where his neighbour – as pale as death and with sunken cheeks – had greeted him. 'What is this place? Where am I? Among friends?'

'Aye, among friends,' muttered the pale man. 'We're all good Czechs here. But in truth, Brother, we are far, far away from our boys.'

'I don't underst—' Reynevan tried to raise himself but fell back with a groan. 'I don't understand. What hospital is this? Where are we?'

'In Oława.'

'Oława?'

'Aye,' confirmed the Czech. 'It's a town in Silesia. Brother Prokop made a truce and an agreement with the local herzog ... Not to ravage the lands here ... And the herzog promised to take care of the Taborite wounded.'

'But where is Prokop? Where's the Tábor? And what day is it today?'

'The Tábor? Far, faaar away ... Heading home. And the day? Tuesday. And the day after tomorrow, Thursday, will be a holiday. *Nanebevstoupení Páně.*'

Ascension Day, Reynevan quickly calculated, *forty days after Easter, falls on the thirteenth day of May. So today is the eleventh. I was wounded on the eighth. That means I was unconscious for three days.*

'You say, Brother, that the Tábor is leaving Silesia?' He continued to pry. 'Does that mean the end of the expedition? That we've stopped fighting?'

'Were you told not to talk politics?' A woman's voice sounded. 'You were. So please do not. Please pray. To God for your health. And for the souls of this hospital's founders. And please remember our benefactors and donors in your prayers. Come on, Brethren in Christ! Whoever can stand, to the chapel!'

He knew that voice.

'You're conscious, m'Lord Lancelot. Finally. I'm glad.'

'Dorota . . .' He sighed, recognising her. 'Dorota Faber . . .'

'It's nice of you to recognise me, m'lord.' The harlot smiled at him sweetly. 'Nice indeed. I'm glad you've finally awoken . . . Oh, and the pillow isn't so stained with blood today . . . So perhaps you'll recover. Let's change the dressing. Elencza!'

'Sister Dorota . . .' grunted someone from the other wall. 'Me leg's hurting me dreadful—'

'There's no leg there, son, I told you. Elencza, over here.'

He didn't recognise her right away. Perhaps it was the fever, or perhaps the time that had passed, but for a long while he looked uncomprehendingly at the fair-haired, thin-lipped young woman with pale, watery eyes. With the once-plucked eyebrows growing slowly back.

It took some time for him to realise who she was. It helped that the young woman clearly knew who he was. He saw it in her anxious look.

'The daughter of Lord Stietencron . . . The Goleniowskie Forests. Ścibor's Clearing . . . You're alive? You survived?'

She nodded, smoothing her apron with a nervous movement. And he suddenly understood where the fear in her eyes came from, where the terrified grimace and trembling of her narrow mouth.

'It wasn't I . . .' he mumbled. 'It wasn't I who robbed the tax collector . . . I had nothing to do with it . . . Everything you've heard . . . Everything you've heard about me is rumour and falsehood—'

'That's enough talk.' Dorota Faber cut him off seemingly sternly. 'Time to change the dressing. Help me, Elencza.'

They tried to be gentle, but in spite of that, he hissed in pain and groaned loudly several times. When they unwound the bandages, he wanted to see the wound but was unable to lift his head. A diagnosis by touch had to suffice. And by smell. Neither diagnosis was promising.

'It's festering,' Dorota Faber confirmed calmly. Her face was bathed in an aura of saintliness in the beam of sunlight shining through the small window. 'It's festering,' she repeated. 'And swelling. Ever since the barber-surgeon removed the splinters of the bolt. But it's better than it was. Better, m'Lord Lancelot.'

Her face was bathed in saintliness, and a bright gold halo also appeared to be framing the head of Elencza of Stietencron. *Martha and Mary of Bethany*, he thought, feeling giddy. *Divinely beautiful. They're both divinely beautiful.*

'My name's not . . .' His head was spinning faster and faster. 'My name's not Lancelot . . . Nor Hagenau . . . I am Reinmar of Bielawa . . .'

'We know,' Martha and Mary replied from the light.

'Where's my comrade? A big man, almost a giant . . . He's called Samson . . .'

'He's here, calm yourself. His head was cut. The barber-surgeons are treating him.'

'How is he?'

'They say he'll recover. He's very strong, they said, and hardy. Supernaturally hardy.'

'Dammit . . . I must see him . . . Help him . . .'

'Lie still, m'Lord Reinmar.' Dorota Faber straightened his pillow. 'You won't help anyone as you are. But you might harm yourself.'

The hospital of Saint Świerad beside the church with the same saint as its patron – one of two in Oława – was subordinate to the town council and run by Premonstratensians from the Church of Saint Vincent in Wrocław. Apart from the Premonstratensians, male volunteers worked in the hospital, and female ones, like Dorota Faber and Elencza of Stietencron. The patients were almost entirely Hussites – Taborites and Orphans – mainly severely wounded or very seriously sick. There were also cripples. All of them in a condition that had compelled Prokop to leave them because of the impossibility of moving them. On the strength of the truce and agreement forced on Ludwik, Duke of Oława, the hospital of Saint Świerad was made available to them. They were being treated there and had been guaranteed unmolested passage to Bohemia. Some of the Czechs being treated didn't overly trust the word of Duke Ludwik and held out little hope regarding the truce and guarantee. The further away Prokop marched, they claimed, the less binding became the truce. Having the Warriors of God at the very gates, and before them the prospect of conflagration and destruction, Duke Ludwik was inclined towards concessions and promises – anything to save his duchy. Now, with the Warriors of God over the hills and far away, the threat had vanished and the promises become hollow. And hollow promises butter no parsnips.

*

The following day, having woken up, Reynevan glanced at the pallet on his left.

Samson Honeypot was lying in it. With a bandaged head. Unconscious.

Reynevan wanted to get up and see how he was. He couldn't. He was too weak. His swollen left shoulder was throbbing with pain and the fingers of his left hand had lost all feeling. The smell of gangrene was intensifying.

'Among my things ...' he groaned, vainly trying to raise himself up, 'was a casket ... A copper casket ...'

Elencza sighed. Dorota Faber shook her head.

'When they brought you here, you had nothing. Not even any boots. They treated you with mercy, but that mercy didn't extend to your chattels. They picked you clean.'

Reynevan felt a wave of heat spread through him. Before he had time to swear or gnash his teeth, his memory returned. And with it, relief. The priceless casket had remained with Scharley. When he was suffering from diarrhoea, Reynevan had treated him with magic, using the sorcerer Telesma's amulets. Setting off on the foray with Puchała, he had left the casket with Scharley.

But the relief was very short-lived. The amulets – though they had probably survived – were now heading to Bohemia with Scharley and the entire Tábor, temporarily out of reach. But he needed them within reach. The festering wound required magic. Left to traditional methods, he risked losing his arm at the shoulder. At best. At worst – losing his life.

'There's an apothecary ...' he grunted, seizing the harlot by the hand. 'There's an apothecary in Oława. He is certain to have a secret alchemic workshop ... Only for a closed circle ... For people from the magical confraternity ... *I* need magical medicine. For *Samson* ... For him, I must have a medicine called *dodecatheon*. For me, for my shoulder, I need *unguentum achilleum*—'

'The apothecary ...' Dorota turned her head away. 'The apothecary won't sell us anything. He won't even let us cross the threshold. All Oława knows who we're treating here. The hospital is under the guard and protection of the duke, but the townspeople revile us. They won't help. No use going ... And it's dangerous on the street—'

'I'll go,' said Elencza Stietencron. 'I'll go to the apothecary's shop. Please ...'

'You'll say the password: *Visita Inferiora Terrae*. The apothecary will understand ... *Visita Inferiora Terrae* ... Will you remember it?'

'I will.'

With great effort, Reynevan managed to focus his gaze on her, even though it kept blurring with the fever. Again, she appeared encircled by a glow. A halo. An aureole.

'The medicaments ...' He felt himself losing consciousness. 'By the name of ... *Dodecatheon* ... And *unguentum achilleum* ... You won't forget?'

'I won't.' She turned her head away. 'I cannot. God must have punished me with an inability to forget.'

He was too sick to notice how bitter it sounded.

'Dorota?'

'Yes, Reinmar?'

'When we met, three summers ago, right here, near Oława, on the Strzelin road ... You meant to go out into the world. As you said, if only to Wrocław. To work ... You didn't get very far ...'

'I went to Wrocław.' The harlot put down the bowl she was feeding him from. 'I resided there and returned. Work, it turns out, is the same everywhere. And it's just as hard everywhere. Then I returned to my old stamping ground, to Brzeg and the Crown whorehouse. I thought, when I die, they can bury me in the same boneyard as they'll bury my mother. And then, when the fighting began, there were plenty of wounded and sick people. The monks in the hospitals needed help ... so I helped. In Brzeg to begin with, at the Holy Spirit. Then I came here, to Oława.'

'You decided on a hospital ... I know something about it, and it's exacting and hard work ... Harder and probably more thankless than—'

'No, Reinmar. Not more.'

Although it was verging on the miraculous, the apothecary in Oława possessed the necessary medicine. Although it was verging on the miraculous, he sold it to Elencza of Stietencron. Although it was verging on the miraculous, the effects were visible right from the first treatment. Yarrow, *achillea millefolium*, the herb which formed the main ingredient of *unguentum achilleum*, not without reason bore the name of the hero of Troy – it healed wounds suffered in battle quickly and effectively. Rubbed on several times a day, the ointment arrested the gangrene, lowered the fever and visibly reduced the swelling. After a day of treatment, Reynevan was able to sit up; after the next two – admittedly not without the help of Dorota and Elencza – to stand up. And to take care of Samson.

After barely one day of *dodecatheon* being applied, a mixture whose effectiveness was second only to the legendary *moly*, Samson opened his eyes. Despite the dose of the medicine obtained from the Oława apothecary's shop being negligible, after two days the giant regained consciousness sufficiently to begin complaining about an unbearable headache. Medicine wasn't needed for that; Reynevan treated his headache with a spell and his healing hands. Samson's pain turned out, however, to be a quite a challenge, and he exhausted himself before alleviating it. Both of them, doctor and patient, lay almost lifeless the entire following day. Until the nineteenth of May.

When problems began.

'Black-haired,' repeated Dorota Faber. 'Dressed in black. Shoulder-length, black hair. A kind of birdlike face. Nose like a beak. And the look of a devil. Know anyone like that?'

'I do, dammit,' Reynevan drawled, wiping away the cold sweat that was suddenly beading his forehead. 'I'll say.'

'Because he knows you. He was with the hospital master and described you exactly. He asked if anyone looking like you was here. Fortunately, the hospital master is a decent fellow, and on top of that has no memory for faces, so he quite honestly denied seeing anybody who looks like you or that anyone like you was staying in the hospice. And when the black bird-man began to demand to be allowed into the hospital, the hospital master didn't give his permission, citing ducal orders and the agreement guaranteeing the Hussites sanctuary. The fellow at first tried to frighten and threaten him, but when he noticed it was in vain, he left. He finally said he'd soon return with the duke's permission, that he'd scour the hospital, and if he found you and it turned out the hospital master was lying, woe on him. Ha, Reynevan, seems to me that bird-man really could be a troublemaker. And even takes pleasure in it.'

'You're absolutely right.'

'Something tells me also that he'll return with the duke's permission.'

'You're absolutely right. I must flee, Dorota. At once. Today.'

'I, too, must leave,' moaned Elencza. She was as white as a

sheet. 'I know that ... person as well,' she stammered out. 'I think he tracked me to Oława. He's hunting me.'

'Impossible,' said Reynevan. 'He's hunting me! He has evil designs on me. I'm his target.'

'No. I am. I'm certain it's me.'

Samson sat up in bed. He was quite lucid.

'I believe,' he said quite clearly, 'that you are both mistaken.'

They left Oława before dusk, unnoticed. It transpired that Dorota Faber had numerous, reliable acquaintances among the right people. The hospital janitor – who made cow eyes at the red-headed harlot – supplied them with clothes and helped them leave the hospital in secret. A burly servant looked at her in the same way as he led them to the stable, helping Samson to walk. Because Samson required assistance. Reynevan wasn't in the best way, either, as a matter of fact. His thoughts turned anxiously to the ride ahead of them.

As it transpired, Dorota and Elencza had given some thought to the matter. With the help of the janitor and the servant, they strapped them on to the saddles so they were able to keep reasonably upright as they rode and wouldn't slide off or fall. It was none too comfortable, but Reynevan didn't complain. He had reason to believe that capture by Birkart Grellenort would guarantee them even fewer comforts.

They left the town through a wicket gate close by the Brzeg Gate, in the south-eastern part of the town. They did it not out of choice, but necessity. Dorota had acquaintances among the guards on sentry duty there. This time, neither her charm nor her beguiling smile were sufficient – more concrete, clinking arguments were necessary. Reynevan's debt with the harlot was growing quickly.

'You may get into trouble,' he said as they bade each other

goodbye. 'They took the money, but they wouldn't hesitate to turn you in. Don't you prefer to come with us?'

'I'll cope.'

'Are you certain?'

'They're only men. I know how to handle them. Godspeed. Farewell, Elencza.'

'Farewell, Mistress Dorota. Thank you for everything.'

They skirted the town from the south and reached the river along a track among some osiers. They found a ford and crossed onto the left bank. Soon the horses' hooves thudded on harder ground. They were on the highway.

'Have the plans changed?' asked Elencza, coping quite tolerably in the saddle, as it turned out. 'Are we heading where we were meant to?'

'Yes. It's this way.'

'Will you cope?'

'We will.'

'Let's ride, then. We'll leave the Wrocław road and head westwards. Quickly! We need to get as far away as possible while it's still light.'

'Elencza.'

'Yes.'

'I thank you.'

'Don't thank me.'

The May night smelled of bird cherry blossom.

By saying they would cope, Reynevan had been lying to Elencza Stietencron. In actual fact, the only things keeping him and Samson in the saddle were the leather straps. And their fear of Grellenort.

The journey through the gathering darkness was sheer torment. Indeed, it was a blessing that Reynevan didn't remember much of it, as he was trembling from the fever again and barely aware of the surrounding world. Samson wasn't in a much better state; the giant was groaning, huddled and hunched over in the saddle, his head nodding onto the horse's mane as though he were drunk. Elencza rode between their horses to hold them up.

'Elencza?'

'Yes.'

'Three years ago, in Ścibor's Clearing ... How did you save yourself?'

'I'd rather not say.'

'Dorota mentioned that later, in December, you survived the massacre in Bardo—'

'I'd rather not talk about that, either.'

'Forgive me.'

'I don't have anything to forgive you for. Keep upright in the saddle, please. Sit upright ... Don't lean over like that ... Oh, God, I wish this night could finally be over ...'

'Elencza ...'

'Your friend is awfully heavy.'

'I don't know ... how to repay you ...'

'I know you don't.'

'What's the matter?'

'My hands are growing numb ... Sit up straight, please. And ride on.'

They rode on.

It began to grow dusk.

'Reinmar?'

'Samson? I thought—'

'I'm lucid. Generally speaking. Where are we? Is it much further?'

'I don't know.'

'It's close.' Elencza spoke up. 'The monastery's close. I can hear the bell ... Morning worship ... We've arrived ...'

The young woman's voice and words gave them strength and euphoria overcame their tiredness and feverishness. They quickly covered the remaining distance to the monastery. Emerging from the sticky, shaggy greyness of the dawn, the world became completely unreal, illusory, mysterious, as though everything was happening in a dream. The nightjars flitting around in the air seemed dreamlike, the monastery seemed dreamlike, the monastery wicket gate with its grating hinges seemed dreamlike. The nun in a grey habit of thick Frisian wool who guarded the gate seemed dreamlike as she emerged from the fog. Her cry as though from the beyond ... And the bell. *The morning worship* ... Thoughts drifted through Reynevan's head. *Laudes matutine* ... *But what about the singing? Why aren't the nuns singing? Oh, it's White Church after all. The Poor Clares don't sing the hours, but say them* ... 'Jutta ... Jutta? Jutta!'

'Reynevan!'

'Jutta ...'

'How are you? What's the matter? Are you hurt? Mother of God! Get him out of the saddle ... Reynevan!'

'Jutta ... I ...'

'Help me ... Lift him up ... Oh! What is it?'

'My shoulder ... Jutta ... Enough ... I can stand ... It's just my legs that are weak ... Take care of Samson ...'

'We'll take them both to the infirmary. Right away, at once. Sisters, help me—'

'Wait.'

Elencza of Stietencron didn't dismount but remained in the saddle with her head turned away. She only looked at him when he called her name.

'You said you had somewhere to go. But perhaps you'll stay?'

'No. I'll be going.'

'Where to? If I wanted to find you—'

'I doubt you would.'

'But I might.'

'Skałka near Wrocław . . .' she said reluctantly and seemingly with effort. 'The estate and stud of Lady Dzierżka of Wirsing.'

'Dzierżka?' He couldn't control his amazement. 'You're staying with Dzierżka?'

'Farewell, Reinmar of Bielawa.' She reined her horse around. 'Take care of yourself. And I—'

'I shall try to forget,' she said softly. When she was far enough away from the convent gate for him not to hear her.

Chapter Twenty-Three

In which time – spent pleasantly and blissfully – passes fleet-ingly for Reynevan during the summer of *Anno Domini* 1428. And one would just love to finish the story with the standard ending: 'They lived happily ever after'. But what one would love and what actually happens are two quite different things.

Reynevan lay in the convent infirmary until Trinity Sunday, the first Sunday after Pentecost. Exactly nine days. As a matter of fact, he only totalled up those days afterwards, since the re-turning waves of fever meant he remembered little of his stay or the treatment. He remembered Jutta of Apolda spending a great deal of time at his bedside, and the stout infirmary nurse, called – most aptly – Sister Misericordia. He remembered being treated by the abbess: a tall, serious nun with bright, blue-grey eyes. He remembered the remedies she gave him, acutely pain-ful and invariably causing fever and delirium. It was thanks to those remedies, however, that he still had his arm and could make tolerable use of it. He heard the nuns talking during the treatments – and they discussed his clavicle, shoulder joint, subclavian artery, axillary nerve, lymph nodes and fasciae. He heard enough to know that the abbess's medical knowledge had saved him from numerous complications. Not to mention the medicaments she had and knew how to apply. Some of them were magical, some of which Reynevan knew, either by their smell or by the reactions they caused. She used both *dodecatheon* – much stronger than the one they had obtained in Oława – and *peristereon*, a medicine which was very rare, very expensive and very effective against inflammation. The abbess used a medicine called *garwa*, the secret of which had apparently come all the way from the druids in distant Ireland, on his wound, which had to be re-opened several times. Reynevan also recognised by its typical poppy-like scent *wundkraut*, a magical herb of the Valkyries which the priests of Wotan had employed to treat the wounded following the Battle of the Teutoburg Forest. The scent of dried henbane leaves betrayed *hierobotane*, and the scent of poplar bark *leukis*, two powerful anti-gangrene medicines. The powder called *lycopodium bellonarium* smelled of clubmoss.

And by the time they started using it, Reynevan could stand up unaided. The fingers of his left hand were no longer numb and he could hold various objects in them. Owing to which he was able to help the nuns treating Samson. Who – though conscious – was still unable to stand up.

Jutta never left Reynevan's side. Her eyes shone with tears and love.

The war, which they had managed to forget about, made itself known soon after Trinity Sunday. On the morning of the first day of June, Reynevan, Jutta and a nun from White Church were startled by the roar of cannons coming from the west. Before precise information reached the convent, Reynevan had guessed what it was all about. Jan Kolda of Žampach hadn't retreated with Prokop the Shaven's army but had remained in Silesia in the fortified position on Sobótka. He and his murderous squad were a thorn in the Silesians' side, too vexing to be tolerated.

A powerful Wrocław–Świdnica contingent armed with heavy bombards encircled the castle in Sobótka and began to fire, calling on Jan Kolda to surrender. The popular rumour had it that in response, Kolda called the besiegers by a vernacular name for the male sexual organs and encouraged them to indulge in sodomy. After which he retaliated from the walls with fire from his own guns.

The exchange of fire lasted a week, and for a week Reynevan all but rode to Sobótka to aid Kolda in some way, for example with sabotage and acts of subversion. He could barely walk, could only dream about riding a horse, but was spoiling to fight. Jutta finally put an end to his agitation and thwarted his military plans. Jutta was firm. She gave him an ultimatum: either her or the war. Reynevan chose her.

Jan Kolda of Žampach defended himself for another week, inflicting such acute losses on the Silesians that when he finally exhausted all his resources, he had a strong negotiating position. The day after Saint Anthony's Day he surrendered, but under honourable conditions, with the pledge of safe passage to Bohemia. Meanwhile, the Silesians razed Sobótka Castle to the ground so that it couldn't be used by the next bloody Kolda.

Reynevan found out all those details from the gardener, who worked in the convent grange and had – apart from good sources of information – a love of gossip and a talent for it. Following the fall of Sobótka, the gardener came with some rather alarming rumours. For Silesia had finally recovered from the Hussite Easter plundering raid. And begun to react. Violently and bloodily. The blood of those who had proved cowards in battle or parleyed with the Czechs dripped from scaffolds. Supporters of Hussitism – and people only suspected of sympathising – sizzled on pyres. Peasants who had informed the Hussites expired on wheels and stakes. Gibbets groaned under the weight of collaborators. Moreover, people who had absolutely nothing to do with Hussitism were also tortured and executed. The usual suspects: Jews, free thinkers, troubadours, alchemists and village abortionists.

The apparently safe sanctuary inside the convent walls suddenly lost its sense of snugness. Reynevan spent his convalescence waking up in a cold sweat to every bell and knock at the gate, and would then fall asleep relieved to hear that it hadn't been the Inquisition or Birkart Grellenort, just the fishmonger with his delivery.

Time passed, and peace, care and medical attention did their job. His wounds healed. Slowly, but surely. After Saint Anthony's Day, Samson began to rise, and after Gervasius' and Protasius' Day to feel well enough to begin helping the gardener with his work. Reynevan, however, had recovered enough for his contact with Jutta through eyes and hands to no longer suffice.

Saint John's Eve came. The Poor Clare nuns from White Church celebrated it with an extra mass. Reynevan and Jutta, on the other hand, followed by the curious looks of the nuns, ran to the forest to search for the fern flower. No sooner had they reached a grove of birches than Reynevan explained to Jutta that the fern flower was a legend and the hunt for it – however romantic and exciting it might be – was in principle pointless and something of a waste of time. Unless they felt a great need to respect the ancient tradition. Jutta quickly admitted that while she did, she'd actually rather make better, more intelligent and pleasant use of the short June night.

Reynevan, who thought similarly, spread his cloak out on the ground and helped her to undress.

'*Adsum favens*,' whispered the young woman, slowly and

gradually emerging from her raiment like Aphrodite from the ocean foam. '*Adsum favens et propitia*; I have come in sympathy and goodwill. Now stop your tears and cease your lamentation; banish your grief. Now by my providence your day of salvation is dawning.'

She whispered and beauty met his eyes. The resplendent beauty of nakedness, the glory of delicate womanliness, the Holy Grail, saintliness. She manifested herself to his eyes as *donna angelicata*, worthy of the brushes of artists he knew such as Domenico Veneziano, Simone of Siena, the Master of Flémalle, Tommaso Masaccio, Masolino, the brothers Limbourg, Sassetta and Jan van Eyck. And of those whom he could not yet have known, who were still to come. Whose names – Fra Angelico, Piero della Francesca, Enguerrand Charonton, Rogier van der Weyden, Jean Fouquet, Hugo van der Goes – a delighted humanity could look forward to knowing.

'*Sit satis laborum*,' she whispered, putting her arms around his neck. 'Let there be rest from troubles.'

Seeing that Reynevan's wounded shoulder was still paining him, she took matters into her own hands. Lying him on his back, she united with him in the position the poet Martial usually ascribed to Hector and Andromache.

They made love like those two lovers. They made love on Saint John's Eve. From somewhere on high came the singing of choirs, quite possibly angelic ones. And all around cavorted sylvan spirits, singing.

The elderflower blooms at Midsummer
Love will be ever more blissful!

During the following nights – and often during the day, too – they didn't bother running to the forest. They made love just outside the convent wall, in a sun-soaked bower among bushes of blackthorn and elder. They made love and – even during the day – sylvan spirits cavorted around them.

Parsley, carrots, celery
Grow in our garden,
The gorgeous Jutta is the bride
She should wait no longer . . .

The convent in White Church was divided into three parts, which Reynevan inevitably associated with the Three Circles of Initiation. The First Circle – which wasn't circular, of course – housed the convent's utilities, including the garden, the infirmary, the guests' and workers' refectory and the converse nuns' dormitory, and also the guests' bedchambers and rooms. The Second Circle – the heart of which was the church – was off limits to guests and included the library and scriptorium, and also the abbess's chambers. The Third Circle consisted of the completely and strictly secluded clausula, and the nuns' refectory and dormitories.

The Poor Clares of White Church observed – on the face of it, at least – a stern religious rule. They fasted strictly and there was no meat in the convent's bill of fare. They kept silent during meals and utter silence was maintained from Compline to the convent Mass. Work, prayer, penance and contemplation took up their entire day; they were only entitled to one hour for their own affairs and rest, with the exception of Fridays, when no rest was allowed. The *conversae* – apart from Jutta, there were four in the convent, all maidens from noble families – followed a considerably tempered version of the rule and their duties were limited in principle to worship and religious study.

However, the longer Reynevan resided in the convent, the more departures from the rule he noticed. What was conspicuous right away was the quite relaxed approach to the clausula. Absolutely inaccessible from the outside, from the inside the clausula wasn't a barrier – the nuns could move through the entire convent. Even the presence in the convent of two men – Reynevan and Samson – didn't limit their freedom of movement. There was only a peculiar piece of etiquette to observe – the nuns pretended that there weren't any men and the men pretended not to see them. This didn't apply to the abbess, who did what she wanted, when and how she wanted to. The sister housekeeper and the infirmarist also had complete freedom of contact.

The more Reynevan was accepted by the nuns and considered trusted, the more he was allowed to see. And he saw that the penance and contemplation ordered by the rule were substituted in White Church by study; the reading of books, writings and postills; discussions; and even debates. But he was not allowed into those restricted areas. Although Jutta had access to them, he didn't.

But the biggest shock was the Mass. Reynevan didn't participate in it. The atmosphere of White Church made him feel safe, so he had no intention of hiding the fact that as a Calixtine and Utraquist he didn't recognise either the papist Mass or Communion.

Once, however, he felt the need and went to Mass, having decided after some thought that it was doubtful whether God had the time or desire to be bothered by liturgical minutiae. He went to the church and received a shock. The Mass was being celebrated by the abbess.

A woman.

After a few days, the abbess unexpectedly asked Reynevan to see her. As he went, he was aware both of the honour and of the fact that he was about to be interrogated. Which he had been expecting for some time.

As he entered, she was reading an incunable lying open on a lectern. Reynevan, as a bibliophile and bibliomaniac, immediately recognised Joachim of Fiore's *Psalterium Decem Cordarum* by its illuminations and engravings. Other works that were lying in eyeshot were: Hildegard of Bingen's *Liber Divinorum Operum*, Saint Bernard's *De amore Dei*, Hesiod's *Theogony*, and Nicholas of Clémanges' *De ruina ecclesiae*. He didn't know why, but the sight of a well-thumbed copy of *Necronomicon* among the books didn't surprise him in the least.

The abbess looked at him for some time over the polished lenses of her spectacles, as though challenging him to endure her gaze.

'An unprecedented thing,' she finally said, and the expression on her face might have been a smile or a sneer. 'An unprecedented thing. Not only am I treating a Hussite in my convent. Not only am I protecting a heretic. Not only have I allowed in a sorcerer – and a necromancer at that. Not only do I tolerate and nurse him, why, I even permit him to indulge in amorous pleasure with a converse entrusted into my care. A converse from a noble family, for whom I am responsible.'

'We are in—' he began.

She didn't let him finish. 'Indeed. In the throes of passion, I'd say. And I wonder whether you've thought about the possible consequences? For even a moment?'

'I am a doctor—'

'Firstly, do not forget that. Secondly, I was by no means only thinking about the possibility of pregnancy.'

She said nothing for some time and played with the linen cord girdling her habit, with the four knots in it symbolising the four vows of Saint Clare, the patron and founder of the Order of Poor Ladies.

'I meant the future.' She pressed a hand to her forehead.

'Something that is most uncertain in today's hard times. I want to know whether you and Jutta think about the future. Whether you, Reynevan, think about the future. No, no, not the details. The simple fact of it.'

'I do, Reverend Mother.'

Her bright, blue-grey eyes held his gaze. Her facial features reminded him of somebody, but he could not think who.

'You claim to be thinking about it.' She tilted her head. 'And what, I wonder, dominates in your thoughts? What is there more of? Jutta and what is best for her? Or perhaps war? The fight for a good cause? The desire to change the world? And if, let's suppose, a conflict arose, if your ideals opposed each other . . . what would you choose? And what would you give up?'

He said nothing.

'It is generally known,' she continued, 'that where the good of great and weighty matters is concerned, individuals mean nothing. They are sacrificed. Jutta is an individual. What will happen to her? Will you toss her away like a stone onto the ramparts?'

'I don't know.' He swallowed with effort. 'I cannot pretend in front of you, Honourable Lady, and do not wish to. I sincerely do not know.'

She looked him long in the eyes.

'I know you don't know,' she said finally. 'I wasn't expecting an answer. I just wanted you to give it some thought.'

Soon after Saint Peter and Paul's, when all the meadows were blue with cornflowers, a long period of nasty, rainy weather arrived. The secluded spot where Reynevan and Jutta usually made love became a muddy pond. The abbess looked on for some time as the pair wandered around the arcades of the garth, as they gazed into each other's eyes – only to finally part and go their separate ways.

One evening, having rearranged the sleeping quarters in the abbey, she summoned them both and led them to a cell, tidied and decked with blossom.

'Here you will live,' she declared dryly. 'And sleep. Both of you. From now on. From this night.'

'We thank you, Mother,' they said in unison.

'Don't thank me. And don't waste time. *Hora ruit, redimite tempus.*'

Summer had come. The hot summer of 1428.

Every now and then, the unflagging gardener unflaggingly brought new rumours. Jan Kolda's surrender and the loss of Sobótka Castle, he said, stamping on some naked baby mice he had unearthed from their nests, infuriated the Hussites. Midway through July, on the Thursday after Saint Margaret's Day, the Orphans, in revenge, attacked and captured Jelenia Góra, razing the town to the ground in a swift foray.

Although it took him more time, the gardener also passed on rumours from Bohemia – the news Reynevan and Samson had been yearning for. The hejtman of the New Town in Prague, Velek Kúdelník of Březnice, recounted the gardener, scraping shit from his pitchfork, struck the land of the Bavarians around Saint Urban's Day. The Hussites burned down Mosbach, the residence of Count Palatine Otto, and marched along the valley of the River Naab to Regensburg. They thoroughly pillaged and utterly ruined the Cistercian abbey in Walderbach. Wagons laden with loot, they returned to Bohemia, leaving scorched earth behind them.

At more or less the same time, said the gardener, picking his nose and looking intently at the contents, the Tábor attacked Austria with a savage plundering raid in order to teach Duke

Albrecht a lesson. Burning, wreaking havoc, sacking, without encountering any resistance, the Taborites got as far as the Danube.
Though only a short distance separated them from Vienna, they
couldn't cross the great river. They shot a few cannons from the
left bank in a show of strength and then departed.

'And our Scharley was no doubt there, too,' Reynevan muttered to Samson. 'Up to no good.'

'No doubt.' The giant yawned, scratching the scar on his head
with his fingernails. 'I can't imagine he'd go to Constantinople
without us.'

The abbess summoned Reynevan again on the Eve of Saint
James' Day.

This time, she was reading a sumptuous and rich edition of
Meister Eckhart's *Book of Divine Consolation*.

'You haven't been to church in a long time,' she observed,
looking at him over her spectacles. 'You might stop by sometime,
kneel before the altar. Ponder over this and that. Give thought to
this and that . . . Oh, I forgot.' She lifted her head and continued
without waiting for an answer. 'You don't have time. You are occupied, you and Jutta, very occupied. Why, I understand you and
don't condemn you. I haven't always been a nun. In my youth,
I'm ashamed to admit, I also paid ardent homage to Priapus and
Astarte, and many times felt that I was closer to God in the arms
of a man than in a church. I was mistaken. But it doesn't prevent
me from understanding those who need time to understand that
error.'

A moment later, she continued, 'We have given you sanctuary
and care. You've no doubt realised that we weren't motivated
entirely by mercy. Nor was our sympathy entirely owing to the
affection and fondness our dear Jutta Apolda feels for you. There
were also other reasons, about which it is time to talk.

'Your sharp eyes have surely also discovered by now that this convent differs a little from other convents. But it is by no means – know you – the only convent of its kind. It's not just you Utraquists who discern the need to reform the Church, not just you strive for that. And though it sometimes appears to you that you are radical in your strivings, it is not the truth. There are those who desire further-reaching changes. Much further-reaching.

'You are familiar, I presume,' she continued, 'with the thesis of the brethren of the Franciscan Order, which drew from the wellspring of great and secret wisdom, the same one fathomed by Joachim of Fiore, under the influence of the sacred will and sacred thought? Let me remind you: our world is divided into three Ages and three Orders. The Age and Order of the Father, which lasted from Adam to Christ, was a rule of harsh justice and violence. The Second, the Age and Order of the Son, began with the Saviour and was a rule of wisdom and mercy. The Third Age dawned when the great Saint of Assisi took up his work and is the age of the Holy Spirit, a time infused by love and mercy. And the Holy Spirit will rule until the end of the world.

'The power of the Holy Spirit, says the inspired Meister Eckhart,' said the abbess, placing her hand on the open book, 'awakens that which is purest, most subtle, most noble, awakens the spark of the soul and raises it up to the very mountaintops in love and glory. It is as a tree: the power of the sun draws what is purest and most subtle in the tree's root and carries it up to the branches where the blossom burgeons forth. In the same way, the spark of the soul is carried out to the light, aroused to its first beginning, and achieves absolute unity with God.

'See wherefore, young man, that the coming of the Age of the Spirit makes the intercession of the Church and the clergy vain and unnecessary, for the entire community of the faithful is enveloped by the direct light of the Spirit. Through the Spirit,

573

it unites and is one with God. Without intermediaries. Intermediaries are unnecessary. Particularly sinful and false intermediaries.'

'Indeed.' Reynevan cleared his throat and gathered the courage to speak. 'We have, it seems to me, similar outlooks and designs. For Jan Huss and Hieronim said quite the same, and before them Wycliffe—'

'And Petr Chelčický said and says the same,' she interrupted. 'Why, then, don't you and yours listen to his words? When he teaches that violence cannot be answered by violence? That war never ends in victory, but spawns a new war, a war that can bring nothing but another war? Petr Chelčický knew and loved Huss but distanced himself from men of violence and murder. He distanced himself from men who turn their faces towards God as they kneel on battlefields among corpses. Men who make the sign of the cross with bloodied hands.

'You climbed the mountains at Easter in 1419,' she continued, before he could protest. 'On Tábor, Oreb, Baranek, Sion and the Mount of Olives, you created a fraternal community of Children of God, imbued with the Holy Spirit and the love of your neighbour. Then you were true Warriors of God, for you had pure souls and hearts, for you zealously carried the word of God and proclaimed Divine love. But it lasted a bare fifteen weeks, my boy, fifteen short weeks. Already by Saint Abdon's Day, on the thirtieth of July, you cast men from windows onto spears, murdered people in streets, churches and houses, and committed rape and slaughter. Instead of God's love, you began to preach the Apocalypse. And the name "Warriors of God" no longer befits you, for what you are doing more delights the Devil. You cannot enter the Kingdom of Heaven up a stairway of corpses. You pass down it to Hell.'

'But yet,' he interjected, reining in his annoyance, 'you said that

Utraquism is dear to you. That you see the need to reform the Church, that you are aware of the need for far-reaching change. When Chelčický called: "The Fifth Commandment: Thou shall not kill!", papal crusades were marching on Prague. Had we listened to Chelčický, who entreated us to defend ourselves with nothing but faith and prayer, had we faced the Roman hordes with only humility and love for our neighbour, they'd have slaughtered us. Bohemia would have run with blood, and our hopes and dreams vanished into thin air. There would have been no changes, no reform. In its triumph, Rome would have been even more haughty, cocksure and arrogant, even more mendacious, even more in opposition to Christ. We had something to fight for, so we fought . . .'

The abbess smiled and Reynevan blushed. He couldn't help but feel that her smile was tinged with mockery, and that the abbess knew what an ass he was making of himself by saying 'we' and 'us', when in actual fact he had watched the ascent of the mountains at Easter 1419 from a distance, in bewilderment and fear and without a trace of understanding. That, shocked by the Defenestration in July, he had fled before Prague in its frenzied revolt, that he had run from Bohemia, mortally horrified by the course of events. That even now, he was barely a neophyte and was behaving like one.

'Regarding changes and reforms,' continued the smiling Poor Clare, 'we actually agree, you and I. But what makes us different is not just the means but also the scope and scale of activity. You want changes to the liturgy and reforms to the clergy on the basis of the principle *sola Scriptura*. We – for I told you there are many of us – wish to change much, much more. Look.'

Directly opposite the abbess hung a painting – the only decoration in the room – a board with a depiction of a white dove, soaring up with outstretched wings into a ray of light falling from above. The Poor Clare raised a hand and said something in a barely audible whisper. The air was suddenly imbued with the scent of rue and verbena, typical for white, Aradic magic.

The ray of light in the painting grew brighter and the dove flapped its wings, flying up and vanishing into the light. A woman appeared in its place. Tall, black-haired, with eyes like stars, attired in a patterned gown shimmering with many hues, now white, now copper, now crimson . . .

'And there appeared a great wonder in Heaven.' The abbess began in a quiet voice to describe the details of the painting as they grew more distinct. 'A woman clothed with the sun, and the moon under her feet, and upon her head a crown of twelve stars.

'The prophet says as he speaks of the Spirit: As one whom his mother comforteth, so will I comfort you. Look. Behold the Mother. *Ecce femina! Ecce Columba qui tollit peccata mundi.* Behold the Third Church. The true Church and in its truth the last. The Church of the Holy Spirit, whose law is love. Which will endure until the end of the world.

'Behold: Magna Mater, Panthea–Triple Goddess. The Regina–Queen, the Genetrix–Parent, the Creatrix–Creatoress, the Victrix–Victoress, Felix–Fortunate One. Divine Maiden, Virgo Caelestis. Behold the mother of nature, the ruler of the elements, *astrorum Domina*, eternal beginning of all things. The greatest of the goddesses, queen of shadows, master of radiant heights, of the sky, of the life-giving breath of the seas, of the silence of the underground. She, whose one, many-shaped divinity is worshipped by the entire world under manifold names and in different rituals.

'*Descendet sicut pluvia in vellus.* She will come down like rain on the grass, like the torrential rain that waters the Earth. During her days, justice and great peace will flower while the

Moon shines. And she will reign from sea to sea, from the River to the very edges of the Earth. And thus shall it be unto the end of the world, for she is the Spirit.

'Bow down before her. Accept and know her power.'

Samson, scratching the scar on his shaved head, listened to the account, acquainted himself with Reynevan's anxieties – as usual without commenting, as usual unemotionally and without the slightest sign of impatience. Reynevan had the overwhelming impression, however, that the giant wasn't the slightest bit interested in the movement of the Builders of the Third Church, or in the cult of the Triple Goddess coming alive again. That he barely attached any importance to the division of history into three epochs. That, all in all, he was quite indifferent as to whether the abbess of the Poor Clares' convent in White Church believed in and put into practice the theses of the Waldensians and the chiliasts, or if she also leaned towards the doctrines of the Brethren and Sisterhood of the Free Spirit. Samson appeared quite unmoved by the Beghards, Beguines and Guglielmites. While as far as Joachim of Fiore and Meister Eckhart were concerned, Reynevan had the feeling that Samson didn't give a tinker's cuss about them.

'I'm going away,' the giant quite unexpectedly announced, having listened politely to Reynevan's reflections. 'You'll have to cope by yourself. I'm going to Bohemia. To Prague. You were present when I was wounded,' he continued, not waiting for Reynevan to recover from the shock or even utter a word. 'You saw what happened when that ball hit my skull. You were a witness; you had the opportunity to see it from close up. I was prepared for something like that. I was told about it and even ... Even advised to do it. Axleben in Prague, Rupilius at Trosky. They called it "returning through death". A means to return to my own universe and to my own ... bodily – so to speak – form is to get rid of my present material shell. In short: the simplest way would be to kill this huge body. To destroy it, to permanently interrupt the physiological processes occurring in it. To put an end to its material existence. The spiritual element – my own – would then be liberated and return to its rightful place. That's what Axleben and Rupilius claimed. What happened on the eighth of May appears to confirm that they were right.

'You can undoubtedly guess where the problem lies. You understand why the method they advise doesn't especially suit me and why I'd prefer something less drastic. Firstly, I don't want to have on my conscience the death of the monastery dullard, clothed in whose body I've been parading around the world for these three years. Secondly, neither Rupilius nor Axleben was willing to give me cast-iron guarantees that it would succeed. And thirdly and most importantly: I'm in no hurry to return. The main reason for that fact has copper hair and goes by the name of Marketa. And resides in Prague. Which is why I'm returning to Prague, my dear Reinmar.'

'Samson—'

'Not a word, please. I'm going back alone. You stay here. I'd be a poor friend if I tried to drag you away from here, separate you from what this place means to you. It's your Ogygia, Reinmar, your island of happiness. So stay here and enjoy it as much and for as long as you can. Stay and act wisely. Separate what is subtle from what is gross. Then you will possess the glory of this world and all darkness will flee from you. I tell you this as your friend, the being known to you as Samson Honeypot. You must believe me, since *vocatus sum Hermes Trismegistus, habens tres partes philosophiae totius mundi*. Listen carefully. The fire wasn't by any means smothered and extinguished, it only died down, the embers are smouldering. Any day now, the world will burst into flames again. And we will meet again. But until then ... Farewell, my friend.'

'Farewell, my friend. Have a safe journey. And give my regards to Prague.'

At the edge of the forest, Samson turned around in the saddle and waved at them. They waved back before he vanished into the trees.

'I'm afraid for him,' whispered Reynevan. 'It's a long way to Bohemia. The times are hard and perilous ...'

'He'll arrive safe and sound.' Jutta clung to his side. 'Don't be afraid. He'll get home safely without losing his way. Somebody is waiting for him. Somebody's lantern will shine for him in the gloom, lighting his way. Like Leander, he will safely cross the Hellespont, because Hero and her love wait for him.'

It was the first of August. The Day of Saint Peter in Chains. For the Elder Folk and witches, it was the holiday of Hlafmas. The Harvest Festival.

Reynevan spent a week thinking over the conversation he needed to have with Jutta. He feared such a conversation, feared the consequences. Jutta had often talked with him about the teachings of Huss and Hieronim, about the Four Articles of Prague, and generally about the principles of Hussite reform. And although she could be quite sceptical regarding certain doctrines of Utraquism, never did she – not with a single word, nor even with the slightest allusion or suggestion – manifest what he feared: a proselytiser's zeal. The monastery in White Church – the conversation with the abbess left him no doubt – was tainted with the errors of Joachim of Fiore, the Builders of the Third

Church and the Sisterhood of the Free Spirit. The abbess, the nuns – and probably the converses, too – venerated the Eternal and Triple Great Mother, which linked them with the movement of the followers of Guglielma the Czech as the female incarnation of the Holy Spirit. And of Maifreda of Pirovano, the first Guglielmite popess. On top of that, the nuns clearly practised white magic, thus linking themselves with the cult of Aradia, the Queen of the Witches, called in Italy *La Bella Pellegrina*. But although Reynevan hovered around Jutta as vigilantly as a crane, seeking a sign or a hint, he never caught anything. Either Jutta was skilfully disguising it, or simply was not a fervent and zealous neophyte of the Joachimite, Guglielmite or Aradic heresies. Reynevan couldn't rule out either the first or the second possibility. Jutta was both clever enough to be able to disguise it and sensible enough not to throw herself headlong into something. In spite of the feelings they appeared to share, in spite of their frequent, enthusiastic and inspired lovemaking, in spite of the fact that their bodies appeared not to have any secrets from each other, Reynevan understood he still didn't know everything about Jutta and was a long way from deciphering all her secrets. And if it were true that Jutta hadn't utterly thrown in her lot with heresy, that she was hesitating, doubting or simply that she had a critical attitude, he oughtn't to bring up the subject.

On the other hand, he oughtn't to delay or stand passively by, either. He still took the Green Lady's words to heart. In Silesia, he was an exile, a wanted outlaw, a Hussite, an enemy, a spy and a saboteur. What he was, what he believed in and how he lived his life exposed Jutta to danger and harm. The Green Lady, Agnes of Apolda, Jutta's mother, was right – if he had even a little decency, he wouldn't put the girl at risk, wouldn't allow her to suffer because of him.

The conversation with the abbess had changed everything, or

at least plenty. The monastery in White Church, the very fact of being there, was actually much more dangerous to Jutta than her relationship with Reynevan. The theses of Joachim and the Spiritualists, the heresy (somehow he still couldn't think about it otherwise, or find another word for it) – the Builders of the Third Church, the cult of Guglielma and Maifreda – all were considered by Rome and the Inquisition to be just as serious an apostasy as Hussitism. In any case, Rome made no distinctions between heresies and apostasies. Every heretic was the Devil's lackey. It also applied – which was downright ridiculous – to the cult of the Great Mother, which was after all older than humanity. And the Devil, which Rome had only just invented.

But the fact remained: the cult of the Triple Goddess, the worship of Guglielma, the errors of Joachim, the Sisterhood of the Free Spirit, the Third Church – each of those things was enough to send her to prison, to the stake or to penitential imprisonment for life in the Dominican dungeons. Jutta should not remain in the convent.

Something had to be done.

Reynevan knew what. Or at least felt it instinctively.

'You asked me in the wintertime.' He turned over on his side and looked her in the eyes. 'You asked if I was ready to abandon everything. If I was ready simply to flee, go with you to the end of the world. I answer "yes" to that. I love you, Jutta, and want to join with you until death do us part. The world, it appears, is doing what it can to thwart us in that. So let's drop everything and flee. If necessary, to Constantinople.'

She said nothing, stroking him pensively for a long time.

'And your mission?' she finally asked, weighing her words slowly. 'You have a mission, don't you? You have convictions. You have a genuinely urgent and sacred duty. You want to change the face of the world, improve it, make it better. What then? Will you abandon your mission? Give it up? Forget about the Grail?'

Danger, he thought. *Caution. Danger.*

'A mission,' she continued, speaking even slower. 'Convictions. A vocation. Sacrifice. Ideals. The Kingdom of God and the desire for it to come about. A dream for it to come about. A fight for it to come about. Are they things that can be given up, Reinmar?'

'Jutta.' He decided to speak, raising himself up on an elbow. 'I can't bear to see you putting yourself at risk. Rumours about what you believe here are circulating – many people know what happens in this convent. I found out about it myself last winter, at the end of last year, so it's no secret. Denunciations may already have reached the relevant people. You're living in great danger. Maifreda of Pirovano was burned at the stake in Milan. Fifteen years later, in 1315, two and a half score Beguines were burned to death in Świdnica . . .'

And the Adamites in Bohemia, he suddenly thought. *And the Picards, tortured and burned at the stake. The cause I've dedicated myself to persecutes dissidents no less cruelly than Rome . . .*

'Every day,' he said, driving away the thought, 'may be the day of your doom, Jutta. You could die—'

'You could, too,' she said, interrupting. 'You could have fallen in battle. You've also taken risks.'

'Yes, but not for—'

'Chimeras, yes? Go on, say it out loud. Chimeras. Women's fancies?'

'I didn't mean to—'

'Yes, you did.'

They fell silent. Outside was the August night. And crickets.

'Jutta.'

'Yes, Reinmar.'

'Let's go away. I love you. We love one another, and love . . . Let's find the Kingdom of God within us. Inside us.'

'Should I believe you? That you'll give up—'

'Believe me.'

'You are sacrificing much for me,' she said after a longer pause. 'I value that. And love you all the more for it. But if we abandon our ideals . . . If you give up yours, and I mine . . . I can't help thinking it would be like—'

'Like what?'

'Like *endura*. Without hope for *consolamentum*.'

'You sound like a Cathar.'

'Montségur lives on,' she whispered with her mouth right by his ear. 'The Holy Grail hasn't been found yet.'

She touched him, touched and stunned him with a gentle but thrilling caress. When she got up onto her knees, her eyes were burning in the darkness. When she leaned over him, she was slowly gentle, like a wave stroking the sand of a beach. Her breath was hot, hotter than her lips. *Samson was right*, came a thought, before the bliss snatched away his ability to think. *Samson was right. This place is my Ogygia. And she is my Calypso.*

'Montségur lives on.' A few moments passed before he heard her loud whisper. 'And will endure. It won't surrender and will never be taken.'

August 1428 was hot, a simply insufferable heatwave that lasted until the middle of the month, until the Assumption of Mary, called by the people the Feast of Our Lady of Herbs. September was also very warm. The weather only began to get slightly cooler after Saint Matthew's Day. Rains fell on the twenty-third of September.

And old friends returned on the twenty-fourth.

*

The first signal of the return of the old friends was supplied – with the mediation of the dependable convent gardener – by rumours, at first vague and not very precise, and gradually increasingly detailed. Somebody had been distributing pamphlets in the town square of Brzeg, portraying a goat-headed monster with a papal tiara on its horned head. A few days later, pictures of a similar kind appeared in Wiązów and Strzelin – on them was a pig dressed in a mitre, with wording that left no doubt: *Conradus episcopus sum.*

A few weeks later, things became a little more serious. Some unknown perpetrators – the rumour multiplied their number to twenty – had attacked and stabbed to death on the Wrocław road Sir Rypert of Seidlitz, the deputy chief of the Świdnica counter-intelligence service, known for his cruel persecution of people suspected of pro-Hussite sympathies. A Grodków town hall scribe who had bragged of denouncing more than a hundred people was stabbed to death. In Sobótka, a crossbow bolt hit the parish priest from Saint Anne's – who was particularly fierce towards his more free-thinking parishioners – as he was giving the sermon.

On the Friday after Saint Matthew's Day, the twenty-fourth of September – before even the rumour about the village headman being stabbed to death in nearby Przeworno had reached the convent – Bisclavret and Rzehors appeared in White Church. They weren't allowed through the gate, naturally, but had to wait for Reynevan in the grange outside the convent by the well. When he arrived, Rzehors was washing the blood off the sleeve of his jerkin in the trough and Bisclavret was perfunctorily cleaning his *navaja* which was sticky with blood.

'Enough lazing around, dear Brother Reinmar.' Rzehors wrung out the cleaned sleeve. 'There's work to be done.'

'Like that work?' Reynevan pointed to the bloody foam dribbling from the trough.

Bisclavret snorted. 'I love you, too,' he sneered. 'I missed you, too, and am glad to see you in rude health. Although a little gaunt, I'd say. Did you lose weight during Lent? Was it the convent vittles? Or the intensive lovemaking?'

'Put that damned knife away.'

'What? Don't like the look of it? Hurts your feelings? I see the convent has changed you. Six months ago, you beat a man to death with your bare hands before my very eyes in Żelazno, near Kłodzko. For personal vengeance. And you dare look down on us, we who are fighting for the cause? You disdainfully turn up your nose at us?'

'Put the knife away, I said. Why have you come?'

'Take a guess.' Rzehors crossed his arms over his chest. 'And when you hit upon it, move your arse. We told you: there's work to be done. The Vogelsang is counter-attacking, and you are still the Vogelsang; no one has removed you from the Vogelsang or freed you of your responsibilities. Prokop and Neplach have issued orders which also apply to you. Do you know the risk of failing to carry them out?'

'I love you, too.' Reynevan didn't bat an eyelid. 'And I'm fucking overjoyed to see you. But soften your tone a little, lads. As regards orders, you are envoys, nothing more. I give the orders. So, therefore, I order you: say your piece and make it short and snappy. That's an order. You know the penalty for insubordination.'

'Didn't I tell you?' said Bisclavret, laughing. 'Didn't I tell you not to talk to him like that?'

'He's grown up,' said Rzehors with a smile. 'The spit and image of his brother. Just like Peterlin. Or perhaps he's even surpassed Peterlin.'

'They know it.' Bisclavret, after finally putting away the

navaja, bowed dramatically. 'Brothers Prokop the Shaven and Bohuchval Neplach, called Flutek, know it. They know what a zealous Utraquist and ardent supporter of the cause of the Chalice Peterlin's brother is. Thus, the above-mentioned brothers – via our unworthy lips – request Reynevan to prove his loyalty to the Chalice once again. The brothers humbly request—'

'Shut up, Frenchman. You speak, Rzehors. Briefly and in plain language.'

Prokop's order for the Vogelsang was indeed brief and ran: reconstruct the spy ring. And do it quickly. Quickly enough for the network to be used during the next strike on Silesia. Prokop didn't specify when the strike would occur.

Reynevan had no idea how he was meant to personally reconstruct something about which he had only a general and rather vague idea – a ring about which he knew almost nothing apart from the fact that it reputedly existed. When taken to task, Rzehors and Bisclavret confessed that they mainly saw his help in the sense that – as they expressed it – three was safer than two.

In spite of the task's supposed great urgency, Reynevan didn't agree to set off immediately. He wanted to teach the Vogelsang some manners and respect for him. But, above all, he had to sort out the situation with Jutta. He thought the second matter much more difficult than the first. But actually things went better than he had expected.

'Oh well,' she said, when the hot wave of anger had passed. 'I might have expected it. Galahad loves, promises and vows for ever and ever. But in truth, only until news of the Grail arrives.'

'It's not like that, Jutta,' he protested. 'Nothing has changed. It's just a few days. Then I'll return . . . Nothing has changed.'

They spoke in church, in front of the altar and the painting portraying – what else? – a soaring dove. But Reynevan had before his eyes the unfortunate Maifreda of Pirovano burning at the stake in the Piazza del Duomo.

'When do you set off?' she asked, now calmer.

'The morning after *festum angelorum*.'

'So we still have a few days.'

'We do.'

'And nights.' She sighed. 'Good. Let's kneel and pray to the goddess.'

On the thirtieth of September, in the morning after Saints Michael, Gabriel and Raphael, Rzehors and Bisclavret returned. Prepared for the journey.

Reynevan was waiting for them. Also ready.

Chapter Twenty-Four

In which the spirit of destruction – simultaneously the spirit of creation – returns, as it were. And Reynevan faces a choice.

In the few years of its existence, the Vogelsang had managed to create in Silesia quite an extensive and many-branched network of sleeping agents, so in principle the basis for its reconstruction was in place. The problem was that the wave of oppression passing through Silesia must have left its mark on the agents. Some of them, one had to fear, had died martyrs' deaths and may not even have left any ashes. Some of those who survived – feeling the unrelenting presence of the Inquisition – might have fundamentally revised their views and come to the conclusion that they'd had enough of sympathising with Wycliffe and loved Huss much less than previously. Among the latter were also those who, of their own free will or under compulsion, had fundamentally modified their loyalties. Having switched their allegiance, they now waited for agents to report to them. And when they did, to inform on them at once to the relevant authorities.

Thus, contacting former agents always bore a considerable risk and could not be carried out without taking suitable precautions in advance. And there was no doubt it was a hundredfold easier for three to take precautions than two.

For over a month, Reynevan, Rzehors and Bisclavret roamed

through Silesia – sometimes in the cold, wet autumn weather, sometimes in bright sunlight and gossamer threads. They visited plenty of places – beginning with large towns and cities, such as Wrocław, Legnica and Świdnica, and ending with villages whose full names were quite forgettable. They visited various people and reminded those various people – using a variety of methods and with varying results – about the vows of loyalty they'd once taken for the cause.

Only four times did they have to make a rapid exit. First in Racibórz, when Rzehors escaped a trap set by the Inquisition by jumping from a first-floor window into the town square, followed by a dramatic chase down Long Street all the way to Saint Nicholas's Gate. Then the three of them fought their way out of a trap outside Ścinawa, when they were greatly helped by a fog that rose on cue from the marshes of the Odra. In Skorogoszcz, they had to gallop like hell to outrun a mounted squad that went after them when a mercenary unit guarding the customs post on the Nysa became suspicious of them. And outside Namysłów, a local cooper was listening to Rzehors and Reynevan when Bisclavret, who was covering them, caught the cooper's son, who had been sent in secret to alert the guard in the town, and hauled the twelve-year-old into the chamber. Before you could say 'Judas Iscariot' three times, the boy was writhing on the dirt floor, stabbed by the *navaja*, the cooper was wheezing with blood gushing from a severed throat, his wife and daughters were wailing at various pitches and the company were hurdling fences to reach their horses which had been left in the thicket.

'In the fight for a good cause there are no ethics.' Rzehors straightened up proudly when, a short time later, Reynevan reproached him, particularly for the boy. 'When the cause demands killing, one must kill. The spirit of destruction is at the same time the spirit of creation. An execution in a good cause isn't a crime, hence one may not shirk from it. Thus, with head held high and a sure step, we enter the stage of history. We are changing and shaping history, Reinmar. When the New Order comes, children will be taught about it in school and all the world will learn the name of what we are doing. The word "terrorism" will one day be on the lips of the whole world.'

'Amen,' Bisclavret added.

Rzehors and Bisclavret found out the name of the Namysłów agent who had turned the cooper and set out to kill him. They stabbed him to death as he returned from a tavern one night and were reunited with Reynevan in two days.

Day by day, it had to be admitted, the spirit of destruction was becoming more and more creative.

'Stop whingeing.' Bisclavret grimaced at the sight of Reynevan's expression. 'One day we'll get an order from Flutek and we'll head off together, the three of us, to stick a knife in the belly of that Grellenort who killed your brother. Or Duke Jan of Ziębice. Or the Bishop of Wrocław himself. Will you be whingeing then, talking nonsense about ethics and honour?'

Reynevan didn't answer.

On the night of the seventh of November, the required in-dividuals came to a meeting at an agreed place, which was a penitentiary cross at the edge of an oak wood in the Tąpadła Pass that separated the Ślęża massif from Radunia. They were the 'reactivated' agents that the Vogelsang considered the most reliable and were needed to accomplish a special assignment. Precautions were taken, naturally – the presence of a turncoat among the agents could still not be ruled out. Only one member of the Vogelsang was waiting for the agents at the Tąpadła Pass – Rzehors was selected by drawing lots. If it went off without any surprises, Rzehors was to lead the group eastwards, to some

shepherd huts where Reynevan would be waiting. If there wasn't
an ambush there, either, the group would continue to the village
of Będkowice, where Bisclavret would be waiting. He had drawn
the shortest straw.

But everything went smoothly and in the course of just a
single night the Vogelsang had increased to nine men. Nine very
different men. A bookkeeper from Wrocław; a stallholder from
Prochowice; a carpenter from Trzebnica; an apprentice mason
from Środa Śląska; a teacher from Kąty; the steward at the monastery grange in Lubiąż; an esquire once in the service of the
Bolz family from Zeiskenberg; a former monk from Jemielnica,
currently a seller of indulgences; and on top of that – in some
ways the crowning achievement – the priest of the Church of
the Heart of Jesus in Pogorzela.

Travelling by night – the unit was too large to be able to ride
by day without arousing suspicion – they reached Rychbach, and
from there headed to Lampersdorf and the Jugów Pass in the
Owl Mountains. There, in a forest clearing outside the village
of Jugów which gave its name to the pass, they met a squad that
had come from Bohemia. The squad consisted of fourteen professionals. It wasn't difficult to guess what profession they were
members of. Reynevan didn't actually have to guess. He knew
two of them by sight from White Mountain, where they were
being trained in the execution department.

The group leader was a friend of his.

'Urban Horn,' said Łukasz Bożyczko. 'The squad was led from
Bohemia by Urban Horn. In person.'

Gregorz Hejncze, *Inquisitor a Sede Apostolica specialiter deputatus* at the Wrocław Diocese, nodded to indicate he had guessed as
much and that it came as no surprise. Łukasz Bożyczko cleared
his throat, judging he could continue with his report.

'It concerned Kłodzko, naturally. Our man was a witness to a conversation between Horn and Reinmar of Bielawa and those other two Vogelsang agents, Rzehors and Bisclavret. Kłodzko, Horn told them, is the gateway and key to Silesia. And added that Sir Půta of Častolovice is becoming an inconvenient icon, a threat to us . . . I mean to them . . . I mean to the Hussites . . . And this time Kłodzko has to fall.'

'Were those our man's exact words?' The Inquisitor raised his head.

'His very words,' confirmed the deacon. 'Our man conveyed those words to our agent in Kłodzko. Who then told me.'

'Go on.'

'The Vogelsang agent Bisclavret said that their colleague Trutwein had survived the turmoil and was again active. Said that he was gathering *oleum*, resin and other ingredients, and this time they wouldn't be short of anything and would start such a blaze in Kłodzko that – these are his words – Sir Půta's whiskers would be singed. And this time, not them but Sir Půta would escape by diving into a shithole. That's what he said, those very words: by diving into a shithole—'

'So the group has been redeployed to Kłodzko,' Hejncze guessed. 'When did the redeployment begin?'

'On the Friday after Saint Martin's Day. They weren't all redeployed at once, but gradually, two or three at a time, in order not to arouse suspicion. Fortunately, our man was in one of the first groups to be deployed, which is why we know that it's true about Trutwein. This Trutwein – Johann Trutwein – is an altarist at the Church of the Blessed Virgin Mary and has been a Hussite spy for years. And it turns out that a fledgling espionage and sabotage cell has been operating around him in Kłodzko since the summer.'

The Inquisitor pushed away a seal he had been playing with.

'Am I to understand that, at this moment, the entire group is in Kłodzko? All of them?'

'All of them apart from Horn, Bielawa, Bisclavret and three more. That group left Jugów on Saint Martin's Day. Our man doesn't know where they went. What are my orders, Your Reverence? What are our next steps?'

The clamour of the town, stallholders quarrelling in the Poultry Market, could be heard through the window. The papal Inquisitor said nothing, rubbing his nose.

'That man of ours,' he finally asked. 'Who is it?'

'Kacper Dompnig. A bookkeeper. From here in Wrocław.'

'Dompnig ... He hasn't been blackmailed. I'd recall it if he had, I don't forget blackmail ... But I don't believe we've been paying him, either. Could he by chance be an idealist?'

'He may indeed.'

'Then keep an eye on him, Łukasz.'

'Amen, Your Reverence.'

'You asked what we're going to do.' Gregorz Hejncze stretched. 'Nothing, for the time being. But should a raid begin, should the Hussites come to Kłodzko, should the town be threatened, our man is to give the whole group away. He is to turn them all in at once to Sir Půta's counter-intelligence.'

'Wouldn't it be better for us to take the credit?' asked Łukasz Bożyczko, smiling. 'Bishop Konrad—'

'Bishop Konrad holds no interest for me. And it isn't the Holy Office's job to take credit. I repeat: our man is to turn the group over to Kłodzko counter-intelligence. It will be Sir Půta of Častolovice who eliminates the saboteurs, and he will thereby grow into an even more terrifying symbol among the Hussites. Clear?'

'Amen, Your Reverence.'

'Reynevan ... Reinmar of Bielawa is not, you say, in the Kłodzko group. He's gone off somewhere, you say. With Horn.

Perhaps to the convent in White Church? For I understand the information about the convent is certain?'

'It is, Your Reverence, I can affirm that. Will we take any ... action ... there?'

'Not for the time being. Listen, Łukasz. Were that Reynevan to return to Kłodzko ... Should he join the saboteurs ... In brief: were he to fall into Sir Pŭta's hands, you're to get him out. Alive and unharmed. Understand?'

'Yes, Your Reverence.'

'Now leave me. I wish to pray.'

The six of them set off to Świdnica – Horn, Reynevan, Bisclavret and the three assassins that had come with Horn. The assassins only accompanied them to Frankenstein. They didn't enter the town but split off and went on their way without wasting any words of farewell. They no doubt had their own goals and tasks in Silesia. Horn may have known what they were, may have known who they were planning to kill. But could equally well have not. Reynevan didn't ask anything. But he wouldn't have been himself had he not made a speech about ethics and morality.

Horn listened patiently. He was his old self again, the one Reynevan had first met, knew and remembered. The Horn in an elegant, short grey cloak fastened with a silver clasp and a doublet braided with silver thread, topped off by a satin chaperon with a long liripipe curling fancifully around his neck. Horn sporting a dagger with a ruby in the hilt and cordovan riding boots with brass-edged spurs. Horn, with his piercing eyes and mouth twisted into a slightly arrogant grimace. A grimace that became more pronounced the more Reynevan expounded on matters concerning morality, ethnic norms and the rules and principles of war, including in particular the use of terror as a weapon of war.

'Terror is immanent in war,' Horn began when Reynevan had finished, 'and war relies upon terror. The very nature of war is terror. *Ipso facto.*'

'Zawisza the Black of Garbów wouldn't agree with you. He conceived of war and *jus militare* differently.'

'Zawisza the Black is dead.'

'What?'

'Weren't you told?' He turned around in the saddle. 'Hasn't word of the death of one of the most celebrated knights of modern Europe reached you? Zawisza the Black has fallen. A loyal vassal, he marched with Emperor Sigismund on an expedition against the Turks, to besiege the fortress of Golubac on the Danube. The Turks defeated them there, Sigismund bolted in customary fashion and Zawisza – also in customary fashion – covered the withdrawal. And perished. It's said that the Turks decapitated him. It happened on the twenty-eighth of May, on the Friday after the holiday of Saint Urban, my patron, which is why I remember the date so well. And thus, Zawisza the Black of Garbów, the good knight, is no longer in this world. *Sic transit gloria mundi.*'

'Much more, I'd say,' said Reynevan. 'Much more than *gloria.*'

As soon as they arrived in Świdnica, they came across a commotion. When they entered the town square after passing through the Lower Gate and along the mud-filled Long Street, they thought they had happened upon a festivity – the cause of the commotion was clearly a source of merriment. Bisclavret moved through the crowd to find out what was happening, while Reynevan was at once reminded of Prague in the summer of 1427, fomented and overjoyed by the news of the victory at Tachov. The associations turned out to be extremely apt, and Bisclavret's face when he returned was extremely sour. The longer Bisclavret's whispered account went on, the darker and gloomier Horn's expression became.

'What happened?' Reynevan couldn't restrain himself. 'What's going on?'

'Later.' Horn cut him off. 'Later, Reynevan. We need to have a meeting now, and some important conversations. Let's go. Bisclavret, find somebody trustworthy and well informed here. I want to know more.'

The meeting took place in a beer cellar in Bowyers Street, near the gate of the same name, and the important conversation concerned the supply of weapons and horses from Poland. And the interlocutor was a Raubritter known to Reynevan, the Pole, Błażej Jakubowski, of the Poraj coat of arms. Jakubowski didn't recognise Reynevan. And no wonder. Some time had passed. And quite a lot had happened.

The conversation was somewhat disrupted by the commotion and the extremely cheerful mood of the guests filling the tavern. The people of Świdnica clearly had a reason to be celebrating. Reynevan wasn't the one to wonder what it was.

'I hear you were defeated?' Jakubowski suddenly interrupted the negotiations, gesturing with his head towards the rejoicing townspeople. 'In Lusatia? At some Kratzau or other? They say Lords Polenz and Kolditz gave you a licking, a sound hiding. Eh? Tell me, Horn, I'd like to hear the details.'

'Now isn't the time to discuss it.'

Just then, Bisclavret returned and the Poraj guessed right away what was happening. And insisted that it *was* the right time. There was no choice.

'Jan Královec's Orphans,' Bisclavret began reluctantly, 'besieged some stronghold or other in Bohemia, my informer couldn't recall which one. Their provisions were running out, the siege didn't look like ending, so they decided to send a few regiments to Lusatia on the pillage. They set fire to Frydland on the sixth of November and on the following days ravaged the land around Zgorzelec, Löbau and Žitava. They loaded their wagons with spoils, rounded up the cattle and set off on the return trip along the road via Hradek and Nysa. And were—'

'—were attacked here, right?'

'Indeed,' Bisclavret reluctantly admitted. 'Královec was too cocksure . . . He disregarded the Germans, underestimated them. And in the meanwhile, the Six Cities mobilised a powerful contingent under the command of Lothar Gersdorf and Ulrik Biberstein. Landvogt Hans of Polenz marched quickly from Lower Lusatia to help and Albrecht of Kolditz approached from Świdnica. They were soon joined by Duke Jan of Żagań and his brother Duke Henryk the Elder of Głogów. Gocze Schaff added his men from Gryf Castle. They set off in pursuit of Královec and at dawn of Saint Martin's Day suddenly attacked the Orphans' marching column. A mile outside Hradek. At Kratzau.'

'And defeated them.'

'Depends what you mean.' Bisclavret wore the expression of a man who had to swallow something foul. 'Královec fled . . . Losing . . . Losing several—'

'Several hundred men,' finished the Pole. 'The wagons. And all the spoils.'

'But plenty of German corpses were left on the battlefield,' snapped Bisclavret. 'Including Lothar Gersdorf.'

'Nonetheless,' muttered Jakubowski, 'Kratzau has shown that you aren't invincible.'

'Only God is invincible.'

'And they who are in God's grace and favour.' The Pole smiled wryly. 'Have you Hussites perhaps fallen from grace?'

'God works in mysterious ways.' Horn looked him straight in the eyes. 'His wonders to perform, m'Lord Jakubowski. His works are not to be predicted. Men are different, their works can. But there's no sense in wasting time on deliberations. Let's get back to our business. It's become important.'

Urban Horn had plenty of other important matters. And the chances for Reynevan – now promoted to the rank of assistant – of a rapid return to Jutta were diminishing.

They didn't stay in Świdnica long but travelled to Nysa, after saying farewell to Bisclavret.

'We'll meet again.' Bisclavret looked Reynevan deep in the eyes as they said goodbye. 'We'll meet again when the time comes. Lest you forget, I shall reappear in your snug little convent and remind you of your duties.'

It sounded a little like a threat, but Reynevan wasn't concerned. He didn't have time. Horn was hurrying him.

They rode towards Opole, a region Horn considered reasonably safe. The heir of the land, the young Duke Bolko Wołoszek, was being taken more and more seriously in matters concerning the Opole and Niemodlin regions. Bolko's antipathy to the bishop and his dislike of the clergy and the Inquisition were widely known. He would not permit any brutality in the Opole region. The bishop and the Inquisitor had threatened the young duke with excommunication, but Wołoszek made light of it.

Horn and Reynevan didn't have a permanent base but were constantly on the move, operating between Kluczbork, Opole, Strzelce and Gliwice, contacting people coming from Poland: from Olkusz, Chęciny, Trzebinia, Wieluń, Pabianice and even Krakow. There were plenty of issues to deal with and pacts to negotiate. Reynevan, who mainly sat in on the transactions in silence, was amazed by Urban Horn's commercial ability. He was also amazed by the degree of complication of issues he had previously thought childishly simple.

No two balls, it turned out, were entirely the same. The handgonnes used by the Hussites mainly shot balls with a calibre of one finger. A finger and a grain of barley was the typical calibre of harquebuses, while the barrels of heavier harquebuses had a calibre of two fingers. The barrels of trestle guns were unified to a calibre of two fingers and one grain. Urban Horn had to negotiate the supply of all the kinds of balls in suitable quantities with the owners of Polish forges.

Nor was all gunpowder alike, it became clear, and it was much changed since the times of Berthold Schwarz. The proportions of saltpetre, sulphur and charcoal had to be weighed out scrupulously, depending on what weapon they were intended for – hand weapons needed powder with a higher concentration of saltpetre, and gunpowder containing more sulphur was needed for trestle guns, cannons and bombards. If the mixture was wrong, the powder was unsuitable and only fit for fireworks – poor ones at that. The gunpowder also had to be precisely granulated. If it wasn't, it separated out during transport: the heavier saltpetre sank downwards to the bottom of the container and the lighter charcoal remained on the surface. Stable and inflammable pellets were created by spraying the ground powder with human urine, and the best results came by using the urine of people who drank much and often. Thus, it was no surprise that powder manufactured in Poland enjoyed a deservedly good reputation on the market and Polish powder mills well-deserved fame.

'I almost forgot,' said Horn as he was returning after completing another transaction. 'Scharley sends his regards. He asked me to tell you that he's well. He's still in the Tábor, in the field army. Jakub Kroměšín of Březovice is now hejtman of the field army, since Jaroslav of Bukovina fell in October during the siege of Bechyně. Scharley was at the siege, he also took part in the plundering raids to Austria and in the attack on the Upper Palatinate. He is, as I've probably said, well. Healthy and cheerful. Sometimes excessively so.'

'What about Samson Honeypot?'

'Samson's in Bohemia? I didn't know.'

They set off for Toszek the following day, to talk to Poles about balls, calibres, sulphur and saltpetre. The matter had begun to bore Reynevan somewhat. He was dreaming about returning to the convent and Jutta. He hoped for something to happen that would take him back there.

And something did.

'We'll have to part,' announced a frowning Horn after returning from the collegiate church in Opole, where he often went, but always alone, without Reynevan.

'I have to go. I hadn't expected . . . I admit I hadn't expected it to happen so fast. Reinmar, war has broken out again. Královec's Orphans have crossed the Silesian border through the Lewin Pass. They're flying along, straight for Kłodzko. You may not manage to reach the town before Královec begins the siege. But you have to go there. Right away. To horse, friend.'

'Farewell, Horn.'

It was the fifth of December 1428. The second Sunday of Advent.

He rode to Brzeg along the Krakow road, and on the way, news caught up with him. Královec's Orphans had wreaked havoc on the Kłodzko valley. Bystřice had gone up in smoke and the townspeople had been massacred. Královec had not yet attacked Kłodzko itself, was not even close, but panic had begun to sweep through Silesia, as it had in March. The roads had become crammed with refugees.

Reynevan hurried. But not to Kłodzko. He rode to White Church. To Jutta.

He wasn't far away now. He passed Przeworno, he could see Rummelsberg. And then – on a forest track – he felt magic.

Beside the road lay a horse's skeleton. It was faded, quite over-grown by grass, undoubtedly a memento of the plundering raid in spring. Reynevan's steed was frightened and started, snorted and danced on the spot. It wasn't the skeleton that had frightened the horse, however, not a wolf or any other animal. Reynevan felt magic. He was able to sense it. Now he could feel it, smell it, hear it and see it in the intense odour of damp and mould, in the cawing of crows, in the browned and frozen stalks of wild celery. He felt magic. And when he looked around, he saw the source.

A thicket of leafless trees concealed a small wooden building. A church, probably made of larch wood, with a pointed, slender bell tower.

He dismounted.

An attempt had been made to burn down the church, which lay right on the route of the Warriors of God. Looking at the charred front wall and very blackened columns flanking the en-trance, Reynevan saw that fire had not completely consumed the building; it had probably been put out by rain. Or something else.

The interior was quite empty, the church having been stripped of everything it contained, which couldn't have been much. The rest had been vandalised. The three-sided chancel at the end of the nave was full of planks and rags, probably the remains of the altar. The marks of fire were also visible there in the form of black patches of charred wood. Had it been a fire of wrath, a fire of destruction and hatred, a fire of blind vengeance for the pyre in Constance? Or just an ordinary campfire, started to heat up a pot of yesterday's lumpy kasha, in a place offering shelter from the rain and cold? One couldn't be certain. Reynevan had seen both kinds of fire in captured churches.

The magic he had felt was emanating from the church. For there was a *hex* on the ground where the altar had once stood. A hexagon plaited from sticks, bast, strips of birch bark and colourful wool and thread, with the addition of yellowed fern, woodruff, oak leaves and a herb called *erysimon*, which considerably increased the *Dwimmerkraft* or magic power. That type of hex was typical for peasant witches or members of the Elder Race. Somebody – either the witch or the Elder One – had brought it and placed it there. As an act of reverence. To show respect. And sympathy.

Something had been painted on the smooth planks covering the walls of the chancel. There were no marks of axe blades on the crude paintings, nor had they been defiled with soot or excrement; the Warriors of God who had camped there evidently didn't have the time. Or the inclination.

Reynevan moved closer.

The picture covered the entire chancel. It was actually a cycle of pictures, a sequence of scenes presented in order.

The *Totentanz*.

The painter hadn't been a great artist. He was actually rather mediocre – and most probably self-taught. Who knew, perhaps for reasons of frugality the parish priest or curate had taken up brush and paint? The figures had been painted primitively, with amusingly distorted proportions. The spindly skeletons – so comical they were terrifying – were cavorting and leading the painting's various *dramatis personae* in a dance of death. A pope, an emperor in a crown, a knight in armour holding a spear, a merchant with a sack of gold and an astrologer with exaggeratedly Semitic features. All of the figures were comical, woefully pathetic and aroused, if not laughter, then smiles of pity. Death itself was pitiful and grotesquely ridiculous in its pose and shroud, delivering its eschatological *memento mori*, written above its skull in angular black letters. The letters were painted neatly and the words were legible – the artist was a decidedly better calligrapher than a painter.

> *Come forth, you mortals*
> *All lament is in vain*
> *You shall have to dance*
> *To my tune!*

The hex unexpectedly pulsated with magical power. And Death suddenly turned its grotesque skull. And stopped being grotesque. It became ghastly. As the church's shadowy interior became even gloomier, the painting on the planks became brighter. Death's shroud shone white, its deathly eyes blazed, the blade of the scythe gripped in its bony hands flashed horribly.

In front of Death stood the Maiden, one of the allegorical players in the deathly procession, stooping modestly. She had Jutta's features. And her voice. It begged Death for mercy in Jutta's voice. Her pleading voice resounded in Reynevan's skull like a flute, like a little bell.

> *I am a beautiful bride*
> *Fair before the world . . .*

When it responded to Jutta's pleas, Death's voice sounded like bones being crushed, like iron scraping on glass, like rusty cemetery gates creaking.

> *Already you are changed,*
> *Now bereft of colour!*

Reynevan understood. He tumbled out of the church, leaped

onto his horse and urged it into a gallop with cries and jabs of his spurs. The cruel voice still croaked in his ears.

Already you are changed,
Now bereft of colour!

He could see from a distance that something wasn't right in the convent. The gate – which was usually securely locked – had been flung open and the shapes of people and horses were visible in the courtyard. Reynevan hunched over in the saddle and forced his mount into an even more desperate gallop.

And that's when they caught up with him.

First a spell was cast, a thunderous jolt of power that panicked the horse and flung Reynevan from the saddle. Before he managed to get up, a dozen men rushed out from ditches and behind trees and fell on him. He drew his knife from his bootleg and with two sweeping cuts managed to slash two of them, stopping a third with a short stab to the face. But the others fell on him. They stunned him with heavy blows and knocked him to the ground. Kicked him. Pinned him down. Overpowered him. And bound his wrists behind his back.

'Tighter.' He heard a familiar voice. 'Pull the ropes tighter, don't spare him! If you break anything, it matters little. Let him have a taste of what awaits him.'

They jerked him upright. He opened his eyes. And trembled.

Before him stood the Wallcreeper. Birkart Grellenort.

Reynevan's head was spinning from a punch in the face and his cheek and eye were stinging as though scorched by red-hot iron. The Wallcreeper swung, hit him again with a reverse blow, with the back of his gauntleted hand. Reynevan tasted blood in his mouth.

'That was just to attract your attention,' the Wallcreeper explained softly. 'To make you concentrate. Are you concentrating?'

Reynevan didn't reply. Twisting his head, he tried to see what was happening beyond the convent gate and identify the riders and pikemen moving around in the courtyard. One thing was certain – they weren't Black Riders from the Company. The men holding him looked like ordinary hired thugs. Beside the thugs stood a small fellow with a round face and clothing identifying him as a Walloon. And eyes revealing him as a wizard. It was that Walloon, Reynevan guessed, whose spell had flung him from the saddle.

'Did you delude yourself that I would forget about you?' drawled the Wallcreeper. 'Or that I wouldn't find you? I warned you I have eyes and ears everywhere.'

He swung and struck Reynevan's already swelling cheek again. His eye, tender from the previous blow, began to water. As did his other. And his nose began to run. The Wallcreeper leaned over towards him. Very close.

'I had the impression you were still not giving me all of your attention,' he hissed, 'and I demand it all. Think hard. And listen carefully. You are caught. You will not escape with your life. But I can get you out of it. I can save your skin. If you promise me you'll take me to . . . You know who. To that astral being who disguises himself as a huge halfwit. You'll save your life if you take me to—'

'I say! M'Lord Grellenort!'

A knight in full plate armour looked down on them from the height of the saddle. He was on a horse in a caparison with a blue and silver chequerboard pattern. Reynevan recognised him. And remembered him.

'The duke demands he be brought before him. At once.'

'Have you decided?' the Wallcreeper hissed. 'Will you take me to him?'

'No.'

'You will regret it.'

The convent courtyard was teeming with horsemen and foot soldiers. Unlike the Wallcreeper's motley and rather ragged thugs, the bowmen and foot soldiers in the courtyard were attired decently and uniformly in black and red livery. Armoured men, both esquires and knights, predominated among the horsemen.

'Bring him here! Bring the Hussite!'

Reynevan knew that voice. He knew the physique, the handsome, manly face, the nape fashionably shaved in the knightly mode. He knew the black and red eagle.

The armoured men in the convent courtyard were commanded by Jan, Duke of Ziębice. In his ducal person, in an ermine-trimmed cloak over Milanese armour.

'Bring him closer.' He beckoned imperiously with a jerk of his head. 'M'Lord Marshal of the Court Borschnitz! M'Lord Grellenort! Bring him here! And get that Walloon out of my sight! I can't bear magicians!'

Reynevan was brought closer. The duke looked down at him from the height of his knightly saddle. His eyes were bright, blue-grey. Reynevan now realised whom the eyes and features of the abbess's face reminded him of.

'The mills of God grind slowly, yet exceedingly fine,' declared Jan of Ziębice nasally and loftily. 'Slowly, but exceedingly fine, yes, yes. You've renounced your religion and the cross, Bielawa, you Judas. You have engaged in witchcraft. You planned to murder me. You will be punished, Bielawa. Punished for your crimes.'

He was already looking elsewhere. Towards the garth. Four nuns were standing there. Including the abbess.

'You have hidden Hussites in this convent!' Jan announced thunderously, standing up in the stirrups. 'You've given refuge to spies and traitors! This shall not go unpunished! Do you hear, woman?'

'You shall not punish me,' replied the abbess in a resonant and fearless voice. 'Not you! You are breaking the law, Duke Jan! Breaking the law! You may not enter the convent!'

'These are my lands and I have power here. And this convent stands here by the grace of my forefathers!'

'The convent stands here by the grace of God and is not subject to either your power or your jurisdiction! You have no right either to enter or to reside here. Neither you, nor your soldiers! Not that scoundrel, nor his thugs!'

'And did he have the right to reside here?' Jan of Ziębice pointed at Reynevan. 'The entire summer? Is it permitted, dear Sister, to conceal heretics here? Heretics like the one lying there?'

Reynevan looked in the direction the duke was pointing. At the point where the wall surrounding the garth met the dry, ivy-covered wall of the infirmary lay Bisclavret. Reynevan recognised him by the tailored calfskin suit of clothes that the Frenchman recently had made and which everyone was meant to admire. Reynevan only recognised him by his jacket, his corpse was so dreadfully mutilated. The fair-haired *miles gallicus*, the erstwhile *Écorcheur*, Bisclavret, must have fought fiercely when caught. And did not let himself be taken alive.

'It is thus, then?' asked the duke with a sneer. 'Did the convent have a dispensation for taking in heretics and criminals? Indeed, it did not! Then be silent, woman, be silent. Display some humility. Lord Borschnitz! Have your men search those sheds! More may be hiding there!'

The Wallcreeper seized Reynevan, arms still bound behind him, by the collar, dragged him in front of the abbess and stood very close to her, face to face.

'Where is his comrade?' he grated. 'The giant with the visage of a simpleton? Speak, Nun.'

'I don't know of what you speak,' the abbess replied fearlessly. 'Or of whom.'

'Oh, but you do. And you'll tell me what you know.'

'*Apage*, O Devil's spawn.'

A hellish fire flashed in the Wallcreeper's eyes, but the abbess's gaze was steady. The Wallcreeper moved in even closer to her.

'Speak, woman. Or I'll make sure you bitterly regret it. You and your little nuns.'

'I say, Grellenort!' The duke didn't move his horse, just straightened up proudly in the saddle. 'What, do you act on your own initiative? I give the orders here! *I* judge and *I* mete out punishments, not you!'

'The nuns are concealing more heretics, Your Grace. I am certain of it. They are hiding them in the clausula. They think we won't enter there and are mocking us.'

Jan of Ziębice stayed silent for a moment, biting his lip.

'Then we shall search the clausula, too,' he finally decided coldly. 'Lord Borschnitz!'

'You wouldn't dare!' screamed the abbess. 'That is sacrilege, Jan! You will be excommunicated for this!'

'Stand aside, Sister. Lord Borschnitz, to work.'

'O knights!' screamed the abbess, raising her arms and barring the way before the men. 'O soldiers! Do not listen to godless orders, do not carry out the will of an apostate and an iconoclast! If you obey him, the curse will fall on you, too! And there will be no place for you among Christians! No one will give you vittles or water! Soldiers, I—'

At a sign from the Wallcreeper, his mercenaries seized the abbess and one of them closed a studded gauntlet over her face. Blood trickled from under the gauntlet. Reynevan struggled and tore himself free from the hands of the astonished servants. He lunged forward and in spite of his bound hands kicked over one of the thugs and shoulder-barged the other aside. But the Ziębice foot soldiers were already on him and knocked him to the ground, where they punched him.

'Search the buildings,' Duke Jan ordered. 'The clausula, too. And if we find any men there . . . If we find even a single Hussite concealed there, I swear to God the convent will pay dearly. As will you, dear Sister.'

'Don't call me "sister"!' screamed the abbess, spitting blood and struggling in the arms of the thugs. 'You are no brother to me! I disown you!'

'Search the convent! Forward, at the double! Lord Borschnitz! Lord Risin! What are you waiting for? I have issued an order!'

Borschnitz scowled and ground out a curse. Many among the Ziębice esquires and foot soldiers looked uneasy. Many were muttering angrily under their breath. The housekeeper began to weep. And the sky suddenly darkened. Duke Jan glanced upwards, as though a little anxious.

'You, Pater,' he said, clearing his throat and nodding at the chaplain accompanying them. 'Go with them, so that the search occurs in the presence of a priest and is suitably religious. So that people don't talk afterwards.'

Soon, the sound of furniture being smashed and shattered could be heard from inside the convent. Screaming, squealing and wailing came from the clausula. And parchment and books began to fall from the windows of the *scriptorium* and the abbess's private chambers. The Wallcreeper picked up a few.

'Wycliffe?' He laughed, turning towards the abbess. 'Joachim of Fiore? Waldhauser? They are read here? And you, Witch, dare to threaten us? You will rot away in the bishop's dungeon for these books. And the excommunication you threatened us with will embrace your entire heretical monastery.'

'Enough, enough, Grellenort.' Jan of Ziębice cut him off

gratingly. 'Soften your tone and leave her be! You assume too much authority here. Master Seiffersdorf, hurry the search along, it drags on somewhat. And gather up those books and scribblings! And burn them!'

'The evidence of heresy?'

'Grellenort. Don't make me bring you to task.'

The books blackened and curled up in the flames. The search was completed. No men or Hussites were found in the clausula. The Wallcreeper's furious expression spoke for itself. Duke Jan's sour grimace suddenly softened into a smile, however, and his handsome face brightened up. Reynevan twisted around in the servants' grip to see what had so delighted the duke. And his heart dropped like a stone.

Borschnitz and Risin were leading Jutta out of the clausula.

'Yes, yes, Bielawa.' The duke's voice seemed to be coming to him from far away. 'I know plenty about you. How do you think I knew I'd find you here? Some Hussite spies were caught in Kłodzko; all were taken alive. One of them – your comrade – knew much. He refrained from talking for a long time, but finally did. And revealed everything. About this convent. About you. And your romances, too.'

As Reynevan had expected, Duke Jan's entourage set off straight along the Ziębice road. Contrary to his expectations, the duke didn't go to Ziębice, but ordered a halt in Henryków. Right beside the monastery. The duke declined the offer of accommodation from the Cistercians who ran out to welcome him, setting up camp instead at the edge of the forest, under a huge oak tree. An enormous campfire of logs was lit, food brought by the monks was prepared and kegs were uncorked. Reynevan watched from his horse, from which he was not allowed to dismount. Three soldiers kept him under constant guard. The ropes cutting into his flesh numbed his body and he began to freeze.

He couldn't see Jutta. She was being kept on one of the covered wagons and not permitted to leave it. During the journey, the duke himself kept riding over and glancing under the tarpaulin. The Wallcreeper also looked into the wagon several times. Reynevan trembled with grim forebodings.

It was soon clear why they had stopped and more precisely why under the oak tree. Horsemen began to ride up and gather at the edge of the village. Knights in full armour with larger or smaller entourages of esquires, bowmen and servants. Hyncze of Borschnitz, the duke's marshal, greeted the newcomers. Jan of Ziębice himself just pouted, tilting his head slightly to acknowledge the greatly respectful bows. Jan only awarded one of the knights with a little more attention. There was a green apple pierced by three swords on his shield, the coat of arms of the Füllstein family.

'Welcome, gentlemen.' Duke Jan finally deigned to speak. 'I owe gratitude to the men you serve for sending you as envoys at my request. I also thank you for your trouble. Welcome to my lands. I welcome Opava and the Duchy of Głubczyce represented by Lord Füllstein. I welcome the Wrocław Bishopric and the town of Grodków in the person of Lord Starosta Tannenfeld. I welcome Wrocław, I welcome Świdnica.'

All those mentioned responded with bows. The envoys from Wrocław bore no devices, but Reynevan recognised in amazement one of them as the Raubritter Hayn of Czirne. Świdnica was represented by a knight bearing the coat of arms with the silver pike pole of the Oppeln family. The bishop's envoy, Tannenfeld, Starosta of Grodków, had fastened to his saddle a shield with a green garland of rue on black and gold bars, an emblem resembling the coat of arms of the Ascanian dynasty.

Hyncze Borschnitz addressed the gathering. 'My lords, you

have no doubt guessed the reason His Lordship the Duke has summoned you. Czech heretics have invaded our lands once again. The town of Kłodzko is once again in danger. And once again, after taking Kłodzko, they will march on us. Thus, it is time to gather our forces. Make a stand!'

'The Hussites will not take Kłodzko,' said the envoy of Świdnica, Oppeln with the pike pole on his shield. 'Sir Půta of Častolovice has reinforced the town and has a strong and valiant garrison. They shall not take it by treachery, either, for he has plucked out the Hussite spies like crayfish from a barrel. Now he has taken them for torture and is interrogating them one by one, having employed our Świdnica executioner. They say, ho, ho, that he has his hands full with the Hussites.'

'And owing to that we have good intelligence,' said Borschnitz, twirling his moustache. 'We know much about our foe! Would you like to say anything on the subject, noble Lord Reibnitz?'

'Only that knowledge about the Hussites is neither secret nor only in your possession,' said the Wrocław envoy, Hayn of Czirne's companion. 'Everyone knows everything there is to know. They're being led by Jan Královec of Hrádek, whom we've already met. He has under him two hundred horse, some three and a half thousand foot and two hundred wagons with firearms. I can guess what we'll be deliberating over here. And I ask: are we able to muster a force capable of challenging him?'

'We shall soon find that out,' said Jan of Ziębice, 'from you, noble gentlemen, since I presume you are sent here with good tidings. Thus, give me those tidings. In turn. You first, Reibnitz, since you've already begun.'

'Your Grace,' began Reibnitz, straightening up. 'Please forgive me, but I ask, I do not talk. I, Jorg Reibnitz of Falkenberg, am a simple hired sword. I do what I'm ordered. And the gentlemen of the Wrocław Town Council ordered me to listen, not speak.

So, I shall first listen to what the others say. For on the orders of the gentlemen of the Council, I must find out who among those gathered here means to battle the Hussites, and who prefers to parley and make truces with them as is customary.'

Füllstein of Opava flushed slightly but said nothing and raised his head haughtily. Jan of Ziębice pouted. Oppeln couldn't restrain himself.

'What's past is past!' he exploded. 'And isn't now! Świdnica proved it could fight the heretics, proved it more decisively than anyone standing here. Who routed the Hussites at Kratzau, gave that same Královec who today stands outside Kłodzko a hiding? We did! Lord Starosta Albrecht of Kolditz and Lord Deputy Starosta Stosz! The Świdnica knighthood fought at the Battle of Kratzau and slaughtered the heretical scum. Don't tar Świdnica with the same brush as those who only fled from the Hussites!'

'Well said.' Duke Jan's resonant voice rose above the hubbub. 'Lord Oppeln has uttered good and weighty words and a weighty name. Kratzau, m'lords. Remember: Kratzau!'

'One Kratzau doesn't make a summer,' observed Tamsz of Tannenfeld, Starosta of Grodków, who had been silent until then. 'A month has passed since the battle, and Královec – though defeated – is again causing us problems at Kłodzko. Kratzau, I don't deny, was a weighty battle, but we should see it rather as a stroke of luck.'

'Or,' said Reibnitz, 'as a godsend.'

The knights guffawed. Oppeln blushed.

'I hear bitter envy!' he shouted. 'You envy Świdnica and Lusatia their fame and glory. Lords Kolditz and Polenz went boldly into battle, heads and standards held high, in a mounted charge, like Richard Coeur de Lion at Ascalon, and since *audaces fortuna iuvat*, defeated the heretics in battle, cut them down, seized spoils and wagons and drove them out of Lusatia. And you envy us that! For your hide was tanned in the spring, when you fled from the Hussites like hares—'

'Heed your words,' hissed Hayn of Czirne.

'What, is it not true?' Oppeln stood with arms akimbo, not in the least disconcerted by Czirne's furious expression. 'Prokop burned down half of Silesia while you in Wrocław trembled in your shitty britches!'

Hayn's cheeks flushed deep carmine and Jorg Reibnitz quickly restrained him, putting a hand on his spaulder.

'At Kratzau, Kolditz and Polenz fell on an overextended marching column made up in part of wagons so groaning with spoils they were barely moving. The sudden charge rent apart the Hussite array, they cut down the dismayed and panicked forces, giving them no time to load or use their arms. Otherwise it wouldn't have been Ascalon, but Hattin. There would have been grief in Świdnica and not merriment.'

'And Świdnica and Lusatia deserve credit for that!' Lord Marshal Borschnitz laughed freely. 'To ably exploit location, time, numerical advantage and circumstances and turn them to one's advantage, striking the foe unexpectedly, surprising him with shrewd tactics ... why, those are features of great leaders. Žižka and Prokop won victories thus; so, praise is due to the Lords Landvogts that they were able to give the Hussites some of their own medicine. I envy them that, I envy them their triumph and glory. And I am not ashamed to say it.'

'The victory at Kratzau,' added Füllstein, 'breathed new resolve into us. Rekindled the hope we had lost. May God give us another like victory.'

'God shall,' proclaimed Jan of Ziębice, sitting up proudly. 'And I shall. I shall lead you into battle against the heretics, to a victory that will eclipse the Lusatians'. I shall lead you, in sooth, to such glory that Polenz and Kolditz will be forgotten. They barely bruised Královec at Kratzau. We shall pulverise him. We shall make a heap from the Hussite carcasses and flay on scaffolds those we capture. This is what I offer you, your dukes, your starostas and your councils. To unify, to strike the Czechs as one and to celebrate Christmas with their demise. Who stands with me? And with what force? Eh? What says Wrocław? Świdnica? Opava?'

'On behalf of Wenceslaus Przemkowic, His Lordship the Duke of Głubczyce and Hradec,' said Füllstein, quickly, as though afraid of being interrupted, 'I pledge five score lances of Opava knighthood. His Lordship the Duke will lead the army himself.'

'Bishop Konrad will field his entire regiment,' said Starosta Tannenfeld after brief reflection. 'Reinforced by regiments from Grodków and Otmuchów. Seventy lances all told.'

'The city of Wrocław,' said Jorg Reibnitz with arms akimbo, 'will send a hundred and fifty mounted men. What of Świdnica?'

'The town of Świdnica contributed much to the victory at Kratzau,' Oppeln proudly declared. 'Since His Lordship Duke Jan promises a victory to eclipse Kratzau, Świdnica will have to be there. We won't let ourselves be so easily overshadowed or erased from the pages of history. Świdnica will field a hundred and fifty horse of peerless cavalry under the command of Lord Deputy Starosta Stosz. All of Świdnica would gladly see the Hussites obliterated. First, though, perhaps His Grace Duke Jan would explain to us what method he means to employ to execute this.'

'Firstly, by using main force,' Jan of Ziębice countered at once. 'From what you've said, I reckon our number at some one thousand horse, of which three hundred are heavy cavalry. Královec has four thousand foot and barely two hundred horse. And since a knight is worth ten wretches on foot, the advantage lies with us. Secondly, we'll tackle them as we did at the Battle of Kratzau. We shall strike the marching column with a surprise attack. Having first ascertained that they are marching into our trap.'

'And how shall we do that?' Oppeln raised an eyebrow.

'We have the means.'

The croaking and banging of the large wallcreeper against the window of the chambers in Nysa Castle of Konrad, Bishop of Wrocław probably surprised the bishop. But the Wallcreeper, to be honest, was probably the more astonished of them. Surprisingly, Konrad wasn't indulging in an orgy, drinking or gambling. Nor was he sleeping off an orgy, drinking or gambling. No. He was reading. Spending his time with a book.

After entering, the Wallcreeper quickly metamorphosed into human shape. He glanced at the book lying on the lectern and shook his head, quite amazed. Not only was it a beautifully illuminated Bible, it was written in German, to boot.

'I know why you came – or rather flew – here,' said Konrad, Piast, Duke of Oleśnica, Bishop of Wrocław and legate of King Sigismund of Luxembourg in Silesia, taking the Wallcreeper aback. 'But you needn't have bothered. I decline your request.'

'Today is the twenty-second of December *Anno Domini* 1428.' The Wallcreeper sat down and reached for a carafe on the chest of drawers. 'On the seventh of November 1427, thus a little over a year ago, here, in this castle, in this chamber, I petitioned, and Your Eminence the Bishop promised me—'

'His Eminence has changed his mind.' Konrad of Oleśnica cut him off. 'And has done so *ad maiorem Dei gloriam*. Reinmar of Bielawa has become a vital pawn in the game, and the stakes have become fucking high. What were you expecting? That I'd give you Bielawa so you could torture him to death? For some vague personal reasons? I'm aware that we once had plans regarding him; he was to be used to cover up the affair of the attack on the tax collector. But now the good of the Church and the country demand something else. I ordered you to collaborate with Duke Jan in the search. I gave Jan permission to enter the convent in White Church. Ha, he'd probably have entered anyhow, since the convent is on his land and the abbess is his sister, but that's neither here nor there. What matters is that Jan of Ziębice is launching a truly great expedition. If the operation is successful – and it has every chance of being so – we shall give the heretics a severe blow, one they haven't hitherto suffered. Do you grasp this, Birkart, appreciate it? First the thrashing at Kratzau, and now the drubbing that Jan of Ziębice will soon treat them to. The myth of the Hussites being invincible in battle will evaporate. Other men will follow our example. It will be the beginning of their end. Their end, my son. I was at the Battle of Prague in 1420, at Sigismund's coronation. I looked from the Hrad at the city, lying in wait across the river like a fierce dog. And when I left that place, I vowed I'd return one day. That I'd see – with my own eyes – that dog's teeth being knocked out, that entire heretical nation being chastened for its crimes. See blood pouring down the streets of that vile town; see the Vltava running red. And it shall be thus, so help me God. And a significant step towards that is Jan, Duke of Ziębice. And the military strategy that I created and Jan will execute. The plan *has* to succeed. God wishes it. And I do, too.

'Thus,' the bishop said, straightening up, 'I categorically forbid you from any action that might thwart my plan. Or even complicate it. Jan is holding Reinmar of Bielawa in a dungeon in Ziębice Castle. I forbid you from taking a single step towards that dungeon, I forbid you from talking to Reinmar, I forbid you from laying a single finger on him. I forbid you categorically and absolutely. I know you're a sorcerer, a polymorph and a necromancer; I know you passed through walls to get to the prisoners in Wrocław. I know of what you're capable and what can be expected from you. But I warn you: if you don't comply you will bring down my wrath upon you. And then you'll learn what *I* am capable of. Do you understand, Birkart, my son? Will you obey?'

'Do I have a choice? Father?'

The bishop puffed angrily. Then snapped the Bible shut and placed a goblet on the cover. And poured spiced Burgundy into it.

'Just between us,' he asked a moment later, quite calmly, 'why did you need Bielawa? It can't just be for the pleasure of revenge and murder? What did you want to get out of him, what did you need from him? What was it? Ha, you probably don't want to say ... Or reveal the details. But perhaps just in general ...?'

The Wallcreeper smiled and it was a particularly hideous smile.

'If you want to know in general,' he drawled through his smiling mouth, 'why not? I wanted to drag out of Reinmar of Bielawa information that would lead me to one of his companions. And I would have wrung further information out of him, acquiring in the process a little knowledge. General knowledge. Among other things, whether the book you were just reading, Father Bishop, is really what it is usually considered to be, or whether it isn't worth any more than the fables of Ezop Fryg.'

'Fascinating,' Konrad said after pondering the Wallcreeper's words. 'Fascinating, indeed. All the same, my orders remain in force. *Ad maiorem Dei gloriam.* And we'll return to the fables in better times.'

The Wallcreeper flew down from the battlements of Nysa Castle and tumbled over, blown by the strong wind coming from Rychleby. He levelled out, croaked and glided off into the night, flying towards the Ślęża massif. But not to Ślęża itself. Ślęża was for amateurs, for dabblers, a somewhat trivial and rather over-rated stage for witchcraft. The Wallcreeper was flying to Radunia, to its elongated peak. To a broad stone bank and a magical rock resembling a catafalque lying in the centre. A monolith that was there when mammoths were striding over the Sudeckie Hills and huge turtles laying eggs on the present-day island of Piasek.

After landing on the rock, the Wallcreeper changed shape. The strong wind ruffled his black hair. He raised both arms and uttered a wild, loud, long-drawn-out cry. The whole of Radunia appeared to tremble at the sound.

In a remote wilderness, at the top of a distant mountain, red flames flared up in the windows of Sensenberg Castle, towering over a rocky cliff. The sky above the old stronghold glowed red. The gates thudded open. There were demonic cries and a tramp-ing of hooves.

The Black Riders responded swiftly to the call.

'I have decided,' said Jan, Duke of Ziębice, playing with a dagger, 'I have decided to give you a chance, Reinmar of Bielawa.'

Reynevan blinked, his eyes painfully blinded by the glare of candles after many hours spent in the dungeon. There were other men in the chamber apart from the duke, though he knew only Borschnitz.

'Although your crimes are grave and call for the harshest penalties,' said the duke, still playing with the dagger, 'I have decided to give you a chance, that you might atone a little for your sins and merit God's mercy with remorse. Jesus suffered for us, and God is merciful; he forgives us our sins and purges us of all immorality. Though your sins be as scarlet, they shall be as white as snow. Everybody may count on the intercession of Jesus and the mercy of our Lord, even a dissenter, blasphemer, sorcerer, demoralised bastard, rat's spawn, chancre, scum, cunt, whoreson and dog's prick like you. But the condition is remorse and a firm resolution. I'll give you the chance to repent, Reinmar of Bielawa.

'The Hussites,' said Jan of Ziębice, throwing the dagger onto a map lying on the table, 'still hesitating about whether to storm Kłodzko, are occupying a fortified camp south of the town, near the village of Rengersdorf, beside the Mezilesí road. You know where that is, don't you? You will go there. Královec knows and trusts you, so will listen to you. You'll persuade him to strike camp and march northwards. You'll tempt him with a lie, with a promise of wealthy spoils, the chance of a crushing attack on the bishop's army, the opportunity to take the bishop himself alive ... In any case, it's your business what deceit you use to convince him; the important thing is that he marches. Northwards, via Schwedeldorf and the village of Rosice, through the Ścinawka valley, and on towards Nowa Ruda. The Hussites won't ever get that far, naturally, we'll deal with them ... earlier. But it's important to ... Are you listening to me?'

'No.'

'What?'

'You won't turn me into a traitor.'

'You already are. Now you're just changing sides.'

'No.'

'Reynevan. Do you know what one can do to a person using red-hot pincers and burning brands? I'll tell you: one can scorch the sides long enough for the internal organs to grow visible behind the ribs.'

'No.'

'A hero, eh?' Jan of Ziębice tilted his head. 'Won't turn traitor, eh? Not even if you're taken to the torture chamber? But what will happen if it's not the hero who is taken there? What if they scorch someone else's flesh? While the hero is made to watch?'

Reynevan, anxious and utterly paralysed in horror, knew before the duke beckoned with a hand. Knew before the servants dragged Jutta into the room. She was pale and didn't even resist.

Duke Jan gestured to have her brought closer. If Reynevan had previously deluded himself with the hope that the lord wouldn't dare to imprison and disgrace Apolda's daughter, that he wouldn't harm a noblewoman, a maid from a knightly family, now the duke's expression and eyes dashed his hopes and dispelled them like dust. A repulsive and cruel smile on his face, Jan of Ziębice touched Jutta's cheek and the girl jerked her face away. The duke laughed, stood behind her and with a sudden movement tore from her shoulders her *cotehardie* and blouse. Before the eyes of Reynevan, who was struggling in the grip of the servants, he squeezed her naked breasts. Jutta hissed and thrashed around, but in vain. She was being held too tightly.

'Before we begin scorching these twin beauties,' said Jan, laughing as he brutally groped the girl's breasts, 'I'll take this maiden to bed with me. And if you continue to play the hero, the maiden will be taken to the town hall cell. Let the fellows there also have their pleasure. For know you, Bielawa, those same warders and guards are still there, that same fraternity who were there when the Burgundian had the misfortune to wind up in the cell. The fellows will get another wench that the duke has grown tired of, ha, ha. And I'll have you thrown into the adjacent cell, that you might hear and picture it. And then . . . Then we'll bring out the red-hot irons.'

'Let her go . . .' Reynevan softly groaned. 'Let her go . . . Get your hands off her . . . Don't you dare . . . Have mercy on her . . . Your Grace . . . I'll do what you ask.'

'What? I didn't hear!'

'I'll do what you ask!'

*

The horse he was given was skittish, nervous and anxious – or perhaps it simply sensed the rider's anxiety. He was escorted to the road beyond the Town Gate by a detachment of knights, including Borschnitz, Seiffersdorf and Risin. And Duke Jan in person.

It was cold. Frozen stalks, covered in frost, crunched under the horses' hooves. The sky to the south darkened, heralding a snowstorm.

'The Hussites,' Jan of Ziębice reined in his steed, 'must march through the Ścinawka valley and onwards along the Nowa Ruda road. So be convincing, Bielawa. Be convincing. May you be aided by the thought that if you succeed, if the Hussites march where I want them to go, the maiden will be saved. If you fail or betray me, you will cause her ruin, offer her up to dishonour and torture. So do your best.'

Reynevan didn't reply. The duke straightened up in the saddle.

'May you be aided in the enterprise also by the thought that by sending the heretics to their ruin you will save your immortal soul. If, thanks to you, we slaughter them, the good Lord will without doubt reward your act.'

Reynevan didn't answer that time, either. He just stared. The duke didn't take his eyes off him.

'Oh, what a look, what a look.' He grimaced. 'Quite like that of Gelfrad Stercza, with whom you must have had so much in common. You won't try to threaten me like Stercza did on the scaffold, will you? You won't say: *Hodie mihi, cras tibi*, what happens to me today, will happen to you tomorrow? You won't say that?'

'I shall not.'

'That's wise. For I would punish you for every syllable you utter. Or rather punish your maiden – one stroke of the red-hot iron for every syllable. Don't forget that, Bielawa. Don't forget it for a moment.'

'I will not.'

'Now ride!'

Beggars, lepers and tramps were squatting in the Town Gate. Duke Jan, greatly pleased with himself, ordered Marshal Borschnitz to toss them a handful of coins. The beggars scrabbled over the pennies as the entourage rode on, the clatter of horseshoes echoing loudly beneath the vault of the gate.

'Your Grace?'

'Yes?'

'If Bielawa ...' asked Hyncze Borschnitz, coughing into his fist. 'If Bielawa carries out ... If he does what you've ordered him ... Will you set the maiden free? And spare him, too?'

Jan of Ziębice laughed dryly. In principle, that laugh ought to have sufficed Borschnitz as an answer. The duke, however, decided to enlarge on it.

'God is merciful and forgiving,' he began, 'but occasionally, He goes so far in His mercy that He doesn't know what He's doing. Konrad, Bishop of Wrocław, told me that once, and the bishop isn't just any village priest, so he knows a thing or two. Thus, before God forgives a sinner, said the bishop, one must make sure that here in this vale of tears the sinner suffers adequately for his sins and crimes. So said the bishop and I think he was right. Thus, Reinmar of Bielawa and his whore will suffer. Adequately. And when, after their torment, they stand before God, let God forgive them if that be His will. Understood, Marshal?'

'Indeed, Your Grace.'

The deep blue of the sky heralded a snowstorm. And something even worse. Worse, for being unknown.

Chapter Twenty-Five

In which Reynevan makes a choice. But not everything ends well.

Reynevan avoided Frankenstein, skirting the town from the south, via Sadlno. He had a dreadful headache, but his spells weren't working, his hands clumsy with anxiety. The pain was making him dizzy.

He rode as though in a dream. In a nightmare. The road, the Kłodzko road, part of the Wrocław–Prague trade route, suddenly stopped being an ordinary road, the route Reynevan knew well. It changed into something Reynevan didn't know and had never seen.

In the dark, overcast sky, a cloud of dense, swirling blackness suddenly billowed, like ink in water. A savage, strong wind blew up, bending the trees over. His horse tossed its head, neighed, whinnied and thrashed around. Reynevan rode, barely able to see the road in the pitch black.

Flaming points glow in the darkness. And red eyes. The moon shines limpidly behind black clouds.

The horse neighs. Rears up.

There's no village where the village of Tarnów ought to be, just a graveyard among misshapen trees. Crosses lean over graves. Some have been stuck in upside down. Fires burn between the graves, shapes swaying to and fro in the flickering gleam. The cemetery teems with monsters. Lemures scrape the graves with their talons. Empusas and necurats wriggle out of the frozen earth. Murons and mormoliks raise their heads and howl at the moon.

Drosselbart sits among the monstrosities, Reynevan can see him clearly. Now, after death, he is even thinner than when he was alive. More cadaverous than a cadaver, he looks like a mummy, dry skin stretched over old bones. One of the lemures is gripping his arm in his teeth above his elbow, biting and chewing. Drosselbart appears not to notice.

'As far as the good of the cause is concerned,' he calls, looking at Reynevan, 'individuals do not count! Prove that you're ready to make sacrifices! Sometimes we must sacrifice what we love!'

'A stone tossed at the ramparts!' howl the lemures. 'A stone tossed at the ramparts!'

There's a crossroads outside the cemetery. Rzehors is sitting with his back against a cross. His face is half-covered and he is wrapped in a shroud, a blood-soaked piece of sackcloth.

'The chariot of history runs on,' he says indistinctly, with effort. 'No power is capable of stopping it. Sacrifice her! You must sacrifice her! For the cause! For the Chalice! The Chalice must triumph!'

'A stone at the ramparts!' croak shretls, hopping, ears flapping. 'Toss her like a stone at the ramparts!'

'In any case, she's doomed,' says Bisclavret, getting up from a roadside ditch. How he spoke was a mystery since there was only bloody pulp where his throat and jaw should have been. 'Jan of Ziębice won't let her go. No matter what you do, you won't save her. She's as good as dead. She's lost.'

Gelfrad of Stercza climbs out of a ditch on the other side. Headless. Holding his head under one arm.

'You vowed,' says the head. 'You gave your *verbum nobile*, your parole. You have to sacrifice her. I sacrificed ... myself. I did my duty. I swore to him ... *Hodie mihi, cras tibi* ... *Hodie mihi, cras tibi* ...'

Horses' hooves strike the earth. Reynevan gallops, bent over in the saddle. The village of Baumgarten ought to be somewhere around. But it isn't. There are bare, ancient trees, a wild forest, a winter wilderness.

'You were a pretty couple,' calls a green-skinned creature with eyes glowing like phosphorous. '*Joioza* and *bachelar*. Oh, you were! You were!'

'A stone tossed at the ramparts!' Pale wights howl as they rise from a hollow. 'A stone tossed at the ramparts!'

Tall, dark-skinned, white-haired alps with pointed ears peer out from behind tree trunks.

'*Tempus odii*.' Their intrusive, clearly audible whispers creep towards him. '*Tempus odii*, a time of hatred ...'

The village of Bukowczyk ought to be there. It is not.

'The New Era!' shouts Krejčíř, the Orphans' preacher, suddenly leaping up. He's completely covered in blood; it is gushing from a stump ending above the elbow and from a dreadful gash on his head. 'The New Era! And may the old world perish in flames! Sacrifice her! Sacrifice her for the cause!'

'A stone tossed at the ramparts! A stone tossed at the ramparts!'

'The Kingdom of God will dawn!' howls Krejčíř. 'The true *Regnum Dei*! We shall triumph! The true faith will triumph, the end of immorality will arise, the world will be changed! For it to happen, you must sacrifice her! You *must* sacrifice her.'

The *Totentanz*, the *danse macabre*, descends the hillside in an unending procession. Hundreds of skeletons attired in shrouds cavort and hop, jiggling in clumsy, grotesque, swinging strides. Ragged standards and pennants flutter and flap. Hellish drums clatter. Bones rattle and teeth snap. And an uneven chorus is sung in screeching voices:

Ye, who are warriors of God
And of his law!

Thousands of crows, rooks and jackdaws circle and caw above the skeleton host. The wind carries a foul, rotten stench.

Bones rattle, teeth snap. There's yelling and hellish wailing. And a song.

Ye, who are warriors of God
And of his law!

A stone at the ramparts. You must sacrifice her.

Reynevan presses his face against the horse's mane and jabs with his spurs.

The hooves thud on the frozen ground.

The nightmare finished as abruptly as it began. The gloom dispersed in an instant. The normal world returned. The normal December sky with a pallid moon hanging over it. The village of Frankenberg was where it ought to have been. Dogs barked. Smoke crept over thatched roofs, rolled over fallow land. Far away to the south, the direction he was riding in, and thus probably in Bardo, they were ringing the Nones.

Reynevan rode. The horse jerked its head, resisting.

His headache subsided.

He passed Bardo, which still bore the marks of fire and destruction. He crossed to the Nysa's left bank. He climbed up a ridge over a bend in the river, rode past the village of Eichau and descended to the Kłodzko valley.

Vespers were being rung in Kłodzko.

He circled the town from the north, once again fording the Nysa. He reached a junction, a place where the Mezilesí road crossed the road leading to Lewin and Náchod.

And there, outside a village whose name he didn't know, he was stopped by a Hussite *hlidka* or patrol consisting of three mounted crossbowmen.

'I'm from the Vogelsang,' he said when asked to identify himself. 'Reinmar of Bielawa. Take me to your leader.'

The Orphans were on the march. Having abandoned their camp outside Rengersdorf, Královec's army was heading northwards. *They're going straight into the Ścinawka valley*, he thought. *I don't have to persuade or convince them. Without my complicity, they're doing just what Duke Jan wanted. Could it be a sign from God? I don't have to do anything or betray anyone. At least not actively. I'll simply stay silent. Keep to myself what happened. Jutta will be saved*
. . .

The column – its flanks protected by the cavalry and infantry – was probably half a mile long, numbering more or less a hundred and fifty war wagons and four dozen wagons carrying provisions. It took some time for the patrol to deliver Reynevan to the hejtmans. To the very head of the column, far beyond Schwedeldorf.

'Reynevan!' Jan Královec of Hrádek appeared extremely surprised. 'You're alive? They said Sir Půta had tortured you to death in Kłodzko. That you'd fallen into their hands, you and Rzehors . . . How the hell—'

'Now's not the time, Brother. Not the time.'

'I understand.' Královec's face was set as hard as ice. 'Tell me what you know.'

Reynevan took a deep breath. *Jutta*, he thought. *Jutta, forgive me.*

'Jan of Ziębice is marching on you from the north with a thousand horse. They mean to strike you on the march. Treat you to another Kratzau.'

At the sound of the name, Královec gritted his teeth. The other hejtmans murmured softly. Jan Kolda of Žampach was among them, as was Matěj Salava of Lípa. There was a man similar to Matěj and bearing an identical coat of arms, no doubt his brother Jan. There was Brázda of Klinštejn, sitting on a huge grey destrier, as usual flaunting the ragged staffs of the Ronovci family crest. There was Vilém Jeník of Mečkov, Hejtman of Litomyšl, whom Reynevan knew by sight. There was Piotr of Lichwin, called 'the Pole', the current commandant of Homole Castle, captured by the Hussites in the spring. And it was Piotr the Pole, hair as black as a raven's, who spoke first.

'What else,' he asked in an evil voice, 'did Jan and Půta order you to tell us? What are you to persuade us to do?'

Reynevan replied with emphasis, face turned not towards the Pole, but towards Královec. 'I was to persuade you to do precisely what you are doing. To march north, into the Ścinawka valley. You are heading into a trap, straight into Jan of Ziębice's jaws. Had I been a spy, as the Lord of Lichwin implies, it would have sufficed to say nothing. But I'm warning you, thereby averting defeat and destruction. You don't even know what it's costing me. If you consider me a spy, kill me. I won't say another word.'

'This is Reynevan,' said Brázda of Klinštejn. 'He's one of us! And he is indeed warning us. What could he achieve by warning us?'

'He would halt the march,' said Vilém Jeník slowly, 'and give the enemy army the time they need. Give time for the villages we are going to ransack to flee with their belongings. I don't know this man—'

'But I do.' Královec cut him off sharply. 'I order the column to stop. Brother Vilém, patrols and forays to the north and towards Kłodzko. Brother Piotr, Brother Matěj, form up the cavalry.'

'Do we build a wagon fort?'

'We do,' confirmed Královec, standing up in the stirrups and looking around. 'Over yonder, beyond that stream, at the foot of the hill. What's the name of the village we just passed? Does anybody know?'

'Stary Wielisław.'

'We shall set it up there. Onwards, brothers! Look lively!'

Reynevan had seen a wagon fort – or *vozova hradba* – being built a good few times, but never so efficiently. Královec's Orphans scurried to and fro and the order and organisation were admirable. First of all, a nucleus was created, a ring of supply wagons, inside which the packhorses and cattle were hidden. The actual *hradba* – a square of war wagons – was quickly assembled around the centre. The wagoners smoothly manoeuvred their conveyances into the appropriate positions. The horses were unharnessed and led into the centre. The wagons were assembled wheel against wheel, with the left rear wheel of the wagon in front chained to the right front wheel of the following one, lending a stepped profile to the barricade of wagons. Artillery – trestle guns and cannons of various calibre – were set up in gaps left every few wagons. Each of the walls was built of fifty war wagons, and the entire *wagenburg* created a square the sides of which measured at least two hundred paces.

Before it began to grow dark, the *wagenburg* was in place. And waiting.

'We were planning to take Kłodzko by treachery,' Brázda of Klinštejn repeated, pensively stopping with his spoon above a pot. 'But nothing came of it. All our men in the town were caught and tortured to death. Rzehors was among them; they say he was cruelly tortured on the scaffold in the town square. And rumour had it that you also met an equally hideous end. I'm glad you survived.'

'I am, too.' Reynevan clenched his teeth. 'But Bisclavret is dead also. They killed him. It's the end of the Vogelsang.'

'You are left. You survived.'

'I did.'

Brázda began slurping his soup again, but only briefly.

'If the Silesians don't come . . . If it turns out that . . . You could be in trouble, Reynevan. Are you afraid?'

'No.'

They said nothing and slurped the soup. Smoke drifted up from the campfires. The horses in the inner ring of the *wagenburg* snorted.

'Brázda?'

'What?'

'I didn't see any preachers with the hejtmans. Neither Little Prokop nor Krejčíř . . .'

'Little Prokop . . .' Ronovci blew his nose. 'Little Prokop is in Prague, advancing his career. He's on course to become a bishop. Krejčíř fell at Kratzau, hacked to pieces along with his sling shooters. There was nothing left of him to gather up. We had one more priest, but he was frail and fell ill. He died. We buried him near Duszniki. It'll be two Sundays ago.'

'You've been left . . .' Reynevan cleared his throat. 'You've been left without spiritual solace?'

'There's always vodka.'

Darkness fell quite quickly and suddenly – it was the twenty-sixth of December after all. And then the patrols, the forays and

Piotr the Pole's cavalry returned. Horsemen began to flood into the square of the wagon fort lit by campfires.

'They're coming!' Piotr the Pole gasped out to Královec. 'They're coming, Brother! That German Reynevan was telling the truth. They're coming! A host of knights, some thousand horse! Silesian eagles on their banners, also the emblems of Opava! They've entered the valley, they're not far from Kłodzko! They'll be here before dawn!'

'Will they strike?' asked Jan Kolda. 'They were planning, as at the Battle of Kratzau, to strike the marching column – when they see that we're at readiness, will they attack?'

'God alone knows,' replied Královec. 'But in any case, we have no way out, we must wait. Let us pray, Warriors of God! Our Lord, Who art in Heaven . . .'

It was cold and a fine, dry snow had begun to fall.

'What village lies ahead of us?'

'Mikowiec, Your Grace. And beyond it will be Schwedeldorf—'

'It is thus time! Time! Bring the banners forward! The banners shall lead the charge!'

The standard bearers moved through to the front. The first banner to stand before the army was that of Ziębice, with its half-black, half-red eagle. Beside it rose up the bishop's banner, bearing black eagles and red lilies. Beside it gleamed the white and red of Opava's standard. Beside it the Świdnica banner: black eagles and a red and white chequerboard. And the black eagle of Wrocław.

The commanders stood alongside Jan of Ziębice in his Milanese armour. The young Wenceslaus, heir of Opava, Duke of Głubczyce. Mikołaj Zedlitz of Alzenau, Starosta of Otmuchów, with a gold clasp on a red shield, leading the bishop's regiment.

The bishop's marshal, Wawrzyniec of Rohrau. The Starosta of Grodków, Tamsz of Tannenfeld. Deputy Starosta Hinko Stosz, commanding the Świdnica contingent. Jerzy Zettritz, the Commander of Wrocław, easy to spot with a red and silver aurochs' head in his arms.

'Onwards!'

'Your Grace! Young Kurzbach, from the foray!'

'Come here, come! And speak! What tidings? Where are the Hussites?'

'They lie . . .' answered the young knight with three gold fish on his shield, still mounted. 'They lie outside Stary Wielisław—'

'They aren't marching?'

'No. They've made camp.'

The commanders muttered. Hinko Stosz swore. Tannenfeld spat. Jan of Ziębice reined his horse around.

'It matters not!' he shouted. 'It matters not!'

'Your spy has clearly betrayed us, Duke,' Jerzy Zettritz declared dryly. 'We've lost the element of surprise. What now?'

'It matters not, I said! We strike!'

'Against the *wagenburg*?' mumbled Wawrzyniec of Rohrau. 'Your Grace . . . The Czechs are at readiness—'

'They are not!' said the duke. 'Bielawa didn't betray us. He could not have! He's a coward and a weakling! He knows we have him by the balls, that I can crush him under my heel, him and his harlot . . . He wouldn't dare . . . Královec, I swear, knows nothing about us, he wouldn't have set up a *wagenburg*, he's pitched a regular camp. Our advantage has grown! We'll arrive before dawn, fall on them in the darkness as they sleep, scatter and slaughter them. They won't withstand the charge; we'll tear them apart! God is with us! Midnight has passed, it's the twenty-seventh of December, the holiday of Saint John the

Evangelist, my patron saint! In the name of God and Saint John, onwards, gentle knights!'

'Onwards!' shouted Wenceslaus of Opava.

'Onwards!' repeated Mikołaj Zedlitz, Starosta of Otmuchów. Possibly a little less boldly.

'Onward! *Gott mit uns!*'

Two and a half thousand Warriors of God were waiting in readiness on, between and under the wagons of the wagon fort. More than a thousand were waiting in reserve, ready to replace the dead and wounded. An assault detachment of Orphans, two hundred light cavalrymen, were crammed in the centre of the square.

The campfires had been put out. Cauldrons of embers glowed red by the wagons.

'They're coming!' the returning *hlidkas* reported. 'They're coming!'

'Ready yourselves!' Královec commanded the hejtmans. 'Reynevan, to me.'

'I want to fight on a wagon. In the front line. Please, Brother.'

Královec was silent for a long time, biting his moustache. It was impossible to make out his expression in the moonlight.

'I understand,' he finally replied. 'Or rather I can guess. I refuse your request. You're staying by me. When the time comes, we shall enter the battle with the cavalry. A thousand horse are coming for us, my boy. A thousand horse. On the wagon, in the field . . . anywhere. Believe me, the chances of fulfilling your death wish are equal.'

The *wagenburg* stood ready and silent. The silence was deathly, barely interrupted by the snorting of a horse, the clanking of a weapon or the coughing of one of the warriors.

The ground began to tremble perceptibly. At first slightly, and then more and more powerfully. The dull thud of hooves striking the frozen ground reached Reynevan's ears. The Orphans began to nervously cough, the horses to snort. The flames of fuses glowed and flickered on and under the wagons.

'Wait,' Královec repeated from time to time. The commanders passed the order down the line.

The thudding of hooves grew. Intensified. There was no doubt. The heavy cavalry, invisible in the darkness, had passed from a trot to a gallop. The Orphans' wagon fort was their goal.

'Jesus Christ,' Královec suddenly said. 'Jesus Christ . . . But it cannot be! They cannot be so stupid!'

The rumble of hooves intensified. The earth shook. The chains connecting the wagons jingled. The blades of gisarmes and halberds clanked and rang as they banged against each other. The hands tightly gripping the shafts trembled more and more. The nervous coughing intensified.

'Two hundred paces!' yelled Vilém Jeník from the wagons.

'Ready yourselves!'

'Ready yourselves!' repeated Jan Kolda. 'Right, lads, arse cheeks together!'

'A hundred paces! Theeey're in view!'

'Fire!'

The *wagenburg* flared up as fire shot from a thousand barrels. A thousand shots rang out.

Amid the squealing of horses, in the yelling, in the tumult and clanking, the darkness was suddenly lit up by fire. At first listless, barely giving off light, it was fanned by a wind that blew up in the dawn and finally exploded with strength and fury. The thatched roofs of the cottages of Schwedeldorf and Stary Wielisław blazed with huge, bright flames, the ricks outside Czerwona Góra and the barns, sheds and shacks on the Wielisławka stream glowed red. Some fires were lit on Královec's order; others Duke Jan ordered his men to light at the moment of attack. The aim was the same: for there to be light. Enough light to make killing possible.

The wagon fort's salvo was deadly. The first line of the charge fell as though flattened by a gale under a hail of balls and bolts thudding against armour; the second line rushed into the swarm of tumbling horses and men trampling them, the charging steeds tripping and falling over the dead and wounded steeds, panicking, throwing their riders in a macabre squealing and whinnying. The cries of horses joined the screaming of men rising up into the night sky.

Only the third line reached the wagons, and although the impetus of its attack was largely slowed, the *wagenburg* still shuddered and shook under the impact of the armoured cavalry. But it withstood the onslaught. And iron rained down on the knights pressed against them. Pushed by their comrades from behind, they couldn't fall back or run away, so they defended themselves as best they could from the blows striking them. Hussite flails, battleaxes and morning stars shattered helmets; halberds destroyed spaulders; battleaxes hacked off arms; and clubs and poleaxes, voulges and awl pikes pierced armour. Hidden under the wagons, the crossbowmen fired bolt after bolt into the horses' bellies, while others slashed their legs with scythes set upright on shafts. Squealing and the thudding of iron and yelling rose above the battlefield, fire reflected red on blades.

The bishop's regiment was the first to withdraw and then flee in confusion. Decimated by a salvo in the charge, they ground to a halt in front of the *wagenburg* and became impaled on the thicket of fixed pikes, gisarmes and bear spears like leaves on a hedgehog.

On seeing it, Mikołaj Zedlitz completely lost heart. Shouting incoherent and nonsensical commands, the Starosta of Otmuchów suddenly reined his horse around, flung his shield with the gold clasp onto the ground and simply rode away. Marshal Wawrzyniec of Rohrau galloped after him. The two men were followed by the entire regiment. Or rather what was left of it.

Wenceslaus, Duke of Głubczyce, son of Przemko of Opava was next. Wenceslaus, an adept of the occult arts, had spent the entire journey pondering over an enigmatic horoscope the court astrologers had cast before the expedition. Now, as the Opava knights began to fall under the blows of Hussite flails, Duke Wenceslaus decided that the conjunctions were unfavourable and the prospects poor. And that it was time to go home. On his order, the entire Opava contingent withdrew. In considerable panic.

Jan of Ziębice, Hinko Stosz and Jerzy Zettritz were hoarse from yelling out orders. The knighthood withdrew from the wagon fort in order to regroup. It was the commanders' final and worst mistake. The Orphans had managed in the meanwhile to load their trestle guns and cannons; harquebuses, handgonnes and crossbows were at the ready. There was a deafening roar as the wagon fort once again spat fire and smoke, and a lethal hail of missiles fell on the retreating Silesians. Once again, balls and bolts cut through armour, once again mutilated horses tumbled down, squealing. And whoever was still able set off in desperate flight.

The Starosta of Grodków, Tamsz of Tannenfeld, fled in panic, overtaking all of his subordinates. Deputy Starosta Stosz ran from the field with the remains of the surviving Świdnica knights. The Wrocław and Ziębice knights, deaf to the desperate calls of Duke Jan and Zettritz, ran away in confusion.

'Now!' bellowed Jan Královec of Hrádek. 'Noooow! Have at them, Warriors of God! Have at them! Death to them!'

Immediately, several wagons were removed from the walls of the wagon fort and the Czech cavalry charged through the gaps. On lighter and fresher horses, less burdened down by armour, the Hussite cavalrymen caught up with the fleeing Silesians in no time. And cut and hacked them down mercilessly.

The infantry left the wagons to rush after the cavalry. Any Silesians who were spared by the cavalry's swords now perished under blows of flails.

'Have at them! Haaaave at theeeem!'

Smoke and the stench of burning crept over the battlefield. The fires died down. But in the east a bloody dawn was rising.

'Have at them!' yelled Reynevan, galloping in the charge between Salava of Lípa and Brázda of Klinštejn. 'Kill them!'

They caught up with the Silesians, swooping on them like hawks, and a massacre began. Swords clanged on armour; sparks shot up from blades. Reynevan hacked with all his might, yelling to give himself courage. The Silesians broke free from the fighting and fled. Reynevan galloped after them.

And then the Wallcreeper saw him.

The Wallcreeper hadn't taken part in the battle, he had no such intention. He had come to Stary Wielisław, riding concealed behind the Silesian army, with only one goal in mind. He had brought his ten Black Riders from Sensenberg with but one aim in mind. Predicting the mishap, they hurtled onto the battlefield like wraiths. Circling and searching.

It was by sheer accident that the Wallcreeper managed to spot

Reynevan in the turmoil of battle, in the wild confusion and the darkness lit by flickering fires. A piece of luck. Had it not been for luck, neither magic nor hash'eesh would have helped him.

Spotting Reynevan, the Wallcreeper screamed an order. The Black Riders reined their horses around as one. Wheezing behind their visors, they hurtled towards where the Wallcreeper was pointing. In a headlong gallop, slashing and cutting down anyone in their way, barging, knocking over and trampling them.

'*Adsumus! Adsuumuus!*'

Reynevan saw them. And went numb.

But accidents and luck could happen to anyone; no one had a monopoly on them. Particularly not that night.

When the Hussite infantry had poured from behind the wagons after the cavalry in pursuit of the Silesians, some of the artillerymen abandoned their cannons and joined in the chase. But not all of them. Others so loved their firearms that they wouldn't go after anyone without them. Cannons, having gun carriages, were ideally suited to that kind of manoeuvre. As luck would have it, three artillery gun crews pushed and rolled their cannons onto the field directly opposite the charging Black Riders. Seeing what was afoot, the cannoneers swung the carriages into position and brought fuses to touch-holes.

The Riders' plate armour was quite impervious to the hail of lead shot, scrap iron and incised nails, which bounced off their breastplates like peas. The elevation of the cannons meant, however, that most of the missiles struck the horses and sowed havoc among them. None of the ten horses withstood the salvo, none of them remained on their feet. Several Riders were crushed, several killed by kicks. The other Riders struggled to their feet, wheezing, looking around with eyes vacant from hash'eesh. They were given no chance to recover.

The last reserve of Orphans rushed out from behind the

wagenburg. Soldiers with light wounds. Wagoners. Blacksmiths and leather workers. Women. Youngsters. Armed with whatever the casualties had dropped. Pitchforks, partisans and gisarmes repelled and downed the Black Riders and the Orphans swarmed over them like ants. Stanchions, axes, clubs, swingletrees and hammers rose and fell, penetrating weak points: visors, plackarts, couters and poleyns. Knife blades, spikes and sickles were plunged through slits in armour. The wheezing turned into high-pitched shrieks.

The Black Riders resisted death for a long time. They fought hard not to surrender their lives. But the Hussites struck, struck and struck again.

As long as was necessary.

The Wallcreeper saw it all and Reynevan saw it all. Reynevan saw the Wallcreeper and the Wallcreeper saw Reynevan. They looked at one another across the bloody battlefield, eyes smouldering with hatred. Then Reynevan roared furiously, spurred his horse and charged at the Wallcreeper, brandishing his sword.

The Wallcreeper dropped the reins, raised both arms in a sudden movement and wove a complicated gesture with them in the air. He was immediately surrounded by a creaking and sparking glow, and a ball of flame began to swell and billow around his outstretched hands. But the Wallcreeper didn't manage to throw it. He wasn't quick enough. While Reynevan galloped, from the battlefield a group of mounted men hurtled towards the Wallcreeper, approaching rapidly. A party of Litomyšl infantry armed with flails and halberds rushed from the wagons. The Wallcreeper screamed a spell and waved his arms. Before the eyes of Reynevan and the astonished Orphans, a large bird took flight from the saddle of the black stallion. Flapping its wings, it rose up into the sky, croaking savagely, and flew out of eyeshot.

'Witchcraft!' roared Matěj Salava of Lípa. 'Papist witchcraft! Ugh!'

In order to discharge his anger, he buried his battleaxe in the black stallion's head. The stallion fell to its knees and then toppled over onto its side, tensing its legs stiffly.

'Over there!' roared Salava, pointing. 'They're over there, the bitches' sons! Over there! Have at them, Brethren! Kill them! For Kratzau!'

'For Kratzau! Kill them! May none escape with his life!'

Having escaped the turmoil of the battle, Jan of Ziębice fled in panic, forcing the last breath from his snorting horse as he galloped.

He was heading northwards, towards the faintly smoking Schwedeldorf. He didn't know exactly where he was going; it was indeed all the same to him. Stupefied with fear, he was simply following the others. Just to escape the slaughter. He caught up with a few knights on staggering horses, necks white with froth.

'Risin? Borschnitz? Kurzbach?'

'Your Grace!'

'Ride, swiftly! We must flee!'

'Over there . . .' panted Hyncze Borschnitz, pointing. 'Across the river—'

'Ride!'

The idea of crossing the river was ill-advised. The worst of all possible ideas. Not only were they plainly visible against the blazing cottages of Schwedeldorf, but the river's banks turned out to be a marsh that never froze. Once the horseshoes had broken the thin layer of ice on the surface, the heavy horses sank in deep, some up to their bellies.

Before they fully understood the danger of their situation, their pursuers were upon them; Hussite cavalrymen in sallets and kettle hats were teeming around. Risin howled, stabbed by spears. Kurzbach sobbed. He cowered in the saddle, struck on the head by a mace, and fell down under his horse. Borschnitz yelled and began to swing his sword around him. The others followed his example. Jan of Ziębice had lost his sword in the flight. At the sight of the Hussites surrounding him, he seized a battleaxe hanging from the saddle and swung it, screaming curses, but in his panic, he swung so clumsily that the crooked handle slipped from his fingers and the battleaxe flew away. The Hussites leaped on him from all sides. He was struck on the back, then on the head. He gave a deafening scream, slid from the saddle and fell to the ground. He tried to stand up, was hit again in the side, then a hammer struck and dented his armour, breaking his ribs, and the duke choked, gulping for air. He was struck yet again, fell over on his back and saw his blood streaming over the shattered ice. He heard Kurzbach's high-pitched scream beside him as he fell under sword blows. And Borschnitz yelling as he was finished off. And then he himself began to yell.

'Mercy! Meeercy!' he bellowed, tearing the armet from his head. 'I am Duke—'

'*Hodie mihi, cras tibi.*'

The duke trembled. He had recognised Reynevan.

Reynevan placed a foot on his chest. And raised what he was holding in his hands. The duke saw what it was. And felt sick to the stomach.

'Noooo!' he howled like a dog. 'Don't! The orders have been issued! In Ziębice! The maid will perish! If you touch me, the girl dies!'

Reynevan raised the bear spear high. And plunged it deep into the duke's belly with all his might. The four-edged, forged blade penetrated the lames of the fauld. The duke bellowed in pain, jerking up his legs spasmodically and grabbing the shaft in both hands. Reynevan pressed him against the ground with his foot and tugged the spear out. Everything around him became blindingly bright, clear and white.

'Ransooom!' Jan howled. 'I'll pay a ransooom! Gooold! Jesus Chriiist! Meeercy!'

Reynevan lifted the spear high. There was a crack as the spear blade pierced a slit between the breastplate and the plackart, entering up to the spur. Jan of Ziębice screamed, choking as blood poured from his mouth and down his chin and armour.

'Meeercy . . . Meeercy . . . Aaaah . . .'

Reynevan struggled with the trapped blade for a while, finally jerking it out. He lifted the bear spear and struck. The blade pierced the plate. Duke Jan couldn't scream any longer. He only groaned. And puked. Blood spurted a yard up into the air.

Reynevan braced his foot against the breastplate and hauled on the shaft, trying to pull out the blade.

'Do you know what, Bielawa?' said Jan Kolda, standing beside him. 'I think he's had enough now.'

Reynevan released the bear spear, barely able to straighten his fingers. He took a step back. He was trembling slightly. He controlled himself. Kolda hawked at length and spat.

'He's had enough,' he repeated. 'Quite enough.'

'Aye, I believe so,' said Reynevan, nodding. 'I believe he has.'

That was the end and epitaph of Jan, Duke of Ziębice, a Piast of the Piasts, a direct descendant of Siemowit and Mieszko, blood of the blood and bone of the bone of Bolesław the Brave and Bolesław the Wrymouth. He fell on the twenty-seventh of December 1428, or as the chronicler said, *vicesima septima die mensis Decembris Anno Domini MCCCCXXVIII.* He fell in a battle fought outside a village called Stary Wielisław, a mile or so to the west of Kłodzko. As some chroniclers have it, he died like his great-great-something-grandfather, Henryk the Devout: *pro defensione christiane fidei et sue gentis*. Others say he was killed by his own stupidity. In any event, he died.

And the male line of the Ziębice Piast Union with him.

The battle raged on. Some of the Silesians, unable or unwilling to flee, put up fierce resistance. Having herded themselves together into a ring, they fought back ferociously against the attacking Orphans. Some fought alone, like Jerzy of Zettritz, the commander of the Wrocław men. Two horses had already been killed under Zettritz, the first right at the beginning of the battle, by the *wagenburg*, and the second in the flight, so he had no way of fleeing. Helmetless, with bloodied hair, Zettritz was also wounded in the leg; a Hussite gisarme had stabbed him in the thigh, piercing his Nuremberg-forged cuisse. Blood now poured down the plates of the cuisse. Resting against a willow tree on a baulk, Zettritz was unsteady on his feet, barely standing, but still valiantly wielding a bastard sword, driving away the attackers surrounding him, hacking more stubborn ones with powerful blows. He was already encircled by a ring of the men he had killed when one of the Czechs finally managed to stab him through the cheek with a glaive, the blow breaking his teeth. Zettritz staggered but stayed on his feet. He spat onto his breastplate, cursed foully, and forced back the attackers with sweeping blows of his bastard sword.

"Pon my word, m'Lord Zettritz,' called Brázda of Klinštejn, riding up. 'Perhaps that'll do?'

Jerzy of Zettritz spat blood. He looked at the ragged staffs on Brázda's breast. And breathed out heavily. Jerzy caught his sword by the blade and raised it as a sign of surrender. And then fainted.

*

'God triumphed,' said Jan Královec of Hrádek in a weary voice. 'God wished it so,' he added, quite without pathos. 'The horn of Moab is cut off and his arm is broken.'

'God triumphed!' Piotr the Pole raised his bloody sword. 'We, the Warriors of God, have triumphed! The arrogant German knighthood is lying here in the dust! Who will stop us now?'

'We have avenged Kratzau!' yelled Matěj Salava of Lípa, wiping blood from his face. 'God is with us!'

'God is with us!'

It appeared that the triumphant yell from more than a thousand throats of the Warriors of God had finally dispersed the gloom and fog. Piercing the smoke rising from campfires, the day dawned and became brighter. *Dies illucescens.*

'I must ride,' repeated Reynevan, using all his willpower to stop his teeth chattering. 'I must ride, Brother Jan.'

'We broke them,' repeated Jan Královec of Hrádek. 'We cut off the horn of Moab. Jan of Ziębice killed, Świdnica and Wrocław decimated. No one can stop us now. We shall take advantage of the victory. Silesia is at our mercy. Do you want vengeance? Come with us.'

'I must ride.'

The sun had broken through the clouds. The day promised to be frosty. The twenty-eighth of December 1428. The Tuesday after Christ's Mass.

Královec breathed heavily.

'Ha, if you must, you must ... Then ride. God be with you!'

A crow sat on the head of the hanged man.

The day, although frosty, was beautifully sunny, almost completely windless. The hanged man only swayed slightly and turned around on a creaking cord, which appeared not to bother the crow at all. Having dug its talons into what was left of the corpse's hair, the bird was methodically and calmly pecking out what there was to peck out.

The tiles on the towers of Ziębice gleamed in the December sun. A column of refugees was heading towards the Town Gate. News of the approaching Hussites had clearly spread fast.

Reynevan patted the horse's frothy neck. He had covered the six miles between Stary Wielisław and Ziębice in a truly remarkable hour and a half. The result was that he had absolutely exhausted the horse. It barely plodded the last stretch of road. And that was with breaks.

The crow flew up from the hanged man's head and away, cawing, in order to alight a little higher, on the horizontal beam of the gibbet.

'Reinmar of Bielawa, I believe?'

He had no idea where the man who asked the question had appeared from. It was as though he had simply materialised. He was sitting on a small piebald horse and dressed like a burgher. His face was ordinary, his accent Polish.

'Reinmar of Bielawa, of course.' He answered his own question. 'I'm waiting here for you, m'lord.'

Rather than answer, Reynevan reached for his sword. The man with the ordinary face didn't even twitch.

'I'm waiting without any evil intent,' he said calmly, 'only to pass on some information. Important information. May I speak? Will you listen calmly, m'lord?'

Reynevan had no intention of agreeing. The stranger noticed. When he spoke again, his voice had changed. There were evil, metallic notes in it.

'There's nothing for you in the town, Reinmar of Bielawa. You rode fast and didn't spare your horse. But still you are late.'

Reynevan fought the despair that suddenly engulfed him. He

fought his weakness. He gained control of his leaping heart. He hid his hands, which had begun to shake, behind the pommel of his saddle. He clenched his jaw until it hurt.

'The maid whom you hurried to rescue is not in Ziębice,' said the stranger. 'Be still! Nothing foolish! Patient, please be patient. Listen to me—'

Reynevan had no intention of listening. He drew his sword and spurred his horse. The horse strained, pawed the ground with a hoof, snorted, then raised and turned its head around. But didn't budge an inch.

'Be patient,' repeated the stranger. 'Don't do anything foolish. Your horse can't move and you can't come any closer to me. Listen to me, please.'

'Speak. Tell me how Jutta is.'

'Miss Jutta of Apolda is hale and hearty. But she has left Ziębice.'

'How . . .' Reynevan breathed deeply. 'How am I to know you aren't lying?'

The stranger smiled unpleasantly. '*Veritatem dicam, quam nemo audebit prohibere.*' His excellent Latin betrayed him as a Pole just as much as his accent. 'Miss Jutta is no longer in Ziębice. We decided she wasn't safe in the hands of Duke Jan, and that the people the duke entrusted her to wouldn't guarantee her personal inviolability. Thus, we decided to rescue Miss Jutta from the prison in Ziębice. Fortunately, we succeeded. And took her, so to speak, *sub tutelam*.'

'Where is she now?'

'In a safe place. Keep calm, young man, keep calm. She's in no danger. Not a hair on her head will be harmed. She is, as I stressed, in our care.'

'Whose care? Whose damned care?'

'You are astonishingly dim-witted.'

'The Inquisition?'

'*Tu dicis.*' The stranger smiled. 'You said it.'

Reynevan once again tried to urge his horse forward, but again the horse snorted and stamped on the spot.

'You burn others to death for using magic,' he spat. 'You fucking hypocrites. I won't ask what you want from me or what the purpose of the blackmail is, I can guess. And I loyally warn you: I've just killed one blackmailing whoreson, and I firmly resolve to kill any more that happen to appear. Pass that on to Gregorz Hejncze. And I shall remember you, O messenger, be certain. You won't know the day or the hour.'

'Be patient, Reinmar, be patient.' The stranger curled his lip. 'Control yourself and your behaviour, since lack of control may result in unforeseen, unpleasant consequences. Very unpleasant consequences.'

'For Jutta? I understand.'

'No, you don't. Sheathe your sword and listen. Are you listening?'

'Do I have a choice? For if not there will be unpleasant consequences. After all, Jutta is in your hands. In your dungeon—'

'She isn't in any dungeon,' interrupted the stranger. 'No one will harm her, lay a finger on her, insult her or stain her honour. Jutta of Apolda is in our care. She is, naturally, in isolation . . . With the knowledge, actually, and approval of her mother, Lady Agnes, the wife of the Cup-Bearer of Schönau. Miss Jutta is residing in a safe place. Removed and isolated from the perils of this world. From certain ideas that once led Maifreda of Pirovano to the stake. And from you. Especially from you. And for the time being, Miss Jutta will remain removed and isolated.'

'For the time being?'

'Until . . .'

'Until when? When will you free her?'

'When the time comes. And under certain conditions.'

'Go on!' snapped Reynevan, still vainly trying to move his horse. 'Get to the point! Tell me! What are the conditions? Who am I to betray this time? Who am I to sell? Turn over whom to their death? And when I do what you want, you will give me Jutta, will you? And perhaps you'll throw in thirty pieces of silver?'

'Be patient!' The stranger raised a hand. 'Quell your excitement, don't rush ahead. I have said what I had to say. Now return to your people. To the Orphans, who, rumour has it, are marching northwards hard and will be here any moment. Go back. And wait for news from us. The Reverend Hejncze asked me to give you these words of the prophet Hosea: the ways of the Lord are right, and the just shall walk in them: but the transgressors shall fall therein. It's time you stopped falling, Reinmar of Bielawa. Time to return to right ways. We shall try to help you in it.'

'I don't doubt you will.'

'Wait for news. We shall find you.'

'Are you so sure you will?'

'We shall.' The Inquisition's emissary smiled. 'Without difficulty. Since you are like marjoram. You often appear. In every dish. My name is Łukasz Bożyczko.'

'I shall remember.'

Łukasz Bożyczko laughed, unconcerned – apparently, at least – by the threat in Reynevan's voice. He threw his cloak back over his shoulder. Reined the piebald around. Spurred it. And trotted off towards the Town Gate. Towards which more and more refugees were trudging.

Reynevan remained watching him for a long time. He was dying of exhaustion and lack of sleep. But he knew there was no time for either rest or sleep. He tugged at the reins and headed back towards Frankenstein. His horse snorted. The road was full of people. News about the Orphans advancing with a plundering raid had spread like lightning, and Silesia was once again seized by panic.

And Jutta was in the Inquisition's hands.

The sky in the south was growing dark, warning of approaching snowstorms.

And much worse things.

END OF VOLUME TWO

Credits

Andrzej Sapkowski and Gollancz would like to thank everyone at Orion who worked on the publication of *Warriors of God* in the UK.

Editorial
Marcus Gipps
Brendan Durkin

Translator
David French

Copy editor
Lisa Rogers

Proof reader
Jade Craddock

Audio
Paul Stark

Contracts
Anne Goddard
Paul Bulos
Jake Alderson

Design
Rabab Adams
Joanna Ridley
Nick May

Editorial Management
Charlie Panayiotou
Jane Hughes

Finance
Jasdip Nandra
Afeera Ahmed
Elizabeth Beaumont
Sue Baker

Marketing
Lucy Cameron

Production
Paul Hussey

Publicity
Will O'Mullane

Operations
Jo Jacobs
Sharon Willis
Lisa Pryde
Lucy Brem

Sales
Jennifer Wilson
Esther Waters
Victoria Laws
Rachael Hum
Ellie Kyrke-Smith
Frances Doyle
Georgina Cutler